The

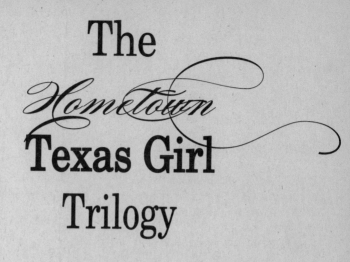

Texas Girl

Trilogy

A Three-Novel
Collection of a Girl Coming
of Age in the 1960s

D0067565

Sharon McAnear

BARBOUR BOOKS

An Imprint of Barbour Publishing, Inc.

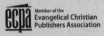

Contents

Corner of Blue

Jemma
Book One

Dedication

For my grandparents,
Rev. Charlie & Addie Williams
DeVerdie & Grace Leathers

Carried Away

Golden-eyed Zephyr
Making up time,
Hear it on the wind,
Better clear the line.

Come, silver chariot,
Long overdue,
Carry me away
To that corner of blue.

Dancing on the track
Until the whistle blows,
Runaway heart;
She comes,
She goes.

—Jemmabeth Forrester

Jemmabeth Forrester just never learns.

Obviously, she shouldn't have picked a fight
with the meanest judge around.
And maybe it wasn't too smart to have
the town's peeping Tom sit for a portrait.
Jemma knows that—now.

But in spite of a pickup load of advice
from most everybody in Chillaton, she remains stubborn,
wanting to go her own way, like the Texas Panhandle wind.

Someday she'll grow old and wise, like her grandmother,
a strong woman of faith,
but Jemma's got a ways to go yet....

Chapter 1
Promises

Rats. She felt it pop at her garter belt tab and zip its way into her shoe. She should've known better than to buy dime-store nylons.

Jemma wrangled the giant Dodge into a parking spot, then checked the run. Maybe Granny's eyesight was bad, and she wouldn't notice. She read the ad again:

> *Floral delivery/Apply in person/Granny's Basket/*
> *Must have a Texas driver's license.*

She admired elderly businesswomen, especially spunky old maids because they could've actually outfoxed any number of men over the years. She might become an old maid herself if she didn't watch out. There weren't many guys left for her to outfox.

She checked her lipstick in the mirror and caught a glimpse of a couple kissing in the car behind her. She drummed her fingers on the steering wheel. The time had come for her to crawl back to Spence, confess what a waste this year had been, and admit that he really was The One. That plan of action would be next on her agenda. At the moment, she needed this job.

A small bell tolled above her as she pushed open the door, and the air inside dripped with the scent of carnations. One bump and hundreds of trinkets would come crashing to the floor from the glass and metal shelves lining the walls. The knickknacks were probably ready to be dusted, too, but not by her. She was going to deliver floral poetry and get paid to do it.

A ceramic fawn caught her eye, and she touched its spotted coat. A buck had jumped in front of Spencer's Corvette once. He would have hit it, too, if she'd kissed him one second longer. Those were the kisses she wanted again. Those were the first ones she'd ever had, not counting family, and as things were turning out, they were also the best. Now he could be kissing somebody else on a steady basis. Double rats. She should send him some flowers and let them do the talking, like the TV commercials advised. Surely employees got a discount. Maybe Granny would offer her a glass of lemonade as they chatted about roses. She could ask about the discount then.

"Don't handle the merchandise." Norman Bates's mother spat out the order. All she lacked was a big knife and a shower curtain to put them on the set of *Psycho*. Jemma was at least a head taller and could see the woman's scalp through her lavender hair. Mother Bates ran her finger along the counter, then examined it with her bifocals. "I assume you are looking rather than shopping."

Jemma had read about projecting a positive attitude at interviews, so she put out her hand. "My name is Jemmabeth Forrester, and I'm your new delivery girl."

"Handshaking passes germs, and you'll get nowhere with sassiness."

"Yes, ma'am." Granny might want to hear about this attitude. It wasn't exactly spunky; it was more along the lines of spiteful.

"I'm The Proprietor and we don't hire girls for various reasons. We use boys to deliver our orders." She moved to adjust the deer, and her shoes squeaked on the linoleum. They were nurse shoes like those Mrs. Bach, Jemma's fourth-grade teacher, had worn. She could still picture Billy Joe Ferris tying Mrs. Bach's laces together as the woman snored through geography. The Proprietor sniffed. "Are you a local?"

"My dad has been the football coach at Wicklow High School for two years, since '63, and I live at Helene Neblitt's." That should carry some weight in her favor.

"Sports are a waste of energy." The Proprietor eyed her for a moment, then checked her watch. "Mrs. Neblitt, you say? I'll call her even though she never trades with us. Grows her own flowers. At least you're big enough to be a boy."

They retreated to a large workroom being minded by a woman chopping the stem tips off carnations with a vengeance and a butcher knife. Her pale blue hair wobbled with each chop as did her hips. Hmm. . .maybe these two were Granny's daughters or some black sheep cousins, and what was a *proprietor* anyway, the manager? Perhaps she should forget about the lemonade.

"Don't touch anything," the chopper said. A vision of Papa's best milk cow, its tail swishing, made Jemma bite her lip. She wiped her forehead, too, quite discreetly. Those cheap stockings clung to her like damp tissue, and the run had to be as wide as a Band-Aid by now.

The Proprietor hung up the phone, then turned to her associate. "Sister, I need quiet for a minute." She rapped her fingers on a counter laden with floral arrangements. "Show me your driver's license." Jemma forked it over. "I assume you know your way around Wicklow since you live with the former mayor's snobby widow. Remove the tickets but leave the sender's card. There is a spray to be positioned on a loved one's casket at the funeral home. You will follow the bereavement spray placement diagram in the car. Any monetary tips are to be given to me immediately upon your return. You should have no questions if you have been listening. Do you promise to follow my instructions to the letter?"

Jemma nodded, but "loved one's casket" swarmed around in her ears until the chopping resumed. Sister knew when a minute was up.

The Proprietor unbolted numerous locks on a sliding door that opened into the alley, then led the way to a Buick Woody station wagon. The butcher knife remained in Sister's hand.

"Remember," The Proprietor said, "I will be calling the delivery addresses to see if there were problems. This is only a test because we are behind on our deliveries. You are not hired yet." She surrendered the car keys and Jemma's license.

The sisters stood guard while she loaded the wagon. Craning their necks like a couple of Papa's chickens, they loomed in her rearview mirror until she turned out of sight. Jemma unleashed a giggle and turned on the radio. She pulled over and did her hair up in a ponytail, then whipped off the stockings and stuck them in her purse. Prepared for an impressive job audition with resultant employment, she sallied forth.

The dreaded casket spray was the only delivery left. The last time she had been in a funeral home was in high school when she and her best friend, Sandy Kay Baker, had to sing a duet for a service at the Boxwright Brothers Funeral Parlor. They were seated behind two heart-shaped floral arrangements that centered exactly on their chests until they stood to sing. Sandy would die laughing when she heard about these sisters.

Cars lined the street and the big semicircle driveway, but a wide space in front of the funeral home was empty. It was perfect for the station wagon. Jemma studied the pseudo antebellum mansion— a poor man's Tara. On the lawn, matching cherubs sputtered water onto concrete slabs. Miss Scarlett wouldn't twitter down these tacky steps with her hoop skirt flouncing, but then Scarlett would have a surefire plan to get Spencer back. If he'd found somebody else, now that she wanted him, it would be the pits.

Right in the middle of a reconciliation scenario, the car died. She pumped the accelerator and turned the key, producing a dismal grinding until a hearse pulled up behind her. One of the men got out and came alongside her. He stuck his round head in the window, cigarette dangling. "You need to get out of the way, kitten. Flowers go around to the back."

"It won't start."

"You've flooded it. Scoot over."

The wagon started on his first try. He flipped his ashes out the window and winked. She drove to the delivery door and slipped inside. Distant groans of organ music greeted her. To the left was a small, roped-off room with an occupied coffin. She cradled the casket spray with *Uncle Dear* written in gold letters on the ribbon, ready to follow The Proprietor's directions. At least somebody's dear uncle wouldn't spring up and spit like Thurman Talley said his wife did at midnight while he sat with her coffin at Boxwright's. That was a perennial Halloween story in Chillaton.

Giving the diagram a quick look, Jemma laid the paper, along with the flowers, on the casket. She avoided viewing the old fellow as she eased the spray toward him, then backed up to the door to check the results. His folded hands were lost among the carnations, a palm branch was curved up against his nostrils, and the diagram rested in an unseemly fashion on his forehead. Otherwise, he looked good. Someone coughed behind her and Jemma, studying Uncle Dear's features, shrieked.

"Shh. There's a service in progress, kitten." The roundhead who had started the car rearranged the spray and handed her the instruction sheet. "Anything else I can do to please you, sweet cakes?"

"No, thanks," she said. She could take him with The Sleeper hold. That would be a good story to tell Spencer, to break the ice.

He put an arm across the door, releasing an unsavory combination of sweat and Old Spice, and his eyes swarmed over her. "Nice to see a girl for a change, 'specially one who's a real looker, like you. I bet you're on a soap opera or somethin', or you could be a stewardess with them long legs." He took a cigarette out of his pocket and stuck it behind his ear. "The sisters always hire boys to make deliveries, due to the fact that they ain't as likely to be scared of the deceased. How 'bout you, kitten? Don't you think it's a little spooky in here?"

She glanced at Uncle Dear. "Not really, but if you will excuse me."

"I'm a generous tipper with the delivery boys, so here's a little somethin' for your trouble." He held up a coin, and as Jemma swept by him, he clutched her arm. "See you real soon, hon," he said, then tucked the coin in her hand. She shoved it in her skirt pocket and raced to the car.

Not only did the station wagon start, but it left a little rubber on the driveway just like Spencer did the night she broke up with him. She turned on the radio and sang along.

Jemma parked the car precisely where she had found it. She left the placement diagram on the dashboard, and she took the keys and the tickets with her. Perfect. She knocked on the alley door.

"Who is it?" Sister asked.

"It's me, the delivery girl."

The door slid open and there they stood, giving her the eye.

"Is there anything you need to tell me?" The Proprietor asked.

"No, ma'am, I can't think of anything."

The sisters exchanged glances. Maybe laying rubber on the funeral home driveway was frowned upon in the delivery business.

"Don't play coy with me. I just got off the phone with Mr. Tiller." The Proprietor's hands were on her hips, fingers together, just like Jemma had learned at cheerleading camp. "I told you that follow-up calls would be made and questions would be asked. Mr. Tiller reported that he gave you a quarter for a tip, and you promised to turn all tips over to me at once."

"Oh, that." Jemma fumbled in her pocket. "It's right here." The Proprietor pursed her lips in victory as Jemma handed it over, accompanied by a weak smile. "I'm sorry. I forgot all about it." She looked to Sister for comfort.

Sister adjusted her bosom. "Young people don't appreciate money these days."

Mother Bates plunked the coin in a Mason jar above her desk. "We run an honest establishment here, but it appears you don't adhere to those standards."

"Because I forgot about the quarter?" Jemma asked.

"Girls always get silly over things. I warned you, we don't hire girls."

Sister clicked her tongue.

Jemma's mind churned. "Ma'am, this isn't fair. I wasn't being dishonest; I just forgot." Then it came to her. "I want to speak with Granny."

The sisters raised their voices in chorus. "Who?"

"The Granny on the window, on the car, and in the ad, too. It's her shop."

"There is no Granny," Mother said. "That's just our business name. I told you, I am The Proprietor. Are you daft?"

Jemma's hands flew to her hips, as well. "Well, isn't this great? You got an afternoon's work out of me, accused me of stealing and lying, and now you're admitting there is no Granny. This job isn't what I thought it was going to be. You can pay me for my hours and I'll go."

"I never said I would pay you. This was a trial period, and it hasn't worked out. Obviously, you don't honor promises."

"You don't even know me! I've gone to church all my life, and I have a boxful of perfect Sunday school attendance certificates to prove it."

Mother's mouth twitched. "Religion is nothing more than a crutch for the simpleminded."

Jemma caught her breath. She was in the presence of a heathen. "Look, whoever you are, ma'am, I delivered your flowers and that alone is worth a stinking quarter."

Sister shifted her weight, possibly wishing she had her knife.

Mother fished the coin out of the jar and held it out to Jemma like a departed slug. "Twenty-five cents for services rendered."

Jemma propelled herself toward the front door, ignoring the offer. The bell jingled wildly as she flung it open, and the ceramic deer caught her attention, his soft brown eyes belying its role as a harbinger of trouble. She slammed the door a little harder than she intended, but the sisters had finished listening to her anyway. Their heads were bent over the workroom counters as they resumed their duties.

Guilt nagged at her, but not because she had tried to keep money from them. She had let a couple of elderly ladies haul out her temper. Papa would say that she should have been more respectful, and Jemma couldn't believe she had been fired, before she was hired, for the only job in the *Wicklow Weekly*.

She languished against the hot bricks outside the barbershop and bawled until the barber came out to ask if there was anything he could do to help. It was too late now for help. Maybe she should have prayed about it. A good, solid prayer couldn't have done any harm. That's what her Gram would've done. Jemma wiped her eyes and stepped off the sidewalk to the Dodge. Across the street the sun sparkled on the glass doors of the solitary law office in town. Gold lettering, edged in black, spelled out the lawyers' names:

Lloyd D. Turner—Stevens P. Turner
Attorneys at Law

A hand-printed sign was taped on the door: PART-TIME POSITION AVAILABLE. MUST BE BONDED.

Jemma undid her ponytail, licked her lips, and opened the door to a rush of frosty air-conditioning. There was no time for stockings. Classical music wafted from a radio and a dish of butter mints rested on the receptionist's desk.

A smartly dressed woman looked up from her typewriter and

smiled. "May I help you?"

Jemma cleared her throat. "I'm here about the job."

The woman gave her some forms to fill out, she met with one of the lawyers, and she was in. It was that simple.

"Are you bonded?" the secretary asked before she left.

"No," Jemma said, "but I want to be."

❧

That night she sat on the steps outside her sticky hot garage apartment, listening to the crickets. Spent clouds masked the moon, but the nearby lights of Dallas made the moonlight pointless anyway. The glow messed up her stargazing, too. In high school she and Spencer had watched the stars and talked about life from the hood of his car, but in the eighth grade they had promised to love one another forever, among other things. Maybe she really didn't keep promises since she had given up his love easy enough. Now she wanted it back. No, she wanted *him* back. It was small comfort that he was somewhere under that same moon, maybe even loving her, still. She should call him, but then if he had a girlfriend, she would just die.

The clouds moved off and she searched the heavens for Orion, like they'd always done. It was no use. Jemma returned to the thick heat of her room. Spencer's senior picture smiled from the dresser, and she touched the little scar, barely visible, on his chin. She longed to touch him in person. He stared back at her with his big gray eyes. She sighed out loud, then sat down at the typewriter. She was running low on sleep, vocabulary, and paper. The old portable didn't help much, either. She gathered her damp hair on top of her head, then put in another sheet.

> *Title: Joy, In Light—Artist's Statement*
> *Medium: oil on canvas*
> *Scenes wash across my path in a kaleidoscope refrain and I am compelled to capture them as they reveal themselves in the light. A delicate line, sensuous curve, or subtle shade of color could release even the most fleeting response in another soul, thereby validating some common ground in the human experience.*

In this piece, the woman's face and the text are illuminat-
ed, capturing the effect of the letter on her heart. One hand is
held midair as in sudden realization, while the other quells the
paper. The tilt of the woman's head and the curl of her mouth
suggest the text is one of joy.
Signed: Jemmabeth Alexandra Forrester, May 9, 1965
Le Claire College of the Arts, Dallas, Texas

She yanked it out and typed it again on her last sheet of paper, translating the title into French: *Joie, Dans La Lumière*. She had looked up the right words at school. Maybe, by some miracle, she would win the competition and Spence would call to congratulate her. Slathering the statement with rubber cement, she positioned it on the back of the canvas. She piled her art history research paper beside it on the floor, wound her clock, said her prayers, and collapsed into sleep.

≺◈≻

Caruso's scratchy voice floated through her window. She sat on the side of her bed for a groggy minute, then splashed cold water on her face and looked down on Helene's backyard. Her English landlady was cutting the first flush of roses and singing along with the gramophone. Jemma threw on one of her daddy's old white shirts and a pair of her painting jeans. She squeezed into her loafers as she descended the stairs where Helene greeted her at the bottom.

"You are up so early, *Zhemma*." Helene pronounced her name in the continental style, further proof that anything sounded better in French. "I have had a brainstorm, dear, and I think you may be quite interested."

"I'll come by later because today is my family's big move to Arizona," Jemma said but couldn't resist the roses. "My mom would love one of those, if you don't mind."

Helene offered her all of the creamy pink flowers. "Give my regards to your family. Tell them I'll look after you. Now carry on, dear."

≺◈≻

Everybody had said that her grandpapa would want her to have his 1957 Dodge, a gas-guzzling, two-toned green monster with fins.

Poking at the pushbutton gear selector on the dashboard, Papa had always been full of advice. "You gotta keep up with the times, Jemmabeth, and pushing buttons is the wave of the future," he had said, looking at her out of the corner of his eye. The Dodge was losing charm, but it still got her around.

She needed to get around to calling Spence, but there remained the problem of what she would say. He was too smart and would pick up on any weak excuses, so it would have to be flat-out honesty. This had been her big idea and, looking back, it was truly dumb. She only hoped that his feelings hadn't changed at all in the last year. She was willing to beg, if necessary, and begging could be good if nobody else had entered the picture. It might also help if she apologized for dumping him. There. That was the rough draft. Not exactly spectacular, but heartfelt.

The sun peeked between the stands of old elm and oak trees, scattering patches of blackish-green along the country lanes. Jemma concocted another tender reunion situation with Spence, loaded with prolonged bouts of kissing, and it sucked her into the other lane around a curve. A delivery truck swerved and honked, but she couldn't help resuming the daydream. After all, it had been a whole year since she kissed him good-bye, and she'd kissed many a dud in the meantime.

Her parents' ranch-style house was set on a knoll and shaded by elms. Her daddy and her little brother had built a tree house in the largest one and she had stayed all night in it with Robby on his seventh birthday just the past week. Now a realtor's sign was nailed to it.

Robby ran out of the house, shouting, "Mom, she's here." He jumped on his sister, spilling a collection of trip entertainment on the steps.

She helped him clean it up and looked into his sky-blue eyes. "You need to lick your lips. There are crumbs and syrup shining under them." She handed him a thick tablet of paper and some of her own colored pencils. "You also have to draw the desert for me, and I mean fill each page."

"Maybe," he said. "Since you're not coming, you have to write me a lot of letters."

She rubbed his buzz haircut, like velvet against her hand. "That means you have to answer every single one, big boy."

"Aw, c'mon; that's too much spelling."

"A letter a month, then," she yelled after him as he was off to watch his bicycle being loaded into the U-Haul.

Alexandra Forrester appeared in the doorway, dressed in her new Arizona outfit, complete with a purple bandana tied at her neck. Her mother knew how to turn heads. People commented that Jemma had become the image of her, right down to their pouty lips, as her daddy called them, but Alex's auburn hair was cut in an Italian bob, and Jemma's was below her shoulders in natural waves. Jemma did have those uncanny golden eyes, too, unlike the hazel eyes of her mother, and she had outgrown Alex by a good three inches. Not exactly twins.

Alex held out her arms. "Come here, sweet pea. I miss you already. Promise you will call us and you'll take your vitamins."

"Sure, Mom." Jemma saluted. "Here's a bouquet to keep you company."

Alex first tucked her daughter's hair behind her ears, then took the roses. "I mean it now."

"Yes, ma'am. It's not like I'm going to prison or something."

"I know a kid whose grandpa is in prison." Robby climbed on Jemma's back. "He was our class pen pal."

Alex and Jemma exchanged glances and giggled.

Jim Forrester set an ice chest, which Jemma knew was full of sodas and pimiento cheese sandwiches, in the rental truck and strode over to hug her. Tall and lanky with brown hair, high forehead, deep-set eyes the color of a lion's, a generous nose, and a toothy smile, he resembled Jemma's grandmother, Lizbeth.

"Daddy, you watch the road and don't be looking around for deer or antelope," Jemma said.

"Or buffalo?" Jim laughed as he inspected their new Rambler station wagon that was hitched securely to the back of the truck. He had made this trip once already with an even bigger load. He wiped the back of his neck and pointed a finger at her. "You be smart, young lady. Watch out for those burly cello players, and you be in church every Sunday."

"Yes sir, I know. I've been learning some wrestling moves from TV." She assumed a stance, hoping for a laugh. None was forthcoming.

"We'll be in Chillaton tonight, so you can call us at Gram's if you want." He opened his wallet and held out a fifty-dollar bill. "You hide this in your sock drawer because it may come in handy. Now don't be shaking your head at me."

"Thanks, Daddy, but I got that cleaning job yesterday."

He stuffed the money in her pocket, along with a quick hug and kiss. "Love you, baby girl. Let's go, troops."

"Wait." Robby came running with a piece of wood. "It's for your hope chest thing. I messed up on the *P*, but Daddy says nobody will notice." It was smooth, gray driftwood, over a foot long, with JEMMA'S PLACE carved into it. The *P* was once backward, but then sanded out to face the right way—there was a reason he didn't like spelling. "It's that wood we found on the beach last summer."

She held him until he wriggled away.

Jim started the U-Haul. "Give Spence a call. Don't let that boy get away from you. I don't think you know which end is up in that department."

Jemma nodded again, like things were under control in every department. She knew that her mother was crying as they pulled out of the lane. "I love you," she shouted and blew one last kiss.

Sunlight glinted off the chrome luggage rack as the Rambler vanished over the hilltop behind the U-Haul. Jemma left without looking back, but her mother's perfume lingered on her blouse. She turned up the radio full blast and sang "Ticket to Ride" with the Beatles. Her new job would start tomorrow, and she would call Spence by the weekend. Life was good. Helene's old red MG was gone when she got home so she set her alarm for eight o'clock, turned on the fan, and fell asleep.

The pouting room was just a whatnot of a room, originally intended as a pantry. Lizbeth Forrester propped open the window, then dusted the shelves and the bulky trunk with its tin, leaf-shaped hinges. The floor was too small to fiddle with, but she scrubbed it on her knees anyway. She laid back the lid of the trunk to get the medals. With tiny, even circles she rubbed the cleanser into the

Purple Hearts. She polished them with a corner of her apron until a bird outside the window caught her attention for a moment. The song was somehow familiar, but it vanished before she could get a look at it. She rested, massaging the bridge of her nose, then stared blankly at the hearts. Such trifles to honor her babies. She returned them to their velvet boxes and the lids snapped shut. This was her private ritual. She didn't know if it made her feel better or worse after all these years, but she had kept it up.

Cameron had never brought himself to look at the medals from the time they put them in the trunk, the soldier box, until he died. Instead, he planted flowers and built fancy little birdhouses to deal with the sorrow. He put them all over their place until folks started driving by just to look at the mass of blooms and birdhouses that filled the yard. Now he was gone, too. Lizbeth closed the window and replaced the little hook on the door just as the 6:23 Zephyr blew by on the tracks behind the house.

She poured herself a tall glass of sweet tea and went to the hollyhock patch. Her dress was already clinging to her skin, so she laid her hand on a metal chair with peeling Getaway Green paint to see if it was still cool enough to sit in. Cam had painted his chair Thunder Red on the screened-in porch one winter day, and the fumes had lingered for a week.

Lizbeth touched the cold glass to her forehead, then rolled her neck on the back of the chair and gazed into the branches of the pecan tree. It was going to make a heavy crop this year and provide plenty of pecans for her holiday pies. A movement in the foliage caught her eye. It was a cardinal, bright red, the same one she had heard outside the pouting room. She had never seen one in this part of Texas, but knew them well growing up along the banks of the Bosque River. The bird shook itself and let out two long, shrill whistles, then a burst of short chirps. It hopped to another spot and was lost in the branches. They saw lots of birds back in Erath County when Cam was courting her, and he could name them all. His birdhouses were trifles, too. She missed the man.

The wind picked up, snapping her laundry on the line and flushing a bevy of birds from the trees. A fly crept around the edge of her glass, leaving a threadlike trail in the condensation. She poured out the last bits of ice and went inside to bake cookies before it got too hot, and especially before her neighbor could bring the mail. The man could eat a dozen before any were offered, but he kept her entertained.

She checked her watch. Her dear ones, Jimmy, Alexandra, and Robby, would be pulling into the driveway in about five hours. Jemmabeth, bless her, was on her own now, but she would make it. Lizbeth had survived, despite all the grief, with the same mettle she had as the only female in her college class. Jenkins girls always did, somehow, and Jemma had just as much Jenkins in her as she did Forrester.

Chapter 2
Snakeskin

The Le Claire College of the Arts was in an older part of Dallas, the area where a squirrel could travel from one tree to another for blocks at a time and never touch the ground. The campus had been a private boys' school at the turn of the century, but it now sheltered minds and hands bent on creativity. The buildings had been refurbished through a generous donation from a patron of the arts now living abroad. Jemma wanted to live abroad someday, too. Maybe Spence would like to live on the French Riviera or in a quaint Italian village. Their children could be multi-lingual, that is, if he took her back.

She read the inscription over the entryway aloud, as always:

Criticism is easy, Art is difficult.
—Philippe Nericault 1680-1754

Art had never been difficult for her, but she liked the quote anyway. He was French.

The smell of paint and brush cleaner saturated the room. Ceiling fans whirred overhead and windows the size of Volkswagens were cranked open, infusing the room with humid Dallas air. The wooden floors, spattered with color flicked in moments of inspiration or frustration, creaked in certain spots. Jemma closed her eyes and inhaled.

Professor Rossi leaned across a counter and tapped on its surface. "Jemmabeth, have you come to bring me your competition piece or are you taking a tour of the school?" His white hair curled around his ears, and his bushy brows sprang up.

She laughed. "I missed you, too. How was y'all's trip to Italy?"

He patted his belly. "Perfect. You should have come with us. Florence would have ignited your senses."

"Maybe next year."

The professor wagged his finger. "Come, give me your painting. The competition will be intense." His eyes widened as she revealed the piece. "Ah, exquisite," he said, kissing his fingers and tossing them in the air. It was his idea for her to enter the contest for the fellowship. He propped the painting on a display ledge that lined the room, then stepped back to scrutinize her work, talking to himself. Jemma smiled and left him to his artistic dissection.

She was late to meet Melanie Glazer, a fellow Le Claireian and concert violinist. Melanie had been invited to play with the Dallas Symphony Orchestra for the summer season, and the two girls had a date to go shopping.

"Over here," Melanie yelled across the fountain plaza.

Jemma waved. "Ready to go?"

"Always willing to spend my hard-earned money."

Jemma pulled out of the school parking lot. "I haven't been shopping since Christmas. I hope I remember how to get to this place."

"Go to SMU, then it's easy. You should know how to get there since you've spent all year checking out the men on that campus."

"Southern Methodist University, where all the good-looking, rich guys are," Jemma said, although she knew better.

"Not always." Melanie flashed her engagement ring.

"I assume Michael is doing well."

"He's my accompanist for the recital. Any luck with Robert?" Melanie asked.

"Clammy hands."

"Clayton?"

"He makes this weird clucking noise when he can't think of anything to say, and his lips fold under or something when he kisses. I just get a lot of teeth."

"Yuck. Now that's what I'll think about every time I see him. He is cute, though. Whatever happened to that guy you dated your freshman year? Wasn't he your childhood sweetheart or something?"

"Yeah. We'd never even looked at anybody else in thirteen years. Well, maybe I looked at a few cowboys, but who wouldn't? Anyway, I haven't seen Spencer since last summer when I said that I needed some time to see if I really loved him." She pulled into a parking spot. They got out and stood before a row of posh shops. "Not exactly middle class."

"Nope. Listen, I found that song you told me about," Melanie said as they surveyed the mannequins.

"Papa's favorite? Isn't it great?"

"It's sweet but melancholy."

"It follows me around."

"Like other things from your past?"

Jemma took a breath. "Let's shop."

She hammered the shiny brass knocker on the door several times in case Helene wasn't wearing her hearing aid. The Tudor-style house was unique in the town of Wicklow. It was gabled with tall windows, half-timbers, and four chimneys. Helene had lived alone in the great house for the last several years until she took in Jemma, her first boarder. She opened the door dressed impeccably in a linen suit. She was a spry, petite woman. As always, she was wearing her double strand of pearls and her emerald earrings.

"Jemma, dear," she said, adjusting her hearing aid. "Let's visit in the kitchen, shall we? Come along." Only at the corners of Helene's brown eyes was there a hint of wrinkles, and her silver hair was forever pulled back into a bun. Jemma followed her through the house, past loaded bookshelves, rich floral fabrics, photographs of Mr. Neblitt and her in exotic places, and paintings of Helene's stuffy ancestors.

Helene went on the whole time about her fat white cat, Chelsea, while Jemma considered how similar the antique mirror above the fireplace was to one at the Chases' house in Chillaton. This home smelled of wood polish and lavender, and recently, toast. At her landlady's invitation over the past several months, Jemma had studied at Mr. Neblitt's desk in the drawing room as Helene read, reclining on a pillow-strewn window seat. They had charmed one another. Helene always wanted a child, and Jemma loved her companionship, style, and spirit. Helene was also a gourmet cook, which didn't hurt anything.

A dazzling collection of china filled every cabinet and shelf in the kitchen. The cookstove was a huge black thing shipped from England, and the breakfast table reminded Jemma of the drugstore tables in Chillaton where she and Papa drank chocolate shakes after the trips home from her art lessons in Amarillo.

"Mom liked the roses," she said, inhaling a vase full of them on the table.

"It was Neb's hobby, you know. I do hope he is watching from some cloud when I tend them because it is backbreaking labor for an old sort like me. Now, Jemma, I have been thinking about your accommodations, and here it is: I would like for you to move in with Chelsea and me. I have two guest rooms, and neither has been used in years. You could keep that oven of a flat over the garage as your studio."

Jemma gawked at her. "Whoa. Thank you, Helene, but I can't afford two rooms. I'm barely paying for one."

"Don't be silly. We are too close for you to pay another penny for anything. This is completely my idea, and it's quite shameful that I haven't suggested such an arrangement sooner. You may choose which room suits you best, and then we shall call your parents and ask their blessing. There you have it."

Jemma shut her mouth. She already knew which room she wanted. It was like a set from a movie. Her mom would croak when she heard about this.

She moved her things as soon as Helene got Alex and Jim's grateful approval. They were thrilled that Jemma wouldn't be living alone anymore. Rose toile wallpaper graced the walls, and the ceiling was at least twelve feet high. The curtains were gold, patterned with hydrangeas. There was a skirted dressing table fit for Miss Scarlett, who might brush her hair there and then leave the room in a huff, overturning the stool. The bed was a four-poster with white linens and needlepoint pillow shams. Jemma could almost see herself in the cherry hardwood floor, she had her own bathroom with a claw-footed tub, and altogether, she was as close to heaven as a twenty-year-old artist could get.

Helene watched as Jemma pushed a large cedar box under the bed. "Whatever is that lovely thing?" she asked.

"It's my hope chest that my grandpapa made for me. It's a

tradition from way back. My Gram had one and I'm supposed to keep things in it for, you know, if I ever get married."

"And so you shall." Helene went to the dresser to examine Spencer's senior picture. "Who is this handsome young man? I didn't know you had a special someone."

"That is Spencer Morgan Chase."

"Ah, the reason for the hope chest."

"Spence and I grew up together. In our first-grade Christmas program nobody would hold hands with Lena Purl Sweeney because they said she had cooties. Spencer let go of my hand and took Lena Purl's. You have to love somebody like that. It was always our plan to marry someday, but we have been dating other people this year." Jemma shrugged at his picture. "He may not love me anymore."

Helene tapped the frame with *Class of '63* emblazoned in gold across the bottom. "If I were a young lady, I would be quite concerned about letting this one loose in the wide world of college women."

Jemma turned back to her unpacking. Everybody was full of advice. She may have learned a few things this year. First off, she missed him more than she had ever planned, and, along that same line, she needed to pray about important stuff rather than asking for help afterward, like she was doing every night now.

Her new bedroom kept her awake, or maybe it was just Spence. She turned on her bedside lamp and reached for her sketchbook. She drew his face, then thumped her pencil on the pad. *Would you* (crossed that out). *Could you* (crossed out). *I miss you so much, and I'm sorry that*. . . She couldn't write it. She got his picture off the dresser and propped it up on her knees. She lay back against the pillow and just told him. It was a very long conversation. She would call him tomorrow night when she got home from cleaning the offices. Maybe her lonesome days would soon be over.

⟨◈⟩

The trash didn't even smell at Turner & Turner's. There were four offices for the lawyers, a conference room, a reception area where the secretaries worked, and two bathrooms. The mahogany furniture, floor-to-ceiling bookshelves, and the lack of windows conjured up the feeling of being trapped, like Papa's hogs must have felt at killing time. She shook off that icky thought and got to work. She polished the wood, especially the conference table, to a perfect shine. There were a few paintings on the walls, but nothing of merit. They were no more than furniture store prints.

Jemma remembered what her mother had taught her—top to bottom—dust, then vacuum. The vacuum cleaner was extra loud so she turned up her transistor radio full blast, pulled her hair back with a rubber band, and made a production of it, singing over the roar and dancing with her metallic partner. Spencer's favorite song, "Mean Woman Blues," was playing. She was barefoot and in the middle of a torrid move when something told her that she had an audience. She turned around and squealed, as much in delight as in shock.

He was almost as tall as the door frame he was leaning against. His black hair skimmed his collar and his eyes, jade green, were boring a hole through her. High cheekbones and square jaw spread into a grin, making him, without a doubt, the most delectable cowboy she had ever encountered.

"That's quite a show, darlin'," he yelled.

Jemma's tongue was as heavy as the vacuum that was still running. She fumbled around for the switch. "What did you say?"

"I said that's some show."

"You're on the photo wall, aren't you?"

"Yeah, I'm one of 'em. Hey, don't let me keep you from your work. I just thought I should let you know that you're not alone anymore."

"Thanks," she said, not knowing where to look. The photo hadn't prepared her for the real thing.

"No thanks needed. You made my day." He turned and went back into the conference room and sat at the table. His jeans were creased and the sleeves on his blue starched shirt were rolled up. Those jeans looked good, but the clincher was the black snakeskin boots. Lucky reptile to end up with this guy. He opened his briefcase and spread papers on the tabletop that she had just buffed to a fine sheen. He concentrated on his work, but Jemma couldn't take her eyes off him. He looked up and winked.

She finished the rooms, raked the shag carpet, washed the coffeemaker, and cleaned the bathrooms again in no time at all, hoping he would come out of that conference room before she had to do it all over again.

He did. He leaned against the door frame again and clicked his pen, staring at her. "I knew they hired someone, but I don't know your name."

"Jemmabeth, but you can call me Jemma. Most people do."

"Pretty name. I didn't see a car outside." Her daddy was six-three, and this guy was taller than that. He looked like a man who knew how to take charge, and he was in good shape, too. There was no wedding ring on his finger. She had checked.

"I walked because my car is basically out of gas," she said like a dumb bunny.

"You shouldn't walk around town at night, darlin'. Where do you live?"

"I live with Helene Neblitt. Do you know her?"

"Sure, the big stone house on the edge of town. When you're ready to go, I'm taking you."

"Actually, I'm ready now," she said, surprising herself.

He opened the passenger door to a baby blue Ford pickup and moved some packages out of the way. "Sorry. I just picked up my laundry." He put on a black cowboy hat. "So, you're a Roy Orbison fan, huh?"

"Yeah, Roy's the best." The hat was almost more than she could bear.

"Where did you learn to dance like that?"

"I like to dance. My mom won a jitterbug contest in college." That sounded stupid. Rats.

"What I saw back there was a far cry from the jitterbug. You were gettin' with it."

"I thought I was alone. You need to turn right here." Jemma pointed. "It's really not that far."

He pushed his hat to the back of his head. "Too far for a pretty thing like you to be walking at night. How long have you lived in Wicklow?"

"My family moved here two years ago, but I moved out last

fall because I wanted to be more independent. My dad was the high school football coach. He has a great job now as an assistant coach at Arizona State College in Flagstaff. Did you play football?" She couldn't shut up, but she might as well have had cotton in her mouth. It was the hat.

"I played back in the fifties. I don't ever remember seeing you at any recent Wicklow games, and I would have noticed if you had been there, darlin', believe me." He drove past Helene's lane and had to back up. They sat in her driveway. As he put his arm on the back of the seat, his fingers skimmed her shoulder. She shifted and squared her back against the door handle.

"I bet you played basketball," he said. "Anybody with your moves and height had to be on the court."

"I had a good jumpshot." She lifted her hair to cool her neck. "I like your hat."

"Why, thank you, ma'am." His voice was like satin. He pulled his hat low over his eyes and smiled. "I wear it when I'm not trying to look like a lawyer."

"I thought good guys always wore white hats."

"That's just in the movies. You can't believe everything you see there, darlin'."

"I know, but I did want to be like Roy Rogers. He was my hero. My grandpapa had a hired hand who was a cowboy. He used to ride up to my grandparents' farm on his horse and pick me up with one arm. We'd go for a ride around their house. I had a crush on him when I was about five years old."

"You didn't want to be Dale Evans?"

"Absolutely not. One Christmas I asked for a Roy Rogers outfit, and Santa brought me a Dale Evans one instead. I was so mad."

"So there are two Roys in your life, huh?" He moved his finger across her arm. "Any other men that I need to know about?"

Every hair on her arm stood up. "No more than a cello player or two." Spencer crossed her mind, but not long enough to stop her.

He walked her to the door and studied her face in the glow of the porch light.

"Thanks for the ride." She avoided his eyes.

He tipped his hat. "Anytime, Roy." He started down the walk, his boots crunching the gravel between the stones.

She took a step after him. "Wait. What's your name?"

He walked back, putting his hat over his heart. "My apologies, darlin'. I'm Paul Turner, son of Stevens Turner. I guess I thought you already knew that."

She was very aware of her own heartbeat since it was drowning out all the crickets in the yard.

His gaze was steady. "I've never seen eyes the color of honey before. You have to be the sweetest thing in Texas, no, in the universe." He moved his finger under her chin. "I hope you have some fine dreams tonight, Jemmabeth Forrester," he said, his perfect lips curving into a smile.

"You, too, Paul Turner," she whispered.

He took a few steps backward, then turned toward his pickup. He gave her one final look over his shoulder before getting in.

"Whoa." Jemma stood staring long after his lights had disappeared. She'd better wait awhile before she called Spencer. After all, she could be delivering flowers for Mother Bates, but she wasn't, so Paul Turner just might be The One.

❧

She cleaned the offices really slow, in hopes he would come, but was about to turn off the last light before his baby blue pulled into the parking lot. She held the door for him and held her breath as well. *English Leather.* Oh man, she was a goner. He had on the works—jeans, white shirt, the hat, and those boots. His eyes were as green as Helene's emerald earrings, and his smile gave Jemma goose bumps.

"Hello, darlin'. How are you tonight?" He set his briefcase on the conference table. "You work late."

"So do you." She couldn't help but notice that his shirt was almost too tight for his big neck.

He sat on the corner of the table with one boot still on the carpet and the other swinging like a hypnotist's watch. "What do you do with the rest of your day?"

"I'm in a summer mentorship at my art school." She glanced into his eyes. "How about you?"

"Law school at SMU." He gestured at the shelves of casebooks as though it were his fate.

"Hey, I went to SMU, too."

"Really, when was that?"

"Cheerleading school, summer of '61."

His laugh was raspy, what Gram called a whisky laugh. "Good one. I bet you were cute in your little cheerleading outfit."

Jemma leaned against the open door. She swayed it back and forth, her hands clutching the doorknob behind her.

"Are you on your way out?" he asked.

Actually, she had forgotten what she was doing. "I think so."

"You didn't walk again, did you?"

"No, I didn't walk. I'm using an old bike from Mrs. Neblitt's garage."

"Let's go." He put the bike in the back of his truck.

"I just keep owing you for all the favors you're doing me," Jemma said.

"I guess I'll have to think of a way to collect. Are you hungry? How about a cheeseburger basket and a milk shake?"

"That sounds good. This is a really nice pickup," she said, knowing nothing about pickups.

He turned up the soul music. "Thanks, I just got it. It's a '66, with an eight-track tape built in."

"So, you're a real buckaroo?" Jemma asked in her best drawl.

"That's right, darlin'. Actually, I just help out the family with our ranching ventures. By the way, you're fixin' to have the best burger in the state. It's down the road a bit, but worth the gas."

She rolled down her window and let the breeze dry her damp face and neck before she undid her ponytail and let her hair fall around her shoulders. She knew good and well that he was watching.

They got their food and sat by the creek that ran behind the burger joint.

The floodlight, which was attracting an assortment of insects, went off. After the last car pulled away from the parking lot, only crickets and bullfrogs filled the humid night air.

"Are you about to graduate from law school?" she asked. That sounded like an old lady question, but his hat was pushed back like Paul Newman's in *Hud*, driving her nuts.

"Yeah, this month. Then I have to take the bar exam. What about you?"

"I just finished my second year in art school at Le Claire. The summer program brings a well-known artist to Dallas who mentors a few lucky students."

He sat way too close to her. "Are you as good at painting as you are at dancing?"

"I've never considered doing anything else. Have you always wanted to be a lawyer?" Her nostrils flared a bit, filling her senses with English Leather and messing with her good sense.

"Pretty much. I decided for sure when I got out of the army. I was in ROTC at the University of Texas. Hey, check out the fireflies over there." He nodded toward the opposite side of the creek.

She jumped up like she'd never seen one before. "Wow! How do they do that?"

"The female puts out the brightest light, but I think only the male can fly."

"I wonder how they decide when to light up for romance?" Jemma asked, teetering on the edge of the creek bank.

He winked. "That's the universal question. The trick is knowing the answer."

A shiver rippled through her. Lashes like his belonged on a girl.

They rode home singing along with his eight-track.

Paul leaned the bike against Helene's garage. "Do you work two or three days a week at the office?"

"I work Tuesdays and Fridays."

"I'll see you on Friday then."

"Okay, but I'm going to look up fireflies and see if you know what you're talking about."

"Good." He ran his finger down the bridge of her nose, touching her lips. "You take care, darlin'."

Jemma swallowed hard. "I'll pay you back for the burgers."

"Don't you even think about it. I like the idea of having you in my debt," he said over his shoulder.

She shut the door and slid down it in giddy anticipation of Friday.

⤜☙⤚

They went again to the Best Burger Stop, talking until the place closed. As the fireflies came out, he popped the question that she'd been thinking about all week.

"Are you in the mood for some romance?"

She gulped.

He ran up the steps to his pickup, leaving Jemma like a limp French fry on the bench. He came back with a tiny flashlight and a jar. "I used to do this at camp, but I haven't thought of it in years." He squatted on the grass by the table and handed her the jar. "Be ready." Then, just like the real thing, he turned the flashlight on and off in short bursts. Another firefly responded to the call and flew right to Paul, landing on his arm. "Gotcha," he said as Jemma put the jar over the bug and screwed the lid on tight.

"It's magical," she whispered.

"Works every time."

They sat on the table, watching the show in the jar. "I guess it's kind of sad, though," she said. "I feel like we've sentenced it to jail."

"Or worse." Paul slid his arm around her waist, making her sweat.

She opened the lid and shook it out. The firefly took off, and they followed its path until it was lost among the others.

"Oh rats!" Jemma said. "What time is it?"

Paul looked at his watch. "Eleven thirty."

"I was supposed to call my little brother because he got home from church camp tonight."

"Close family?" He pulled her to him.

Her pulse rocketed. "My parents met at the University of Nebraska. Daddy was on a football scholarship, and my mom was a cheerleader, the daughter of a big shot newspaperman in St. Louis. Daddy joined the army after Pearl Harbor, and they got married as soon as he got out. My grandparents weren't exactly thrilled about her marrying a farmer's son."

"I take it they weren't football fans, or they would have liked your dad. Did love last for them?"

"Of course it did. Daddy always says that he was a lucky man to find a Midwestern girl with all the charms of a Southern belle.

He likes to tease."

"You're the cutest belle I've ever shared a milk shake with, darlin', and that's the truth."

"Aw, shucks," Jemma said in her Scarlett accent. "You stop that, or I just might swoon."

Paul laughed and moved his hand toward an unauthorized spot.

"I think it's bedtime for me," Jemma quickly deflected his move.

"Well," he whispered. "We don't want you sleeping out here. Unless I am with you, and then what would people say?"

He walked her to the door, and Jemma wanted him to kiss her so bad that her lips quivered. Paul took her hand instead, kissed it, and looked her in the eye.

"You know that I think about you all the time," he said. "I want to see you more than twice a week. How about if I come by here tomorrow night?" He was so close she could taste his breath in the midnight air.

"I can't wait to see you either. Come every night."

He grinned down at her. "I'll be having some sweet dreams about you tonight, darlin', guaranteed."

Jemma watched from the door until she couldn't see his lights on the road. She took a long bubble bath and went to bed, hoping that maybe tonight she wouldn't dream about Spencer Chase.

Chapter 3

Against Her Heart

Jemma was, perhaps, smitten. That's all she could come up with. When she least expected it, a word or a touch would remind her of Spencer, but Paul's green eyes and snakeskin boots hustled those memories right out. How could her plans turn around so quickly? It was only over a week ago that she was dying to talk to sweet Spence. Now words came out of her mouth to which she hadn't given much thought until she heard them. Rats. She was tumbling into a wild hole with this cowboy, but he made the trip so easy on her. Spence could be engaged to some debutante by now. That was a troubling thought. She considered how it might feel to see Spencer with some other girl, but then she considered the fact that Cowboy Paul still hadn't kissed her. If he were a rotten kisser, well, what a waste of those perfect lips. There was nothing better than a great kiss, and she needed a sample by the end of the month. Then again, Spence could also be missing her kisses right now rather than being engaged. Double rats on her lifelong weakness for cowpokes, but, oh well, she was in this curious hole too deep to crawl out just yet.

❧

"The French have a name for this time of day that is more romantic than our 'twilight,'" Paul said. "They call it *L'heure bleu*, the blue hour."

Good grief, he speaks French. "I love the way you said that," she said, then suddenly recalled Spencer was learning French the last time she saw him, too.

"Why thank you, ma'am. I had to take some kind of foreign language at college. Girls always seem to like French, so I took it. How's your mentorship going?"

Jemma tossed a kiss into the air. "Fantastico!"

"So you like Italian, too."

"I'm having so much fun in my class. We examine classic paintings with a magnifying glass to see what technique the artist used. After we figure it out, we try the same technique and paint a toss-away piece. Isn't that great? Eet is zee European way."

"You've never told me your favorite artists."

"I hate that question because there are so many, but I'll try. There's Vermeer, of course. Frank Benson, Mary Cassatt, and Andrew Wyeth are wonderful. The painting of the last Russian tsar's wedding is dazzling; it's by Laurits Tuxen. Oh, and I just did a paper on William Bouguereau. I love that man."

"Maybe I'll have to learn about some guy you love."

She looked away, and he put both of his nice arms around her. Jemma's mouth suddenly felt parched.

"You are something else," he whispered. His lips touched her ear as he spoke, then he turned her chin toward him and kissed her. It was perfect, just like she had imagined. He had made her wait on purpose. Only an unexpected twinge of guilt kept her from floating off with the swarm of fireflies. He rubbed the back of her neck. "I can't quite figure you out. You've got those bedroom eyes, but you keep giving me a Sunday school smile. How about we stop by my apartment on the way home, darlin'?"

She drew back. "No."

"A good girl, huh? I kind of figured that, but you can't blame me for asking."

"Yes, I can."

"I'm glad you said no. I really am. You might be the darlin' that turns me into a one-woman man." His eyes were half-closed as he smiled at her. For an instant, he resembled a cobra emerging from its charmer's basket in a cartoon that Jemma had seen at The Parnell with Spencer.

She blinked. "So, normally, you are not a one-woman man?"

"If I had somebody like you, I could learn that life. I just need a woman with your looks and your morals because I already know that I like your style."

"My style?"

"Yeah, innocence and something extra."

"I am innocent."

"Yeah, but you've got some stuff seething in the wings, darlin', right down to that husky voice of yours. I know it when I see it."

Jemma looked at him hard. She'd never had a conversation remotely like this one with anybody except her mother or sort of with Spencer. Paul knew how to twist things around, and he was not yet a solid part of her heart. Spencer still was, though, and the promise they had made about not fooling around was very much intact.

"You're making me uncomfortable." She stood.

He grabbed her hand. "Let me tell you that the feeling is mutual. So, let's talk about something else. I have to know everything about you."

Jemma hesitated, then flopped down on the wooden steps. He was smart to let her cool off, and he extended the timeout by stroking her hair as though she were Helene's cat, Chelsea.

"I love flowers," Jemma said. "Someday I'm going to have fresh flowers all over my house. I'll grow my own roses, especially the old ones that smell so good. I'll have Asian lilies, peonies, lilies of the valley, lavender, sweet peas, but no carnations."

He eased his arm around her again. "What do you have against carnations?"

"They remind me of funerals." She moved his arm away.

He bumped her with his shoulder. "I like carnations. They smell like cinnamon. Something about you sure smells sweet."

"It's probably my shampoo."

"Hmm. . .what's your favorite perfume?"

"I haven't found one I really like. My Gram wears something called Moonlight Over Paris. That sounds intriguing to me. I like mysterious fragrances because I don't want to be like everybody else."

"Darlin', I don't think there could be anybody else like you."

"Thank you, cowboy." She looked at his watch. "We'd better start back."

It was a quiet ride to Helene's, but she did sit next to him, and unless he was shifting gears, his arm stayed around her shoulder.

"I've never known any girl named Jemmabeth."

"I'm named after my daddy, Jim, and it's become a tradition in his family to add 'beth.' My great-grandparents named my Gram, their firstborn, Lizbeth. Then came Annabeth, Marybeth, Sarabeth, and Julia—the Jenkins girls."

"Julia doesn't fit the pattern," he said.

"We call her Do Dah. That's how my uncles said her name when they were little. Papa said that Gram's parents had worked so hard to have a boy that when Do Dah came along they were all out of 'beth'—get it? My grandparents raised Do Dah because her mother died giving birth. She was born about the same time as my uncle Matthew. My grandpa, Papa, was from a Scottish family. He wore his father's kilt on holidays or just to aggravate Gram. I spent every summer with them on their farm while my parents finished college. There. Now it's your turn."

"You already know my dad and my mother died when I was in high school. I have two sisters who live in Dallas. Say, how'd you like to go dancing? There's a place in Kensington called the Handle Bar that has a great band. Let's go tomorrow night."

"What should I wear? Is it a dress-up place or what?"

"Not exactly." Paul smiled. "Wear jeans." He leaned across the seat and kissed her. She did have to watch out for those buckaroo hands of his.

❧

He picked her up with his snakeskins polished and ready. She wore her jeans and a long-sleeved, muslin shirt that her mom had given her. He didn't seem to mind that her red boots were a little on the shabby side.

"Every guy there'll be jealous of me tonight," he said, making her scalp tingle. He cranked up the eight-track player, and they sang along until he turned off the road and into a parking lot already crowded with cars.

"Wait." Jemma's eyes were like two fried eggs. "This is a bar."

"Yeah. Remember, I said it was the Handle Bar."

"I thought it was the handlebar, like on a bike or a moustache. I've never been to a bar."

"Oh, come on, darlin', I thought you told me you'd been dating every man in Dallas this past year."

"I don't drink," she said flatly, staring at the flashing neon signs.

"Really? Well, you don't have to drink. Just dance and it'll be fine. I know you're going to love this band, and old Paul will protect you from whatever dares to mess with you, I promise."

Inside, the Handle Bar was stale with smoke and beer. Jemma's twitchy smile waned as the bartender called Paul by name. They had just been seated at a table by the dance floor when the band broke out with "Treat Her Right." They moved onto the floor with several other couples. After the first few notes, Paul couldn't keep up with her. They danced every dance until he was tired and let other guys cut in, but she kept on until the band took a break. Paul ordered her a soda and winked at the waitress. Jemma needed to dance again to forget where she was.

"You're sure tearing up the floor, darlin'." He winked at her, too.

Another cowboy dragged up a chair and straddled it backward. "What's up with you, Turner? I thought you were going to call me about our Vegas trip." He nodded at Jemma and stubbed out a cigarette.

"Sorry, Kyle. Something's come up," Paul said.

The cowboy turned to Jemma. "Are you the something? You gonna break this bronco and put him out of his misery?" He took a swig of beer and planted the mug on the table.

Jemma said nothing, but watched the little bubbles slide down the insides of the glass. Her mother and daddy would be shocked to see her at this place, and Gram would disown her.

"Jemmabeth, meet my friend, Kyle, who considers himself a dancer. How about you show him a thing or two?"

Jemma turned to the husky fellow with dark blond hair and bloodshot eyes. She paused but gave in to his crooked smile and outstretched hand. The band was playing "In the Midnight Hour." Kyle was big, but he was smooth and quick. Her daddy would have used him as a linebacker. He kept up with her, but nothing compared to Spencer. She was aware of Paul's eyes on her the whole time.

She went to the bathroom when the song was over. A platinum blond was checking her makeup at the mirror, and she gave Jemma a long look before she spoke. "You're quite the little dancer, aren't you? Paul's fixin' to come unglued."

Jemma blushed. "Actually, I've never been to a place like this before."

"Drinking from the devil's cup tonight, then?"

"What do you mean?" Jemma asked as her hands dripped on the floor. "I don't drink."

"Paul Turner is what I mean."

"I like Paul." Jemma's stomach turned queasy.

The blond arched an eyebrow. "We all like Paul, kiddo. I've been down a few roads with him myself. Every woman here would die to be his only darlin', and believe me, he's a real prize. Just watch yourself. That's all I can say, because I don't think you know what you're up against." She blotted her lipstick, then left.

"The devil's cup?" Jemma whispered and looked in the mirror, blinking back tears and now feeling a solid swell of nausea. It would break Papa's heart if he could see her right now. She only hoped the world didn't come to an end in the next five minutes before she could get out of that place. But, first, she had to throw up.

It was a humorless trip home. She had drunk two Cokes, chewed a whole packet of gum to free her taste buds of barroom air, and had kept her head in the open window to rid her hair of cigarette smoke.

Paul took off his hat and put it on the seat between them. There was plenty of room, too. He ventured a comment. "I loved watching you dance tonight, Jemma."

She kept her eyes off him for once. "Isn't that what you do in places like Las Vegas?"

"I'm not following."

"If you're not going to dance with me, I'm not dancing."

"Looks like I've missed something here."

"Yeah, well, you could be missing me after tonight."

He reached for her hand, but it was quickly withdrawn. He drew a heavy breath.

"Look, darlin', I'd like to settle down. It would make my family very happy and probably be good for my health, but I'm going to need somebody to lay down the law and keep me on the straight and narrow. What do you say?"

"You want me to be your mother?"

"Heck no, I want you to be my woman."

Jemma chewed on her lip. "Just how bad are you?"

"That's not the point. The issue is that I want you more than anything, and I can see that's going to force me to be good."

She touched the brim of his hat. It couldn't hurt to bring in the Lord. "I know the Bible says not to judge people."

"Well, there you go, darlin'. I'm your man." He moved his fingertips across her cheek.

"Lesson number one is never take me to a bar again." She looked him in the eye. "And I mean it."

"Understood." He crossed his heart. "Am I forgiven?"

"Maybe," she said, half smiling. "I don't know what to make of all this stuff I've heard about you tonight. How do I know if you're really serious?"

"I'm serious all right. Don't worry about my past. It just makes me a better kisser." He gave her a sample.

Jemma sat up, moving his hands away from her. "Kissing doesn't cure everything."

"Well, it might help what's ailing me right now, my darlin'. Have mercy and give me one more."

⁂

Jemma came in from school and Helene met her at the door. "You have some lovely flowers, dear. They are quite intoxicating."

Jemma walked down the hall to the dining room. Four large vases of lilies, roses, delphiniums, and lily of the valley lit up the room with color and sweet perfume. She opened the envelope and pulled the card out just enough to see his note.

> *Hope this fills your senses for now.*
> *See you tonight.*
>   *P.T.*

"I assume they are from your young man, Spencer."

"No, ma'am." Jemma blushed at his name. "They're from Paul."

"Ah, someone new for the hope chest. Let's move them to your room."

Jemma bit her lip. "Let's leave them here." Nobody had said anything about Paul sharing her hope chest, but the flowers were an impressive start.

She raced upstairs to change. The evening could not come soon enough.

⌘

She finished cleaning around dark and drew cowboys in her sketch-book until she heard his truck. Her temples tightened when he opened the door. He was a shiny red apple in that Stetson, like the cowboys who came into Chillaton for the Fourth of July dance.

He grinned at the sight of her, sitting cross-legged on the floor. "Hungry?"

"First, I have something for you." She held out a small package. "It's just a little thank-you for one of the best surprises I've ever had."

He tore off the tissue covering and held up the painting. "You did this? It's not a Monet or something?"

Jemma giggled. "The flowers were stunning. This is only a little watercolor."

He looked right into her eyes. "No, darlin', you're the one who is stunning."

"I think you call all women 'darlin'."

He shrugged. "Could be, but when I say it to you, it's different. Remember that."

⌘

Sandy Kay called her from an army base in Germany, where her husband, Martin, was stationed. Jemma reported that it was the most thrilling summer of her life, and that her time with Paul was romantic but never juvenile. She didn't mention that he made every attempt to fool around and that she had to stay on her toes to keep the eighth-grade pledge to Spence. After all, a promise was a prom-ise, regardless of the circumstances or participants. She didn't report that information to Sandy because, within twenty-four hours, it would have been all over Chillaton and melting like butter on the sizzling tongues at Nedra's Beauty Parlor and Craft Nook.

⌘

"Aren't you getting a little carried away with this guy?" Jim asked her during their weekly phone call. "I sure hate to hear that. Maybe you should at least call Spencer, just to see how it feels."

"I don't know, Daddy. I really like Paul and I think you will, too." She didn't mention that he was almost ten years her elder, a fact she didn't dwell on herself.

"Don't rush into anything," Alex said. "You have plenty of time."

Robby was more succinct. "Cowboys are goofy, Jem. Spence is cool."

If she had never kissed Paul, things would have been easier because she did admire a great kisser. Spencer probably had himself a good kisser by now, too. Rats. That thought continued to thwart her otherwise perfect summer.

It wasn't as though Paul was everything to her. Art was her first love. At least that's what she'd told Spence the night they broke up. That memory carried her off for a few seconds, but then she snapped out of it and chose the fattest brush from one of her first-grade cowboy boots. She loaded it with white and splashed broad strokes across the canvas, giving her the base coat she wanted for the outdoor setting. She checked her notebook to study sketches of the stone walls of the garden and the Tiffany rose that would serve as background for Helene, then drew it in. She positioned Helene's head, neck, and torso on as well, then stepped back to see if she liked the composition. She added clusters of lupines and delphiniums to break up the line of the wall behind the roses. Helene would be pleased. She jotted notes in her book, selected her color palette, and opened up her portable stereo, the last gift Spencer had given her. He flitted through her brain again for a second, which wasn't unusual, but rather unprofitable, in light of the last couple of weeks.

Jemma put on her favorite Fritz Kreisler song and dipped her brush in the glistening mixture of pigments. She guided the bristles across the knobby texture of the canvas. Her fingers pulsated with the initial sensation of bringing form to fiber. She dashed and tipped the color against the canvas, as it responded to her touch, interpretation, and design. The music was inside her. The bristles struck in bursts, like milk hitting the side of Papa's bucket in the barn, then softened as the paint absorbed into them, settling into strokes like the ebb and flow of the surf when she slept on the California beach with her family. Nothing compared to re-creating life on canvas. She had known since that day in the second grade when the school principal hung her watercolor painting in his office, that her talent was a gift from God.

❧

"Talk to me about your hometown." Paul straddled the bench like a horse. They didn't even have to place their orders anymore because the cook knew what to do when the baby blue pulled in.

"Well, Chillaton isn't nearly as big as Wicklow. It's about sixty miles from Amarillo, the biggest town between Dallas and Albuquerque. Main Street and The Boulevard are paved with bricks, and we have trains that fly through town about four times a day. That's what Wicklow needs, a train."

Paul shook his head. "Once there are train tracks, it opens up all kinds of social issues."

"Surely you don't think that's the train's fault. Social issues are people problems. The tracks are merely an excuse."

He sensed trouble again. "Tell me more about this Chillaton."

She was somewhat perturbed, but his smile was so inviting. "My Gram's house is one of two houses on the last street before crossing the tracks, about eight blocks away from The Boulevard. Lots of Papa's friends tried to talk him out of buying a house so close to the tracks. Gram took a liking to it, and nothing would do but for Papa to get it for her. It's a great location if you love trains like I do."

"There are always nosy people in small towns," Paul said.

"I guess you could call them nosy, but it's more like a huge family. If you're having trouble, you'll get prayed for in various prayer circles around town, and if somebody gets sick or dies, there will be a steady stream of casseroles at your door within an hour. The postmistress, for example, knows everybody. You can write a letter to somebody in Chillaton with just a first name on the envelope and Paralee will get it to the right person. We should try it. Let's send a letter to Lester, Gram's next-door neighbor, and see if he gets it."

"I don't know as I like you writing to some man."

She laughed. "Lester is an old man. So, I can't write to any men, huh?"

He pointed a French fry at her. "You can if you want to. I just

45

wouldn't like it. I want you all for myself."

Jemma leaned over and looked him in the eye, nose to nose.

"What are you doing?"

"I have to look people in the eye when they say something important."

"You'd be a good horse trader because nobody could fool you."

"Say it again."

"I want you all for myself, darlin'."

She stayed in his face. "What exactly does that mean?"

"It means I'm hoping you won't be going out with any more piano players."

"Cello."

"Them, too."

"Are we going steady, then?"

"It's been a long time since I heard that, but yeah. If you'll have me, it would make me happier than I've ever been in my life."

Jemma kissed him like he was her steady. He did take the prize for wandering hands. The cook's radio crooned in the background.

"Oh, listen. 'True Love's Ways,' my favorite Buddy Holly song," she said.

"C'mon, then." Paul put both arms around her waist and held her close, bending low to dance cowboy style. Jemma closed her eyes, her temple against his cheek. When the song was over they danced in place anyway. Paul kissed her neck, sending those chill bumps all over her.

"I can't believe you've never had a serious boyfriend," he mumbled.

"I, uh, had the same boyfriend all through school, since the first grade."

"And?"

"He still likes me, I guess."

"Likes?"

"There's a chance that he loves me."

"How do you feel about him?"

"Oh." She stumbled over the words. "I don't know. We're kind of like brother and sister."

"Puppy love."

"How about you?"

"I do like the ladies, darlin'. Remember, I warned you that I have a reputation."

"I keep hearing that."

"I hope you aren't in love with that kid."

She responded with only the slightest negative movement of her head.

"Good."

"It's getting late," she said.

He drove home singing along with the radio. It was just as well because she was thinking about the golden-haired boy who had loved her most of her life, and that she should have had a firm answer to Paul's questions. She didn't, though.

And to top it off, when she dreamed, it was still of Spence.

Their favorite place soon became Helene's garden, and occasionally, her conservatory. Helene made herself scarce when Paul came over, but Jemma never asked about it. She was more curious, however, as to why she never got to meet Paul's family. He talked of his sisters' visits to the family home, but Jemma was never a part of the gatherings. She figured that maybe they had something against artists.

"This is a great old place." Jemma tilted her head back and scanned the gilded ceiling of The Grande Theater in Dallas while they waited for *Doctor Zhivago* to begin. "Hey, want to go to a concert? The violinist is a good friend of mine."

"I suppose I have to wear civilian clothes."

"Do you have some? I figured you wore cowboy boots even when you played football."

He grinned. "Naw, the cleats kept falling off."

Jemma could not imagine a more romantic movie to complete their night. Back in Wicklow, they held hands on the marble bench in Helene's garden.

"Close your eyes," he said, then draped her hair over her shoulder. She felt something cool and light around her throat, followed by Paul's kisses, warm and soft. "Okay, open." Even in the starlight, she could see the silver rose. "I know how much you love flowers so I thought this would be perfect for you."

"Paul, I don't know what to say." Jemma lifted the rose, then raised her eyes to his.

"Say that you won't love anybody else, ever, darlin'." He kissed her with such tenderness she knew he was becoming a one-woman man. "You and I were meant to be, and I hope this sweet feeling never ends."

"Me, too," she whispered.

"I remember the first time I ever touched you. We were sitting in the pickup right over there, and I put my arm on the back of the seat. I wanted to kiss you, but we'd just met, so I touched your shoulder, just to connect. That was a whole new attitude for me."

"I wanted you to kiss me," she murmured.

He took a deep breath. "I have to really watch it with you, and I'm not used to that. I've always had it easy with women, but you are a tough one. You've got me feeling like I'm sixteen again."

"I love the necklace," she said. Rats. What a pitiful response.

"Could you miss church next Sunday? I have to take some horses to the hill country, and I really want you to come with me. We'd be gone all day."

"Just tell me when to be ready."

He twisted a lock of her hair around his finger. "How about four?"

"In the morning?"

"Yeah, it'll be all day, darlin'."

"I can't wait." She kissed him good night, then watched him drive away.

She switched on the light in her bedroom to see her new necklace in the mirror. Spencer's senior picture was looking right at her, staring at the rose. She picked him up and touched his lips. He had to have a girlfriend of his own after a whole year. She closed her eyes and held him against her heart for a moment, then tucked the photograph, facedown, into her hope chest.

She said her prayers and asked God for some kind of big sign if Paul wasn't The One. She lay in bed, trying her best to concentrate on him and their special evening but saw instead Spence's sweet face. She didn't even try to hold back the tears. They made a slow, steady descent into her pillow.

Chapter 4
A Big Sign

The red brocade dress with the mandarin collar that her Grandmother Lillygrace had sent when Jemma was Homecoming Queen was only a tiny bit snugger. She did her hair up in a cascade of curls and wore a touch of red lipstick, the necklace, and ankle strap heels. Paul whistled when he saw her. Helene and her elderly neighbor friend, Sophia, were already seated as Jemma waved from their front row seats.

Paul slid his arm around her. "Every man in here is looking at you, darlin'."

She knew every woman in the concert hall was looking at him. Even in his civilian clothes, he was something to brag about.

She didn't hear anything else once Melanie began tuning up backstage. The house lights went down and Michael slipped in and sat at the piano. Melanie entered and nodded to him. The music began. Her long, red hair flew around her like a lighted torch.

Melanie's passion became Jemma's, and she, too, was exhausted when Melanie took her bow.

She was also unaware that Paul's eyes had never left her during the performance. He was under a spell of his own. She clung to his arm as Helene and Sophia approached.

"Delightful," Helene said. "I am so glad we came, Jemma."

"I knew you wouldn't be disappointed."

Helene turned to Paul. "What do you think, Mr. Turner?"

He kissed Jemma's hand. "She's something else."

Helene and Sophia exchanged glances and excused themselves to get some punch. Melanie played a wild gypsy song after intermission, then the final three pieces included Clayton Burgess, the cellist that Jemma had gone out with a few times. He of the folded lips did know how to play the cello.

Melanie caught her eye just before she raised the violin to

her shoulder for an encore piece. Jemma held her breath for self-preservation. It was Papa's favorite song. The Scottish tune sang from his fiddle every holiday that she could remember. Papa's cousin had played it, too, at his funeral. Jemma was a wreck, but she loved Melanie for choosing it. She hustled Paul backstage to thank her and to show him off. Melanie gave a wide-eyed nod of approval when his back was turned. They moved to the foyer where Helene and Sophia waited, but Paul was ready to leave. They passed right by the two women and Jemma could only smile.

"These shoes are killing me," he said as they raced to his pick-up. "Listen, I have to help my uncle and my dad tomorrow. We're working on a big case at the office all day because the trial starts Monday."

Jemma stopped. "Could you come by Helene's for lunch? She's teaching me to cook, continental style."

"What else can you do continental style?"

"You mean like, zee French kiss, monsieur?"

"Yeah. Cook me up one of those, darlin'."

"Maybe next year, if you've been a good boy."

"I'll keep that in mind," he said and kissed her while they walked.

Jemma, though, was lost in thoughts of Spencer at that remark. It was too close to a private joke they shared from a line in *Hud*. She broke away and ran ahead of Paul, to clear her mind, like that would matter to her heart.

❧

There was so much green in the Texas hill country, making it a complete contrast to the Panhandle. Jemma took it all in for future paintings. They had delivered two horses to a ranch that sprawled alongside the Guadalupe River. She was singing harmony with Wilson Pickett when Paul pulled off the road. He led her through a pasture that sloped down to the river.

"Nice, huh?" He rested his chin on her head. "My dad and Uncle Lloyd own five hundred acres through here. Over those hills is a spot called Rustler's Roost where stolen cattle got zapped with bandit brands. I think there's even a boot-hill cemetery over there. Someday, I'm going to build a cabin in this meadow. What do you think about that?"

"Perfect," Jemma said, not referring to the land. She could marry him if he asked her at that very moment, and she would build the cabin for him, too.

"Maybe you could paint this for me sometime." He folded his arms around her, and she held his hands to keep them out of trouble.

"I'd love to do that."

"Good. In the spring, this pasture is full of bluebonnets. The only thing that could make it more perfect would be to see Jemmabeth Turner standing in the door."

That particular combination of names roused a tender longing first engaged in junior high when she wrote *Jemmabeth Chase* and *Mrs. Spencer Chase* on every page in her diary. She looked away. He pulled her down beside him on a rock and kissed her so hard that it was almost a relief when it was over.

"Darlin', you know I've fallen for you big-time, and I'm more than ready to pop the question. I've never been so sure of anything in my life. Problem is, I have a lot on my mind right now, and I need to see some stuff through before we go over the brink. This sounds crazy coming from me, but I can't do squat for thinking about you, Jem, and I need a clear head to take the bar exam."

"You're not saying that you don't want to see me anymore, are you?" she asked, big-eyed.

He returned the look like a spooked horse. "What? Good grief, no! You own my heart, and I have no intention of ever giving you up. I just need a couple of weeks to study." The sun was gone, leaving a shimmering mix of pinks and oranges behind. They were fast becoming a part of the night. He took a deep breath and looked straight into her eyes. "I might as well say it, Jemma. I love you. I've never said that to a woman and meant it, but I do now, and with every breath I take, I love you more. I only want to cool off long enough to pass the bar."

"I suppose I can wait two weeks," she said.

He held her until the stars came out. She closed her eyes so she wouldn't look for Orion. They left the river and headed for the truck, but she had no idea how she could stand to go two weeks, even two days, without him. It was very late when they got home.

He leaned against the gate at Helene's. "Got a question for you.

What's your middle name? I can't believe I don't know that."

"Alexandra, after my mother. What's yours?"

"Jacob."

"Nice name. Paul Jacob Turner; it'll look good on a law degree."

"And on a marriage license. I like yours, too. It's beautiful, like you."

"Why are you asking about my name?"

"I need it here." He thumped his heart. "I want all of you, even your middle name." He reached for her, his hands massaging her spine until she thought she was going to melt.

"Paul," she said, catching her breath. "Do you believe in prayer?"

He frowned. "What brought that up?"

"We've never talked about religion. I've been told all my life that the Lord answers prayer, and I've started praying about us."

"Oh yeah?" he said, letting her go. He propped a boot on the railing and folded his arms. "I prayed for God to make my mother well, but He didn't. I'm not really into religion, darlin', although I'll have to start thanking God for your precious self."

"You don't get *into* religion, Paul. It's always there, as the heart of life." She needed something. "Do you read the Bible?"

"All I know is that I love you, and if religion is a part of the package, so be it. We can talk about this some other time. I just want you to remember one thing. You are mine forever, and I'll do whatever it takes to keep you. You are my one and only woman." He kissed her like he had done at the river, and Jemma's lips hurt like they'd met hot metal.

He moved his finger under her chin. "Good night, Jemmabeth Alexandra Forrester. You remember what I said tonight and I'll see you in two weeks. It'll be smooth sailing after that." He laid his English Leather cheek against hers. "I do love you, darlin'," he whispered, "like no other man could."

He walked to his truck but stopped, like he was looking for something in the gravel. She thought he might come back and kiss her again, but he didn't. Instead, he saluted her from the brim of his hat. His lights disappeared down the road, and Jemma went to her room, her head full of romance and her heart full of love, or something close.

There was one more day to go, but she couldn't wait. She loaded the painting into her car and headed to the office. All the lights were on. Her plan was to take the piece inside the office and surprise him, but his baby blue was not the only car parked in the lot. She decided to set it in the pickup. The overhead security light was not exactly museum quality, but it would be sufficient for her surprise as it beamed through the windshield and onto the canvas of the Guadalupe riverbank, replete with bluebonnets. Jemma opened the back door to the building.

A pretty blond sat in the conference room looking at a magazine. Her bare feet were propped on the table, displaying hot pink toenails. She glanced at Jemma and flipped a page.

"Well, who let you in?" she asked and made a popping noise with her chewing gum. Her makeup was flawless, and her Wind Song perfume packed the air.

Jemma smiled. "I'm sorry to bother you, but do you know where Paul Turner is?"

The blond popped her gum again but gave Jemma her full attention as their eyes met. "Well, of course I know where Paul Turner is, darlin'. I'm his wife."

Chapter 5

Tara

Helene assumed that Jemma was working in her studio and was quite surprised to find her sitting on the stone bench in the garden. Chelsea jumped in Jemma's lap, expecting a good petting, but got nothing more than a blank stare. They sat in silence while the caged lovebirds in the conservatory chatted away.

Helene adjusted her hearing aid at this somber sight. Jemma's puffy eyes and tear-stained cheeks were cause enough for alarm. "Is it your family, dearest?" Helene asked. "Has there been an accident?"

Jemma blew her nose. "Not an accident, more like a major disaster. Helene, I have to go to Chillaton for a while."

"Oh my." Helene put her hand to her chest. "Then I shall make you a boxed lunch for the journey. It won't take but a moment."

"No, really, it's okay. I meant to leave sooner, but I just couldn't." A wounded look swept over Helene and Jemma relented. "On second thought, yes, ma'am, a lunch would be nice."

They went inside and Helene puttered around in the kitchen, taking much too long to prepare a sack lunch. Finally, she turned to her. "Tell me, dear, is it that Turner man?"

Jemma bit her lip and nodded.

"Men can be such beasts. Even my dear Nebs would shut down without warning." Helene sighed and nestled the lunch in Jemma's hands. "Please give my regards to your grandmother. Chelsea and I shall miss you terribly." Jemma nodded again, but Helene lifted her young friend's chin. "We are all but a breath away from joy or disappointment. Such is life. You know that my heart goes with you. Now, carry on, dear."

Jemma lost it and collapsed against Helene's double strand of pearls. They dug into her face as Helene guided her to the little kitchen table.

"I'm sorry," Jemma wailed into a tissue. "It's just so embarrassing."

"Nonsense. You sit right there and let me make you some tea. You know, dear, sometimes it helps to talk."

"I have to get going, Helene, but thank you." Jemma picked at a spot of dried paint on her jeans. "Paul is a big fat liar. Actually, that's an understatement. He's a devil because I met his *wife* last night." The words hung in the air.

Helene gasped. Jemma took the neatly folded bag from the table and did her best to smile as they walked to the Dodge. Belongings were stuffed every which way inside. "I love you." She kissed Helene's cheek. "I just can't talk about it now. Sorry."

"You are dear to me," Helene said, her voice unsteady. Scooping up Chelsea, she retreated into the house. Jemma sat for a minute, then backed down the lane. Miss Scarlett went home to Tara, and she could go home to Chillaton.

The worst shame she had ever known until this was 'fessing up to the Sunday school superintendent when he asked if she'd been the one to scramble all the numbers on the hymn board in the sanctuary. That was a long time ago. Now a sickening thought ran ice cold through her brain. If Spencer heard that she was messing around with an old married cowboy he would lose all respect for her. That would be far worse than never seeing Mrs. Turner's husband again. If Jemma had anything left to throw up, she would have. That seemed to be her special way to deal with things these days.

As though she weren't distracted enough, it began to rain. She rolled her window down halfway to keep the windshield from fogging up and to keep her awake. Papa could have eased her guilty pain. He always claimed that he could fix anything but the weather.

When walking from one chore to another, he would set his straw hat on the back of his head and examine the sky. She would ask, "Are those rain clouds, Papa?"

Usually, he responded with, "I hope so, the coos need a wooshing."

Jemma would giggle at the old saying that he had learned from his Scottish Granny about the cows needing a washing. As she grew up, it became apparent that no weather was specifically intended for the Panhandle. Most of it had no particular place to go between the West and the Midwest, so it wandered in, sort of like Mr. Turner.

A beat-up blue pickup passed her. Rats on the devil's cup. There must have been more warning signs along the way that she missed, like that woman at the Handle Bar "going down a few roads with him." What an idiot she'd been. Her mom would know how to help. No, she couldn't tell her parents. She would tell Gram. Maybe.

The pickup was just ahead of her, its taillights guiding her through a downpour. Papa and Gram used to have a pickup. It was red and black with yellow wheels. In the hottest part of summer they'd leave it in the tractor's turn rows, and spend the day chopping weeds and Johnson grass out of the cotton. If necessary, they hired Negro field hands to help. Whole families would work until sunset, then they crammed into the back of Papa's pickup and he drove them home to colored town.

Little Jemma had been in the fields, too, in her makeshift tent off the bed of the pickup. She played with Papa's old dog that was there to fend off rattlesnakes while she drew in her Big Chief tablet. The old fellow was grateful for the shade and usually dozed while Jemma drew portraits from photographs in the *National Geographic* magazines that Gram left for her. The people in the photos seemed to know things that Jemma wanted to know. Secrets sparkled in their eyes, so she whispered make-believe secrets to the people in her drawings so that their eyes would shine even brighter. It was a little girl's game, but now the devil's secrets were another matter.

An hour away from Chillaton, the rain stopped and she turned on the radio. There was nothing but country music and scratchy radio evangelists. She turned it off and sang some of Roy's songs. The starry water tower finally came into view. It was always Christmas in Chillaton because the framework of two giant stars attached to opposite sides of the tower could be seen year-round. The day after Thanksgiving, they would be plugged in to rev up Chillaton's holiday spirit. Chubs Ivey broke his hip changing the bulbs in 1959, so the town council had voted never to replace the bulbs again. In a few years it would be pretty much dead, like she was now. Folks might as well start bringing in the casseroles for her family.

Just outside the city limits, she turned down the Farm to Market county road, past the Chase castle, to the Citizens' Cemetery. The sun was beginning to set as she rolled to a stop at the Forrester family plot. She sat in the car a few minutes before moving to the wrought-iron bench. There were fresh flowers in the sunken pot that she and Gram had put there at Easter. She stared at the headstone.

Cameron Andrew Forrester
Born to Andrew & Mary on February 10, 1887
Departed this earth on September 12, 1962
A Scotsman Glory Bound

It had been her daddy's idea to add the last line so that future generations could share Papa's pride. She ate the grapes and bread from Helene's boxed lunch, but the cheese had begun to sweat; she knew the feeling. There was nothing between her and the glitzy sunset, save a scrawny cloud and a windmill on the horizon. Movie directors sometimes came to Connelly County to catch a sunset and splice it into their films. Rats. If only the last twenty-four hours had been a movie. What happened to the big basketball captain who was cool and calm no matter what? For the last two years, she had jumped into the middle of things with no prayerful consultation whatsoever. That wasn't the way she was raised, but now the Lord might click His tongue at her prayers since this mess with Paul. She was no better than the women so disdained in the gossip at Nedra's Nook. Good grief, she had even danced in a bar, but at least she hadn't done it on the counter, half-naked, like Missy Blake did at the Western Tavern in Amarillo.

The bullfrogs by the cemetery pond began their nightly chant. She couldn't put it off any longer. She laid her hand on the tombstone and asked the Lord that if Spencer ever heard about this, the news would come from her own lips. As she drove past the Chase castle, she looked to see if his Corvette was there, but it wasn't. Good. She needed to get herself back together, big-time, before she faced him.

⋘⋙

Lizbeth's phone had rung while she was still asleep and before she had her teeth in, scaring the wits out of her. Jemmabeth had spoken so softly that Lizbeth wasn't sure what she was saying. It seemed that she wanted to come and stay with her for a reason she didn't reveal or Lizbeth couldn't hear. It had to be this new boyfriend, the one she talked about all the time and wanted everybody to meet. Lizbeth had always hoped that Spencer would be the Lord's intended for her granddaughter. There was something in Spencer's eyes that made her know he was a golden boy, but she didn't mention her preference to Jemma even when the child had announced, over a year ago, that she was going to go out with other young men.

Lizbeth had dry-mopped and dusted the front bedroom, changed the sheets, and emptied out the chest of drawers. Jemma did not say how long she would be staying, and it was very peculiar for her to leave college like this. She loved that art school so much, and she was surely their star pupil. Maybe Jemma would put some new paint on Cam's sad birdhouses. She had come at Easter and followed Lizbeth around for two days, pencil and sketchbook in hand, then mailed her a Polaroid of the final painting. It was of Lizbeth reading a letter from her baby sister, Julia. The painting was as good as anything Lizbeth had ever seen in a book. She kept the photo propped up on the television set.

❧

Gram had not asked why her eyes were puffy, but she had made her eat some toast and drink a 7-Up, the standard cure-all. Papa's clock was striking three when Jemma crept to the pouting room off the dark kitchen and lifted the hook. The door creaked as she ducked under the door frame and felt for the soldier box lid. The moonlight cast a thin beam onto the contents. She undid the necklace, felt her way to the bottom of the box, and let it drop. She stood over the trunk for a moment, then closed the lid and left. She sneaked out the back door and walked to the tracks. A watchful dog barked on the other side. She sat on the rails, the icy steel penetrating her thin nightgown. She didn't care. Maybe a freight train would come along and squash her like the worm that she was.

Chapter 6
Lost Lamb

Lizbeth got up early, thinking it would be a good time to polish the medals while Jemma slept. The child needed some rest. She looked just like she did when she had the Asian flu and ran a high fever, worrying everybody for a week.

She cleaned the pouting room and opened the soldier box. As she reached for the velvet containers, something odd caught her eye at the bottom of the trunk. She lifted out the necklace. The silver rose glinted in the early morning light. Lizbeth sank to the floor and leaned her head against the wall for a good while. She struggled to her feet and put the necklace back where she had found it, then poured herself some strong coffee. She had polished mementoes long enough. Lord willing, her granddaughter wouldn't pick up where she left off and start polishing something of her own.

❦

Jemma shot up in the bed, bumping her head on the quilt frame that Gram kept tethered to the ceiling. She hadn't a clue why she was there, but then it came back like an avalanche. She slumped down to her pillow. The curtains moved with a sudden breeze that bore the sweet perfume of honeysuckle from the front porch.

Gram tapped on the door, then sat beside her on the bed. "You know that you are welcome to stay, sugar, but you should call your folks. They'll be worried."

"Yes ma'am. I will." She paused. "It's just that I think I was in love, and I got my heart hurt pretty bad."

Gram stroked her hair. "Well, I'm here if you want to talk about it, but for now, let's get some food in you."

❦

Jemma walked around Chillaton and wound up across from her family's old house, wishing for the days when she and Spencer were the king and queen of hearts and nothing hurt for very long. What if he pulled up right that minute and looked her in the eye? He would know. She jumped as a horn sounded in front of her. Shy Tomlinson waved as his pickup disappeared around the corner. Shy had filled the bed of his pickup with dirt thirty years ago and still grew things in it, including a blue spruce. *Only in Chillaton*, she thought, and trudged home.

She called her parents, saying she needed some time off to work on her portfolio. Her daddy was adamant that she should either get back to school or come to Arizona. Her mom was more sympathetic, and they finally agreed that she could stay with Gram if she got a job and went back to school after Christmas.

When he was a toddler, Robby ran from room to room in Lizbeth's house, opening and shutting the bevy of doors, much to the adults' aggravation. To get from the living room to the kitchen, it was necessary to pass through the *good* bedroom. Before Cameron died, it was their bedroom, but since his death, Lizbeth could not bear to sleep there. She slept, instead, in the cozy shed attached to the house that Cam had enclosed the same year he passed away. The bathroom, pouting room, pantry, and a screened-in porch all branched out from the kitchen. Beyond the porch was Lester Timm's driveway that led to his garage and Lizbeth's backyard where the hollyhock patch, pecan tree, storm cellar, and the car house all beckoned to an adventurous little guy like Robby.

Jemma was comforted by the scent of coffee brewing and Gram's perfume that seemed to find its way into every corner of the house. The extra bedroom opposite the living room was hers now. Tall windows were propped open in the summer with broom handles that Cam had sawed in two. Crocheted pull rings dangled from the shades, and in the center of the ceiling was a bowl-shaped light fixture adorned with golden tassels. The wall switches were hefty pushbuttons. Lizbeth's tethered quilting frame was used once a month when she took her turn as hostess for the North Chillaton Quilting Club.

Quilting didn't interest Jemma at all. She craved instead the ground-jarring rumble of the train. That opportunity now presented itself less than a hundred yards away. Dancing on those tracks had always given her a thrill. No secrets could lurk there, and she knew just when to jump out of harm's way. However, instead of growing up safer and smarter, it appeared she was even dumber than she used to be. She had developed into a genuine nitwit.

She spread the *Chillaton Star* on the kitchenette, as Gram called it. The yellow Formica-topped table had come from Sears with its own matching vinyl and chrome chairs. There were two ads. Byron Blankenship was hoping to trade a homemade trailer for a rifle scope, and an anonymous person had lost a license plate near Farm to Market Road 2485. Jemma grinned. That bumpy dirt road led to The Hill, local parking spot for teenagers.

Lizbeth was busy making biscuits on the wooden countertop while Jemma moved around the room, touching things. The black-and-white-checkered linoleum was laid over the uneven wood floor where Robby had scooted his metal cars. She stopped at the framed print of a lamb lost in a snowdrift with a sheepdog howling for his master to rescue it. She used to think of herself as the rescuing dog, but now she was the lost lamb, plain and simple.

"Gram, do you know of any jobs in town?"

"Lester knows what's going on, and he'll be over soon, once he smells these biscuits."

Jemma was well aware that the latest gossip was all that was ever going on. The citizens of Chillaton liked to stretch out an event until it was only a shadow of the truth. That common trait probably came from enduring the wicked Panhandle wind all their lives. It had whipped them into a gentle orneriness. Lizbeth's neighbor, Lester Timms, was the best storyteller in the county. Cam had called him Windy Timms. He was a "long drink of water," according to Lizbeth, meaning he was taller than she was. Lester was skinny enough to be carried away by a chicken hawk, but his heart was golden.

Lizbeth concentrated on her Sunday school lesson after she put the biscuits in the oven. She indulged Lester unless he got on her nerves, then he had to watch it. Cam always got a big kick out of him, but since Cam's death, Lester had his heart set on Lizbeth.

She had never learned how to drive, so he took her on all her errands. He beat a path to her door two or three times a day under the guise of bringing her mail from the post office. The mail was only put up once a day, so Lizbeth knew that he was holding some back and doling it out. Were it not for the sake of good manners and lack of company, Lizbeth would have put a box on the porch and asked him to put the mail in it, but she didn't, and Lester was a patient man. Jemma knew, though, that he didn't have a chance with her Gram. Papa's robe and slippers were hanging in their closet and his shaving set still rested on the shelf under the bathroom mirror.

As predicted, Lester showed up at the screen door. "Mornin', ladies. Here's the mail crop, Miz Liz." He loved to say her name that way, drawing out the vowels in typical Texas style. He took off his hat and sat down, his silver hair reflecting the kitchen light. "Well, Jemmerbeth, it's sure good to see you. How are things down to Dallas? Run over any armadillers lately?"

"Jemma is here to stay with me until Christmas," Lizbeth explained. "She's going to be painting."

"Is that a fact? Well, sir, you got yourself in a dangerous business then. I worked on a paintin' job one time and like to have died. We was paintin' a water tank over to Cleeber, and I got up right near the top and run out of paint. I hollered down for a refill just as my rope come loose. I was scramblin' around that tank like a chicken on a windmill. Yes, sir, dangerous business." Lester helped himself to some coffee.

Lizbeth ignored his story. He knew good and well that Jemma was an artist.

"I'm looking for a paying job, Lester," Jemma said. "Do you know of any?"

He rubbed his chin. "I seen a help wanted poster at the fillin' station, but that ain't no place for a young'un like you. The Judge has that poor little child with polio. Eleanor Perkins stays nights with her, and a right nice colored woman took care of her for years, but she passed away. Her girl took over for a while, but she broke her hip, so then the granddaughter come on, but I heard she up and quit."

"I'll talk with him," Jemma said.

"The Judge stays down to his office all day or he could be holding court," Lester warned.

"Then I'll talk to Eleanor," Jemma replied.

Lester tapped his foot on the linoleum. "Jemmerbeth, you watch your step around that old McFarland goat. He's the meanest judge in six counties."

She smiled. "I just want a job. I'll go tomorrow."

After supper, the phone rang and Lizbeth held it out to her. "It's that fellow," she whispered. Jemma hung up the phone and went to sit on the porch swing. He called about the same time every night, but it was no use. She would not talk to a married man.

Chapter 7
Carolina

She sat on the tracks as the sky faded from flat cobalt to sparkling tangerine, then transformed into a blue-white spray, silhouetting the trees like a multitude of Creatures from the Black Lagoon. The wind that had kept her awake all night now mustered the tree row of elms into a frenzy of leaf and limb, summoning the arrival of the 6:23. Jemma moved off like a deaf old dog to let it pass. Sleepy-eyed passengers blinked at her wild hair and threadbare chenille robe that stirred in the force of the great Zephyr. The silver lady with the golden eye could do her a great favor now and melt away little pieces of shame in the sparks of her steel, but then it always had been a lopsided relationship. This magnificent thing enchanted her, frightened her, but never did her any favors. All Jemma could ever do was get out of the way.

Later, as she walked to The Judge's house, Pud Palmer honked at her. He was on his way to man the Chillaton Volunteer Fire Station. Pud's job was to blow the tornado warning whistle every day at noon, just to make sure it was working right. Most adults still recalled that early morning in June of '37, when a twister came through town and killed eight good Democrats. After that, everybody with a lick of sense dug some kind of a storm cellar. They got in it, too, if the whistle blew and it wasn't high noon. Folks outside the range of the whistle had to rely on radio weather bulletins and their own two eyes—or just one eye in the case of Bernie Miller, the town barber and WWI veteran.

She made her way to The Boulevard. There, separated from the rest of Chillaton by ornate wrought-iron fences, remained the trappings of wealthier days when ranchers built townhomes to display their good fortunes. The Boulevard was wide and paved with bricks all the way through Main Street. In the middle of The Boulevard were patches of blacktop where great old trees once stood. In a rash decision, they were removed to make way for motorized traffic, but it had been a super place for bike riding when Jemma was a little girl.

Although once grand, Judge McFarland's house was now in sore need of care. A three-story beauty, it was accessed by a long walkway with cedar bushes lining both sides. The porch made a horseshoe around the front of the house. Jemma had seen The Judge's little blond daughter sitting in a wheelchair on that porch many times as she walked to her dreaded piano lessons. She remembered her slightly from the first grade, too.

Eleanor Perkins had the absolute largest bosom in the county. Gram said that you could see her coming around the corner a full five seconds before she actually did. Now her double-chinned face appeared at The Judge's door. Her little pea eyes were totally lost as she flashed a toothless grin at Jemma. She whipped open the door with one hand and planted her dentures on her gums with the other.

"My stars, hon, I'd know you anywhere. You sure are a good looker, just like your mama. I know your grandma, too. She's a fine quilter, the best in the county. I remember when you was born. Now you just call me Eleanor. I knew that ever who we found to watch over our Carrie would be ever who the good Lord wanted. And there you were on the phone. Come on in and let me show you around. You can start tomorrow." She dusted off a side table with a tea towel slung over her shoulder, then clicked her teeth.

Uneasy at this sudden employment, Jemma hesitated. "I haven't talked to The Judge at all. It wouldn't be right to assume that he would hire me."

Eleanor poo-pooed that suggestion. "Don't you worry none about that, hon. The Judge and me go way back to kingdom come. If I want you for the job, he'll go right along with it, rather than listen to me talk."

That self-assessment made Jemma giggle. She drew her first taste of McFarland air, a heady mixture of cigars, disinfectant, and freshly baked sweet rolls, then followed chatty Eleanor around the house. The rooms were laid out just as she had imagined. There was a great staircase going up the middle of the house, and on the left was a parlor and to the right, a dining room. The foyer extended on both sides of the stairs and met behind them with one door to the kitchen and breakfast room, then double doors that opened into The Judge's study. On the stairs was an odd chair mounted to a platform. A track wound around the bottom of the banisters all the way up to the top of the stairwell.

Eleanor caught Jemma looking at it. "Here, hon, I might as well show you how The Crawler works. Have a seat." Jemma angled onto the foam-covered chair. "You don't have to buckle in, but you'll want to make sure our Carrie does. Of course, she'll be downstairs during the day, you know, but she needs the lung about sundown and sometimes during the day and all. Anyhoo, you'd best get used to this contraption." She pressed a button on the side of the chair and it began to crawl up the track like a snail. Robby would love it.

Huffing with each step, Eleanor gave a tour of the second floor of the house, too. Faceless ballerinas danced across the wallpaper in a corner bedroom. It was an odd little girl's room with a white canopied bed, dresser, numerous stuffed animals, and an ominous iron lung. The metallic monster resembled John Glenn's space capsule, and Jemma listened intently as Eleanor explained how to use it.

There were several closed doors, but the one she assumed was The Judge's bedroom stood open. A massive bed and antique wardrobe filled the space. There was very little art to be seen in the whole house. A portrait of the late Mrs. McFarland hung in the dining room, but it was only a cut above a truck stop print in Jemma's eyes.

The tour ended on a screened-in porch, where Carrie sat in a wheelchair. Her body, like a stem of baby's breath, was bent over a book. Her pale blue eyes met Jemma's with no hesitation.

Eleanor patted her arm. "Carrie, this is your new helper, Jemmabeth Forrester. Ain't she pretty? I've knowed her since she was a baby, and she's gonna take fine care of you, so get acquainted ever how you want to. I've got to check on something in the kitchen."

Carrie sized Jemma up with a quirky grin. "I've seen you in the *Star*. Homecoming Queen, cheerleader, all-state basketball, and Miss Chillaton High School. You and your ex-boyfriend were the darlings of everything." Her blond hair was cut very short, like a boy's. A long smock hung on her and made her look like a paper doll whose clothes could be changed on a whim.

Jemma caught the *ex*-boyfriend reference. "I'm not exactly sure that I have this job because I haven't talked with your father at all."

Carrie's eyes were intense, making Jemma look away first. Surely she didn't know about Mr. Turner. That hadn't made the paper yet.

"Sorry I was staring, but you used to take lessons from Miss Mason next door," Carrie said.

Jemma laughed. "Yeah, for some reason, my parents thought I was going to be a great pianist, but after a few years of lessons, they gave up. I remember seeing you on your front porch."

"I hope you don't get bored around here. It's not exactly scintillating fare. You should bring books or something."

Jemma, impressed with Carrie's straightforward approach, nodded. "I might read, but I'll probably draw. I'm an art major. Or at least I was." It was the first time she had admitted that status to herself.

"Oh yeah. You won some kind of national competition. Are you a college dropout now?"

"I suppose you could say that. I think I'll just call it a semester off. How do you spend your time? Apparently, you read the *Star* a lot."

Carrie shrugged. "I'm not exactly helpless like Eleanor makes me sound."

"So, you *were* rolling your eyes a minute ago."

"Well, obviously I can't dance, but I do play the piano. I took lessons from Miss Mason, too. She came twice a week, sort of like a house call. I think my father paid her big bucks to make the effort."

"What kind of music do you play?"

Carrie pointed to a leather ottoman. "Open that thing up and take a guess."

Jemma peeked inside. It was filled with classical sheet music. "I have a friend in Dallas who is a concert violinist. You two would get along great."

"Someday I want to break out in a rock 'n' roll frenzy. I can pick up songs by hearing them once. Do you have any records? Eleanor listens to country-and-western music, and Dad never plays music at all."

"I'm loaded with records and a portable stereo."

"Bingo." Carrie stuck out her hand. "It's good to meet you, Jemmabeth. I think our destinies are sealed."

Jemma clasped the slender fingers in hers. "Call me Jemma. What's that you're reading?"

"*The Feminine Mystique.* I have to hide it from my father."

"Really. I didn't know anybody in Chillaton would read that one."

"I like to live on the edge of propriety."

Jemma laughed, liking her even more. "I'll see you tomorrow."

In the kitchen, she addressed Eleanor's broad back. "What time should I come in the morning?"

Eleanor wiped her hands. "Oh, my lands, hon, I should have told you that. Get here by eight, then you can leave ever when I come back. Now, we'll both be here of a morning, but I'll be doing housework. Plus, I can't miss my shows. I don't have a TV set at home, you know." Eleanor stirred a steaming pot as she spoke. She raised a spoon to her lips, then shook her head. "I shouldn't do that 'cause just a spoonful of beans sends me higher than a kite. I'm right up there with that astronaut fellow. Gas, you know. It's a good thing that you're a strong Panhandle girl, because you've gotta do things around here—ever what comes up." She went into The Judge's office and came right back with his typewritten instructions.

"Is Carrie her real name?" Jemma asked as she folded the paper and put it in her purse.

"Let me see." Eleanor's lips puckered in concentration. "We've called her that for so long. She was named after one of them states, ever which one her mama was from. The Judge calls her by it when he's of a mind to."

"Carolina?"

"Why just look at you, figuring that out so quick like. I think you're gonna be real good for Carrie. Law knows she needs something, poor thing."

"Thanks for the tour." Jemma skipped down the front steps.

Eleanor pushed open the screen door. "Hon, this ain't none of my business, but I sure did hate to hear that you cut things off with the Chase boy. He's had a hard time of it, what with his mama being a drunk and all. Maybe you'd better think on it. He's such a sweet one."

Jemma's head bobbed in agreement. *Welcome home.*

She walked home against the wind, holding on to her skirt so it wouldn't blow up. Dirt peppered her bare arms. Panhandle winds could blast a fleet of ships across the Atlantic in one afternoon. Papa always said that a smart man would spit every five minutes just to make room for more grit to sift into his mouth. Even the trees that lined the highway were bent from years of yielding to the wind. On the other hand, it kept windmills whirling and thus water flowing for farmers and ranchers. Only on hot summer nights, when it was actually welcome, did the wind die down to nothing. Kind of like love.

Lizbeth had the table already set for supper.

"I have the job, I guess," Jemma said as she filled her plate with tomatoes and fried okra. She added a small portion of meat loaf to keep Gram happy.

"It'll be all over town tomorrow," Lizbeth said. "Eleanor's quite the gossip. Did you meet The Judge?"

"No, ma'am. Did you know that his daughter is a pianist? I can't believe that she still has to sleep in that iron lung. Good grief, we have sent monkeys and people into orbit. Haven't we learned anything about polio?"

Lizbeth was thinking about something else. "When you were about five years old, we all went to hear the governor give a speech. It was after the Fourth of July barbeque and you were playing with your dolls on the courthouse lawn. The Judge's little girl came over and the both of you were having a good time until her mother came looking for her. I guess she'd wandered away. You probably don't remember that she was in your class in school. It was the next summer after your first-grade year that her mother died in that wreck, then the child got polio. Such a shame. Most folks believed she caught it when The Judge sent her down South to stay with her mother's people for a while."

Jemma moved the meat loaf around her plate. "It doesn't seem fair. Why her; why not me?"

"All I know is that we can't be second-guessing the good Lord. He is our Creator and we are His creation. We mustn't forget that."

❦

The Judge was still at the table, reading the Amarillo *Globe*, when Jemma arrived early for her first day of work. He filled the chair with his dark brown suit. Jemma could detect a partial comb-over, too.

Eleanor was fussing around in the kitchen, so Jemma walked right up to him. "Hello, sir, I'm Jemmabeth Forrester. I hope that you approved of Eleanor hiring me to help take care of Carrie. That's sort of funny—*care of Carrie*."

The Judge folded his paper and looked at Jemma over the top of his glasses. "My daughter's health and comfort are not a matter for childish humor, so I assume you will take your responsibility seriously. I pay a dollar twenty-five an hour, and I expect you to remember that you are an employee, not a guest, in my home." He stroked his beard, his eyes boring through hers, like she'd already messed up. He scooted back his chair. "Eleanor, that was a fine breakfast, as usual. Good day, Miss Forrester."

"It's, ah, good to meet you, sir, and don't worry; I'll take great care of her." Jemma extended her hand, but he ignored the gesture.

"I'll be the judge of that," he said and left the room.

Chapter 8
Latrina

Her wimpy plan was to leave the Dodge at home and walk everywhere in case Spencer happened to be driving around. She'd probably hide if she saw him, but it was worth a chance. Maybe she could pretend to faint or something. She'd just crossed the street that ran behind the tennis courts at the high school when she spotted a tall black girl shooting baskets on one end of the courts. She couldn't resist.

"Hey, want to play some one-on-one?" she yelled, pulling her hair up into a ponytail.

"Sure," the girl shouted back.

It felt good to play her old sport again. After about half an hour, though, it was a draw.

"Let's quit," Jemma said, panting. "I'm so out of shape, I may faint. You're good. What's your name?"

"Trina Johnson. That's some jumpshot you've got, girl. I'd be outta shape, too, but I've been playing on a junior college team," she replied with a dimpled grin.

"That makes me feel a little better. I'm Jemma Forrester." She wiped her forehead, and like any good artist, studied Trina's face. Her eyes were like slanted almonds and her lashes were extra long, like Paul's. "I always wanted dimples like yours. In the first grade, I drew them on with my mom's eyebrow pencil, but they looked like moles. Do you live in Chillaton?"

Trina jerked her head toward the tracks. "Right over yonder, all my life."

"Really? We could've used you on our basketball team. That would've been fun. We came in second at state my senior year. When did you graduate?"

"In '63. I went to the colored school over in Red Mule."

"Whoa, that's an hour from here."

"Hour and forty-five minutes on the bus, one way, what with stopping to get kids."

"You're kidding." Jemma chewed on her lip. "I'm really sorry you had to do that. Listen, I need to get home, but I live near the tracks myself, with my grandmother. You want to walk with me?"

"Thanks, but I need to shoot some free throws. I'll see you around." Trina resumed her dribbling.

"Maybe we can play again if I get in shape," Jemma shouted.

Trina flashed her dimples and waved. Jemma walked home, thinking of what she would have done for almost four hours, round trip, to get to school and back for twelve years. It was a ten-minute walk, even against a stiff wind, from her old house to her own high school.

After supper, Lizbeth took her quilt pieces out of the cigar box and glanced at her granddaughter. "Are you doing math, sugar?"

Jemma read from her page of figures. "Around eight thousand— that's about how many hours those kids sat on a school bus for twelve years, just to get to Red Mule and back. Over a year, wasted. I can't believe that happened in this country."

Lizbeth put her sewing aside. "Well, honey, we let them do it. We probably felt real smug that we were even sending colored children to school."

"It never even crossed my mind. I went about my big social life and never gave it a thought. Where did I think they were going to school? At the Dew Drop Inn?" She wadded up the paper and pitched it on the coffee table, then slumped on the couch. "I'm ashamed of myself. I could have written letters to Congress. I should have done something. Rats."

"I'm not sure folks would have paid you any mind," Lizbeth said, clearly heavy with her own fresh sense of guilt. "It was a part of life that nobody talked about. Why didn't I say something? I knew where all those little children were going to school. We've been boxed up in our own little world, but maybe things will change now."

Jemma went outside. She sat on the rails surveying the ramshackle houses on the other side until the sun went down.

"Boy howdy, it's so hot, I seen dirtdobbers carrying an ice cube into their nest," Lester announced. "Don't see that every day." He waited for a laugh, then proceeded. "I'm thinking about sleeping on my porch tonight in my new swimming shorts. Got the pinkin' shears and whacked off about two feet of my oldest overalls. Maybe I'll run through the sprinkler, too."

"I trust you'll be in your backyard for that," Lizbeth said.

He closed his eyes and inhaled. "I smell a piece of heaven done come down to earth."

Lizbeth tried not to smile. "The pie has to cool, Lester."

"No offense, Jemmer, but you been giving any thought to the Chase boy?" he asked.

"Lester. That's none of your affair," Lizbeth chided, but she kept a close eye on Jemma's reaction.

"I'm too busy with my job and painting for boys," Jemma replied. Now she could add lying to her list of sins. She jangled her car keys. "I think I'll run to the grocery store before it closes. Do you need anything, Gram? Remember, I'm sharing the bills around here."

"I'll go with you." Lizbeth deposited her sewing on the end table. "I'm making a new recipe to take to the quilting club tomorrow."

"Well, now, looks like I'd better get on home myself," Lester said. "Gotta get things set up for my sleepin' arrangements tonight, but I could sure use a piece of that pie when you get back."

"Don't fall off your porch, Lester," Lizbeth said. "We'll see about pie later."

⋘⊛⋙

Jemma, fresh from the bank, stood in the middle of the kitchen, sizing up the walls. "I want to paint something different."

Lizbeth looked up from her reading. "Not another picture of me, I hope."

"No ma'am, I want to paint a room. I know that you like blue."

"Help my life, you are your Papa's child. I don't think this old wallpaper will hold up under paint."

Jemma waved her hand. "Oh, I'm ripping that off. We're going to do this right. I've got it! We can do a *trompe l'oeil* and knock the socks off your quilting club." Jemma ran her hands across the wallpaper.

"A what?" Lizbeth had seen this behavior before when Cam would get a wild hair.

"It means to fool your eye. It's a mural, only very realistic. What would you like? A countryside, a garden, a river?"

"Sugar, you are making my head spin. I need to think about this."

Jemma put her hand over her mouth. "I'm sorry, Gram. Maybe you like your walls just the way they are, and here I'm trying to change them."

"No, no, it sounds like a fine idea. I'll sleep on it, and we can talk in the morning. Maybe you could paint something that your papa would have liked. He loved flowers and he loved his farm."

Jemma grabbed her sketchbook. "I'll do both or whatever you say. I can make the background from wall paint and I'll do the details with the acrylics Helene sent. Maybe just one corner could be a mural. I'll use lots of blue since that was his favorite color, too."

Lizbeth was not listening. She watched as the wind rippled through the pecan tree. Jemma stopped yakking and kissed her grandmother's cheek. "I know you miss the farm, so maybe this is not such a good idea."

"I miss him, honey, but the old home place was a part of him. Once he had that heart attack, the doctor said no more farming. Cam couldn't live on that place and not farm. You know all that. I'm just going on, showing my age." Lizbeth poured her coffee into the sink and wiped the table. She leaned against the counter. "Flowers. We need flowers in this room. I don't have to wait until morning to see that."

⋘≫

Working with Carrie had to be the best job anybody could have and still get paid. Carrie was smart, quick-witted, well read, and could play the piano like nobody's business. She watched the TV soaps with Eleanor, who got into the characters and plots like they were for real while her false teeth soaked in a jar by the breadbox. Jemma brought her portable stereo every day so Carrie could listen to rock and roll.

Carrie was in the "circus cannon," as she called it, for a scheduled breathing session, so Jemma brought the stereo into her bedroom.

She moved the lamp table to reach the outlet and spied a necklace on the floor. The clasp was broken, but a small locket was still attached to it.

Jemma held it up to the cannon. "Is this yours?"

Carrie shook her head.

"There's an *L* on it. Who would that be?"

"Latrina," Carrie whispered.

Jemma put the locket in her purse. On her way out that evening, she stopped in the kitchen. "Eleanor, how could I find Latrina, the girl who was here before me?"

"Law, hon, just go across the tracks and her mother's house is on the first street to your right. You'll know it by all the flowers out front. Why are you askin'?"

"I found her necklace, so I thought I would take it to her." Jemma shut the door.

Eleanor turned back to her work. "Just don't go after dark, is what I say."

❧

Jemma had been "across the tracks" with Papa when he went looking for day workers. He drove around the neighborhood until someone came outside to the porch of a house. Then Papa would stop and talk with the grown-ups while she sat in the pickup and stared at the kids who appeared from nowhere to stare back at her. She was too young to pose any abstract social questions. Life was concrete—she was in the pickup and they were on their porch. The differences in skin color did puzzle her. Once in a while she would see some of the children and teenagers going up the balcony stairs at The Parnell on Saturday night. She even asked her daddy why she couldn't sit up there, too. Yet, even now, the cluster of shacks, outhouses, the Negro Bethel Church, and the Dew Drop Inn store remained a murky reality.

She scanned the street for dogs and spied a scrawny one emerging from under a porch. He barked a few times, then retreated. The house with all the flowers was easy to spot. Anything that would hold soil was full of petunias. Old boots appeared to be a favorite, and some looked better than Jemma's own. She made her way up the hard dirt path leading to the house. A homemade sign was nailed to a porch post—Does Ironing and Guarantee Her Work. It shimmied in the wind. A sturdy rocker and two odd chairs rested on the plank porch, and inside, a radio was tuned to the same station Papa had liked. On the screen door were scattered puffs of cotton held there by bobby pins. Jemma knew about those human-crafted spider webs designed to scare off flies. She touched one.

A stocky young man appeared in front of her. "What do you want?"

Jemma stepped back. "I'm looking for Latrina. Does she live here?"

"Trina, some white girl's here," he yelled.

"What's the matter, Weese, don't you have any manners at all?" Trina pushed open the door and grinned.

Jemma shook her head. "Dumb me. I didn't make the connection. We played basketball last week."

"Yeah, I know," she said. "You wore me out."

Jemma motioned toward the kitchen. "Is that your brother?"

"Weese?" Trina laughed. "Naw, he's one of Mama's strays."

"I think I have something that belongs to you." Jemma handed her the locket.

Trina clenched the locket in her fist and moved to the path, glancing over her shoulder. "My boyfriend thought that Latrina sounded too much like a latrine and he said he dug way too many of them in the army to kiss one." She took a few steps into the street and lowered her volume. "I thought I might've dropped this somewhere in her room. Thanks."

"You're welcome." Jemma followed along. "How weird that we both worked with Carrie."

Trina exhaled. "I miss seeing her. She made me laugh."

"She says the same thing about you. Why did you quit?"

Trina looked toward the house where Weese had perched on the steps. "Carrie wasn't the problem."

"Ah, His Honor. He's such a grump, and he keeps Carrie shut up in the house like she has leprosy or something. Did you have a fight with him?" Jemma asked, watching Weese, too, though she didn't know why.

"Something like that," Trina said.

"Well, if you ever want to talk about it, I live just across the tracks. You can see the big pecan tree from here."

"I know. Mama told me."

"Come over and we'll get a Dr Pepper at the little Ruby Store. I guess I'd better be getting back. I try to paint every day and I don't want to get behind. See ya." Jemma moved to the high grass by the tracks.

"Hey, wait," Trina yelled and caught up with her. "The Judge, well, you don't want to be around him by yourself if he's been hitting the bottle heavy."

Jemma nodded. "I thought as much, but thanks for the warning. Is that what happened with you?"

"Yeah. He kind of got friendly with his hands, if you know what I mean."

"I can guess," Jemma said.

"My mama doesn't know, so please don't tell anybody, okay?"

"I won't say a word."

"It's just that The Judge has been real good to Mama, and she would be upset if she knew that he was messin' with her baby."

"Did he hurt you?"

"That old tub of lard? He didn't do much of nothin' except blow his whiskey breath down my shirt. Claimed he liked my necklace and wanted to get a better look at it."

"Well, if he ever tries anything like that with me, he's going to get a surprise. I've seen my share of *Saturday Night Wrestling* on TV."

Trina laughed, then clamped her hand over her mouth as Weese moved off the porch. "I don't think The Judge will mess with a white girl. He probably doesn't even remember."

"So, that guy you mentioned, is he still your boyfriend? What's his name?"

"Nick Fields. He's in Dallas, studying to be a doctor, and I'm stuck here. Mama said your boyfriend was that Chase boy, but that you dropped him. Mama irons for the Chases when their housekeeper is out of town."

Jemma sighed. "News sure gets around in Chillaton."

"So you're looking for love, huh?"

"I don't know what I'm looking for," Jemma said, meaning it.

The screen door flew open and a large woman wearing a feed sack dress and a white, starched apron held it back with a cane. "Latrina, who you talkin' to out here?" she shouted.

"Mama, I thought you were gonna take a nap," Trina said. She turned to Jemma. "C'mon, now you've gotta say hello."

Jemma smiled and walked up to the porch. "Hi. I'm really glad to meet you. I'm Jemmabeth Forrester." They clasped hands, and Jemma was struck with a feeling of sweet honesty at Willa's touch. There were no dimples, nor were her eyes slanted like Trina's, but they met hers straight-on.

"I'm Willa Johnson. Ain't you a pretty one. We seen you grow up, child. Ever time your grandpap come over looking for hands, I'd peek out the door and see how much littler you were than my Latrina. Now it looks like you two are just about the same."

Jemma's smile wavered. "I'm sorry that I never met y'all until today. That makes me mad at myself."

"Well, we can't do nothin' about the past, can we?" Willa proclaimed. "All's we can do is keep on walkin' the road that Jesus give us, and try to do right by each other in the here and now."

"Mama, she doesn't want to hear a sermon. Thanks for coming over, Jemma," Trina said.

Willa stood in the doorway. "It's good to say hello and see you all growed up, face-to-face like this. You come back any time."

"Thanks. I will." Jemma walked to the tracks and looked back. She had missed out on something over the years, and it had left a vacant corner in her life that she had never noticed. Rats. She vowed right there on the tracks that things would change.

Chapter 9
Assumptions

"Did I ever tell y'all how my second wife died?" Lester finished off his bowl of Golden Vanilla ice cream and set it on Lizbeth's front porch. "Well, sir, we had a storm come along 'bout dinnertime, and I'd just gone to shut up the henhouse. The missus was still at the table when I left. The rain was movin' in fast, so I was tryin' to move even faster. All of a sudden my arm hairs—excuse me, Miz Liz—come hence to pricklin', then BAM, this ball of fire knocked me plumb to the ground. When I come to, there lay the missus, flat-out in the dirt no more than ten feet from me with one of the milkin' buckets atop her head. She was a goner. For the life of me, I still hadn't figgered out why she come outside with a metal bucket on her head like that. Beat all I ever seen. Ruint my bucket, too."

"How many times have you been married, Lester?" Jemma asked.

"Well, let's see. First there was Bertie, who died with the flu. So I married Mae Ella, the one I was just talkin' about. Then here come Zippy. Of course that wasn't her real name. It was somethin' like Zipporah. My last, Paulette, was part French. I ain't sure which part. Anyhow, she had a bad ticker and keeled over one mornin' with a dad-gummed heart attack. I hated to see her go. She was a ringtail tooter."

"You were married four times?" Jemma asked.

"I reckon that's right. Truth is, Zippy run off, and after a few years batchin', I went before The Judge and he figured she was a goner, too. So I married Paulette. She had a good bit of money from her first husband. Thanks to him, I can live on my railroad pension. Paulette was workin' at the drugstore when I met her. She was makin' malteds and whatnot, but she didn't need the money. Maybe that old Zippy will show up here one of these days, and I reckon we'd still be married."

Lizbeth cleared her throat, and Lester changed the subject. "I don't know if y'all know it, but I heard down to the post office that Shorty Knox is lookin' in windows again. He must be near seventy by now, and he's been peepin' in windows for sixty of them years. Back in the Dust Bowl days, folks come hence to askin' Shorty when the next duster was comin'. He could predict them nasty things. I reckon he had extra sense about that kind of stuff 'cause he knew it was coming before the radio did. Anyway, you ladies best keep your doors locked up tight. 'Course Shorty don't do nothin' but look in. He's got himself a foldin' stool now. The sheriff took his old stool away the last time they hauled him in. I reckon that's hard on a fellow to be a peepin' Tom and himself no taller than a cookstove. He took a fancy to one of them high school teachers last year and come hence to starin' in her window at school until the principal had to call the sheriff. Shorty heard the police car comin' so he climbs up on top of the announcer's stand at the football stadium and won't come down for nothin'. Only come down when the sheriff promised him a new stool. That takes the cake, our own sheriff helpin' a criminal. I guess y'all know I'm just a holler away if y'all ever need a man to protect you."

Lester clicked his tongue in Lizbeth's direction. She, of course, didn't look up.

Eleanor stayed late to shell a bushel of black-eyed peas. She dumped the contents of a basket on the kitchen table and gave Jemma and Carrie each a lapful to work on. "Jericho McKinney is in the hospital up to Amarillo. Do you know her, hon? Lives over by the old skatin' rink." Eleanor's teeth were in the jar, so every *S* whistled, like Sylvester the Cat.

Jemma grimaced at the peas in her lap. "Yes, ma'am. I know her."

"Jericho was at the football game on Friday. They follow all them games even though they never had any kids at all. Ever where the team goes, they go. I don't know why she ever give that man of hers the time of day. Law knows he's chased ever who wore a skirt in this town and even got Vela Crane p.g. down to Cleebur. 'Course he can't hold a candle to Max Chase, but Mr. Chase never got nobody p.g. that I know of, exceptin' Mrs. Chase. Law knows how she puts up with him, 'course they had themselves that sweet child, Spencer. Now, that boy is a wonder."

Jemmabeth flushed at that revelation and wondered what Eleanor would say about her if she knew about Mr. and Mrs. Turner.

"Anyhoo, Jericho was at our own football stadium, and you know all they've got is them dinky little bathrooms. It beats all I ever seen how they can build a fancy ball field, then throw up them scrawny necessary rooms, thinkin' ever what's built is good enough to do your business in. They're probably nasty, too. Well, she was in one of them stall things, and it seems she had on a new kind of girdle that's got legs in it, not like the good kind that's shaped like a water hose. There's no tellin' how much them new ones cost. Ever how much that man of hers makes over to the light plant, it can't be enough to put up with him anyway. Now where was I?"

"Jericho had a new girdle," the girls said in unison.

"Law, yes, hon. Anyhoo, she hitched up her dress, got that thing halfway down, lost her balance, and slipped clear down to the filthy floor. I heard she hit hard, too, but she didn't just hurt herself. She got her feelings hurt. Went down between the commode and the cinderblock wall and couldn't get up to save her life or reach her dress to cover certain things up. She was stuck like a wienie in a bun. She let out a holler for help, but it all happened toward the end of the game when the score was tied and everybody was carryin' on so loud that you couldn't hear nothin'."

Eleanor burped softly and went on with her story. "Sheriff's deputy, Faylon Price, was having to go himself right next door, and heard the racket that Jericho was makin' so he busted in the door. She had it latched, you know. He claims that he shut his eyes as soon as he saw her state, but I figure he had himself a good peek."

"Faylon saved her then," Carrie prompted.

"Law, no, hon. It took a plumber to do the job. They had to take the toilet out and her with a smelly locker room towel draped over her while they did it. Ever how you look at it, Jericho had a bad deal. She was mortified to the point that the poor thing won't even talk now. I bet she burns that girdle riggin' as soon as she gets home. I know I would, plus I'd throw her mister on the pile, too. They say she cracked a couple of ribs, but I think she's havin' a nervous breakdown, myself."

Eleanor collected the shelled peas and rinsed them in the sink. "I'm takin' a loaf of bread over to her mister and I sure hope he don't try nothin' with me." She sighed and stared out the window. The girls didn't dare look at one another.

Eleanor cut herself a generous slice of bread. "Now Jericho herself runs a nasty kitchen. I personally seen her cat walk around on the table just before they come hence to eatin'. That cat was lickin' the gravy only five minutes before I had a servin' of it. When folks ain't clean in their kitchen, they ain't clean in life. That's what my mama said. Of course that don't mean she deserved to have a nervous breakdown. Jericho's been packin' on the pounds lately, and that's why she was tryin' a new girdle. I reckon she squeezed into a large, on account of wishful thinkin'. I'm out for comfort myself." Eleanor hoisted her significant bosom right onto the tabletop. "Anyhoo, you given any more thought to the Chase boy, hon? He's a keeper."

"Uh, maybe," Jemma said. She didn't mention that she drove by the Chase castle every day to see if his car was there. She didn't have a clue what she would do if it showed up.

"Did y'all have dances in high school?" Jemma asked Trina as they sat in the sunny hollyhock patch, painting their toenails with Rose Sensation polish and listening to Jemma's transistor radio. They were easy company and had shared most of their secrets.

"We had the best," Trina said. "The school over in Monroe would come, too."

"Monroe? Isn't that a hundred miles from here?"

"Yeah, from here, but not from Red Mule. They had some fine-looking boys."

Jemma rubbed baby oil on her arms and legs. "We had ours at the old WPA barracks across from the feed store. They knocked out some walls, and it was just one long, rocking place. Once we got started on the Chillaton Stomp, the light bulbs would swing like crazy. Sometimes you could taste the dust from the thirties falling out of the ceiling and into the punch."

"What's the Chillaton Stomp?"

"The jitterbug and bop combined. You know how Chillaton is. It's always behind any new style of dancing, clothes, or you name it. I think they just heard about hula hoops last week." Jemma laughed.

Trina gave her a sidelong glance. "You really think I knew how things were across the tracks?"

Rats. Jemma took off her sunglasses. "Trina, I hate it that you were just right over there and I never knew you. I am ashamed of that. Honest."

A sudden breeze caught Lester's wash on his clothesline, flipping a dozen socks into motion.

"I always wondered why the good Lord didn't leave everybody as skeletons. Then we could all be alike," Trina said. "Nobody would be a different color or too fat or real ugly."

They giggled at the idea.

"Good one, but then my art would be really boring. Didn't you feel weird every time you saw how different things were across the tracks? It's so unfair and unequal. I think I would've been angry at the injustice."

Trina raised her brow. "Like Weese? Naw, Mama wouldn't put up with that kinda attitude. She's got her own way of living and behaving. It doesn't matter to her who you are or where you live. That's why folks are always sending their lost sheep to her. She makes 'em toe the line."

"So you toed it."

"I never really wanted to step off it. Mama has a good handle on the Scriptures and that's the way she raised me. How about you?"

"I've been going to church all my life, every Sunday."

"Going to church doesn't mean you really live by the Scriptures, though."

"I'm a good girl. I believe everything that's in the Bible, and I say my prayers every night."

Trina shook her head. "I'm talking about the Lord taking care of every day. I mean flat-out giving it over to Him, on purpose. Even when things don't seem to go the way you're hoping, you still read the Scriptures, do what they say, and tell Him your worries. He'll do what's best for you. That's living by the Scriptures."

"Then why pray if God's going to take care of everything?"

"We're supposed to thank Him and praise Him. It doesn't hurt to ask for your way, too, but you have to be willing to live with His answer. I don't make a move without listening really good first."

Jemma gave that some thought. "How'd you get to be so smart?"

"Mama, Grandmama, and Brother Cleo," Trina said.

"I think I must not have been listening in church. I was probably thinking about Spencer." Jemma got lost in that memory for a minute.

"So, how come your team didn't win the state basketball tournament?" Trina asked.

"Rats. I hate this story. We were behind one point with five seconds left in the game. I got the ball and jumped one in with three seconds on the board. They threw the ball down court, picked up a foul, and won with two free throws. It was the pits. I should have waited and run out the clock before I shot. You would've thought of that."

"Maybe." Trina shrugged. "Sometimes two heads are better than one. I guess it wasn't meant to be."

The 3:37 Zephyr blew its horn, punctuating their thoughts.

⌘

That night Jemma bought everybody burgers from Son's Drive In, and they ate them on Willa's porch. Weese left his in the sack.

"What we need around here are more fireflies. Did you see many fireflies in Dallas, Trina?" Jemma asked.

"Yeah. We called 'em lightning bugs. I guess they're the same thing."

Weese spat a wad of chewing tobacco. "Why you bringing food over here? Just give us the money instead."

"Weese!" Willa banged her cane on the porch. "Mind your manners, young man."

"There are all sorts of bugs that can light up," Jemma said tentatively. "There's a beetle in Europe that can shine, but only the male can fly. The females spend their whole lives crawling everywhere they go."

"Sounds just like people to me." Trina shot Weese a look. "Men strutting around showing off, and the women down on their hands and knees, scrubbing."

Willa planted her cane and stood, ready to call it a night, but first she fired off a few choice comments. "Just like them little bugs makin' their own light, you can't wait on nobody to take care of you. If'n you crawl 'round on your belly all your life, don't be puttin' blame on nobody else. Ask the good Lord to show you the way, then pull yourself up and work it out. If you get to fly, well then, that's Him puttin' a blessin' on you and helpin' you along. Good night, girls, and you watch your mouth, Weese."

Weese stepped off the porch, spat another glob of tobacco near Jemma's foot, and ambled down the dirt road.

⌘

Lester was on his third cup of coffee. It was so hot that he poured it in the saucer and sipped it like soup. "I bet Jemmer don't know about the big floods we used to have around here. Some fields was taken as fishin' holes by city folk. Scratch Mason's outhouse floated clean out in the middle of his field with himself yellin' out for dear life from the roof. Beat all I ever saw. 'Course we ain't had that much rain in twenty year or more. Not since the Republicans got into the White House."

"I believe JFK was, and LBJ is, a Democrat," Lizbeth said, rolling out piecrust.

Lester tapped his foot and looked out the window. "That Kennedy feller was a Catholic, though."

"There are a lot of good Catholics in this world," Lizbeth added, "the same as with any other church."

Lester sniffed. "Used to have whoppin' sandstorms, too. When the sky turned black with dirt and it was the middle of the day, we called it a duster. A feller could see one comin' for a hundred miles off. 'Course Shorty knew it first. The wind come hence to howlin' for two or three hours, solid, and the sand would pile up and wedge itself between your teeth and your gullet. It was like a swarm of chiggers on your bare skin. If the missus left the wash on the line, it'd look like you drug it behind a plow horse. That sand would drift plumb up over barbed wire fences. Why, half our dirt's bein' plowed in Oklahoma right now. The other half got here from New Mexico yesterday. That's why farmers gotta work so dang hard to make a living. It ain't even Texas dirt."

"Lester, you're giving me a headache."

He lowered his voice. "Well, now, I'm just trying to educate this young lady here. 'Course nobody can ever forget what happened to old F.G. Powers durin' one of them big dusters."

Lizbeth sighed as she cut slits in the top crust. "Jemmabeth doesn't even know F.G. Powers."

That was all the invitation Lester needed. "Well, sir, him and his missus were leavin' church when one of them dusters let loose and turned day right smack-dab into night. He come hence to yellin' for the wife and she was yellin' right back, to get their bearings. Old F.G. climbed up into his wagon, all the time still hollerin' over to the wife to make sure she was in the wagon. The Powers place was just down the road so their old mule lowered his head and pulled them up right by the front door. Now this is the gospel truth. F.G. helps his wife down and into the house. They get inside and, lo and behold, if F.G. don't give his wife a little celebration hug only to find out that he's got ahold of old lady Pinkerton instead of the missus. Old lady Pinkerton claimed she was as surprised as F.G., and that she couldn't tell for sure which wagon she was gettin' into. 'Course everybody knew that she was lookin' for herself a man and had been for near fifty year. Her face stopped many a decent clock."

Lizbeth reached for the aspirin on the rack above the kitchen sink. She shook it, too, for effect, but Jemma wasn't sure if Lester even noticed.

"Hi, cutie pie." Jemma gave Lizbeth a kiss on her cheek. She hung her purse on the hall tree and set the table. "I'm so excited about using the car house as a studio. Lester is going to help me do a few things to it tomorrow."

Lizbeth cleared her throat. "A letter came for you today; it's on the table there. The return address is that law office in Wicklow. I thought it might be your last paycheck."

Jemma circled the kitchenette twice then sat at the opposite end from the envelope. She recognized the handwriting. Besides, only Paul would know he could get by without a post office box number. Lizbeth was mashing potatoes at the counter. She didn't turn around but spoke instead about the weather.

Jemma interrupted. "Gram, I'm not going to open it. Would you mind putting it in the soldier box?" For what purpose, she had no idea.

"All right." Lizbeth wiped her hands on her apron and unlatched the pouting room door. Jemma closed her eyes when she heard the trunk lid close with a thump. Only Lizbeth's occasional humming leaked into her head during supper.

Afterward, they sat in the porch swing. The extra bit of chain on the swing made a clinking with each movement, and a dust-settling sprinkle came up from nowhere to cool things off.

"Whatever is in that letter can just wait at the bottom of the soldier box with all those other sad things," Jemma said. "Someday I'll throw it away."

Lizbeth laid her hand on Jemma's arm. "It's getting chilly out here. I think I'll go in."

Jemma stayed on the swing with her legs pulled up under her chin until the sun went down, then she went inside. Lizbeth had lit the flame in the gas heater.

She laid her head on Lizbeth's shoulder and fixed her eyes on the flickering reds and oranges behind the patterned grill. "Gram, I'm ready to talk about Paul." She inhaled warily, but let it out in rapid fire. "I went to his office to surprise him with a special painting I'd done. There was a woman sitting in the office, and I asked her if she knew where Paul Turner was." She glanced at Lizbeth. "The woman told me that she was his *wife*."

Lizbeth caught her breath. "His wife! Are you sure?"

"Yes ma'am. I knew it was true because I could see it in her eyes. They were cold."

"Oh my." Lizbeth held her close. "How you must have felt, honey. I wish you could have told me sooner."

"I just couldn't because I think I loved him and he was married."

"You didn't know."

"So what could he have to say in a letter—that he was sorry I met his wife? The rat. I am so embarrassed."

Lizbeth took her hands. "The good Lord knows your heart and everything that happened."

"If Spencer finds out, I'll just die."

"God doesn't give us anything we can't handle. He has a plan for you, Jemmabeth, and it will come for you in His own good time. Your job is to be patient, trust Him, and pray for His guidance. Listen to Him and you'll see."

They watched the flame from the little stove as it warmed the room around them. Jemma sniffed into a tissue. "Gram, today is Spence's birthday, and I don't even know where he is."

❧

She could hear them laughing in the dark as she arrived with a carton of Dr Peppers. Willa waved at her. "Jemma, come and set yourself down. This here's Brother Cleo. He's been our preacher for about forty year. He knows more about Jesus than old Paul himself."

Brother Cleo took off his fedora. He was a big man, almost bald, and carried himself well. His voice bellowed like a fine-tuned bass. "I don't know about that, Miz Willa, but you are right about me preaching the Word of God, but for more like fifty years. That's a long time for folks to be listening to an old codger like me."

"I'm glad to meet you, Brother Cleo." Jemma shook his hand. She didn't see Weese in the doorway behind the screen until he kicked it open and stood on the porch, lighting a cigarette.

Willa pointed her cane at him. "Don't be kickin' my door, young'un."

"Maybe that's not all I'm gonna kick," he mumbled, then took a swig from a bottle.

"When did you start smoking?" Trina fanned the fumes away. "I thought you were chewing these days."

"And what are you drinkin'?" Willa frowned at him. "That don't look like no Dr Pepper."

"I wonder what these mosquitoes do if they can't find a warm-blooded animal to feed on. Maybe they just die," Jemma said, hoping to change the subject.

"They just move back and forth across the tracks," Trina added.

"There's lots of warm-blooded animals over here to feed on, always has been, always will be." Weese flicked ashes on the porch. "Just one more thing owed us."

"I'll show you who owes who if you burn down my porch with

them ashes." Willa shoved at the glow with her cane.

Brother Cleo took out his handkerchief and wiped his forehead. "My way of thinking is that folks of every color have to find their own way in this world with the guiding hand of the Almighty."

"You're so full of it, old man." Weese hissed and moved to the grass. "You still livin' on the massa's place."

"Weese!" Willa jammed her cane onto the porch floor. "You mind who you talkin' to." She narrowed her eyes. "Don't you be usin' that kind of sass with Brother Cleo."

Jemma knew it was her presence that caused the outburst, not the venerable preacher. Even in the dim light she felt Weese's glare.

The words oozed from his mouth like sour milk. "Gov'ment comes along and says we can go to school in our own town, then do-gooder whites like you poke your nose across them tracks and say, 'We got coloreds livin' around here? Where are they? Come over here, you dirty little black children and let us give you our old clothes and junk. Now you be sure and give us a smiley thank-you right out of your poor little hearts.'"

"That'll be enough, young man." Brother Cleo's voice echoed down the street.

Willa struggled up and cracked her cane against the porch post. "I'll not have you talkin' that way in my house, Weese. If you know what's good for you, you'll be tellin' Jemma just how sorry you are for them words."

Weese jutted his jaw. "She knows I'm right."

"It's okay, Willa. I know what Weese is talking about," Jemma murmured. "I hope you don't think that about me, though."

"I don't care about you." He turned toward the tracks.

"Where you off to? Jemma brought us some Dr Peppers. I know I got my mouth all set for one," Willa called after him. "You're gonna be sorry."

Weese disappeared into the dark but not before he tossed his cigarette. Everybody watched it glow in the grass.

Trina broke the silence. "Good thing it looks like rain."

"I swear, sometimes that boy ain't got the sense that the good Lord give a one-eyed pee ant," Willa said. They all heard the sound of a bottle as it hit the packed earth and rolled to a stop. "That boy's done shucked my last cob."

"He's just baring his teeth, Miz Willa. Nothing's gonna come of it," Brother Cleo said.

Willa exhaled. "I done all I can do for that boy, so it's up to Jesus now. He's either gonna get himself throwed in jail or else he gonna get struck by the Holy Ghost and turn his sorry self around." The wind stirred around them and the first fat drops of rain pecked at the roof.

"Yes ma'am," Brother Cleo said. "You've done more than his own mama would've. I'm gonna have to say good night, y'all. I don't want to get caught out in a storm, though I do like the smell of wet earth."

"I think I'd better go home, too." Jemma smacked another mosquito. Lightning sliced the sky and thunder rattled the ironing sign.

Willa gave one last look down the road. "You're fixin' to get soppin' wet, child."

"I'll see y'all tomorrow." Jemma took off. The rain came on hard. She quickened her step through the tall grass and sunflowers. She and Trina had almost worn a path up to the tracks, down the other side through the tree row, and across the vacant lot behind Lizbeth's house.

A great flash of lightning revealed that she wasn't the only one on the trail. A crouching figure shared the path. It had to be Weese. Her scalp tingled, and she broke into a run off the trail, then bounded up the tracks in a new spot, hoping to avoid him. Adrenaline coursing, she paused between the rails, then jumped at a noise behind her. The blinding headlight of the 9:04 pierced the darkness only yards away. Jemma screamed and stumbled off. She slid down the slick right of way, taking rail-bed rocks with her. The train horn blasted and the ground shook as the train shot past. Sparks hissed in the water and a gush of heat from the driving metal on the rails enveloped her. She lay in the mud and watched the cars flash by. A few passengers were lingering over their late evening meal in the dining car, unaware of her brush with death.

Her head pounded in rhythm with the clamor on the tracks and her stomach was in her throat. How stupid of her to come within a few feet of her own funeral. She slipped again, as she thought she heard something on the tracks. Her mind was a jumble, her clothes were soaked, and she had a big scrape on her arm. To make things worse, she upchucked the burger and fries. Jemma was a muddy, stinking mess when she at last pulled open the screen door. She halfway hoped Lizbeth was still awake, and then again, she hoped not.

"Jemmabeth, I was a little worried," Lizbeth whispered. "That was a cloudburst."

"Sorry, Gram. I'm okay, but I think I'll take a bath."

Jemma stayed in the water until it was cold. If Lizbeth knew about her close call with the train, she wouldn't be snoring—"cooling potatoes," as she called it. Jemma would tell Trina tomorrow and together they would confront Weese. That would've been a nice headline in the *Chillaton Star*: FORMER MISS BIGSHOT RUN OVER BY TRAIN. She didn't even jump off the tracks; she stumbled.

Spencer, her sweet Candy Man, was better off without her.

It was half past seven when she woke up the next morning. She was gulping down breakfast when Lester came in with the mail.

"Mornin', Jemmerbeth." Lester nodded. "Where's Miz Liz?"

Jemma pointed to a note. "She took a casserole to Mrs. Schneider."

"Oh, the Germans," he said. "Old man Schneider's always laid up with somethin' or the other. I just wanted to let her know that Shorty's at it again. I heard down to the post office that he was peepin' in windows last night. You know he lives in a dugout just over yonder across the tracks. Sheriff spotted him out in that little storm we had, runnin' the rails right back here behind us, carryin' his metal step stool on his head. Pitiful feller. He could've got lightin' struck pullin' that kind of stunt, like my Mae Ella."

Jemma gave him her full attention. "I'm sorry, Lester. What did you say?"

"I said Shorty Knox was prowlin' around the tracks durin' that storm we had last night."

Jemma washed her hands and face in the kitchen sink, something she'd never done before but had seen Papa do many times after a rough day in the field. "Thanks, Lester, I'll be sure and tell her about Shorty."

She exhaled in the morning air, rubbing the bandage on her arm. It was a brisk walk to work as she considered the trouble that she could have caused an already bitter young man.

Chapter 10
Good Enough

Well, well, if it's not Jemmartsybeth. So, big-city college was just way too much for you."

Jemma turned to face the wickedly beautiful Missy Blake.

"Moved in with your granny, huh?" Missy pushed her pink sunglasses back on her head. Suntan lotion and Chanel No. 5 served up a pungent blend. Her signature high-cut shorts and very low-cut top showed the best of Missy—drum majorette legs and cleavage that belonged on a fat girl.

"Missy. I didn't know you were in town," Jemma managed.

"Oh, I'm here all right. What happened to you and that art school in Dallas?" Missy's indigo eyes scanned the sidewalk for other victims.

"I'm taking a break." Jemma noticed a big hickey on the otherwise perfect neck before her.

Missy waved at someone across the street. "Come on," she said to Jemma. "Let's go to the drugstore and get a Coke."

"I don't have time," Jemma said. She'd sooner be chased by a big snake.

"Yes, you do, because I want to talk about *Spence*." At that, Jemma allowed herself to be dragged away. Missy's nails gleamed in a sugary pink. "Do you like this color? It's called Cotton Candy. Oh, and I'm called Melissa now. I'm dumping 'Missy.' It's so juvenile. I assume that you and Spence have called it quits forever because he and I had several dates this summer. He was very interested, but it was me that didn't want to get serious. I'm way too busy at UT for a steady right now, but he was a temptation. Spence has gotten even cuter and everybody's talking about him."

Jemma flushed and focused on a display of antacids. Rats. She didn't know he would go out with CHS alumni, most particularly,

Missy Blake, and most especially several times. She drew a face on the side of her frosty glass. "I haven't seen him yet so we haven't talked."

Missy cocked a perfect eyebrow. "Really. I thought he told me that he was coming home early this semester or something weird like that. I have a good feeling about us, so I know we'll be going out again." She was distracted mid-sentence by a well-toned delivery-man who was giving her equal attention. "Now that Spence is a free man at last, anything can happen and it usually does, with me. I have. . .what's the word. . .uh. . ."

"I don't know what you're trying to say."

"You know, that stuff that JFK had," Missy prompted.

"Back pain?" Jemma suggested. "Intelligence?"

"No. The stuff that made people want to be around him."

"Money?" Jemma said, enjoying the moment. Missy suffered from a limited vocabulary. It was her only flaw—that, and her personality. Jemma caved in. "Are you trying to think of *charisma*, Missy?"

"Yeah, cha*ris*ma," she said, as though she'd heard it at least once before.

Jemma sipped her soda. "So, what keeps you so busy at the University of Texas?" she asked, not caring at all.

"My sorority, of course. Is there such a thing as an art sorority? I mean, for parties and meeting guys and all that good stuff? I just love my sisters. I have really found myself. We have the same interests and goals. You wouldn't believe what serious f-u-n we have. You know, party time." She made circles in the air with her finger. "And the guys." Missy rolled her eyes. "If you are a Delta, you have more frat boys than you can handle. So, what did you do for fun in Dallas? Do you still play basketball and make your famous leaping shot or whatever you call it? I bet you don't have to write those boring term papers and junk like that at art school."

Missy folded her arms, sipped the last of her Coke, and rambled on. "It's so cool that you aren't going to start dating Spencer again because I'm thinking about my future." She put on fresh lipstick that matched the nail polish. "I can tell when a guy's, you know, interested in fooling around with me." She shook back her hair as the deliveryman passed by again. "Spence is hard to read, which is weird because he is just so hot. Did I say everybody is talking about him, only I've got dibs, if you know what I mean."

Jemma swallowed a big chunk of ice and tried to make eye contact with Missy to see if she was telling the truth about Spence fooling around.

"I heard that you were taking care of some crippled girl." Missy's nose wrinkled up like she smelled a hog farm. "Do you have to, you know, change a bedpan for her or does she wear diapers?" She leaned back in her chair and ran her fingers through her thick, flaxen hair. She looked like a TV commercial for shampoo, and she knew it.

"The girl's name is Carrie. She is smart, funny, and really pretty. Her hair is the same color as yours and that's her natural shade. She was in our class and in my Brownie group, before you moved here."

"How weird. I also heard that you're hanging around with a colored girl, but I couldn't believe it. I mean, that's too tacky for words, even for you. Oh, and Miss Priss Sandy's wedding was kind of cute, in a hokey way. Marty's not good looking, but he's something else on a date. We went out once when she was mad at him. He only had one thing on his mind. Uh-oh, promise you won't tell Sandy that. It's just me—I bring out the passion in guys. All of them." Missy looked at her watch. "Didn't you say that you have to be somewhere?"

"Sandy and Martin are in Germany," Jemma said, "so I doubt she's worried about a date that he had with you when he might have to go to Vietnam, and yeah, Trina Johnson lives across the tracks. She's one of the nicest friends I've ever had. If you'll excuse me, I need to pick up Gram at the beauty shop." Jemma scooted her chair on the wood plank floor.

Missy's jaw dropped, and she slipped some Dentyne into it. "How completely weird. Oh well, to each his own. Your hair has gotten so long. I guess you're trying to go for my length, but it does sort of help tone down your height. You should try this thing I read about in a movie-star magazine. Daddy gets them because of all the theaters we own, I guess. Anyway, you put mayo in your hair. I know that sounds crazy, but it makes your hair shine."

"Really?" Jemma paused. "Mayonnaise?"

"It sounds goofy, but it's so healthy for your hair roots or something. I'm trying to be more health conscious. Have you rolled your hair on o.j. cans yet? They are the coolest for long hair. It might help with those weird waves you have, too."

"Orange juice cans and mayo. I guess I'll have to try that."

"Yeah, just leave the mayo in. Don't rinse it out." Missy sized up Jemma's silk blouse and long skirt. "You're still trying to get by with the bohemian look. I guess I love fashion way too much to go that route."

"Bohemian?"

"Yeah, you know, artsy, backwoodsy, like those cowboy boots you used to wear with everything. I guess there are guys who could overlook that, but not the fratties, trust me." Missy tapped her long nails on the tabletop. "Spence looks like James Dean's twin brother now. It's so freaky. I probably don't know him as well as I could because y'all were like Siamese twins or something in school. Did you know that he joined a fraternity? He told me all about it. We were so close. Listen, if you're ever in Austin during school, call the Delta house and ask for me. Maybe my sisters and I could give you a makeover or something. It would be a cool project, but you might bring some extra money to pay us back."

Missy propped a rhinestone-studded sandal on her chair and frowned at a mosquito bite that dared to spoil her bronzed leg. She flashed her faultless smile at Jemma. "Thanks for letting go of Spencer. You did him a big favor and me, too, for that matter."

"Good-bye, Missy."

"*Melissa.* High school just seems so long ago." Missy took out her compact and checked the corners of her mouth and her eyeliner.

"Right," Jemma said, forgetting the question.

Missy swiveled away like she was still leading the band. "Say hi to Sandy. Anything you want me to tell Spencer the next time we're out?" She yelled it so everybody could hear.

"No." Jemma turned down the sidewalk to Nedra's, her nose and eyes burning.

Rats. If Spence took Missy to The Hill or to the river, she didn't know what to think about him. Maybe Fraternity Brother Spencer would do that. Maybe dumb Jemmabeth would do that with Mrs. Turner's husband. Everybody in their class did not call the only girl who could afford braces "Missy." Most just called her The Cleave, for obvious reasons.

≈⚓≈

Subsequent to The Cleave encounter, Jemma was wishy-washy about seeing Spencer. It was driving her bananas to think he might know about Paul. His whereabouts remained a mystery, and she was too ashamed to ask anybody. She stopped driving by the castle, but each time the phone rang, she jumped. Like just now.

"Jem, can you hear me?"

"Sandy? There's lots of static. How's married life?" Jemma asked. "I had a disaster with Paul," she added, waiting for the sarcasm.

"Mr. Perfect Cowboy?"

"This is just between you and me, okay? I met his wife."

"Cheezo! The rat fink. I can't believe that he was married. What a cheating liar."

"I feel like dirt."

"How could you have known he was married?"

"I guess I could've asked him."

"Oh sure, that comes up a lot on a date. He's not worth worrying about." Sandy always shot to the heart of things.

"He called for a while and now he writes me twice a week, but I'm not opening the letters."

"Burn them. He's only digging himself a deeper hole. Good gravy! If Marty ever did that to me, I'd kill him. That poor wife."

"I think I loved him, Sandy."

"More than Spence?"

"I don't know if I really loved Spence. You know that."

"You never knew what you had with Spencer, Jem. You two were like that Jacob's ladder experiment in science where the voltage shoots across from one side to the other."

"I wasn't gah-gah like you were with Marty."

"Oh yes you were. Don't forget who you are talking to here."

"Yeah, but I was crazy all the time I was with Paul. I mean crazy. He was so smooth. He was not your average buckaroo."

"Just a cheating married man. Jem, how many times did we run

97

the bulls on the Fourth of July? I know you. Once you see a cowboy hat pulled down low over dreamy eyes with long lashes, and that 'howdy, ma'am' attitude, you're done for. Tell Spencer to get him a Stetson."

Jemma lay back on the good bed. "I'm not sure he's still interested in me. Besides, I don't want to mess up and hurt him."

Sandy snorted at that. "That's big of you since you already hurt him. I've heard he's been dating everything in sight since you broke up, like you have. Aren't you the least bit jealous? Haven't you missed him?"

Jemma closed her eyes. "Yes to both."

"He was always my second choice for a boyfriend. Remember our list? You and Spencer need each other; it's been too long. My phone time's about up. I'll call you next month. Get off the guilt train about the cowboy."

"Say hi to Marty. Oh yeah, Missy said your wedding was kind of cute."

Sandy laughed. "The Cleave said that? Well, that's exactly what I was shooting for—kind of cute."

"Spencer went out with her several times."

"Jemmabeth."

"Okay." Jemma hung up. Maybe she shouldn't have told Mrs. Blabbermouth about Mrs. Turner.

⚜

It took her just a week to save up enough orange juice concentrate cans to cover her head. She bought o.j. for everybody on the condition that she got the cans back. She also bought a large jar of mayonnaise and got all set to have hair like a sorority sister and good enough for a certain fratty, should he ever show up. Jemma shampooed, then dipped her fingers into the oily mixture. "This had better be worth it," she said under her breath. The mayonnaise made the cans slippery and she winced at the smell. She had to use about four bobby pins per can to make them stay in place.

Lizbeth watched the proceedings with grave misgivings, as did Lester, who gaped at Jemma as though she were wrapping her hair in hundred-dollar bills. "I reckon you know what you're doin', Jemmerbeth, but I ain't never seen nobody put food in their hair, on purpose, excepting babies."

"It's okay," Jemma muttered with bobby pins in her mouth. She rolled the last greasy section onto a can. "I've heard of people using lemon juice to lighten their hair."

"Now that you mention it, Paulette, my little Frenchy, used to put beer on her hair. Of course, I never asked where she got the stuff," he said with a righteous look.

She sat outside to hasten the drying process. The wind whistled through the cans. She wore her sweater and sat in the hollyhock patch, knowing full well that Gram and Lester were taking turns watching her out the window and snickering. It would be worth it because she was going to have luxurious hair. After the first hour, she tested a strand, but it remained limp and greasy. She rolled it back on the can and propped her feet up in the extra chair. She closed her eyes, thinking about Spencer and his possible reaction to her new look.

"Girl, what planet did you come from?" Trina's voice woke her up and the cans clinked together like a bagful of garbage.

"Trina, you scared me to death," Jemma said.

"Well, now you know how I felt when I saw you." Trina giggled. "What are you doing?"

Jemma shoved a chair toward her. "I'm trying something new on my hair." She unwound another can to check it.

"You been eating sandwiches or potato salad?" Trina waved her hand in front of her nose.

"No, why?" Jemma clipped the bobby pins back to the can.

"Something stinks."

"I think it's my hair. I put mayonnaise on it."

"Like for a baloney sandwich? Girl, you've lost your marbles. Have you ever seen that stuff after it's been setting around all day? It separates and looks like chicken mess. You wouldn't find me putting that stuff on my dog if I had one."

Jemma was perturbed. She unrolled the cans and let them drop on the ground. "What do you think?" she asked, running her fingers through the gooey mess. Trina erupted in laughter as Jemma ran inside to look in the mirror. Her hair was a clump of seaweed, glistening with mayonnaise and dumped by the tide in Chillaton.

Tricked by The Cleave. Rats.

Lizbeth stood in the bathroom door, laughing and covering her nose. "Honey, I've been thinking about this," she said with great control. "I've seen Nedra give some kind of oil treatment, but she does it a little differently, seems like. I think she rinses the oil out before she does anything else."

"Oh." Jemma looked in the mirror again and started to giggle, despite her consternation. "Well, I guess this is what happens when bohemians try to join the ranks of sorority girls. Would you mind asking Trina to come in? I've got to wash my hair."

"I was hoping you would." Lizbeth handed her a towel. Jemma used up her bottle of shampoo and her hair finally smelled like flowers again, like it did that night with Paul.

Chapter 11
The Candy Man

Nedra Porter could intercept a tasty tidbit of gossip from thirty yards upwind. The sign in her beauty shop window—HAIR'S WHERE IT ALL BEGINS—spoke to the heart of Nedra's real business. She didn't pump her customers for information during a shampoo and set in order to run home and whip up a casserole or form a prayer circle. Nedra was pumping for the sheer thrill of knowing things first or secondhand or at least a good third.

Twila worked part-time at Nedra's Nook. She caught the tail end of gossip after Nedra herself had snooped it out. Twila Trout was in Jemma's class, but she married Sandy's older brother, Buddy Baker, two days after high school graduation. She was the one that Jemma and Sandy could count on to be on their side in a girlfriend spat. She was sweeter than she was smart, could cook better than their home economics teacher, and hadn't missed any meals. Her dark blond hair was cut in a Nedra Helmet. That's what Jemma and Sandy called the hairstyle until Sandy got one, too.

"Guess who's in town?" Twila asked, broom in hand as Jemma came through the door.

Sweat beaded instantly on Jemma's upper lip. "The cast of *Gilligan's Island*?" she asked, her heart swirling around.

"You're so weird. It's Spencer, and he's even better lookin' than he used to be. I mean really cute, Jem, and so nice," Twila said with a big sigh.

"I'm going to tell Buddy you said that."

"Hey, just because I'm married doesn't mean I'm blind. I don't see why you have to be so stubborn about Spence. He's cute, he's rich, he's so smart, and you were such a cute couple."

Jemma pouted. "If you say cute one more time, I'm leaving."

"He still loves you. Everybody knows it."

"He's dated all the girls in this town and several other towns, I'm sure, since we broke up. Just sell me some shampoo." Jemma opened up her purse.

"You told him to get lost. Everybody in Chillaton knows that, too." Twila shut the cash register drawer. "Buddy got a call from Sandy. I sure miss her. She makes me laugh, but I bet she gets lonesome so far away from home. They were a cute couple, too, but not as cute as you and Spencer."

"That's it," Jemma said with the snap of her purse. "Good-bye, Twila. Say hi to Buddy for me."

"Well, if it's not the long-lost darlin' of Chillaton." Jemma turned at the word *darlin'* to the waiting arms of Nedra Porter herself. Her frosted Helmet was backcombed and sprayed solid atop her long neck like a ripe dandelion, ready to blow. She dusted hair from her pink smock and smiled, revealing a tiny smidge of orange lipstick on her front tooth.

"You have come back for him, haven't you?" she asked. "I knew you would 'cause y'all are just made for each other. It's like a movie. Now you take that Missy Blake, for instance. Nice hair, big busted, but the angels must not have been holding their mouths just right when they made her. She ain't never easy to take, being so sweet on herself, plus she's too forward with the boys. Throws a basketball like a girl, too. Nothin' like you, hon. You coulda been on a college boys' team with that jumper of yours. I wouldn't worry too much about her and Spencer. Missy must bathe in #5, and a little of that goes a long way. Spencer's Corvette probably still reeks with it. Now are you gonna let me do up that nice head of hair before you see him? I could fix it just like mine. What do you say, hon?" Nedra stubbed out her cigarette.

Jemma flashed a smile and shook her head.

"Well, you give me a call if you change your mind. I could work you in."

Nedra moved back to the chair where Betty Kate Richards, towel-wrapped and poised for curlers, resumed reading her magazine, as did the rest of the hungry Nook patrons, most of whom had lifted their hair-dryer hoods so as not to miss a word.

Jemma swore she would never wear Chanel.

He called that night.

"Hi, Jem." The sound of his sweet voice stirred a yearning in her, deeper than she ever expected. She wilted onto the dresser stool.

"Oh Cassanova." What a stupid opener. After all the ideas she had practiced, too. She twisted the cord around her finger and chewed on her lip.

"Hey, it wasn't my idea to break up," he said.

"I can't believe you went out with Missy." Rats. It came out earlier than she planned.

He ignored it anyway. "Your year was up a long time ago, so let's go to the movies tonight."

"You've seen me before, and the last time we agreed that would be the last." Dumb, dumb, dumb.

"You agreed all by yourself, Jemmabeth. Right now I miss you, and I want to be in your presence."

"Smooth talker."

"Heartbreaker."

"Frat boy."

"Siren."

"Truce." She wanted to see him so bad that she ached.

"I'm coming over because I've missed Gram," he said in his cute way. Twila was right about that.

"Fine. Maybe I'll be here."

She was, and she had picked out the least bohemian thing she owned—a tailored, violet pantsuit from her mother. Her heart hammered when she heard the Corvette in Lester's driveway. She stood just inside the foyer so she could see him before he saw her. What if he knew about Paul? She hadn't been this nervous in a year.

He stood at the front door a few seconds, then pulled the little knob that substituted for a doorbell. Jemma took a couple of deep breaths and opened the door. She tingled from her scalp to her knees at the sight of him. It was the same Spencer, but oh, he did look fine. His sandy blond hair was parted and still cut short. He had that gentleman's nose, high cheekbones, a full mouth—she wanted to kiss it—and the tiny scar on his chin. His eyes were the color of old pewter and she looked into them briefly. He was still taller than she was. Always the smart dresser, he was wearing tan slacks and a black shirt. James Dean never looked so good. Her tongue wouldn't work.

"Hi." She smiled.

He stepped in and stood very close to her, but she didn't recognize his aftershave. It was probably something he got in Europe.

"Hello, baby," he said, just above a whisper. Neither knew what to do with their hands. He played with his car keys and change in his pockets. "You look beautiful." His eyes twinkled.

Yes, yes, he still called her *baby*. "You don't look so bad yourself." She wrung her hands behind her back.

"I've missed you."

Jemma nodded. All she could think about was the way they used to kiss. Her heart was about to fall on the floor, but they simply stood there like abandoned marionettes.

"Hey, I want to say hello to Gram," he said at long last.

She led the way to the kitchen, where Lizbeth politely lingered over her coffee.

"Spencer! Give me a hug, son." She patted his back. "It's a real treat to see you, but I think you've lost weight."

Spencer patted his trim stomach. "Maybe a little. It's the food back East. I need some of your cooking."

"Do you have time for cobbler? I just made it this afternoon."

"Thanks," he said, eyeing it, "but we are off to the movies. Do you want to go?"

"Let me get my purse." She laughed and hugged him again. "You two have fun."

They walked to the car in silence. She was ready to check it for Chanel, but it was the latest Corvette Sting Ray convertible and candy-apple red.

"When did you get this one?" Jemma asked, remembering the way he walked.

Spencer touched her arm as he opened her door. "Today. It's my 'welcome home' gift and belated birthday present from my dad."

His touch didn't go unnoticed. "What's showing at the movies?" Jemma asked, too jittery to think of anything else to say.

"*Mary Poppins*." When he backed out of the driveway, he put his hand on the back of her seat to check behind him. His eyes darted into hers for a second.

She held her breath until he moved his hand. "I've already seen it."

"Me, too. So, what do you suggest?"

"What's at the drive-in?" she asked, like she really cared. She did care about who he took to see *Mary Poppins*.

Spencer peeled out at the first stop sign. He always did drive a little fast for Chillaton and had his own share of warnings from Sheriff Ezell. He pulled up to the marquee, creating a small dust storm behind him. *Darlin'—starring Julie Christie* was on the marquee. "The Chillaton spelling," he said and laughed. She didn't. "What do you think?" he asked, watching her.

"It's up to you." She had almost forgotten how he made his smile. It started with his eyes, not his mouth, and she liked that.

Spencer made a U-turn and headed toward the Salt Fork of the Red River.

"Whoa, what happened to the movies?" she asked.

He threw it into another gear. "I want to talk."

Jemma got a colossal knot in her throat. Rats. He must know.

He turned off the road onto a little dirt lane that she knew all too well, then pulled up to their river spot. The clock and their synchronized breathing made painful little explosions in her ears.

"Look at that sunset," she said, buying time.

"Be honest with me, Jem. We broke up so you could see if there was more out there than what we had. Did you find it?"

"I don't know. Why the third degree so soon?"

"Look at me, baby."

She kept her eyes on the gearshift. "Maybe."

He stopped breathing. She licked her dry lips.

"Why are you here?" he asked.

"You drove us here." She knew that kind of logical wordplay drove him nuts. "I also needed some time to work on my portfolio." It was not a total lie.

"Jemmabeth."

She closed her eyes. "Okay. I got caught in a bad situation, and I decided to come home."

"What kind of bad situation?"

"A relationship." Maybe he didn't know. "I was in a relationship, and it went bad." She watched the rise and fall of his chest but didn't dare look him in the eye again. "Spence, I didn't want to tell you this, but you are making me."

"Did you love him?"

"I don't know." She laid her hand on his arm, setting off fireworks in her stomach. He let it rest there a few seconds before touching her fingertips. When he did, every nerve she had overloaded.

"Spence," she began.

He held her hand, the one she painted with. "It's okay. Do you want to go home?"

"Only if you do."

He started the Corvette and adjusted his rearview mirror.

Her heart sank. "Wait. Stay awhile."

He turned off the motor.

She traced the scar on his thumb where Sandy's cat had scratched him in the third grade. "Let's start over, Spence, okay? Pretend we don't know each other's every thought, habit, and memory. Just have fun. What do you say?"

He shook his head slightly. "I don't think I can do that. I'm afraid I've already lost you. I never thought you would find..."

"I missed you so much."

"Where did I go wrong? At what point did you decide it was time to look for somebody new?"

"You didn't ever go wrong, Spence. You couldn't. It's my fault because I always wondered what would happen if we got married and never really knew for sure that we were meant for each other. We had never even kissed anybody else."

"I didn't need to." His eyes glistened.

"I know, but I did. I'm just made that way."

"There had to be some point, though, when you thought I wasn't enough."

She exhaled and looked out at the river. "All right, but remember, you asked for it. At Le Claire they have a May Day celebration."

"The pagans."

"I went with my friend, Melanie. She was trying to get a date with the guy that's her fiancé now, and I sort of went on a double date with her."

"There's no sort of."

"I went along as a part of her plan."

"You liked it."

"I guess, but I didn't kiss the guy or anything, honest. But it was kind of exciting to be all new with somebody."

"Was he a *cowboy*?"

Her stomach flipped when he said the word. "No. He was a cellist."

"Brought down by a cellist."

"I wish I hadn't done it, really I do." There she went, sounding like Miss Scarlett. "We could start over, though. Pretend I'm a new kid in town." She watched him out of the corner of her eye, then turned her head to look squarely at him. He loved that look. He could never turn it down, even when she asked if they could date other people.

He exhaled. "You're a mean woman, Jem. What choice do I have?" She grinned, and he couldn't resist. "So, new kid in town, what do you want to do now?"

"This." She yanked him to her by his shirt and kissed him like she hadn't kissed anybody all year. He came alive, and she got her lightning bolts without even planning it. It was so easy to kiss him again and so very excellent. The Sting Ray was far too little for that kind of stuff.

Spencer got out and opened her door. They stared at each other, barely able to breathe, then he pinned her against the car. "Welcome to Chillaton, baby," he said and kissed the dickens out of her until their jaws ached.

They lay on the hood of his car and found Orion. She reached for his hand. "Whenever I looked at the stars last year, I pretended that you were watching them at the same time. Actually, it made life bearable without you."

"Was it really better than what we had?"

"It was different. I did worry that you had found somebody else."

"I want nobody else, Jem. I love you."

She suddenly wanted to say it back to him but couldn't. "You are precious to me, Spencer," she whispered as tears rolled down her cheeks and onto his.

On the way home, they stopped off at Son's, the local drive-in hamburger joint.

"Why did you join a fraternity?" she asked after a loud slurp of her soda. "We always made fun of them."

He laughed. "How did you know about that? It's the American Institute of Architecture Students, not exactly a wild bunch."

"Oh." She had smelled like potato salad for nothing.

She dug in her purse and took out a small package. "Happy birthday, Spence. You have always been my best friend."

"Not exactly what a guy wants to hear, baby." He unwrapped it and lifted out a blue moon on a leather cord. "Hey, thanks."

"I made it for you in my ceramics class. Remember our last date, how we danced in the moonlight at the river? Now you will always have the moonlight with you. I wrote something on the back, too."

He turned it over and read aloud. *Near or far, I am where you are.*

"I really mean it," she said.

He draped it over his mirror. "I had to talk myself out of calling you every night. I nearly went crazy."

"I wish you would've called." She attempted a smile. "What are you doing home this time of the year?"

He grinned. "I needed to work on my portfolio. Actually, I'm doing an apprenticeship with an architect in Amarillo," he said, twirling the moon.

"All year?" Her heart jumped at the thought.

"I just finished orientation and I have to go back in May for culmination seminars." He gave her a sideways look. "Jem, I already knew that you had a boyfriend before you told me."

Rats. The question was how much did he know. "But you've been out of the country."

He drew in his chin. "Come on. . .Sandy, Buddy B, Twila, Nedra, Mother, telephone."

"Oh yeah. The Chillaton chain of command," she said with a dry mouth. "What was it like for you the first time you kissed somebody else?"

"A big zero. I kept thinking that you were kissing somebody, somewhere."

"I know. It was the same for me." She didn't add *until I met Paul*.

"I missed your look." He kissed her hand, palm up, knowing she loved that. "I never realized how much I liked it until you dumped me. I hope you didn't give it to anybody else."

"I didn't do it on purpose if I did, and I didn't dump you. That's an awful way to put it." She knew that was precisely what she'd done.

"Anyway, that little look makes me want to kiss you every time you do it," he said. She did it again with a great giggle. He reached for her. "Pucker up, woman. You asked for it." Spencer leaned against the horn as it happened.

The carhop appeared mid-kiss. "Do you want something or not?" she asked, arms folded.

"Nope, I've got everything I need now," Spencer said, coming up for air.

❧

"I don't like this." Trina tiptoed her way down the cross-ties on the track.

Jemma stretched out her arms and balanced on the rails. "You'll get used to it."

"Why can't we just walk in the street like other people?"

"I like the tracks. They give you direction and security."

"Security? Girl, you've got a screw loose. We could get smushed like bugs on here."

"Tracks are wings. They can carry you off into the blue." Jemma demonstrated her theory.

Trina peered down the rails. "Most people use a plane for that."

Jemma wasn't listening anymore. She was dancing and humming a French song she'd learned at Helene's. They shot some baskets, then went to play board games with Carrie. On the way home, they were making good time until Jemma took a seat on the rail. The wind picked up, lifting her hair from her shoulders.

Trina reluctantly sat next to her. "Now what?"

"I'm waiting for the 3:37." Jemma pushed wisps of hair out of her eyes.

"You're crazy if you think I'm gonna sit here and wait for a train to come, girl. What if you get your foot caught or you faint or something?"

"I won't." Jemma put her ear to the rail.

"Okay; this is weird. I read a story once about robbers who listened to the metal so they could tell exactly when a train was on its way. Is that your plan?"

"Yes. Now you're an accomplice because you know my secret."

"See, you're cuckoo. C'mon, I've got work to do for Mama."

They walked to the elm tree row and parted. Trina started down the trail to her house. She looked back and smiled at Jemma, who stood with her face to the sun and her eyes closed, dancing again. Spencer was in her life.

⟨⟨⟩⟩

Some nights Spencer sat in Papa's car house with her while she painted. He read or did paperwork for his apprenticeship. Whatever else he was supposed to be doing, he mostly just watched her paint and she loved it. They usually ended up shooting baskets under the lights at the tennis courts, then eating something fried at Son's. It was in the war that Son Shepherd claimed to have invented the *spork*, a cross between a fork and a spoon, for General MacArthur. It had become the logo for Son's Drive In—a giant spork, flashing in red neon.

"Jem, you know that I love you or else I wouldn't let you eat in my new car," Spencer said.

"Yeah, me and ten other girls." She made a face at him.

"Why do you always say things like that?"

She shrugged. "Because it's true. Everybody in this town can't wait to tell me about your love life."

"I needed to keep my mind off you, but that's all it ever was. I'm still your Candy Man, if you'll have me. I can wait as long as it takes for you to love me like you used to."

"I can never love you like I used to," she said like an ignoramus. "People change, love changes; there's always the test of time."

"My love has stood the test."

Spence was staring her down and she knew it. He was like a faithful old dog that wouldn't stay put if you drove thirty miles away to drop him off in the next county, but that was part of his charm.

"Do you mind if we go up to The Hill?" he asked. "Just to talk."

He started the Corvette and every head at Son's turned. It was The Car in town. Even Son, burger flipper in one hand and cigar in the other, stood in the doorway to watch them leave.

When they pulled up to their old parking space on The Hill, heads turned again, then went back to their business. A breeze moved the warm night air and Jemma fanned at a mosquito. Spence caught her hand in mid-flight and held it. "I want to make you a deal like the one you made me at the river."

"Always the car salesman," she said, but with a touch of nerves.

"Just listen and stop being so sarcastic. You're not Sandy."

She pretended to focus her attention on a white mare grazing in the pasture just over the barbed wire fence. Spencer turned her chin. "Jem, I love every single thing about you, even your temper. When you get tired of fooling yourself that you can find someone who'll love you more, I'll still be waiting for you. I want you to know that I'm keeping the promise that we made in the eighth grade. All the dating and all the good times, that's all they are. If we get married, it will be even more special to me."

She drew back, wide-eyed. "I'm keeping it, too. Did you think I wouldn't? Good grief!"

He had the same look the night she broke up with him. "All I ask is that you give me a chance to win you back before next spring. That's my deal. What do you say?"

Jemma was thirteen again, playing Spin the Bottle at Fountie Clark's birthday party. Spence did have a way with words, so she blinked and did the only thing she could do. She leaned over the gear-shift knob and kissed him with more affection than she originally intended. "I'll keep it in mind," she whispered.

Spencer held her face in his hands, backing up his deal with warm kisses that Jemma had known and loved since the seventh grade.

Chapter 12
Common Ground

Lizbeth carried the basket through the chest-high Johnson Grass and up to the railroad right-of-way. Train tracks made her nervous ever since she and Cam lost a milk cow on them years ago. The silly thing had wandered through a downed fence and ended up dead, a mile away on the tracks. She had yelled like a banshee the first time she saw Jemmabeth dancing on these tracks, but the child would have her way, claiming some foolishness about dancing to make the trains come. That prompted Lizbeth to memorize the schedule, just to be safe. Now she made sure of solid footing before taking a step. She surveyed the small houses and shacks facing the tracks. One, in particular, stood out from the rest. Petunias lined the dirt path to the unpainted house. She made her way to the sign that Jemma had told her about and knocked on the door.

"Yes ma'am?" A large woman smiled through the screen door. "You got some ironin'?"

"Hello. I'm Jemmabeth's grandmother, Lizbeth."

"Mercy, Miz Forrester. What a surprise. Come on in and make yourself to home." Willa pulled out a chair from the small kitchen table and unplugged her iron.

Lizbeth looked around. The room was dense with the smell of starch and damp fabric. "I thought you might like these," she said and set the basket of plums on the table. "They are from our old home place."

"Why, bless your heart," Willa said. "I know your home place. My man and me worked it a few times. Jemma took us out to your creek on a ride just the other day. These plums will make good eatin'."

"They're good for cobbler and jellies, too," Lizbeth said.

Willa wiped her forehead with her apron. "There's nothin' like a cobbler to make a place smell good."

Lizbeth nodded, noting the stack of ironing to be done. "You must keep busy with your business."

"Ain't much business to it. Sure don't take no brains to speak of," Willa said.

"Jemma told me that you are fond of petunias. My husband, Cameron, was, too."

"Yes ma'am. The old-style ones. My mama worked for The Judge for a good long while, and tended his 'tunias, too. The Judge don't cotton much to things that's cheerful, so he had 'em dug up. She chewed him out real good and told him she'd take 'em home, and that's what we got now. Mama never was afraid to speak her mind. The 'tunias are doing real good this year. I seen your house, and it looks like a picture book."

A fly buzzed across the table, and both of them took a swat at it.

"Would you like a Dr Pepper?" Willa asked. "Jemma brought me some. I gotta hide 'em from the neighbor kids." Willa reached behind a washtub, pulled out a bottle, and emptied it into two small jelly glasses. "Sorry it ain't cold and we ain't got one of them freezers to keep ice. How 'bout we go sit out on the porch, Miz Forrester. That might cool us off." Willa grabbed her cane. "There ain't no breeze in here today, but sometimes a stray one will come along outside."

"Please call me Lizbeth," she said, holding the door. "Would you look at that? I haven't seen rope bottom chairs since I was a girl."

"They're sturdy as a boot, too. They gotta be strong to hold up this old caboose." Willa laughed. "My man and his pap used to make 'em to sell in Amarillo."

"Is that so? I wish I'd known that. My father made them, too, when we lived in the hill country. Have you ever been to that part of Texas?"

"Law, no, Miz Lizbeth, I ain't never been past Amarillo or Red Mule. I bet you miss them hills."

"I do, but of course Cam and I have lived in Connelly County so long that it seems like home. How about your family?"

Willa tapped the porch post with her cane. "I was born in this house in 1927. My pap and his brother built it, and it took them near three year to get it done. My mama and pap come from Georgia. Their folks was plantation workers, but my husband's family come down here from way back in Harlem."

"New York?" Lizbeth asked.

"Yes ma'am. My husband's pap was a Buffalo Soldier in France—they was all colored boys, you know, then he come home and hauled his family clean across to Texas. I'm thinkin' his money run out in Chillaton," Willa said. "No other reason to stop on this windy stretch."

"I've heard of those Buffalo Soldiers," Lizbeth said. "They did themselves proud. I surely do like your daughter. Is she your only child?"

"Yes ma'am. Latrina's daddy got hisself killed way over to It'ly. That's his picture there on the wall. He was a Buffalo Soldier, too, with the 92nd Infantry. His mama named him Samuel, but we called him Sam."

"I'm so sorry." Lizbeth looked at the military issue photo much like her own boys' pictures.

"That's all right. I done cried a creek full of tears over losin' him, but he's gone to a better place. He was a righteous man, that one. Jemma told us that you've plumb near lost all your menfolk, too."

"Yes," Lizbeth said. "We had three boys, all good sons, and we raised my baby sister, too. My oldest boy is buried in Italy and his brother rests in Africa. Only Jemma's daddy is left. His name is James, Jimmy to me."

"That's gotta be a powerful pain, what with your husband gone now. He was always more than fair when our folks worked the fields for him."

"I'm not sure I'm up to it sometimes." Lizbeth smoothed her cotton dress over her knee.

"I know the feelin'. I get the blues real bad sometimes, but I believe the good Lord give womenfolk the backbone to carry heavy loads. That's what my mama always held with. She said men take to hidin' behind the bottle or the barn when they got troubles coming down around them."

"What do you suppose she meant about the barn?"

Willa's brow creased. "I reckon she was talkin' about workin' themselves to the bone. How did your man handle hisself when you lost your boys?"

"The barn. He wasn't a drinking man. He farmed until he had a heart attack, then he kept busy with his flowers and birdhouses from dawn to dusk after we moved into town. He never stopped."

"Was he a serious man?"

"Goodness, no. He was a talker and a joker, too, but very spiritual."

"Yes ma'am, I figgered that. How'd he pass?"

Lizbeth twisted her wedding band. "He came in the kitchen gray-faced and perspiring one morning while I was making biscuits. He made it to the refrigerator and got some nitroglycerin tablets to put under his tongue, then passed out. He never came to, so I didn't get to say good-bye. I think the last thing he heard from my lips was a scream, and I do hate that."

"Well, where he is now, it don't matter about that, Miz Forrester. The Lord don't want us dwellin' on them things. My goodness, how did you hold up under such a lot of grief?"

"I tend to sweep my sorrows under the rug and go on," Lizbeth said quietly.

"To my way of thinkin', folks need to lay open their hearts until all that sadness and misery is spilled out so they can move on with livin'. It's gotta get out of you one way or another, so that it don't eat you up like the devil that it is. I've seen too much of that in my day. Coloreds and whites chewin' on this and that until that's all they think about. Just listen to me. I might as well get me a pulpit." Willa slapped her leg and laughed.

Lizbeth smiled. "There's a lot of sense in what you are saying. Jemma told me that you are a wise woman."

"That Jemma. I don't know when I've enjoyed anybody's company as much as your grandbaby. She's got a good heart and a gift straight from heaven. Them paintings beat all I ever seen. Why, some of 'em are better than real life. My Trina and her sure are havin' themselves a time. I figger there's folks on both sides of the tracks wonderin' why them two parade around town like there's nothin' funny about it. Good thing is, they don't seem to care. What do you say about it, Miz Forrester?"

"I say it's high time. If I would have stepped across that silly track years ago and met your mama and bought a chair from your father-in-law, we'd all be the better for it."

"Well, yes, that's the truth, ain't it? I guess you and me are just little specks when it comes to the whole country. We can't undo what happened up to now." Willa tapped her cane, and they watched as a butterfly lit on the lavender petunias nearest the porch, its wings opening and closing over the blooms.

"Do you ever wish you could visit your husband's grave?" Lizbeth asked.

"Yes ma'am, I reckon I'd like that. I'd just like to reach out and touch it. It'd be a comfort to say a proper prayer over it, too."

"That would be nice. I don't think my Cam wanted to see our boys' graves. We didn't talk about it much, but I think that's why he wanted them buried where they died so it wouldn't ever be final, like it was a dream and they could walk in the door and we could hug them again. It's my opinion that funerals and cemeteries give us someplace to go and know it's real."

"I know it's real 'cause I got that old yeller letter in there from the Gov'ment."

"I have too many things like that in my soldier box." Lizbeth covered her eyes as a big dust devil blew down the road. "It's really only an old trunk that Cam and I had. It was his mother's, but when we lost the boys, I couldn't bear to see anything that belonged to them, so we put all of it in there. One day I got out their Purple Hearts to polish them, and from then on, I felt like I was doing something. Where do you keep yours?"

"What's that, Miz Forrester?"

"Your husband's Purple Heart."

Willa shrugged. "He didn't get no heart that I know of."

"That's odd. The Purple Heart is a military medal given for being wounded or worse," Lizbeth said.

"I don't know nothin' about no hearts. I just got that old ugly letter and a chain with his name on a piece of metal." Willa's voice trailed off.

Lizbeth frowned. "That makes no sense."

"They's lots of things I don't understand in this world. I reckon my man had to die way across the ocean so Latrina could go to college."

"That doesn't make you miss him any less," Lizbeth said.

"No ma'am, it don't. That man could make me laugh until I was fixin' to pop. He was a dancer, too. I wasn't as big as a barn back in them days, and we did cut ourselves a rug on the dance floor." Willa's eyes crinkled up.

"Jemma moves around like silk when she's dancing. Of course our church isn't real big on dancing, even now, but that child has a mind of her own."

"Well, I figure the good Lord wants us to dance, or He wouldn't have give us Elvis." Willa tossed her head back and howled with laughter, and Lizbeth couldn't help but join her.

"I've had such a good time visiting with you, Willa. Let's do this more often. We have a lot in common, you know, despite our age difference. Now I hope that you'll come over and visit me sometime." Lizbeth rose and extended her hand.

Willa clasped it and smiled. "That's mighty nice of you to invite me. I appreciate the plums, too."

"I mean it. Please come over and I'll show you around Cam's garden. Maybe you can give me some advice because I'm no flower gardener."

"It takes me a good while to get around, but I'll come. I like puttin' a face to your name, Miz Forrester."

"Call me Lizbeth."

"Yes ma'am, Miz Forrester," Willa said. "I'll sure try."

Chapter 13

Silver

Jemma dried her hands on the dish towel and grabbed the phone. She said hello a few times.

"Jemma? It's Helene here. How are you, dear? Just a moment, these horrid hearing aids are ringing in my ears. I'm missing you terribly, and telephone chats won't do. I would like to visit your little village, but I want to consult with your gram before proceeding any further."

"Great! We would love to see you."

"Now, I insist that you tell her every meal is to be dined out, and I shall stay in a hotel. There you have it."

"Okay, I'll be right back." Jemma found Lizbeth sitting under the pecan tree. At her news, Lizbeth stood, ready to receive Helene at that very moment. Jemma ran back to the phone. "Come as soon as you can because we can't wait."

"That's lovely. I shall get my ticket and be there next weekend, if all goes well."

"It will." Jemma beamed. "We'll have fun."

"I want to meet Lester, and I do hope he will have some stories for me."

"Lester is never without stories. If nothing else, ask him about trains."

"Ah, a railway man. Lovely. Now, can you make arrangements for my hotel room?"

"We haven't had a hotel in Chillaton since the thirties, Helene."

"No? Then there must surely be one of those motor hotels," Helene said.

"A motel? We have one called That'll Do."

"What do you mean by that?" Helene asked.

"I mean that's the name of the motel. You might as well give up, because we want you to stay with us. Gram has a guest room waiting for you. If you stay at That'll Do, you'll be all alone."

"Such an odd name for a guesthouse. Are you certain it won't be an imposition?"

"I'm certain."

"I suppose that will do, then. Good-bye, dear. I'll call back with the schedule."

Jemma suppressed a giggle at Helene's unintended play on words. "Good-bye. See you soon."

⁂

The great silver engine creaked and moaned its way to a stop. The Zephyr, like mercury halted in a hasty rise on a thermometer, waited impatiently for Helene to disembark. The smell of hot metal and well-oiled mechanisms permeated the air. The conductor put out a little step, then offered his hand to Helene, who was dressed as though she were meeting The Queen. Her silver hair was done up in a French twist and her cerise linen suit was somehow unwrinkled. Her pearls and emerald earrings lent a decidedly regal tone to the station. Jemma wrapped her arms around her. The conductor set Helene's baggage on the platform and signaled to the brakeman. The Zephyr disappeared down the tracks.

Helene held Jemma back by her shoulders. "Let me look at you. Good. You are happy and it shows. That sets my mind at ease."

"I'm much better than the last time you saw me," Jemma said.

"Nothing could make me happier. Now, I must meet your gram straightaway." Helene peeked around Jemma to spy Lizbeth.

Jemma introduced them, her two favorite silver-haired women. They hit it off, and she followed them around the rest of the day. Lizbeth and Helene went over each of her paintings, comparing observations. By nightfall, Helene had spent more time with Lizbeth than with Jemma. She insisted they go out for supper, and took it as great fun that the only place for a sit-down meal was the truck stop. Lester came over later for pie and coffee. He had his eye on Helene because he wasn't quite sure what to make of an Englishwoman in the house. He was quiet, but Helene had a good memory.

"I am quite fond of the railways," she announced. "In England, they were our main method of transport. I lived just outside London, but I once rode five hours to see my cousin in northwest Wales.

It was lovely to chat with all sorts of travelers and see the country-side without the bother of a motorcar."

Lester shifted in his chair. "Well, sir, I reckon I know a thing or two about trains."

"Oh, and how's that, Lester?" Helene asked.

"I worked for fifty year down to the station. I done everything from sweepin' up to sellin' tickets. I know the Burlington Route like it was the back of my hand. I even rode me some rails when I was a young'un. I took boxcars out to California and back, then all the way to Chicago. I caught me another line that went to New York City itself. I must have been on one train or another for two weeks, give or take a day."

"How clever of you," Helene said, giving him her full attention. "Those must have been adventurous times."

Lester tapped his foot. "It was just life on the rails."

"Do give us an example," Helene urged.

"Well, sir, first thing that come upon me was just about Grants, New Mexico. I seen this right nice-lookin' woman in a boxcar by herself, so when the train stopped, I figgered I might as well have me some company. I hopped in her car and I was doin' my best to be friendly and all, but then she come hence to moanin'. I figgered her for a gypsy fortune-teller or somethin', and I give considerable thought to gettin' out of there. There ain't much to slow up a freighter across New Mexico, though, if you know what I mean. Of course, I walked all over France, and there weren't much happenin' there neither, except the Big War."

"So, this young lady was not amusing?" Helene asked.

"Well, sir, somethin' was going haywire because she worked herself up into a tizzy, then got kind of quiet-like. I thought maybe it was over. I give her a quick look, and I'll be Uncle Johnny if she wasn't sittin' in the corner like a bullfrog. She let out a coyote howl, and the next thing I knew, she was holdin' a young'un and wipin' it down with her skirt. Beat all I ever saw. She just looked at me and grinned. I come hence to sweatin' and shakin' all over. That seemed to tickle her funny bone because she was laughin' and that baby was wailin'." Lester shook his head. "My ma had a similar story when she was in a family way. She'd been cleanin' out the chicken pen, and it struck her to pay a visit to the outhouse—no offense, ladies. We had us a two-holer just in case things got busy. Not many folks had a two-holer in them days."

Helene's eyes widened, and Lizbeth hid her smile behind her coffee cup.

"Ma took a seat, but come hence to feeling woozy. She decided to sit on the floor until she got her bearings. That's when I come into this world, smack-dab on the floor of the two-holer. Ma said she reckoned she'd about had enough young'uns when they started droppin' in the outhouse. I figger I'm a lucky man because if I'd come a few seconds earlier, I could've been at the bottom of the two-holer instead of eatin' this fine custard pie with you ladies. Now, back to my rail-ridin' days."

"Helene, let me refresh your coffee," Lizbeth said.

"How about some more pie?" Jemma asked.

Helene got the picture. "Lester, thank you for sharing these fascinating bits of history with us." She stifled a laugh.

"I've got plenty more, ma'am, whenever you're ready." Lester took a chance and winked at the Englishwoman.

❧

No matter if company was in town, Nedra wouldn't change a long-standing appointment. So, Jemma took Helene for a drive while Lizbeth was getting pumped for information as she got her hair done. Helene was interested in the farms, asking questions and taking photos. "Parts of this country remind me somewhat of the moors in England. Nevertheless, I am sure that working the land gives one a different perspective."

"I know that my papa loved it," Jemma said. "He believed farming was a kinship among the earth, the forces of nature, and the wisdom and labor of the farmer."

"Nicely put." Helene looked out at the rows of struggling, dry land cotton.

"We also have some big cattle ranches around here." Jemma turned away from the farmland and took the road to the sprawling Bar C Ranch, which belonged to Spencer's family.

"Jemma, have you heard from Paul?" Helene asked.

It took her a few seconds to answer. "He writes me every week, but I won't read letters from a married man."

"I am quite puzzled concerning that revelation," Helene said. "You were openly dating, dear. It was no shady tête-à-tête. Although he did strike me as a man who was familiar with the art of romance."

Jemma swallowed. "I'm glad to be here now. I love being with Gram and living in my hometown. I have discovered people who have been here all my life and I never knew them, and, of course, I have Spencer."

"I see." Helene looked out at the vast acres of sagebrush and mesquite trees. "Does Spencer expect to share the hope chest with you?" She continued to observe the scenery since her question went unanswered. The ranchland gave way to farmland, and soon they were back on the streets of Chillaton.

Jemma parked the car in front of Nedra's Nook and toyed with the steering wheel. "Spencer loves me."

Helene adjusted her hearing aid and took Jemma's hand. "And how do you feel toward him?"

"I feel safe and happy, like it's going to be blue skies forever around him. That sounds silly, I guess."

"On the contrary, dear. It sounds like love."

Jemma opened the door. "I'll be right back. I think Gram wants to show you the old home place."

Helene touched her shoulder. "Do be mindful of the suffering heart, Jemma. You mustn't become a passage for pain in your indecision."

Jemma nodded. How could she cause him pain? He was still her Candy Man.

❦

For a while, Jemma sat in the car sketching the two women as they strolled through the field. She decided to walk up a small rise and make other sketches of the place while Lizbeth and Helene continued to meander around, talking. They made an interesting pair because Lizbeth loomed over the diminutive Helene.

"This is where you lived during the war?" Helene asked.

"Yes. When all of them were overseas, I'd sit at the south window and listen to the wind moaning through the cottonwoods. It was the same window where I watched for their school bus every day when they were little. See the windmill near the house? The boys played many summers in the shade of it." She smiled. "Once, they tied a rope from the platform at the top down to the fence below and rigged up a washtub with my baby sister in it. I can still hear her squealing as she slid down. Those three boys were full of the dickens."

Helene shaded her eyes. "I'm sure that you felt cheated when they died. I know I would have."

"My Cameron kept up a brave front for the both of us. He took a stand that our boys died in a noble cause. I supported that, and I wanted to believe it, but they were so far from home and very young. I just wanted to hold them one more time. I know that mothers all over the world felt that pain."

"This is not much consolation, Lizbeth, but my family suffered through the London Blitz. Many Europeans wondered what took America so long to get involved in the war, but my father said, 'Be patient. Liberty will call America to battle as it did her forefathers; then she will fight with extraordinary vigor because her people burn with freedom.' He was right. Just look at your sons. No one in my generation will ever forget the sacrifice made by them and our own British boys in those horrid wars."

Lizbeth stopped. "Thank you for those words. They were fine young men with high hopes for the future, but I believe that in God's Great Plan, they were born to be warriors in the name of freedom."

"Well said, my friend." Helene took Lizbeth's arm in hers, and they walked down a turn row.

"Now tell me about Mr. Neblitt," Lizbeth murmured.

It was Helene's turn to smile. "I called him Nebs. You know we English love our nicknames. I think he was much like your husband—very outgoing, full of energy, ideas, mischief, and quite the romantic. We traveled extensively because of his profession. He was a freelance geologist for a consortium of oil companies, and quite successful. Nebs died the same day that he suffered a massive stroke, poor darling. To my deep regret, we had no children. I know he would have been a good father, but part of it was our own fault. We kept postponing the decision to have children at all. Then, when we decided we could drag the little things around the world with us, I couldn't seem to get pregnant."

The women rested on an old cedar bench that Cameron had built and placed under an elm tree so he could eat his lunch and look out over the crops. It was in good shape to have endured so many Panhandle winters.

Lizbeth ran her hand along the wood. "Do you have family still in England?"

"Sadly, they are all gone. My grandfather was a member of Parliament and my father was the British diplomat to France. I grew up in Paris, but after his retirement, we took up residence near London. You know, Jemma is rather taken with the French language. Like her, it is beautiful—so expressive and romantic."

"Did you know this Turner fellow?" Lizbeth asked.

"Evidently, I did not know him well enough. His family is quite upstanding in the community, and I simply cannot believe that he would have been having a lurid affair with Jemma. He was very much the charmer, that one, and oh, so splendid on the eyes. She seems content now with her friend, Spencer."

Lizbeth smiled. "You'll have to meet him. Spencer is the kind of young man that you want for your daughter. He's like a member of our family. Everyone thought that they would marry someday, and I know he loves that girl. I pray that she is not giving him false hope."

Helene looked toward the little knoll where Jemma sat, intent on her work, and seemingly unaware of their presence. "She is a rare child who will become well-known for her art, Lizbeth. We shall see her work in New York, Paris, and London galleries."

Lizbeth raised her brow. "My, my. Well, as I said, I do believe that the good Lord has a plan for all of us. It will be a true pleasure to see Jemmabeth succeed. She has brought such joy to her family and friends."

"I believe joy follows the child around," Helene said, still watching her.

"And joy sometimes follows pain," Lizbeth added.

❦

Helene's last day included a tour of The Boulevard and a visit to meet Carrie, who played several classical pieces, finishing with the two of them in an impromptu duet. Their next stop was Willa's, where they lingered for an hour on the porch while Helene laughed until she cried at the irrepressible wit and wisdom of Willa.

Lizbeth declared it would be an insult if Helene didn't allow her to prepare just one home-cooked meal; therefore, supper was a feast. She pulled out all the stops to show off some real Texas cooking. Jemma invited Spencer, and Helene was very much taken with him. They talked on and on about Europe and architecture. Spencer was buoyant. His family never talked with him about things close to his heart.

"What are your plans after you graduate?" Helene asked.

"I'd like to work in a large city, but live in a small town, like Chillaton. Sometimes I think it would be great to work in Europe, too," he said, glancing at Jemma.

She knew his plans backward and forward, and truly believed that his love for architecture began when they played with blocks in the first grade. Spencer could talk all the kids out of their blocks then build something that would prompt Mrs. Hardin to stop the class and have everybody look at it and clap. He was the smartest and most motivated person she had ever known. Somehow Jemma had ended up in his heart, and she knew it was a sweet place to be.

"You're my hero, Spence," she said as they washed the dishes.

"C'mon, don't mess with me. Since when did you think that?"

"Since the first grade. Girls always say you are so cute, but I know your heart, my handsome, Candy Man hero. They know you're cute but only hope that you're sweet, too. That's the way girls think."

"So, you don't think like most girls?"

"Nope. You should know that." She put a dab of dishwater bubbles on his nose.

He wiped it off. "It's because you've had cowboy fever all your life. It's weakened your brain."

"Don't start." She flicked a handful of suds at him, giggling.

He hit her with the dish towel, and it was a standoff around the kitchenette.

"Let's finish this conversation in the hollyhock patch." She ran out the door into the night.

❦

In the living room, Helene was ready for more of Lester. "You know, Lester, there is something about you that reminds me of my husband. He had the same silver hair, but it's something about your eyes. Of course Nebs had a moustache, always did. How is it that you remain a single gentleman?"

Lester basked in the compliment. Maybe his foolhardy wink had paid off. "Well, I had me some fine womenfolk in my time. Now I go around doin' good deeds here for Miz Liz. I figure it's worth it just to get a smile out of her, and that's all I'm askin' in my old age."

Lizbeth sniffed.

"Do you have children?" Helene asked.

Lester scratched his ear. "No ma'am, never did. I reckon the good Lord figured on me bein' a husband several times over and havin' no time for young'uns. I had me some good dogs, though. Had me a mutt named Floyd that could gather eggs from the henhouse."

Lizbeth, being well acquainted with farm chores, snickered at that notion.

Lester leaned forward in his seat. "I ain't jokin'. Most folks used to keep hens and a milk cow no matter what they did for a livin', even here in town. When I'd get up of a mornin', I'd set me a basket by the henhouse door and by noon Floyd would have her filled up. Now you may think old Lester's full of beans, but I wagered a buddy of mine that Floyd could do it, so we spied on him. He wiggled the latch on the door until it come open, then in he went and sure enough, a few minutes later out he came holdin' an egg as gentle as you please, between his teeth. He did it over and over until the basket was full."

"Did Floyd milk the cow, too?" Lizbeth asked.

"No, Miz Liz, not in his youth, but as he come hence to losin' his teeth, he give 'er a try a few times." Lester tapped his foot and grinned.

❦

Helene insisted she had things to do in Wicklow that couldn't wait, so she bought a ticket on the 6:23 Zephyr. Jemma hugged her tight.

"Promise you'll come back to see us."

"How could I refuse such delightful company? Thank you, Lizbeth, for your lovely hospitality and companionship. Jemma, I dreamt that I saw your work in a London gallery."

Jemma laughed. "That would be a miracle. I love you, Helene, and you are always in my prayers."

The Zephyr roared into the station and screeched to a halt. Helene read the name on the silver engine and turned to Jemma. "Do you know the meaning of *Zephyr*, my dear?"

"No ma'am. I never thought about it."

"It means a west wind, something that just passes through, much like a summer romance."

Jemma nodded, staring at the metallic letters. Helene blew a kiss and boarded the train. Jemma bit her lip. Okay, so the definition might be appropriate, but this Zephyr didn't smell like English Leather and it didn't have eyes like. . .a big rat.

Get over it. Carry on.

Chapter 14
Old Moves

H ave you ever had a boyfriend?" Jemma asked as she got Carrie ready for the cannon.

"I did," she said, "in the first grade. His name was Fountie Clark. I claimed him as mine when he swallowed the class goldfish the first day of school. Why are you asking me about boyfriends? You must have somebody in mind for me that had polio, too. Maybe he and I could line up our circus cannons and stare at each other."

"Stop it. If you get out into the world, you'll find love," Jemma said.

"Ah, but will it be true love, the kind you're still whining about? I thought true love is what we watch on *As the World Turns* every day."

"What *you* watch," Jemma countered.

Carrie spoke now in regulated gasps as the iron lung did its work. "So, you really think that some pitiful guy could fall in love with me?"

Jemma wagged her finger at Carrie. "Not a pitiful guy. He would be your Prince Charming. I don't see how it can happen in Chillaton as long as your father hides you in this house."

"I know."

"Maybe I'll talk to your father sometime."

Carrie smiled. "You're nuts."

Jemma smoothed Carrie's hair. "Nah, I just don't like it when people aren't fair."

The cannon took over the conversation for a while.

"Why do you keep fighting the fact that you've found your true love?" Carrie asked.

"I don't know. I need a big sign to come down from heaven that says 'He's the One.'"

"You're not fair to Spencer."

"You need to be quiet now." Jemma turned off the lights and moved to the window. A stray cat sat in the light from the street lamp, then jumped up to capture a moth. It played with it for a few seconds, then moved on down the dark Boulevard, leaving the moth to flail hopelessly on the ground. Jemma chewed on her lip; she was not being unfair to Spence. Carrie just didn't understand.

The static on the line always gave her away. "Sandy?" Jemma asked.

"Hey, Jem, how are things in good old Chillaton? Twila told me that you and Spence are going out again. That's the best news I've heard."

"We're having fun. How are y'all doing?" Jemma flopped back on the good bed.

"All Marty talks about is Vietnam. Did Spence go for the cowboy hat idea? Is that what changed your mind?"

"I didn't fall for Paul's clothes."

"Really. Well, that's behind you anyway."

Jemma hesitated. "I guess."

"Hold it right there," Sandy said. "The guy was married."

"My head knows that, but my heart is still a little tender in that department."

Sandy's tone changed. "You'd better not hurt Spencer again."

"See? I'm in trouble if I don't go out with Spence, and I'm in trouble if I do," Jemma said.

"What does he know about Paul?" Sandy asked but received no answer. "I see. Just as much as your parents know. Buddy said that you have a new friend."

"Yeah, Trina Johnson. You'd like her."

"You relish the gray area, don't you? Always ready to dispense Jemma justice."

"That's not it at all. I hate the fact that Gram's house was so close to Trina and her family all this time, but I never knew or cared about them. She's funny, talented, wise, and a good person. They've had a hard life, Sandy."

"Do you think Chillaton is ready for that kind of thinking?"

"It had better get ready. Anyway, remember The Judge's house that you always wanted to skip at Halloween? I'm working for him now, as a sort of companion to his daughter. She's smarter than anybody in our class, except Spence, of course, and you should hear her play the piano. She's another one that I should have taken more interest in. I was too wrapped up in myself in high school."

"We all were, Jem. You don't have a corner on guilt. I assume you're still painting. Are you going back to Le Claire?"

"Next fall, or Daddy will kill me."

"I wish we could come home for Christmas. Just pray they don't send Marty to Vietnam because we are hearing horror stories about that place. Gotta go. Say hi to Spence for me. Love you."

"Love you, too." Jemma hung up the phone and sat on the side of the bed, thinking about Mr. and Mrs. Turner. Good grief.

The Parnell actually had a line at the ticket window. It was their first showing of *Torn Curtain*. Paul Newman had a following around Chillaton ever since *Hud* was filmed just down the road. Jemma and Sandy had stood around the *Hud* set so long that he walked right by them—after they got out of his way. His eyes were the same sky blue as Carrie's.

The theater was built just before the Depression, not grand by any means, but it had a certain flair that Jemma liked. The maroon floral carpet was now worn and the beveled snack bar mirror had a small crack down one side. The signs that read COLOREDS and WHITES ONLY had been removed from the restrooms, water fountain, and the stairs leading to the balcony. The wallpaper was still vivid where the handmade notices had once hung. The only bad thing about the Parnell was that The Cleave's dad owned it.

After the movie, they sat on the hood of the Corvette and ate fries with their jackets on. The moon cast ribbons of light in the slow moving waters of the Salt Fork, and the stars were brilliant. One streamed across the sky.

"Make a wish," Spencer whispered.

Jemma crossed her fingers and held her breath.

"So, what was it?"

She held up a fry and lowered it into her mouth. "You can't ask that."

"Did it involve your Prince Charming?"

"Maybe you're my Prince Charming." She meant it to be funny, but looked at Spence, his blond hair ruffling in the breeze, then exhaled. "Okay. The guy's name was Paul. He was a law student in Dallas, and he was older than me." She bit her lip and turned away. She did not dare mention that he was a cowboy, of sorts.

"How much older?"

"About ten years."

"Ten?" His voice pierced the otherwise quiet night and bounced against the rocks. "You're in love with somebody over thirty?"

"I didn't say I am in love with him."

"What are you then?"

"I don't know, Spence. I don't want to talk about this anymore."

"You haven't anyway."

Jemma got off the car and walked to the riverbank. Spencer followed her, easing his arm around her waist. "I just want to know where I stand. Look at me, baby." Jemma stared at the ground instead. "I love you, Jemmabeth. If you are hurting, no matter the reason, it hurts me, too."

She put her arms around him, playing with the short hairs at the nape of his neck, and their muffled conversation mingled with the sounds of the Panhandle night. She had never felt so close to anyone.

Dr. Huntley hadn't missed a day to check on Carrie. She only had a cold, but for her, that was major. Anxious to cheer her up, Jemma wanted to take her into the parlor right as the sun was making its way through the big windows. It was Jemma's favorite time of day and she wanted to share it.

"How was your nap? Do you feel any better?" she asked.

"Maybe," Carrie whispered.

"Do you feel like going downstairs?"

"For five minutes."

Jemma strapped Carrie into the crawler, then lifted her into the downstairs wheelchair and rolled her into the parlor. "See how the shadows on the wall look like a leaf dance? The light plays with the wind and we get to watch. It's great."

"That was my dream—to dance in the spotlight. I took lessons in Amarillo when I was only three years old. We saw the New York Ballet perform once and my mom said, 'Carrie, you'll be up there someday,' and I never forgot it. The room next to mine upstairs was my practice room. Dad even had a bar and mirrors installed, but of course the door is locked now. I've checked."

"Can you move your legs at all?" Jemma asked.

"A little, if I really concentrate."

"I suppose you've had all kinds of therapy."

"No, Dad doesn't want me to be disappointed."

The rhythmic dance pattern faded before them. Jemma sketched as Carrie watched the final shadows. "I can still dance or I can even fly, Jem. It's all up to me and what I choose to put in my head."

Jemma kept drawing. "Do you ever wonder why this happened to you?"

Carrie shot her a look. "All the time. Miss Effie, Willa's mom, said it wouldn't change things to sit around and wonder why this or that, but she wasn't the one sitting in this chair. She'd say that the Lord's in charge and He knows what he's doing. He uses all of us for something."

Jemma quit drawing. "Has God used you?"

Carrie coughed. "I don't know. Miss Effie said we might go our whole lives and never figure that out. I read the Bible, but as you know, I don't get out much to apply what I learn. Miss Effie was my preacher, I guess, because I never go to church. Dad forbids it."

"Your dad has a lot of nerve. Maybe too much. Oh yeah, I got you those books you wanted; hang on." Jemma was nearly to the doorway but glanced over her shoulder. Carrie was still watching the wall, though the light had long left. In about ten minutes it would be time to get her into the cannon. Jemma sat on the floor and took out her sketch pad again. Her hand flew over several sheets of paper until Carrie wheeled up next to her.

"Where are the books?" Carrie asked, coughing. "You just can't get good help these days," she said with some effort, but sounding more like herself.

Jemma jumped up. "Sorry, I wanted to catch you in that light. I'll grab those books right now."

Carrie clutched Jemma's sleeve. "Just get me upstairs before I croak." Jemma took her up the stairs herself and put her in the cannon. Carrie closed her eyes. "You think you're Wonder Woman, don't you?"

"No ma'am. I think you are," Jemma said, then called home. "Gram, I am going to stay with Carrie tonight. Please ask Spence to come over, if he can." She went back to the cannon, but Carrie was asleep, her breathing controlled by the lung.

Life wasn't fair. Maybe sometime she would have to sneak Carrie into church. The Judge had never told *her* that it was forbidden.

⁂

They were the first ones in the church the very next Sunday. Carrie could not stop smiling through the service.

⁂

Spencer and Jemma went to the Chillaton Homecoming celebration and danced every dance. The Buddy Baker band was, naturally, playing only Buddy Holly. The last dance was "True Love's Ways." Jemma put the Best Burger Stop out of her mind, which was easy to do with Spencer holding her so close, but Buddy B had one more song.

"Ladies and gentlemen, I know you'll enjoy a little Roy Orbison to finish off the night, by special request," he said. As Buddy pulled out his harmonica, Spencer led her back onto the gym floor. Jemma knew what was up. He was not only a smooth talker, but Spencer was the smoothest dance partner she'd ever had. This song belonged to them in high school. Every time it was played, the floor cleared for Spencer and Jemma to strut their stuff. They had their own particular interpretation of the Chillaton Stomp, worked out in Jemma's living room when they were in junior high. Buddy belted out his version of "Candy Man," which wasn't too bad for a garage mechanic, amid wolf whistles and cheers. The old moves came back, and the eye contact they were giving each other was obvious to everybody in the gym. The crowd joined in, still giving them wide berth.

"You are in so much trouble, Spencer Chase, I mean big trouble," she shouted over the music. "How much did you pay him?"

"Just hush up and dance, so I can get my money's worth."

Jemma did love to dance with him. When the song was over,

he held up her hand during the applause. Turning it palm up, he pressed it to his lips, looking her straight in the eye. She felt a lightning bolt shoot up her arm and straight into her stomach. Maybe he was The One.

Chapter 15

Arizona

Something had bothered Jemma all night, then the call came at breakfast. "Hi, sweet pea." Her voice was all wrong.

"Mom, what's happened?" She paced around Gram's dresser as far as the cord would allow.

Alex sighed like she'd been up all night. "He's okay now, but your daddy fell off the roof and broke his leg. It's a bad break, so he'll be in the hospital a few days. He just had to get that silly Christmas star up before the Festival of Lights tour this weekend."

"Good grief! Can I talk to him?" Jemma asked.

"He's asleep, thanks to the pain medication. We're lucky he didn't break his neck."

"I guess y'all won't be coming to Chillaton."

"I'm sorry, Jem. You know we were looking forward to it. Robby is so disappointed. Now we're hoping you two could come here."

"I'm afraid the Dodge won't make it. Spence thinks it needs to go to the shop."

Alex sighed again. "Well, keep your chin up, honey. There'll be other Christmases. Let me talk to Gram. We love you."

Jemma gave the phone to Lizbeth, then slumped on the couch, tears welling up. She looked around the house. Spencer had bought a tree in Amarillo, and they had spread soapflake snow on its branches. All but one of Papa's bubble lights were ready to shine in Robby's eyes.

❧

She took the car to Chase's Cadillac & Chevrolet the next day. Buddy called her at The Judge's house with more bad news, which she relayed to Lizbeth. "It's going to cost at least seventy dollars to fix the Dodge," Jemma said, "and the worst of it is that they have to order some part that will take a week to get here. Spencer already said he'd pay for it, but I'm scared it'll break down again."

135

"Help my life," Lizbeth replied. "I guess we could ride the train, but that would cost more than the repair bill."

"What about the bus?"

"I just got off the phone with them and there are no seats left. It's the holidays."

"Rats."

"We could go for New Year's Day," Lizbeth murmured halfheartedly.

"Maybe. I guess I'd better get off The Judge's phone. I'll see you later, Gram."

"You never know what the good Lord has in His plan for us, sugar."

During supper, the Lord's plan showed up at the back door. He was still in his suit.

"Come in this house, Spencer," Lizbeth encouraged. "Have a bite to eat with us."

He was all smiles. "I have a proposal for you ladies. I would like to see Arizona this Christmas, and I need some company."

Jemma squealed.

"I get off day after tomorrow, and I'll be ready to hit the road if you are," he offered.

The ladies each planted a big kiss on his cheek, like grateful bookends.

Lizbeth pulled out a chair. "Now, eat, son. That's the least we can do for you."

"What about your family?" Jemma asked. "Won't they be upset if you are gone for the holidays?"

"Mom is oblivious to the holidays, and Dad will be relieved he doesn't have to stay home on Christmas Eve, trust me."

"I do trust you." Jemma kissed him on the lips while Lizbeth's back was turned. She grinned at him the rest of the evening. Everything about him was perfect, right down to his French aftershave.

Flagstaff's mountains and pine trees surprised her. There was a dusting of snow on them at sunrise, so naturally, she went out in her pajamas and coat to sketch.

"You look cute in your jimmy-jams," Spencer said, sneaking out when she wasn't looking. "Mind if I watch you think?"

Jemma gave him a dirty look. "You aren't supposed to see me in my pajamas. Gram would have a fit."

"That coat is thick enough for a blizzard," he said, pulling her collar up around her ears. "I think you're safe in it."

"I wasn't expecting company. Missy told me that I had a bohemian look. What do you think?"

"Since when did you care what Missy says?"

"Since you went out with her more than I wanted to hear about."

"*Voila!* I've found the way to your heart. It's through The Cleave."

"Don't you dare try that route. Let's go in. I'm too cold to draw."

"Not until you give me a kiss, you bohemian."

"I haven't brushed my teeth yet."

"Me neither," he said, moving in closer.

She kissed him just as her mother opened the door.

"Good morning. Anybody out here want breakfast?" she asked.

"You bet," Spencer said and walked inside, holding Jemma's hand.

"Hmmm." Her mother raised her eyebrows a couple of times as Jemma passed by.

It was a lazy day. Lizbeth and Robby played dominoes and checkers while Jemma and Alex made pies. The men watched football in the den, with periodic wails and whoops.

"I know the time's going to fly, and you will be on the road again," Alex said as they relaxed in the living room.

Jemma put her head in her mother's lap. "I miss you."

"I miss you, too. By the way, that wasn't a sisterly kiss you gave Spence this morning," Alex noted.

"True, but don't draw any big conclusions from that. You know I have to love him in some way. It's just that I don't know if I love him above all others."

"You mean above Paul?" Alex mouthed his name.

"Mom, Paul made me wild inside, like my senses were starved or something. I think I loved him," she whispered, "but I never said it, even to myself."

"It was probably a physical attraction. That can be powerful at your age. You hadn't been attracted to anybody else in such a long time. Does Spencer know all about him?"

"I can't talk to Spence about that. I know he must feel about me the same way I felt about Paul."

"Felt?"

Jemma shrugged. "I haven't seen him in over four months. Maybe I need to see him again so I can sort things out."

"You haven't told me why you broke it off. Was there somebody else?" Alex asked.

Spencer appeared in the door. "I'm being sent out to get burgers."

Jemma jumped up, covered with guilt.

"That sounds great!" Alex gushed with enthusiasm. "I'll set the table."

"So, what hot topic have you been chewing on?" Spencer asked as soon as Alex left the room.

"Girl talk." Jemma straightened the throw pillows. Spencer caught her as she turned and kissed her. Jemma's conscience made it a good one, too.

◈

She knew that her daddy had questions. Talking to her mother was one thing, but she wasn't sure how she would hold up with him. He was a "look you in the eye" man. That's where she got it. Spencer offered to drive them around Flagstaff to see the Christmas lights, but Jemma stayed with Jim, to get it over with.

"I'm already tired of this cast," he said, laboring to sit on the couch. "Now, what's the deal with this Paul guy? Your mother and I thought you were going to call us any day and say you were bringing him to meet us and plan the wedding. The next thing we knew, you were calling from Chillaton to say you weren't going to school and you were going to live with Mama. Did this guy break your heart overnight?"

Jemma chose her words with great care. "There was another girl, a woman."

"I see. He was a jerk. Then what's going on with Spencer? You know that we love that boy. He may have money, but he's had no real love in his life, aside from us. I'm not saying that our feelings for him should make any difference to you, but he's a great kid and I don't want to see him hurt, especially by my own baby girl."

"I know." Jemma felt like she did when she was six years old and told the whole class that Eddie Parker had fleas, making Eddie cry and hide in the boys' bathroom.

"So, is Spence your boyfriend now?"

"I guess."

"Not much of an answer."

"I'm sorry, Daddy."

Then the tears came, but Jim was used to this. He handed her a box of tissues. "Come over here." She inched her way across the couch, not wanting to make his pain any worse. He put his arm around her. "Now, tell me why you left Wicklow like that."

Jemma could not bring herself to say the words that would send Mr. Turner straight into eternal fire as far as her daddy was concerned. "I just couldn't stay."

"How'd you give up your school? That was the biggest shock to me."

"I'm going back, Daddy, but not until next fall, if that's okay. I know y'all said for me to go back after Christmas. You should see all the paintings I've done, and I have made some really good friends in Chillaton. I think the Lord wanted me to go there." There she went again, using the Lord after the fact.

"Well, I know you've been good for Mama, too. I already heard about the change of plans for school, but back to Spencer. You're a good girl, honey, but I think you underestimate yourself when it comes to the effect you have on boys. You're like your mother in that department, so you must use your power for good."

He shifted his leg with a moan. "When you played ball in high school, Digger Randall told me that he never worried about losing a close game. He just needed you to get the ball. All it took was one good jumpshot from you and the game was in the bag. You were always in control. Second place at state wasn't your fault. Digger takes the blame for that one." He grinned at her with some amount of coaching pride. "The thing is, you are in control of more than a game now. You have to watch out for Spencer's heart. Life is not a basketball game despite all the analogies we coaches like to draw from it. Remember that. Deal?"

Jemma exhaled. "Deal." She had escaped the third degree.

"Good. Now let's talk about something else. Tell me about these paintings you've been working on before these painkillers kick in, and I fall asleep."

❧

She opened Spencer's gift and touched the gold Florentine heart; a diamond dazzled from its center. She laid her head against his chest.

Since he was a little boy, he had loved giving her things. "It's in the Etruscan style and diamonds are your birthstone. There's something on the back, too." He watched her face as she turned it over to see *Always* engraved there. "Don't forget that, baby."

He had endeared himself to her again. "Thank you so much, Spence. I love it, and I thank you for this trip." She kissed him before she had to choose any more words with such care. "Now open your present."

Spencer slipped off the wrapping paper and blinked at the painting inside.

"It's my first self-portrait as a grown-up." Jemma wrinkled her nose as she waited for his response. "Well, almost grown-up. I've done some others, but nobody's ever seen them."

"You are an incredible artist." He shook his head in disbelief at the painting. "I don't understand how you can do this."

"I do it because it is given to me. I don't know how."

"Could you marry me, Jem? This is not a formal proposal, but I need to know if it's even a possibility."

It was a solid hit to her heart. "Let's not do this tonight. I. . . don't understand my feelings for you right now." She was sorry as soon as she said it.

"Is there hope?"

Jemma could hear her daddy's words, and she didn't know what to say. "Spence, I know that we could get married and live happily ever after, but I don't want to marry anybody right now." There. That should buy her some time in this silly game she had created.

"Then promise that you will tell me when you are ready to marry—anybody. Promise?"

"Okay. I promise." She winced even as she said it.

❧

They all played board games late. Lizbeth went to bed, but Robby was entranced with the model airplane kit that Spencer had given him.

"We'll take it out tomorrow, okay, Rob?" Spencer said.

"'Night, Jem. You, too, old man Chase." Robby yawned. "I like the plane."

Jim got up on his crutches. "Hey, I'm beat. Y'all excuse me, but my pain pills just took over again for the evening."

Alex drew Jemma and Spencer to her. "Merry, merry Christmas, you two."

Then they were left alone in the lights of the tree.

"Happy Christmas, baby," he said.

She put arms around him. "You, too."

"Thanks for the portrait."

"I didn't just give it to you. I painted it for you. There's a difference." She touched his chin.

He tucked her hair behind her ear and kissed her neck. "Do you think they have a parking hill in Flagstaff?" he whispered.

"Probably, but why go out in the cold when we can stay here?"

"You're right." He walked her backward until her legs hit the couch. "Sit down, woman, and let's smooch until Santa comes."

Giggling, she did, and for a while, forgot her deal with her daddy.

❧

Christmas morning, Robby flipped on the light and jumped on Jemma's bed with her stocking. "You got the fattest one." His red-and-white-striped pajamas made him look like an electric candy cane in the bright light.

She sat up. "What time is it?"

"Almost six o'clock." Robby checked his new watch while he continued to jump.

"Good grief." Jemma flopped back on the pillow. "Can't we do this later? You're going to wake up Gram."

"She's already up, drinking coffee with Daddy." Robby crash-landed next to her. "You'll hurt Santa's feelings if you wait."

"The sun's not even up yet."

"C'mon, Jem. Please."

She tried to focus on the lumpy stocking in her lap as Robby crawled in bed with her. "Let's see," she said. "Here's an apple, and oh, look, an orange."

"I saw that apple on the dining table yesterday. See, it's got a dent in it right there."

She turned her sleepy eyes on him. "Hey, Santa put these in here. Who cares where he got them?" She pulled out a plaid tam with a pompon on top, matching scarf, red mittens, and a bottle of French perfume she'd never heard of before. "I bet you didn't see these on the dining room table yesterday."

"No, but I saw Spence getting all of it out of his suitcase last night."

Jemma put on the tam. She used her best Scottish accent. "Did ya, now, my wee laddie? Well, goot. Did you see this a-coming, too?" She threw back the covers and tickled him until he couldn't breathe.

"Jem, stop! I gotta go to the bathroom."

"You'd better run, or I'm gonna get you again." She yawned.

Robby streaked out of the room and down the hall.

She turned off the light and got back in bed, hoping for sleep, but she got more little brother.

"So, how did God make the world?" he asked.

"Good grief, Robby. It's too early for this."

"My friend told me that He used electricity."

Jemma buried her face in the pillow. "Go back to sleep. You can stay in my bed if you want."

"Okay." He snuggled close to her. "You know what else? He said God was a teenager when the dinosaurs were alive."

Jemma cleared her throat. He lay still for a whole minute.

"Are you in love with Spence?" he asked. "I saw you kissing him last night."

"It's none of your snoopy business. Let me sleep a little longer."

Robby covered his head with the sheet. "My girlfriend wants me to kiss her."

Jemma turned over and pulled the sheet back. "Who's this girlfriend?"

"Kimmy Sutton. She has short hair that goes all the way around her head like zurrrp." He made a halo around his head in the faint light. "She wears a different-colored bow every day, and her hair is yellow like Spence's. Mom says she's cute, plus she draws me pictures of monkeys. I'm going to get a real one someday."

Jemma laughed. "Girlfriend or monkey? What does Mom think about you kissing a girl?"

"Mom says kissing is for high school, but Kimmy says I have to kiss her so she'll know I love her."

"Are you going to?"

"I don't know. I think I should because she's my best friend, and I want to make her happy. Jem, are you asleep?"

"Nope. I'm wide awake," she said, thinking of her own best friend since the first grade, asleep in the next room, and that Santa's helper had better get up to stuff Spence's stocking.

※

After lunch, Spencer took Robby to the school playground to fly the model plane while Alex and Jemma went for a tour of the college.

Lizbeth and Jim had visited for an hour, enjoying the empty house.

"It was a real blessing to see you, Mama," Jim said. "I'm sorry that I was all banged up for your visit."

Lizbeth patted his arm. "I'm glad you are better, son. I've had a fine time."

"I think you and Jemmabeth are good for each other, don't you?" he asked.

"You and Alexandra have done a first-rate job raising that child. She's a joy, and I am not the only one who thinks she is going to be famous someday. You wait until you see the paintings that she has done in Chillaton, and to think that she did them in that dusty old garage."

"Do you know why she left Wicklow?" Jim asked, hoping luck was with him for an answer.

"She had some hard grief that she couldn't hold up to, James."

He tried again. "I don't suppose you would share that information with me, would you?"

When Lizbeth puckered her lips, Jim knew that look very well.

"Well, I guess I'll just have to put my trust in the Lord to take care of her," he said.

Lizbeth smiled, at last. "That's always the best place to put it."

◈

Robby and Jemma finished up a jigsaw puzzle while Alex loaded the stereo. She and Jemma took turns jitterbugging and bopping with Spencer. The young people were dancing to "Mean Woman Blues" when Lizbeth entered the room. If her brow could go any higher, her eyes would have popped out on the floor. She could say with some certainty that Cam would not have liked seeing his little Jemmabeth move around like that to music. It wouldn't have even mattered that it was Spencer who was her partner. Alex and Jim didn't seem to think anything of it.

Lizbeth returned to the kitchen for more pie and coffee. She peeked out at the snow-covered mountains and wondered if Jemma had danced like that with this older man, Paul. No wonder he kept writing her letters. Jemma, with her looks and chaste ideals, would be irresistible to a man of the world. Things were so different when she was young. In her college physiology class, the professor pulled down a chart of the human body on the first day and the girl sitting behind her fainted. She thought of her own courtship with Cam. There were no dances at all. They went to socials where stern-faced church deacons and their poker-faced wives stood over them like crows watching the corn grow. She and Cameron played silly games and longed to be together, walking in the moonlight, bravely holding hands.

Cam had kissed her full on the lips once during their courting days. It made her so angry that she didn't speak to him for nearly two years. Had he not come to her school and played his fiddle under the window, she might have still been an old maid. He had to propose in front of her students so she wouldn't yell at him. School-marms couldn't be married, so she gave up her career for him, and it was the best thing she ever did.

She washed her dishes and went to the linen closet to get a clean dish towel. She opened the door to find Jemma and Spencer kissing. Red-faced, they stepped out.

"Hi." Jemma grinned.

"Sorry, Gram," Spencer said. "Watch out. There's some mistletoe in there."

Lizbeth couldn't help but smile back at them. Her own heart was full of youthful memories at the moment, now well over half a century old.

Jim leaned on his crutches and watched them load the car. Robby sat on Jemma's lap just like he had done when they left Wicklow nearly seven months ago when Alex reminded her to take her vitamins. Only this time, Jemma wasn't left on her own. She had Spencer. Now she needed to figure out what to do about it.

Chapter 16
BB & Scarlett

Jemma shook snowflakes out of her hair at the post office counter. Paralee Batson, the postmistress, gave her stamps and change. "We've sure had us some sorry basketball teams since you graduated, Jemmabeth. None of them girls will ever have a jumpshot like you. It took the cake. 'Course nobody is as tall as you either." Her face was white with powder and set off with two rounded splotches of rouge. Joan Crawford had inspired the use of her eyebrow pencil, and tight brush curlers peeked out of a hairnet. A column of smoke rose from an ashtray on her desk.

Paralee leaned over the counter to check both ends of the lobby. "Hon," she whispered, "are you in some kind of legal trouble? I know it ain't none of my business and I shouldn't be talking about it, but I've known you since before you were born. Nobody gets a letter a week from a law office, so I've been worried about your state of affairs." Paralee's cat, H.D., raised his head from his perch by the scales in anticipation of Jemma's reply.

Jemma blushed. "I'm all right, Paralee. Thanks for worrying about me, though. I worked for that office, and I guess they want me back." It could be the story.

Paralee thought for a second. "Well, I'll say. You must have made a good impression on somebody. I'm sure glad to see that you and Spencer are having another go at it. You two could make some cute young'uns, after you're married, of course."

Jemma turned red again and reached to give H.D. a pat on the head. She couldn't think of a response to that. Chillaton—no secrets. Well, maybe one.

⌘

The snowy New Year came in at the country club dance. The Buddy Baker band was rocking and Spencer brought his mother. He had stewed over it for a week. Jemma came by herself so that he could spend most of the time with his mom. Mrs. Chase, fresh from Nedra's Nook and her own makeup drawer, was probably a smooth dancer in her younger days, before the drinking. She was still pretty, despite all that alcohol had done to her. Spencer kept his mom on the dance floor as much as possible. Jemma knew he was steering her away from the spiked punchbowl. He danced with Jemma only at midnight, then took her to say hello to his mother before they went home. She had dreaded it all night. Rebecca Chase had never liked her, not even when they were in grade school.

"Hello, Mrs. Chase. It's good to see you," Jemma fibbed, then clamped down on her lip.

Mrs. Chase glared at her. "So, did you find yourself a new boyfriend? My Spencer wasn't good enough for an overgrown, stuck-up hussy like you, I guess."

Spencer was humiliated. "C'mon, Mother, let's go. I'll see you later, Jem."

"You'd better not ever hurt him again, you little. . . !" She yelled something horrible as Spencer whisked her outside. The party turned silent for what seemed like forever.

Back home, Jemma's cheeks burned as she sat in Papa's chair waiting for Spence. Not only did Mrs. Chase dislike her, now she was calling her vile names in public and threatening her, too. Jemma closed her eyes. She truly didn't want to hurt him ever again. She heard his car and ran to open the door.

He was loosening his tie. "Sorry I'm late, baby. Mother got sick. She's asleep now, but I need to go back out and stay with her. I just wanted to apologize."

"I'll come, too," Jemma said, getting her jacket. "Are you sure she's asleep?"

"Jem, about what she called you. . . ," he began.

"Let's not talk about it now. I'm over it, really." She fibbed again.

"I don't know, maybe she's caught the flu or something. I shouldn't have taken her, and I'm so sorry about what she said."

"I deserved it." Jemma smoothed his hair. "She looked pretty, and y'all were great on the dance floor."

Every light was on at the Chase castle. Jemma hadn't been in the house for a couple of years. Everything about it said *money*, although nobody ever saw it except the three of them and their housekeeper.

They sat at the top of the big staircase, just outside his mother's room.

"This could be where Rhett carries Scarlett up the stairs," Jemma said, keeping her volume low.

Spencer almost smiled. "Don't ask me to carry you up it tonight."

"I think I must be like Scarlett because I am so bad."

"You are anything but bad. Mother didn't know what she was saying."

They sat thinking of things they couldn't talk about.

She took a deep breath. "Your house belongs in a magazine."

"Not in my opinion. An interior decorator redid it last year and got it in *Southern Comfort* magazine, but it's the palatial design that I hate."

"Everybody around here thinks it's magnificent."

"They don't have to live here." Spence took her hand. "Come on, I'll show you my room." He ushered her down the hall and into a large, very organized bedroom that included a drafting area.

"My goodness." Jemma walked around looking at the numerous photographs of her. "You have way too many pictures of me."

"Nope. I can never have too many until I have the real thing. There's my favorite." He pointed to a black-and-white photo of a practically toothless Jemma in braids, her now famous cowboy boots, and a frilly little dress.

She picked up a framed drawing of a fox. "I can't believe you have these from grade school. They are so funny, but where did you get all this artwork, may I ask?"

"Your desk." He leaned against the door frame.

"You stole my drawings out of my desk in school?"

"Yup. They are in safekeeping until you are famous. Then we can publish them in a book."

"Spencer, you love me too much." She kissed him.

"Let's get out of here," he said and took her home.

Lizbeth heard the delivery truck pull in Lester's driveway. "Honey, let Kenneth in, please. I'm on the phone with Do Dah."

Jemma opened the door. "Hi, Kenneth. Just set the groceries on the table."

Kenneth Rippetoe's claim to fame was that one of his eyes was brown and the other blue. Their senior year in high school, Kenneth had outbid Spencer for her box at the student council's box supper. Kenneth, who was just a freshman then, paid fifty dollars to eat fried chicken and potato salad next to Jemma while she stared daggers at Spence. Spencer said he was giving him the thrill of a lifetime, but it must have cost Kenneth over two months' worth of delivering groceries. He wasn't all that bad looking. He was just one of those guys who didn't fit in, coupled with the fact that he had a silver front tooth, and Gene Autry–style pants with the cuffs rolled up. He was undersized, but bigger than a cookstove.

"Jemmabeth, I've been hoping to catch you at home so I could tell you that you're looking more like BB every day." He moved his eyebrows in an impressive series of lifts. "Actually, you're prettier than she is."

"Thanks, Kenneth, but isn't Brigitte Bardot a blond?"

"I wasn't talking about her hair. I was talking about her lips. . . I mean, her mouth or something." He turned bright red at that revelation.

Jemma signed the delivery slip. "It's sweet of you to be thinking of me when you see BB."

He lingered at the kitchenette. "What I was wondering was, if you'd come to my Eagle Scout award ceremony."

"I didn't know you were going for your Eagle. Congratulations, Kenneth. When is it?"

"Seven o'clock, Thursday night at the Methodist church. There'll be cake and punch, too."

"I'll be there. Thanks for asking me, and here's a quarter from Gram."

"Thank her for me." He headed for the door. "Wait. Have you noticed that my blue eye looks like Paul Newman's now?"

"Really." She bent down to check. "Not quite, but that's a nice line."

Kenneth grinned, his silver tooth glinting in the noonday light. "See ya Thursday." He tossed the quarter in the air and caught it.

⬥

On Thursday Trina came over to Carrie's, and the three of them were still playing Clue at a quarter to seven.

"I gotta go if I'm gonna shoot some hoops," Trina said. "You're too good at this game, Carrie."

"I'm just a lucky gal." Carrie patted the arms of her wheelchair.

Jemma made a face at her. "I think you cheat."

Carrie cupped her hands and shouted, "Eleanor, come and throw these people out of the house."

Trina grinned. "She can't hear you; she's hanging out the wash. We'll leave quietly."

Trina dribbled along the sidewalk, taking care to miss the cracks and buckles. "Want to shoot some?"

"Sure." Jemma stole the ball and dribbled across the road. "Did you swipe this basketball? It says Metro College on it."

"My coach gave it to me when I left. He said for me to practice and try to walk-on for a team at a four-year school."

"Did you?" Jemma popped in a long shot.

"Nah. That was about the time that Mama broke her hip, but I'm still working on my game. Brother Cleo fixed me a goal by the church, but this is better dribbling. Anyway, I don't know if I still want to play on a team."

"That's because you're in love," Jemma said.

"No more than you are."

Jemma took another long shot and missed.

Trina laughed. "Rattled you, didn't I?"

"I don't love anybody." That sounded tough.

"Sure you don't. You should see the way you look when you talk about Spencer or when somebody says his name."

"Maybe you need glasses." Jemma missed a jumper.

"Maybe your jumpshot's getting rusty." Trina swished one through the net.

"You're on," Jemma said, popping one in herself.

They battled it out until they were both tired and thirsty.

"What time is it?" Trina wiped sweat on her shirt.

"It's seven thirty. Rats!" Jemma took off, tucking in her shirttail. "I'm late. I'll talk to you later," she yelled.

She stood outside the church and faced the wind to evaporate the sweat. She dusted off her jeans, undid her ponytail, ran her fingers through her damp hair, then pushed open the door.

In the choir loft, a whole troop of Boy Scouts was ready to sing. Explorer Scouts held flags at attention and Kenneth was in the middle of his speech. Jemma eased herself into a pew at the back of the church. He smiled when he saw her. The Boy Scouts sang "God Bless America," then the color guard walked down the middle aisle with the flags and it was over.

Kenneth came right toward her. "Thanks for coming."

"Kenneth, I am so sorry that I was late. You gave a good speech."

"I made my mom cry."

"I'm sure she is very proud."

"Come and meet her."

Everybody was dressed up for the ceremony, but Jemma didn't even look bohemian. She looked like a field hand.

Mrs. Rippetoe hugged her son. Her thin arms held him for a long minute. Then she turned her attention to his guest.

Kenneth grinned. "Mom, I want you to meet Jemmabeth Forrester."

Jemma shook her hand. "Congratulations on your son's accomplishments," she said, hoping his mother didn't notice that her hands smelled like a sweaty rubber ball. She recognized Mrs. Rippetoe's dress as one that had belonged to her own mother.

"You're Alex and Jim's daughter, aren't you? Your mother is one of the nicest people I've ever known. She cleaned my house for me when we lost Kenneth's father. She brought us food and called me several times to see how I was doing."

"My parents are very kind," Jemma said. "I hope that I can be like them someday."

Mrs. Rippetoe's voice was soft and tender. "I've heard nothing but good things about all the Forresters, and it sure means a lot to Kenneth that you came tonight."

Jemma smiled. "It was my pleasure. I've never been to an Eagle Scout ceremony."

"Then I'm glad you got to see mine first. Now let's eat. Mom made cowboy sheet cake."

They ate the chocolate cake in the fellowship hall.

"Aren't you a senior this year?" Jemma asked, having her second piece.

"Yeah," he said.

"Going to college?"

"Junior college, at least I hope so. I applied for a bunch of scholarships, but my grades aren't real good."

Jemma scraped the last bit of icing off the plate. "I bet you'll get one. I'm sure your Eagle award will impress them. What do you plan to study?"

"I'd like to study business because I think I've got a good head for it. I want to manage a nursing home. My granny was in one that she hated, so I'd like to change that. I'd make it something special," he said, looking right at her with his blue and brown eyes. "I'll tell you my ideas sometime, if you want."

Jemma's heart melted. "You keep trying for those scholarships. Something good will happen." She set her plate and cup on the table. "Your mother is a great baker."

"Thanks. I'm glad she's out with other folks because she's been sad too long."

"Well, I'd better be getting home," Jemma said. "Gram will wonder where I am."

He stuck his hands in his pockets. "You probably don't remember this, but when you were in junior high and I was still in grade school, you said a poem over the loudspeaker one morning, right after the pledge."

She thought for a moment. "I do remember. It was a Dickinson poem. She's my favorite poet."

"One of the lines is about helping a fallen robin into his nest again. That's what I'm gonna do at my nursing home, and I'll put that poem on a plaque and hang it above the door. Life should be about helping others."

Jemma stared at him. "I can't believe you remember that day."

"I remember everything about you." He looked at the floor. "Spencer is a lucky guy."

"You are a special person, Kenneth. You'll make a woman very happy someday."

He glanced at her.

Jemma started to leave, paused, then bent down and kissed him right on the lips. Kenneth drew back a second, then responded. She left him, stunned, at the church. She walked past the courthouse just as The Judge was getting into his car. She waved, but he ignored her. She smiled anyway at the thought of Kenneth, his dreams, and his eagle moment in the sun.

Lizbeth sat in her porch swing waiting for her family to arrive. The honeysuckle vine behind her was in its first flush before summer. She broke off a stem and savored its sweet fragrance. Too bad the blossoms didn't keep their fragrance longer off the vine. At her age, even a flower could set her thinking about the brevity of life.

Things seemed to revolve around arrivals, departures, and uncertainties. "Who Can Know What God's Great Plan Will Reveal?" That had been the title of her father's sermon when she and Cam had their first date on a warm spring day in 1905. It was about a year later that he messed up with the kissing business. She quickly realized that she had been too hard on him for that, but in those days it wouldn't have been proper for her to contact him and apologize. He proposed by asking in a great Scottish voice, "Will you stand with me, Lizbeth Jenkins, in front of God and man, and say that you will love me forever?" In spite of all schoolmarm etiquette, she had promised loud and clear, in front of her students, "I will stand with you, Cameron Forrester, forever and a day, and I will love you."

The Great Plan, though, had waxed hard, and she longed for the days when all her menfolk were with her, when joy was within reach. She didn't consider herself a bitter woman. It was just that she had nothing left to give, save small gestures of Christian kindness. Each day was the same now. She just went through the motions, playing out the past in her mind. Jemmabeth had brought a glimpse of the old joy back into her life.

She watched as a whirlwind caught a tumbleweed and sailed it skyward. They had named their sons from the New Testament—Matthew, Luke, and James. Cam had wanted to use Scottish names, Angus being a particular favorite. She had prevailed by choosing a scripture for each son and Cam liked that idea. Lizbeth's faith in the truth of those scriptures remained, but two of her three boys were gone, buried in far-off places she had only seen in an atlas.

She had adopted a verse of her own now, James 1:2–4: "My brethren, count it all joy when you fall into various trials, knowing that the testing of your faith produces patience." She was still standing, as promised, but in the shadow of a sorrow she did not want to confront. Maybe it was time she did. Jemmabeth was not the only one in the family who could do with some advice. Lizbeth recognized that she needed to count the joy, to take the advice of the Lord. The crunch of gravel in the driveway stirred her into a smile. They had arrived, signaling the onset of yet another sad parting.

Jemma ran out of the house to pick up Robby. "Goodness, you have grown." There was a knot of conversation and laughter for several minutes.

"What's new out here?" Alex looked around at the yard. "You've painted the birdhouses and planted more bulbs. I see the honeysuckle is in bloom."

Robby tugged at his sister's arm. "C'mon, Jem, show me the bird's nest." The group migrated to the nest tucked in a cluster of branches in the pecan tree.

"Jimmy, it's a cardinal's," Lizbeth said.

"I don't ever remember seeing one around here." He squinted up at it.

"I saw one last year, the day you moved to Arizona. First, I heard it outside the pouting room. Then I saw it in the pecan tree. It's a cardinal all right."

"Let's see these paintings we've heard so much about," Jim said. Jemma and her daddy took the bar off the car house door. Alex gasped when she saw inside.

"Baby girl," was all Jim could say, over and over.

Alex clasped her hands to her heart and cried. Jim slipped his arms around his wife and daughter, but nobody said anything more.

Robby broke the silence. "Wow! This is just like that wax museum in California. Hey, there I am, almost." He pointed to the one unfinished piece.

"I can't believe I gave birth to you, sweet pea," Alex said.

Jim chuckled. "Papa's bragging would have been impossible to deal with."

Leaned against the walls were paintings so detailed that their subjects appeared to be waiting their turns to speak. There were so many—Willa in her rocking chair, fanning and laughing; Lester, hat in hand, concocting his next story with an eye on the train tracks; Trina bent over her old Singer sewing machine; Eleanor's hands in bread dough and her teeth in a jar; Lizbeth and Helene walking arm in arm in the sandy turn row; and Carrie engrossed in a piano piece while leafy shadows danced on the wall behind her. There were also landscapes of the home place and the Salt Fork of the Red River; a pastoral piece depicting two laborers, one black and one white as they hoed a field of cotton; a sunset behind a windbreak of perverse, leafless trees; a small bird on a wrought-iron gate in a snowstorm, its black eyes piercing the swirls of white; the North Chillaton Quilting Club members hovering over their work; the half-completed one of Robby under his tree house; and a big one of Spencer on the hood of the Dodge, watching the stars.

Her family discussed each piece, lingering over their favorites. Robby was the first to leave, running to visit Lester. After an hour or so they went inside.

"Heavenly days," Alex said when she saw the kitchen. "I bet this is the only *trompe l'oeil* in Chillaton. Jemma, it's truly a garden."

"See, there's the home place. The sun is shining right on the windmill." Lizbeth pointed with pride to the house. "Now I can look at it any time I like."

Jim shook his head. "I have to say that you haven't wasted your time, baby girl. This is something."

"Robby can sleep on the cot in my room," Jemma said, holding their bags.

"Thanks," Jim replied. "I need to get my circulation going again."

"How's your leg?" she asked.

"It gets a little stiff riding that far. How's Spencer? Are things okay with you two? I sure like that painting of him."

"Things are good, Daddy."

"Are there wedding bells yet?"

"Jim," Alex said, "aren't you being a little nosy?"

"Hey, I'm getting tired of waiting, and I'm sure Spence is."

Jemma played with her necklace. "Daddy, you will be one of the first to know because I'm sure that, whoever my future husband is, he'll do the right thing and ask you for my hand."

"That doesn't qualify," he said. "Give me a simple yes or no."

"I don't have an answer," Jemma declared with some impatience.

"Let's go look at the flowers," Alex prodded. "There'll be time for questions later."

❧

The guys went fishing at Pearl Lake about fifty miles away while Jemma took Alex to meet her new friends. She was so proud of her beautiful mother. She watched her talk with Willa and Trina like she had known them all of her life. As they walked back to Lizbeth's, Alex stopped on the tracks and took her daughter's hand.

"Jemma," she said, "I want you to know that I'm ashamed that I never reached out to the black community in all the years we lived in Chillaton. The most I ever did was send food and clothing to the Bethel church. That's inexcusable. It's my loss and my family's. I set a poor example for you."

"I know the feeling, Mom." Jemma squeezed her mother's hand. "We have a second chance now."

Carrie was dying to meet Alex. Jemma had never seen her so nervous. She fretted over her clothes, her hair, and which song to play for her on the piano. There was no cause for worry because Alex breezed in and took Carrie's breath away. Carrie was hungry for a mother, and Jemma was eager to share her own. They laughed and played the piano while Jemma talked with Eleanor, who was doing double duty to give her time off with her family.

"Jem, would you please help me get Carrie on the sofa," Alex asked from the hallway.

Carrie couldn't take her eyes off Alex. They sat together on the sofa talking about things that Jemma couldn't hear. She didn't want to intrude, so she went for a long walk. When she returned, Carrie had fallen asleep on her mother's shoulder and Alex had been crying. Neither spoke of it. When Carrie woke up, Jemma left her mother to say good-bye in private.

"Thank you, honey," Alex murmured on the way to Lizbeth's. "I don't know when I have been so touched by such a starving, sweet spirit."

"I know," Jemma said.

Alex blew her nose. "She needs a mother."

"I'm glad she had you, even for a little while."

Spencer, who couldn't help himself, walked with Robby and gave him hints about where to find the candy eggs that he and Jemma had hidden for him. Alexandra sat with her daughter in the hollyhock patch. "I recall when your second-grade class had the big Easter egg hunt in the park," Alex said as they watched Robby race around yelling each time he found another one.

Jemma sensed a lesson coming on. "I remember. There was a prize for finding the most eggs and for finding the fewest, too."

"You wanted to win so much that Spencer gave you some of his to fill your basket."

"Typical Spence, always looking out for me."

Alex kept on. "Somebody else had found more eggs than you. So, all the way back from the park, you kept dropping eggs out of the car window."

"I thought maybe I could get the prize for having the fewest," Jemma explained. "I know what you are going to say, that I was the loser all the way around because Eddie Parker won that prize for being late and not even getting to hunt."

"Now that you're a big girl, do you see any life lesson there?" Alex asked, taking her daughter's hand. "Maybe that's something to think about, Jem."

Alex took a box of clothing to the Rippetoes. Jemma meant to go with her but took Robby to the park at the last minute.

They decided to end the week with a cookout at the river.

Spencer and Jim bought the groceries and Jemma went to invite the Johnson ladies.

Willa waved. "You young'uns go on. I'll stay here and get some work done."

"No, Mama. You're going with us. You never go anywhere," Trina said.

"It's true, Willa," Jemma declared. "You rarely go when I invite you to do something."

Willa chuckled. "I'm just a homebody."

"Then I won't go either." Trina plopped in a kitchen chair.

Jemma rolled her eyes. "Well, this is just great. I want both of you to come, and if you don't, I'm going to have to tell everybody it's because you don't like eating with white folks. How do you like that?"

Willa and Trina exchanged glances, then Willa burst into laughter. It was one of her rolling, roaring ones. She slapped her leg and shook her finger at Jemma. "You are a sneaky one, Jemmabeth. You come here and give me a hug. I'll go."

Trina grinned. "Mama will make some cobbler."

Jemma found her daddy in the good bedroom. He was in the rocking chair, eyes fixed on the big portrait of Papa.

"Want some company?" she asked.

"Sure," he said, blowing his nose. She sat in his lap. "That's a perfect likeness of him. It's almost too much."

"Thank you, Daddy. I wanted him to be watching us out of the corner of those blue eyes, with a twinkle in them, of course."

"You did well. That's the way he disciplined us kids in church. It only took one look. Of course we knew that he was thinking of some mischief of his own the whole time he was giving us the eye. I sure miss him."

"I think about him a lot, especially when I hear a fiddle."

"I don't know if I could bear to hear that old song he loved again," Jim said. "It got to me at the funeral, and I always wondered how Mama stood it. She never flinched. It was the same at Matt and Luke's memorial services."

"You never talk much about your brothers, Daddy."

"I keep it all here." He patted his heart. "If I didn't have your mother back then, I don't know what I would've done. We were so close, and to have them both erased from my life in the same year, well, it was tough. It must eat Mama up sometimes."

"I think Gram is changing. I think she's letting go a little."

Jim shifted his leg. "Is she feeling okay?"

"She never mentions anything. Why?"

"Mama's always been healthy, but age is creeping up on her and I'm not around. You be my eyes, Jem, and remember, as much as you miss Papa, it's the Lord who always has His eye on you."

"I will. How's your leg?"

He shook his foot. "Right now it has no feeling in it at all."

She jumped up. "Oh no! Do you need to go to the doctor?"

"I just needed you to get up. You must weigh a ton."

Jemma put her fists on her hips. "I do not. I run to work nearly every morning. You have to take that back."

He laughed. "Okay, okay, but you aren't exactly my baby girl any more, are you?" Jim stood and studied the portrait again. "You find yourself a man like Papa, Jemmabeth, and you don't need to look very far."

She leaned against his shoulder. "I know, Daddy, really I do."

So many people she loved were together in the same spot. She watched them as they joked and unloaded the cars. Spencer worked harder than anybody as he built the fire. He looked across at her, smiling, and she saw it all. He was so worthy of love, but she still needed to know if it was the marrying kind.

"You eat up these big productions, don't you?" he asked.

Jemma grinned. "I do. Hey, where's Mom?"

"She's on her way."

As they spoke, Alex drove up in the Rambler with Carrie.

Jemma ran to the car. "How did you swing this?"

"You could say that I used my womanly wiles on The Judge, but she can't stay long, so make the most of it." Spencer got Carrie out of the car and into a lawn chair, but first he took her to the river and dipped her feet in the water. She giggled and was the queen of the party until Jim and Alex had to take her home.

Robby, who built a whole city in the sandy banks, ate four hot dogs. Jemma and Lizbeth had no idea that an April girls' birthday celebration was in the works. Spencer had bought a fancy cake in Amarillo. It looked a lot like Sandy's wedding cake. Lester played his favorite song, "Red River Valley," on the harmonica, and they all sang along to whatever else Lester could play around the big campfire. Jemma watched Spencer work his charms on Willa as he talked her into singing a solo of "What a Friend We Have in Jesus." How could anybody resist him? Only a nitwit like herself could accomplish that.

"You'll get my present when it's your real birthday," he whispered to Jemma when it was time to go. She knew it would be something special.

❧

They left the next morning before the sun came up. Robby was still asleep when Jim put him in the backseat.

"You know everything that I am going to say to you, sweet pea. Be wise and listen to the Lord," Alex advised.

"Bye, Mom. I love you."

"Love you, baby girl," Jim said. "You'd better be registered for school next fall. No more extensions."

Lester's light came on just as the Rambler's taillights disappeared down the street.

"I'm going back to bed." Jemma yawned.

"I think I'll stay up and do a little reading, sugar. You go on." Lizbeth reached for her Bible. Her father had given it to her when she learned to read. She turned to the first Psalm and read the words under her breath. "He is like a tree planted by streams of water which yields its fruit in season and whose leaf does not wither. Whatever he does prospers."

She laid the Bible across her heart and ran her fingers along its leather spine. Jimmy was the last of her men. They had all been trees planted by the water, but he was the only one whose leaf did not wither and die.

She closed her eyes. *May he prosper, Lord, and may his wife and children reap the fruits of Your Spirit. Amen, Sweet Jesus.*

Chapter 17

A Whirlwind

It was May Day, and Jemma had wasted a page in her sketchbook, doodling. Exactly two years had passed since she had agreed to go along with Melanie on a double date. That was her first sip from the devil's cup. She felt weird about doing it even then. Now look where it had gotten her.

Lizbeth bent over the mail and tore open an envelope. "Uh-oh."

Jemma looked up. "What?"

"Julia is coming next week."

"Great! There's nothing like a dose of Do Dah."

Lizbeth laughed. "Julia is so much like my mother—boss of the world. She's nothing like Father. He was a man of few words until he got in the pulpit. Preachers in his day were fire and brimstone men, but he believed in following the Lord's example of teaching in parables. He taught us that life is like a jealous crop we must always be tending. Some of us have a short row to hoe and some have a long one. Regardless of the length, there will always be an abundance of work to be done. Mercy me, sugar, I've gone and preached a sermon to you."

Jemma put her arm around her. "What did your father think about discrimination?"

"Oh, there was plenty of that when he was alive. It's a mystery how even good people justify prejudice. He used to say, 'We are all sinners, even if our sins are ones of omission, but it's never too late to change.'"

"I think we get used to things being a certain way and get lazy."

"I suppose." Lizbeth put on her apron. "I know Cam said that the devil loves a lazy man."

"Or woman. Does Do Dah get along with Lester?"

"Lester?" Lizbeth laughed again. "That man is hard to find when she comes."

"Then Lester doesn't know what he's missing."

Lizbeth smiled. "Maybe so."

⌘

Julia came in like a whirlwind. "Let me look at you, Jemmabeth. You've got Jim's height and Alex's good looks. Those are his eyes, too, but you look out of them like your mama. Now, what are you doing here in Chillaton with Lizbeth when you should be in Dallas, painting? A man, I presume." Julia was not known for her tact, but for her generosity of opinion, affection, and money. She was shorter than Lizbeth but had the same gentle eyes and high cheekbones. Her hair was dyed a little too red, and Lizbeth was right—she was building herself a front porch that she camouflaged with classy clothes. Lizbeth might have one, too, if she had a cook and a maid.

"I am painting. I'll show you my studio in Papa's car house." Jemma grabbed her great-aunt's arm and caught a wink from Lizbeth.

"I never could get Cam to call it a garage," Julia said. "He did things just to aggravate me sometimes, the stinker."

Jemma lifted the homemade bar and let it swing aside, and Julia entered the odd studio. "Mercy," she said. "You need to get a padlock on that door. Somebody could rob you blind the way it is now. Oh my!" Her head swiveled as she stepped around the garage, and her high heels made little dots on the canvas tarp that Lester had spread for a floor. "Jemmabeth, this is sensational! Why, I've got friends at home who would pay a fortune for one of these. You can't leave them out here in this outhouse of a studio. You have to take them inside. They should be in a vault somewhere. I'm serious. Where do you get money for these huge canvases?"

"I have a friend in Wicklow who buys the materials for me, and I make the canvases myself," Jemma said, moving her easel out of the way.

Julia looked at her. "That Dallas boyfriend bought the materials?"

"No. Helene was my landlady."

She lingered at a new portrait of Carrie. "This one is so sweet."

"It's a gift for a friend," Jemma said.

Julia whistled. "Amazing. They show such personality, and I like that. It gives me a connection. That has to make you feel good, as the artist."

"Yes ma'am, it does. I hate to break into that connection, even a little. That's why I don't like to put my name on the painting itself. I'd rather sign the back of the canvas."

Julia sniffed. "You have man troubles, sugar. I can spot it a mile away. We can talk about it because I know a thing or two about men. I'm not an old fogey, you know."

"Nobody would ever think that about you, Do Dah," Jemma said, not knowing how this was going to turn out.

"Oh heavens, call me Julia. Only in Lizbeth's house does anybody still utter that silly name."

"It's cute. Mom calls me sweet pea."

Julia waved that notion away with one bejeweled hand. "Speaking of cute, what happened to Spencer? I hope you didn't run that boy off. He's a winner if there ever was one. Maybe you're looking for greener grass on the other side. It usually turns out to be crabgrass, by the way."

Julia was hard to keep up with, especially when she was sniffing out an injustice.

"Spence and I were taking a little break, but we're seeing each other now."

"Well, all righty, then. Now tell me the truth about my sister's health."

"Daddy asked me the same thing. Should I be worried about Gram?"

"I'm not talking about her physical health," Julia said. "I mean, does she still mess around with the old trunk in that pouting room?"

"The soldier box? I'm not sure," Jemma said.

Julia hopped up on the painting stool and kicked off her heels. "It's not healthy the way she holds her feelings back about those boys. It broke all our hearts, but Lizbeth never shed a tear, that I'm aware of, and I was living with them. When Cam died, Dr. Huntley told me that she went in the pouting room and threw a fit, excuse me, sugar, from you-know-where. She screamed and hollered and beat on the walls and kicked that puny little door until it came loose from its hinge at the top. It never has hung right since."

"Gram did that?" Jemma stared at her. "Surely she cried then."

"Nope. He said she came out of there wild-eyed but composed.

Lizbeth needs to let go and grieve like the rest of us." Julia pointed her finger at Jemma. "She's going to have a stroke one of these days."

Jemma's scalp tingled. "Oh, surely not, but then I've never seen her cry about anything."

"Well, I'm no psychiatrist, but it can't be healthy not to shed a tear over three losses."

"Why didn't they bury Matthew and Luke in Chillaton?"

"The government said they would bring them home, but Cam wouldn't have it. He said Rest in Peace means just that, so they were buried in the closest cemetery to where they gave their lives. I think it would've been good for both of them to have those boys out there in Citizens' Cemetery, but what's done is done. Now Matthew is way over in Italy, and Luke is in Africa. Who would have ever thought that?"

"Africa?" Jemma had never heard anybody mention that before or maybe she just hadn't been paying attention.

"Tunisia." Julia stared at the tarp. "Luke died in an air raid on the Ploesti oil fields. He was a gunner in a fighter plane. You know, at first, they told us that Matt was Missing in Action. About a month later, they sent another telegram saying. . ." Julia's voice broke. "That Matty was dead."

Jemma put her arm around her great-aunt.

"If Lizbeth would go," Julia continued, "I would take her to those graves. You know that we love traveling to Europe, but I've never been to their graves either. They might as well have been my brothers."

"Have you ever asked her?"

"I have not. She won't even fly down to Houston to see our sisters. She rides the bus. That's why I flew them all here for her birthday last spring. She uses that old joke about the Lord saying: 'And lo(w), I am with you, always.' I know what she would say about flying across the ocean. She won't leave him." Do Dah stood in the door, watching the stars. "I hear you're making some new friends across the tracks."

Jemma pulled the chain on the light bulb and swung the big wooden bar into place. "Yes ma'am, and I wish I'd done it a long time ago. I can't believe that I never even considered it."

They walked arm-in-arm to the front porch. "In the bigger world, there's not quite as much prejudice toward people of color," Julia said. "Places like Chillaton, where it's no more than a wide spot in the road, old thinking runs deep, but that will all change in your generation, I hope. Who are these new friends?"

"Willa and Trina Johnson, they live straight across the tracks from here. Trina and I graduated the same year, we both played basketball, we like the same music, and *To Kill a Mockingbird* is our favorite book. Do Dah, I used to walk those tracks all the time and never once acknowledged their existence. It's like I had a gift that I never opened."

"I know, honey. Don't forget that I grew up here, too. Blacks were just a part of the landscape back then. None of us would've considered crossing those tracks for social purposes. It's the shameful truth. I also heard you've been working for Judge McFarland. You know I dated him for a while in high school. I don't suppose Lizbeth told you that."

Jemma's jaw hung open. "No! What was he like?"

"Let me see, I would give Johnny about a five out of ten. He was like a king with no kingdom as far as social graces went. With me, he was more like a benevolent dictator, always keeping emotional score until I just quit. He was smart and nice to look at in his youth. It's too bad about his wife and little girl. What's she like?"

"His name is Johnny? I can't believe you actually dated him. He is such a fuddy-duddy." Jemma giggled. "Carrie has to be her mother's daughter in every way. She's so funny and talented. We were in Brownie Scouts together, and we both took piano lessons from Miss Mason."

Julia stopped. "Brownies? It could be that I have a picture of you girls. Maybe of a fund-raiser or something for the Negro church, I don't know for sure, but I remember there were some black children in it, too. I'll check when I get home and send it."

"All three of us were there?" Jemma asked. "Now that would be a real coincidence."

"We'll see. I just know I have a picture. I'm amazed at your art, and I don't get that way often. You should paint your old aunty a picture. Whatever happened to the one you did of Lizbeth reading the letter from me about her birthday party?"

"I'm not sure where it is. Maybe in Dallas, at my school," Jemma said. "Ask Gram, please. She might surprise you."

"To go to Europe? When the time's right and if you'll come to see us in Houston. Now tell me what happened in Wicklow, and I'm not buying anything but the truth."

There was no use tiptoeing around it. Jemma released the bomb. "I think I fell in love with a married man."

Julia made a slight noise in her throat. "Sounds like you didn't meet him at church. Are you sure the passion bug didn't blind you? I bet he used all the tricks he had, and you just got a little carried away with things. Let's stay out here for a while." Julia took a seat in the wicker chair, and Jemma sat in the porch swing, pushing off from the cool concrete with her bare toes.

"Tell me about last summer," Julia prompted.

They talked until Gram's light went out in her bedroom, then Julia paced around the porch, sifting through the story. She stopped at the swing. "Scoot over, honey. Now I don't like all these letters. It's only common sense that if you send a few letters and they don't get answered, you try something else. This smacks of a Brontë novel. What did your parents say?"

"I haven't told them the whole story because I'm afraid Daddy would pound him."

"And you haven't seen this guy or written to him or anything?"

Jemma halted the swing. "He has a wife. You know me better than that."

"I didn't mean in a romantic way. I meant to chew him out or something. Let that Jenkins's temper fly."

"No ma'am. I haven't done anything. It wouldn't be right."

"Sugar, I'm glad you told me. Love can be a mean old thing, and I speak from experience. I had my share of love stories before I met Art, but it's worth it all when you find the right man. This Paul business should show you that it's all the more reason to stick with the Chase boy. He's gold."

Jemma nodded blankly. Everybody was so sure.

"I know what you're thinking," Julia said, "that nobody under-stands. Well, I gave your papa fits with my love life. Cam was a patient man. Anybody who's a farmer knows patience. Of course he also learned a lot of that raising me. Those were exciting times, but he might have called them something else. I had boyfriends who made me break a sweat with their romancing, and a few whose idea of romance was to agree with me in an argument. When you pack on a few pounds and makeup won't cover your wrinkles, you can get down on yourself, but if your man tells you that you're beautiful, talented, smart, and he can't wait to see you in the morning, you know you made the right choice. Arthur still dances all the slow ones with me, sugar."

Julia slept in the next morning. She claimed it was part of her vacation routine.

"Good morning, ladies, what's the plan for today?" she asked, wearing her Chinese robe and slippers into the kitchen.

"I want you to meet Carrie," Jemma said.

"Good. I'd like to see how old Johnny Mac turned out."

Much to their disappointment, The Judge was not at home. Julia made Carrie laugh, though, with tales of her brief courtship with her father. Next they drove across the tracks so Julia could meet Willa and Trina. After listening to Julia and Willa trade jokes and stories for a couple of hours, the younger women went to Lizbeth's for supper. Julia came home during dessert, still laughing.

On her last day, they hit Amarillo hard for some shopping. Jemma figured her favorite great-aunt must have spent over three hundred dollars. Lizbeth protested at each purchase, but her sister paid no attention to her and did as she chose. "That's why I drove, Lizbeth," she said. "When I fly, I can't splurge on you the way I want because there's no place to put the booty."

"I have the Dodge," Jemma reminded her.

Julia flicked her hand in the air. "That old thing needs to be put out of its misery. It's going to conk out on you one of these days."

"Maybe I'll start driving it when Jemmabeth gets a new one," Lizbeth said.

Julia threw back her head and guffawed, attracting everybody's attention in Woolworth's coffee shop, her favorite. "That'll be the day."

Lizbeth sipped her coffee, then excused herself to the restroom.

"I think maybe I'm in the doghouse now," Julia whispered. "She didn't like me laughing at the idea of her driving."

"Don't you think she could learn?" Jemma asked.

"Honey, there is nobody in this old world that I admire more than Lizbeth. She is my mother, for all intents and purposes, and she is one strong woman. Did you know that during the Depression she had to have most of her teeth pulled? They were rotten, but we didn't have enough money to get dentures made. She went almost a year without any teeth and never complained, poor thing. It nearly killed Cam. Finally, he started selling off the furniture to get a dentist in Amarillo to fix her up. Now, if that's not strength and humility, I don't know what is. She simply doesn't take teasing well, and I learned how to tease from the master, your Papa Cameron."

"Are you still entering contests, Do Dah?" Jemma asked, changing the subject as Lizbeth returned.

"Goodness, yes." Julia left a ten-dollar bill on the counter for the two cups of coffee and a soda.

"I don't know why you go to all that trouble when you already have everything you need," Lizbeth said.

"Once in a while, I win, and that keeps me going. When I pass away, I want everybody to think of it as me winning the Big Contest in the Sky."

"Julia!" Lizbeth set her cup down hard.

"Let's get on home." Julia winked. "Lizbeth is all tuckered out."

The next morning, Julia sneaked out before they got up. She put an envelope on the kitchen table with a hundred-dollar bill in it for her sister and a note for Jemma.

Sweetie Pie,

I believe that once you pray about something and you sleep on it, then you go with what your heart tells you. How else is the Lord going to talk to you? I don't think that I've made so many bad choices in my own life. If I did, it seems more likely to me that the circumstances, when I happened upon them, were lacking in stability. If I'd had more information, I could've done even better. The same is true for you. I'm certain sure that you've been on your knees about your love life. Now you need to make a choice, Jemmabeth, and embrace it with all you've got. Choose Spencer. Thank you for introducing me to Willa and Carrie. I loved being with you and seeing your art. You make us all proud.

 Hugs and kisses,
 Julia a.k.a.—unfortunately—Do Dah
 P.S. I want a painting!

Chapter 18
Lucky Ducks

Their table at Cattlemen's, the Amarillo penthouse restaurant in the Golden Spread Building, was graced with a bouquet of twenty-one roses and a silver box tied with a black satin ribbon beside Jemma's plate.

She untied the bow and lifted out a porcelain music box. The top was adorned with a replica of Van Gogh's *Starry Night*.

"I wanted to remind you of our stargazing," he said.

She opened the lid and it played part of a song that she had heard on the radio, "I Will Wait for You." Inside the box was a pair of earrings—tiny flowers of pink gemstones and pearls.

"They're supposed to be sweet peas," Spencer explained, "your birth flower."

Jemma was afraid to look at him. When she did, the tears had made it to her chin. "How do you think of these things?"

"I bought the box in Paris for your birthday last April, but you said to leave you alone for a year. So I had it inscribed when I got back to New York." He read her the inscription under the lid: *I think of thee*. "That's all I could do."

Her tears got fatter. "How did I get so blessed to have you love me?"

"If things were different, I would ask you to marry me tonight. That was always my plan, to propose on your twenty-first birthday."

Jemma closed her eyes.

"I won't, but you have to remember, you're going to tell me when you are ready, no matter the circumstances."

"Spence, you deserve better than me." She leaned across the table and kissed him. It was the first of many before the night was over.

❦

"Jemmabeth, are you brave enough to teach me to drive?" Lizbeth asked, her lips puckered in dread.

"Sure. I'll teach you where I learned."

Lizbeth's glasses slipped. "The cemetery? Oh my. Well, I suppose no one could see me there. This driving business is to be our little secret. Don't tell a soul."

Jemma couldn't wait to tell Spencer. He could keep a secret.

Lizbeth had her first lesson that afternoon while Lester was at the barbershop. She wore her paisley headscarf and held her Sunday purse in her lap on the way. They had agreed that she would not practice anywhere near Papa's grave. That meant they would have the lessons in the oldest part of the cemetery. "Do you think this is awful, driving around these graves with no intention of paying our respects?" she asked.

"No ma'am. I think it will liven up the residents' day," Jemma replied.

Nobody was at the cemetery except Scotty Logan, who was mowing in the newer section. Jemma pointed out all the stuff on the dashboard and made a circle around a section heavily wooded with cedar bushes to show her how things worked. She made a second loop around the reflecting pond and the Chase mausoleum. Then it was Lizbeth's turn, but first, Jemma took her picture with the Brownie camera. It was not unlike a photo for a reward poster. The engine grated and screeched as Lizbeth held the key to start it after it was already running. She let go with a gasp.

"You're doing fine," Jemma said. "Just put your foot on the brake; no, the other pedal. That's it. Now press the button with the *D* on it." Lizbeth did, and at Jemma's direction, she lifted her foot off the brake. The Dodge began to roll. She gripped the steering wheel and Jemma braced herself. "Now put your foot on the brake again and press it real easy so you can turn up by that big cedar bush."

"Which way?" Lizbeth asked, her voice like Tweety Bird's.

"Either way," Jemma said, trying not to laugh.

She turned without slowing up at all and ran over the curb. Both their heads bounced up and hit the ceiling of the car. Lizbeth's eyes were like Ping-Pong balls behind her glasses. "Oh, help my life. This was a bad idea."

"Try giving it a little gas with the pedal on the right." Lizbeth found it and the car shot forward past several plots safely enclosed with rusty iron fences.

After an hour, she was making turns. When it was time to go, she chose to drive by the Chase mausoleum and all the way back to the arched entrance, past the pond. Scotty was putting the mower away in the caretaker's shed. He looked twice as the car crept by.

"Fiddlesticks," Lizbeth said. "Scotty and your papa were good friends. I hope he doesn't say anything."

"Gram, everybody will be amazed that you are learning to drive," Jemma replied as she took over the wheel.

They were at the cemetery every day, provided Jemma could get home before dark. Sometimes they stopped at the pond so Lizbeth could feed bread crumbs to a duck family that had taken up residence there. The pond was full this year, not like some years when there was no rain and it was more like a sandy bog, full of cattails. The Chase family had bought all the plots running down the incline from their mausoleum decades ago and created the pond as part of the memorial to the patriarch of the Chase family, Morgan Chase. Their mausoleum was probably the only replica of the Pantheon in the Panhandle. It was a good spot to wait out the rain, which they did one evening. Jemma read the inscriptions.

The Honorable Morgan Ashton Chase
Banker, Philanthropist
Member of the Senate of the Great State of Texas
Born—New York, New York—March 9, 1868
Died—Chillaton, Texas—August 19, 1954

Margaret Phelps Chase
Beloved Wife & Mother
Born—Teaneck, New Jersey, June 3, 1870
Died—Chillaton, Texas, May 1, 1949

"Did you know them?" Jemma asked.

"I knew them, but we were never in their home. They were money folk. He came out to the Panhandle to get into the cattle business, best I recall. His family owned some banks back East. I heard Mrs. Chase came from old money and that she also survived the *Titanic*. She was never happy here, poor thing, even though he built her that castle."

"Spencer doesn't like his grandparents' house. He thinks it's out of character with the land or something like that," Jemma said.

"Well, it didn't help anyway. I believe she died of boredom."

Jemma nudged her. "Gram."

"That's what folks said."

"This stone must have cost a fortune." Jemma glided her hands across the cool marble.

"They had it to spend."

"I wonder why they moved so far away from New York? I'll have to ask Spence more about his grandpa. It looks like he was a bigshot. Too bad his dad is such a jerk."

"Jemmabeth Alexandra."

"It's true, Gram. He's had fifty different girlfriends, and he knows nothing about Spence. All he does is give him cars."

"Don't judge someone's heart, sugar."

Jemma decided to take a chance as they headed back to the car. "Have you ever wanted to visit Uncle Matthew's and Uncle Luke's graves?"

"I've given it some thought," Lizbeth said. "I used to feel I couldn't do it even when I had Cam, but it's nonsense to talk about that anyway. They rest on other continents." Lizbeth drove to the Farm to Market Road and reached for the door handle.

"Do you want to try driving home?" Jemma asked.

Lizbeth pushed her glasses up. "Do you think I'm ready?"

"I do indeed."

The car rolled onto the pavement. "So much sadness out here," Lizbeth said as she turned toward town.

Jemma smiled as an old tractor passed them. "There's one tombstone that's not too sad. It's the one that says, 'Here lies Bodie Farlow's right foot. The rest of him is in Erath County.'"

Lizbeth had to agree.

The phone was ringing as they walked in the house.

"Jemmabeth? It's Kenneth Rippetoe."

Jemma could feel him blush through the phone. "Hi, Kenneth.

What's up?"

"I wanted you to be the first to know that I got a scholarship to Amarillo Junior College," he said.

"Way to go! I'm so happy for you."

"Thanks. My mom said that maybe sometime you and Spencer could come out to our place and have supper with us. She'd make that cake you liked."

"We'll do it, Kenneth. Thanks for sharing your good news."

He dropped his voice. "Thanks for the you-know-what, Jemma. It was the highlight of my day"—he hesitated—"of my life." Then he hung up.

※

Jemma wiped off the TV trays and put them away after Hoss slapped Little Joe's back and guffawed, just like Do Dah, bringing up the happy ending music. *Bonanza* was Papa's favorite show. Lester, who usually joined them for it, had gone to see a John Wayne movie by himself this particular night. Lizbeth paced to the kitchen and back, arms folded, head down.

Jemma followed her. "Are you having a spell, Gram?"

"No, but I need to get my driving license. I don't want to break the law any more than I have already."

"You'll have to study for the written test, pass a vision test, and you'll need to parallel-park with an officer."

She quit pacing. "Surely I could pass a test. I was first in the state teaching exam, and my glasses are like new. Now, I don't know about the parallel parking."

"The Dodge is too long. I have trouble with it myself. Maybe we could borrow somebody's car. How about Lester's?"

Lizbeth shook her head. "I don't want him to know yet."

"Maybe Spencer could get us one. He knows you can drive."

Lizbeth waved her finger at Jemma. "You weren't supposed to tell."

"I only told Spence. Besides, he'd love to help."

Lizbeth took up the pacing again. "I'm being too much trouble with all this driving business."

"You are not. I'll go by the courthouse tomorrow and get a driver's manual for you."

Lizbeth took off her glasses and rubbed the bridge of her nose. "I haven't studied much of anything but a Sunday school lesson and the Scriptures in nearly fifty years. The good Lord has His work cut out for Him."

~❦~

Lizbeth sat at the kitchenette, staring at the manual. The State of Texas had spent a lot of time making up driving rules. With the Lord's blessing, she might get the feeling again, that she could work hard and change things, like the Lizbeth before all the sadness had done. That person had hunkered down somewhere inside her ever since she had become acquainted with grief. She had wept at the death of her mother when Julia was born and for her father's long journey home to heaven, but that wellspring of sorrow had gone dry and she could not see clear to bring it back. Grief had hollowed out holes in her that she longed to patch up, and overcoming her fears was a part of her plan. As silly as it might seem to her family, driving a car had always been a great fear for her. She wanted to win at least one battle.

Cam would have fainted to see her take this test. She smiled at the thought of those blue eyes crinkled in laughter over her parallel-parking skills. Nobody had been able to help her do it right. Poor Jemma, bless her heart, had surely tried, too.

Lizbeth stretched and drew a weary breath. She wandered into the bedroom that she and Cam had shared. His portrait dominated the room. She wished Jemma were not so talented because Cam looked as though he were about to speak. It was bad enough to think of sleeping in the bed where he took his last breath, but to wake up and see him watching her, well, that would be too much. She smoothed the old chenille bedspread and adjusted the cross-stitched pillows that Annabeth had sent last Christmas. The room was never bright enough to suit Cam. "We should be able to cut off the lights in broad daylight," he had said at least once a day. Maybe Jemma was right. She should let her paint the room the color of butter, put a pretty quilt on the bed, and take down the heavy drapes. Nobody was going to look in her house anyway, except maybe Shorty Knox.

Lizbeth crossed the room to their closet and took down the

wedding ring quilt top that was almost finished. It would be a quilt for newlyweds, whenever that happened, and if she were reading Jemma's heart correctly, she knew who would be sharing the quilt with her on cold winter nights. That's why Lizbeth had embroidered their initials in the heart at the center of the rings. It would stay in the closet, though, until Jemmabeth got her head straight and Jimmy gave his approval. It was the old-fashioned way, but she liked it.

❦

"I've got a car for Gram," Spencer said as they walked to the car house. "A '64, two-speed, Powerglide, automatic Corvair."

"Does that mean she doesn't have to shift gears?"

"There are no buttons to push except on the radio, and it's much smaller than the Dodge." Spencer opened the door and turned on the lights. "She'll need to practice driving it." He sat in the rickety armchair Lester had loaned them and watched as Jemma made preparations to paint. "I told my dad that we needed the car for a couple of weeks."

"Thanks, Spence. It's nice of your dad to help us out." Jemma mixed her colors and applied them to her palette.

"He doesn't care. I doubt he was even listening. He'll sell it when she's done and make a good profit. I do have to pick it up in Lubbock, though." Spencer stretched out his long legs and folded his arms behind his head. "I'm hoping that you'll go with me in Buddy's truck and we can tow it home."

"Sure. I'll work it out with Eleanor." She turned her attention to the painting in front of her, and he watched with everlasting admiration.

❦

After two weeks' practice, Lizbeth had a cheering section when she emerged from the courthouse with the testing officer. She had even allowed Lester to come since he had discovered her hapless efforts to parallel-park in their alley. Now the official parking poles were set up next to the curb by the shady lawn. The officer stood outside the Corvair, writing on his clipboard. He opened the door and slid in the passenger side. Lizbeth inched the car away and was out of their sight for a long fifteen minutes.

She came creeping back on the other side of the courthouse. The officer got out of the car and Lizbeth pulled up next to the two upright yellow poles. Jemma couldn't look. Lester held his breath, then moaned. Lizbeth had parked between the poles, but at least eight feet away from the curb. Even the officer was laughing as he continued to write on his clipboard, then they disappeared into the courthouse.

Anxiety ran high as Lizbeth emerged, but she was practically skipping. "I did it, help my life, I did it! Can you see this, Cameron Forrester?" She held the paper overhead, laughing. "There's only one thing," she said after the clapping died down. "I failed the parallel-parking. The officer said he would overlook it, but for me to stick with driving in Connelly County. It seems there isn't a parallel-parking space in it."

The next day, Willa and Trina agreed to go for a celebration ride in the Dodge. Lizbeth treated everybody to soft-serve ice cream at Son's, then headed to the cemetery, her old training ground.

"I've never been here," Trina said. "White folks sure do spend a lot of money on fences out here. They must expect an escape."

Willa laughed. "I come here once with Mama to Miz McFarland's service. You know, The Judge's wife. There was a whole slew of cars out here then."

"Let's show them the ducks," Jemma said. "Just pull in there by the mausoleum, and we can walk down."

Lizbeth eased up next to the marble structure and stopped, angling in, as was her only parking style.

Jemma leaned in the back window. "Don't you want to come, Willa?"

"Y'all run on," Willa said, "I'll keep the car company. It would take me a whole hour to get down there."

"We won't be long," Lizbeth called over her shoulder.

The trio walked to the pond, the girls on either side of Lizbeth, to keep her safe on the incline. Jemma had a packet of sunflower seeds in her purse, and she and Trina tossed them to the waiting ducks.

Willa watched as best she could from the backseat. She shifted around to get a good view, and the springs groaned at her every move. With considerable effort, she leaned up over the front seat to flip the sun visor out of her way, then plopped back with a resonant grunt. There was a slight movement in the car itself, a creaking sound, followed by the soft crunch of gravel beneath its tires.

Trina was the first to see it. "Look out—Mama's coming down the hill!"

"Oh no!" Jemma took off right behind Trina.

Lizbeth froze in her tracks. "Have mercy."

The whole thing was over in seconds.

The Dodge came to rest where the water stood midway on the cattails just as the ducks lifted off at this extreme invasion of privacy. Its headlights were underwater, like a duck taking a drink.

Willa was sprawled across the seat when the girls got to the car. Her Sunday hat was willy-nilly at the side of her head and her purse was upside down on the floorboard.

Trina shook her. "Mama! Are you hurt?"

Willa's eyes popped open. "Now that's a whole lot faster than I figgered I could make it."

Jemma found Scotty Logan, the caretaker, still mowing on his tractor. He hooked a cable to the Dodge and pulled it out of the pond. Lizbeth was mortified. She half-expected Sheriff Ezell to show up and take her new license away. It didn't help that Scotty grinned the whole time he was helping them.

"I thought I'd seen you driving around here, Mrs. Forrester," he said, smoothing back his white hair.

"Well, I'm never doing it again, Scotty."

"I reckon you pushed the neutral button instead of the park button. It's a natural mistake in them Dodges. It could've happened to anybody."

"But it didn't. It happened to this old woman. I'm just lucky that my friend didn't drown."

Scotty and Willa exchanged nods as she fanned herself with her hat.

"The way I see it, Miz Liz, them's lucky ducks that they didn't end up on your cookstove," Willa said, then hooted with laughter.

"How much do I owe you?" Lizbeth asked stiffly after everyone had a good giggle.

Scotty wiped his hands on his overalls. "It was no trouble. Just my good deed for the day."

"I meant how much do I owe you to keep this quiet?" Lizbeth whispered.

Scotty chuckled. "Ma'am, I could write a book about some of the things that go on in this graveyard, and it's sure not the residents that I'm talking about. They're well-behaved. It's the visitors who get restless after they come through them arches yonder. Don't give it another thought, Mrs. Forrester. I was very fond of your Cameron. On his honor, I won't breathe a word."

"Thank you." Lizbeth extended her hand. "I'll make you some plum jelly, Scotty."

"Sounds like a deal," he said and drove off. Soggy cattails clung to the big tractor tires.

Willa loved being the center of attention. She was still roaring about it when they pulled up to her house with Jemma at the wheel.

"Miz Lizbeth, don't fret about this no more. I ain't had that much fun since a mouse run up Brother Cleo's britches when we was cleanin' out the fraidy hole. I mean it, now."

Lizbeth forced a smile. "I'm glad you didn't get hurt, Willa. You'll never want to ride with me again. Not that I'll be doing any driving anyway."

"Hush puppies. The good Lord holds my life in His hands. He don't want me to be foolish, but He don't want me to sit around on my caboose all the time neither. I'll ride with you. Just honk and I'll come limpin' out." She was still giggling when she got to her porch.

Trina shook her head. "See y'all later."

That evening, Lizbeth pieced quilt squares in the living room while Spencer and Jemma played chess in the kitchen. Jemma braided her hair and twisted rubber bands around the ends as Spencer contemplated his next move.

"Do you think she'll get over this?" he asked.

"She's just embarrassed," Jemma said, countering his move.

"I don't like those pushbutton controls. They are confusing. Anybody could hit the wrong one by accident."

"I see now why they had a pouting room," Jemma whispered.

"It's weird to see your own grandmother in a big snit like this."

"I'm giving her the Corvair. I'd get you any car you want, too, if you'd let me."

Jemma kissed him. "Nope. It was Papa's."

"Let's go watch the stars." He pulled on her braids.

At the river, they put a quilt on the hood of the still warm Corvette. They kissed, as was their stargazing ritual, then lay back, arms folded under their heads.

"Tell me about Paris," Jemma said, finding Orion.

"I want to show you Paris, baby."

She touched his chin, the way she'd touched his picture for that whole year.

"Spence, if you captured a firefly in a jar, would you keep it there, just to watch, or would you let it go?" She had no idea why she'd posed such a thing to him.

He turned his eyes on the heavens. "I think that there's a secret about fireflies, Jem. It's the firefly's heart that gives off light, and if we hold such hearts captive, even for a few seconds, they must always be set free to rise above the earth and become the stars."

Whoa, whoa. The wind fluttered his hair at that very moment, and she was in awe of him. How many more incredible things like that did he have inside his head, or even better, in his heart?

Lizbeth stood over the flower bed where Jemma was perfecting her weeding skills. "Honey, I'm worried about Lester. He hasn't come over in two days."

Jemma took off her gloves and wiped her forehead. "I thought maybe he was in the doghouse with you or something. Have you been over to his place?"

"No, but would you mind going with me to do that now?"

"I'll go, Gram. You stay here." She got no response when she knocked on either of his doors. She checked his garage and shed, too. "Do you know if he has a spare key?" she yelled.

"I think there may be one in the clothespin bag on his clothesline."

There was. Jemma opened his back door and stepped inside.

"Lester?" She rummaged through the old mail on the table. The dishes were clean in the drainer and his bed was made up. There was nothing unusual in the house. She put the key back and found Lizbeth wringing her hands in the driveway.

"I should have checked on him sooner, but I was busy on a quilt. Shame on me," Lizbeth said.

"He didn't say anything to you about leaving?"

"Oh sugar, he talks so much he could have told me that he was running off to become a missionary and I wouldn't have noticed."

"You want me to ask at the barbershop?" Jemma asked.

"No, I don't want to scare folks. It's just not like him, poor old thing."

"Let's give him one more day."

Lizbeth nodded, but doubt lingered in her eyes. During the supper blessing, she said a special prayer for Lester, and Jemma heard her get up several times during the night and open the back door to see if Lester's car was in the driveway.

Two mornings later, as Cotton John rattled on about the price of pork bellies on his radio show, the back screen door opened.

"Morning, y'all." Lester stood in the door sporting a Panama hat, a Hawaiian shirt, and flip-up sunglasses. Lizbeth and Jemma looked at each other. He came in and set a paper bag on the kitchen table.

"Howdy do from the sunny state of Californ-i-a." He hung his hat on the chair next to him.

Lizbeth switched off the radio and folded her hands on the table. "Where in this world have you been? We've been worried sick about you."

"Beg pardon, Miz Liz?"

"Don't call me that."

"Missus Forrester, ma'am, I sat right here last week and announced my intentions to head out to California to learn the chinchiller business."

"The what?" Lizbeth asked.

Lester's voice was shaky, like a one-room student sent to the corner. "The chinchiller business. I'm gonna raise the little critters to sell. I told you the whole plan right here in this kitchen."

"Chinchillas?" Jemma asked.

"That's the ticket," he said. "Chinchillers. I expect everybody downtown knew where I was off to."

Lizbeth was in no mood for excuses. "Take off those ridiculous things."

Lester fumbled with his flip-ups. "Well, sir, I don't know nothin' else to say. If I caused y'all to worry, I'm sure sorry."

"You gave us a fright," Lizbeth added.

"Then, I'm askin' forgiveness, from the both of y'all." Lester's nose was scalded.

Jemma smiled at him. "It's okay, Lester. We're just glad you're back."

Lizbeth was not so quick to let it go. "You're fixing to start peeling, too. A man your age shouldn't be out in the sun getting blistered like that."

Lester was a turtle, hopelessly abandoned on his back.

"Tell us about the chinchilla business," Jemma said. "I thought California had too many Republicans in it to suit you."

"It's gonna be my ship comin' in," he explained, skipping the political comment. "I'm startin' off with a few newlyweds, then they'll be doin' the expandin' of my business for me."

"Where are you going to keep them?"

"In my shed. I got me some cages ordered and a heater so they won't get too cold in the winter."

"What exactly are chinchillas?" Lizbeth asked.

"Well, I have to say the little critters favor their cousins, right smart."

"I have no idea who such cousins would be," Lizbeth said.

He got quiet. "Mouse family."

"Help my life." Lizbeth cradled her head in her hands. "You mean to tell me that you've gone all the way to the Pacific Ocean to buy mice to multiply, practically in my backyard?"

His face drooped. "There's good money in chinchiller ranchin', Miz Liz."

"Mr. Timms, don't you ever bring one of those rodents in my house, no, not even anywhere on my property, and I don't want to hear a single word about them either. I detest vermin," Lizbeth scolded. "You might as well be raising snakes, in my book."

Jemma poured Lester a cup of coffee. "Are you going to be a rancher, Lester?"

He took an audible sip. "That's my plan."

Lizbeth arched an eyebrow and pointed at him. "Those folks saw you coming a mile away."

Lester gulped more coffee and Jemma bit her lip. The words lingered in the room until Lizbeth's shoulders began to tremble with laughter. "Since you're going to be a mouse cowboy, I suppose you'll have to brand them, too." She took off her glasses and wiped her eyes. "You can borrow some of my knitting yarn for the roundups, or maybe you could just set out some cheese and they'd come running." She took a deep breath but started laughing again. She looked at Lester, then headed for the bathroom, blowing her nose behind the closed door.

Lester's ears had turned the color of the Corvette. He picked up his hat and left without another word.

Lizbeth opened the bathroom door.

"Lester went home," Jemma said.

"Fiddlesticks," Lizbeth muttered and rushed out after him.

Jemma looked in the bag that Lester had left behind on the table. Inside was a giant conch shell and several peaches. In a few minutes, Lizbeth came back with Lester in tow.

"Jemmabeth, could you start some fresh coffee? I want to hear more about Lester's business, don't you? Oh, and get out the bread and dewberry jam, please. Here, Lester, have a seat. Let me take your hat."

Jemma hid her smile. Gram was probably right. Dewberry jam could be good with crow.

Chapter 19

Restoration

S pencer left for a weekend conference in Dallas, and Jemma got up her nerve. "Gram, I want to ask you a favor. If you don't want to do it, it's okay."

Lizbeth poured the rest of her coffee in the sink. "I'll be happy to help."

"When I was a little girl, you told me that someday you would show me the things in the soldier box. Do you think we could do that now?"

Lizbeth's fingers pressed into the yellow vinyl on a kitchenette chair. "I suppose so."

Jemma unhooked the latch and pushed the creaky door. She moved the TV trays out of the way. "Who named this the pouting room?" she asked, making an extra effort to sound cheerful under the circumstances she had created.

Lizbeth took a big breath right before she ducked under the doorway. "Oh, that was your Papa. When we first married he said I needed a place to pout when we quarreled. When the boys and Julia came along, that's where we would send them to settle down if they got into mischief. On the home place, the pouting room was more like a real room where Papa did his paperwork for the farm. This little nook has served the purpose, though." Lizbeth blinked at the soldier box. Her visits had always been private.

"Should we move the trunk into the kitchen?" Jemma asked.

"No, no, I like it here. We can sit on the floor, if you'll help me up later." Lizbeth opened the trunk and set Paul's letters aside, as though they were not there. She took out two velvet boxes. "I used to polish these medals, but that seems a little strange to me now."

Jemma opened the containers and traced around the hearts with George Washington in the middle. Lizbeth lifted out more velvet boxes: Distinguished Flying Cross, Air Medal with Oak

Leaf Cluster, Bronze Star, and Good Conduct Medals, among others. She carefully placed three mustard-colored telegrams in her granddaughter's lap. Jemma unfolded one, curious at first, then a chill crept over her as she realized how it must have felt to open them for the first time. *The Secretary of War desires me to express his deep regret that your son. . .* Not wanting to read the other two, she touched Lizbeth's arm. "We don't have to do this, Gram. It was rude of me to ask."

"It's all right. I need to show you." Lizbeth withdrew several notebooks tied together with ribbon. "These were Matthew's Bible study notes. He planned to enter the ministry when he got home. Bless his heart." Lizbeth untied the ribbon and opened the top notebook. The penciled entries were organized by chapters of the New Testament. Pages were meticulously numbered and cross-referenced with notations in the margins. There was also a large, leather-bound Bible. Lizbeth held it for a moment. "This was my father's. We gave it to Matthew on his sixteenth birthday. He was always a serious young man, very caring. His girlfriend's name was Eileen Jeffries. I heard she's married now and lives in California with her family, but she used to write to us." She exhaled. "Here are some of Luke's drawings. What do you think about them, sugar?"

It was like taking her uncle's hand. It was easy to see that he was good. The sketches were very detailed with no apparent erasures or second attempts on the subjects. They were all portraits of young women with each personality revealed in elegant detail. Most were suppressing a grin, some peering over their shoulders, a la Betty Grable, but all their eyes were fastened on the artist. "These are excellent," she said.

"Luke had a way with the young ladies. He was so outgoing and full of nonsense, like his pa." She opened a heavy photograph album filled with laughing babies growing into teenagers. Jemma looked over Lizbeth's shoulder as she turned the pages on their lives: chubby infants in lacy gowns; towheaded, grinning boys and a tomboy girl dressed up for church; and lanky, barefooted kids on the train tracks. Other photos showed the foursome hiding their teeth with watermelon seeds, building snowmen, riding mules, climbing the home place windmill, forming a human pyramid, and wearing soldier uniforms with their arms around their pa. The last was of all the boys standing at attention, saluting Julia.

"Was Matthew more like you?" Jemma asked.

"Oh yes, and Luke like Cam."

Jemma thumbed through a few photos that had come loose from their mountings. "What about Daddy?"

Lizbeth rested against the wall. "He is some of both, but they were all good sons. Your daddy, being the baby, took a lot of foolishness from his big brothers, but he was a good sport. He and Julia carried a heavy burden when we lost them. The government sent Jimmy home after we learned that Matthew was not just missing, but gone. Sometimes I forget how those two must grieve. Julia is open about everything, but Jimmy hides it. At least he has Alex and you children. He was my baby, but now he and Julia are my Gibraltar."

Jemma leaned into the trunk and felt around for something else to talk about. She took out two stacks of old letters tied with ribbon. One look at the return addresses and she laid them aside. She would not intrude on precious correspondence between parents and departed sons. There were several cigar boxes held together with rubber bands and filled with ribbons from track meets, little wooden toys, a miniature metal horse, and two high school rings. She found several pages of poetry written by Luke and a program from a play.

"Whose rock is this?" Jemma asked, giving Lizbeth a white, pitted stone.

Lizbeth turned the rock over in her hand then placed it back in the trunk. "That was a birthday present from Luke to Matthew on his birthday. Luke must have been about three years old then and Matt about five."

There were several shirts at the bottom, wrapped in tissue. Jemma looked through them. "No wonder you treasure all this, Gram. It's like pieces of your heart."

Lizbeth touched the paper, then retreated. She cleared her throat. "I couldn't throw those shirts away, but I couldn't bring myself to seeing other youngsters wearing them, either."

"Let's stop for now. We'll finish some other time." She replaced everything, closed the lid, then helped Lizbeth to her feet. They left the trunk as they had found it, like the Chase mausoleum. Lizbeth had done it and survived. They had both seen the necklace at the bottom, but neither had mentioned it.

❧

It was Friday and Jemma was in a fizz, almost late to work. "Gram, I've been thinking about those shirts," she said, downing a glass of juice. "You've made quilts before out of old dresses and shirt scraps. Wouldn't it be nice to make one for your bedroom and use Matthew and Luke's shirts?"

Lizbeth folded her newspaper on the table. "I suppose. I know they aren't doing anybody any good in that musty old soldier box." She managed a smile. "Thank you for thinking about it."

Jemma waved and was out the door. Lizbeth blinked after her.

❧

Lizbeth didn't feel like eating a noon meal. Instead, she made a pot of coffee and drank most of it, staring at the pouting room door. She set her cup in the sink and got the shirts. There were seven in all, plus a skinny rag doll she had made for Julia from one of her old petticoats. Matthew's shirts were dark blue and brown, made of sensible and sturdy cotton. Luke's were cotton as well, a plain khaki, a bright blue, and the other a green plaid. There was one small item that all the boys had worn, a cream-colored baby's undershirt. At the bottom of the stack was Jimmy's favorite shirt from high school—a faded red corduroy. She tried to brush aside visions of the three of them bounding over the fence to catch the rattletrap school bus, their hair still wet from the windmill pump, with Julia tagging behind. Those grinning, freckled faces with hands stretched high to catch the wind would reappear as they raced home from school at day's end. Lizbeth swallowed hard, thinking she shouldn't have drunk so much coffee. She rested, hoping the queasiness would subside.

She took the shirts to the good bed and spread them out, cutting each into squares and saving the buttons in the nightstand drawer. Her hands made quick work of it, but her mind was overflowing with the past and it seemed to disconnect from the working parts of her, as though she had snipped the final thread that had secured her composure over the years. She tossed out the little bits of fuzz left over from her assault until only the baby shirt remained. Its fabric was cotton soft, worn almost to the fiber by use and washings. There were no buttons to remove, just small satin ribbons once tied across fat tummies. A stain on one sleeve was barely noticeable, but she knew it was there. Lizbeth stroked the tiny arms and positioned the heavy blade of the scissors under the widest part of the shirt, but her hand would not move the metal. It trembled instead with such violence that she let the scissors drop on the bedspread. She sank down to the throw rug beside the bed in the fear that she might faint, then leaned forward to let the moment pass.

She moved to the oak chair that was her mother's and caressed the fabric as she rocked. She lifted the shirt to her face with the desperate notion that some fragrance of her babies might still linger. The chair creaked in gentle rhythm with her body as the tempo increased, then came to a sudden halt, like a bird shot in mid-flight. The misery rose through her chest and throat until a pitiful moan shuddered out of her. Then, in waves of unrelenting sobs, she wept. Her cheeks became slick with tears until her glasses fell in her lap and she buried her face in the soft folds of the shirt.

The clock chimed another hour. Lizbeth steadied herself and went to the portrait on the wall to touch it for the first time. The brushstrokes of oil were hard against her fingers, the same as his dear face just before they laid him to rest. The faintest hint of violets and roses, like those she wore in her hair on their wedding day, crept through her senses. She looked into the blue eyes on the canvas and whispered, "I'm still standing, Cameron Forrester. I am still standing."

She folded the baby shirt between two sheets of tissue paper and tucked it back in the soldier box. She shut the pouting room door and washed her face in the kitchen sink.

❧

Spencer called Jemma right after breakfast. "Hey, let's go to Amarillo for dinner, a movie, bowling. . .whatever you want."

"Putt-putt golf."

"I'll see you at five."

The evenings were getting warmer. They ate Mexican food and

played eighteen holes at the Amarillo Fun Park. Spencer was in top putting form and won a banana split bet.

"You hate to lose, don't you?" he said, blowing his straw wrapper into her float. "Have you thought any more about us getting married? I need to know so I can propose and not get turned down."

Jemma was caught off guard again, even though she had thought of little else for weeks.

"We aren't just best friends, Jem." He leaned across the table. "Not the way we kiss."

"Remember, I'm not ready to marry anybody." It was probably the ice cream that zapped her brain as she spoke.

"I'm not going to sit by while you daydream about your summer romance. I know that you love me, but you're too stubborn to admit it. I'll refresh your memory. My conference at Syracuse is in three weeks, then I'm off to Italy."

"But you'll come home for Christmas."

"Maybe. It depends on you. I can stay in Florence and finish my degree or come back to Syracuse and graduate there. How far away do you want me? I can be in Europe or New York."

"I thought this was a study abroad program."

"If the program is as great as they say it is, I might stay. The university also has an impressive school of art, Jem. After all, it is Florence."

"You'll find some Italian bombshell and forget about me anyway." She could have talked all day and not said that.

He narrowed his gray eyes. "I want to spend the rest of my life with you, baby."

She pushed the float aside. "I don't know what else to say, Spence. I'm just not ready yet." There it was, a second zap to her brain.

Jemma lay awake that night considering the next year without Spencer. It didn't take a genius to make a commitment to the sweetest man in the world. What could she possibly get from Mr. Turner that she didn't already have with Spence? It had to be the hat and the snakeskins. She was so pathetic. She went to the living room and sat in Papa's chair for a while, sketching familiar faces on Lizbeth's lined stationery until she fell asleep. She awoke in the morning with a quilt spread over her.

Lizbeth was drinking coffee at the kitchenette. "Good morning, honey. I hope you slept well."

"Thanks for the quilt." Jemma yawned and got ready for work. It was going to be a late one. Eleanor's gall bladder was acting up.

⟨≈⟩

The Judge let her go home a few minutes before midnight when he got back from his poker game. She tiptoed inside and hung her coat on the hall tree. Lizbeth was still up and reading in bed. "It's way past your bedtime," Jemma scolded.

Lizbeth closed her Bible and swung her feet to the side of the bed. "I want to show you something," she said and headed to the good bedroom. She flipped on the light switch then stood back to watch Jemma's reaction.

"Oh, my goodness, it's beautiful!" Jemma caressed the shirts from the soldier box, now blended together with stitches in the Lone Star pattern. "It has a blue corner. That's Papa watching, isn't it?" She turned to Lizbeth, then gasped. "Oh Gram, I've never seen you cry. I know it was so hard for you to create, but it truly is a masterpiece."

"No, it's just a bunch of cotton, but it was my life, our life." Lizbeth rubbed her forehead. "I need to get some sleep. Good night, sugar." She paused in the doorway. "Jemmabeth, would you keep me company if I sleep in here tonight?"

"I'd be honored."

Lizbeth folded back the covers and reclined between the sheets. Jemma lay down beside her, still in her jeans.

"Sweet dreams," Lizbeth said. "Say your prayers."

Cam's portrait was faintly illuminated by the moonlight filtering into the room. Jemma's eyes rested on his and it came to her. "Gram, I've been thinking Papa's portrait is too big for this room. Would it be all right if I add it to my portfolio?"

Lizbeth sighed. "I do admire that painting, but I feel like he is standing in here, actually out of his resting place. Oh my, don't tell anybody I said that."

Jemma reached for her hand. "I'm sorry that I did that to you."

"Hush now. You can't help being good at what you do. The way he's looking, well, you caught the little blue corner, too."

"Daddy says it was always on them, making them behave."

"It was, but with a twinkle. He was a special man."

"I'll take it to the car house in the morning."

"Thank you, honey." The gratitude offered was for much more than Jemma could ever realize.

Chapter 20
Unto His Nest Again

Her transistor radio was blasting, but she sensed someone watching her. She let a brush drop on the tarp and, as she bent to pick it up, glanced at the window. Shorty Knox was barely visible at the window's edge, but for some reason, he didn't frighten her at all. He stayed about ten minutes. She did hear him leave and she watched out the window as he darted down the alley, step stool in hand. He came again the next three nights. After a week, he was on his stool for at least a half hour, watching various paintings evolve, not her. Jemma angled her easel to give him a better view, and she hadn't said a word to anybody—especially Spencer. He would have a cow.

Shorty came the same time every night. On the last Friday of the second week, she left the car house lights on but stood in the shadows of the pecan tree. Shorty arrived as usual, setting up his stool under the window. She had never realized how tiny he was. Lester was right about Shorty being the height of Gram's cookstove.

"Would you like to come in, Shorty?" Jemma asked. He tumbled off his stool, then backed up on all fours.

"Didn't do nothin'!" he shouted.

"No, no, you didn't do anything at all. I would like to paint your picture, like I did this little boy. He's my brother. Please let me."

Shorty was halfway into the alley before he stopped. "You callin' the sheriff on me?"

"No, I'm not. Let me draw your picture and then, if you like, you can watch from the window while I paint. It'll just take a few minutes, but I need the light to do it."

Jemma opened the door to the car house and stood back. "It's okay. Please sit on my stool over there. It won't be long. See, no phones in here."

Shorty came in like a sick pup, but he smelled much worse. Jemma took shallow breaths and got her sketchpad. Shorty spent the time surveying the other portraits around the room, but her stool was too tall for him. His feet dangled, sporting two different kinds of boots with no laces. He was gotch-eyed, which had to make his peeping Tom business difficult, and he used his mouth like an antennae to detect sounds. His head was topped off with a tattered fedora perched on flapjack-sized ears.

"All done," she said. Shorty hopped off the stool without a word and evaporated. She added detail to her sketches and left the door open for some fresh air. Anything for art.

She began his portrait the next Monday. A cold snap hit the Panhandle and brought much-needed rain with it. He didn't come that night, so she did the background work. He was there the next night, standing on the stool for almost an hour. Jemma would have worked longer, but she took pity on him as he shivered in the chilly air.

The next night she left one of her winter jackets under the window. He came as usual and the coat was gone when she went to bed. The piece was coming along, but she had no idea what Shorty thought about it. He never made a sound, but lasted each night as long as she did. He left abruptly once when Spencer showed up and knocked on the door. Jemma went outside immediately to talk to him since she wasn't quite ready to explain her latest work to anybody.

"Hi, baby," Spencer said. "It smells like something's cooking in there. Are you staying warm?"

"It's just that old camp stove," she said. "I got cold so I fired it up. It stinks, but I'm fine. What brings you out during my work time, you naughty boy? I thought we agreed that I can't paint with you in the room anymore."

"I miss you. I drove over for a kiss."

She gave him one worthy of his trip across town.

"Could I come every night for one of those?"

"You may, and here's one for the road. Now, scram."

"Is Gram awake? I thought I might visit with her awhile."

"I don't know." She eyed him. "See if her light is on."

"Love you, Jem." He stood there for a few seconds, then walked away.

Jemma went back to her work, but changed her mind. She cleaned her brushes and went into the house. All was dark, Gram was asleep, and Spencer's car was gone.

She grabbed her keys and found him at Son's. "Tell me what's going on."

"You're supposed to be working."

"I'm almost finished with the piece anyway."

"That's good news." He avoided her eyes.

"Let's go back to Gram's and talk, Spence."

"I'll be there in a minute," he said, gesturing with his burger.

They drank cherry lime Dr Peppers, a specialty of Son's, and Jemma gave him a shoulder rub. "Is it your family?"

"Yeah. The usual. They set an all-time high for being nasty tonight, and I just couldn't take it anymore. It's not like when we were in high school, and I was so busy doing sports and stuff that I could be away from the house until they went to sleep. Living with them now is the pits. Mother yells and screams, and tonight she was throwing stuff around. She actually started swatting at Dad with a lamp. It's a wonder somebody doesn't get hurt. I'd call Sheriff Ezell if he hit her back, but he's not made that way. Mother's the fighter. I guess it's sort of unfair that I don't call the sheriff on her, but when I have the nerve, I'm getting her into a treatment center. She needs help bad."

"I'm so sorry, Spence."

He leaned back against the couch and looked at her like a little boy. "Hope I didn't ruin your night, baby."

"You could never do that."

"I miss your papa," he said. "I always wanted to be like him—a friend to everybody. He was the last of his kind, wasn't he?"

"Yeah. My daddy is pretty special, too."

"Sure, but he has some coaching persona, too. Papa was just himself. He made me forget about my problems. I like the portrait of him that you did for Gram. Would you paint me one sometime?"

"I will. I'm working on a few things right now, but I will this summer, I promise."

He yawned. "Thanks, Jem. Sorry to be so down."

"I'm sorry that I paint at night."

"I guess it's time I moved out on my own," he mumbled, eyes closed.

That thought gave her a chill. It shouldn't have, but it did.

He soon fell asleep. She kissed his forehead and covered him with a quilt.

He was gone when she woke up the next morning, and the quilt was neatly folded on Papa's chair.

❧

The nights warmed up again and Shorty and Jemma continued their vigil until the painting was done. On that night, she turned to the window and smiled at him. "May I keep this, Shorty? I want to take it to my school, but I have some drawings for you. They are in that folder by the window. Thank you for letting me paint your picture."

He blinked at her then bobbed his head. She hung the painting on the wall next to the one of Robbie. A couple of times a week he came by to look at it. Jemmabeth acted as though she didn't see him so he would feel welcome.

❧

Carrie had just beat her soundly in Scrabble.

"Hey, want to go to Son's for a Dr Pepper?" Jemma asked. "I have the car today."

Carrie giggled. "Oh my gosh."

At Son's, two teenage boys in the car next to the Dodge flirted with them as they sipped their drinks.

"Can you believe that they are looking over here?" Carrie asked.

"They have to be on their lunch break from high school," Jemma said.

"They must be looking at you, Prom Queen."

"Nope. It's you and your blond hair. It's getting long, by the way."

"They'd change their minds if they could see all of me." Carrie watched them as she twisted a lock of her hair around her finger.

Jemma started the Dodge. "That will have to remain a mystery because it's time to get you home."

"I hope they don't follow us." Carrie waved at them and grinned.

"Then they would see me get out."

"Nah. They have to get back to school."

"That was so cool. Let's go back tomorrow." Carrie peeked over her shoulder.

"It's a date." Jemma waved at Twila, who was walking home from work.

Carrie gave Jemma a sidelong glance. "Tell me what it's like to kiss a guy."

"Well, it can be the highlight of the day," Jemma said, thinking of Kenneth's remark. Rats. She and Spence hadn't been to visit the Rippetoes yet. Maybe she'd call them over the weekend.

"You told me that you dated half of Dallas last year. I bet you kissed them all," Carrie teased.

"Hey, I didn't say that I kissed all of those guys. Some of them were real creeps."

"So, who's the best kisser, Paul or Spencer?"

Jemma didn't really like hearing their names linked up like that. "The cowboy was smooth, but he's been around awhile. Spence gets this look in his eye just before and, well. . ."

"Is that all you do, kiss?" Carrie asked.

"Of course. We made a promise. No monkey business until after the wedding bells."

Carrie raised her brow. "What about Paul?"

"What about him?"

"You said the agreement was with Spencer."

"I couldn't promise that to Spence and give in to somebody else. I guess it never occurred to us that we would be dating other people. You're getting too nosy. Let's get you in the cannon." Jemma lifted Carrie out of the car and into her wheelchair.

"Do you think I'll ever kiss anybody?"

"If you can ever get out of this house for more than an hour." Jemma sat by the window and watched Carrie doze off in the cannon with an overwhelming urge to give her the joy that she deserved. This was worthy of a prayer. Jemma asked the Lord to show her what to do. He was probably surprised to hear her asking for help before a wild idea rather than afterward.

Lizbeth stood on the front porch and tilted her face skyward. "I don't like the feel of this. The sky is green and there's no wind."

"At least it's not raining yet," Jemma said. "I'm going over to Trina's, but I'll be back in an hour, okay?"

"You keep your eye on these clouds, honey."

An eerie calm hovered in the air as she walked across the tracks, but the 'tunias seemed bright and perky. Willa was standing on the porch as Jemma walked up. "I ain't no weatherman, but something's brewin'."

"You sound just like Gram. Is Trina busy?" Jemma asked.

"She's makin' a dress for Miz Lewis's girl and she's a big 'un, like me." Willa laughed.

Trina didn't look up from an ocean of pink taffeta when Jemma came in.

"I keep forgetting to ask you, where is Weese these days?" Jemma asked, watching Trina guide the fabric under the needle.

"Somebody told Mama that he got into trouble in Amarillo. The police thought he stole some money, but they couldn't prove it. That boy's meaner than dirt and about half as smart. He came slinking around the house the other day and told Mama that he was joining the army."

"They'll send him to Vietnam."

"Maybe that'll straighten him out," Trina said over the whir of the old Singer. "Too bad we couldn't put him in the cannon. That'd teach him a lesson if he spent a few nights in there."

Jemma studied a postcard of the Eiffel Tower that was tacked to the wall. "I wonder how long it's been since Carrie has been to a clinic. Did you know that she's never had any kind of physical therapy? She might be able to move her legs for all we know."

"Mama told me that The Judge doesn't trust doctors."

"Really?" Jemma turned to her. "Maybe I'll say something to him."

"Oh boy, here we go." Trina shook her head and refilled the bobbin.

"What does that mean?" Jemma asked.

"It means, The Judge better eat his Wheaties."

The wind came up and Jemma shut the windows, but it still rattled the roof. They joined Willa on the porch. Gusts whipped the branches of the elm trees and rippled the Johnson grass in wanton, choppy waves. The sky was a canopy of moss-colored pearls.

"You girls get my 'tunia boots." Willa held the door while the girls brought in all they could carry.

Rain blasted the tin roof like the heavens just opened up.

Jemma held up her hands. "Listen." Through the pounding on the roof, they heard it.

"Oh, law!" Willa shouted. "That ain't no noon whistle. Get to the fraidy hole!" She threw a dish towel over her head, grabbed her cane, and headed out the door. The girls followed, steadying her as she grunted down the steps.

"I'm going home," Jemma yelled.

"No, you're not," Trina yelled back. "You're helping me get Mama into the fraidy hole."

The whistle never stopped. Jemma glanced in the direction of the tracks. The elms thrashed and the rain turned to hail, pelting their arms. They leaned into the wind and half dragged an exhausted Willa to a metal door protruding out of the ground behind the church. Willa beat on it with her cane until the door cranked open. It took several young men to shut it again as the women made their way down the steps. Brother Cleo helped bolt it with a heavy piece of lumber.

They quickly adjusted to the somber mood in the musky darkness. Lit by two coal oil lanterns hanging from the crossbeams, the room was crammed with people. Jemma stood out from the crowd, her face even whiter in the lantern glow. Brother Cleo gave her a hug.

"Sorry I'm so wet," she said.

"We're all sopping," he said and went to talk to Willa.

The noise overhead was deafening. "Over here," Trina yelled from a corner. They sat on stools fashioned from metal tractor seats. Trina shivered. "Aren't you freezing?"

"I just hope Gram is okay," Jemma said. "Surely she went to the cellar. I should have stayed with her."

"Lester will take care of her," Trina shouted, tucking her ponytail back into its rubber band. Jemma shook her wet hair. "Hey, cut that out, girl," Trina said as she brushed the extra dose of water off her arms.

"Sorry," Jemma yelled. A clap of thunder reverberated down the metal door. A little boy about Robby's age edged his way over to Trina and crawled in her lap. Jemma smiled at him as he nuzzled up to Trina with his fingers in his ears. The air was fraught with dust, damp clothing, sweat, and apples. In the shadows of the lamplight, she could see bushel baskets of old clothes, broken toys, canned goods, and overripe fruit.

"That's where we keep stuff for folks having a hard time," Trina screamed in Jemma's ear. It seemed to Jemma that everyone in the cellar could qualify. Something major walloped the door, causing shrieks from the children. Within seconds of their screams, another monstrous blow vibrated the room. Dust sifted from the rafters, and Jemma jumped up, her heart racing. The same violent tremors undulated above them that she had encountered with the Zephyr. The beams shook with such force that a lantern popped off its hook and crashed to the floor. Jemma grabbed Trina's arm and the little boy ran to his mother.

Brother Cleo's voice pierced the pandemonium. "Brothers and sisters, let us gather in prayer."

The girls joined the circle and held hands with the others.

"Lord God Almighty, Creator of heaven and earth and all who dwell upon it, we ask that You hold us in the palm of Your great hand, and, like the story in the Scriptures, we ask You to calm this tempest and deliver us to do Your glorious work until the day of reckoning. Amen."

A mother hummed "This Little Light of Mine" to her crying child and soon they all joined in singing. They were to the part about "won't let Satan blow it out" when a hush fell over the room.

Brother Cleo took the lantern off its hook. "Women and children move back yonder to the far corner. Men, come this way." The group did as they were told. Brother Cleo moved up the steps to examine the door. Jemma could hear the men straining until something heavy clattered down the stairs.

"Everybody all right?" Brother Cleo asked. There were reassuring responses, so the grunting and shuffling resumed, coupled with an intermittent pounding. Something was being used as a battering ram against the door. The sounds of metal being bent against its will were somewhat reassuring. Finally, a tiny shaft of light shot across the room, and collective sighs of relief rose up from the captives. "Now folks, we're going to see what can be done with the door. Stay where you are until we make sure it's safe out there."

Jemma said a prayer of her own. She would never forgive herself if anything had happened to Gram. At least Spencer should be home by now if he didn't get caught in this mess. The men spent another half hour working to remove something from the entrance, then the group filed silently up the steps and out through the twisted remains of the door.

The scene above ground was sickening. The little church was no more than rubble. A giant cottonwood tree was split into pieces with a big chunk of it sprawling across the fraidy hole and what was left of its door. Brother Cleo reached under a splintered piece of wood and pulled out part of a hymnal. Others did the same, gathering up what they could salvage, which wasn't much. Willa and an older woman held one another, crying.

Jemma picked her way through the shambles toward home. The tornado had taken a crooked, wicked path. Willa's house had a gaping hole in the roof. Jemma raced through the trail, dodging odd mixtures of muddy clothing, paper, chunks of metal, slivers of wood, and tree limbs. Several elms were down behind Lizbeth's house, their roots sticking up like Medusa's hair. Lizbeth's pecan tree was still there, as was her house. Jemma's shoe came off in the sludgy mess that had collected in the alley, so she was standing on one foot when her heart stopped. The roof of the car house was gone as well as one wall. She raced to look inside, then collapsed on her knees, breathless. All the paintings she had done over the last year were gone.

Lizbeth and Lester rushed toward her. They huddled together, stone-still. Jemma's grasp was so tight on them that they couldn't have moved anyway. Lizbeth wiped her eyes. "I'm so grateful you are safe, but I can't tell you how sorry I am about the paintings. We should have moved them inside like Julia told us. It's all my fault, sugar."

Lester stared at the hapless remains. "That car house had a good roof. I helped Cam put 'er on in '61. Devil's work, that's what it is. A dang shame. There was a million dollars' worth of art in there, at least."

"Honey, you know strange things happen when a twister comes. Maybe we'll find them around the neighborhood." Lizbeth stroked Jemma's damp hair.

"I'll look for them tomorrow," Lester said, out of hopelessness. "I'm just as sorry as I can be, Jemmer girl."

❧

Jemma sat on a splintered limb. Devil's work? Was she forever aligned with him? If she started now, maybe she could paint some of them again by August.

Where was God's plan in this? It was too painful for her to sort through and find some spiritual lesson. Maybe she was being punished for stepping foot in the Handle Bar. She picked up bits and pieces of the little birdhouses that were strewn around the yard, then wandered around to the front porch. The swing was impaled in the honeysuckle vine, but still in one piece.

They had water, and that was it. Whatever Lizbeth had in the fridge they took to Willa's. Once there, Lester shifted his weight and sighed repeatedly. He had never paid a social visit to a home across the tracks. "Sorry about your church and all. I lost my chinchillers."

"Well, that's too bad," Willa said. "Losing critters is worse than me losing part of my old roof. I reckon the good Lord will take care of us."

"Jemmerbeth lost ever one of her paintings," Lester said.

"Oh no, sugar pie, come give me a hug." Willa stretched out her arms.

"Girl, you didn't lose them all, did you?" Trina asked.

Jemma raised her chin. "Willa, what can we do about your roof? You can't sleep with it open like that."

"You're welcome to stay at my house," Lizbeth offered, "and Lester has an extra bedroom if your neighbors need a place."

Lester looked at her like she had just announced she was a Republican.

"We'll be fine, Miz Lizbeth, but thank you kindly," Willa said.

"I'm just glad it ain't rainin'."

"Lester, the tarp that was in Papa's car house is in the backyard. Couldn't we nail it up on the roof to keep the rain out?" Jemma asked.

"I think I could get up there." Trina sized up the hole.

"That'll work," Lester said. "I'll get my ladder."

"Mama, we'll be right back, okay?" Trina said.

Willa joined Lizbeth, who was already making sandwiches. The sheriff was there when they returned.

"He's been here before, talking to Weese," Trina said as they dragged the tarp to the back of the house. They set up Lester's ladder and Jemma climbed up halfway with a corner of the thick canvas. Trina followed her with more of it, until they pulled it up the whole way. It was heavier than they thought. "My grandpap built this old house," Trina said, struggling with the weight.

"He did a good job," Jemma noted. They stretched it across the hole as best they could, then drove nails through the tarp and into the tin. It looked awful, but it covered the hole and they didn't break their necks like Lester said they would.

"I could use a bath." Jemma wiped her face on her arm.

Trina brushed mud off her arms and legs. "Me, too."

"What did the sheriff say?" Jemma asked as they tied the ladder to the top of Lester's car.

"The road is closed to Amarillo, but he said the tracks are cleared off, so they can get supplies in," Lizbeth said.

Jemma frowned. "That means Spence is stuck up there. I hope he's okay."

Willa poked at a stray petunia blossom with her cane. "There's gonna be some Gov'ment fellas here tomorrow to see if we need help."

"Well, that's not too hard to figure out." Trina slumped on the steps.

Lester cleared his throat. "The sheriff said that some folks were killed over to the river."

Jemma looked up. "Who was it, Lester?"

"Well, sir, the only ones they knew for sure were Wilma Rippetoe and her boy."

Lizbeth covered her mouth. "I always liked that young man and his mama, too. They had a hard life. Such a shame, oh, I do hate to hear that."

Jemma leaned against the side of the house. "Kenneth was an Eagle Scout." She slipped down to the ground, her shoulders shaking.

It was after midnight as she sat on the cold steel, waiting for the 9:04. As it passed, blowing its horn, she screamed with all her soul, the kind of scream she thought an eagle might have made, long and loud. The Lord had taken them unto His nest, but they did not die in vain. Jemma would see to that if she never accomplished anything else. She took a somber bath by candlelight and went to bed. The devil may have brought the tornado, but not getting around to having supper with Wilma and Kenneth Rippetoe was nobody's fault but her own.

Chapter 21
Rescues & Risks

Jemma woke up at the sound of Spencer's voice, just as Lizbeth knocked on her door. "Honey, get up quick and put something on. We have company."

She threw on her old robe and padded out of her room, numb and depressed. Everybody scurried around rather suspiciously.

She ran to hug Spencer, but stepped back. "Are you okay?" He smiled and turned her shoulders. "Oh my gosh!" she said, then held on to the sides of the door frame and bawled. "Thank You. Thank You, Lord. Where were they?"

"Lined up on the front porch." Spencer dusted off his hands.

"Oh my goodness, they're all here." Jemma jumped from painting to painting, touching each one. She squealed when she came to her brushes, still in the little cowboy boots. "How is this possible? Lester, where did you find them?"

"Well, sir, truth is, I hadn't even started looking for them, no offense, Jemmerbeth. I don't know how the Sam Hill they got there. I worked on that porch swing last night and there weren't no paintings out there then."

"This calls for a celebration," Lizbeth said. "I'll make blueberry pancakes." She and Lester went inside, exchanging theories about the paintings.

"Any ideas about this?" Spencer took Jemma's hand. "There has to be a logical explanation."

"I don't have a clue. Look at my brushes and the boots. They're in perfect shape. It's all too weird."

They took the paintings to the living room and examined them.

"That must have made you sick, baby, to think that all your art was gone." Spencer frowned at the portrait of Shorty. "When did you do this one?"

"A few weeks ago," she said into a yawn.

"You didn't do this from seeing him around town."

Jemma tried to sound casual. "He posed for me."

"Are you crazy? Where did this all take place?"

"In the car house. He was watching me paint so I asked him to come inside and let me sketch him. He did."

"Jemmabeth Forrester, you need a spanking. That guy is not right in the head, and you were alone with him in the car house at night? Tell me that you will never do anything like that again."

"Okay, okay; I'm sorry, but he was like a lamb."

Spencer studied the portrait. "Doesn't he live close to Willa?"

"Yeah. He lives in that old dirt cellar at the end of her street." Jemma touched the painting of Papa.

"Look at this, Jem. There's sand on these canvases, but only on the bottom. You don't suppose that Shorty could have taken them to his place before the tornado hit, do you?"

Jemma's eyes widened. "I guess it's possible because I haven't painted the last two nights, and Lester said that Shorty could predict the weather when he was young. Oh Spence, bless his heart. He even saved my boots."

"Let's not tell anybody, baby. Shorty did you a great favor. I'll think of some way to make it up to him, but he doesn't need a bunch of hoopla, okay?"

"He's like Boo Radley, in *To Kill a Mockingbird*, helping me," she said.

They talked about Kenneth and then sat looking at the paintings and the blotches of Panhandle dirt, most likely from a cellar across the tracks that had become an earthen stronghold against the devil's work. She would never forget Shorty's kindness nor Kenneth's sweet invitation she let slip away like it didn't matter.

Lizbeth was in the final stages of making her famous pecan divinity. She poured the hot corn syrup and sugar mixture into the egg whites while Jemma beat it in a heavy iron pot. Spencer had just left, and Lester watched from the kitchenette as he drove away.

"I sure do like that young'un, but I never could hold with his old man, Max-a-million Chase. His folks come from back East somewhere, big money people. Right there's the problem. That shifty feller's got money to burn. I bought a Ford truck off him about ten year ago. He was asking seventy-five smackers for it because it was supposed to be in such fine shape and he even showed me what low mileage it had. I was flabbergasted, so I bought it. Well, it wasn't worth a plug nickel. I went straight back to get shed of the thing. He come right out and told me a bald-faced lie, too. Said he got it off Buford Watson in Cleebur, who bought it new and only drove it to church. Seeing as how I went to school with Buford and knew he hadn't darkened a church door since he was in diapers, I paid my respects to him and the missus. Then I got the truth. Buford got that Ford off an old boy named Leroy Jessup during a trade for two blue ribbon sows way up to Sweetwater in '51. Leroy's son drove it to work in Abilene every day until the packing plant closed in '60. Plus, Buford and the missus took it on a whole slew of trips to Arkansas themselves. Why, it was on its last set of legs when he towed it into Chase's place behind his tractor. *Only drove it to church*, my foot. Bald-faced lie, just like I figgered."

"Was that the end of it?" Jemma asked.

"Nope. I drove right up to his car lot and waited 'til he come out for a cigarette break. I got so close I could tell his brand of smokes. He come hence to drinkin' a sody pop and took a few gulps with the bottle turned up right in front of my nose. I said to him, 'I'm drawin' back on your sorry hide, Max-a-million Chase. The truth ain't in you because Buford Watson done told me the truth. So you'd best draw back right now and may the best man win.' I was ready for him, too." Lester jumped up and assumed his boxing stance. He punched the air a couple of times then sat down. "Yes, sir. He's one sketchy cuss." He tapped his foot and Lizbeth and Jemma exchanged glances.

"Lester Timms," Lizbeth said, throwing up her hands, "you beat all I ever saw. What happened next? You get your audience all riled up, then quit at the most exciting part."

"Yeah, did you sock him?" Jemma asked.

Lester scratched his ear. "I drew back on him and I reckon that's all it took, 'cause my punch landed in thin air. He tucked tail and run off into that fancy office of his. Couple of days later, a check come in the mail for seventy-five big ones, and I kept the truck, too."

"Then you won the fight." Jemma couldn't wait to tell Spencer the story.

"You could say so." Lester nodded. "Fact is, I also took a spill on the concrete when I tried to land my punch. I kindly broke my nose," he said, sniffing. "That wasn't the only time I broke it, neither. First time, I must've been about eight or nine, me and some other young'uns was seein' who could throw a brick the highest. I probably won that match too, but the dang thing landed right across my nose while I was doin' my calculatin'. All the same, I throwed it up a good ways. Yes sir, this old arm's been right decent to me."

Jemma had been thinking about the painting of Robby. She set it on the bed, leaning the canvas against the wall.

Lizbeth stood back and admired it. "It gives me a chill, sugar. He is the image of your Uncle Luke. I just don't see how you can make those little dabs of paint put our Robby by that tree. It's like I'm looking out the window and there he is. I've seen him sit like that so many times, with his knees all drawn up. He looks like he heard a little bird or something in the branches, doesn't he?"

"Gram, I am going to send it to the Lillygraces. Do you think that's a good idea?"

"Why, yes, honey, I do. Goodness, it is a big painting, isn't it? They'll have the perfect place for it in their grand house."

"I feel a little guilty because down deep I want them to regret the way they've ignored him."

"Well, they'll never know why you sent it. It'll be your heart that has to reconcile your motives. You need to forgive them, Jemmabeth. Some money folk have a hard time showing love."

"They could at least send him a birthday card once a year." She moved the painting off the bed and went to Papa's chair to write the letter.

A package came from Julia, and Lizbeth held up a polka-dotted driving scarf. A black-and-white photo fell to the floor. Jemma picked it up and got goose bumps. It was the picture Julia had told her about. She recognized the Negro Bethel Church and the big cottonwood tree. Standing to the left was Jemma's Brownie troop. In the front row was a little blond cherub looking straight into the camera. There was no mistake; it was Carrie. It was impossible for Jemma to miss her own smiling face in the back row. Then there was also an undeniable image of Trina Johnson with her slanted eyes and dimples. She stood in a cluster of little black girls, each holding a can of food. Brother Cleo was shaking hands with the troop leader, and Sandy Kay was holding a poster that read:

TROOP 814—FOOD FOR THE POOR DRIVE—1951

She couldn't believe it, but there it was.

"Jemma, telephone. It's your Grandmother Lillygrace," Lizbeth announced.

"What? It's not even Christmas." Jemma took the phone as Lizbeth swatted the seat of her pants. "Hello."

"Jemmabeth, dear. Your grandfather and I just received your letter, and we are sending a check to cover the cost of shipping for the painting. It sounds like you have been busy with your art. We are anxious to see the portrait of little Robert."

"Thank you, Grandmother. I didn't mean that y'all needed to pay for the shipping. I merely wanted permission to send it."

"I'm sure it is nice, dear. Little Robert is a pleasant child. He writes to us now and then. So, it's all settled about the shipping?"

"Yes ma'am. Thank you. I'll get it ready to go."

"We'll be glad to have it."

"Robby is a great little guy. I wish you could get to know him." Jemma threw that in just to be ornery.

"Yes, well, families live so far apart these days. Give my regards to Lizbeth. Oh yes, and Trenton was here this weekend. He sends his love."

Jemma hung up and sat on the bed. Trent didn't love her. He didn't even know her. During the war, her mother's only sibling, Ted, was in the Air Force. His wife gave birth to Trent while he was overseas, but she took off when the baby was only a few weeks old. She gave him up to the Lillygraces to raise. "She simply wasn't the type to be a proper mother," her grandmother Lillygrace had explained, "too nervous." Jemma overheard her mother say once that the Lillygraces had paid the baby's mom a sizeable amount for her to divorce Ted. The baby, Trent, then became the object of all their attention and affection when Ted made the Air Force his career. It was as though they had no other grandchildren. They were not at all pleased when Robby came along after such an embarrassing space of time. Jemma knew Trent about as well as she knew her grandparents. He had just received a degree from Stanford in structural engineering and, reportedly, had a great job in New York City. How could she say that Trent "sent his love"? Maybe that's how rich people made themselves think they care about each other.

Lester was rosy with news. "Sheriff Ezell was down to the post office this mornin', and word has it that Shorty Knox done come up with a color TV for himself."

"How on earth could Shorty afford a color television? I don't even have one," Lizbeth said.

"It was bought and paid for by an anonymous person or persons. That's straight from the sheriff."

Jemma grinned and finished up her oatmeal.

Lester went on. "I'd sure like to see Shorty in his dugout with a color TV. It's got a big antenner stuck in a slab of concrete right by the door, too. Even got its own generator. That just don't seem natural. Must've cost somebody a pretty penny."

"Maybe if Shorty has a television to watch, he won't be looking in windows," Jemma suggested.

Lizbeth nodded. "You could have a point."

"Well, be that as it may, that's not my best news." Lester beamed and waited for a query. He tapped his foot on the linoleum.

"Do we have to guess it?" Lizbeth said.

"Nope. Here it comes. Some feller down to the barbershop was going on about his young'un winnin' first prize for his school science project. Seems he showed how a varmint could follow a trail in a box or some such thing. Well, sir, he come hence to tellin' how the young'un found the varmint under the porch and it wasn't scared of them at all. They was pettin' it and the young'un was sleepin' with it."

"Are you thinking it is one of your chinchillas, Lester?" Jemma asked.

"It's Bruno. I figured it out right quick like when he said that the little critter likes to get under the pillow when he sleeps. Yes siree, that's my Bruno." Lester got a melancholy look in his eyes. "Them folks just live two blocks over."

"You don't mean to tell me that you slept with those things?" Lizbeth asked.

"Well, not ever single night, Miz Liz, but a feller has to have some company ever once in a while," Lester said, sipping his coffee.

Jemma waved good-bye to Lizbeth, who looked as though she had encountered a rat in her house.

❧

Lizbeth rarely got to answer the phone anymore, but she got a kick out of seeing Jemma run to get it before the first ring finished.

"Jemmabeth? Robert Lillygrace here, ah, your grandfather. I trust all is well with you and your grandma Elizabeth. I'll get right to the point. We received the painting today. I'm not sure what we were expecting, but often, with a subject matter such as you have chosen, the results are saccharine and rather clichéd. We were delighted and quite frankly, astounded with what you have done. It has a unique and fresh perspective, and I look for that quality. Your mother has spoken of your art many times, but, well, we had no idea of the depth of your talent. We just got off the phone with your parents to share our accolades with them."

Jemma smiled to herself. "Thank you. I'm glad you like it."

"We were discussing your educational plans with your parents. As you know, I consider myself to have an eye for artistic talent. You may recall our collection from your visits."

"Yes sir, I do." Each visit, she had memorized a different painting and tried to replicate it with crayons on the trip home.

"What I am trying to say, dear, is that your grandmother Catherine and I would like to make you a proposition. As you know, we have been generous patrons of the arts and find it quite satisfying to discover such giftedness within our own family. Our obvious reaction is to embrace your efforts. We are, after all, your grandparents." He cleared his throat. "We want to fund the remainder of your education."

Totally stunned, she groped for words. "Even if I want to finish at Le Claire?"

"We can look at all options. I have acquaintances at numerous schools of art."

"Mom and Daddy know about all this?"

"Indeed. They consider it an opportunity to develop your talent without financial worries for any of you."

"Wow! This is such a surprise. I'll have to think about it, not that I don't appreciate it, but I like to sleep on things. Thank you and thank Grandmother for me."

"She's right here."

"Jemmabeth, dear." She sounded all smiles.

"Grandmother, I don't know what to say."

"The pleasure is ours. The painting is enchanting, and it is very touching that you sent it to us. We had no idea that our grand-daughter was capable of such work. We cannot think of anyone else in the family with even the slightest flair for creating art," she said.

Jemma was quick with the answer. "My uncle Luke, on my dad-dy's side, was an artist."

"How interesting. Well, then, we shall be talking with you very soon."

"Jemmabeth, it's Grandfather here again. The likeness of little Robert is brilliant. Is portraiture your forte?"

"Everybody calls him Robby, and yes, I am fascinated by it."

"Catherine and I have considered sitting for an updated portrait ourselves. Would you accept such a commission? You could come here and stay with us for a couple of weeks before the autumn term begins. That way we can become better acquainted, and it would give us a chance to finalize your plans for the future."

"Yes sir, I guess I could do that. Everything is happening so fast."

"I will call you first thing Monday morning. Another thought. Would you like to have little Robert, Robby, come and visit at the same time? And perhaps Trenton, if he can get a weekend off?"

Jemma was about to pop, but she kept her cool. "That would be nice. Thank you."

"I'll call your mother and work it out," he said. "Until Monday then."

She bounced on the good bed before leaping into the kitchen.

"Child, what's happened?" Lizbeth set down a steaming pan of potatoes, and Jemma danced her around the rippled floor while Cotton John compared fertilizer brands on the radio.

"You're not going to believe this," Jemma said. "The Lillygraces have offered to foot the bill for the rest of my college. All because of that painting I sent to bug them about Robby."

"Well, praise the good Lord."

"Papa would say to sleep on it, right?"

"It was his policy."

"That's what I told Grandfather. They also want me to come to St. Louis and do their portrait."

"St Louis, my, my."

"Oh, and they are inviting Robby to come, too, and Trent. That should be interesting." She frowned. "I wonder what kind of control they'll try to have over me if they're funding my education. Good thing I asked to sleep on it."

Lizbeth said a prayer over their food while Lester played his harmonica on his back porch.

"God is blessing me, Gram," Jemma said, "and I wasn't even looking for it."

Lizbeth filled her plate. "We must always be looking for blessings, so we will be prepared to accept them. Cam was my greatest blessing, but I chose to make him wait and accepted him in my own good time. Looking back though, I could have been with him longer. I should have grabbed that blessing as soon as it came to me. Now I'm sorry for it."

Jemma reached for Lizbeth's hand. She touched the slender gold band, still worn on her wedding finger. "You think I'm being stubborn about Spence, don't you?"

"It's not that simple, Jemmabeth. You've muddied the waters with this man from Wicklow. I think you need to look this Mr. Turner in the eye so that you can get on with your life. I don't think you are being fair to Spencer." The clock chimed, interrupting a lecture that had been building for months. "It's a Forrester trait to look folks in the eye when it's serious business, but I think the time has come for you to look yourself in the eye, too, sugar. You need to do some serious business in your heart."

Jemma dragged her fork through her mashed potatoes. "I can't tell Spence that I love him as long as I have a single thought about someone else. If I ever see Paul again, I might be bowled over by my feelings for him. He electrified me even though I shouldn't have been dating him. My brain is all tangled up, and I just can't love anybody like this."

Lizbeth considered this rationale. "That doesn't say much for Spencer. As bad as I hate to admit it, you two weren't exactly acting like Sunday school children at Christmas. Granted, I'm an old lady, but that dance you were doing was electrifying enough. Love doesn't have to muddy the waters, honey. It can clear them up, too. I had to choose between being a teacher and marrying your papa because only single women were hired by school boards back then, but being with him would have made me a better teacher, I just know it. Blessings multiply when you act on them. I learned that and tried to raise my boys with that in mind."

Jemma sighed. "I'm not ready to marry. I need to sort out my feelings first, to be fair to everybody." She laid her hand on Lizbeth's arm. "You're a blessing to me, Gram."

"I came with the territory. You'll have lots more coming down your road."

"I think I will accept my grandparents' offer. I can live with Helene again. I know she would want me to."

Lizbeth didn't respond at first. She took off her glasses and pretended to have something in her eye. "I know that she will love having you with her because I surely have. . ." Her voice failed her.

Cotton John never missed a beat as he updated the price of pork and beef. Then again, old Cotton wasn't fighting back tears.

Chapter 22
Chances

"Let's do something crazy," Carrie said, wheeling herself in circles around the parlor. "Dad doesn't go off like this very often and for you to be here instead of Eleanor is great. I hope he doesn't find out, or he'll have a conniption fit."

"Let's redecorate your bedroom in polka dots or a Beatles theme."

"Oh sure. Dad would really freak out then."

"Then what would you say if Trina and Spence come over and we play Password and listen to records?" Jemma asked.

"I would say yes, yes!"

Jemma wore a blue sundress that her mother had sent. They played board games for a couple of hours, and then she couldn't stand it any longer. She took all the records off and loaded a new stack, heavy with Roy's songs. Spencer danced the Stomp with Trina. Jemma loved to watch him, but she loved to dance with him even more. When "Candy Man" came on, they didn't even have to think about it. Every subtle movement was built on the one before it. Carrie and Trina watched, googly-eyed. When it was over, Spencer kissed Jemma on the lips and whispered in her ear, "Baby, if you ever wear that dress again, I'm not going to make it through a dance with you."

Carrie and Trina giggled and busied themselves making a sign. They held up their creation: He's the One!

Jemma made a face at them.

"Girl, if you don't marry that man, you are one dumb woman," Trina whispered. "You told us that you needed a sign, well, now you've had one."

Spencer scooped Carrie up in his arms for her last dance. The Everly Brothers sang their "Dream" song for them.

"All she needs is a glass slipper, plus she's going to be hard to deal with after dancing with Spence Charming," Jemma whispered to Trina. The hallway clock chimed right on cue for Cinderella's bedtime. "Time for the cannon," Jemma announced.

"I'll do it," Trina said. "You stay here."

Spencer set Carrie in the crawler and kissed her forehead.

"If I could, I would steal him away from you, but you've been too good to me, Miss Forrester." Carrie pointed at the discarded sign and glided up the stairs.

They were alone in the den and Roy was singing "Crying."

"May I?" Spencer asked, taking her hand.

"Of course. Are you wearing new cologne?"

"It's my magic potion. It puts ladies in a trance and they do whatever I say."

"Ladies—plural, hmm. . .then what is your wish, oh great one?"

Spencer lifted her chin. "Marry me."

"I keep it in mind." Jemma kissed him until the music stopped. She walked him to his car and they sat on the hood. "I'm going back to Le Claire, Spence," she said, straight out. "My grandparents said they would pay my expenses anywhere, but that's where I want to finish. I love it there."

He looked away. "Whatever you want, Jem, but I wish you would come to Florence with me. It could be something special. You might be surprised."

"Le Claire is so good for me. I've learned to be fearless and to trust my instincts. Last summer I was in a mentorship with a French painter. We studied famous artists' techniques and I learned so much. My last semester I wrote a paper on William Bouguereau. His work impressed me, but I identified even more with his passion. I actually memorized a little reflection he wrote on his work. Anyway, I think I have my style down now."

"So, what was the quote?" Spencer asked.

She closed her eyes and recited:

"Each day I go to my studio full of joy. In the evening, when obliged to stop because of darkness, I can scarcely wait for the morning to come. My work is not only a pleasure, it has become a necessity. No matter how many other things I have in my life, if I cannot give myself to my dear painting, I am miserable."

"Now I know what to do when you are miserable. Put you in front of a blank canvas with some good lighting," Spencer said.

"That, or this," she said and kissed him in the moonlight.

❧

Late Sunday night the phone rang as Jemma was fine-tuning a sketch of Carrie.

"Jem, it's Buddy B. Listen, I need your help. We are going to have to cancel our big chance to get a two-night gig at Amarillo Junior College. Some of their homecoming organizers are coming to the Chillaton prom next week to sort of audition us. Now it may not happen."

"Why not?"

"It's Leon. He wrecked his dumb motorcycle. He's banged up, but he'll live long enough for me to kill him."

"Sorry, Buddy. Can't you do it without him?" she asked.

"Are you kidding me? Leon is lead guitar, sweetness. I do well to play rhythm and throw in some harmonica. I'm what we in the business call a vocalist."

"What about Wade or Dwayne?"

"Obviously, you've never heard those yahoos without Leon. Listen, I was wondering about that guy in your class who moved here your senior year. Leroy somebody. He was good."

"Leroy Sapp? He joined the army right after graduation. I don't know anything else about him. Surely you can find a guitarist."

"In five days? Nah, I'll just call and tell 'em what happened."

Jemma got an inspiration. "Buddy, what would you say to another instrument playing the lead?"

"What are you suggesting? We only do Buddy H.'s stuff."

"Buddy H. used strings on some songs and all kinds of weird percussion stuff. Do you want to get that college thing bad enough to take a chance?"

He sighed. "Okay, let's hear it."

"I have a friend who can rock out on the piano."

"I don't know about a piano. How good is he?"

"She's great."

"Is she good looking?"

"She's very pretty."

"Does she have some moves?"

"She's in a wheelchair."

After profuse begging by Jemma, Buddy agreed to come by on his lunch break and listen to Carrie play. She had to spend even more time talking Carrie into it. When he arrived, however, she could see the mischief return to Carrie's eyes. Jemma had done her hair in a flip, and she looked like an angel.

"Buddy, this is Carrie McFarland. Carrie, meet Buddy Baker. We call him Buddy B so as not to confuse him with Buddy Holly, Buddy H."

Buddy smiled cautiously, then took a seat on the big leather sofa. He ran his hand through his hair, freshly dyed black to maintain his professional persona, and waited. Carrie rolled up to the piano, laid her fingers on the keys, then busted out a medley of Buddy Holly songs. Buddy B's mouth hung open. He jumped up, whistling and clapping. "Hey, I think this might work. Can we practice here or what?"

. Carrie flinched.

"No," Jemma said. "You'll have to practice at the gym. Do you think you could arrange it? If not, I could talk to the principal. He won't mind."

"I'll call him. Maybe we can rehearse tomorrow and Thursday night. Where'd you learn to play like that?" he asked.

"Miss Mason, next door," Carrie said.

"Aw, I know that old hen and she didn't play rock and roll. My sister took lessons from her and so did she." Buddy jerked his thumb at Jemma.

Carrie giggled. "Well, I sort of learned that on my own."

Buddy lifted one blond eyebrow, sorely in need of a dye job. "And the style?"

"Hey, I do what I can to keep my charge enlightened," Jemma said.

"Good for you, sweetness," Buddy said. "I'll see you ladies tomorrow night, but I don't think it was chance that brought us together. It was fate." As soon as he left, Jemma ran to Carrie and grabbed her around the neck, screeching for joy.

Carrie's eyes danced. "Do you think I can last through a rehearsal?"

"Or a performance?" Jemma asked. "I sure hope so. We're in too deep to back out now." She smiled at the fresh zing in Carrie. So, the Lord was going to use Buddy B—interesting.

❧

Jemma arranged to wheel Carrie out at five for a walk. They went down a block and turned toward the high school, then circled back to the side entrance to the gym. Buddy had laid some wide boards for the wheelchair to make it up the steps. Once inside, Jemma and Buddy lifted her chair to the stage. The band had been forewarned by Buddy to keep a civil tongue and cut her some slack. She blew them away on the first song. The rehearsal actually went faster than Jemma had thought, and she had Carrie back and ready to get in the cannon by seven. The Judge was asleep in front of the television with his bottle nearby.

"At least he'll be gone Saturday night," Carrie whispered, drinking a soda.

"I told Eleanor that I was going to sleep over. We are just going to have to rely on the Lord and the power of poker. How late does he stay out?"

"It varies. Sometimes he stays until two o'clock, sometimes midnight, and sometimes he doesn't go."

"Don't tell me that. The dance starts at seven. I'm going to have to get Trina and Spencer to help us with this."

"Actually, I'm not too tired," Carrie said.

"That's just the Dr Pepper talking," Jemma said as she fired up the cannon.

❧

The Judge left the house with two brown bags at 6:45, just as Trina and Jemma rolled Carrie out the front door. Then, when his car disappeared around the corner, they pushed the wheelchair across the street to the side door of the crowded gym. Spencer picked her up and whisked her through the boys' dressing rooms, out the storage room, and up the stairs to the stage. Trina met them with the wheelchair and Jemma got her set just right at the piano. As planned, Buddy went in front of the closed curtain to do his introduction. Carrie grinned at Jemma then took a deep breath. The curtain and the applause went up and Buddy B blasted out "*Wellllll. . .*" and Carrie came in right on cue.

The gym floor was alive with teenagers dressed in clothes that had set their parents' checkbooks back a month, but it was prom. Carrie was on fire. Her crew stayed backstage the whole time. At the break, they brought her some prom food, then Jemma and Trina carried her to the restroom.

"Are you worn out?" Jemma asked.

"This is the life." Carrie beamed.

"You are some kind of piano player, girl," Trina said.

The trio made their way back up to the stage. By ten o'clock Jemma was keeping a close eye on Carrie.

❦

At the back of the gym, near the exit, another eye was on Carrie, too, an eye glistening with pride and old fears. During the final slow dance, The Judge slipped out the exit and made his way across the street to his empty house.

❦

Carrie got the biggest applause of the evening. Jemma and Trina were in tears and even the guys in the band said nice things to her.

Buddy gave her a big peck, right on the lips. "Sweetness, you just got us a two-night performance at the Amarillo Junior College Homecoming Weekend next fall."

Carrie was jubilant. Spencer carried her home and up the stairs. "Do you think your father is here?" he whispered.

"I don't care. Let him see me coming home with a man."

Trina got the cannon going while Jemma said good night to Spencer.

"You always come through for me, don't you?" she said. "Thanks for fixing the car house for me, too. You're the best."

"I try," he said. "Sweet dreams, baby." A sudden breeze lifted her hair between them, and he tucked it behind her ears.

"Good night," she whispered. She gave him a superb kiss, then watched as he drove away. For a split second, the baby blue wiggled through her brain as the Corvette's lights disappeared around the corner. Rats.

❦

Eleanor woke them up Sunday morning. "You girls gonna sleep all day? You better scoot home, Jemmabeth. Your gram may not like you being late to Sunday school. I don't know ever who your teacher is, but I've been in your gram's class before, bet you didn't know that. Anyhoo, she's got a head full of Bible learnin'."

Jemma scrambled out of bed. She and Trina flew down the stairs to the Dodge. Eleanor was right. She was late, but it had been worth it.

❦

They were sitting in The Parnell, waiting for the movie to start, when Spence broke the news. "My dad told me that The Judge was at the prom the other night. He said The Judge was drinking and bragging at their poker game about how well Carrie played at the dance."

Her heart skipped a beat. She didn't know if it was bad, or half-way good, news. "Yikes. I'll have to tell Carrie."

"It was just a matter of time until he would have found out anyway. This is Chillaton," Spencer said.

"Maybe it's best that he saw her. Now he knows what she is capable of doing."

"We'll see. At least Carrie had a ball."

❦

Lizbeth walked over the little path to Willa's house with a pro-posal in mind. She got right to it. "Willa, would you like to have a memory quilt in honor of your husband? I made myself one not long ago."

Willa wiped her brow. "Well, I'm no quilter, that's for sure."

"Now that's where I come in," Lizbeth said. "I guess quilting is my calling in life."

"Well, that's a different story." Willa leaned in to hear more.

"If you have saved any scraps from his shirts, I could get started."

Willa considered the assignment. "Law, seems like I saved some of Sam's things, but we'll have to look around."

"Have Trina bring them over this week, and I'll get going on it."

"Thank you kindly," Willa said, her face already lit up with memories.

Trina was at the door with an armload of fabric the next morning.

"Come on in and let's see what you found," Lizbeth said.

"It's sure nice of you to do this for Mama. She's real excited."

They dumped the fabric on the good bed. There was a pair of threadbare overalls, several bandana scarves, and a set of feed-sack curtains.

"Mama said this was all she had. The overalls and bandanas were what my daddy wore when he was working the fields. She didn't have any of his shirts, but the curtains were the ones hanging in their bedroom before I was born."

"These will all do just fine, Trina. You should help me choose the pattern. I know that you are handy with needle and thread."

"Yes ma'am. I like to design dresses."

"Well, there must be scholarships for that kind of thing."

"I'm not sure many colored girls go into that business."

"Now you listen to an old woman, Trina. I went to college. It was hard enough back then, but nowadays, there are money folk who will help you along no matter whether you call yourself a Caucasian or a Negro. Now let's look at some of these patterns."

"Actually," Trina reached in her pocket and pulled out several sheets of paper, "I have an idea." She laid the cutouts on the bed. "Here's a drawing of it when it's finished."

Lizbeth examined the samples and nodded her approval. "It's a fine idea. Let's get to work."

"I have some things to do for Mama, then I gotta get over to The Boulevard to clean a house. I could come afterward."

"We'll start tonight, then."

"Thank you, Miz Forrester."

"Trina, please call me Gram."

Her dimples went deep. "Thank you, Gram."

They worked well together. Lizbeth showed Trina something once and she had it. Lizbeth stayed up way past her bedtime each night, knowing that Trina had already put in a full day of work. She taught her all the tricks of master quilting. Trina's were tiny, even stitches, the kind so valued in quilting circles. On their last night of sewing, Jemma went to bed before the two of them were finished. She had to sleep in the little side bedroom since the quilt frame was lowered over part of her bed.

"Gram," Trina asked, "did you ever think you'd be sitting up at midnight making a quilt with a Negro girl?"

"Sugar, the good Lord surprises us all with His plans. I'm just proud that we got to know each other well enough to make this quilt for Willa. If you keep it up, you are going to be a whole lot better at this than I am. You'll be able to pass your skills on to your grandchildren." Lizbeth lowered her voice. "I don't think my little artist in there is going to be passing along any quilting skills."

"I heard that," Jemma yelled.

The quilt was finished right before Papa's clock struck two. Lizbeth hadn't stayed up that late since Jim was a baby.

The next morning, they walked ceremoniously over the tracks together to give Willa the quilt. Jemma followed along with Lizbeth's camera.

Willa greeted them with an anxious grin. "Well, what are y'all waiting for? Show me what you got."

"Close your eyes, Mama." Trina spread the quilt over the kitchen table. "Okay, open."

Jemma had never seen Willa speechless, but this was close. She ran her big hands over the fabric and stitches and then backed up to look at it again. Trina's design was just the thing.

"That must be the most beautiful batch of 'tunias ever made by human hands. Sweet Sunday morning, how did you do it? Miz Lizbeth, I gotta hug you because this is a blessed quilt and I know it mostly come from your hand. I'll never be able to thank you proper."

"Call me Lizbeth and that'll be thanks enough," she said.

Trina and Willa held up the quilt and Jemma took a whole roll of pictures.

"It's a beautiful tribute to your husband," Jemma said.

"Our baby girl here is the beautiful one." Willa hugged Trina to her side again. "Don't really need nothin' else, but this quilt sure will keep me warm when the wind is howlin'. I can snuggle up in it like a big ol' baby. Latrina, your daddy would be awful proud. You done good."

Chapter 23
A Matter of Opinion

The artist carried the big canvas into the parlor, then stepped back from the painting. "Drumroll, please," she said.

Carrie thumped her knuckles on her wheelchair. "Let me have it."

Jemma untied the blindfold.

Carrie blinked. "That's not me."

"Well, thanks a lot. I guess that puts the artist in her place."

"But you've painted my face on another girl's body. She's a dancer."

"No, no, I painted the spirit I see in you." Then she noticed the tears and dropped beside the wheelchair. "Oh rats. Carrie, I didn't mean to make you cry. I was hoping to make you happy. You told me that you could do anything in your head. So, you dance."

Carrie wheeled herself right next to the portrait. "I do love it."

Jemma followed her. "You're not going to do anything crazy, are you?"

"You mean like slit my wrists with a letter opener and fall across the painting?"

"Yeah, something like that."

Carrie touched the ballet slippers. She closed her eyes and hummed a song she had been playing on the piano lately. She moved her body, within the confines of the wheelchair, not unlike Melanie's dance with the violin. Jemma looked away so as not to intrude.

"Dad won't like it because he's a complete realist," Carrie said.

"It's your painting, not his," Jemma insisted.

"I didn't say he would throw it out the window. You painted it for me, and I couldn't love it more. Thank you."

"You shouldn't thank me, Carrie. I owe you."

"You aren't going to tell me how my weakness has become

your strength or something."

"That's not what I was going to say."

"What, then?"

"I believe my art is a mirror of physical and emotional realities. I only take liberties with light and shadows and I try to paint from my heart, but this time I painted from yours, and, for opening up a new perspective in my work, I thank you."

Carrie looked away. "It's Dr Pepper time. Forward, Jeeves."

Jemma rolled Carrie across the parquet floor, but she grabbed the door frame as they passed and twisted in the chair for one more look.

"You're welcome," she said under her breath and then smiled up at Jemma. "It gives substance to my fantasies."

❧

Monday morning, Jemma arrived for work as usual. The house was much too quiet. Eleanor didn't yell out to her, and Cotton John was not squawking from the radio, but more importantly, Carrie was not at the kitchen table.

Jemma dropped her purse on the floor and bounded up the stairs.

"Miss Forrester!" The Judge's voice catapulted behind her. She jerked around and came down hard on her bottom. He made no effort to help her up or inquire as to her health.

"Sir, where is Carrie?"

"Come to my study." He turned and disappeared around the dark-paneled wall. Jemma followed him, rubbing the seat of her jeans. His back was to her as he stared out the bay window behind his desk, and he didn't seem in any hurry to talk. An annoying clock above the fireplace ticked off the minutes, and leftover cigar smoke fouled the air.

"Has something happened to Carrie?" she asked.

"I knew your grandfather," he said. "We were on the bank board together. He was a good man, and it was very sad about his boys. Your grandmother has had more than her share of grief."

Jemma glanced around the room. The painting of Carrie was propped against the wall of bookshelves.

"I see that you have the painting. Where is she?"

"Sit down, Jemmabeth."

She remained behind an armchair. "If she's sick, why didn't somebody call me?"

"Carolina is out of town." He pulled out his big desk chair and lowered himself into it.

Jemma narrowed her eyes. "How far out of town?"

"She's in Houston." He leaned back and put his hands together like a church with a steeple. "Miss Forrester," he said, dragging the steeple through his beard, "I appreciate the spirit you have awakened in my daughter. I know you meant well and that you two have become very close. I have no malice when I say this, but it's time that you move on."

"Are you firing me?"

"Call it what you will. However, Carolina is a very sensitive, special person, and she is quite vulnerable in most respects. You have ignited a kind of hope in her that has no future."

"Are you talking about the prom? You sent her away because she played the piano at a dance? She had a fantastic time. I only want Carrie to enjoy living and not spend every waking minute in this house wheeling around wondering what her life could have been like. I love Carrie."

"Those who love her guard her against false hope." He raised his brow and then leaned forward, his pudgy fingers pressing on the glass top of his desk. "Dispensing false hope is not an uncommon trait in your family."

Jemma came out from behind the chair. "I did not give her false hope. She isn't a memento from your past to put away in some old china cabinet. She's a talented, vibrant person. Carrie has something to offer the world." She paced around the room, gesturing like Professor Rossi. "How can she do anything cooped up in here? You won't even let her have physical therapy. She could walk for all we know."

The Judge rose up like Godzilla emerging from the sea. "Sneaking her out of the house to a huge gathering like that was unauthorized and endangered her life."

"She did fine. I would've asked you, but Carrie wouldn't let me. She didn't want you to say no."

He jabbed his finger toward the portrait. "No friend would paint her like that."

Jemma's cheeks burned. "It's how I see Carrie, her spirit. She told me that she could do whatever she wants in her head, so I translated that power to canvas. Ask her. She understands."

"I find it a mockery of her."

"The painting is a confirmation of her, who she is inside that body."

The Judge looked past her and toward the painting. "Then it is an unfair portrayal, and it breaks my heart." His breath was short.

Jemma had a sudden, yet fleeting, compassion for him. She did lower her volume. "I disagree, and I am the artist. I believe it is spiritual justice, but maybe you aren't familiar with that kind, sir."

He turned his icy stare on her. She knew how it must have felt to stand before him in court, awaiting sentencing. He aimed his finger and erupted. "You have no right to superimpose your vision of Carolina onto canvas in the face of her reality and expect it to be interpreted as any type of justice whatsoever. It remains a haunting reminder of her handicap."

"It shouldn't be a reminder of her physical condition, but of her spirit."

They stood, unrelenting. The Judge's breath emerged in snorts as Jemma held hers.

He jerked out his chair and slammed his bulk into it. "I have kept quiet long enough about a number of things that have happened in my home since you came. I tolerated them, thinking it might bring joy to my Carolina. However, you have begun to make decisions outside my control. Now you have toyed with my daughter's mind. Whether you approve or not, we are a family, and you are merely in my employ. I realize the merit of your argument, but the fact remains that we need a rest from you, Miss Forrester."

She wiped her cheeks. "Why is she in Houston, and who is with her?"

"Carolina is with experts in this type of polio. They, not you, know what is best for her. I am flying down today."

"How long will she be there?"

"Indefinitely." He fumbled through a stack of papers. "She is there for long-term treatment. You are not the only one concerned with her happiness. I admit that she has missed opportunities due to her confinement and that she might be more mobile than first thought."

"Why did you send her over the weekend?" Her voice broke. "We didn't even get to say good-bye."

"I've had these arrangements in the works for some time now, ever since your little church excursions. She left you a letter. It's with your final wages." He held out an envelope. "I know that you care for her, Jemmabeth, but you have exceeded your boundaries. I am not a cruel man, despite what you think. A young woman with your obvious talent will not remain in Chillaton very long, and those left behind suffer most in these cases."

"This is not one of your cases."

He extended his hand to her. "My regards to your family." Jemma could not accept it, and his fingers curled into his palm. "Very well," he said, withdrawing. "Take the painting as you leave."

"That belongs to Carrie. Ask her what she wants to do with it." She took a step toward him. "Sir, somebody has to take up the slack from you leaving Carrie stuck in that wheelchair to the point where she is up on a stage playing rock and roll. Who do you think will do that when I am gone? Eleanor?" Jemma paused for a moment, knowing that he didn't have an answer. "Carrie is my friend, and you can't fire me from that." She turned to leave but stopped in the hallway for one more look at the painting. The Judge lit up a fresh cigar and resumed his position at the bay window.

Jemma turned on her heel. "She wanted to go to church. Will you keep her from God as well?" she shouted down the hall, the words echoing into the rooms. She grabbed her purse at the foot of the stairs and saw Eleanor in the kitchen. It would be hot news by noon, but Jemma didn't care. She slammed the door on her way out. Her head ached with a creeping sense of permanent loss. She walked to the tennis courts, sat on the bench, and opened the note.

Dear Jem—I'm off to Houston in case you didn't know it.
Dad says that I am going to have a bunch of tests with some
specialists. Maybe they can actually help me. It's all happening

so fast that I can't believe it. I'm flying down there, and I can't help but think of your Gram's motto about flying. Ha, ha, I don't know when I'll be back—maybe next week. Tell Trina and Spence 'bye for me, and I'll see y'all soon. I guess you can get some extra painting done. I love my portrait, but Dad hasn't mentioned it yet.

Love you, Carrie

She refolded the paper and stared at a scrawny weed growing in the middle of the concrete. Carrie was smart and the Lord would take care of her, but what was His plan? It was probably all her own fault. Typical Scarlett. Someone across the way was running scales on a piano. She should've taken his hand. That would have shown some class, even though he didn't shake hers when she first met him.

Jemma walked home the long way, through the park and back up Main Street. She went past Gram's and down to the Ruby Store. Lester straightened and waved from his rocking chair as she approached the porch.

"What's going on, Jemmerbeth? Are you 'tard,' but not feathered?" He slapped his leg at the joke.

Jemma handed him a cold Dr Pepper. "Lester, tell me some stories. I've had a bad morning."

❧

"I think I'll look for work in L.A. this summer. My uncle has a beach house near there," unemployed Jemma said as she watched Willa and Trina work.

Willa set the iron down with a thud. "Jemmabeth Forrester, I expect you got flowers in your heart and fertilizer in your head. Runnin' off to Los Angeleez ain't gonna solve nothin'. You're pulling Spencer around by his tongue that's hangin' out after you. Now, don't deny it and don't give me that look. I've seen many a lovesick child and he fills the bill. Marry that sweet man right now or get a job." She hung another crisp shirt on the line. "You'll find there's plenty of work once you start lookin'. Latrina has to turn folks down all the time in her housecleanin' business. You can help with that, if nothin' else. Now, c'mon over here and give me a hug."

The damp warmth from the steam iron was still fresh on Willa's neck. "There ain't no shame in being mixed up about things, sugar," she said, looking Jemma in the eye. "The shame's in leaving it to fester."

Chapter 24

A Very Blue Corner

It was Lizbeth's idea for them to picnic at Plum Creek on the old home place. Jemma had been there a hundred times with her family. Papa always invited Spencer, too. Her favorite place as a little girl was a shady spot under the cottonwoods where the creek ran clear. Sometimes, when rain swelled the waters, a little island formed that Robby had claimed as his own. The creek would definitely be a good place for their last date.

As he drove under clear blue skies, Spencer talked about a Parisian chapel, the Sainte-Chapelle. "I want to take you there. You will feel God's presence in every square inch, I promise," he said. His smile was so easy and always part of his speech. She traced around his ear with her finger. He lifted his shoulder to defend himself. "Hey, you don't want me to have a wreck, do you?" She proceeded to nibble on his earlobe.

"That does it." He slammed on the brakes, causing an explosion of dust behind the Corvette. He grabbed her and planted a red hot one on her.

"Whoa!" She caught her breath.

"Let that be a lesson to you," he said and resumed his lecture about the chapel.

They set the cooler under the cottonwood that bore their initials, threw off their shoes, and waded into the ankle-deep creek. The water was cool, even in the heat of the afternoon sun. Jemma wore her favorite silk skirt and a cotton peasant blouse Alex had sent. It was, without a doubt, bohemian. The silk was wrinkled and clingy against her skin, and she bunched it up to keep the hem out of the water as she scanned the creek for minnows.

"Jemma," Spencer called.

She looked up, pushing locks of hair out of her face with one hand as he snapped her photo.

231

"Stay right there," he said, taking several shots.

"Nice camera." She kicked water at him.

"Nice legs." He sloshed over to her and took a close-up. "You look like a million bucks. Let's eat."

Jemma had packed a lunch of fried chicken, potato salad, and peach cobbler. Lizbeth had made it all. Spencer brought a big thermos filled with cold, sweet tea. Sitting on one of Lizbeth's picnic quilts, they ate until their faces and fingers were greasy with fried chicken. They washed up in the creek, and Spencer followed her every move, making memories for Florence.

"Sorry about Carrie," he said, "but I know you did the right thing by showing The Judge that she can do more than he wants to allow."

"Yeah, well, I thought that it was all a part of God's plan."

"It could be, Jem. Remember, the verse that says His ways are mysterious."

"I hope so. Right now it's a mystery how I'm going to get a job."

"If we got married, you would never have to do anything but paint."

"Spence."

"Let's have our own secret wedding right now."

She dug her toes into the sandy creek bottom. "What do you have in mind?"

"The honeymoon," he said with a smile like his third-grade school picture.

She leaned over, peering into the clear water. "Look, minnows."

The little fish scattered before he could see them. He led her back to the big tree and they relaxed against it. Her hair spread out over his shirt like ribbons of mahogany silk.

Spencer sighed. "I think that getting married might make us spontaneously combust."

"Gram says that marriage can clear the water rather than muddy it."

"Hey, I'm talking about fire here, not water."

"I know, but Gram waited to marry Papa and she regrets it now. If I were going to marry someone, which I'm not, I would want to wait until I was thirty."

"You're kidding, of course."

"No. I think thirty would be a good age."

"Jem, do you know how ugly you're going to be at thirty?"

"That's okay. It's what you have in here that counts," she said, pointing to her chest.

"Oh really." He gave her a sneaky look. "Well, I'm not too familiar with that particular spot on you."

"Very funny. I was talking about my heart." She smiled like she loved only him, and, at that moment, it felt like she did. "Did I tell you that Gram is going to Europe with Do Dah?"

"Nope," Spence said, not particularly wanting to change the subject.

"Do Dah talked her into it, and I helped a little. They are going to visit my uncles' graves. I think it will help her heal after all these years."

"That would be something, to run into them in Italy."

"Maybe they could visit you. Do you know where you'll be staying?"

"Not yet, but I'll call Do Dah before they come."

The cottonwood leaves quaked in the breeze and she closed her eyes. Spencer went to the Corvette and came back with a guitar.

"What's this?" she asked.

"I spent all last year learning. I had to do something with my time, and I've finally got these two down, so here goes."

He sang "Candy Man." She moved her shoulders to the music and watched his long fingers move across the frets. Spencer was the only football player with enough guts to sing in their school choir. She danced barefoot under the tree as though she was alone on the tracks, but then it had always been Jemma's nature to dance anytime the music moved her. It was just one more thing that he loved about her.

"What else did you do last year?" she asked, settling beside him.

"Rode a motorcycle all over Europe."

"No! Tell me you didn't do that. You know how I feel about motorcycles. Remember what happened to the Kelseys?"

"Baby, they could have died in a car wreck. You wouldn't have me stop driving a car, would you?"

"Mom and I weren't the first ones to come up on a car wreck. At least in a car you have some protection."

"I have another song."

"Changing the subject, huh? Is there anything that you can't do? You really are a Renaissance man."

"Apparently, I can't make you love me." He played some chords. "You can't dance to this one. You have to listen," he said, and sang Roy's "Running Scared" with more emotion than she was prepared to hear. She got the message. There was nothing to do but hold him when the song was over.

"Do you like pipe music?" she asked.

"Uh. . .you mean bagpipes?"

"Nope, the Uilleann pipes. Remember, Papa's cousin, Angus, drove all the way from North Carolina to play the Uilleann pipes at his funeral? I miss Papa's fiddle music. I wish you could have heard my friend, Melanie, play that song he loved at her recital."

"I wasn't invited."

She exhaled. "Do you remember the first time you ever touched me?" Not really a fair question and she knew it.

"The first time I ever touched you was at our first morning recess in the first grade. We played Red Rover and I busted through you and Randy Jordan. I didn't like him holding your hand."

"I meant when you first touched me in a loving way."

"That's easy. It was noon recess the same day. I grabbed your hand as soon as you got to the playground to play Red Rover again. Afterward, when nobody was looking, I kissed my palm where you'd touched it."

No other guy could have come up with that. He was truly a rare, beautiful man.

The bullfrogs warmed up for their evening chorus and a mourning dove cooed in the plum thicket. In the distance, cattle called for feed. Spencer and Jemmabeth sat on the banks of Plum Creek, under the generous branches of a cottonwood tree and a peach-colored sky, soaking in one another but avoiding the obvious.

"You'll go with me to the airport tomorrow, right?" Spencer asked when they got home.

She nodded.

"Jem, you know this is going to be hard for me. I'm leaving you again with no idea about our future."

"I don't want to think about that right now," she said. It came out wrong, and she was too chicken to fix it. Rats. He was pouring his heart out to Miss Scarlett.

❦

She had dreaded this day ever since she kissed him on that warm night at the river, a winter ago. Jemma wore the blue sundress he liked, the heart necklace, and the earrings. She tied a blue velvet ribbon in her hair, humming *"Un Coin Tout Bleu,"* "A Very Blue Corner," one of Helene's favorite songs. The morning was sunny even though Cotton John had predicted cooler weather. Spencer was cool already. He hadn't looked at her since she got in the car.

"Well, here we go again," he said just as they passed the city limits sign. His jaw was tight, like it was when his mother was yelling obscenities at the country club.

"I know," Jemma said, "and I'm sorry."

"Tell me what you want to do because you can't tell me how to feel."

"Spence, I don't know what to say. I have loved every minute with you these past months." She reached for his hand. He let her hold it, but he didn't kiss it. She had come to expect that.

"So, you still want to date around." He took his hand out of hers and gripped the steering wheel. "Looking for Mr. Skyrocket?"

Her mouth went dry. He wasn't like this even when she broke up with him. "I just have to see how things are when we're apart one last time. I'm not horsing around with you, Spence. If we are meant to be together, then I promise I'll make a commitment. You don't want me if I have any doubts, do you?"

"Doubts? It's us, Jem. It was us at Flagstaff and Plum Creek and dancing in the moonlight at the river. We aren't the prom king and queen anymore. This is grown-up love and you know it." He turned back to the road. "I'm curious how you'll figure all this out to your satisfaction. Let's see. . .maybe you'll record how many times you think about me and track that data on a calendar. Or I suppose it could be more like a rating system to measure the intensity of the thoughts. Well, I'm sorry, but I can't stand to think about you kissing anybody but me. Does it bother you at all that I will be with other women?" He gave her a look, his eyes piercing into hers. "Go with your heart, baby. Let our relationship be like your art—fearless and instinctive—but that can't happen because it's him, isn't it? The almighty Paul."

Jemma chewed on her lip and watched a cluster of sparrows on the high line wires beside the highway.

"I know that he's a cowboy."

It shot through her.

"You're still running the bulls, aren't you? Hemingway would be so proud. Only this is one bull at a time."

"Who told you he was a cowboy? I never said that."

"What difference does it make? You've found your fantasy, and nothing else matters. He's a wild, barhopping womanizer. That's fine. He lied to you. That's okay. He even forgot that he was married—not a problem. Good grief, Jem, married!"

Jemma's face tingled. Rats. Rats. Rats. The ceramic moon swayed wildly.

"So, that's it. You are waiting on Paul. Maybe he has kids and you can be a little mama sooner than you thought. You've just been killing time with me until he's a free man. Well, I can guarantee that I'll be dating every knockout that I find because I don't have anybody waiting on me. Enjoy your cowboy with a clear conscience, my friend. I won't be around to watch you like a hawk, so do as you please. I'm staying in Italy."

He stopped the car and put the top down so that the only thing they could hear was the wind. She couldn't look at him. This was not her Spence, the one who cried when she broke up with him, and this was certainly not the sentimental drive to the airport she had expected. Teardrops spotted her pretty blue dress.

"I can't say good-bye like this," Jemma said as they waited at his gate.

He turned to her, his face solemn, his gray eyes cool and glassy. "I'm sorry, Jem, but for the first time in our lives, I feel like I don't know you. How could you even consider loving somebody like him? It's not only your cowboy fixation; it's that you could mess with me all these months. You should have more respect for me or for yourself. You must take me for a fool."

"That's not fair. You are dear to me, and I didn't mean to hurt you." Her voice cracked. "I thought you understood last fall. I don't know how I feel about us, but I never, ever meant to cause you more pain. I want you to be happy. I want us to be happy. Can't you wait a little longer for me to make up my mind?"

"I have waited almost two years for you to make up your mind." He blew out his breath and hugged her to him. "For once, I wish I didn't love you," he said, his voice husky. "This is it, though. I've humiliated myself for the last time." He looked right into her golden eyes. "I can't play your game anymore."

She put her fingers on his lips, then struggled to say the words. "Spence, you and I are pieces of each other. The best that I am, I owe to you, and we can never be separated. We will never be far from one another's heart or mind, ever. Remember the quote on the moon. I must love you because I want to so bad. All the time I dated him, it was you I dreamed about. Just give me until Christmas to sort out my feelings so I can look you in the eye and say that I'll love you, and only you, forever and always. Just that long. I'll give you my answer then. I promise." She choked up. "Remember, we started over. I should get a little more time."

"No, baby, you should know by now." He wiped his eyes. "I won't be back," he whispered. "I can't do it. For you to choose between him and me is like cutting out my heart."

"Spence, listen. I promise I wasn't waiting for him."

His flight was announced, and she gripped his arm. He stroked the length of her hair, untying the velvet ribbon to fold in his hand, then cupped her chin and kissed her. It was a fireball kiss that stopped her heart. "Good-bye, Jemmabeth," he said. Then he was gone.

"Call me, okay?" she yelled, then covered her mouth. "Please call me, Spence," she whispered into her hand.

Jemma watched the plane lift off from the runway. She ran to the parking lot and squinted at the silver speck heading northeast. Her foolish lips still tingled. She was Frankenstein's bride getting the jolt that awakened her from the dead.

She drove home with the purr of the motor and beat of her

anxious heart to keep her company. Even the ceramic moon was gone. She parked the car at the dealership, gave the keys to Mr. Chase's secretary, and walked home. Jemma knew that she had painted herself into this very blue corner.

Chapter 25
Quicksilver

The summer blew in, literally, keeping her busy with work and painting. She teamed up with Trina and put her cleaning skills to work again. They landed the Farmer's Union Bank custodial job at night for a steady income, and she helped Trina with private homes during the day. She dropped off bags of food at Shorty's dugout every week and could hear his television blaring.

Spencer never called. Her head was clear on that because he had said as much. She deserved it, too, but her heart hoped otherwise. Her heart hoped many things—most of all, that she had not lost him forever. She even prayed about it, remembering a sermon about the mercy of God. Maybe He didn't just reserve mercy for kings and nations. Surely there was a drop left for complete nitwits like her.

She hadn't seen Eleanor Perkins since the day The Judge fired her. That is, not until she was paying for a half gallon of Golden Vanilla ice cream for Lizbeth at the grocery store.

Eleanor abandoned her cart and walked right up to her, bosom heaving. "Well, here you are, hon, out and about. Ever who says to me these days, 'Iddinit a shame about the Chase boy running off to It'ly, and leaving poor Jemmabeth,' I say, 'Hold your horses right there. We ain't talking about Max Chase here because Spencer Chase is a perfect angel.' Anyhoo, the shame's on you for having yourself a high time with that sweet young man, then turnin' him down flat when he proposed marriage."

Jemma raised her head. "Who said Spence proposed to me?"

Edith Frame, sitting comfortably at the cash register, drew in her pointy chin. "Law, sugar pie, some things go without sayin'. Did you think he was just gonna date you forever?"

Eleanor went on. "Hon, you give up a good, good man ever how you look at it."

Edith clucked her tongue and opened the register, but Jemma was gone before Edith could count out the change.

⇜⦿⇝

Next to the Cotton Festival, the Fourth of July was Chillaton's crowning glory. The same citizens organized both events and took their jobs dead serious. Depending on the event, they were in charge of the Cotton Queen pageant, town barbeque, parade, rodeo, and the cowpoke dance at the old skating rink. The Cotton Festival acknowledged a bountiful harvest, and the Fourth celebrated America's independence from the British and dependence on beef.

All Jemma had ever cared about was getting a gander at the cowboys. The Fourth was a hat and boot jungle for one whole weekend, but then the cowboys disappeared to their ranching duties and reappeared en masse the next Fourth. They were a breed unto themselves, and she wasn't the only one that felt that way. They were of interest to every breathing female who would admit it. That's what she hadn't been able to resist and one thing, among others, that Spencer had tolerated about her. In high school, Jemma and Sandy put on their cowgirl outfits to mosey down to the rink without their boyfriends and check out the buckaroos waiting for the dance. "Running the bulls" is what she and Sandy had named their pilgrimage.

It was their expert opinion that if any decent-looking male put on a pressed pair of jeans, a starched shirt, boots, and a cowboy hat, he could pass as the good Lord's gift to women for five minutes—ten, if he wore English Leather or a Stetson. The real ones came across as so wantonly feral. It was the way they stood around in those jeans, like they could wrestle any large animal with one hand tied behind their backs and never mess up that crease. Or maybe it was the hat. A cowboy sure knew how to make a girl feel special. She got roped for real once, and several times she had given in to a dance or two if they scored high enough on her buckaroo rating scale. She felt a need to do it one more time. Maybe it would cheer her up.

She pulled on her jeans, beat-up red boots, a long-sleeved white shirt, and Papa's old straw hat. Lifting her chin, she walked straight past the prime candidates who leaned against the outside of the building. She walked through the appreciative, verbal crowd and into the rink. She turned down some good invitations to dance all night, but it was nothing. Then she waited under the rodeo announcer's stand to meet a reluctant Trina, as planned. If only there had been just one blond with gray eyes and a tiny scar on his chin. If only.

The day took a turn for the worse. A sports car idled at the curb and the Voice of Doom called, "Hey, over here!" The Cleave waved to her from the car. Jemma hesitated but walked over and leaned in the window. Great idea.

"That's some outfit, cowgirl." A stranger pushed his sunglasses up on his head and grinned at her from behind the steering wheel. He winked and took a drink from a bottle. "Wanna have some fun?"

"Chad, this is Jemmartsybeth Forrester," Missy said, eyeing Jemma's boots. "She's sort of the town's token hippie."

"Hi, Chad." Jemma eked out a smile.

He puckered his lips and kissed at her. "Missy may not last all the way to Amarillo. Why don't you hop in?" He jerked his head toward the tiny backseat.

The Cleave turned to Chad. "Jemma doesn't have fun. She's a Sunday school girl, and, remember, it's *Melissa*, not Missy." Her *s*'s were slurred, and her breath foggy with beer.

Jemma drew back. "Y'all are in no condition to drive anywhere. You should just stay in Chillaton."

Missy flipped her mane over her shoulder. "I heard you and Spence are splits—for good this time. I guess he finally figured out that you're not Miss Perfect after all. Now it's my turn."

"Good-bye, *Missy*," Jemma said. "Good luck, Chad."

Missy gurgled a noise resembling a bored horse. "Oh, shut up. You're the one who needs some luck. Everybody knows you had a cowboy in Dallas and managed to lose him, too." Missy's laughter blended into the squeal of the tires as Chad threw the car into gear and sped away. A Greek fraternity decal glowered from the back window. Jemma clamped down on her lip and waited for Trina.

❧

The phone rang and she raced to it as though Lizbeth might try to get it first.

"Carrie! Where are you?"

"I'm still in Houston in a physical rehab program. I miss you so much."

"I miss you, too. I would write, but I doubt your dad would give me your address and Eleanor claims she doesn't know it."

"I'll get it for you. Just a second." Jemma heard a male voice in the background, then a stranger came on the line.

"Hello there," he said. "Got a pencil?"

"Sure, I'm ready." Jemma wrote the address and Carrie came back on.

"So, is that your boyfriend?" Jemma teased.

"Yeah."

"Whoa. I was just kidding."

"I'm not," she said with a giggle.

"So, what's the deal? Is he cute or what?"

"Are you cute or what?" Carrie asked the boyfriend. "He says he is in the *or what* category."

"See, it didn't take you long to find somebody."

"It just happened, Jem. He is the head of physical therapy here, and we fell crazy in love. He doesn't even care about my other boyfriend."

"The cannon?"

"Yeah. His name is Philip Bryce, and I'm so happy."

"What does your father say about this?"

Carrie lowered her voice as though he might be listening. "Dad doesn't know. Isn't that funny? Phil plays the drums. We could have a weird band if you wanted to be our singer."

"Did you know your daddy sneaked you out of town to get you away from me?"

"I kind of figured that out. I'm sorry you lost your job."

"We had words, but what's important is that you are in good hands now."

"How's Spence?" Carrie asked.

Jemma fidgeted with her necklace. "He's in Italy."

"Oops. I forgot about that. When's the wedding?"

"We parted hard."

"Oh, c'mon, y'all are in love."

"It's my fault because I can't get rid of Paul."

"You gave up Spencer for that guy?"

"I just want to know for sure. I told Spence that I would make up my mind by Christmas."

"What did he say to that?"

"He said he wouldn't come home for Christmas, but I'm afraid he meant something else."

"Like what?"

"Like he is tired of messing with me."

"You can't blame him, Jem. If you were on *As the World Turns*, the writers would give you amnesia about now, and you'd be sent off to an island."

"I guess we've known each other too long and too well. It's like we've been married all our lives."

"I wish I'd known Phil all my life. He's my hope for happiness. Remember when we talked about that?"

"I do, and I'm glad for y'all. I promise I'll write, but don't tell your father. He hates me."

"He doesn't hate you. You scared him."

"Carrie, you keep the painting. I did it for you, not him."

"Don't worry; we've already talked about it."

"I'm going to send you another one, and I hope you'll like it even better. It's from my heart to yours."

"I can't wait. Love you. Tell Trina about Phil."

"I will. Love you, too."

"Don't mess around and lose Spence, because y'all were magic. You were so right about kissing being the highlight of your day. I'll talk to you later, Jem. I'm the happiest girl in the world."

"Good for you, Carrie." Jemma hung up the phone and cried.

It was propped up on the kitchenette between the salt and pepper shakers.

Jemmabeth Alexandra Forrester
c/o Her Grambeth
Chillaton, Texas

"It's time you dealt with this," Lizbeth said, her tone firm.

Jemma knew she was right. An odd sensation, layered in swirls of emerald and black, snaked up from her stomach. The answer to all her doubts could lie in front of her. The almighty Paul. He had messed with her life and, therefore, with Spencer's. She grabbed the envelope before she could change her mind and took it to the living room. She turned on the lamp by Papa's chair and ripped it open.

Sweet Jemmabeth,

How you must feel toward me, I can never know for sure because the hurt I have caused is your private pain. Why I didn't have the guts to tell you about my situation is beyond me. It would have saved us from all this grief.

Shelby is the woman that you saw the night you came by, and she was, technically, my wife. She and I met in college. We were both bad kids, and we got married our senior year. Things went from wild to worse. We were stepping out on each other even before our first anniversary. We said it was over, but my dad wanted us to make it work. I had been in ROTC so I began my service right after graduation and stayed in a few extra years. You already know all about that. Shelby was with me for part of my service, then she stayed with her folks. At least that's what she said.

When I came home, it was like old times for a while, but it just didn't work. We were both ready for something else. When I met you, I was living alone and nobody knew where she was living, but we were legally separated. She called up one day and wanted a divorce. When you saw her, we were meeting to file. That was the first time I had seen her in over a year. The divorce was granted on Valentine's Day, and I am no longer a married man.

I should have told you this last summer. You were so perfect, and I was not proud of the whole Shelby mess. I know you are a spiritual person and in your eyes I was out of line to be dating you or anybody else before I was divorced. My only excuse is that I must be weak when it comes to you, Jemma. Even your name gives me a chill.

I joined my dad and uncle in their law firm, but nothing else matters if I don't have you in my life again. Let me ask your forgiveness in person so that I can look you straight in the eyes. I know how you feel about that.

My feelings have only grown stronger for you, my darlin', and I will never rest until you're mine. I mean that.

I love you,
Paul

Jemma stuck it back in the envelope. Old pangs of guilt and shame seeped through her. She moved to the porch swing and pushed off, longing to be rocked by something or someone.

❧

The next morning, before Lizbeth woke up, Jemma crept into the pouting room and opened the soldier box. Lizbeth had bundled up the letters and put big rubber bands around them. She sat on the floor wielding Papa's shiny letter opener until she decided they were not letters at all. They consisted of a couple of lines jotted on the back of his business cards:

Jemma, please call or write to me.
I have to talk to you.
Love, PT

How embarrassing. These bits of nothing had shared the soldier box with dear letters from her daddy's brothers. She pitched the cards in a cigar box and squeezed it into the corner of a shelf. She stood for a few seconds, looking into the open chest, then felt around the bottom of it until her hand touched the chain. She took out the rose. It was as beautiful as the night he gave it to her. It glittered in the first light of the day that filtered through the little window. She draped the necklace around the shade of her bedside lamp. In spite of everything, she still needed to see him, to be sure. Time had healed her pain, but now there was this solid longing for Spence. He was not tucked away in a corner of her heart—he filled it up, or so it seemed.

⟨❧⟩

Each time the phone rang, her heart skipped two beats, thinking it could be either of them. She was truly hopeless. This call was full of static.

"Sandy, hi!" Jemma said. "I've got news about Paul."

"So what? He's got problems," Sandy tossed back.

"I don't think so. He was legally separated when we dated and he still loves me."

Sandy exhaled. "Jem, he's weird, I'm telling you, and he's got history. Nobody needs history; it's no fairy tale when you get married, trust me."

"You don't know him."

"Obviously, you didn't either."

"I need to see him."

"You used Spence, didn't you?"

"I did not."

"What would you call it? As soon as the lonesome stranger comes riding back into town you drop Spence like he was nothing. 'Ooh, he still loves me.' What a bunch of bull. You are plain mean, Jemma. You were born to hurt him."

"I was not. You were the one who begged me to start dating him again. Everybody wanted me to get with Spencer. He and I talked about our feelings for each other."

"I'll bet you did. You probably spent time on The Hill, too, and at your not-so-secret spot on the river. You probably danced your little heart out with him every chance you got. Don't be trying to blame me for anything. You're the girl who's been on this big campaign against injustice. All you need to do is look in the mirror. Excuse me, but I have to go now."

Jemma hung up and fell back on the bed. This was a solid hit with the double whammy from *Saturday Night Wrestling*. Sandy always had a good handle on things. That's something the two of them had in common since the first grade, and Sandy was right, despite the sarcasm. Rats. Maybe she had just unleashed her hormones with Spencer, or maybe she loved him.

She tore half a page from her sketchpad and wrote the note. It was short and to the point: *Paul, We need to talk. Jemma.* She figured that was equivalent to the back of a business card. She took it to the post office herself.

Paralee stamped the letter with a lifted Joan Crawford brow. "I heard that Spencer is off in It'ly. I kinda thought you'd be whippin' out a letter a day to him by now." H.D., her cat, stretched and looked Jemma right in the eye before jumping off the counter.

"Yes ma'am, I should do that," Jemma whimpered and left. She sat in the car and blinked back tears, but the letter was mailed and Paul would come.

The hollyhocks were in full bloom. They didn't have the sugary aroma of honeysuckle, but they were heavy with pink blossoms. She leaned back and closed her eyes. A warm breeze moved through her hair.

"Jemma?" His voice surged through her like quicksilver, and fond memories regained their throne.

"Paul!" She gasped at the sight of him and shot straight up, her heart pounding as she looked into his startling green eyes—just like when she froze in the lights of the 9:04 Zephyr.

"I am so sorry, darlin'. I was stupid and wrong." He kissed her hand, sending her into a familiar spin.

She didn't even think about it. "I forgive you." Good grief.

He kissed her a long one. It was nice, but she was cool enough to know that some of the feeling came merely from pressing her lips against any man's after three months of abstinence.

Paul moved the chairs together and took her hands. "Did you get my letters?" he asked, almost innocently.

"Only the last one was a real letter."

"My father finally convinced me that you were worth risking the truth over. I hope that what I said explained things. I've missed you so much," he said, looking her over like she forgot to dress. "So, you're wearing perfume now, huh?"

"Someone gave it to me."

They sat for a while, breathing in rhythm with the swaying and bobbing of the hollyhocks.

"Why did you wait so long to tell me?"

"I don't know. The longer you were away from me, the more I

felt like you weren't going to listen."

"No, I mean from the start."

"Like I said, I was ashamed of it."

"I don't see how you could keep such a thing from me," she said.

"Why wouldn't you talk to me on the phone?"

"I thought you were married, and actually, you were."

"I guess there's a lot to forgive."

She nodded, fiddling with the heart necklace. "So what do we do now?"

"It's up to you."

She'd heard that enough to last a lifetime.

"Did you date after I left?" Curiosity, nothing more.

"I didn't for a while, darlin', but, well, I got lonesome."

The thought of him with other girls didn't have any impact on her at all.

He traced around her wrists and hands, like a blind man. "This morning, when I told my dad that I was coming here, he said he hopes you're the one to be the mother of his grandchildren."

He seemed older, heavier than she remembered.

"What are you thinking?" he asked.

"Do you still wear your hat?" Great choice.

He grinned. "What kind of cowboy do you think I am? Of course I wear my hat."

How weird. He had grown wrinkly lines around his eyes over the winter.

"What's your horse's name again?" she asked. What an idiot.

"His name's Cinco. Jemma, do you love me? You've never said the words, and I need to know." He was serious, but she couldn't say it. She had made such a big deal about him for all this time, and here he was, wanting answers she couldn't give. Just like Spence. "Do you love me?" he asked again, this time with a kiss.

She pulled away. "I don't know. You and I had something, but I don't know what it was. I'm not thinking straight. This all seems like a dream."

"I understand, darlin'. It's been a long time. I just thought that maybe down deep, things hadn't changed."

"People change, Paul. Love changes. I don't know how I feel

right now." Yikes, there were those words, too. She kissed him because she didn't know what else to do. He knew exactly what to do because Paul was, after all, a ladies' man.

Lizbeth was gracious, and Lester came over for supper and told stories. Jemma, though, was edgy. It was not right, somehow, for Paul to sit in the chair where Spencer had left that quilt so carefully folded. At Lizbeth's suggestion, Lester invited Paul to stay overnight at his house.

"Gram, I'm going to take Paul to meet the Johnsons," Jemma said.

"You young folks run along. Say hello to Willa for me." She gave Paul a polite smile. "We're glad you came," she said, meaning more than he knew.

The lights were still on at Willa's house. Paul waited in the baby blue while she knocked. She wasn't sure how this would go over.

Willa opened the door. "Mercy me, child. Why are you gallivanting around at this hour?"

"What's going on?" Trina asked, yawning.

Jemma led them off the porch and along the 'tunia path. Paul got out of the truck and stood beside it. "Paul Turner, meet Willa and Trina Johnson."

He took off his hat and bowed.

Trina stammered and stared at him with a silly grin. "Glad to meet you," she said, then looked to Jemma for help.

Willa pursed her lips. "You in town for long?"

"I'm here for one reason." Paul pulled Jemma to him.

Willa and Trina knew too much. "I just wanted you to meet him," Jemma said. She really wanted them to see what she'd been up against.

Willa read her mind. "It's good to put a face to a name." She turned toward the porch. Her cane whacked the path with each step.

"Bye, Paul," Trina waved. "Nice to meet you." She lowered her brow at Jemma.

"Y'all watch out for the 9:04," Willa said over her shoulder. "Be a downright shame to mess up that pretty pickup."

~◆~

Lester pulled in his driveway with the morning paper and found Jemma sitting in the porch swing, wrapped in her old robe.

"Jemmerbeth, you're up early. Did you already milk the cow?" he asked, chuckling.

Jemma gave him a weak smile. "I'm just thinking."

"That lawyer is still asleep. He seems a bit peculiar around the edges. Sort of drifts off while a feller's talkin'."

"I miss Spencer," she said.

Lester settled into the wicker chair. "I know what it's like to be without your sweetheart, and I've got lots of them to fret over. I loved 'em all, too, even the cranky ones." A rooster crowed across the tracks. "Yes, sir, the only thing worse than being in love is being plumb out of it."

"I think I'm going crazy, Lester. I have no control over my heart. It's separate from me, running wild."

"Well, sir, you know, back in the thirties, we had a runaway train come thunderin' through here. The engineer had hisself a heart attack, and there wasn't nobody else with him at the time. That runaway was full throttle through four counties. Folks was gettin' off their deathbeds to see it fly by. The sheriff and the Texas Rangers was trying to beat it down the road to clear the tracks. It had a mind of its own, too. Them kind of runaways have to hit somethin' to put 'em out of their misery. This particular one run smack-dab into Eugene Richey's cotton trailers. He was pullin' a double load behind his tractor, right close to Cleebur. It rained cotton for a whole hour after the collision. Eugene got throwed thirty foot in the air, and his wires was crossed after that, poor old feller. He should've jumped off when he seen it comin', but he wouldn't leave his cotton, I reckon."

"I don't have any excuses," she said.

"How's that, Jemmer?"

"Helene warned me that Paul was only a passing fancy. I thought I was so smart, but it looks like I am no better than Eugene, when it comes to jumping out of the way of a real Zephyr."

Lester couldn't add anything to what she'd said. He tapped his foot and looked out over the yard.

Jemma gave him a kiss on the cheek. "I'd better get dressed. Thanks for the conversation, Lester."

⊰⊱

Paul and Jemma drove out to the river, but not to The Spot.

"Does this creek have a name?" he asked.

"The Salt Fork of the Red River." Jemma scanned the horizon.

"Sounds western, but it's not much of a river though."

She scowled at him. "It's ours."

Paul put his arm around her. "Seems like you're ticked off, darlin'. Surely you don't want me to confess every detail about my past. We could be here for a week." He laughed—that same old whiskey laugh—then crossed his heart. "No other secrets worth repeating, Jem. The only truth that matters is that I was hooked on you that first night at the office. Any man alive would've been, but you were such a good girl that I knew I was going to have to straighten up. Then I realized that I really loved you and had to have you to love me back. That was the first time I'd had thoughts about a woman from my heart, and I knew I should tell you everything. When I opened my truck door and saw the painting, I cried like a two-year-old. . .anyway, my dad and I talked for hours that night. He was hacked off at me for messing up again. He said I deserved a good kick in the pants for hurting you."

"He was right."

"I saw your car at Helene's, but I couldn't bring myself to face you. I don't know why I fell apart like that. I let you leave town, thinking the worst of me. I will always regret that, darlin'. Always."

She watched the water as it curved around and made a little pool below them. It could be a spot for minnows to scatter if she and Spence went wading there. He was probably asleep now, across the Atlantic. She hoped he was having sweet dreams.

Paul lifted her hand to his lips. "I think you have become even more beautiful, if that's possible."

"A good heart is more important than good looks," Jemma said. As though that was why she fell for him.

"You do have a good heart, and I'm sorry I caused you pain."

"Nobody goes through life without pain," Jemma said. "The pain that Gram has endured makes mine insignificant. My friend

Carrie has gone through physical and emotional pain, but she still has an amazing spirit. Trina and Willa, well, they know pain on a daily basis."

"Black people are resilient," he said, playing with her hair.

She drew back. "Excuse me? Black *people*? We've wronged each individual. It makes us feel better to think of people in groups, and then we put the groups in boxes, like mementos. It makes us comfortable. We close the lids and open them up occasionally for our own purposes. We need to face the people inside the boxes."

"Hey," he said, fending off the verbal barrage with his hands, "I wasn't inferring anything. I just meant, as a race, they have shown a remarkable ability to survive. It was a compliment."

"As a race? Like there is something in their blood?"

"Now hold on here a minute, darlin'. I'm not a racist. I was only making an observation."

"Integrity. That's what Willa and Trina have. When you ride the bus four hours every day when you're only six years old, there's nothing in your blood that says 'be strong.' It was Trina who got on that bus every day because she loved to learn. Willa does ironing for people across the tracks who won't do their own because they're too lazy. If she could've been on that bus like Trina, maybe she could have realized her dreams, too. You and I did that to her, our parents did that to her, and our grandparents, too, because we put people in boxes to keep our consciences comfortable. You were not making a compliment and you know it."

"Is this the temper you told me about? Are you about to throw something at me?"

"No. I throw stuff when I'm only a little mad. I was throwing things from my heart just now."

"Come here." He pulled her toward him. "Let's talk about the scenery," he said, nuzzling her ear. "There sure is a lot of flat land around here, except for some draws and a few hills."

She shrugged. "I guess it grows on you, like the desert."

He pushed his hat back on his head. "Dry land cotton, I suppose."

"Some farmers have irrigation wells, and there are ranches, too."

"Ranching's good, but farming seems like a hard way to make a living in this country."

"My papa and Gram did it."

He moved his fingers under her chin. "It's interesting that someone like you came from a one-horse town like this."

"What's that supposed to mean?"

"Your art. It's way too sophisticated to have been nurtured by Lester, for example."

"Grammar has nothing to do with character or good sense," she said, daring him to say more.

Paul chuckled. "Well, you have to admit that he's quite the bumpkin."

Jemma looked him in the eye, ready to pounce. "Don't ever say that about my friends. What you see in them is exactly what's inside me."

Paul exhaled and readjusted his hat. The wind kicked up from the west. "Is it that I was married?"

"You have to be kidding me." Her hands sprang up in the air. "The problem was that you were *married and dating me!* Good grief. All this talk about love was going on while you had a wife and didn't have the decency to let me in on your little secret."

"I was afraid I'd lose you."

"You did anyway."

"I get the feeling now that you wished I hadn't come."

"No. I needed to see you to get my heart straight."

He touched her cheek. "I'm so sorry I hurt you, but I can't change the past, Jem. I don't believe in living like a monk, either, and I know your opinion of that. It's just the way I am, but I promise you, on my mother's memory, that I've never loved anybody but you and I never will."

The sun moved behind coral-edged clouds, changing the color of the river. She touched the heart necklace. "You're right. Some things never change," she said, "and they shouldn't."

"Just give me another chance. I won't push you or stand in the way of your art. If you need to finish your education, that's okay with me. We both have things we need to do. I've got a career to get off the ground, and besides, we can get to know each other again. Have fun like we used to." He touched her lips. "What do you say, my golden-eyed darlin'?"

"I think I still love Spencer, my high school boyfriend." Jemma's heart sank when she said his name, as though she had summoned his ghost and he was with them now, watching.

Paul laid his hat on the rock. Then his lips curled into a grin. "Well, I'm in this for the long haul, so I suppose I can handle a little competition from some kid." His arms were tight around her, and he wouldn't let go. "I love you, Jemma," he whispered. "You'll always be mine." He kissed her like a man determined to start a fire with wet wood.

There they were, only a football field away from Jemma and Spencer's parking spot. A cinnamon-colored hawk sailed above them, its shrill cry startling her. She broke away from Paul's kiss and sat up, watching as the hawk circled, then flew into the sunset. She could still hear it on the wind as Paul wiped her tears, thinking they were a good sign.

❧

It was time for his return to Wicklow. "If there were any way to swing another night, I would," he said. "I realize we have some more talking to do. Problem is, I have a court hearing tomorrow morning, and nobody else in the office knows the case."

"I leave next week to spend the rest of the month with my Lillygrace grandparents in St. Louis," she said.

He stood by the door, touching her hair. "I do know about commitments, but I'll miss you and I'll call. One more thing I need to ask. Do you know anybody who would hire a detective to follow me around and then quiz my family and friends about my character and personal life?"

"A detective?" Jemma asked, suddenly interested. "I don't know. Unless it could have been my great-aunt." She couldn't help but smile. "I bet you've been Do Dahed." At least that's who she hoped it was. He held her, cowboy-style, as they kissed good-bye. She should have told him right then that there was no hope for them, but being the Queen of Bad Choices, she didn't.

Chapter 26
Fallow Ground

English Leather was still on her skin as she painted, even after playing basketball for an hour with Trina. Paul dazzled her last summer when she was ready to love again, but it was Spence she needed then and now. The initial surge of emotion she felt when she first saw him in the hollyhock patch was not worth the grief she had caused Spence and herself. It was neither earth-shattering desire, nor was it love. She had only been running the bulls, but this time she had tripped and let herself get caught up on a big horn.

She took a break from painting and walked the rails. Cotton John had predicted scattered showers. Only at the vanishing point of the rails was there a hint of blue. She smiled at Shorty's TV blaring across the tracks. Funny, how wood and steel could come to dictate social status. How easy things would be if all lines were so clean and clear cut as the tracks, creating tidy boundaries, boxes, for sorting souls. She knew now that lines must be blurred for people to achieve their dreams. Those were the gray areas. There was no gray area for love, though. She either loved Paul or Spence, and she knew the answer.

"Let's drive out to the cemetery and then to the home place," Lizbeth said after church. Jemma picked flowers from the garden and put them on Papa's grave. The stiff wind flipped the petals like broken pinwheels. Lizbeth kissed her hand and laid it on the tombstone. She said a prayer, then waited in the car.

"Papa," Jemma whispered, "I'll make it up to Spencer. I promise. I do love him." Saying it out loud, at last, made her feel better. It might be nice if she told him, too.

Lizbeth drove to the little rise on the far northeast corner of the home place. In the distance, the windmill next to their farmhouse was a prism, spinning and sparkling in the blazing sun. Lizbeth tied her scarf under her chin and got out of the car. Jemma followed her to the edge of the barren field, left unplanted for a growing season by the tenant.

Lizbeth surveyed the horizon as the wind flapped her thin, cotton dress about her legs. "Your papa liked to let the land rest now and then, too. He said it worked hard giving us a living and needed time to regain its strength. He always talked about this place like it was a person. 'Let it go fallow for a while and it'll come back twice as strong,' he'd say and he was right. We had some fine crops over the years."

She gathered a handful of dirt and sifted it through her fingers. It sprayed back against her dress. "That's how he tested the fallow ground. Claimed he could feel if it was ready to taste life again." She put her arm around Jemma. "I sometimes think that I am like this old place." They stood together, wavering in the wild gusts that hissed through the fencerow grass. "You drive back, sugar," Lizbeth said, dabbing at her eyes with her hanky. "He was full of joy. I do so miss that man."

On the way home, Jemma admitted to herself that all she needed was a hoop skirt. She couldn't go back to Tara anymore. She was already there. She couldn't sift the dirt through her fingers and know when the fallow ground was ready to taste life again. She had Spencer, gave him up, wanted him back, got him, and gave him up again. She was not even worth being called fallow ground.

❧

She heard the phone ringing as they drove up. She raced to it on the outside chance it was Spence.

"Hi, Jem."

"Sandy. Okay, I was wrong, and you were right. I'm so sorry."

"Yeah, well, it may not matter now. I hate to be the one to tell you this, but Spencer has a serious girlfriend."

Jemma crumpled to the floor, stomach churning. "No, no, no." Her fingers went to her lips where his good-bye kiss still smoldered.

"She's in that study abroad thing with him in Italy, and I guess they are quite the couple. Mrs. Chase said that he is bringing her home for Christmas. She was showing pictures to everybody at Nedra's."

"He hasn't been gone that long."

"Hey, it only took you a summer to fall in deep love, remember?"

"It was a mistake."

"Looks like the mistake of a lifetime. She's from New York. Twila saw the pictures and said that she is completely gorgeous. Remember when we used to do the Zephyr Dance on the tracks? You were always the last one to stop dancing, and you wouldn't jump off until the train blew its whistle. You just waited too long this time. It was bound to happen sometime. Well, hang in there, Jem. I have to go."

Scarlett barely made it to the bathroom to throw up. Afterward, she sat on the bathmat and unleashed a deluge of sobs.

Lizbeth heard it all from the living room, but decided to let nature take its course. She had already heard the gossip at Nedra's. Unfortunately, it was the talk of the town.

Jemma stayed in the bathroom until dark, then when Lizbeth tactfully went to bed early, Jemma crawled onto her own bed and stared at the ceiling. The teardrops filled her ears, then trickled through her hair and soaked into the pillow. She was swallowed up with misery, the surly kind that gnawed with each breath to remind her that it was all her own doing.

Rain plinked into a watering can left on the front porch as the curtains billowed out with the damp breeze. She took the broom handles out of the windows, letting them slide shut, then she wandered outside.

It was a quiet shower that would rinse leaves and give the birds brief puddle water. She rubbed her arms at the sudden cool air. The knot that had lodged itself in her throat began sifting down to her heart, to a gloomy corner that harbored comfortless and pointless loss. She stepped into the rain and lifted her desperation to the Lord in prayer, but it was the night that pointed its soggy finger at her. She was without him—her hero, her best friend, and her own true love.

⬥

Most of her paintings were gone, shipped to Le Claire in carefully packaged crates, designed and crafted by Lester, who knew a thing or two about shipping on trains. She was going on with the work at hand. Spencer had warned her that he was going to do it. Rats. Not just gorgeous, but completely gorgeous. Jemma blew her nose. "I won't come home for Christmas," she said to the walls. "I'll go to Arizona." She got the paintings and walked across the tracks.

"Hey, girl, what's with the puffy eyes?" Trina asked as she opened the door.

"Spence has a girlfriend in Italy," Jemma said. She knew she was in for a sermon.

Trina shook her head. "I hate to say it, but everybody saw it coming, even though that cowboy was really something to look at. Man, you sure can pick 'em."

Willa made the face that mothers get just before they give a lecture. "Give me a hug, sugar. Now, you'd better get yourself some backbone. Just because Spencer's got himself a honey don't mean he's outta love with you, even though you were fiddlin' around with that pretty boy."

"Mama, don't start preaching," Trina said.

Jemma propped the painting up on the kitchen counter. "It's okay. There's nothing you could tell me that I haven't already beaten myself over the head with anyway. Here's my surprise."

Trina's eyes widened. "Oh Jem," was all she could say.

"I painted three of them and I already sent one to Carrie. The one of Papa is for Spence, so would you take it to his housekeeper's for me? She'll make sure he gets it." Jemma might as well have been talking to the ironing board even though Trina nodded politely.

Willa wiped her eyes. "Jemmabeth Forrester, you are the sweetest child I ever knew outside of my Latrina. I need another hug."

The painting enchanted the Johnson women. The three little girls were dancing on the tracks with the wind in their hair. The smallest was a pretty blond with eyes the color of cornflowers, the tallest was a beautiful little black girl with slanted eyes and dimples, and in the middle was an auburn-haired beauty with pouty lips, freckles, and golden eyes. All were laughing—heads back, arms akimbo, like there was no tomorrow.

"I gotta go," Jemma said. "I'll see you in the morning for the 6:23."

As she trudged home, something pink caught her eye. She

pulled it out from an old pipe, sheltered by the cellar door. It was the remains of a candy Easter egg, wrapped in cellophane, a survivor of Robby's egg hunt and the tornado. Spencer had hidden that one. She put it in her pocket. Now she understood playing both ends against the middle and losing again. Like that did her a lot of good at this point. She called her family to get chewed out and get it over with.

Alex answered the phone. "Sweet pea, you knew this was coming if you didn't make a commitment to him. He needs to be loved."

Her daddy was less tactful. "I don't know what to say, Jem. I'm happy that he has someone now, but it breaks my heart that it's not you. You'll just have to deal with it, baby girl. You're the one who let it happen."

Only Robby had anything encouraging for her. "I bet Spence is just teasing you. He likes to tease me. I'll see you tomorrow at the airport."

She stared at the stack of records under the dresser. Roy was calling to her. She might as well make herself as miserable as possible. She put on his album but couldn't make it past the first song. Eleanor and Edith were right. She'd had her time with a sweet man and tossed him aside, like those practice pieces in her mentorship. Even in Chillaton, there were no comforting casseroles for this particular brand of pain. She would have to buck up alone.

Paul had called every night. He talked for a half hour each time, droning on about his work. Jemma's ear was sore from it and from hearing *darlin'* every other breath. He had never even asked to see her work when he came. She should have thrown out those letters with the table scraps. She took the rose necklace off the lampshade and dropped it again, without ceremony, into the depths of the soldier box. She wrapped the letters in the *Amarillo Globe* newspaper and dumped them in the trash barrel, along with a whole pack of lighted matches from the truck stop. The flames danced as tidbits of the ashes floated away. The 9:04 Zephyr flashed by on the tracks, quite appropriately. Jemma stood beside the barrel until nothing was left but a whiff of smoke.

⊰◈⊱

On the morning she left, they sat in the porch swing, holding hands.

"I don't want to leave you, Gram," Jemma said.

"I know. I won't be able go in your room for a while," Lizbeth admitted.

"You know I'll come to see you every chance I get."

"You're a joy to me, Jemmabeth, no matter where you are."

Jemma squeezed her hand. "I hope that I can be a strong woman like you someday."

"It was a hard row that brought me here, sugar. I pray that God's Plan will be an easier one for you. Nobody sets out to be weak or strong. Life simply falls in your lap, and you have to do something with it."

"Remember when Papa would say that we can ask the Lord about one thing or the other when we get to heaven? I could imagine this long line of people waiting to sit in God's lap and ask their list of questions, like the Santa line at a department store."

Lizbeth laughed. "Surely that's not the way it will be."

"I want you to live forever. Say that you will."

"I will, honey, but not on this old earth, thank the good Lord. You take care to guard your heart, Jemma. Sometimes the paths we consider are not the ones the Lord intends for us to follow."

"I've lost Spence. I hurt him again, and now he has somebody else."

"That's your pain, and you'll have to bear it. You need to quiet your heart now, so you can hear the voice of the Holy Spirit leading you. Here, this is for you." Lizbeth took a package from her sweater pocket. Jemma opened it to find a small white Bible. It was encased in a leather cover with a zipper and a tiny cross as the fob. Her name was written in gold letters on the cover, as was a Bible verse—*Proverbs 3:5–6.*

"It's beautiful, Gram. Now it's your turn." She took a bundle from under the swing and put it on Lizbeth's lap. "Go ahead, open it."

Lizbeth pulled back the paper and hooted with laughter. It was her own grimacing face, teeth bared, behind the wheel of the Dodge. The ends of her scarf were bent back in the wind and her knuckles were white on the steering wheel. They were still laughing when Lester walked up the porch steps.

"I figured I'd find y'all bawlin' like babies, but here you sound like a couple of settin' hens," he said. Lizbeth pointed at the painting propped up on the wicker chair. Lester lined up his bifocals and leaned over for a good look. "Jemmerbeth, you are something else. You look downright scary, Miz Liz, no offense."

That set them off again.

Jemma loaded her bags in the car. "Just a second." She ran to the tracks and gathered pebbles from the rail bed, then stopped at the honeysuckle vine and picked off a solitary blossom and pressed it between the pages of her new Bible.

Lester drove especially slow to the station, giving her plenty of time to think. "Gram, would you keep my mail for me? I might get some registration stuff from school. Just open it and call me if it's important."

"I'll do that. Tell Robby that the cardinals are doing fine, and give your grandparents a chance to show their love for you in their own way."

She wasn't too sure about that idea. "I can't wait to hear all about your plans for the trip with Do Dah."

"Oh mercy. Don't bring that up."

"Gram, if you learned to drive a car, you can handle sitting in a plane."

"Lord willing," Lizbeth said.

Trina and Willa were there to see her off. No more tears, Gram had said, but she was the one waving backward so Jemma couldn't see her cry. The Zephyr was on time. The conductor looked at his watch and brought in the step. She pressed her face to the window to get one last look. The sun was not quite up, but the Chase castle stood silhouetted against the horizon. It suddenly occurred to her that she used to call him "babe" when they were in high school. Since Paul, she had denied Spencer even that morsel of affection. *Selfish hussy.* That's what Mrs. Chase could've called her.

In six hours she would be in Dallas, then on a flight to St. Louis and the elegant Lillygrace mansion. Things would not be quite the same at all, what with someone to cook and clean, and a gardener who lived in a caretaker's house the same size as Gram's.

The Zephyr rocked along as the sun cast a red-orange glow on the fields. Jemma leaned her head against the cool window and watched the "man on stilts," as Robby had named the passing rows, striding to keep pace with the speed of the train. Each row helped the stilt man along like a cartoon flip chart.

She squinted into the sunrise as farmhands waved at the train. Weese would never know that life. Maybe he would send Willa a photograph of himself in his uniform, just before he shipped off to Vietnam. If Spencer married his new girlfriend, she would lose him and become a wretched old maid, but if she lost him to a war, that would kill her.

She took out her sketchbook and wrote him a note.

Dear Spence, I promised that I would tell you when I am ready to marry. Oh, I am. Let's go back to Plum Creek and invite the whole county.

She wadded it up. She couldn't write those words to him when he had a girlfriend. So she drew his face as he looked on the trip to Amarillo. After scribbling off a poem about her runaway heart, she put the book away. She was not born to hurt him, like Sandy said. She was born to love him.

⁂

Lizbeth stood on the porch and watched the swing move in the wind. Jemma had been gone for the better part of a week. The soldier box now held the overflow of her granddaughter's hope chest. Her prayer was that Jemmabeth's trials would not increase, and that her menfolk would not come into life to be warriors, dying in far-off places, nor would they leave in her screaming presence.

She walked out back to the hollyhock patch. There were two cardinals living in the pecan tree. Jemma had painted them for her and hung the piece where Cam's portrait had been. Lizbeth liked seeing them first thing when she woke up. They made pleasant company. If those stray little birds could adapt to a harsh existence in the Panhandle, surely she could find joy in her own solitary life. The 6:23 Zephyr passed, blowing its whistle. At least she didn't have to worry about Jemma dancing on those tracks anymore. She reached in her pocket for a tissue.

"Miz Liz, would you mind a little company?" Lester stood

outside the patch, hat in hand.

"Help yourself."

"I've been thinkin' about Jemmerbeth. If I could've had me a child, I would want her to be like Jemmer. She made me feel good, always comin' and goin'. I kinda think she's the one that's like that Zephyr, but not silver, 'cause she has them gold eyes like yours, no offense, Miz Liz. I looked forward to being around her every day. We don't have too many things like that in our old age, do we?"

"No, we don't, Lester. We'll just have to get along without her. I knew she would leave someday. She's headed for bigger things."

"A feller wishes though, that she could've stayed here and painted them pictures. I reckon she'll get famous and they'll be hangin' in museums."

"Helene thinks so and she should know." A squirrel scampered across the grass, catching their attention. It hesitated, then, with a swish of its tail, ran up the pecan tree.

Lester cleared his throat. "I've got a real lonesome feelin' today, so I was wonderin' if you would like to go for a little drive."

"That's a fine idea. Let's drive until we run out of gas, Lester. What do you say to that?"

"Now, Miz Liz, when I was in my courtin' days, runnin' out of gas was just an excuse to spark."

Lizbeth pushed up her glasses. "Mr. Timms, my sparking days were only with one man. You and I are friends, like Willa and I are friends, understood?"

"Yes ma'am. Your plain speakin' always reminds me of Paulette, my last wife. I think you must be part French, too."

She smiled and picked some flowers to put on her only sparking man's grave.

❧

Lester brought in the morning mail and sipped his coffee, going on about mail-order brides. Not finding much of an audience for his story, he left for the barbershop.

Lizbeth turned down the radio and went through her mail. There was a letter for Jemma from her school in Dallas. She slid Cam's letter opener under the flap.

≪≫

August 18, 1966

Dear Miss Forrester,

We have just received official notice that you have been awarded the Girard Fellowship at Le Academie Royale D'Art in Paris. The award was based upon your portfolio, staff and mentor recommendations, and, of course, your competition piece, Joie, Dans Lumière. *This prestigious prize carries a full stipend for all expenses incurred during the Fellowship. Additionally, your work will be featured at the Academie's public gallery throughout your attendance.*

We are honored, indeed, to have sponsored you in this international competition. You are the first American student to receive the Fellowship and it is only the second time a woman has won in over seventy years. We are fortunate that the competition date only recently expired and the award came within the time limits of your attendance and intent to re-enroll at the college. Your portfolio must be updated, and we shall be in contact with your liaison at the Academy. There are many details that must be addressed.

Again, the faculty joins me in extending our warmest congratulations and most sincere appreciation for the attention this award will undoubtedly bring to our own program. We look forward to seeing you soon. Please do contact my office immediately.

Yours truly,

Dr. Edmond Crowder, Dean
Le Claire College of the Arts
Dallas, Texas

The sun glinted through the honeysuckle vine and its lacy shadows flickered across the letter in her lap. The Great Plan had begun for Jemmabeth. An odd tear slipped down Lizbeth's cheek and pooled in the fold of the paper. She blotted it with her finger, then touched it to her lips. Its taste conjured a long-abandoned sensation. With a cleansing breath, she dialed the long-distance operator, then waited while she connected her with St. Louis. Jemma herself answered.

"Lillygrace residence, Jemmabeth speaking," she said.

Her formality made Lizbeth smile. "Jemma, it's Gram. You have some mail."

"Something bad?"

"No, sugar, something of joy."

Chapter 27
Being Still

*C*riticism is easy, Art is difficult—*Philippe Nericault 1680–1754.* Jemmabeth read it and exhaled. Her heart hadn't found a steady beat since Lizbeth's call. She was beside herself with the thought of studying in Paris. Her Grandfather Lillygrace had given her a French dictionary and phrase book to read on the flight to Dallas, but she had barely looked at it. Instead, she had memorized the foldout map of Europe that showed France and Italy, and she had marked Florence with a red heart.

"Jemmabeth!" Professor Rossi was waiting for her at the top of the steps. He held out his arms. "Bravo! Bravo! The school is buzzing with the news of the Fellowship. I am so proud of you. Now the world will learn what we have known all along—beautiful woman, beautiful art."

Jemma laughed. "I missed you, Professor, and I have missed Le Claire. I wanted the smell of paint in my nose and the sound of pianos and violins in my ears."

"No, no, Jemma, you have not lived until you see Paris and it becomes a part of you. That will be your new love, believe me. Now, when you are there, you must go to Italy, no questions asked. It will ignite your heart. I shall give you the name of my friend who teaches in Florence and you will stay with his family. They will love you."

Jemma's throat tightened at the name of the city. "Thank you so much. I'm a little overwhelmed right now, and I have to meet with the dean."

"Yes, yes, don't let me keep you, but my wife and I will have you over for dinner to discuss these plans. Where are you staying?"

"Mostly with my friend, Melanie Glazer. I won't be here very long, but I do have to get my portfolio ready. Will you help me?"

"I am your servant, Jemma."

Le Claire was so eager to get the school's name in the international media that every effort was made to assure she made it to Paris. She was shuffled around from office to office while the staff took care of her. She had to get a passport quickly. Calls were made. There was so much paperwork to sign that someone joked that a lawyer would be helpful. An attorney appeared. It was a fun, mind-joggling experience. At day's end, Jemma and Melanie sat in the student center, eating and going over the excitement.

"You have caused all this, you know," Melanie said.

"What? The paperwork and phone calls and names I can't pronounce?" Jemma said with her feet propped on an empty chair.

"No, I mean the anxiety about your boyfriend."

Jemma sat up. "I know. I wasted a year on a wild cowpoke lawyer."

"Was he worth it?"

"Not really, but at the time it was like a rodeo poster—chills, thrills, and spills."

"What's your plan? I assume you have one."

"My plans are worthless. I only know that I'm scared," Jemma admitted.

"Isn't it possible that this girlfriend is just a rebound thing?"

"Spence is not one to take romance lightly."

"You have to talk to him. If he knows your feelings, then it's his choice."

"It all comes down to Spencer getting to make the choice. That's poetic justice, and I'm so big on justice, you know."

"It'll work out. Look at my life. I just finished a world tour with a major orchestra, Michael and I are headed for Juilliard, and we will be getting married after that. Two years ago I was only hoping to teach violin lessons and find a boyfriend who wasn't too pathetic. Besides, what happened to the old Jemmabeth who wasn't afraid of anything? Are you scared to let go of this problem? You do realize that the God who created the universe can figure out your little life."

"I know," Jemma said. "I only hope I'm not in the doghouse with Him, too."

❧

Paul knew she wanted to tell him *adios*. He was, after all, a lawyer and knew when he had a losing case. They had discussed it at great length on the phone before she left St. Louis. He had said he would meet her at The Big D coffee shop at Dallas Love Field. Jemma had given him the date and time of her flight. She called him from Helene's when she spent the weekend there, but he didn't answer.

❧

Jemma got to Love Field two hours early so they could talk, but Paul never showed up. After an hour passed, she called his office. The secretary said that something had come up, and he wouldn't be back until the next week. Jemma asked, on a hunch, if his friend Kyle had gone with him, and the response was affirmative. They'd gone to Las Vegas.

She hung up and stared at the jets taxiing into the terminal, thinking about those words at the Handle Bar—*Drinking from the devil's cup tonight?* She should've said her good-byes then.

❧

She had no idea that she would be hanging in the sky for thirteen hours, all flights totaled. Across the Atlantic, she watched the sun rise above a carpet of clouds, like puffs of pink whipped cream piled below the jet. As the sunlight spilled across the heavens, she noticed a sprinkling of ice crystals on her window. They cast tiny star shadows on the window frame. She could have still been finding Orion with Spence. As they dropped altitude the crystal stars evaporated, the clouds cleared, and Paris came into view. If she never got to set foot in it, just seeing it with her own eyes was enough to make her cry.

She had practiced French phrases until they sounded reasonable to her, but once she tried them out on the airport staff, she realized there was going to be a problem. To her relief, most of them spoke English. Her liaison met her at the baggage claim area, as planned.

"*Bonjour,* Miss Forrester, I trust you had a good flight. Permit me to introduce myself. I am Peter Neville, and I am ready to assist you in your acquaintance with the Academie."

Jemma liked his style. He reminded her of her cousin Trent—

short, slender, very well dressed, and equally well mannered.

She shook his hand. "*Bonjour.* I'm Jemmabeth, but please call me Jemma. You'll have to forgive me, because I'm in a dream world right now and can use all the help I can get."

"You have a nice Texas accent, Jemma." He pronounced her name like Helene did, *Zhemma.*

"How do you know about my accent?"

"My wife and I go to many movies, particularly cowboy movies. You sound somewhat like the woman in the movie *Hud.*"

She clapped her hands. "I can't believe you said that. It was filmed not far from my hometown. Paul Newman actually spoke to me. Oh, there's my luggage." She pointed to her new matched set, courtesy of the Lillygraces. "Have my paintings come yet?"

He lifted her suitcases onto a cart. "*Oui,* they have arrived. What did Mr. Newman say to you?"

"He said, 'Excuse me.' I was sort of in his way as he left the set. I know that's not much, but it is when you are in high school and you have a crush on him."

"What do you mean 'crush'?"

"Oh, you know, an infatuation. Surely you French know about that." She did, for sure.

"Ah, now you are speaking in the language of love. I am certain that you have had many young men with these crushes for you, Jemma," he said with a French grin.

Jemma flushed. "How far is it to the Academie?"

"We will be there within the hour. Here is where you should wait for me. I will bring the car and collect the luggage and you," he said, then blended into the crowd.

In Peter's car, she could neither sit still nor could she stop talking. She didn't even care that he drove fast, much like Spencer. He was gracious and smiled at her enthusiasm.

"I can't believe that I am here," Jemma babbled. "Paris is too beautiful to be a city. They should call it a museum; then every corner could be a painting. Can you believe the vanishing points? Where do all these people work? What is the name of that building? Where are we, approximately? Is that the Seine? Paris! I can't believe it!"

They went to her apartment on the third floor of an old building within walking distance of the Academie. The ceilings were high, as were the windows. The room, plain white, was furnished with the essentials: bed, dresser with a mirror, bench, desk and chair, an umbrella stand, chest of drawers, and a wardrobe—no closet. Next to the door was a coat hook. There were shades on the windows, but no cabbage rose prints like at Helene's. She would have to do some fixing up to make it her own. Below was a courtyard with scattered trees, roses, benches, and a bicycle rack. Jemma's room was at the rear corner of the building with two sets of double windows. One pair looked down on the courtyard while the other looked out over the jumble of buildings in that part of the city. Across the rooftops, she could see a hill with a gleaming white structure at the pinnacle.

"Sacré-Coeur?" she asked with her nose against the glass.

Peter joined her at the window. "You have studied well. May I help you with your baggage?"

"No thank you. I will manage just fine. Could you help me with one call later? It's collect to my grandparents."

"That is no problem. It will be a joy to hear you talk."

Peter was her constant companion throughout the day. He took her to the Academie and showed her the basics. The double doors at the entrance dwarfed them, but the classrooms were similar to those at Le Claire.

"All art schools must smell the same." She took a deep breath. "It's the best perfume."

They toured the Gallery, too. She couldn't wait to get her materials and get started. He showed her the neighborhood markets and cafés, but she was amazed by the amount of dog poop on the sidewalks. Papa would have gotten a big laugh out of that. It was no different than dodging chicken mess, but she didn't mention that to Peter. He was very good at avoiding it. They stopped for lunch at a café near her apartment.

"Do you have someone in your life at the moment?" Peter asked, taking her off guard.

She blushed. "He's in Florence, but he doesn't know that I'm here."

"I see that you are in love. You are quarreling?"

"How did you know?" She recalled hearing a story about French fortune-tellers. "Are you a gypsy?"

"I am a Frenchman," he said, laughing.

"Spencer and I grew up together and we've always been in love. Now he's seeing another woman."

"He could not be in love with her as long as you are alive."

Jemma smiled. "No wonder the French have such reputations. You have a way with words, don't you?"

"As I said, it is the language of love. We created it. Now tell me this story." Jemma gave him the basics about Paul. He listened, watching her face almost to the point of distraction. He raised a finger. "This is the plot of another American movie, correct?"

"No, unfortunately, it's my story."

"Everyone makes mistakes in life, Jemma. If one never does anything, one never does anything wrong."

"I hadn't thought of it like that."

"I am certain that you are weary. I'll take you back to your apartment so you may call your family, then rest. I shall see you in the morning. Sleep late, Jemma. You may suffer some of the jet lag," he said, arriving at the telephone near her room.

She made her call with his assistance. "Thank you so much, Peter. You've been wonderful."

⌘

It was the first time she had been alone in a year. She looked around her room and unpacked a few things, but the sleepless flight was getting to her or maybe it was the rain that had begun to trickle down the windowpanes. She managed to move the furniture around, and she hung the driftwood Robby had carved for her on the hook by the door. On the dresser, she spread her great-grandmother's lace handkerchief and put Spencer's picture on it, and beside it, the music box.

She set out a picture of her on the tractor with Papa and the pebbles from the train tracks. Yawning, she opened her new Bible and read aloud, "Trust in the Lord with all thine heart; and lean not unto thine own understanding. In all thy ways acknowledge him, and he shall direct thy paths." *Trust*—that was the key word. She underlined it and fell asleep on the bare mattress before she could finish her prayers.

In the lonesome early morning hours, she woke up with a pounding headache and serious rumblings in her stomach. The trip had caught up with her. She went to the window and looked out over the rooftops. The moon was a big snowball in the sky, like those she had made for Carrie to throw at her last winter. In its light, the mishmash of Parisian structures rose like ancient, pastel Monopoly houses up to the gleaming Sacré-Coeur. Jemma smiled. *Moonlight Over Paris.* Gram would be reading the mail by now and trying not to laugh at Lester's stories.

At least Spencer was somewhere on the same continent with her now. He said that he wanted to show her Paris, but that was before he found out the truth about Paul. A wave of nausea overwhelmed her, and she ran out her door, down the hallway to the toilet, and lost her first French meal. She was back to her old ways of dealing with life.

She returned to the window and chewed her last stick of American gum. Arizona was a zillion miles away. Robby was most likely teasing some little girl, her daddy was almost certainly yelling at his football team, and her mother was probably worrying about her. For sure, the Lillygraces were having something served to them.

St. Louis had been such an odd experience. How her warm, generous mother and her uncle came from that stilted couple, she hadn't a clue unless it was due to their nanny. Something was done right because Trent turned out well, too. He resembled her uncle Ted with his dark blue eyes and gentle smile. Trent was not arrogant, as she had once thought, but reserved, with a very dry wit. It was Jemma's full intention to open some kind of cousin door to him, and Robby was the key to that plan. Nobody could resist her little brother because he was such a tease, and Trent played along with him on everything. They found their family link in their funny bones.

She went back to the mattress. Tomorrow she would buy some sheets and a duvet, but she could live without those. Her greatest dread was finding out what it would be like to live without Spence.

Her morning sleep was interrupted by an argument. She sat on the side of her bed, collecting her thoughts. Meanwhile, the shouting intensified outside her window. She looked down on a young couple standing in the open alcove of a ground floor apartment. The man was shirtless and barefooted. He ran his hands through his already rumpled hair and leaned into the face of a woman in a satin nightgown. She stood her ground with her hands on her hips. Her hair was pulled back and tied with a ribbon. Jemma couldn't understand a word of their conversation, but she didn't need to. A little boy with a mass of curly hair pedaled up between them on a tricycle. He asked something, appealing to them both for a response. The man clenched his fists and turned away. The woman lifted the child from his seat and carried him into the house. She returned, speaking in low tones to the man, then slipped her arms around his chest and laid her head on his back. He turned to embrace her and took the ribbon from her hair. Jemma slid to the floor and cried.

"How's my girl?" Julia's accent sounded so comforting on the phone. "Did you survive the trip? Everybody is still busting with pride over this fellowship thing. Now Lizbeth can't wait to get over there, just to see you. Sit down, sugar. I've got something to tell you because Spencer just called."

Jemma's stomach went bananas. "Oh no. What did he say?"

"He was calling with information about Florence so we can meet him there. He said he got Papa's portrait, and he liked it, I could tell. I told him about you winning the fellowship and all, but he didn't say squat. There was nothing but those pregnant pauses."

Jemma bit her lip. "Somebody told him that I was dating a married cowboy."

"Well, be that as it may, I couldn't stand it. I told him that even though it was none of my business, I had hired somebody to check out that man in Dallas and that he was from a good family, but wild as an acre of snakes and divorced to boot. I told him that you broke things off with him before you went to Paris. That's right, isn't it?"

"Yes ma'am."

"Well, it's all been said now. You know I'm not going to let my little girl suffer any more than she has to."

"Did he sound happy?" Jemma asked.

Julia hesitated. "Oh, polite and sweet, as always."

"That's not the way he sounded the last time I saw him. Do Dah, I'm just like Scarlett. I want too much, I choose all wrong—if I make up my mind at all, I don't learn from my mistakes, and now my man has left me."

"Well, if that's so, sugar, don't forget what Scarlett said at the end," Julia said.

"You mean to go home to Tara? I already tried that."

"No. Scarlett said she would think of some way to get him back. Don't mess with your aunty, Jemmabeth. I know that movie backward and forward."

"I guess I forgot about that," Jemma said, "but then again, you can't believe everything you see in the movies." Like someone who wore a black hat once told her.

"No, you can't, but you can't believe everything people say when they are angry, either, honey."

"Did he sound like he was in love?" Jemma asked.

"Oh my, you are pitiful, aren't you? You know your papa always said that when you are between a rock and a hard place, remember that your rock is Jesus."

"Yes ma'am. I know."

"Don't go turning into some French free thinker on us now. Listen, I mailed you some folding money to spend however you want."

"Thanks, Do Dah. I love you. Call Gram for me and tell her I miss her."

"Jemmabeth, you are not Scarlett. Bye, now."

Jemma hung up the phone and went to her room. She stood at the window for a minute, then went to the dresser and got her scissors. She gathered a lock of her hair and clipped it. She tied a bit of ribbon around it and laid it in the music box. She said her prayers and asked the Lord for His will to be done. She promised to take it like a big girl, whatever it was.

Her schedule included a meeting with the Academie Director, Monsieur Lanier, to discuss the Girard Fellowship and her obligations. He was a thin, balding man with a trim moustache. His

English was impeccable and his praise for Jemma's work was extensive. Her portfolio pieces had arrived intact. Lester's handmade containers were preserved in a tidy stack in a cavernous storage room. She had not seen the painting of Gram in over a year. She smiled, remembering that particular letter from Julia, and enjoyed the remarkable likeness created by her own hand.

Another faculty member joined Jemma and the director. He was Louis, the head portraiture instructor, and Jemma's advisor for her tenure as a Fellow at the Academie. The three of them spent hours going over the pieces, sustaining technical discussions and heated points of view. Jemma loved every second of it. She was both exuberant and articulate about her art, and their fresh perspectives had stimulated her creative juices. It was apparent to her that she had entered a higher level of exploration in her work. They briefed her on the timeline for the Girard Fellows Exhibition in October. It was traditionally the opening exhibit at the Academie gallery, and Jemma asked if she could add one more piece to her portfolio.

Her assigned workspace was in the west section of the Academie studios. She liked it because the afternoon sun was best there. She shared the area with a young Frenchman. He did not speak English, which suited her just fine. She had carried the brushes Helene had bought in her purse. The rest were packed in an old suitcase filled with her art supplies. She unpacked brushes, oils, acrylics, and watercolors. She checked them all to make certain that each had survived the journey in good condition and put the brushes, always wood down, into her first-grade cowboy boots. The Frenchman raised his brow at the boots, but smiled.

The Academie required all students to spend time in the shop making stretched canvases each week, but then they were allowed to use the canvases as needed. She had selected a large one for this piece and paced around it several times, brushes in hand. Then, like Melanie tuning her violin, she brandished strokes across the canvas with a dry brush. She had not painted in weeks and this one was to be perfect. She loaded the brush and began. It rushed back to her just as the old steps had come when she and Spencer had danced to "Candy Man" at Homecoming. She worked on it at a breakneck speed, not stopping to eat the first day. She had to force herself away from it, but when she wasn't at the canvas, she was thinking about it, and when she wasn't thinking about it, she was thinking of him.

❧

Jemma was in the middle of an especially nice dream when a pounding at the door woke her up. A girl down the hall pointed to the telephone. She wrapped her old robe around her and picked up the phone.

"Jemma? It's Sandy."

"Sandy, can you believe I'm in Paris?"

"I can," Sandy said. "I knew you were going to hit it big someday, but I had no idea it would be in Paris. I'm so proud to know you."

"They eat, breathe, and sleep art. I love it."

"Nobody has heard from Spencer in a long time, Jem."

"I was afraid of that," Jemma said.

"I do know where he got his information about Paul. I know you said not to tell anyone, but I let it slip to Buddy, and he thought Spencer knew all about Paul. He said that the morning Spence left, they were sitting around talking at the dealership. Buddy made some comment about how he would like to horsewhip your wild cowboy and I guess that's all it took. Spencer grilled him about everything."

Jemma closed her eyes. "Oh no. Bless his heart. He must think the very worst of me."

"He probably just thinks you would rather be with an old married guy than with him."

"Thanks, Sandy. You're making me feel worse, if that's possible."

"Sorry. Let's meet somewhere for the day, okay? I really want to get away."

"Ask me next month. I have this big art show now and I'm so nervous. I need my mommy."

"Yeah, right. You've never needed anybody when it comes to your art."

"Maybe so, but this is Paris. I'll talk to you next month." Jemma paused. "Today is Spence's birthday, but I can't call him, not with the girlfriend."

"Hey, you did it to yourself. 'Bye, Jem. Oh yeah. Buddy swears nobody else knows."

She went to her room and sat in front of the big window. Sacré-Coeur rose above everything else. She wondered if Spence had ever been there. She got dressed and walked up the long, narrow streets to the church. The view of Paris was incredible, but Jemma went inside and got on her knees. She thanked God for letting Spencer love her all those years and for sending him someone to love him back. Those last words came hard. She sat back on the pew and peered up at the stunning mosaic of Christ. How silly of her to think that the Lord of the universe would not know what was best for her. It was time that she grew up in her faith, and she meant to do it, too, with all her heart.

❦

Louis, her advisor, dropped by on a daily basis. His suggestions were brief and well received by Jemma, who was never one to bristle at technical criticism. As the piece neared completion, Jean-Claude spoke briefly with Louis, who acted as interpreter.

"Jean-Claude inquires if the man in your painting is your love?" Louis asked. Jemma glanced at Jean-Claude, who grinned and raised his brow, as seemed his habit.

She nodded. "*Oui.*"

Louis translated again. "He says that that the work flows from your brush with such emotion he knew that you must be in love with your subject."

"Tell him it has been so for a very long time, but only recently did I come to realize it," Jemma said.

"Ah, the best kind. True love."

Chapter 28
I Think of Thee

The Girard Fellows Exhibition was scheduled for the middle of October. Jemma finished the piece on the last day of September. She stepped away from it for a final appraisal: Spencer reclined against the old cottonwood, strumming his guitar. His head was turned toward what Jemma knew was Plum Creek, and a faint smile played about his lips, tugging at her heart even from the canvas. The sun danced on the cottonwood leaves and in his golden hair. She did love him so.

Jean-Claude stood beside her, kissed his fingers, then tossed them toward the painting, just as Professor Rossi had done.

"*Merci beaucoup*," Jemma said.

"Title?" he asked.

Jemma drew her breath. "*I Think of Thee*." Jean-Claude did not comprehend the words, but he did understand the look in her eyes.

※

Peter met her for lunch. "You have exhausted even me with your attention to your new piece, Jemma. I assume it is of your Spencer. Is there some secret about the painting?"

"No secrets, just regrets, like I told you before."

"Regrets can be mended. We are all very anxious to open the show with your work. Louis and I agree that you must take a brief holiday and see our beautiful city. My wife and I would like for you to go with us to a concert tonight."

"I love concerts!" she said.

"It will be in the Sainte-Chapelle, our secret jewel of Paris. Most memorable, I assure you."

She smiled slightly. "Thank you, Peter, but I'm not ready to go there yet."

"The painting, I presume?"

"Yes. I have to go to Florence." The words made her shiver.

On Saturday, Peter took her to the train station. She had never seen so many trains in one place. She half expected Monet to materialize and set up his easel in the early morning light. The shrill whistles were more like Robby's toy train compared to the Zephyr, but she didn't care. Each clack of the wheels took her one more step closer to him. She would fall at his feet, if necessary, and apologize.

The last hour of the long trip, she couldn't breathe right. Her greatest fear was that she would see them together—Spencer and Miss Completely. She didn't want to cause him any embarrassment or worry, but she had to tell him that she was ready. As the train moved into the Florence station, she could hear her own pulse above the noise of the crowds and the trains. Peter had written phrases for her to use. She managed to catch a cab to the university.

After asking, in Texas Italian, for the location of the School of Architecture, she finally found it on her own. She walked past classrooms, thinking how she would react if he appeared in the hallway. She located the office and got out Peter's notes. She read something to a secretary, hoping she had asked where Spencer might be.

"Ah," the woman said in clear English, "Mr. Chase is not here. He is with the field group in Greece. He will return next Friday. You are his sister, perhaps?"

"No ma'am, I'm not his sister," Jemma said with prickles rising on her scalp. "Could I leave him a message, please?"

"Yes, yes." The woman gave her a pen.

Jemma tore a page from her sketchbook. She didn't have to think about it, but her hand was shaking.

Dearest Spence,
*   I know this is bad timing, but please forgive me. There was never a choice to be made. I love you and only you. You said to tell you, no matter the circumstances, when I am ready. Oh, I am, babe, I promise. I need to look you in the eye, if that's something you would like. If not, then may the Lord bless you both.*
*   Always,*
*   Jem*

She took something from her pocket and folded it in the letter. It could be the last part of her that he would ever hold. The woman offered an envelope. Jemma sealed the note inside, then kissed it, right in front of everybody.

"I will see that Mr. Chase gets it," the woman said and put it in her desk drawer.

Jemma lingered at the door but finally stepped away. She could relax now. He was in another country with the one who could speak four languages, or was it five? She knew the secretary had assumed that she was his sister because he already had a girlfriend. She bit her lip and repeated her new prayer of accepting the Lord's will. It was not easy. Jemma decided she would learn French. The first thing she would master would be the word for *fool*.

Professor Rossi had given her the phone number of his friend in Florence, Mario Grasso. He and his wife, Carlena, spoke English as well as Jemma, and they insisted that she spend the day with them. The couple took her in and treated her like family. She had fun in spite of herself. They gave her a guided afternoon tour of their city. It was full of all the things Spence loved—masterpiece sculptures and elegant buildings with extraordinary details, Gothic churches with brilliant stained glass, graceful bridges, and an amazing number of museums. Jemma was spellbound by the art collections in Florence. All that beauty, and she hadn't been with him to share it.

Jemma wolfed down Carlena Grasso's sumptuous food until she was miserable. They went for one more stroll, this time along the Piazza della Signoria. When they returned to the house, she used her colored pencils and sketched Mario and Carlena sitting on a bench at the Piazza as a gift. She propped it up by a vase of flowers on the kitchen table along with a note of thanks.

She caught the midnight train back to Paris and slept most of the trip. A sense of relief that she had made the effort was better than having no sense at all.

Peter picked her up at the station and took her to their usual café for a late lunch.

"Success?" he asked.

"No, he was in Greece," she said. "I left him a note."

"Ah, a love letter. *Très bon*. Now you must begin preparations for the show. The opening will be a very formal affair. Have you brought with you anything suitable to wear?"

Jemma considered her wardrobe. The closest thing she had was the red dress from high school she wore to Melanie's recital. "I don't have a thing."

"My wife, Ami, thought you might like to go shopping."

A sweet thought came to her and she nodded. "*Oui, oui,* monsieur." She checked her mail, hoping it would be there, and it was—a plump letter from Julia. She took half of the money and put it in her purse to exchange at the bank. The other half she folded up in a pair of socks and put them back in the drawer. Her daddy would be proud of her. She knew also that Do Dah would approve of her spending the money somewhere along the Champs Elysees in Paris.

❧

All former Girard Fellows were invited to show two pieces of work and Jemma could show up to a dozen, but she had to title and write an artist's comment for each piece. It took her two days to do that with the help of a translator. The most difficult was his portrait. She asked for permission to let that title stand as sufficient statement for the work. It was small comfort. The big comfort would have been if he had called her from Florence.

❧

The day before the opening, Jemma was in her jeans and Le Claire sweatshirt helping the gallery manager make display choices.

"Miss Forrester, you have guests," an assistant called to her.

Jemma turned to the foyer, her heart racing. Surely Spencer wouldn't bring Miss Completely to her show. She blinked and caught her breath.

"Mom!" she squealed and ran like crazy. They hugged and cried and jumped around, much to the staff's amusement. Her Lillygrace grandparents stood by, smiling and inspecting the gallery.

"Sweet pea, you look so thin. Have you been taking your vitamins?" her mother asked, holding her at arm's length.

Jemma laughed. "I can't believe this. I'm so happy to see you."

"Your daddy sends this hug and this kiss to you," she said, complying with his wishes, "and Robby says to tell you that he is now saving up for a pet lizard. You have your grandparents to thank for this surprise. It was their idea."

Jemma hugged them both at the same time. Their stiff arms relaxed in hers, but there was no jumping.

"Thank you forever!" she shouted.

Her grandfather almost laughed. "Our pleasure, Jemmabeth. We are very proud of you."

"Yes, congratulations, dear," her grandmother said. "We wouldn't have missed this, and we couldn't let Alexandra either." Her grandparents quickly became distracted by her art because they had seen little more than their own and Robby's portrait until now. They engaged in an animated side conversation with the manager, in French, and her grandfather proceeded to take over the placement decisions on Jemma's behalf. For once, she didn't mind.

Jemma turned to her mother and clamped her arms around her. "Come, look at my work." They went from piece to piece, reading her artist's comments. Alex was moved by the painting of the three girls. She looked at it for several minutes, sniffing into a tissue at the statement. When they came to Papa's portrait, they both cried at her reflection on the piece, *Corner of Blue*. Jemma kept an eye on her grandparents to see their reaction to her very personal reflection about him. They read it without reaction and moved to the next painting.

Alex patted her arm. "I'm glad you brought it over. I think it was too painful for Gram to have in her house."

"I feel like Papa is here and I like him watching over me. Here's my last piece, Mom," Jemma said, standing next to it.

"Oh honey, *I Think of Thee*. The title alone breaks my heart. Have you heard from him?"

"No ma'am," she said, touching the painting. "I went to see him in Florence, to apologize, but he was on a field trip to Greece, so I left him a note. I thought that was better than nothing. He hasn't answered, Mom, and I know he's back by now."

"After all that has happened, it must be in the Lord's hands, sweet pea."

"I know. The Great Plan. Well, I'm ready to accept it, whatever it is." Maybe saying it would help her believe it.

"So, I assume this is the Chase boy?" her grandfather asked, looking closely at the painting.

"Yes sir," Jemma replied.

Her grandmother read the French translation. "*Je Pense au Vous.* I see a longing in his eyes. Well, it has been some time since we had a wedding in the family. There is nothing that your mother and I would like more than to plan a wedding." She slipped her arm around Jemma's waist. "Oh yes, and Trenton will be here tomorrow. He will serve as the family photographer. He's quite good, you know."

"That's great," Jemma said. "He can be my date."

❧

Trent arrived early the next morning. Jemma and her mom were already up, making decisions about shoes. Nobody knew more about footwear than Alexandra Forrester.

"I read an article about this show in the *New York Times*," Trent said. "There's even a paragraph about you, cousin. Oh yeah, Dad sends his congratulations and says it's nice to have a celebrity in the family."

She shrugged. "I'm just me. God gave me whatever skills I have."

"It involves more than skill," Alex said. "You see details overlooked by most, letting us revisit life's joys, Jem. You see with your heart."

Jemma lowered her eyes. They should all know that her heart was blind.

"This is for you." Trent tickled her chin with a white rose wrapped in tissue.

"Perfect," she said. "I'll wear it tonight."

❧

Parisians knew how to throw a party. Great towering baskets of flowers, glimmering candelabras, elaborate tables of *hors d'oeuvres*, and a string quartet playing chamber music had transformed the gallery. Reporters, cared for with ease by Peter, took as many photographs of Jemma as they did of her work. The Lillygrace men wore tuxes, and her grandmother was decked out in a black Chanel gown. Alex stayed close to her daughter's side. She wore an emerald gown purchased the day before, courtesy of her parents. She looked better than Jackie Kennedy.

Jemma's new dress was periwinkle blue satin. She and Ami had searched until they found an evening gown similar to the sundress she wore when Spencer said that if she ever wore it again, he wouldn't make it through "Candy Man." She wore her hair loose with the white rose pinned in it.

The attendance was elbow to elbow, and the ever-patient Peter had to translate the many questions about her paintings.

"I wonder what these folks would think if they saw Papa's car house and knew that's where most of these were painted," Alex said. "I bet none of them have even seen a dirt floor."

Jemma smiled, thinking of their sojourn in Shorty Knox's dugout as well. Shorty was probably watching his color television as they spoke.

Alex went suddenly pale and clenched her daughter's arm. "Jemmabeth, look."

Jemma gasped. "Spence!" she yelled like a true cheerleader, then picked up her skirt and flew to him.

He turned from his portrait at the sound of her voice. "Hi, baby," was all he got out. She kissed him an embarrassing length of time while light bulbs flashed around them. Spencer locked his arms around her and lifted her off the floor, returning the kiss tenfold.

She drew back and looked him in the eye. "Do you love that girl?"

He laughed, laying his head against hers. "What do you think?"

"Please say you forgive me, Spence. I've loved you since the first grade. I loved you then, I love you now, and all the time in between. I'm yours forever, if you'll have me."

"I keep it in mind, always." He inhaled the scent of her hair, then gathered her in his arms. She said something soft and low in his ear, making him grin. "Dance with me until the sun comes up," he said, "then I'm showing you Paris, you crazy woman."

The string quartet never missed a beat. The patrons, quite amused, resumed their festive endeavors, but Spencer and Jemmabeth danced through the crowd and her delighted family. It just so happened that some of their sweetest words came in whispers, quite near the portrait with the twinkling corner of blue.

Touch of Silver

Jemma
Book Two

Dedication

For
Dwight

Lifted

꧁⊱꧂

Dance now in sunrise or moon-cast shadow,
Music sprung from love—a sweet melody.

Be lifted to the stars, my one and only,
And fret not of melodies unsung for me.

To far constellations, I shall whisper no sonnets,
Nor secrets—my dear, my dearie thee.

For you are with me always—the brightest star,
And forever the best part of me.

—Jemmabeth Forrester

The charming Jemmabeth Forrester
has painted her way
into the hearts of two men.

One she tries to avoid.
The other she's hoping will offer her "The Ring."
Neither will be an easy task. . . .

Chapter 1
Blessings

Paul Turner wedged the quart of milk between the other containers of liquid refreshment in his fridge. He tossed off his Stetson and ran his hand through his thick black hair. He wasn't all that hungry anyway. His dad's parting words as they had left the office still hung in his ears. "You're one sorry disappointment, son," he'd said, without humor. Not exactly something a grown man wants to hear, but it was better than some of the things his dad had called him in college. He knew the old man wasn't talking about his work in their legal practice because Paul was carrying that off with style. His dad was referring to Paul's private life, and he was right—it was slime.

Paul had considered buying a few more groceries so he didn't have to eat all his evening meals out or maybe taking his little sisters up on their constant offers to cook for him. Neither of those options was appealing. If he went to one of their places in Dallas for supper, it would haunt him for a month. They were both married with kids, and that was the root of the disappointment he'd brought to his dad.

Paul settled for cold cereal. He pitched his boots at the front door, then parked himself in front of the television to eat. He hadn't been to the Best Burger Stop in Texas since Jemma had left Wicklow. It was their place, and he wouldn't go back without her. He didn't need his dad to tell him what he'd lost when he had messed up with Jemmabeth Forrester. She had been his one treasure in life, and he had botched that relationship at every turn. She most likely was with that puppy love of hers right now in France. Maybe the kid would get drafted and shipped off to Vietnam.

Something solid shifted through the couch cushions. Paul felt around and pulled out a gold bangle bracelet. It probably belonged to the loudmouth redhead from the night before or one of the crazy blonds from the past Saturday. He sailed it across the room and into the trash can. "Bingo," he said aloud and returned to his cereal. If his mother had lived, he might've turned out different. She was spiritual and smelled like flowers, too, like his darlin' Jemma. But God had other plans.

The painting Jemma had made for him hung behind his desk at the office. Most days that was his sole motivation to go in to work. He liked to imagine that they were together again, back in the hill country, watching that very spot from the riverbank, and that Jemma was safely in his arms.

Paul set his bowl in the sink. He needed more of her paintings so he could have some at the office and others at home. Her art gave him hope and a chance to look into her pretty head. He stared blankly at a sparrow scratching at the fresh leaves on his lawn, then wiped his eyes. She was bound to come back to her school in Dallas sometime, and then he would have a chance to prove his love to her in ways that really mattered. Until that day, he would fill his evenings with whatever came along, because nobody could ever fill his heart like Jemma did.

He could wait forever for her because she was his solitary blessing from God. She was inside him, in his bones, and there was nothing anybody could ever do about it.

In the golden bath of dawn, a pigeon with feathers the color of rust and wings striped with red, moved around the great gargoyle. A shimmering white female caught his eye as she spread her wings and glided, embracing the cool air, to feed on the ground below. The male followed, settling near a bench. Puffing out his neck feathers, he circled her, then lowered his head and bowed. She would be his mate for life.

Jemmabeth watched the feathered dance as she and Spencer sat on the bench outside the grand Notre Dame Cathedral, holding hands. They had walked the streets of Paris all night, catching up on their lives since their hard parting five months earlier in Texas.

Jemma rested her head on his shoulder. "Do you think pigeons ever make stupid mistakes?"

"I guess if one showed up in a pie, he would have made an error in judgment somewhere along the way."

"Yuck, but I bet even a pigeon knows the difference between real love and infatuation. Look at that pigeon couple there. Do you think she's cooing to him while all the time that one over there is her true love? I doubt it. That makes me dumber than a pigeon. I'm the ultimate birdbrain," she said, then jumped up. "Dance with me."

"Fast or slow?"

"Roy's 'Candy Man.' We'll make our own music." She took right off on the song.

The pigeons flurried skyward as a gardener began his work near them. Jemma's golden eyes were fixed on Spencer's as they worked out their own version of the Chillaton Stomp—the dance that had made everybody in high school know they would get married someday.

When they'd sung their last note, the gardener applauded. Jemma bowed, not at all embarrassed, then stepped up on a bench and made an announcement to the returning birds. "As of today, October 15, 1966, I publicly declare that I never loved Paul Turner, not even a little bit." She gestured toward Spencer. "This man is my dearest and best cowboy. He's my hero and my one true love."

The pigeons ignored her, but Spencer didn't. He grinned and helped her down. "Enough adjectives. Those were just half truths anyway, because if there's one thing I'm not, it's a cowboy."

Jemma danced circles around him as they toured the grounds. "So, this Michelle person from New York, was she a good kisser?" Her voice came out like she was still in the first grade when she gave him her answer, that yes, she would be his girlfriend. "Everybody in Chillaton thought you were about to propose, and I know you wouldn't marry someone who couldn't kiss."

"I assume this information about proposing came from Nedra's Beauty Parlor & Craft Nook."

"How else? You know her motto: *Hair's where it all begins!* Gram saw the pictures and Twila saw them, too. Twila said that Michelle was completely gorgeous, whatever that means."

"Pictures don't mean anything," he said. "Who knows what Mother was flashing around?"

Jemma wasn't through with it. "Then why did you go out with

her for nearly five months?"

"Jem, what else was I going to do? For all I knew, you were making wedding plans with the cowboy."

They leaned against the Pont au Double. The sunlight filtered through Spencer's blond hair, creating a halo of sorts and making her smile. "I know it was stupid the way I handled it, but I didn't want to have him floating in my brain when we were together. I needed to get rid of Paul, like a toothache, and I had to see him to do that."

"So, is the great Paul out of the picture forever?"

"He is gone. Complete history."

The cathedral bells tolled, adding a nice touch. She took the wilted rose from her long, auburn hair. Her cousin had given it to her the night before, for her first exhibition as the only American art student ever to be named the Girard Fellow at Le Academie Royale D'Art in Paris. She dropped the white petals, one by one, into the Seine. "I want to mark this night. It is the best one in my life."

"Nope, you just wait, baby. I have plans for when we finally say 'I do.'"

Jemma put her arms around him and looked into his eyes, black-rimmed pewter. "Should I be feeling guilty about that girl?"

"I didn't make any commitments to Michelle, but I suppose you could manage a little guilt about making me wait while you made up your mind."

"Hey, I'll never let you go again." She yawned. "But right now I'm ready for bed."

"What about our eighth-grade promise?"

She giggled. "Silly boy. I'm exhausted and I need some rest. Did you sing 'Michelle' to her?"

"She sang it to me, I think," Spencer said.

"Rats. I love that song; now I'll always associate it with her."

"She's not the French type, baby. Don't worry about it." He pulled the collar up on his jacket that she had been wearing since midnight. It almost fit her. Their kids would be basketball players, for sure.

They walked along the Seine as shopkeepers opened their

doors and set up for the day. He got a cab as she continued her interrogation.

"Was she as pretty as everybody said?" she mumbled.

"Nah, she was nowhere near as beautiful as you, inside or out, and she can't even kiss as good as Missy Blake."

Jemma woke up. "What? The Cleave entered your brain as the pinnacle of kissers? Now I'm mad!" She folded her arms and set her mouth into a Shirley Temple pout.

Spencer was still laughing as the cab pulled up in front of the hotel where her family was staying. "Hey, time out. You know you're the best. I just thought maybe the solid way to your heart would be to bring up Missy."

"The way to my heart is a straight line from yours, Spencer Morgan Chase. My Scarlett O'Hara days are behind me." Jemma wrapped her arms around him and kissed him until even the passing Parisians took notice.

⌘

Lester Timms was having himself a good laugh at one of his own jokes when a hefty gust of Texas Panhandle wind showered him with sand and lifted his straw hat off his head. He had to spit. "Them flowers just keep on bloomin', don't they, Miz Liz?" he asked through a gritty smile. "Don't see that on nobody else's grave. I think it's 'cause your Cam had a way with plants." He picked up his hat and waited for her to look away and she did, just in time, too. He wiped his mouth on his sleeve.

Lizbeth Forrester dusted her hands, then shaded her eyes to check around the cemetery. "I suppose you're right, Lester, but there's not much glory in farming from the grave, now is there?"

Lester planted his feet in case she needed help getting up, but she didn't. She was a tall, slender woman, and limber for her age.

Lizbeth smoothed her dress. "Why don't we drop by your wives' resting places? I'm sure there's work to be done on those graves, too." She retied her headscarf to keep the Panhandle wind from fiddling with her fresh hairdo.

"Well now, that would take us a few days, Miz Liz, seeing as how I got me three of 'em fillin' graves out here. That old Zippy could be passed on somewheres, too, for all I know. 'Course she run off and I didn't have to bury her."

Lizbeth patted her husband's headstone. Lester knew that meant to hush up while she prayed.

"Lord, I give You thanks for Cameron Forrester. He was my best blessing, and I praise Your name for the years we had together and the children we raised. I ask now that You have mercy and help me, Lord, to keep on working to Your glory. Amen, sweet Jesus."

They walked to Lester's black-and-white '62 Buick. He always waited for her to start talking again. She was the finest woman he knew, but he didn't have a lick of a chance with her. He considered himself lucky to be her neighbor and that she let him bring over her mail and give her a ride now and then. She'd been married to Cameron for fifty-five years and she still grieved over losing him to a heart attack the same year Lester had bought the Buick, fresh off the delivery truck in Amarillo.

"Thank you for bringing me out here today," Lizbeth said as they reached the cemetery entrance arch. "My car should be fixed by tomorrow. It's just a broken headlight."

"It's never a problem, Miz Liz, you know that. No offense, but if you'd let me drop you off at Nedra's like you used to, maybe your car wouldn't be in the shop right now." Lester glanced at her as he turned down the county Farm to Market Road. That could have been a dangerous comment he'd just made.

"What's that supposed to mean—that I'm not a good driver? I'm as good or better than any other new driver in the county." Lizbeth shot him a look then watched out her window as a dust devil whipped through Myrtle Gist's white sheets hanging on her clothesline. Myrtle would have to wash them again.

Lester tapped his fingers on the steering wheel, thinking fast. "Well, sir, I reckon the city ought not to keep them old hitchin' posts on the sidewalk anyhow. Nobody ties up horses these days." He faked a chuckle. "I was fixin' to ask you how Jemmerbeth is doin'. Wasn't her big art show in Paris last night? We should've heard somethin' about it by now."

"It's no use to change the subject, Mr. Timms. You know good and well that it was last night and you know also that it costs too much money to call from France. Alexandra will phone me when she gets back to Arizona." Lizbeth hummed the chorus of a hymn as they entered the city limits, a further sign that he had irritated her. "Jemmabeth didn't know that Alex was coming to Paris," she volunteered. "The Lillygraces bought tickets so their whole bunch could attend. Too bad Jim and little Robby couldn't have gone, but it should cheer Jemmabeth up to have her mother there. Alex is so full of fun. I do hate it that Jemma's been depressed, but it seems Spencer's in love with that New York girl in his architecture class."

Lester jumped on the topic. "I've got my money on Spencer. He's known that Jemmer is the sweetest and the prettiest gal he could find ever since they was young. Not to mention she's gonna be famous someday, like Cam said. She's twice as good as Norman Rockwell and that's saying a lot."

"She is, Lester, but all the same, Jemma didn't do right by Spencer and we have to keep that in mind."

"The way I see it, Jemmer never should've give that lawyer the time of day. He was a real good-lookin' feller, but smart-aleck. I sure didn't cotton to him. Lawyers do make a right good livin', though. I always heard that money don't buy happiness, but it sure helps iron out the rough spots. 'Course them Chases have got more money than all the rest of Chillaton put together." Lester stopped the car in the middle of the road. "Would you like to drive out to your old home place and check on your renter's cotton crop?" He knew she couldn't turn down such an offer.

"Why, yes, Lester, that's a fine idea."

Lester backed up and turned onto the graveled shortcut through Windy Valley. His description of Jemmabeth was easy to come by because her grandmother Lizbeth had the same golden eyes, and was sweet, too. . .at least when she was in a good mood.

❧

That evening, Lizbeth set out two fruit pies and two lemon custards for the North Chillaton Quilting Club to enjoy the next morning. She would have to hide them before Lester came over for *Bonanza*. He ate twice as much as her Cameron had ever eaten, but you couldn't tell it by Lester's scrawny frame. Cam loved desserts. He liked to sneak a slice of fruit pie before breakfast but always denied it. She could look in those twinkling blue eyes of his, though, and know what happened.

Their three boys and her baby sister had enjoyed her lemon custard meringue pie the last time they were all together. They had sat in the home place kitchen, laughing and kidding around. That same day at the train station was the last time she had seen her Matthew and Luke. Only Jimmy had returned from that awful war.

Now she baked for what was left of her family on holidays or for old quilters like herself and shut-ins. Sometimes Lester would get the last piece, if he was lucky. He talked so much that he gave her a headache, but just as often, he made her laugh. Nobody could get her tickled like Cam could, but he had passed on without ever uttering a word one morning while she was making biscuits. His heart just played out.

"Sure smells like heaven in there," Lester said outside the back screen door.

"Aren't you early?" Lizbeth quickly laid a cloth over the fruit pies but left the meringue ones exposed.

"Nope. It's eight o'clock, on the nose." He checked the gold pocket watch given him by the Santa Fe Railroad Company. "You're cookin' awful late."

"Now don't get your hopes up for any pie. These are all for my club tomorrow. Go ahead and get *Bonanza* going. I'll be there directly." She could hear Little Joe throwing the first punch in an all-out brawl when her telephone rang in the good bedroom. She took off her apron and picked up the phone.

"Gram? It's Jemma."

"Jemmabeth, honey, how was your art show? Did your mom surprise you?"

"Yes ma'am, she did, and the exhibit was fantastic. I have someone else who wants to say hello."

"Hi, Gram. This is Spencer."

"Spencer, help my life. Are you in Paris? I thought you were in Italy."

"Well, I'm in Paris with my girlfriend."

"Oh." Lizbeth's heart sank. "We heard about the girl in your architecture school. Your mother had photos at Nedra's Nook."

"Well, my real girlfriend is the famous artist from Chillaton,

Texas. You know her, don't you? We want you to do us a favor. Make it a point to tell everybody at Nedra's the next time you get your hair done that we are back together. Talk loud and long, especially if my mother is there. Dig out some old pictures of us and pass them around."

Lizbeth laughed. "I will indeed. Good-bye, you two. Blessings." She turned to Lester, who stood in the doorway, hat in hand.

"Good news, Miz Liz?"

"Lester, let me cut you a piece of pie. Do you want lemon custard or fruit? How about a piece of each?"

"Them young'uns seen the light, huh? Well, sir, I was hopin' that would happen. I expect I'll have me a slice of your lemon custard."

Lizbeth cut them both generous pieces and made coffee in the percolator. They sat across from one another at the yellow and chrome kitchenette because Lester made it a point to never sit in Cameron's chair.

"Do you think there'll be weddin' bells for them two?" he asked.

Lizbeth's smile widened. "I do indeed. It could be this summer or next because they both have their schooling to finish. I'm just glad that Jemma got her heart still, long enough to listen to the Lord."

"Well, sir, He's blessed her with the Chase boy and a whole lot of talent to boot." Lester ran his fingers across his upper lip. "Not to change the subject, but do you hear much from that Englishwoman friend of yours?"

"Helene calls once a week. Why do you ask?"

"I wondered if she's ever comin' back to the Panhandle to see you again."

"Are you hoping to show her your new moustache?"

His ears turned cherry red. "Why, no, Miz Liz, I just think she's a fine lady, and a nice complement to your company. I know she'll want to know about Jemmerbeth and Spencer, since Jemmer lived with her for a good while."

Lizbeth gave him a sidelong glance. "If Helene decides to come, I'll let you know." She ate a bite of pie. "Do Dah is coming in about a month."

"Well, sir, truth is, your baby sister gives me the same looks that

Zippy was prone to givin'. I try to steer clear of her, no offense."

"Lester, any man who's been married as many times as you have should be able to handle Do Dah."

"Well, sir, have I ever told you about the time that Zippy shut me up real good? She'd been actin' peculiar all week, so I excused myself to the privy after supper one night, just for a little peace and quiet—no offense, Miz Liz. I was readin' the Roebuck catalog and come hence to hearing shufflin' noises outside. I give a yell and nobody answered. The next thing I knew, there was a good bit of poundin' on the door. I kept on sayin' that the privy was occupied, but it didn't make no difference. The poundin' went on until I give the door a shove, but it wouldn't budge. Zippy had nailed 'er up good and tight." Lester tapped his foot on the black-and-white-checkered linoleum.

"Well? What happened next? You always do this to me, Lester. You consider yourself to be such a storyteller, but you leave your audience hanging about half the time."

"My apologies, Miz Liz. You're as right as rain. I shouldn't have started this one because it gets to me every time."

"Meaning what?"

"I never saw Zippy again. She up and left me in the outhouse and took off to parts unknown. The only good thing is, that if The Judge hadn't said he figgered her for a goner, I'd never had my number four, pretty Paulette."

"I suppose there's more as to how you escaped a nailed-up outhouse."

"Well, sir, I was in there a good while, but I got my neighbor's attention when he come out to his own privy. That would be the feller who sold you and Cam this house. He got his hammer and pulled them nails out. It took him awhile, too, seeing as how he was up in years. He like to have had himself a stroke for laughin' the whole time, too. I failed to see the humor in it myself, but then, like I said, if Zippy hadn't took off, I wouldn't have married my Frenchy. The very next year the town council passed a rule that everybody on this side of the tracks had to have indoor plumbin'. Old Zippy would have a hard time nailin' me in the indoor privy that I got now."

Lizbeth had stopped listening to him. She moved to the window and looked out toward the tracks where Jemma used to dance on the rails. She had taken pure joy from their news but was troubled with another feeling, too. She went to the closet in the good bedroom and took down the quilt top that she had made last spring. It was the wedding ring pattern. In the middle she had added a heart with their names on it. When she knew the date, she would add that as well, but for now, it gave her the comfort that she needed just to touch it. "Thanks be to You, good and gracious Lord." She replaced the quilt and returned to Lester, who was still talking.

Alex was absorbed in a French magazine when her daughter woke up. They looked enough alike to be sisters.

"Good afternoon, sweet pea," she said. "How are things?"

"Things are perfect. Spencer is perfect."

"Jem, don't put that burden on him."

"I know, but he's close." Jemma stretched and sat up. "I think I've ruined my new dress by walking around in the rain all night."

Alex picked up the blue satin gown. "There's nothing here that a good dry cleaner can't fix. Let's see what I have that you could borrow for the airport."

Alexandra was a fashion queen, but not on Jim's coaching salary. Her high-society parents were always generous to their daughter even though they still felt she had married beneath herself when she'd married a farmer's son. Jemma watched her mother search through the neatly packed suitcase.

Alex held up her choice. "Try this on. Everybody needs a simple black dress. It'll be short on you, but miniskirts are the style these days."

Jemma took her mother's hand. "I'm glad you were here for all this good stuff, Mom. I've been a fool."

"No. You've been foolish, but all is well now."

"I sure hope so." Jemma touched the gold heart on her necklace.

"You made your mark on Paris with your show, cousin," Trent said as her extended family waited at the airport. "I should have bought a painting myself, as an investment, like Grandfather did."

Her Grandfather Lillygrace perked up at the mention of the show. "I assume the gallery will retain some of the proceeds, but you should have a nice nest egg," he said, all business. "We are very pleased with our purchase." Her prim grandmother nodded in agreement.

Jemma didn't care. She only wanted to be alone again with Spencer. They couldn't keep their eyes off each other. The flight was announced, and Jemma passed out hugs and kisses. "I love y'all. Mom, give Daddy and Robby my love," she said as Alex waved and vanished down the gate corridor.

Spencer didn't waste any time. He cornered Jemma in the waiting area like they were already alone. They headed to her apartment. Jemma thought she was going to die before they could get there. She could barely get the door unlocked.

"Wait," Spencer said with his hand on the knob, "how are we going to stand this? I don't know if I can be in this room with you, baby."

"Spence, I have to be alone with you without Paris. That's all I ask. I need to hold you and tell you some things, okay? Just five minutes."

"I could go berserk in five minutes."

She giggled. "I won't allow it."

"Let's go to that little courtyard I saw as we came in. I don't want to lose control after all these years."

She grinned at him, at the idea that he would lose control, then relented. He was the most composed human she had ever known. "Okay. Good grief. Do you realize that I've loved you since the first grade? What would that be in dog years?" she asked as they smooched and talked under the trees.

"About one hundred and five years."

"That's too old to get married, huh?"

"Hey, you promised Papa that you wouldn't marry until you got out of college. Do you think he would hold you to that if he were still alive?"

"No, but can we make it a whole year, being over here in Europe, all by our lonesome?"

"I can if you can," he said. "Now, let me show you my favorite things about Paris while it's still daylight."

⁂

They crammed his favorites into an afternoon, and he saved the best for last. They entered the lower level of Sainte-Chapelle while it was still light. Jemma was already impressed, thinking that they were in the main chapel.

Spencer led her up a small stairwell in the corner. "Close your eyes," he said when they neared the top. He held her hand and took her to the center of the chapel. "Now open."

Jemma caught her breath. "Whoa. It's like being inside a kaleidoscope. I can't believe this." She walked around him, captivated by the brilliant stained-glass windows. "I don't know where to look."

"This is the best of Gothic architecture." He scanned the windows. "Louis IX had bought what he believed was the Crown of Thorns and a piece of The Cross, so he had this chapel built to house them and probably to show off. The relics cost him three times more than what the chapel cost to build. During the war, they actually took all the stained glass out and stored it so it would be safe. Extraordinary, huh?"

They sat on the floor in the bare room, soaking in the panorama of color and light. The sun went down, leaving them still absorbed in the jeweled walls. They stayed until workers began to set up for a concert.

"Jem," he said, looking up at the windows, "do you know Psalm 37?"

"No." She barely knew any scriptures by heart.

"It's been my hope."

"I'll look it up. You're a better Christian than I am, Spence. I have all those Sunday school perfect attendance certificates, but I've never just hung on to a scripture because that's sort of scary and hard. Nobody ever tells you that."

"I'm not a better Christian than you are. I'm just older and wiser."

"Oh brother. You're right though, about the wiser part."

He drew her close.

"Good-bye, beautiful place," Jemma said as they turned to go. "I had a chance to attend a concert here last month, but I wanted to wait and see if you still loved me so we could come together."

Spencer stopped on the stairs. "Jemmabeth, did you read the back of that necklace you're wearing?"

"I know," she said. "*Always.*"

"I meant it."

"I'm so glad."

They ate ice cream and took a tourist boat down the Seine.

"You know I have to go back to Florence tonight," he said. "I'm on the last flight."

"When will I see you again?"

"I'll be right here every weekend, unless you want to come to Florence."

"I don't want to see her, Spence. What do you think she'll do? Does she know about me?"

"She knows. I told her on our first date. I wasn't looking for a girlfriend, Jem, just entertainment. Michelle has her own plans, and I came along at the right time. I'll take care of things. Don't worry."

"Speaking of worrying, what do you think about Vietnam? Sandy says it's quicksand. Martin is convinced that he'll get sent there. You don't think they'll draft you as soon as you graduate, do you?"

"I don't know. We'll take what comes. Maybe I'll get a master's degree, but even graduate school doesn't guarantee a deferment."

"Should I be worried about the draft?"

"You should worry that we can keep our eighth-grade promise." He stopped at the hallway phone in her building. "Here's the plan, Jem. I'll call this number and let it ring just once and hang up. Then you'll know that I made it back okay or maybe that I'm thinking about you, but then I guess I'll be calling all the time."

"I'm at the Academie from seven in the morning until about nine at night."

"You keep long hours."

"Well, I have classes, then I paint—a lot."

"I really have to go, baby. I'll see you next Friday night. The best day of my life will be our wedding day," he whispered. "It's been an unbelievable weekend." He skipped down the stairs, two at a time.

She couldn't stand it. She ran down the steps and caught him on the last landing, almost knocking him to the floor. They held one another until the taxi took him away. She had never kissed so much in twenty-four hours.

Jemma returned to her room and looked up the verse he'd mentioned. "Delight thyself also in the Lord; and he shall give thee the desires of thine heart. Commit thy way unto the Lord; trust also in him; and he shall bring it to pass." She looked toward Sacré-Coeur, then got on her knees. "Lord, only You could have kept Spencer loving me all this time. I'm glad You and I are finally on the same track. Amen." It was probably a weird prayer, but it was to the point.

She sat on the floor in the hallway sketching park benches, pigeons, gothic churches, kaleidoscope windows, and him. A few minutes before midnight the phone rang once. She caught it before it finished ringing. "Spence?"

"Hey, you aren't supposed to answer, but I'm glad you did. Go to sleep and dream about us trying to catch those minnows in Plum Creek."

"You dream about our names carved on the cottonwood tree there."

"I love you," he said.

She hung up the phone and danced down the hall to her room. As was her habit, she wound the Starry Night music box Spence had given her on her twenty-first birthday and got in bed. She was asleep before "I Will Wait for You" wound down.

Chapter 2
Shick

Their weekends were crammed with fun, and they took advantage of all nooks and corners in Paris. It wasn't quite the same as their special spot at the Salt Fork of the Red River or their parking place on The Hill back in their Texas Panhandle hometown, but it served the purpose. She quit asking about Michelle Taylor, Miss Completely Gorgeous, as Spence's mother had called her, but she still wondered.

Since the exhibition, Jemma had painted several pieces. Her favorites were of the café owner standing in his doorway near her apartment, and a couple arguing in the foreground of the tangle of buildings visible outside her window. Spencer was so good for her. Gram was right. Love could clear muddy waters.

She was working on the third painting when the Academie's gallery manager came to visit her workspace. "Mlle Forrester, a word with you, please."

"*Oui*, madame." Her French was inching along.

"It is about the proceeds of the exhibition. You have not yet inquired as to the sales. The patrons paid a total of 31,375 francs. The Academie retains a small portion of those funds, but the majority of it is yours. We have set up a bank account for you with this money. When you wish to withdraw funds, all you need to do is notify Peter. He will take care of it for you. Your work sold exceptionally well. Our congratulations."

"*Merci*, ma'am, but how much money is that in American dollars?"

"Perhaps about seven thousand dollars."

Jemmabeth whistled. The last time anybody had paid for her art was in the third grade when her best friend, Sandy Kay Baker, gave her a nickel to paint a picture of her mean cat.

Lizbeth sat at the kitchenette with Julia, looking at brochures of Europe.

"You know that I'm scared to death of being in an airplane, Do Dah," Lizbeth said.

Julia yawned. "You have never been in one, my dear. Furthermore, please don't be calling me that silly name all over Europe." Her red-orange hair stood out a little funny on one side.

Lizbeth smiled at her. "I'll try to remember, but I'm the old one, so keep that in mind."

"You are also the one with the college degree, so you can remember things."

Lester knocked on the door with his hat pulled low over his brow.

"Mr. Timms," Julia said as she opened the door, "I never see you around much when I visit. Why is that?" Julia never beat around the bush about anything.

"Well, sir, I figured y'all would like to have your time alone to hash out one thing or the other. I ain't good for nothin' but bringin' the mail."

"Sit down, Lester, and have some coffee." Julia pulled out a chair, then ushered him to it.

"Here's something for you," Lizbeth said. "Just look at those pretty French stamps."

Julia opened the letter and took a money order from its fold.

Paris, November 11, 1966

Dear Do Dah,
    Gram said you were coming to Chillaton, so I hope this gets to you in time. I am sending part of the money that I got from the art show, and I want you to do something for me.

Julia finished the letter and disappeared into the bathroom, just off the kitchen, and blew her nose. Lizbeth and Lester stared at one another until she returned, sniffling.

"What did Jemma have to say?" Lizbeth asked, eyeing her sister.

Julia cleared her throat. "Jemmabeth and Spencer are coming

home for Christmas, and she sends her love. Anybody need a refill?" she asked, bringing the coffee percolator to the table.

Lizbeth decided not to press. "Lester, you've been to Europe. Am I wrong about the plane ride being just awful?"

"Miz Liz, that plane ride was about the least scary thing that happened to me in the Big War. I wasn't thinkin' about nothin' but keepin' body and soul together long enough to see a cotton field again."

She sighed. "I suppose that wasn't a fair question."

"The main reason we're going is to visit the boys' graves, Lizbeth Forrester. You keep that in mind when you start turning chicken on me." Julia drank her coffee at one of the tall windows, looking toward the train tracks that ran just beyond the alley.

"Well, I guess if I'm going to go, I'd best hush up, but sometimes I wonder if I shouldn't just wait and see my boys in heaven."

"I'm thinkin' the Bible says we won't know our family in heaven, Miz Liz. I'm bankin' on that, seeing as how I've got me three or four women waitin' up there," Lester said.

"Lizbeth, you're going and that's that. It's high time that you see the rest of the world. There are actually places where cotton is not the main topic of the day." Julia poured what was left of her coffee in the sink and resumed her seat at the kitchenette.

Lester shook his head. "No, sir, I don't think we'll know family in heaven. We're gonna be there just to worship the good Lord forever. I've heard many a sermon on that in more than one denomination."

"Where were you in the war, Lester?" Julia asked. She was well aware of Lester's penchant for telling long tales. Cam's nickname for Lester was "Windy." Cam should have known, too, since he could tell a few tales himself.

"In France, mostly—Battle of the Marne, the second one. It was there that I met up with the gypsies. Now they were a fearsome lot. I was more afraid of them than any airplane. Not meanin' to change the subject, but I keep hearin' about this Vietnam War havin' gorilla warfare. Now what in the Sam Hill could a gorilla do in a war?"

Julia laughed. "Y'all are going to have to excuse me. I need to say hello to Willa and Trina; I'll be back shortly. Don't get up, Lester. You keep on with your story." Julia slipped on her fur coat and walked over the tracks to what many still called "Colored Town."

Lizbeth and Lester watched her make her way through the little trail that had been worn through the weeds.

"That's what I was talking about, Miz Liz. Zippy would up and walk out, just like that, while I was talkin'."

"Don't let it bother you, Lester. We have to keep in mind that she's from Houston, and that she and Arthur are money folk."

"That looked like a chinchiller coat she's wearin'. See, if that old twister hadn't tore up my chinchiller ranchin' business, I could've been livin' in high cotton by now. Exceptin' for Bruno. I couldn't have parted with him for his fur. He was my sleepin' buddy. How come your sister got to be called that strange name when you and Annabeth and Sarabeth and Marybeth all sound alike?"

"She's wearing a mink coat, Lester, and her nickname is a family joke. Her real name is, of course, Julia. They tacked *beth* onto our names to make up for no middle name. The joke has it that my father wanted a boy so much that he just ran out of 'beth.' When my dear mother died giving birth to her, Cam and I took Julia to raise. We already had Matthew, and the other boys came along right afterward. They couldn't pronounce Julia, and it came out Do Dah. She is not fond of it, as you can tell, and I do believe we've had this conversation before."

"She's sure bossy. No offense, Miz Liz," Lester said, taking a chance since Lizbeth was in a talkative mood.

"Julia has her own way of doing things. That girl nearly was the death of Cameron. I don't know how she got to be so stubborn and sassy. We loved her, though, like she was our own little girl."

"How'd she come to meet up with a big shot like Mr. Billington?" Lester asked. "She have that kinda hair then, too?"

"Julia was so downhearted after we lost the boys, Cam thought it might do her good to visit my sisters in Houston for a while. She lived with Annabeth, Marybeth, and Sarabeth for a short while, but she couldn't get along with them. She talked about going to college, too, but she didn't have the funds. That's when she got a job at Billington's. They only had the one store back then, and she worked her way up to being a manager in the cosmetics department. That's when she changed her hair color and that's how she met Arthur.

She's sharp and always about ten steps ahead of everybody else. She got that from our mother, too, even though she never knew her."

"Mr. Billington bought some hair color from her? Ain't that kindly odd?"

"Lester, really. Julia wanted to make some changes in the merchandise, so she made an appointment with him. He says it was love at first sight. He liked her spunky ways. Of course she was a cute little thing in those days, too, before she got that front porch around her middle."

"Why didn't they have young'uns?"

"Art is twenty-odd years older than Julia. Besides, I think they like being free to trot around the globe. Now help me pick out someplace to visit in Italy before she gets back."

"Wherebouts is your boy buried in It'ly?"

"Near Florence, that's Matthew, bless him. Luke is buried in Africa at a place called Carthage."

"Africa? Miz Liz, I don't know nothin' about Africa."

"All I know is that I'll get to see their names chiseled into those crosses, and I can stand on the same dirt that they gave their lives for."

"Yes, ma'am. You deserve that, Miz Liz, at the very least."

"Miz Julia, come on in this house." Willa Johnson opened her door wide and gave Julia a hug. She cleared a basketful of ironing off a chair and smoothed her starched apron over her own generous middle. "Latrina, we got company. Stop that sewin' machine for a minute and get on in here."

Latrina, a tall girl with dimples and almond-shaped eyes, emerged with a big grin for Julia, who had made her laugh since the first time she met her, a little less than a year ago. "Hi, Do Dah. Have you heard from Jemma?" she asked with a hug.

"I just got a letter from her, and I need to talk to you two," Julia said.

"Well, set yourself down." Willa pointed at the table with her cane. "There's not trouble again with them two lovebirds? I'm gonna give that girl a spankin' myself if she's done gone and fiddled with that boy's heart again."

"No, no, I think we'll be hearing wedding bells before we hear of anything like that ever again. Jemmabeth has learned her lesson."

"What's going on then?" Trina asked.

"Jemma sold most of her paintings at that art show in Paris. She got a pretty penny for them, too, and she wants to use some of it to send you two to Europe with Lizbeth and me."

Their jaws dropped. Julia might have just as well announced that Lady Bird Johnson was coming for high tea at their house.

"That girl is plain crazy," Trina said.

Willa rubbed her face. "Now I know for sure that Jemma's gotta be the sweetest white child in this world. How come her to think of such a thing, Miz Julia?"

"Jemma *is* the sweetest white child in the world, and she won't take no for an answer. She got that from my side of the family."

"What would become of my ironin'? Folks would find somebody else to do it, and I'd be out of business."

"Oh Mama, they'd come right back to you. Nobody else can please them," Trina said. "I can't believe that Jem. She'll be home Christmas, right?"

"Yes, but she wants this all settled before she gets back. She figured on Willa giving me trouble. Are you going to give me trouble, dear?" Julia asked.

Willa moved around the table, her heavy steps accentuated by the tapping of her cane. In the distance, the noon whistle blew at the fire station. "Law, law, Miz Julia. You reckon a plane could get off the ground with this big old caboose inside?"

Julia laughed. "I reckon. Now you two will need a passport. I'll take care of that, but I'll need your birth certificates."

"Trina's grandpap got her a birth certificate, but I ain't got one. I got my Pap's Bible with my name in it. He had the preacher to write it."

"Good. We'll get you passports one way or another," Julia said.

"When are you going, Do Dah?" Trina asked, her heart thumping.

"You mean, when are *we* going? I like to go in the spring. Things will be so pretty over there. Does that sound okay with you?"

Willa and Trina looked at each other and shrugged, still in shock.

"I need to get back to Lizbeth for now. I'll come over and get you girls, and then we can sit down and do some serious planning at her house. Would this evening work for y'all?"

"We'll be ready after supper. Thank Jemma for us and tell her I said that she's too much." Trina walked Julia to the door, then ran back to throw her arms around her mama's neck. "Wait 'til I tell Nick. He's gonna flip."

"Sugar, do you know what a pass the port is?" Willa asked, wide-eyed, as Trina skipped away.

"Don't worry, Mama," Trina hollered from her room, "it's just a way to identify us as Americans." She took down the yellowed postcard that had been thumb-tacked to the wall beside her bed. She had never imagined that she might someday see Europe, and maybe even the Eiffel Tower that was on that card. God was so good to her.

Jemma left school early on Friday to get ready to meet Spencer at the airport. She had already laid out the clothes she was going to wear for the evening and was gathering things to take a bath when she heard the phone ring. She waited to see if it only rang once, his signal that he was about to leave Florence. It kept ringing, though, and she answered.

"Jemmabeth Forrester, please," requested a male with a distinct English accent.

"This is Jemma."

"I am a friend of Spencer Chase's. He wanted me to call because he is ill and will be unable to come to Paris."

Her pulse rocketed. "What do you mean, ill? Is he in the hospital?"

"No, actually, he is in his flat. It's most likely a nasty bug he's picked up."

"Thank you for calling me. What's your name?"

"Lawrence. Lawrence Miles."

"I'll be on the next train."

"Our flats are only two blocks from the School of Architecture, and I'm in number eleven. Just ring for me."

Jemma threw some clothes in her bag and called Peter, her

liaison with the Academie. At his suggestion, she bought a ticket to fly to Florence. Peter and his wife, Ami, drove her to the airport. Rather than thirteen hours on the train, the flight only took three. She took a cab to the apartment house. Lawrence, a slender, pale young man, answered.

"Is he any better?" Jemma asked as they went upstairs.

"He seems the same to me. Just a warning; he has company. It's Michelle. She has been with him since Wednesday."

Her insides turned to ice. "Oh? How did she know Spence was sick?"

"Our classes are quite small and Spencer is, of course, a dynamic component. I know that you and he are, shall we say, a couple. Michelle is tenacious, though. If you need me, I'm right downstairs. Where are you staying?"

"I'll be staying in Spence's room, on the floor, if necessary."

"I see," Lawrence said with a smile. "Good luck, Jemma. Lovely meeting you."

Jemma didn't even knock; she opened the door and walked right in. Spencer was asleep, his face glistening with perspiration. In an armchair, curled in slumber, was Michelle. Her blond hair was pulled back with a clip. She wore slacks and a sweater. Her shoes were on the floor beside his bed. She was completely gorgeous, as advertised. Rats. Jemma's heart pounded as she sat within inches of the woman who had almost stolen Spence's heart.

His room was organized and light. Her first self-portrait and the photos he had taken of her at Plum Creek were framed and on his desk. Papa's portrait was propped against the wall, atop his dresser. The place reeked of sickness. Spence turned over, moaning. She touched his burning cheeks.

Michelle awoke and vaulted out of the chair. "Hey, what are you doing in here?"

"I might ask you the same thing," Jemma said, rising to her full height, which was at least three inches above Michelle. "I'm Jemma, Spencer's girlfriend, and you are. . . ?"

Michelle stared a hole through her, then smirked. "Let's just say that I'm the one caring for him so you really aren't needed."

"I am here, though, aren't I? So probably you're the one who's not needed." Jemma chewed on her lip and checked out Michelle's bluish-green eyes. Cat eyes.

Michelle took out the clip and shook her hair. "Spency and I have a relationship, and it's very special. I don't know what he's told you, but things haven't changed between us even if he does see you in Paris."

Spency? Jemma's nose burned. "Really? Are you napping with him while he is passed out with a fever?"

"His temperature does rise with me, but not because he is ill." Michelle raised her chin.

Jemma raised hers as well. "Look, I'm not buying this at all. You're wasting your breath." She could take her down with one good *Saturday Night Wrestling* move.

Michelle shifted her weight. "What *are* you anyway—one of the Harlem Globetrotters? You must descend from giants. Are you familiar with the term *shick*? It's what we call a she-hick like you where I come from."

"Are you familiar with the French term *imbécile de New York*? That's what we call New York smart alecks where I come from."

Word had it at Nedra's Nook that Michelle spoke several languages. Apparently, French was among them. "Amazing that you know a few words in a language other than your native hillbilly. Look, I'm not leaving and I don't think you want to share Spency with me, do you?" she asked in simple English.

"Well, then, are you going to carry me out? Because I'm not going anywhere. *Spency* would prefer me to stay, I guarantee," Jemma said, thinking that maybe The Claw would be the best move, to get her attention.

"Michelle," Spencer whispered, "thanks for your concern. I'll see you around."

Jemma smoothed his damp hair.

Michelle's face twitched, but she picked up her purse and her leather jacket. "Good-bye Spency," she said, stroking the blanket where it covered his leg. She shot Jemma a look with her feline eyes. "Remember, he's with me five days a week, shick, and we share much more than the same architectural philosophies."

"Watch where you put your paws on my man and get out."

Jemma raised her hand in The Claw formation.

Michelle slammed the door behind her. Jemma turned back to Spencer, who opened one eye and smiled weakly at her.

"That was almost worth having this crud, you little spitfire," he said. "I wish I could laugh, but right now I'm feeling a little shick myself."

Jemma found a washcloth and went down the hall looking for water to cool his face. When she got back he was asleep again. She opened the windows a little and picked up a book about architecture that was on his desk. Lawrence came by and brought some food for her and soda water for Spencer.

"Try to get him to drink some tea. There is a kettle and hotplate in his room. Did you meet Michelle?" he asked with an odd grin.

"You could say we met, I guess. It was more like a sparring."

"She's nice to look at, but not worth the bother. I went out with her for a while last year before Spencer came. She is relentless."

"Thanks for the food. Surely he'll be better by tomorrow," Jemma said.

"Yes, well, I know he's glad that you are here. I'll be off now."

She curled up in the same chair where Michelle had been, but awoke to more groaning. "What are you doing?" she whispered.

"If you arc going to make me drink all that tea, I have to go to the bathroom." He shivered in his pajama bottoms and undershirt.

"Let me help you," she said. "Here—put on your robe so you won't freeze. It's cold in that hallway." Spencer looked like a little boy again, but his breathing was easier and his skin felt cooler to her touch.

"Is this our first whole night together?" he asked when she put him back in bed.

"I hope not."

"If you get sick, too, I'll never forgive myself," he said, his eyes already closed.

"I wasn't with you the first few days, so maybe I won't get it."

"Michelle was. She'll probably catch it and sue me."

"Yeah, especially since she was sleeping with you in the bed."

"Was she? I hope I didn't hallucinate and think it was you."

"Are you serious?"

Spencer smiled. "I'm very serious. I heard that whole conversation you had with her. I like your French comeback. When did you learn the word for *fool?*"

"When I thought I had lost you."

"You will never lose me, baby, ever," he mumbled, then drifted away.

❦

The next morning Jemma opened the windows wide, changed his sheets, and sent him off to shower and shave. He was on the mend. In two weeks, they would be in Chillaton for Christmas. They talked about art and architecture, music and love, being careful to keep an arm's length apart. Lawrence appeared with more food.

She got up her nerve. "Spence, I saw a motorcycle parked outside, and it hasn't moved since I came. I don't suppose you know anything about that."

He rubbed his chin.

"Well?"

"I have to have some transportation, but it doesn't get used every day. Italians love their cycles."

"Spencer Morgan Chase, you know my feelings about those machines. You have no protection whatsoever when you ride it. I can't believe you haven't told me before."

"I wonder why."

"If you'd seen the Kelseys lying in the road like Mom and I did, you'd never get on one again."

He sighed. "I'm sorry, baby. I just happen to like motorcycles. It's like your cowboy thing."

"I gave that up."

"I'll be careful. It's just a rental."

"Thanks." She took his hand. "I called the Grasso family and they invited me to stay with them tonight. They're friends with Professor Rossi in Dallas. I don't want people getting the wrong idea about us."

"Could we at least hug before you leave?"

"I suppose so, but that's it. I'll come by in the morning with breakfast."

"I love you, Jemmabeth. I dreamed you were running the bulls again. That won't happen, will it?"

She was not expecting this topic. "Babe, I promise that I'll never go back to the rodeo dance and walk through the cowboys to get a thrill. I have no desire to do that. Remember, you're my cowboy now. You're my dearest, my only one." She meant to give him a small kiss but had to pull away. He was getting well. "Don't you let Michelle in this room. Promise? I don't want to have to put The Claw on her, *Spency.*"

He laughed. "I keep it in mind," he said, using a line from a Paul Newman movie that had become their private joke.

Chapter 3
Stetson Sunrise

I t seemed to her that half of Chillaton was waiting for them at the Amarillo airport, and it was a giddy Jemma who flung herself into their waiting arms. Everything and everyone seemed fresh and beautiful to her. She was pleased and surprised that Helene, her former English landlady, had come to share the holidays with them. Neither of Spencer's parents showed up, but he was used to that. Lizbeth's house was all decked out with lights, cedar boughs, and ribbon. Helene was sharing the culinary duties, and beautiful pies were stashed all over the house. It was a curious mixture of English and Texas Panhandle fare.

Jemma's eight-year-old brother, Robby, hung on to Spencer like a magnet, and it was difficult to say which one of them enjoyed it more. The three of them sat on the cold wrought-iron bench beside Cameron's tombstone while she told some funny Papa stories. Jemma's giggle was the same one she'd had all through grade school that had gotten her into trouble more than once.

"Let's visit your grandparents' mausoleum," she said.

The Chase mausoleum was a smaller version of the Parthenon and stood out somewhat in the Chillaton Citizens' Cemetery. Robby was off, running down the hill to the pond to see the very much alive cemetery ducks.

"Tell me about your grandparents again," Jemma said as they sat inside the pillared, marble extravagance, overlooking the pond.

"I don't remember my grandmother much at all," Spencer said. "She died when I was little, but I went with Granddaddy to church every Sunday. We had lots of fun together. When he died, I was ten years old and he left his estate to me—the ranches, the office buildings back East, trusts, stocks, cash, the banks. . .everything except his house and one hundred acres surrounding it. That place was all he gave my dad because his womanizing embarrassed Granddaddy, especially since he was a state senator and an elder in his church. I don't get into that business much. His lawyers in New York take care of everything for me, but now that I'm over twenty-one, I guess it's time I started learning about it."

"Whoa. You'd make a good catch for some lucky girl. Was your grandmother really on the *Titanic*?"

"Yeah. It left her kind of strange, but then, my whole family is strange. That's why I want in your family, and why I want to have a family with you."

Jemma's scalp tingled at that thought.

Robby burst inside, skidded to a stop, then crept around the mausoleum. "Hey, this is cool. It looks like the place where the gladiators fought."

"I think that was the idea." Spencer grabbed Robby and put him on his shoulders. "Let's go. I have to meet my dad."

Jemma dropped Robby off at home, then took Spencer to his dad's car dealership to get his Corvette. Mr. Chase came out grinning and shook his hand. "Welcome back, son. I guess you and Miss Forrester are riding double again, huh? I thought you had yourself a New Yorker there for a while, but I guess hometown girls are best," he said, winking at Jemma. He lowered his voice. "Your mother still thinks that other girl is coming with you for the holidays. You'd better get home and straighten her out." He lit a cigarette and went back to his office.

Spencer kissed Jemma and walked to his car. Just as he opened the door, she yelled at him. He came right back and leaned in the window, but she couldn't look up. "Now don't give me a lecture, but I have to know," she said. "You didn't have anything going with Michelle, did you? She acted like y'all were messing around, but I assume that was a lie."

Spencer exhaled. "Baby, we made a promise in junior high to not fool around before we married. Do you think that I would waste my promise on anybody but you?"

She halfway shrugged.

"Did I ask if you and that old cowboy broke our promise? No, because I trust you."

She sniffed, then started to cry, full steam. He opened the door and held her. She was talking and crying, but he was used to it.

"I didn't want to believe her, but she made me doubt. I was so mean to you last spring and she was so sure of herself. I'm sorry, babe. Really, I am. I do trust you. Please forgive me. Say you do." There she was, sounding like Miss Scarlett O'Hara again.

He smiled at her, at those golden eyes full of tears and those pouty lips contorted in remorse. She was the love of his life, his only love, and the only one he would ever give himself to—the only one.

◄◊►

Jemmabeth waited until everybody was asleep. She put on her wool coat, hat, and mittens and walked up to the tracks. A freight train was due soon. She just knew it. A freighter wouldn't be as good as the Zephyr, but it would have to do. The wind whipped around her legs as a dog across the tracks spotted her and wouldn't hush. The last time she stood there, it was to grab some stones from the rail bed to keep with her on a journey to St. Louis. Now those stones were in Europe, thrown in rivers to mark her presence. She picked up a few more in case she visited another water of some significance.

She heard the train coming, but it did not have the smooth, pulsating sound of the passenger train. It was a wobbling dissonance that smacked of empty cars and sluggish, grinding connections. The light from the engine shone yellowish white like a jar full of fireflies. Jemma stood her ground and waited for it to pass, blowing its irreverent horn. It was a poor substitute. She needed the Zephyr to make her feel that all had come full circle and she was truly forgiven.

◄◊►

Early the next morning, she walked across Chillaton to her parents' former home, where she had lived most all her days. She leaned against a big elm tree next to the sidewalk. It wasn't too long ago that she didn't know which end was up in her life. Back then, she had sat on that very curb and cried, but now Spencer's enduring love had changed all that.

The house looked much the same as it did when her parents sold it and moved to Wicklow, Texas, for a while. They had fixed the place up over the years, and Jemma hated moving away from it.

One Christmas, the Lillygraces had sent documents showing that they had paid off the loan on the house as a gift. She would never forget the look on her daddy's face that morning—a mixture of gratitude and hurt pride.

She wasn't close to the Lillygrace family. Her mother's folks had never paid much attention to her or Robby, until now that she'd won the Girard Fellowship in Paris. It always puzzled Jemma that her mom was such a generous, kind, and unaffected person because her mother's parents were cool, formal, and very rich. Not that being rich was necessarily a bad thing. Spencer probably had a bigger bank account than they did.

She went to see Willa and Trina and straightened the crooked shingle on Willa's porch post that served as her business sign: DOES IRONING AND GUARANTEE HER WORK. It swung right back like it was.

Willa unplugged her iron. "Jemmabeth Forrester, you and I are gonna go round 'n' round until you quit being such a sweet child to Latrina and me. You shouldn't be givin' up your paintin' money like this. You're throwin' away money so's an old fool like me can get on a plane and fly to kingdom come and back. What do you have to say for yourself?"

"I say that people pay way too much money for art, and I want to spread my little fortune around as it pleases me. I want y'all to go, and it'll hurt my feelings if you don't."

"Does your mama and daddy know that you're gonna do this?"

"Yes, ma'am, and they like the idea."

"You really are something else, girl." Trina hugged her. "Nick says I better not come back with a Frenchman."

"I don't know; those Frenchmen are very debonair," Jemma said.

"Now don't you be coming home with that kind of talk," Willa chided.

Jemma laughed and went with Trina to see her latest dress designs. "How are things with you and Mr. Fields?"

Trina laid out her sketchbooks on the bed. "The same. Nick has to get through his internship before anything can change."

"Have you written to any design schools yet?" Jemma flipped through the multitude of pages.

Trina lowered her voice. "I can't leave Mama. She still can't walk good from breaking her hip. Besides, it would tear her up if I left."

"You left once before to go to junior college. You are talented, Trina, and you should be given a chance to have a career at what you are good at. If you don't write to schools, then I will, and I'll sign your name."

"And mail them from Paris? Yeah, right." Trina laughed.

"We'll see," Jemma vowed.

"I can't trust you, girl. You would just as soon do that as to look at me."

"That's right. C'mon, I want to walk the tracks and play some hoops."

❦

They walked down the rails to Main Street and up the brick-paved Boulevard to the high school tennis courts and its single, net-less basketball hoop. Jemma had her eye on Judge McFarland's house. It was dark and dreary, like The Judge's personality. As such, it stood out from the neatly kept Queen Anne–style homes that lined both sides of the street. Jemma had tried her best to bring some joy into the old place for a while when she was a day companion to Carrie, his invalid daughter.

"I was thinking about that sulky Weese kid that your mama tried to reform," Jemma said. "Remember when we talked about putting him into Carrie's iron lung? Whatever happened to the burglary case they had against him, anyway?"

Trina rolled her eyes. "A judge in Amarillo gave him the choice of the army or jail, and he picked the army. So it was just like we figured—Vietnam. I know in my heart he stole that money, but they never found it. Mama got a letter from him a while back."

"Have you heard from Carrie?"

"Last week. She's still in love with her physical therapist in Houston."

"Good. Let's go see The Judge."

Trina shook her head. "I'll shoot some free throws until you get through with him. Remember, that old geezer tried to kiss me when I was working for him."

Jemma walked to the front door and knocked. She hadn't been

320

to his house since he sent Carrie to Houston for rehabilitation and fired Jemma as her caretaker for being more trouble than she was worth. The Judge opened the door and drew back when he saw her.

"Miss Forrester. What brings you here?" He stroked his beard.

She could smell whiskey. "I just wanted to say hello and tell you that I'm sorry."

"An apology coming from you? If it's about the portrait you painted of her, I've changed my mind about that. Carolina loves it and whatever she loves, I have to tolerate, somehow, but that doesn't mean I agree with your interpretation."

"No, sir, I want to apologize for not shaking your hand when you offered it on the day you fired me. I wondered if you might give me a second chance. My aunt Julia says that you were well mannered in your youth."

A smile worked its way around The Judge's mouth. He considered Jemma's outstretched hand, then clasped it. "Apology accepted. Now you can go on with your life, Jemmabeth. Give my regards to your aunt Julia and your grandmother."

Jemma turned toward the street. She heard the door close as she was nearly to the gate. Carrie would like the fact that Jemma had the guts to apologize to her father, the meanest judge in the Panhandle. She would also be interested to know that he had to tolerate whatever Carrie loved. Surely that must extend to boyfriends as well as paintings. She would call her as soon as she got home.

"Jem, I never have told you this, but when we were in junior high, I used to see you dancing around on these tracks," Trina said as they walked home. "I know for a fact you still do it."

"Really? You should've joined me." Jemma stretched out her arms and lifted her face to the sky. "You might have liked it."

Trina smiled at her friend. There was no way on earth that she could have joined her back then. Jemma wouldn't have cared, but Trina wouldn't have had the nerve to share something so free-spirited with a white girl. Besides, the tracks made her nervous even now, and in more ways than one.

❧

Twila Baker called to invite Jemma and Spencer to a party at their new trailer house. It was a used one, but new to them. Twila worked as a helper at Nedra's Nook. Her husband, Buddy B, as everybody called him, was not only Sandy's big brother, but head mechanic at Chase's Chevrolet & Cadillac and lead singer in the Buddy Baker Band. Nedra's Beauty Parlor and Craft Nook offered the women of Connelly County a choice of two hairstyles: the bubble (a.k.a. Nedra's helmet), or a French twist. Both were guaranteed to last a week. She also offered an outlet for local handicrafts, on consignment, of course. Most of her crafty customers never sold anything because nobody wanted to part with their hard-earned money for stuff that they could make just as well or better. Juicy bits of gossip, however, were Nedra's real handiwork, and those outlasted her hairdos.

Jemma was relieved that Missy Blake wasn't at the party. Missy was at the top of Spencer's dating list the first time Jemma broke up with him which, at the time, seemed like a clever move on his part. In high school, Missy was known as The Cleave, due to her abundant bosom. Every boy in town had been out with her, and now even Spencer had joined that dubious club. Missy's family owned all the rural movie theaters across six counties, so she got in free on dates, but the boys always had to pay. She was also Jemma's rival in every high school election, and her well-publicized dream was to have Spencer for her very own. Quite aware of that fact, Jemma had just picked up some fresh moves from *Saturday Night Wrestling* on Lizbeth's TV.

"Missy is comin' with her new boyfriend," Twila whispered as she set out chips and dip. Jemma sucked in a pout as Buddy B put on some records and she and Spencer started dancing. They were taking a break when The Cleave and her date arrived. Missy's dress was so low-cut that if she were to lean over, every male who knew what was good for him would shut his eyes. She went straight to Spencer and surprised him with an embrace and a pucker that landed right on his lips, not to mention that she had to lean over to do it. Her skirt was extra short to show off her drum majorette legs.

"Spence, how are you?" she purred. "I haven't seen you in forever. I heard that y'all were back together. How long do you think this will last? Here, meet Kent Hall, my fiancé. He's a medical student at UT.

We might get married sometime, or not," Missy said, shaking back her mane of lustrous blond hair. She looked Jemma up and down. "Hello, Jemmartsybeth. I see you're still going for the bohemian look and creeping across the tracks to find friends. How low can you go?"

"Well, I suppose I could call you one of my friends," Jemma said.

"I don't think so. We are like people who know each other, but would never be friends. . .you know that word. . .appli. . .admi."

"Acquaintances?" Kent said.

"Yeah, that's it. Here, take care of this."

Missy handed Jemma her black mouton jacket. Rather than hang it up, Jemma let it fall on the floor and stared daggers at Spencer.

He knew that look, and he would have to do something about it, quick. Buddy started the next stack of records.

The Cleave wasn't finished. "C'mon, Spence, let's dance, for old times' sake," Missy said, pulling him out of his chair like a loose tooth.

Jemma choked on her chip. By the time they were on the floor, she was fuming.

Spencer gave her a helpless look.

"I guess that leaves you and me." Kent offered his hand. Kent could certainly dance and Jemma took full advantage of it. "Devil with a Blue Dress On" was playing, and the two of them rocked. Jemma hoped that Spencer was watching, but she never looked at him to see. When the song was over, The Cleave was ready to go in for the kill, but Spencer's attention was on Jemma. Kent held on to her for "Wild Thing," and they were moving on when Spencer cut in. He was out to prove who was the better dancer and the luckiest man. When the song was over, he dragged Jemma into a bedroom. His shirt stank of Chanel No. 5. A skunk might as well have sprayed it as far as Jemma was concerned.

"I know what you're going to say, and you are absolutely right. I should have defended myself, okay? She tackled me, but you got me back good because I was dying while you danced with that guy. I got what I deserved."

"You give in to pushy women and even after what she said about Trina and Willa! Aren't you tough enough to resist the strong arms and loud mouth of The Cleave? You were the bigshot quarterback. Maybe Missy should've been on your team, and then we might have won more games. Don't try to make me smile, either." Out came the pout. After all, she had the lips for it.

"You know, she does remind me of a fullback. I think she's packed on about ten pounds since high school, don't you?" It was a nice pass, but not as well received as he would have liked.

"Why did you let her kiss you like that? Good grief."

"I knew she was leaning toward me, so I shut my eyes. I didn't see the kiss coming, baby."

After about ten minutes, he'd talked himself out of trouble and made her laugh. She was never any good after he got her tickled.

Buddy B probably did it on purpose to help Spencer, but their song was up next on the stereo. As soon as the harmonica played, everybody moved back. It was a tradition to let Jemma and Spencer start this one alone. Roy Orbison sang the first line of "Candy Man" and Spence curled his finger at Jemma, and their version of the Chillaton Stomp was rolling. The best part was when somebody said "umm-humm" low and soft on the record because Jemmabeth always sang that part along with the music and all the boys waited for that to happen. They still had the electricity, too. Spencer was forgiven. He could see it in her eyes. They ended with a kiss since there were no football coach chaperones in sight.

"You two are good together," Kent said at the punch bowl. "I think y'all must be in love."

"Yeah." Jemma watched Spencer talk to a group of laughing guys. "We've been in love for most of our lives."

"Time to get married then," Kent added as Missy yanked him away.

❧

Jemma and Spencer went to their parking spot at the river. They got their old quilts and climbed on the hood of the Corvette to watch the stars as they had done for years, no matter the season. They kissed, then leaned back on their arms.

"I'm really sorry about Missy tonight. I should have spoken up when she made the reference to Trina, too. That was pathetic of me."

"Yeah, well, I forgive you, but keep your guard up around her.

I know her better than you do."

"You said that I am a better Christian than you, but I've never made an effort to get to know anyone in Chillaton who's been treated like third-class citizens. That was you, Jem. I followed your lead."

"I've done nothing special. All I want is to make up for lost time and missed friendships. That's it."

They listened to the night sounds for a while, thinking about the past.

"Tell me why you always liked cowboys so much. I know those days are behind you, but I'm curious."

"Rats. I wish you'd forget all those times when Sandy and I flirted with the buckaroos on the Fourth. I don't know. Cowboys were like forbidden fruit, so I guess I was intrigued. They stood around like wild horses, pawing at the ground."

"Hmm. Why do you love the train tracks?"

She paused. "A long time ago, I used to pretend that the trains would only come if I danced on the rails. Sometimes I still feel that way. It's like a blank canvas before I touch it with my brush. The tracks just sit there, waiting for me to bring them to life."

He leaned on his elbow to look at her. "I know you have a thing about Missy, but she really did catch me off guard tonight."

"I suppose that after all I've put you through the last two years, dancing with The Cleave was a drop in the bucket." She grinned at him. "Just don't ever do it again."

They watched the heavens, but she couldn't help but remember a comment made to her in the ladies' room at a bar, of all places, about drinking from the devil's cup. She had no call to get high-and-mighty with him. "Spence," she said, reaching for his hand, "promise you'll never, ever leave me, no matter how bad I am."

He kissed her hand, palm up. "Promise already made."

Christmas Eve night, Lizbeth's house was packed and noisy. Lester played his harmonica, and Willa led Christmas carols in her booming voice. Spencer wanted to wait until Christmas Day to exchange gifts with Jemma, who had bought presents in Paris and was dying for him to open his. She'd found an ebony cuff link box that played "Yesterday," his favorite Beatles' song.

Christmas Day began, as always, with Robby waking Jemma up to dig in to her stocking before dawn. "No, Robby, not this year; have mercy. Wait two more hours," Jemma said into the pillow, but it was useless to try. He was using the bed as a trampoline. "Okay, okay. You're going to break this old thing."

"I got a magic set. Look." He showered the whole works on the bedspread.

She snickered at his attempts to do some of the tricks. "Merry Christmas, Robby," she said, giving him a peck on the cheek.

"Daddy says it's time for you and Spence to get married."

"Aren't you the little tattletale?" she asked, sitting up with her stocking.

"Show me what you got."

"Well, let's see. Here's a candy cane and another candy cane and another. What's the deal? It's full of them."

Robby made a face. "That's no fun. I like my magic set better," he said, running off to practice in the living room.

Jemma poured the stocking out on the bed. It was full of peppermint canes and a note at the bottom:

Meet me on the tracks at eight.
Always,
Your Candy Man

Racing to the kitchen window, she looked toward the tracks. The sun wasn't quite up, so she couldn't really see anything. She took a bath and heard the 6:23 Zephyr blow its horn. After changing clothes twice, she finally settled on her white turtleneck and a long paisley skirt and boots. She brushed her hair and checked herself out in the mirror. Not everybody could be blond and have a gigantic bosom.

She watched Robby practice his tricks. Her family got up and she set the table for breakfast, then began to pace. Papa's clock was about to chime as she went out the back door and walked up on the tracks. She didn't see him anywhere, but there was a box wrapped in gold foil paper and tied with a red ribbon in the middle of the cross ties. She opened it to find another note.

Look to the East.

She turned to see a handsome cowboy wearing a gray Stetson pushed back on his head, a long black duster, a red scarf at his neck, and shiny new boots. He was walking toward her.

"Spence?" She shaded her eyes.

He grinned. "Care to dance?" His eyes shone like sterling silver. She giggled at first as they danced down the tracks and back again to their phantom waltz. Eventually, the only sound was the shuffle of their feet on the wooden ties and packed earth. Their gaze was set on each other. The dancing stopped when Spencer took the blue velvet ribbon out of his pocket that Jemma had worn in her hair the day he told her that he wouldn't be back. He was back, and now the ribbon was threaded through a ring, the likes of which Jemma had never imagined.

Spencer put his Stetson on the ground and got on his knees. "Jemmabeth Alexandra Forrester, you mean more to me than my own life. I have loved you since the first time I saw you, and it's my life's joy just to be with you. The only way that I could be happier is if you would marry me. What say ye, Jemma?"

Jemma knelt with him and cried. It took her a minute to get her voice back. "Everybody knows that I don't deserve you, Spence. I realize that it's an honor being loved by you all these years, but it will be my life's greatest blessing to be your wife."

They kissed, amid tears and shouts of joy from Lizbeth's backyard and Willa's front porch.

Chapter 4
Murmurings

Peope she hadn't heard from since high school showed up to see her ring. It was as though they could all now move on with their lives because Spencer and Jemmabeth were getting married. Jemma considered that fact every time she looked at him. How did she ever get so involved with Paul? It must have been the way he twisted words around. Who was she kidding? It was his eyes. He had snake-charmed her. Rats on him. Nobody would ever come between Spencer and her again.

"The Ring," as Alex called it, was a rare, purple diamond set between radiant blue sapphires with a row of tiny white diamonds encircling the band. Spencer had had it made in Italy. Jemma didn't even know there were colored diamonds. Lester said it must have been hijacked from royalty.

"I want you to feel like you are at Sainte-Chapelle every time you look at it. It had to be extraordinary, like you," Spencer said as they sat on the floor in the cramped pouting room where Lizbeth used to go when she was upset with Papa. They kissed until they heard Jim and Alex in the kitchen, then emerged amid grins from her parents.

"Well, I guess we'll have to rename it the smooching room," Jim said.

Spencer blushed. "Sorry; we just needed to be alone."

"Why don't you kids go for a walk?" Alex asked. "We'll have supper ready by the time you get back."

"I want to help," Jemma protested. "I don't want to be called a princess or something."

"Off with you, Princess Jemma," Helene said, bursting into the room as she tucked her silver hair into a bun. Jemma loved the way she said her name—*Zhemma*. Helene winked at Spencer. "We have too many cooks in here already," she added. She and Lizbeth set to work on their latest culinary project.

Alex handed them their coats.

"When you get back, will you watch my magic show, Spence?" Robby asked. "I'll turn Jemma into a toad," he said, then escaped into the living room, laughing.

They walked across town to the park and sat on a chilly concrete picnic table. A rusty old pickup rolled past and honked. In the bed of the pickup was a blue spruce tree, lit up with Christmas lights. Shy Tomlinson, the driver, had grown the tree for decades in the dirt-filled back of his truck.

"Merry Christmas, Shy," they shouted. He yelled back, then turned the corner.

Jemma leaned on Spencer's shoulder. "Things are too perfect. It's like when the camera moves in behind the actor in a scary movie. I have this feeling that something bad is going to happen."

"It's just the season. They say that more people get down at Christmas than any other time."

"What do your parents say about us being engaged?"

"Well, Mother hasn't been sober long enough for me to tell her, and Dad slapped me on the back, then asked if we needed to have a little talk about the birds and the bees."

"Your mom hates me, Spence. Remember last New Year's Eve? She cussed at me for breaking up with you, and don't say it was only the liquor talking."

"None of that matters because it's just you and me now. I'm closer to Harriet than I am to my parents, anyway."

Jemma jumped off the table. "Then let's go see Harriet. She lives around here, doesn't she? I want somebody from your family to be as happy as we are."

Harriet O'Connor lived a block west of the park. She was a small woman with delicate features and a twinkle in her eye. She had a high, light voice, quite Irish. "Spencer and his lady," she said, untying her apron. "How good to see you. Are things all right at home? Your father gave me the holidays off, you know, but I did so want to see you two. How are you, Miss Jemmabeth?" She took their coats and served them pumpkin pie and cider.

"We wanted you to know our good news." Spence held Jemma's hand.

"Now, let me guess. I don't have to wonder too much since that stunning ring is on your finger, dearie," she said with a sweet smile. "My congratulations to the both of you." She embraced Spencer, then moved to Jemma, taking her hands. "Of course I always hoped that my boy would marry you, since that's all he's ever wanted, so now I can call you my girl, if that's all right."

"I would love that," Jemma said.

"Spencer is like my son, you know. My husband died in Korea and I never remarried. Taking care of Mrs. Chase and Spencer has been my life."

"Then you have outdone yourself," Jemma said.

"Well, I grew up on a ranch, and I tried to bring this boy up under the cowboy code. I think he's turned out to be a fine young man. You probably agree with me, don't you, my girl?"

Jemma beamed at him. "There is nobody finer in the world than your boy."

"I think I've heard about enough of all this," Spencer said. "We're supposed to be home by now."

"Do come back to see me, won't you, dearie? Spencer, I expect to see you tomorrow at your folks' place."

"I guess I'll be there," he said.

Harriet raised her brow at him.

Spencer closed the gate in front of Harriet's house as a '57 Chevy rolled past, then backed up. Wade Pratt stuck his head out. "Where's your 'Vette, Spence?" he asked, flicking cigarette ashes.

"I'm trying to get it in shape so I can take y'all on if I have to," Spencer said.

Dwayne Cummins, the driver, got out and came around to shake Spencer's hand.

"I see you've still got the most beautiful girl to ever come out of this town." Dwayne nodded toward Jemma. "I'm available, ma'am, if you ever need a backup."

Spencer laughed. "I know, I'm a lucky guy. How are you boys doing since you got out of the army? Are you still playing in Buddy B's band?"

Wade answered. "Shoot, yeah, but we could sure use your girl-friend's voice if you could spare her sometime."

Dwayne leaned against his car. "We tried to get on at the power plant. Leon Shafer's makin' some big bucks over there, but they ain't hirin' now. So, we've been doing this and that. Wade's been pumpin' gas at old man Sykes station, and I'm helpin' my daddy get in his crop. How about you? You still gonna be a. . .architecture or whatever you call it?"

"I'm working on it," Spencer said.

"Maybe you'll get famous someday and give us a job, you know, rememberin' the little people that helped you along," Wade added.

"Wade, you never did nothin' to help nobody along, unless you mean runnin' off good-lookin' women. . .am I right about that, Jemma?" Dwayne clicked his tongue at her, then turned to Spencer. "Me and Wade were about to whup up on old Chubs Ivey the other day for sayin' y'all was gettin' too thick with the coloreds."

Spencer scowled. "What do you think he meant by that?"

"Same thing everybody in town thinks. Y'all are overstepping the friendly churchgoer thing," Dwayne said. "Coloreds is coloreds, and whites is whites. That's the way God made us."

"We ain't agreein' with you or nothin'," Wade added quickly. "We just didn't want your good-lookin' girlfriend's name to be thrown around."

Jemma raised her chin. "I can take care of my own name, thank you. And skin color doesn't have anything to do with brain size or personality. Did y'all know that?"

"Now don't be pickin' on Wade 'cause he's got a small brain and a bad personality. He can't help it." Dwayne punched Wade's shoulder, then turned to Jemma. "You give us a call if you ever dump Spence."

"Yeah, I'll do that," Jemma said. These two yahoos had been flirting with her since she was in the seventh grade and her daddy was coaching them in high school football. Their claim to fame was that they hid in the high school boiler room one night in order to sneak into the social studies classroom and steal test answers. They used them the next day on their sophomore civics exam. The answers were to a senior world history test. What a pair.

Spencer, ever the diplomat, suggested they stop by to see him at his dad's business later in the week. "I've got to get Jemma home. Y'all take care."

"Tell Coach that we said howdy," Wade shouted as the '57 spun out.

Jemma and Spencer walked at a brisk pace to get home before dark.

"Do you think the whole town thinks like Chubs and those two?" Jemma asked.

"I don't really care, do you?"

"Nope. At least they didn't offer us a ride. My hair would've smelled like cigarettes for two days," Jemma said. "Hey, it's faster if we walk down the tracks."

"Let's go, then." Spence took off ahead of her.

"You were in the Gene Autry Club, weren't you?" Jemma asked, running to keep up.

"Yeah, and you were in Roy Roger's," he replied over his shoulder.

"Do you think that was the cowboy code that Harriet was talking about? I think it's funny that Harriet raised you by the cowboy code, then you looked so handsome when you proposed to me in your Western outfit, but you've never even been on a horse."

"Well, don't get your hopes up. That was a once-in-a-lifetime deal just for you, baby. Now come on, before the chuck wagon runs out of vittles and we miss the magic show." He took off in a sprint with Jemma, ever the competitor, close behind.

"I know, let's decorate a little tree and put it by old Shorty Knox's dugout. I bought some socks and gloves for him," she yelled. "I still owe him."

He grinned back at her, at his sweet love. "You bet. Someday, though, I'm building Shorty a real house."

⚜

Helene was due to return to her home in Wicklow. Jemma sat with her on the sofa in the living room.

"This has been delightful, my dear," Helene said. "Your parents are charming, and I would take little Robby home with me if they would allow it."

"Helene, could I stay with you again next year when I return to Le Claire?"

"Of course, dearest, I would like nothing more, but I assumed that you and Spencer would be getting married before then."

"I know. That's what we would like, but I promised Papa I wouldn't marry until I got my degree, and I always keep my promises."

"Have you discussed this with Lizbeth?"

"No, ma'am. It was a promise between Papa and me."

"From what I know about your papa, he was a compassionate man. To see you and Spencer together, dear, would surely have brought him great joy. One has to believe that he would advise to carry on with your wedding plans. Now, I must see your sketchbook. I do so regret that I was unable to come to the exhibition in Paris." Helene went over each page with her.

She left on the Zephyr that afternoon, headed to Dallas, a short drive from her home.

"Y'all come on," Jim shouted. "We're going out to the old home place, and Mama's driving!"

Robby cut short his magic show matinee, and they all piled into the Rambler.

"Now, let me get acquainted with this." Lizbeth frowned at the gearshift.

"It's easy, Mama. Just pull it down for forward and up for reverse," Jim said.

Lizbeth started the car. "The last time I took a group for a spin, the car ended up in the cemetery pond."

Alex giggled, but Jim gave his mother a dubious glance. She did fine, though, and soon pulled into the driveway of her old farmhouse.

"Boy, the house sure looks run-down, Mama. Why don't you lease it out and let the renter provide some maintenance?"

"I couldn't do that. Renters would just tear it up."

"Well, it couldn't look much worse than it does now," Jim said.

Alex and Jemma sat in the car while the rest went on an inspection tour of the place. "Your daddy is so happy for you, honey."

"He's happy for himself, too, Mom. He's always wanted me to marry Spence."

"Can you blame him?" Alex asked. "Tell me about living in Paris."

"It's different. I long to hear more English and eat Mexican food. I don't think I have picked up much French, but I love to hear it. I mostly paint and wait to see Spencer on the weekends. As far as my work goes, I know that I have grown as an artist because I see things with a different eye."

"We're concerned about Spencer getting drafted, Jem. Does he talk about it?"

"No, but surely that won't happen. What would they do with an architect in this thing that's not even called a war?"

Alex looked out at the harvested field. Scraps of the cotton still clung to the stalks. "I assume they would put a gun in his hands and push him out the door."

Jemma's face flushed at that thought. "Spencer is about the least aggressive person I know."

"That doesn't matter when Uncle Sam calls, sweet pea. Your daddy's brothers were gentle, sweet young men, too."

"Mom, don't say that. Look at what happened to them."

"I'm sorry, honey. I just have a bad feeling about this war."

The sun slipped behind a solitary cloud in the sky.

"I know," Jemma whispered.

⁂

"Well, baby girl, looks like I'm going to be walking you down the aisle soon, huh?" Jim pulled onto the highway, giving Lizbeth a rest from driving.

"I don't know, Daddy. I promised Papa that I wouldn't marry until I graduated from college."

"Well, Papa didn't know that you were going to drop out for a whole year like you did." Jim adjusted the rearview mirror.

"I painted the whole year, Daddy. That's how I made all that money from the show."

"Yeah, Jemma's loaded," Robby said, not even looking up from his comic book.

Jim pointed at her. "All I know is that you don't want to wait too long."

"What does that mean?"

"It means that Uncle Sam is going to be knocking on Spencer's door, baby girl. He'll be out of school and available," Jim said in a voice tinged with old pain.

"James," Lizabeth began, "the time that Jemmabeth stayed with me in Chillaton was a gift from the good Lord. It was part of His great plan for me and for her. I don't want any more talk that insinuates otherwise." Her voice was clear and strong. "Jemma, your papa loved you and he loved Spencer. If he concocted that promise, it was only because he wanted you to be a success. Look at what you have done with your art, sugar. He would be proud and satisfied. Of course he would want you to finish your degree, but he wouldn't want your hearts to suffer because of it. Married women go to school. There's too much pain in this old world as it is, for you to feel it coming from Papa's grave. He would want you to be happy. I know that for sure."

The rest of the way home, the only sound in the car came from Robby's comic book as he turned the pages.

❧

Lizbeth and Jemma sat on the bed in the side bedroom that was once a shed. Their long legs were drawn up under their chins, and their arms were folded around them.

"I read the Bible that you gave me every night, Gram, and I'm trying to let the Lord lead my life, honest."

"Memorize some verses, sugar. If you have them right up there in that pretty head of yours, they can carry you through hard times. I meant what I said in the car today. I know how you feel about promises, Jemmabeth, but this is one you can let go. I speak for your papa."

Jemma hugged her. "I miss you so much."

"I miss you, too. It'll be hard when everybody leaves. For some reason, an empty house gets me to thinking about the brevity of life. Now, don't tell your daddy that."

"You have Lester to cheer you up."

"Oh, he's a good man, but he's even older than I am and he'll be gone one of these days. I do have the trip with Julia to look forward to. I suppose it'll be good to see the boys' resting places."

"Gram, if Spencer gets drafted, I don't think I can stand it. Marty says that Vietnam is not like other wars. He says it's not a winnable war."

"You'll bear whatever comes your way, sugar. You're a strong woman. It's in our Jenkins's blood. Let's not dwell on this war talk. You should be thinking about wedding dresses and such. You may need Julia to manage things for you. She knows all the right people."

"Did you know that Do Dah, I mean. . .Julia, came to my show the second week? She was disappointed that all the paintings on display were already sold. She's so much fun. Everybody has us planning the wedding, and Spencer and I haven't even had a chance to discuss anything."

"Well, you'll have lots of time to talk about it on that plane ride over the ocean. Oh, I do dread that."

"I love you, Gram. You're always in my prayers."

"It's the same with me, sugar. Now, let's see what's going on in the kitchen."

❦

"Baby girl, I'm sorry if I came down on you too hard yesterday," Jim said as the Rambler idled in the driveway, ready for their trip home to Arizona. He hugged her to him. "I just want you and Spence to be happy and have a good life. I wish Matt and Luke could've had that. I think Mama is right, though; Papa wouldn't hold you to the promise. You were probably ten years old when you made it anyway."

"Actually, Daddy, it was the year he died, so I was almost seventeen. I think that's part of my problem. I made him that promise, and he died the next week. It's hard for me to let it go."

Jim held his daughter's shoulders and looked her in the eye. "Papa didn't know there was a war coming where boys like his own would give up their free will and go fight. You can explain yourself to Papa in heaven, Jem, but you have to grab this blessing of a happy life while you can get it."

Jemma nodded and stared at the floor, but if she didn't keep this promise, then what good were others she had made in her life?

She held Robby in her lap for as long as she could, even though he was half asleep. Alex cried with her, and then they were gone, just as though they had never come. But they had come, and her life's direction was taking a joyous turn, straight to Spence. Jemma couldn't shake off the melancholy from the change, though, nor could she shed the thought that her Candy Man might leave her to go carry a gun. Roy Rogers had guns in his pretty holster, but it was only to wing the bad guys, not to kill or be killed.

⇜≋⇝

Buddy B took them to the airport because it was snowing and Spencer didn't want just anybody driving. Buddy ran Chase's tow service, too, in a four-wheel-drive truck. Today he had a full load of people.

"Hope y'all don't mind Dwayne and Wade hitchin' a ride," Buddy apologized. "Dwayne's car broke down in Amarillo and they need to pick it up."

Wade snickered. "Y'all two lovebirds probably wanted to be left alone, huh?"

"This is fine with us. Jemma will just have to sit in my lap." Spencer winked at her as they all crammed into the front seat.

"Your daddy had to fire Wade's little brother last week," Dwayne said.

"Yeah, they don't come any dumber than him." Wade cleaned his teeth with a guitar pick. "Buddy got him a job washin' and polishin' the cars on the lot, but the genius took a nap in one of 'em. Your daddy was showin' it to some old people and they opened the door on him, snorin'. Like to have scared 'em to death."

Dwayne shook his head. "Old people get scared too easy."

"Not them old people—he scared my brother. Remember that time we shut him up in your locker and he lit a cigarette while he was in there?" Wade snorted at the memory.

"Yeah, yeah." Dwayne slapped his leg. "The principal saw smoke coming out of the locker and called the fire department."

"He lit up all your biology cheat notes. That's what was making most of the smoke."

"That makes me wanna light up." Dwayne reached for his cigarettes.

"Not in my truck, you don't," Buddy B said and turned up the radio. Jemma was more than glad to sit in Spencer's lap even if it had meant stinky, cigarette-smoke hair.

⇜≋⇝

On the flight to Paris, they talked at last.

"We don't have to rush, Jem. If you want to keep your promise, we'll wait."

"You and I are the only ones who feel that way. I didn't listen to anybody's advice about us last year and I'll regret that forever. I want to marry you on this plane," she said. "I just feel funny about Papa."

"And I want you to have the wedding you've always talked about. I would marry you in Shorty Knox's dugout, but whatever you decide is fine with me. You think you're the lucky one; wrong. I am that person."

She kissed him behind the airline emergency instructions card. "Let's get married this summer." She got goose bumps just saying the words.

Spencer grinned and shoved his fists in the air. "Yes!" he yelled, causing a stir among the passengers. It was the only excitement on the whole flight. . .for them, at least.

<hr />

She was jet-lag weary, but she had to at least start the painting. She'd missed the smell of the studio and the light that poured in from everywhere. She found the largest canvas in the workroom and put the base coat on it. It was a luminous palette with the sun bursting up from the vanishing point of the tracks. She sketched him in with life-sized proportions. His hands were on his hips, the long fingers curved slightly. She didn't need a sketch for reference. Every detail remained in her heart.

The night janitor was arriving just as she had the basics done. She stood back and the janitor joined her. He smiled and nodded toward the painting. "Zee Duke?"

Jemma laughed, assuming he meant John Wayne. "No, it's my own cowboy."

He shrugged and went about his business. Jemma yawned and held her hand up to see his ring of love sparkle in the studio lights.

<hr />

Spencer wanted to show her Florence, but she was still nervous about another encounter with Miss Completely Gorgeous. He assured her that Michelle was after a new guy, an Italian. Jemma stayed with the Grasso family at night and with him all day. Listening to him as a tour guide was all she wanted to do, but the city was distractingly beautiful. Spencer rented a car so they could see the countryside and so he could try out his new travel rod and reel. As they drove alongside the River Arno, he found a spot he liked.

"I've wanted to fish this river ever since I came here," he said.

"I don't have to clean them, do I?"

"Nah, I'll let them go."

"Do you want me to wait in the car?"

"Are you kidding? You are going to be my good-luck charm."

Even so, she followed him at some distance, remembering her daddy's admonitions to "stay back" when she went fishing with him. Spencer walked quickly through the narrow meadow that ran down to the river. She loved the way he moved, like he was in high school again, keeping the ball and running across for a touchdown. How did she ever even think of loving anybody else?

To see him from afar, independent of her, and so focused on the moment at hand, gave her a peek at his life all those months with Michelle. A sudden weight in her chest changed her breathing. Guilt. Her eyes filled with tears. Those were lost months that she could have been sharing his sweet company instead of making him wait. Rats.

A few grazing cattle raised their heads as Spencer passed. Jemma clamped her hand over her mouth when he slipped at the river's edge, but at least he didn't fall in. Rising up from the wet mass of undergrowth, he threw out a practice cast. There was a soft whirring of his reel and then the lure floated perfectly in the water. Jemma climbed a small knoll to watch. He lifted the rod a little and she could see his shoulders and biceps tense up, then relax through his shirt. Did he ever go fishing with Michelle? Or for a long walk? Did he kiss her four or five times in a row? Double rats. All her fault.

He reeled in the line, then cast it again. No sooner than the hook broke the surface, it was grabbed by a gray, splashing streak. A tug at the line brought the realization that a fish was ready for a fight.

"Got one," he yelled. In a flash of energy, he swept the rod and line upward and toward the bank. The fish lurched out of the water, then back in again. He repeated the move while taking the slack out of the line. This time it worked. The fish lay just beyond his feet, glinting and flopping in the sunlight. Spencer was breathless but smiled up at her. He dangled his catch before him. Jemma wiped at her tears, then applauded and whistled. This would become a painting, for sure. He tossed the fish back into the water and motioned for her to join him. After he washed his hands in the river, he kissed her.

She covered her nose. "You smell like a fish."

"Yeah, it's great, isn't it?"

She turned to the water and reached in her pocket. "There," she said, plunking a small pebble into the Arno. "From Chillaton to Italy, with love."

❧

They visited the American cemetery just outside Florence where her uncle Matthew was buried. Without Spencer's encouragement, she wouldn't have made it to see his grave, one of many in the rows of white crosses. It was too sad. They laid a bouquet of flowers on it and stood in silent prayer for her daddy's gentle big brother and all the others laid to rest so far from home. Jemma could only think of her great-grandfather's Bible with Matthew's study notes tucked inside, and the yellowed telegrams sent to Papa and Gram telling them of their sons' deaths. She could not imagine enduring that pain. She squeezed Spence's hand extra hard.

❧

Jemma sat in the Grassos' conservatory, much like Helene's in Wicklow, eating Italian ice cream.

"I've never tasted anything like this in my life," she said with a mouthful.

Spencer grinned. "It's like your kisses—sweet and habit-forming."

She gave him The Look, cutting her eyes in his direction, then turning her head to look at him.

"Hey, when are the ladies coming from Texas?" he asked.

"In April. Oh, and Helene is coming, too."

"That's going to be hilarious. Do Dah will be bossing Gram around, and the others will be trying to keep peace. Willa is going to have the time of her life."

"I almost forgot. Sandy and Martin want us to meet them somewhere. Do you have time to travel?"

"You are the one with the big art show coming up. Are you ready?"

"Of course I am. What do you think I've been doing until midnight every night? Sandy wants to get away, and Marty has a few weeks coming up so they want to meet us in Brussels. I think his folks sent them some money. He's about to get shipped out to Vietnam and the military is giving him some time off. Big gift, huh?"

"Brussels it is. I'll fly to Paris and we'll go together."

Jemma and Sandy had been friends since they were toddlers. Sandy was always on the honor roll and won the state typing contest and the Sew It with Wool contest their senior year. Sewing with wool in cotton country didn't get much respect, but Sandy's parents kept her trophy on their mantle even after she got married. Jemma always thought that Sandy resembled her final doll that Santa had brought: pale skin, blond hair, hazel eyes, and extra-long lashes. She was famous for her makeup that she had been allowed to wear since the sixth grade. It was fun to see it smear during basketball games. Due to that fact, Sandy wouldn't put out the extra bit of hustle that could keep her a spot on the starting squad. They never talked about the makeup, though. It was one of those things friends let go about one another.

Martin was in the best shape he'd been in since high school. He was a stocky gorilla guy with curly hair. His brown eyes, normally looking for trouble, seemed to have lost their zip. He'd been in and out of dilemmas in high school and was rarely in good standing with Sandy's family. He was two years older than Spencer, but they had played sports together, at least when Martin was not on probation with the coach for one thing or another.

Sandy squealed when she saw The Ring and the girls giggled like they were in elementary school again. They spent the day touring the city. Spencer and Jemma were engrossed in the art and architecture. Sandy and Martin were happy being off the base. The girls practically had the wedding planned by nightfall. As if Jemma needed any help.

"So, are you guys, you know, going to stay in the same room tonight?" Sandy asked at supper.

"Hey, that's their business." Martin shot her a hard look.

"Well, I just wondered since you are way over here on another continent. Nobody would know or care." She shrugged. "Unless you're still keeping your junior-high vow of celibacy. You are, aren't you! Cheezo, y'all are grown-ups now, in case you haven't noticed."

Spencer took Jemma's hand. "It's our choice, Sandy. It's all about anticipation." He kissed Jemma right in front of them, and it was no junior-high peck.

"Spence, are you going to call on some of your family's old friends in D.C. to get a deferment when you graduate?" Martin asked, clearing the moment, but with a suspicious eye.

"I'll take whatever comes my way. I don't want to, but I will."

"Man, this southeast Asia mess scares me," Martin said. "I'm just hoping to come out of it alive."

Sandy frowned. "I don't want to talk about it. I want to go dancing. Have you been running the bulls anymore, Jem?" She never did know when to shut up.

Jemma bugged her eyes at Sandy. "Not recently," she said through clenched teeth. "Actually, I gave it up for my own cowboy." She batted her eyelashes at Spencer.

"Spence's no cowboy," Sandy said. "Anyway, let's go somewhere and watch Jemma get crazy."

They found a discothèque playing British pop music. Jemma and Spencer got going and couldn't stop. "You Really Got Me" by the Kinks was blasting out when Sandy and Martin decided to join them on the dance floor. Jemma had observed a few things about disco dancing and was springing them on Spencer. He already knew them, making her wonder about Michelle again. The four of them were representing Chillaton quite well, so well, in fact, that an overexuberant French tourist cut in to dance with Jemma. He was singing along, in loud French. Spencer cut back in front of him, shouting over the music, "*Prends ta proper femme, celle-ci est la mienne prenez votre proper femme.*"

"What did you say to that guy?" Jemma yelled. "How did you get so good at French for a CHS graduate?"

"I told him he had a nice voice."

"You did not. I caught one of those words."

"I told him to find his own wife, that you are mine."

"I don't recall us getting married yet, big boy."

"It happened the first time we kissed, baby. The deal was sealed."

They slept in separate rooms and Sandy never gave up talking about it, either. She wasn't known as the class blabbermouth for nothing. The next morning was cold and rainy, so they headed for the museums.

Sandy whispered in Jemma's ear at lunch, "Jem, pray for Marty and me, and not just about Vietnam." She drew back and said in a perky voice, "I'll be coming back to Chillaton, so I guess I'll see you there. I can help you with the wedding. What's the timeline?"

Jemma gave her the schedule and a perplexed look. "Spence graduates in the middle of May, but my term isn't over until June. The wedding is at the end of July."

"The hottest time of the year in Texas?"

"That's the only time Daddy can get off. He has one weekend between the high school football camps he hosts and his own college fall training camp. Don't worry; it will be a morning wedding, before it gets too hot." She didn't mention that it would be early enough that Sandy's makeup wouldn't run.

"Pray for us. Don't forget," Sandy said when the guys were paying the bill. "Marty's not himself these days."

Actually, Jemma thought he was a good deal nicer. "I will pray for y'all, I promise, but you practice keeping a civil tongue for our wedding. No more talk about sleeping together and running the bulls. Got it?"

"Yes, ma'am," Sandy said.

Only two weeks to go before the Academie's spring exhibition. She'd sold three more paintings since the opening exhibition in the fall and was saving that money for the wedding. Most of the pieces for the spring show were portraits of people she didn't know personally but had seen on the streets between her apartment and the Academie. There were twelve paintings in all. Her favorite, of course, was of Spencer on the tracks. *My Cowboy* she had named it. After their trip to Brussels, she painted her second favorite, a watercolor of Sandy and Martin sitting on a bench—Sandy leaning on his shoulder and Martin in uniform. Marty was hunched over, arms on his knees and hands clasped, staring at the ground.

Another was of two small children feeding pigeons below the rose window of Notre Dame. She worked through Friday night on a watercolor of Spence fishing in the River Arno, then she was done. They were due at the gallery the next morning, so she went home for a couple of hours of sleep, repeating a Bible verse as she walked. She was trying to memorize scriptures, like Gram had suggested, by Easter. She'd learned eight so far, unlike when she was in vacation Bible school and could learn two or three a day. She said her prayers, wound the music box, and went to bed. Spencer would be on the first flight out of Florence in a few hours to help transport the paintings.

❦

"I'm having weird feelings about this show," she said to Spencer. "Some sort of anxiety about you, like at the fall show, I guess, when I thought I'd never see you again."

"Ah, but this time I will be here before the doors open. There will be no drama, just art," Spencer said as they wrapped her last painting for the trip to the gallery.

"Spence, I want to send Trina to design school. I have been putting money aside for her, but she would have a hissy fit if she knew. How can I do it so she won't know?"

He smiled. "You're always surprising me. We'll figure something out."

Spencer watched her at the gallery, talking with the staff. Her conversations were animated, like an Italian's. The way she closed her eyes when she laughed, which was often, enchanted him. It always had. She could be stubborn one minute and then give in completely the next. He knew her better than she knew herself. He could have told the gallery manager that the portrait of her cowboy would have to be the focal piece. Jemma was not budging on that point. The manager wanted a painting of two elderly women laughing on a park bench in that spot, but Jemmabeth won. She usually did when it came to her work. The cowboy piece was too near her heart. Spence just hoped it wouldn't hang in their living room

344

someday with a spotlight on it. He had only bought that Western stuff to make her smile and maybe get it out of her system at last, but that procedure could be a challenge. When Jemma was six years old, her papa had given her a pair of red cowboy boots. She had worn them every day for a year, even when they pinched her toes. Now she used them to hold her brushes. Spencer wondered if she would ever recover from cowboy fever.

He had decided a long time ago that watching her move was even better than watching her talk. She walked with such grace and self-confidence, probably because she was a dancer at heart. Her hair swung when she walked, and she was constantly looking around for something new to paint. Seeing her dance, though, was the ultimate. Movement came to her like her art—smooth, creative, and elegant in detail. It wasn't provocative; it was captivating. He knew all the guys liked watching her when she danced, too, but they knew better than to say it around him. He had missed her so much that to be with her now and to enjoy her company without giving himself to her was maddening, but that was the way it was going to be. He didn't know how he would feel toward any other woman. He had never had the desire to find out, nor did he care. Jemmabeth Forrester was worth waiting for.

She wore a purple silk dress to match her ring of love, the sweet pea earrings, and heart necklace, all gifts from Spence. Once again, the art patrons of Paris were delighted by her work. She was the most talked about artist in town. Her work was "in." Every piece, except the one of Spencer, which was reserved, sold to high bids. The total came to over eight thousand American dollars. Jemmabeth was amazed that people would pay that kind of money for her art, but she was glad of it since she had two more projects to fund. She explained them to Spencer as they sat in her favorite bakery for breakfast.

"I'll never forget the look on Willa's face when we came out of the storm cellar and their church was nothing but scattered splinters and rubble. This money is going to repair some of the pain caused by that tornado. When the new church is done, I want to build a chapel onto the old rest home in honor of Kenneth Rippetoe. Remember how he wanted to run a nice nursing home? At least the chapel will smell good and it will be a place of hope."

Spencer sighed. "What a way to go—in a tornado. I'll have some time in May and June to finish up the design for the church and then I'll get started on the chapel. Have I ever told you how much I like you?"

"Yup, but I like you more. You're my hero. Remember?" She melted him with a smoldering, movie-star kiss.

"Are you sure your dad can't get off any sooner than the end of July?" he asked, out of breath.

"You told me that you liked the wait," she said, giving him The Look. That was one of the best things about Paris. Nobody cared if you kissed like crazy anytime, anywhere. And they did.

Chapter 5
Reckonings

Lizbeth settled into Cam's chair. She moved her fingers over the worn patches of maroon velvet where his arms had rested. They had bought it just before Pearl Harbor and their plan was to save up for the matching sofa. The war helped them decide to use the money for Matthew's seminary fund instead. Cam would like it that she was taking this pilgrimage to the graves. It never occurred to her that she might fly across the ocean, but she'd learned to drive last spring, hadn't she? Still, she had no idea how she could get on a plane and stay on it for more than a minute. Julia would be watching her, though, and despite the fact she had raised her like a daughter, Julia remained her little sister and a teaser. Flying was for birds, but then surely the good Lord wouldn't have given the idea for humans to build airplanes if He didn't approve. Julia had said she could give her a pill to go to sleep. Perhaps, then, they could carry her on like a suitcase.

❧

"Miz Liz?" Lester shouted from the back door.

"I'm at the front of the house," she yelled back, adjusting her hat. Her bags were packed and on the porch.

Lester was in his Saturday khakis. "We'd better get along to Miz Johnson's. Is this all you're taking? I thought you were gonna be over there two weeks."

"That's none of your concern, Mr. Timms. You just make sure that Cam's flowers get watered and my ivy doesn't die. I'm expecting an important letter in the mail, too, so take care with it."

"Yes, ma'am," he said, recognizing her tone as one not to be trifled with.

They picked up Willa and Trina, who had even less luggage than Lizbeth. Lester chattered the whole hour to a solemn audience. Silence prevailed in the waiting area at the Amarillo airport, too.

"So you'll pick up the rest of your bunch in Dallas?" Lester asked, hoping for some kind of conversation.

"Yes, sir," Trina obliged. "Helene and Do Dah will meet us there."

"Well, all I know is that when you ladies step off that plane, it's gonna look like heaven has done taken itself a recess."

"How's that, Lester?" Trina asked.

"Why, 'cause all the best angels will be vacationing in It-ly." He grinned. He had been waiting to pull that one all morning. A wobbly chuckle made its rounds with the ladies.

Lizbeth remained in continual prayer before takeoff. She tried deep breathing like Jemmabeth had recommended. Willa and Trina were like swivel-headed owls. Trina had made them both several new outfits for the trip. They looked good, but that was of little consequence to their jitters.

A stewardess, pasted-on smile intact, came by to assess their anxiety level. "It's a perfect day for flying, and our pilot has twenty years' experience."

"Doin' what?" Willa asked, making Lizbeth and Trina shake with laughter.

It was a good start to uneventful flights. Lizbeth even managed to look out the window a few times. She closed her eyes and tried to visualize a field of white crosses by the Mediterranean Sea, and another field near a wooded hillside in Italy. Jemma had been there with Spencer and she said it was beautiful. Even if Lizbeth survived these airplanes, she feared she might not hold up to those fields of white.

The five of them, wilted and weary, stepped away from customs.

"I don't know about you ladies, but I need me some food," Willa said.

Trina rolled her eyes. "Mama, you just ate on the plane."

"Nobody could make a meal outta them scraps." Willa eyed a pastry shop in the Rome airport.

"Do Dah, how far are we from Nettuno?" Trina asked.

"About forty miles. Remember, I'm only answering to Julia on this trip."

Lizbeth exhaled. "I am so glad to have my feet on the ground. I was getting restless there toward the end."

"But you made it, dearest. I knew you would," Helene said.

Julia put on her glasses and took a list out of her purse. "Here's the plan. We eat something, grab a short nap, then we'll do a quick tour of Rome."

"Now just hold on, Miz Julia," Willa said. "I don't do nothin' quick. My caboose will only go so fast." She patted her behind.

"Mama and I'll do what we can," Trina said. "Y'all just go on."

Helene raised a brow. "Nonsense. We shall take a cab to all the sights, and you may move about at your own pace, dear."

"That's right. Nobody is going to be left behind. We are the five musketeers," Julia shouted, gathering their hands.

"Are you talkin' about them Mickey Mouse kids?" Willa asked. "I ain't wearin' no funny hat," she said, adjusting her own Sunday best that had gone askew on the flight.

They checked into a lavish hotel overlooking Rome, courtesy of Julia and Helene. Trina felt like she had stepped into a movie, and Willa thought she had stepped into heaven. Lizbeth commented it was way too extravagant, but enjoyed the fuss over the least little thing. She was ready, though, to get on with the reason for the trip.

They barely fit into the cab that was to take them to the Sicily-Rome American Cemetery. Helene spoke fluent Italian so there was no trickery on the fares with the taxi drivers. Upon arrival, Julia and Trina went to ask the location of the grave. Willa was already breathing hard.

"Are you doing all right?" Lizbeth asked as she put her arm around Willa's broad shoulders.

"Would water help, dear?" Helene asked.

"No, ma'am," Willa said, her voice breaking. "I just need that man who's out there somewhere in this I-talian dirt. The closer I get to him, the bigger my hurt."

Lizbeth turned away and closed her eyes. Willa's pain would soon be her own. Already, she could feel it tugging at her heart. The dread of those crosses with her sweet boys' names on them was strong. Trina and Julia returned, cemetery map in hand.

"Are you ready, Mama?" Trina asked quietly.

"I'm as ready as I'm gonna get, child. Your daddy's been waitin' long enough for us to say a prayer over him. Let's go." Willa and Trina moved slowly along the path to the main group of graves. Trina looked over her shoulder at Lizbeth.

"Oh my." Helene drew a deep breath. "What we do to one another in times of war."

"Jemmabeth did a fine thing, arranging it so they could come here," Julia said.

Lizbeth walked to the edge of the path, shading her eyes to see them. They had stopped, most likely to let Willa rest.

Helene and Julia went for a walk in the garden, leaving Lizbeth alone on the bench. She could barely see Willa and Trina, but she could see plain enough that they were at his cross. She couldn't help but cry, knowing how Willa must feel at the sight. Trina would weep, too, even though she had never chopped weeds out of some white man's cotton with him or pulled a lead-heavy sack of the stuff down a row next to him until their fingers bled from the burrs. Lizbeth was afraid that when it was her turn to say prayers and touch the letters in the stones, her façade might crumble and she herself would come completely undone.

They were there for a couple of hours, but nobody cared about the time. It was Italy and it was a glorious day, despite the sadness. Julia had convinced Lizbeth to walk with them to the museum. It was a place of honor paid to lives lost, but never forgotten.

When Trina and Willa rejoined them, it was Helene who greeted them first, arms outstretched. "My friends, please know that no one will ever forget what your Samuel did for freedom in that hideous war."

Willa wiped her face on a well-used handkerchief and Trina stared at the path. "Yes ma'am," Willa said. "I ain't never been one to question the good Lord's business, but I sure wish He would've took me before He took my man." Her lip quivered. "I guess, though, my Latrina wouldn't be here, would she? Sam never got to see our baby. He wrote to her but never got to hold her."

Lizbeth put her arms around them. "Bless you," was all she could say.

"We'll be staying in the village tonight, Willa, so that y'all can come back this evening and again in the morning, if you've a mind to," Julia said.

"Thank you, Miz Julia; I'll do that."

❧

Lizbeth withdrew from the rest of the group on the long train ride to Sicily. Julia wanted them to fly, but she was voted down. Trina and Helene read while Willa napped. Julia sat by her sister, holding her hand. They took a boat from Palermo, Sicily, to Tunis, on the tip of Tunisia in Africa. How odd, thought Lizbeth, to float on waters that the apostle Paul had traveled. She recalled that he was in Malta, below Sicily, and Syracuse, before traveling to Rome. She had taught about his journeys in Sunday school. Surely his eyes must have looked upon some of the very same Mediterranean coastline, and she took some comfort in that.

❧

The American Military Cemetery in Carthage overlooked the sea. The seabirds dipped and called around the fountains. It was a beautiful, serene place. They went first to the visitors' center, then Lizbeth and Julia walked to the first white cross of their journey.

Lizbeth clenched the paper. How peculiar it was to need a map in order to find her baby with the bright blue eyes of his papa. She read it again:

S Sgt Luke J. Forrester, Plot D, Row 1, Grave 8.
68th Bomber Squadron, 44th Bomber Group, Heavy.

It listed all those medals that she had kept in the Soldier Box. When the telegram came to them on that hot August morning in 1943, it was the beginning of the pain that had shut her heart to grief. She had promised to stand with Cameron through everything, but he had left her to walk this hard row without him. Julia was beside her now, holding her arm like Jimmy did when Cameron died.

The briny scent of the Mediterranean wafted on the cool breeze. Only a few hours earlier, she had been on the deck of a ferry with that wind in her face, dreading this passage. She considered for a moment that the salty air would eat away at his name over the years. Lizbeth read each cross as they walked, thinking it might soften the sight of his. There were no references to birthdays or carefully worded sentiments, only names, numbers, states, and dates of passing. All were equal in death.

Julia's arm twitched when they reached it. A sudden calm spread over Lizbeth and she knelt, feeling the warmth of the earth under her. She traced the letters in his name with her finger, to make them her own doing, and then embraced the cool marble. Julia stood over her, crying. Lizbeth could not weep the day that telegram came, but now tears fell from her chin in clusters. He was her artist—nothing like Jemma, but good enough.

His mischief had often caused her to hide her laughter as best she could in order to discipline him. He was much too handsome for his own good, and the girls had chased after him in a time when it wasn't done. All that love and joy bundled up and sent to Europe to die in the clouds. It had to be a part of God's Great Plan, as her own father had said in his sermons. Luke and Matthew were born to give their lives in the name of liberty.

She reached for Julia's hand. Her baby sister had helped them keep their sanity when the boys had died and was with her now, within six feet of one of them. She drew a long breath. "Will you pray with me, Julia?"

Julia got on her knees beside her.

"Father God, I give my son, Luke Jenkins Forrester, into Your holy hands, at last. I trust he is as much a joy to You in heaven as he was to us on this earth. Thank You for allowing his papa and me to love him for a while. Amen, sweet Jesus."

Lizbeth took an old pill bottle out of her purse. She removed the lid and fished out a slip of paper. Clearing her throat, she read as her father had done at the pulpit, "From the book of Luke, chapter 11, verse 36, 'If thy whole body therefore be full of light, having no part dark, the whole shall be full of light, as when the bright shining of a candle doth give thee light.'" She rolled it up and replaced it in the bottle, snapping the lid.

Moving back the grass with her slender fingers, she dropped the bottle between the base of the cross and the earth. It was Luke's scripture. It was the one that she and Cam had picked for him before he was born, and it should remain with him in this foreign land. She dusted her hand and stood, with Julia's help, then kissed her fingertips and touched the cross. He was their bright candle. "Come, Julia," she whispered, "I have nothing left to give this place."

⟨◊⟩

Lester reshuffled the papers. He had not planned on so much work for himself. Nobody ever asked him such questions. Everybody in three counties knew he was a Democrat. What in the Sam Hill did that have to do with getting a wife? He looked at her photo again. She sure was a beauty. Maybe the Republicans that ran the magazine would switch her out with somebody on the homely side, seeing his strong stance in the Democrat Party. No, surely even a Republican wouldn't pull that kind of business.

There couldn't be any harm in a man his age taking on a new wife. He laid down his pen and went to the front porch to sit a spell. Miz Liz's petunias looked better than usual. She had been his hope for a companion. That dear woman would have been his crowning glory, but he couldn't see clear how to make her turn his way. She was still set on Cam, her dearly departed. Lester had tried every trick he knew, too. He wanted someone to cozy down with at night, but that was never going to happen with her. The closest he had ever come to even touching her was when she almost slipped on the ice getting out of the car at Nedra's Nook. Even then, she had grabbed the door handle and not his arm. No sir, it was going to have to be a foreigner, a woman who came in the mail, just like his pension check.

He went to the pantry. He had stocked up on pork 'n' beans, Vienna sausage, Spam, and canned tamales. He grabbed himself a handful of store-bought cookies. That was the best he could do since Lizbeth was over to Europe. He hoped that foreigners ate baked goods and that this woman knew how to make them. Maybe he'd give Tillie Shepherd a call and order some fancy Avon perfume as a welcome present for his bride-to-be. He poured himself a glass of cold milk and resumed his paperwork with fresh vigor. The advertisement said eight to ten weeks and he would be in matrimony once again. It had to be better than cuddling up to a now-absent chinchilla.

❧

"Spence, where are you?" Jemma pressed the phone to her ear. "I can barely hear you."

"I'm about to leave Venice. I just wanted to say hello. Are you sure you can't come?"

"I can't, babe, my class leaves in the morning for Giverny, and I am required to go. Do Dah called and said they will meet you in Florence tonight. I talked to Gram about it, and I think she's okay. I'm so sorry."

"Don't worry. I'll take care of her. You have fun in Monet's garden. I know you've always wanted to see it. Be sure and throw a Chillaton pebble in his lily pond. I'll miss you this weekend."

"I miss you right now. Is Michelle with you?"

"Jem, she's in the same program with me. Don't worry. She has a boyfriend. All she does now is give me dirty looks."

"Tell her the shick says hello. No! Don't talk to her."

He laughed, and she did love it when she could make him laugh. She closed her eyes and thought she could smell his aftershave.

❧

Willa did not know that such beautiful things existed as she had already seen in Europe, but she wasn't quite sure if she liked them. "Them statues is all so old. These I-talians need to get some new stuff. I sure did like that big David, though. He's my kind of man."

"Mama." Trina giggled along with the rest of the group as they waited in the Piazza.

"Spencer said five o'clock, and it's five thirty," Julia said, always the dutiful guide.

Lizbeth wasn't worried. "He had to rent a car and drive from Venice. His class has been studying there."

"Looks like they could just go to the library. Ain't that what it's for?" Willa asked.

Helene liked all of Willa's jokes. She knew Willa was a sharp cookie behind all that kidding around. "There he is now." Helene waved.

Spencer gave each lady a good hug. He was the darling of the evening. They ate at a bistro and finished with the gelato that Jemma so relished.

Lizbeth walked with him as they headed back to their hotel. "Son, would you go with me tomorrow? Julia doesn't think she can. She was very close to Matthew and took it real hard when he left us."

"Yes ma'am, it'll be an honor," Spencer said.

Lizbeth sighed. "Since Tunisia, I know what's coming."

Spencer put his arm around her. He was a strong young man. Maybe he could hold her up when she had to face the cross of her firstborn.

⁂

A steady drizzle accompanied them as they rode to the cemetery. Julia sat in the backseat, silent. Lizbeth could not remember a time when her sister had spoken as little as she had in the last twelve hours. It had rained the day they buried their father, too. Matthew was so like him. Her boys were all tall like their grandpa, but it was their grandmother who had given Matthew and Jimmy their golden eyes. Matthew had gotten his degree on a basketball scholarship, and his plan was to enter the seminary when the war was over. She still had all his Bible study notes at home. His fiancée had her teaching degree, the wedding plans were set, but God's plan was otherwise.

It was a short trip from Florence to the impressive gates of the cemetery. Just as Jemmabeth had said, it truly was a field of white, like cotton ready for harvest. Lizbeth gripped her Sunday purse. Matthew had spent every summer helping Cam in the fields. He had come home from college on weekends during the picking season to help get the crop in. Acres of solid white could mean a bale and a half of cotton to the acre, making life a little easier through the rest of the year. This sight, however, turned her stomach. The windshield wipers came to a sudden stop as Spencer turned off the engine at the car park. "I'll stay here for a while, Lizbeth; you two go on ahead," Julia said.

"Are you sure, Do Dah?" Spencer asked.

"I'm sure," she said, not correcting her nickname.

Spencer came around to Lizbeth's door with the umbrella. The map was easy to follow. They walked for about five minutes, then stopped at his row. She shivered and turned away toward the lush crepe myrtles, heavy with sodden blooms, along the path. Matthew had brought her a bouquet of pink cotton blossoms when he was old enough to know that girls liked flowers. She never saw another one without thinking of him. Walking out from under the umbrella, she broke off a cluster of blossoms from a bush. The grass was standing in water. Every step they took splashed up on her legs and the cuffs of Spencer's trousers.

Lizbeth saw his name on the cross before she realized how far they'd gone. It didn't help at all that she had seen Luke's grave already. The choking sound that had rolled up through her almost a year ago, when she had first been able to weep over her boys, rose again.

Spencer dropped the umbrella and covered her with his raincoat. She laid her head on his shoulder and wept for gentle Matthew. She'd had this dear child inside her before she'd really understood about life. With him, she came to know the sting of birth and the joy of mothering. Without him and his brother, she had come to endure all the dark sorrow a mother's heart can stand without giving out altogether. She had nursed them from her own body, only for them to become warriors, filling early graves in foreign lands.

Yet knowing that fact earlier would not have changed anything. She still would have read them poetry and taught them how to sew on their own buttons and make scratch biscuits. She had told Cameron that she would stand before God and man and say that she'd love him forever and always. She did not say that she could stand to bury all but one of her menfolk.

Lizbeth sensed that Julia had joined them. She reached for her hand and Julia grasped it. "I have something I must do," she said, kneeling in the wet grass.

Spencer knelt with her, as did Julia.

"Father, here lies my boy, Matthew Cameron Forrester. I give him up to You in the same way You gave him to me, in great pain. You are our Lord, and we love You and trust in Your ways. I pray that my life will be as great a blessing to You as this child was to his father and me. Amen, sweet Jesus."

She took out a second small bottle and removed the slip of

paper, taking care to keep it dry, and read Matt's scripture. "From the fifth chapter of Matthew, verse 8, 'Blessed are the pure in heart: for they shall see God.'"

Julia could not hold back her pent-up grief any longer. Spencer held both of them as the drizzle turned to rain, making dull thumping sounds on the upturned umbrella. Lizbeth pushed the bottle into the narrow space between his cross and the sod. She embraced the stone, leaving the crepe myrtle blossoms to wilt under his name.

"Good-bye, sweet Matty," Julia whispered, and they walked away.

"Gram," Spencer said as they shook off the rain at the chapel door, "Jemma wanted you to see something." He led them inside to the mosaic behind the altar. "She thought this was very peaceful and that you would like it."

Lizbeth nodded at the beautiful artwork and smiled, thinking of her granddaughter. They sat in a pew for a while. "I have to show you this, too. It's from an ancient poem," Spencer said as they left the chapel by way of a courtyard. He read an inscription—one of several—on a granite panel: *The love of honor alone is not staled by age and it is by honor that the end of life is cheered.*

Lizbeth had never been convinced in her heart that their passing was truly an honor. She read the words again and considered if *honor* crossed their anxious thoughts on the mornings of their deaths. Knowing her boys, it did.

The rain had lessened somewhat as they eased past Matthew's row. Lizbeth wiped her eyes and touched Spencer's arm. He stopped the car and she walked alone to the cross once more, turning to face the east. This would be the closest she would ever be to him in this life. If the Lord came tomorrow, she wanted to look with her own eyes at what her eldest son might see when he rose up from this place so far from home. She traced his name in the stone and gathered a few pink petals from the ground. The seeds of honor had been planted in her heart.

Chapter 6
Postcards

"Mama, you better hurry up and pick out someplace you want to go or everybody else is gonna do it for you," Trina said as the train rocked along near Paris. The women had been writing postcards for the last half hour.

"Child, I'm just glad to be here," Willa said. "If we were home, I'd be sweatin' over a pile of clammy shirts, then hurryin' to iron 'em before they 'dewed. It don't make me no never mind what we do. I'm ready to see Jemma and thank her again for makin' it so I could pray over your daddy's grave."

"Willa, what did you like best about Italy?" Spencer asked as he played cards with Trina and Julia.

"I'd have to say that old statue of David. What I can't get shed of is why that fella made him so big 'cause, in the Bible story, Goliath was the giant, unless everybody in them days was big."

Julia piped up. "Maybe he was showing us that David's faith made him bigger than life, and it gave him power."

"It is an impeccable sculpture," Helene proclaimed. "I first saw it with my husband many years ago. Nebs was a great admirer of Michelangelo. He told me that the statue was originally designed to be on top of a building; that's why it is so large."

"Is that a fact? I think I like Miz Julia's story better," Willa said.

"Oh my," Lizbeth whispered. They all turned to see the top of the Eiffel Tower coming into view.

Trina's eyes were glued to it. "I can't wait to get there."

Lizbeth knew it was time for her to put the sorrow aside and enjoy the days ahead. She studied Julia's face. She seemed like her old self again, laughing and bossing. Most likely, she needed to shop, and Paris was probably a good place to do it.

Jemma met them at the train station. She lined the group up like kindergartners and hugged each one. Spence, she hugged twice and kissed him on the lips in front of them all. It was going to be a good week.

The Hotel Lutetia in the Saint-Germain des Pres District was a great hotel in the Art Deco style, as Spencer pointed out. Only the under-forty crowd was hot to go out that night. They set off to find a bistro with a band, and that was an easy chore. The girls took turns dancing with Spencer, so whoever was sitting out was asked to dance by Frenchmen. Jemma always declined. Trina was shy about it at first, but then she gave in and had her own partners, probably just to let Jemma and Spence dance every dance together. They ended the evening with a soul group that played some good Pickett and Redding.

Trina didn't say a word on the walk home until prodded.

"How's Nick doing?" Jemma asked.

Trina grinned. "He's good. I don't think he really believed me when I told him we were coming over here. He's such a nice guy."

Jemma leaned her head on Spence's shoulder. "We both have nice guys."

"What are your plans, Trina? Are you going back to school?" Spencer asked.

"I don't know. I want to get my degree, but the only thing I'm interested in is fashion design. The schools I can afford don't offer that."

"Have you thought about scholarships?"

Trina shook her head. "I don't want money for my education to be paid for by somebody who doesn't know me from Adam—like blind charity. I'd rather not go. That sounds crazy, but it's the way I feel. I'll just keep sewing for folks and cleaning houses until Nick gets enough money for us to get married."

"Did you bring your sketch book with you?" Jemma asked.

"Don't you take yours everywhere, girl?"

"Let me look, then."

They went to a coffeehouse and talked about college and life in general, until it closed. They walked Trina to the hotel, then Spencer took Jemma to her apartment. They sat on the floor in the hallway.

"We'll tell her it's a loan. I think her pride would allow her to accept that idea, don't you?" Spencer asked.

"Maybe. At least I hope she will, but enough of finance. I didn't give you a proper hello yet." She pulled him by his shirt and left him breathless. "I liked dancing with you tonight," she said with a grin.

He inhaled. "Whoa. Me, too. You were such a good girl, not taking any offers to dance with anybody but me."

"I told you that you are my last cowboy, sir. You are permanently in my heart, got it?"

"I keep it in mind. I'll see you in the morning."

"You keep this in mind," she said and laid another smacker on him.

They spent the next day at The Louvre, waiting almost an hour to see the *Mona Lisa*.

Jemma led a discussion over it during the evening meal. "What did you think about da Vinci's masterpiece, Willa? He painted it on a thin piece of wood, but it's probably the most famous painting in the world."

"All that fuss over a paintin' that you could've done a whole lot better," she said.

"Why, thank you. Did you notice how her skin looked real, like it changed as you moved, sort of transparent? It is a technique of blurring the lines in a painting by blending tones. He did it with layers of glaze and turpentine. It's called *sfumato*."

"Very interesting," Helene said. "How do you pronounce that again?"

"Ss-foo-mah-toe." Jemma stretched out the word.

"Sounds like dessert to me. Anybody interested in some French pastry?" Julia asked.

Jemma and Spencer gave them the grand tour of Paris. Willa, her Sunday hat perched just so on her head, enjoyed much of it from a taxi. Lizbeth began leaving her hat at the hotel. She didn't want it to get wet, and it seemed to rain every day. Helene and Julia left the group periodically to duck into various odd little shops. They all rode the tourist boat for an hour down the Seine, telling

Jemma the details of their trip.

Back on land, Lizbeth, Trina, and Willa got lost looking for a public bathroom. After finding one, they took a wrong turn and ended up in the opposite direction from the meeting place. Willa was tuckered out.

"I'll just ask in this store," Lizbeth said. "Surely somebody can speak English."

Willa and Trina waited outside.

"No luck. Those folks acted like I was speaking a foreign language or something," Lizbeth said, giving the storekeeper a look from the sidewalk.

"I'll try." Trina disappeared into the shop but came out just as fast.

"We'll all try this one." Lizbeth arched her brow and led the way into a stylish shoe salon. "Pardon me, but we are trying to find the Eiffel Tower," she said with a Texas smile.

Two mannequin-faced saleswomen looked at each other, shrugging. *"Veux-tu acheter des chaussures voulez-vous acheter?"* one woman said, then they both laughed and made faces like they had no clue what Lizbeth had asked.

Willa drew back as though they were cussing at her.

Lizbeth asked again, with exaggerated enunciation. She was careful to say *towh-wer*, not *tire* like Lester would have as she built a tower in the air with her hands.

The salesladies again snickered behind the counter.

Willa was hungry as well as sick of hearing French. She suddenly raised her cane and smacked the top of the lacquered counter. The sound bounced off the walls. The women shot up out of their seats.

Willa leaned forward, her Sunday hat quite near their slack-jawed faces. "Ei–full–Tie–er–now! Please," she threw in. Both women pointed across the street. The three weary travelers made their way through the traffic to investigate the spot. Between the buildings, Trina spotted it. The landmark could not have been more than two blocks away. The rest of the crew was waiting for them on the steps.

Trina's heart pounded. It was just like the postcard that her mama had kept pinned up on her bedroom wall all her life, and that she had brought with her from Chillaton, tucked in her purse. She took it out and compared it to the real thing, then turned it over. It was postmarked August 15, 1944. She read the words for the millionth time. *We will be together soon. Love, Your Daddy.* There were things worse than never knowing your daddy, but she hadn't lived through those. She kissed the handwriting and put it back in her purse.

Willa dabbed at her eyes with her hanky. She knew the postcard had been taken off the wall. The spot where it had hung was now a small, bright rectangle. The card was about all that her baby had of her daddy—that, and his almond-shaped eyes and dimples.

❧

Spencer treated them to an elegant farewell meal, and Willa had a thing or two to add about the stingy French food. A violinist came to their table and played for Lizbeth's early birthday celebration. They had all pitched in, some more than others, and bought her an antique sewing basket, most likely found by Julia and Helene on their shopping sprees. Lizbeth would miss her old cigar boxes, though. Cam had gotten them for her from the drugstore for as long as she had been a Forrester.

❧

The concert began at eight. They arrived at Sainte-Chapelle an hour early, since that was the Chillaton style. The changing light on the stained-glass panels was an awesome sight.

"It is truly a moving experience," Helene whispered. "I am not a religious person, but I could become so, under these circumstances."

"Now, what's that supposed to mean, 'not a religious person'?" Willa whispered back, giving her the eye. "Are you telling us that we've been sleepin' in the same room with a heathen?"

"I wouldn't call myself that, dear." Helene adjusted her hearing aid.

"Well, either you join up with the believers or you join up with the heathens. There ain't no middle section in that choir, sugar."

Trina and Jemma exchanged glances.

Lizbeth could see it coming, too. "I think what Helene means is that she's a believer, but doesn't get to church as often as she would like."

Julia smiled behind her program. Her big sister was very good at being a peacemaker when she wanted to. Even so, Willa gave Helene only the slightest benefit of a doubt.

Spencer missed out on that repartee. He was watching the light from the windows reflecting in Jemma's eyes—those golden eyes created with *sfumato* from heaven.

❧

After the concert, Spencer and Jemma said their good-byes and rode home in a taxi, necking in the backseat. The driver smiled and adjusted his mirror so he couldn't watch.

"We have a date next weekend to celebrate your birthday," Spencer said.

"Where do you want to go for our honeymoon?" she asked.

He grinned. "I was thinking about the That'll Do Motel in Chillaton."

"We can't put that on the society page of the *Chillaton Star*."

"It has a society page?"

"It's on the page with the high school sports and beef prices. Anyway, I have a honeymoon place in mind."

"I hope it's on a beach. I want to see you in a bikini every day."

"Nope. Scotland."

"Scotland? Doesn't it rain there every minute of the year?"

"I don't know, but I want to do it for Papa since I'm breaking my promise to him."

"No bikini then?"

"Maybe in our room."

"Deal," he said and kissed her with a thrashing heart.

❧

The next morning the kissing resumed, but only with their eyes and at the waiting area of the airport.

Lizbeth cleared her throat as she approached them. "Thank you for everything you did for us on this trip. You'll have to let us give you both hugs now."

Willa gave Jemma an extra-long one. She pulled back and started to speak. She just couldn't because her lip began to tremble.

"Thanks, Jem," Trina said, "from both of us."

Good-byes over, they boarded the once-dreaded plane, bound for Texas.

❧

Spencer's idea of a birthday dinner date was at the restaurant at the *Tour Eiffel*—the Eiffel Tower. She wore a red dress, and Spencer looked like Prince Charming again, like he did when he took Carrie out of her wheelchair and waltzed her around The Judge's study. He didn't have to dress up to look that way to Jemma anymore. They held hands across the table, eating now and then.

"Jem, I couldn't bring your present. It's being shipped home, but here's a picture of it."

She took the tissue off the photographs. There were two circular stained-glass windows, looking much like kaleidoscope designs. "You said you felt like you were inside a kaleidoscope when you first saw Sainte-Chapelle, so I thought you would like to put one in the little church and another in the chapel for the nursing home."

Jemma clapped her hands. "What a fantastic idea and a beautiful present!"

"Actually, I have one more thing," he said, giving her an envelope. She slid her finger under the flap and took out the documents.

Her jaw dropped. "Ten thousand dollars to build the church and the chapel!"

"I think we can do something really special if we put our money together. Happy birthday."

"Thank you." She lowered her head and blinked out fat tears. "How do you keep doing these things, Spence? God made you perfect and I am not worthy of you."

He lifted her chin. "I am not perfect. Now hush, and let's see if we can stargaze from this place." They moved to the observation deck.

She kissed him under a cloudy Paris sky. "I've missed finding Orion with you, but seeing all these city lights is kind of like watching the stars from your car, isn't it?" she asked.

"Yeah, in a topsy-turvy world," he said. "After we get married, I was thinking we could move into Nedra's rental apartment above her shop. . .you know, to give her something to talk about. What do you think?"

She laughed. "I would live anywhere with you, Spence, even your parents' house, and that's saying a lot. Just tell me that you won't get drafted."

The breeze fluttered her hair across her face. He didn't answer but tucked her hair behind her ear and kissed her neck. She tilted her head a bit to make it easier for him and because it felt so good, like everything was going to be all right.

The graduates walked through the streets of Florence in their caps and gowns and congregated at the University Plaza. Each school then paraded to its respective area and the graduates' names were called out. There were no long speeches, only long celebrations. Spencer Morgan Chase was officially a graduate of Syracuse University via Florence. He left for Chillaton a week ahead of Jemma. The beginning of the end of Jemma's sojourn in Europe had begun. It would be a busy, happy summer, at last.

Le Academie Royale D'Art had opened her mind to subtleties, nuances of perspective and technique, and unparalleled joy—or maybe that part was just Spence. She had developed a close friendship with Peter and his wife, Ami. Her studio partner, Jean-Claude, spoke very little English and Jemma's French was spotty, at best, so their relationship was one of mutual respect as artists, shared glories as well as frustrations, and food. They made each other laugh trying to communicate in charades.

Her final pieces as the Girard Fellow were six nighttime watercolors. Jean-Claude had given her some suggestions since she had helped him with his portraiture efforts. Peter and Ami dragged them away from the studio for a farewell dinner at a lively bistro that Jemma had never heard of before. It served American burgers and shakes along with a rock-and-roll band. Jemma vowed to bring Spencer here if they ever came back to Paris. She was dying to dance. She knew Spence wouldn't care if she danced with Jean-Claude as long as he didn't have to watch. Jean-Claude was not a great dancer, but he had fun, and he was fascinated by Jemma's style on the dance floor. It was a good way to bring her journey to a close, dancing her way out.

Jean-Claude and Peter shared a laugh. Ami interpreted for her. "Jean-Claude says that if you grow weary of painting, you could work as a go-go dancer."

Jemma rolled her eyes. "That might be a way for a starving artist to eat."

"*Au contraire.* You will never have this worry with your art," Ami said.

Peter winked at his wife. "I think we should take you home, Jemmabeth, before a queue forms to enjoy your company," he said, nodding in the direction of several young men looking her way.

Jean-Claude spoke again.

"He says that it is a good thing that you are leaving for America or he might try to steal you away from your fiancé," Ami said.

"Nope, that's not possible." She gave Jean-Claude a gentle shove.

"We shall miss your cowboy talk," Peter said, "and your élan."

"Well, I'll miss y'all, too, podnuhs," she said, flattening out the vowels.

They tried repeating her words. Jemma laughed so much it hurt.

❧

She was early for an appointment with her advisor, Louis, the next morning to discuss her progress during the term.

"I asked Louis to meet in my office because I have some exciting news for you," Monsieur Lanier, the Academie director, said as he opened the blinds in his art-filled office. He handed her a magazine.

"*Nouvelle Liberte?*" She stumbled around the words.

"It means New Freedom," Louis said. "It is a very respected publication here. You may not be familiar with it in America."

"I think I've seen it at the newsstand down the street," Jemma said, puzzled.

Monsieur Lanier came around from his chair and sat on his desk near Jemma. He was a small man, balding and fond of playing with his moustache. "My dear," he said, "the magazine bought one of your paintings. They wish to use it as cover art for an issue."

Jemma shrieked. "Fantastic! Which painting?"

"As you might imagine, it is the watercolor of the couple on a bench. The young man is in an American military uniform."

"Oh, the one of Sandy and Martin, my friends. Wait 'til she hears this."

"It is customary to get the artist's permission to reprint the painting, even though they now own it," Louis explained.

"The Academie's legal representative read the document and sees nothing improper about it," Monsieur Lanier said. "It is a mere courtesy to you."

"Sure, I understand. Just show me where to sign. When I was a little girl, I liked looking at the *Saturday Evening Post*'s cover art. They used lots of Norman Rockwell's work. I would draw them, too, and have a completely different perspective than his."

"Ah, but your perspective elicits many emotions, Jemma," Louis said. "It has been an honor to explore your thinking this year. I cannot tell you how much I admire your work. You have been the, how do you say it? Aha—the icing on my cake. I will refer to your art for many years to come with my pupils." Louis kissed her cheeks in the French way.

Monsieur Lanier kissed her hand. "In my years at the Academie, Jemmabeth, I have not enjoyed watching a pupil work as much as I have you. Your passion and concentration are as remarkable as is your gift. We wish you well, but your presence in these halls will be missed. I shall see to it that you are posted several copies of the magazine when it is issued. Enjoy the honor."

She smiled. "I have loved being here. You have made me reflect and consider other interpretations and techniques. I'll always be grateful to you and your staff. If you ever come to America, please find me. I will have a new name then, Jemmabeth *Chase*." She smiled again. It was the first time she had said it aloud to anybody except Spence, and she liked it.

Her paintings were ready for shipping in Lester's fine crates. Jemma said her good-byes. She took a break from her packing and stood at the window, thinking of her prayerful pilgrimage to Sacré-Coeur almost a year ago. She had begun her time in Paris in sadness, but those days were gone. The Great Plan was with her and with Spencer.

❦

Lizbeth sifted through the mail that had collected while she was gone. The letter that she had hoped to receive was at the bottom of the stack. She read it twice.

Thank you for your interest in this matter.
We suggest that you contact your congressman
for advice concerning posthumous awards.

So be it. She knew who her congressman was and she would not give up. Just as she sat down to write the letter, Trina appeared at the door to use the telephone.

"I need to call Spencer," Trina said.

"Help yourself, sugar." Lizbeth hid her mail.

Trina dialed the number. "Spencer, what's up? Mama said you came by the house to talk to me. Is Jemma okay?"

"She's great. I just got off the phone with her. How about a burger for lunch? Could you spare a few minutes? I could swing by and pick you up."

"Sure. I have to clean a house at two o'clock, so I'll just wait here at Gram's."

❦

Spencer was his usual charming self, but Trina couldn't help but notice there was a hint of sadness about him, plus he left his cheeseburger half eaten. He was most likely missing his fiancée.

"I need to talk to you about somebody we both know and love," he said.

"Let me guess. Is she out of the country right now?"

"Slightly. Jem wants you to go to design school. She has more money than she's ever had in her life, and she has her heart set on paying your tuition. I don't think you can change her mind. We both know how stubborn she can be. What do you say?"

Trina exhaled. "Wow. This is a surprise. Well, I have all these ideas in my head, and I'm dying to learn how to make them sell. What can I say? I want to go to design school real bad. Did I talk too much in Paris and sound like a charity case or something? I'm so sorry if I did."

"Nothing like that would enter Jem's head. She wants you to do what you love, like she and I are able to do. Look, Trina, if Jemma didn't do this, I would. She just beat me to it. When money will buy some joy, don't mess with the plan. It will make both of you happy. Let her do it."

Trina's eyes glistened. She looked out her window as the wind gave flight to litter along the train tracks. "Jemma is the best friend I've ever had. I know her pretty well now, and how she feels guilty about being a white girl. But I know also that her heart's in the right place. This is a real sweet thing she's doing. You don't suppose she's one of God's angels, do you?"

Spencer smiled. "I've occasionally wondered that myself, but then you've never seen that temper of hers."

"Nah, but Mama always says that when waters run really deep they're bound to kick up some rocks ever once in a while. I guess that just means she loves you a lot."

He nodded, and Trina thought she saw a glimmer of a tear in his eye, too.

"So, what's your answer?" he asked.

"That girl just gets crazier all the time, so I'd better take her up on this before we have to put her away." Trina sniffed. "Tell her that I love her, Spence, and I'll make sure her money doesn't go to waste," she said, then flat-out bawled into her napkin.

⁂

Jemma's flight was over three hours late. He held her so tight that she knew something was wrong. She drew back to look him in the eye and realized the problem as soon as she did. Her heart sank. She leaned against the wall and cried. He had gotten his draft notice. They sat on the floor at the airport and talked, oblivious to the crowded terminal.

"Why did they jump on you so soon?"

"Who knows, but it doesn't matter now. We can still get married. It's not the end of the world. You can live with me on the base, I think, like Martin and Sandy did."

"You mean until they ship you off to Vietnam?"

"We don't know if that's what will happen."

"Oh, come on, Spence." She didn't mean to sound so sharp. "How long do we have before you go?"

"I have to report for my physical in three weeks."

She pitched a wad of tissues in the trash then turned to him. "I hate this stupid war. It makes no sense. Rats! They don't even call it a war, for Pete's sake."

There was no sparkle in Spencer's eyes. He was suffering enough without her pitching a wall-eyed fit. Willa had told her once to get some backbone. She could, now, and help her sweet man. She just didn't want to lose him like Gram did her boys, but then she didn't even want him to go, period. She eased her arms around him and felt the veins in his neck pulsing against her cheek. This war could not take life from him.

"I have to do this, baby, it's my duty," he whispered.

She could not stand to hear the words. She laid a finger on his lips, then shook her head. They walked to the car, arms full of luggage. She saw the letter on the dashboard and turned away. He drove straight to the river, and they lay under the full moon and searched the starry heavens for consolation. Jemma tried to recall the scriptures she had memorized. The only one she could think of was Psalm 46:10: *"Be still, and know that I am God."*

She couldn't let him go to his house and be away from her. Lizbeth made up the bed in the little side room, and he stayed the night. They talked until Papa's clock chimed three and she woke up again at dawn, her body still in Paris. Everyone else was snoring. She went outside to hear the early morning sounds of late spring in the backyard.

She heard it coming and ran to the tracks. It raced by, blowing its familiar horn. Jemma held down her robe and walked up on the rails to watch the Zephyr disappear into the sunrise. How dare the government take him from her! Spencer would go, too. He would not run off or plead some defense. He would go and let them give him a gun, put him in harm's way, and teach him to kill or be killed. Her dear Spence. She had to choose, though, whether to become a part of his burden in all this, or to be his refuge and joy. She closed her eyes and danced as the wind rustled the tall grass by the tracks.

❧

Trina was ironing Mrs. Lacey's new dress when she saw her. She grinned and slapped the iron down on its stand, ready to squeeze Jemma to death for giving her the money and to say that she had applied to Le Claire, but something told her to leave her friend be.

There was no joy in her dance this morning. Trina saw the sadness instead and sat on the porch, hoping it was not what everybody had feared.

Somehow, though, she knew that it was.

Chapter 7
Whispers

S he vowed to buck up and be his joy. After all, they had their wedding and marriage to look forward to. Jemma spent every waking minute with Spencer, drinking up any detail that she thought she might have missed in all years she had known him. She watched him work on the church plans. He was so detail-oriented, like her.

The Bethel Church congregation had approved his design for the building wholeheartedly and offered the muscle to build it. Willa had lifted Spencer off his feet to give him a big smacker kiss, and Brother Cleo, the pastor, wrote Jemma and Spencer a touching letter of appreciation.

Spencer passed his physical and was to report for basic training at Fort Bliss two weeks after the wedding. Jemmabeth would miss another of his birthdays. The wedding was less than a week away. Alex, Julia, and Helene were camping out at Lizbeth's house, as would Jemma's Le Claire friend, Melanie Glazer, when she got there. Rollaway beds and old army cots were in every room. Lester already had Robby at his house, but he was prepared for the second crew that was scheduled to arrive in two days. Jim—Jemma's daddy, cousin Trent, and Uncle Ted—Alex's brother, would stay with Lester, but Uncle Arthur—Julia's husband, wanted to stay at the That'll Do Motel. He thought it would be fun. Julia told him that he would be sleeping alone. The Lillygraces, of course, had reservations in Amarillo. Lizbeth's sisters, the *beth* ladies, would fly in the day of the wedding.

Blabbermouth Sandy was back in town. She threw Jemma a bridal shower for the younger set and another was hosted by some of Alex's friends.

Trina had gotten up her nerve and made an appearance at Sandy's shower. Jemma ignored the whispers and stares as she introduced her newest friend to her lifelong friends. Trina wasn't oblivious to the reserved politeness, but she kept up a good front for Jemma's sake. She had designed the wedding gown and veil from sketches Jemma had drawn in high school. They had gone through every bridal magazine and didn't find anything more perfect. It was waiting for her when she got home.

The only things left to be done were the finishing touches on the bridesmaids' dresses, and Jemma needed to pick up some last-minute items including the reception souvenirs in Amarillo. Buddy B had all the portable equipment he needed for his band, and Spencer had hired a caterer from Amarillo to feed everybody. Jemma planned to make the bouquets herself. She just needed ribbon, florists' wire, and tape. Only the good Lord could provide some decent weather and a windless morning.

Sandy finished her soda and tossed the can in the trash as they cut voile squares for the rice packets. "I hate to tell you this, Jem, but nobody goes to Scotland for their honeymoon," she said. "People go to Padre Island or Colorado or even Hawaii, but not a dreary place like Scotland. Is Spence going to wear a kilt?"

"I think he's all English, but Scotland will be a beautiful place for a honeymoon. I've seen pictures. We're going to a Highland village near the Isle of Skye where Papa's family lived."

Sandy lowered her voice. "Okay, nobody can hear us. You have to tell me what the rules were for 'no fooling around.'"

"Nope. Private."

"Cheezo, you'll be married in three days. Tell."

"I love you, Sandy, but you're a Big Mouth and you don't even realize it."

"I won't tell this. I have my scruples. Just tell me part of it, and I promise I won't say a word to anybody."

"You've had a bad attitude about it ever since we decided to make the promise."

"I just didn't see how you could keep it. What good is a vow if it is doomed before you even make it?"

"Ah, but we lasted to the end, so you were wrong."

"Tell me, or I won't be in the wedding."

"Oh, all right. Swear you will never speak of this again. You can't even tell Marty."

"You don't have to worry about that."

Jemma leaned toward her and whispered in her ear, "I'm never going to tell you because it's just between Spence and me."

Sandy rolled her eyes. "Well, thanks for that news flash. So, you won't even tell your best friend. All I know is that nobody else could've kept whatever those rules were."

"I'm dying for it to be over."

"Never an infraction?"

"Nope."

"Not even with the cowboy? I can't believe that. Wasn't he like ten years older than you?"

"Yeah, but I've never let anybody break the rules. It's all in the hands. You have to be faster than they are and always on guard."

"Cheezo. I don't know how you did it or why. I hope it was. . . you know. . ."

"Worth it? Yeah, it was. We're moving to a whole new level of love."

Sandy put the last of the rice in the squares. "Maybe it'll help with the fights, and there will be plenty of those, believe me."

"Nah. It will help with the making up," Jemma said, tying the final ribbon.

"Spence was my second choice, remember?" Sandy said with a little too much pride.

"You say that all the time, but I don't remember you picking him second. I think he was your first choice, too."

"Who was your second choice?" Sandy asked, skipping the inference.

"I picked Spencer for all the slots. I can't believe that we will be married in three days. I'm scared now that Uncle Sam has him."

"Marty says Spence will get a desk job or something noncombatant. It's not like they will take an architect and teach him to fly a helicopter or something."

"Good grief, Sandy; I hadn't thought of a helicopter pilot. That has to be the most dangerous job in Vietnam."

"Marty calls it the suicide assignment, but then Marty says that about everything over there."

Jemma wasn't listening. She pushed open the screen door and stood on the porch. A cluster of sparrows darted around the telephone wires, then disappeared into the clear summer sky. She would feel better about everything in only three short days.

Jim, Robby, and Spencer decided to get out of the way by taking a fishing trip to Pearl Lake—a man's day out the day before the wedding. They were to leave before the sun came up and get back before it set, scouts' honor.

Spencer took Jemma for a moonlight picnic at the river the night before. "They are making good progress on the church. Have you been over there?" he asked.

"No, but I'll go tomorrow. I have to run up to Amarillo and pick up some things. Spence, why did you give me a power of attorney?"

"So you could use my bank account for the church or something."

"You aren't having a premonition, are you?"

"Yeah, it's about you and me in a Scottish hotel room."

She giggled. "What's the latest? Are your parents coming or not?"

"Dad says he's coming, and he's going to make a speech, heaven forbid. I don't know about Mother. She could wind up making an embarrassing scene."

"Your mother still hates me for breaking up with you."

"Mother is a pitiful person, Jem."

"Well, nothing can spoil the next two days."

Spencer touched her cheek. She hadn't mentioned the army much since the night he told her, but he knew her better than that. He could see it in her eyes. He only had to keep his hands off her for forty-eight more hours, then their deal was history and she was his, forever. Every dream he ever had was about to come true.

"Come here," she said, lying back on the car. "Spence, if I could, I would erase some things."

"It's okay, baby," he murmured, before she put her fingers on his lips.

"No, hear me out. I would erase in the seventh grade when I said that you just liked me because my daddy was the high school football coach. I would erase running the bulls with Sandy every

Fourth of July and dancing with Martin's wild cousin at his graduation party to spite you. I would get rid of that year when I was lost in space thinking that I needed to find out if I really loved you. But most of all, babe, I would wipe out Buddy telling you about Paul right before our disastrous trip to the airport last year. If ever there was a fool on this planet, you are looking at her, and I apologize from the bottom of my heart." She choked up. "You are the only, only one I have ever loved."

He held her. "I just pretend it was research, Jem. You measured me up against the masses and I put them all to shame. Think of it like that."

"I keep it in mind," she said.

Spencer got off the car, humming a little of "In the Still of the Night." She smiled and joined him. They sang and danced like ghost lovers in the moonlight on the banks of the Salt Fork of the Red River.

❧

Her last stop in Amarillo was to pick up the New Testaments from the bookstore. Each one had their wedding date on it. Papa would have approved, and she liked to think he was watching from some fluffy cloud. The Testaments were white with gold foil edges on the pages. Jemma stopped at a filling station just outside Amarillo and bought gas and a Dr Pepper.

After a couple of tries, she got the cantankerous Dodge going, then pulled onto the highway where blasts of Panhandle wind buffeted the car. She hoped the wind would blow itself out and calm down by morning. Across the train tracks, an old green pickup stirred up a cloud of dust as it sped down a dirt road alongside a wheat field. "Try a Little Tenderness" was playing on the radio, so she turned up the volume, then pulled the ring on her drink. The cold liquid spewed everywhere, and she dropped the can.

"Rats," she yelled as it sprayed over her legs like a volcano until the can tipped and rolled under her feet. As she groped around for it, her hair blocked her vision for a fraction of a second. She blew it out of her eyes just as a semi loomed up in front of her. She jerked the steering wheel to get back in her lane, but it was too late.

The eighteen-wheeler careened across the highway, its cab

slamming into the Dodge. The sound of the big rig's brakes and crumpling metal blended into her scream.

⋘◈⋙

A shiny hubcap spun wildly, then wobbled to a halt on the black-top just as the truck driver crawled out of his steaming cab. The stench of burned rubber filled the air. He stumbled to his feet and blinked. The other vehicle lay upside down in the ditch with its wheels still rolling. He couldn't see anybody as he scrambled on his knees, shouting for help from the crowd of people who had stopped to look.

"Over here!" a teenage boy yelled, running down the embankment.

The truck driver knew as soon as he looked at her. "Don't touch her 'cause she's hurt bad. I'll get an ambulance."

He ran to his cab and placed a call for help, grabbed a blanket, and went right back to her. She was barely breathing and stone-still. He put the blanket on her real easy and checked to see if all the blood was just from the gash on her head. He found another ugly wound on her arm, not to mention all the smaller cuts and scrapes everywhere else.

"Is she dead?" the young man whispered.

"I don't think so." The driver took off his shirt, ripped it apart, holding the plaid bandages in place with solid pressure on her head and arm. He touched her cheek to get rid of the tiny pieces of dirt and rocks that were stuck there.

The boy stood over them, out of breath and staring at Jemma's face. "Are you hurt, mister? I saw the whole thing. She went right over the line in front of you."

"I've got a couple of scratches. . .nothing like her, though. Man, she's messed up. I need you to double-check inside the car to make sure nobody else is in there," he said.

The kid went straight to the Dodge, his shoes crunching the shards of glass that littered the area. "Nobody," he yelled.

The wind ruffled her auburn hair as it mingled with sunflower petals, now smashed and saturated with blood. There were dozens of little white books strewn between her and the car. Some of them were open, their pages flipping and glinting in the wind.

The truck driver was feeling light-headed. "Bring me one of

377

them little books, would you, young feller?" he said to the kid.

It was a New Testament with the next day's date stamped in gold on the cover. He had one similar to it that he kept in the truck. He took a breath, then leaned down close to her, whispering his favorite verse in her ear. It just seemed like a good idea.

❧

Buddy B stood on the porch, his face drained of color and his tow truck still running in Lester's driveway. He blew out his breath when Julia opened the door. "Ma'am, I need to talk to the toughest person in this family."

"Let's say you're looking at her right now," she said, her mouth going dry.

Tears trailed down his cheeks. "It's our Jemmabeth, ma'am. She's been in one horrible wreck outside Amarillo. And, well, things look real bad."

Chapter 8

A Lit Candle

The Golden Triangle Hospital was sixty-eight miles from Chillaton. Julia Billington drove it in thirty-five minutes with a car full of silent passengers. Sheriff Ezell, his patrol car lights flashing, had to step on the gas to stay in front of her and the others. The group filled the emergency room waiting area. Trent and Ted headed to Pearl Lake to break the news to the rest of the men.

Every time a door opened, they all rose up like a choir in case it was somebody who knew something. No tears yet, not even from Alex. She wouldn't sit down, but paced, as though suspended in a surreal nightmare. A nurse came out and told them that it might be another half hour before they could talk to anyone.

Lizbeth stood at the bank of windows, staring vacantly at a group of crows pecking at the lawn. She had memorized "The Raven" by Edgar Allan Poe in her high school English class and recited it in an assembly. She had learned it because Rachel Moore said the poem was too long for anybody to memorize, but she had done it. Sometimes the lines crept into her thoughts, like wayward sheep. *And my soul from out that shadow that lies floating on the floor shall be lifted—nevermore!*

The Lord would surely hear her prayers and lift this shadow from Jemmabeth. She herself could not stand to lose another piece of her heart to fill an early grave.

The doctor came to them at last. Lester stood close so as not to miss a word, as he molded and remolded the brim of his hat.

"Who is the next-of-kin here?" the doctor asked in a crisp manner.

Alex moved forward. "I'm her mother," she said, trying to read the doctor's face.

"Your daughter is alive, but she has lost a considerable amount of blood. She is undergoing a transfusion and a second one may be necessary. Our gravest concern is that she has a fractured skull and is not responding to stimulation at this point. We are doing all that we can for her."

Alex shuddered and held on to Lester's arm to keep her balance. "May I see her?"

"Her face is swollen, she has multiple abrasions, and we had to shave part of her head to examine and treat the injuries. Perhaps you should wait. The next twenty-four hours are critical."

"I want to see her," Alex said firmly.

"Very well. We'll send for you."

"I need to come with her," Julia announced. "I'm her great-aunt."

"Only two from the immediate family may come and only for five minutes."

Julia stiffened. "She can't go alone. Look at her."

"Only this once." The doctor disappeared into the emergency room complex. Collective sighs spread across the room.

"This just can't be." Lester blew his nose and headed outside.

Buddy B arrived with more of the wedding party. Trina knew from the hushed group how bad things were. Willa dropped in a chair and cried. It was as though the traffic light had turned green because everybody let loose. Sandy sat away from the group, her streaked makeup even paler in the hospital lights.

The Lillygraces kept near their daughter, not knowing how to console her except for cups of water that Robert Lillygrace relentlessly provided. The ICU nurse led Alex and Julia out of the waiting room and down the shiny hallway to the room where Jemma lay, comatose. They put on surgical masks and went in. Alexandra took one quick glance and fainted. Julia tried to hold on, but she staggered out of the room as soon as she entered. They should have waited like the doctor said.

The sheriff pulled into the emergency entryway again, this time with Jim right behind. Spencer jumped out of the moving car, leaving the door open, and burst into the waiting room. Trina threw her arms around him, but everyone else had moved to the Intensive Care area. He listened, wild-eyed, as she told them everything the doctor had reported. Then he turned to the ICU desk. "I need to see Jemmabeth Forrester. I am her fiancé."

The nurse got Jemma's chart and shook her head. "Hon, you don't want to see her. It'll break your heart. Just let us take care of her."

Jim and Robby stood next to Spencer. "I'm her father, and we want to see her now, if at all possible," Jim insisted.

The nurse tapped her pencil on the desk, looking at Spencer. "Let me check, but the boy's too young." Trina took Robby's hand, and they left.

Jim and Spencer still smelled of fish and bait. The nurse came back and had them scrub up and put on masks and gowns. "Only five minutes, gentlemen," she said and took them to her.

They stood by the bed, holding on to one another, weeping into their masks. It was plain to see that she was full of tubes and monitors that couldn't be covered up with sheets. He closed his eyes and pictured this beautiful body moving like silk when she danced. He would look nowhere but her face, so swollen that he could not see any part of her eyes. There were tubes in her nose and in her battered mouth. Crimson fluid oozed into her from a bag overhead and wheezing from a respirator filled the room. The wavy hair that had tickled his nose the night before had been partially shaved into a grotesque Halloween wig. This could not be his Jem because she was going to be his wife in twenty-four hours. He swallowed the urge to throw up.

"Is she going to make it?" Jim whispered to the nurse.

"She's in a real bad way, hon. I'd be calling the prayer hotline if I were you. Your time's up now. Go get some rest. It will be a long shot for this child to live through the night."

"May I wait in the hallway?" Spencer asked.

"No, sugar," she said, looking into his gray eyes. "The rules in here are real strict. We need to move fast sometimes and you'd be in the way." She lowered her voice. "I'll come talk to you on my break, okay? I'll watch her real good." She patted his shoulder.

"Could we say a prayer before we go?" Jim asked.

The nurse hesitated. "Hurry, then. You really do need to leave."

Jim put his arm around Spencer and prayed aloud for his baby girl. He didn't make it through the prayer, and Spencer couldn't finish it for him. It just hung in the air without an "Amen."

Jim left, ashen-faced, but Spencer lingered. He touched his fingers to hers, and his eyes followed the delicate path of veins on her arms. Her sweet, stubborn heart was doing its best to keep her with him. He longed to see her smile like she did in grade school. It was her special grin that always made his heart jump.

He went straight to the nurses' desk. "Jemmabeth Forrester and I are the same blood type. I want to donate the blood she uses."

"We use the blood bank for emergencies, but we never turn down donations," the nurse said.

He looked her in the eye. "This is important to me."

"I'll try, sir, but I can't guarantee it." The nurse left him standing at her desk, but he wasn't moving until he got an answer. He pulled out his wallet and removed his Red Cross blood donation card. The nurse came back with a form.

"If you want to be a directed donor for your fiancée, we'll need proof of your type," she said. Spencer gave her the card and filled out the form. She called the hospital blood bank. He leaned against the wall until a young woman about Jemma's age came to get him. He lay on the table and watched the bag turn red. It was the only thing he could give her for now.

About midnight, the ICU nurse came out. Nobody had left.

"Her heart signs are steady and the second transfusion is underway. Other than that, you will have to talk with the doctor."

"Has she moved?" Alex asked.

The nurse shook her head. "No, sweetie, that's not happening."

"Does she. . ." Spencer stopped.

The nurse smiled at him. "She has your blood in her veins, son."

"May I see her?" he asked.

"Let me talk with my supervisor," she said and disappeared through the swinging doors.

"I don't see how you can stand to look at her, Spence." Alex put her head on his chest. "I'm not sure I can go back."

"Do you need me to go with you, son?" Jim asked. "I think I can."

"I would like to go by myself, if that's okay. I need to suffer with her," Spencer mumbled.

Lizbeth held Robby's head in her lap. He had cried himself to sleep. It wasn't this way for her boys. She didn't even know they were hurt until they were gone. Jemmabeth was not going to die. Lizbeth could feel the Lord in this place.

Brother Cleo and his wife came in the room, his booming voice attracting everyone's attention. The atmosphere changed to one of hope as soon as he organized them into a circle and led a hand-holding prayer. Lizbeth watched Jemma's Lillygrace grandparents clasp the hands next to them with awkward reluctance. Jemma would have appreciated that scene.

Brother Cleo's voice demanded that even the angels listen. "Almighty God, we come to You as sinners, pardoned through the blood of Jesus. Hear our prayer of intercession for the life of Jemmabeth Forrester. She is a worthy child, Lord, and we look to You to spare her to us, full of joy, as she was before, if it could be Thy holy will. Be to us like a lit candle in this cavern of anguish. Amen and amen."

The nurse motioned to Spencer, and the room fell silent again, as everyone considered what he would have to endure. He scrubbed up and put on the mask. She hadn't changed. He held her fingers this time and bent to kiss them. His blood would make her stronger. She would live and smile at him again. He kept his eyes on her face because it would be a sacrilege to look at the rest of her like this, plus it would make her mad, and it would be breaking their promise. He squeezed her fingers, hoping otherwise, but knowing that she couldn't respond.

Her fingers were slender and delicate, like Lizbeth's. They were stained now with antiseptic solution. Since the third grade, they were always stained with bits of paint. He related the smell of paint and turpentine with her, but she also smelled like flowers. This was where he wanted to be, not down the hall where he couldn't tell if her fingers were warm. He shouldn't have been at Pearl Lake. He should have gone with her to Amarillo. He was probably laughing with her daddy and her little brother when something cracked her skull and stole her away from him.

"Time to go now," a new nurse said, checking the monitors and changing things around. "Is she your wife?"

He shook his head. "She would have been today."

The group remained all night, crumpled up in chairs and on the floor. The Lillygraces had gone to their hotel in the early hours. Only Spencer and Alex were awake all night. He saw Jemma every time they would let him. No changes, but she was still alive.

Robby came to sit in his lap. "Is Jem going to die?" he asked, looking up at Spencer with eyes just like Papa's.

Spencer took a breath. "Only God knows that. We can only ask Him to see things our way."

"Why would He take her to heaven?"

"His ways are not our ways."

"Probably so she could paint stuff for Him. Did you see the monkey she painted me for my birthday? It's so cool. He looks like he is gonna jump on you."

The doctor appeared and everyone stirred at her voice. "Things are stable for the first twelve hours. The tests show that there is swelling in her brain, which is normal for a fracture of this type. We are watching now for blood clots or any leakage of brain fluid, which would require surgery."

Spence did not like the way she talked about Jem in a textbook tone. Her incredible brain would not leak.

"Has she moved?" Alex asked again.

"No, she isn't responding, but that is to be expected in this situation. I know that seems frightening to you, but the most important thing right now is that we are aware of complications. I suggest that all of you go home and get some rest. We will give her the best of care," she said in her monotone.

"Ma'am, many of these fine folks are here for her weddin'. Do you think there's gonna be a buryin' instead?" Lester asked when no one else would.

The doctor blinked and looked at Spencer, realizing the situation. Her voice softened. "If there are no complications by tomorrow evening, I think she'll survive."

"So there's hope. I'm obliged, ma'am," Lester said. "Praise the Lord."

Nobody took the doctor's advice. They did take turns going to a nearby hotel room that Julia rented just to shower and nap, and they rotated to the cafeteria for food. Spencer wouldn't go anywhere and he couldn't sleep. Alex finally went to see her with Jim and didn't faint. Lizbeth wouldn't go, but she and Brother Cleo kept a prayer vigil in a far corner of the room. Carrie arrived about noon with her boyfriend and stuck with Trina.

Melanie Glazer had not seen Jemma in months and was prepared for a joyous occasion. Instead, she took her violin to the cafeteria and played for an hour to honor her friend. The diners had no idea a world-class musician was entertaining them. They just knew she was incredibly good, and that her long red hair was like the flame atop an exquisite candle when she played. She visited with each member of the family, giving special attention to Spencer, whom she had never met.

"Jemma was so worried that you were in love with someone else last year," she said.

"I could never love anybody but her," Spencer said, his voice raspy.

"She's a creature of the arts, and we don't think like other people. Jem has been so good to me, and I've really missed her. I believe it will all work out."

"Do you?" Spencer asked, looking up at such optimism.

"I do." She could see why Jemma didn't want to lose him. She saw honest compassion and uncommon goodness, despite this torment, in his eyes. Such qualities had to stem from a heart overflowing with love.

Lizbeth kept a curious eye on Alex's parents. She thought they might break down and cry like everyone else, but not so. She herself was well acquainted with hiding pain, and wished she had the nerve to talk to them about it. Instead, she went to sit with Lester, who tapped his foot and stared out the windows at a man mowing the hospital lawn.

"Lester, I need to have a word with you."

He stirred in his chair and straightened himself. "Help yourself, Miz Liz. Is there news about Jemmer?"

"No, but I want to apologize to you for the way I acted about your chinchilla business last year. It was downright mean of me to poke fun at you about it. Will you forgive me?"

"Oh Miz Liz, no need to ask that. Didn't never take off anyhow, did it? I kinda liked the critters, though, and I might could've made me some spendin' money if that twister hadn't scattered 'em all over town. It's just as well. I ain't sure I could've stole their hides off 'em anyway. I heard just the other day that one showed up in the basement of the Catholic Church. Don't that beat all, considerin' my feelings toward the pope?"

"You've been a fine neighbor, Lester. I know that Jemma loves you, and I'll be sure she knows that you stayed up here all this time, worrying about her. You're a sweet man." She patted his arm and went back to her seat.

Lester blushed. Maybe he was too hasty when he sent off for the mail-order bride. He should've heard back from his application by now but hadn't for some reason. None of that foolishness mattered now that Jemmerbeth was at death's door.

He held on to the arms of his chair as he stood and stretched. He crossed the room and got a drink from the water fountain. A Mexican family nearby bowed together in prayer, most likely over their own loved one.

Life is full of worries. Don't matter who you are, Lester thought. He had a sudden urge to talk to young Mr. Chase.

Spencer nodded off and awoke with a gasping breath. He looked around the room. Carrie was in a far corner of the room talking with Trina. She had avoided him since their initial conversation, but he was too drained to get up and see why. He sat on the floor, watching the clock.

Lester laid his hand on Spencer's shoulder. "Son, I wonder if you mind taking a little stroll?"

"I don't know if I can, Lester. I'm not feeling too hot. Could you sit with me instead?"

"Sure thing." Lester didn't know when was the last time he'd sat on the floor, but he couldn't turn down this pitiful young man. He eased his way down beside Spence. "Son, I wanted to share a tale with you that I'm hopin' will give you a ray of sunshine."

Spencer rubbed his unshaven face and looked at Lester. "I'd appreciate some sunshine right now."

"Well, sir, you know I sure liked Cam Forrester. He was about the best man I ever knew. Had them crinkly blue eyes and a big old belly laugh. He was right proud of Jemmer, as he should've been. Him and me was sitting on my porch one day and he come hence to tellin' me about a dream he had the night before. Now, mind you this was before y'all was in high school, probably around '58 or so. Anyhow, in Cam's dream, the president of the U. S. of A. asked Jemmerbeth to paint his official picture. She did, and it was hung in the capitol buildin' way up to D.C."

"That's a great story," Spencer said. "Jemma could do it, too, if she gets through this. Who was the president?"

"Well, sir, that's the spooky part. When he told me, I didn't think much of it. Truth of the matter is, we had a good laugh over it."

"Why's that?"

"The president that she painted was that actor feller, Ronald Reagan, the one who just got to be the governor of California. In 1958 he was still making them silly drive-in movies. Don't that beat all?"

A chill spread over Spencer. "Papa was a man of God, Lester. Maybe his dream meant more than he realized."

Just before one in the morning, Carrie McFarland rolled over to a sleeping Spencer with Philip, her boyfriend, at her side. They put a blanket from a nearby chair over him. Carried tucked in the corners as best she could. Then they left.

Spence woke up a couple of hours later and scrambled to the nurses' station, behind the sacred doors. His heart was pounding. "Anybody here?" he asked.

A familiar nurse appeared. "You aren't supposed to be in this area, young man."

"I have to know how she is. I fell asleep."

"She is the same—no better, no worse."

"May I go in?" Spencer asked.

The nurse sighed. He was a hurting man and she had seen them before, but this was such a heart-wrenching case. All the staff was talking about it.

"I tell you what. Let me get somebody to take you to the hospital locker room. You take a shower, put on some surgical scrubs, have a little breakfast, and maybe I'll let you see her. You're a sight right now. If she were to wake up, you'd scare her back into a coma."

Spencer was in no condition to argue. He did as he was told. When he came back, she smiled. "Now, she doesn't look any better, but it's been almost thirty-six hours and there are no complications yet, so that's good. You scrub up and get that mask on."

The nurse was right. In fact, Jemma looked worse in some places. There were purple bruises on her face that he hadn't noticed before. He held her hand in his and stroked her palm. She was so ticklish there. Maybe the next time she would respond to it. He went back to his spot by the door even though his tailbone hurt.

Jim came over, yawning. "I'm going in. Any change?"

Spencer shook his head and looked around the room. It was like an airport with major flight delays. Even Willa was flat-out on the floor, two blankets covering her hefty frame.

The wedding seemed so frivolous now. They should have eloped; at least that way he could have kept her safe. Her uncle Ted and Trent were helping Buddy B get the wedding stuff returned to the rental places. They had such good friends and family.

"Spence?" Trina whispered.

His body jerked to attention. "What? Has something happened?"

"No, no. I just wanted to sit here."

Spencer nodded. "How are you doing?"

She started to say something but choked up. Spencer put his arm around her.

Jim passed through the waiting room and headed straight outside.

Spencer turned to Trina. "Follow me," he whispered. He held out his hand and she took it, glancing around as he pushed open the doors that led down the hallway toward Jemma's room. No nurses were in sight. She stayed right behind him, her pulse thumping against her temples. Spencer pulled a mask out of his shirt pocket and handed it to her. She put it on and entered the room. Unprepared for what she saw, Trina reached for the side rail of the bed. She touched Jemma's hand just as a nurse appeared in the doorway.

"Hey, only immediate family or special permission. Out."

The nurse's sharp tone drew a response from Spencer. "I'm sorry. It was my idea."

Trina glanced at Spencer and turned to the nurse. "I'm her sister," she said through the mask.

The nurse snickered. "Oh really, and I'm the pope's daughter."

Trina looked her in the eye. "I'm adopted."

❧

A Texas State Trooper was in the waiting room when they returned. A nurse pointed to Alex and Jim, but Spencer met him at the desk. "Sir, are you here about Jemmabeth Forrester?"

The officer removed his hat. "I just need to ask a few questions. Are you related to her?"

"She is my fiancée. We were to be married last night."

"I'm sorry, son." He got out his pen and clipboard. "Let's have a seat over here."

The officer gave them the details of the accident, according to witnesses. He also told them about the truck driver, his kindness, and the first aid he administered to Jemma. Jim told him to take the old Dodge to the junkyard and send him the bill. He never wanted to see it again.

The Lillygraces came to say good-bye. Alex had asked for special permission for them to see Jemma.

"I cannot, Alexandra, I have a bad heart, you know, and I don't think I should risk it," her father said. Alex hadn't heard much about his bad heart until this.

"Mother, would you go with me?" she asked.

Her mother cleared her throat. "Yes, I'll go," she said, surprising them all. "I am quite fond of Jemmabeth."

They put on the required apparel. Alex and her mother held hands as they approached the room. The nurse gave them the usual warning.

"Oh, my sweet girl." Catherine Lillygrace covered her face with her hands and wept. When it was time for them to leave, she kissed her fingers and moved them across Jemma's arm. Alex could not remember the last time her mother had let anybody see her cry.

Catherine hugged everybody in the waiting room like she meant it. "She's going to be all right. Look at all these good people praying for her," she said.

Then they left in a waiting taxi.

The group began to shrink. People had to go about their lives. Jemma remained the same and Spencer stayed at the hospital, as did Alex. Ted and Trent took the older ones back to Chillaton, even though Lester didn't want to leave, and Lizbeth would only go to change clothes.

Carrie and Philip came to the hospital before flying back to Houston, and she went straight to Spencer with a long hug. "Spence, I'm sorry I didn't talk much to you the other day, but I didn't know what to say. I was so upset and it broke my heart to see you in such pain. You know how I feel about Jemma. She was my salvation, and I owe her for having a semi-normal life." She gestured toward her boyfriend. "I want you to meet my own long-awaited Prince Charming, Mr. Philip Bryce. Phil, this is my first Prince Charming, Spencer Chase."

Philip was a slight man with thick reddish hair and green eyes. He looked at Spencer and smiled. "First Prince, huh? Should I be jealous?"

"He has been in my bedroom more than once and carried me up the stairs to get there," Carrie added.

Spencer smiled weakly. "Carrie and Jemma say a lot of things just for the dickens of it, Philip. You'd better straighten him out about that, Carrie, or else he might want to have a duel or something."

A nurse, accompanied by a heavy-set, black cowboy, interrupted. "Excuse me. This man would like to talk to Miss Forrester's family."

The cowboy put out his hand. "Name's Joe Cross. I'm the driver of the truck that hit your girl. I'm sure sorry, but there just wasn't nothin' I could do. She came right at me." Cuts on his face and arms were stitched up, and he had a bandage on one hand.

"We're sorry, too," Alex said. "The trooper told us that you took care of Jemma until the ambulance got there. I can never thank you enough for that. Did she say anything to you?"

"No, ma'am, she was out when I got to her. How's she doin' now?"

"She's in a coma," Spencer said.

"Man, I knew it was bad. I was afraid she'd broke her neck. At least that's not the case. I brought some things that I thought you folks might want. I'll go get 'em."

He brought in a couple of large paper bags. "Yesterday must have been a special event for somebody."

"It was supposed to be our wedding day," Spencer said quietly.

"Well, that explains it. Bless her heart. These were scattered around the wreck, and I know how people will just steal things. . . it's kinda sick like, but they will. These looked important, so I gathered up all I could. Listen, I've got to hit the road now. I'm headin' home to Sweetwater. God bless."

Neither Spencer nor Alex wanted to look inside the bags. Carrie rolled her chair over to one and reached inside. She held up a dusty little New Testament stamped with the wedding date. She quickly replaced it. The second bag held more of the same, but there was also a leather-bound King James Bible, still in its box, on top. Carrie reached for Philip's hand and read the inscription.

To Spencer from Jemmabeth
July 23, 1967
Philippians 4:13

Spencer took the Bible from her and traced his finger over the gold letters. He took it with him to his spot on the floor and read the scripture. "I can do all things through Christ which strengtheneth me." It was appropriate now, even though she was probably thinking about Vietnam when she placed the order. He went to the nurses' desk and asked if he could go in. He had to touch her.

Chapter 9
The Hardest Thing

After a week, they moved her to a room crammed with flowers. Even The Judge had sent roses. Spencer's father brought an elaborate arrangement in person and hugged Alex, albeit a little too long for her comfort. Alex slept in a recliner and Spencer was in a sleeping bag on the floor. Jemma looked somewhat better. The swelling was down and they had cleaned her hair, but she was still unresponsive. Spencer didn't know how he could leave her, but he did know that he would be on some kind of military transport in nine days to report for basic training.

"Jem," he said, close to her ear, "are you in there, baby? Let me know. Hit me, yell, wrinkle your nose, do anything." He had tried so many things, but he again massaged and kissed her hands, tickled her nose—nothing worked.

Alex sang to her and read works by her favorite poet, Emily Dickinson.

"She will come around when her brain is ready, but it is good for you to keep trying," the doctor had said. Alex and Spencer suspected that she was giving them busywork. Jim and Robby came to take Alex out for supper since they were leaving for home, Flagstaff, the next morning.

Spencer held Jemma's hand, and just for himself, started humming "Candy Man," their song, the one that she could dance to like a wild woman. He started out low, but closed the door, took her hand again, and sang loud enough for anybody to hear him. He sang it three times and started on the fourth when he felt her fingers curl inside his own. His heart leaped.

He slipped his little finger into the curl and let her squeeze it. "Do it again, Jem," he said, and she did.

He pressed the call button and a nurse came running. Jemma did it for her, too. He tried her other hand and she did it again, even though the doctor had warned there might be some nerve damage where the lacerations were on her arm. Spencer was half crazy with joy.

Her folks were thrilled, too. Robby drew a happy face in the palm of her hand, making her fingers twitch. Jim talked to his daughter alone for a while, then Alex walked them to the car to say good-bye. It was an encouraging sendoff. While they were gone, Spencer did what he'd wanted to do since he left to go fishing; he kissed her lips. He thought he heard her make a sound. "Jemma, it's me. I love you." He saw her eyes move under her lids. He called for the nurse again. A couple of them came and checked her out.

"These are all good signs, right?" Spencer asked. "She's waking up?"

"They are good signs, but it is a slow process," one of the nurses said. "Take it a day at a time."

"You don't know my girl. She's quick," he said. "She was all-state in basketball."

Alex came back as the nurses were leaving. "What's happened?"

Spencer opened his mouth to answer, but froze. Jemma was looking right at him.

"Jemmabeth!" Alex screamed.

Spencer walked around the room, and she followed him with her eyes. That was it for the night, but what a night. They couldn't turn off the light as long as her eyes were open. Just before midnight, she began mumbling in her sleep. It was the most beautiful sound they'd ever heard.

The scriptures started a couple of days later, and Lizbeth was there when it happened. The first was the inscription on his Bible and she repeated it like a religious robot, as well as Psalm 37. Then the others came like a waterfall. "Let not your heart be troubled, neither let it be afraid."

There was no emotion, just the Word of God. "Be still, and know that I am God" was a particular favorite. "Blessed are the pure in heart, for they shall see God... My brethren, count it all joy when you fall into various trials, knowing that the testing of your faith produces patience."

Lizbeth smiled. She knew what her girl was doing, and now it was healing her broken head. "If thy whole body therefore be full of light, having no part dark, the whole shall be full of light, as when the bright shining of a candle doth give thee light."

In the midst of all the scriptures, she whispered his name, and Spencer cried like he was six years old again when he heard it. On the fifth day since she first opened her eyes, the doctor sent her home. She could move her head and say "yes" and "no" when asked a question. She was still taking medication and looked ghastly, but they let her go.

Spencer's dad drove up to get him. It was the second nice thing that he'd done since the accident. Spencer didn't say much until they approached the spot where the wreck had been. "I need to stop here, Dad."

Deep ruts remained in the ditch. Spencer plucked a strand of ribbon that was caught on a barbed wire fence, then walked around the area where he thought the Dodge might have come to rest. He sat on a protruding stone, trying to get a sense of peace for all that had happened to her beside this nondescript asphalt. A dark-stained area near a clump of droopy sunflowers caught his attention. He squatted beside it, then went to his dad's car and opened the trunk. There wasn't much there, except a roadside tool kit. He opened it and took out an ice scraper.

The window hummed as Max opened it. "What's wrong, son? Do you need some help?"

Spencer shook his head.

⋘◊⋙

Max watched his boy go down the embankment and get on his knees, pounding the ice scraper into the dirt. Spencer worked for fifteen minutes making a hole and burying the dark soil in it. It finally dawned on Max what his only child was doing. He hadn't cried since his own father died, but he let the tears come on down his face. He would have to have a heart of bricks to have done otherwise.

⋘◊⋙

With only a few days of freedom left, Spencer slept on the couch at Lizbeth's house. Trina sat with Jemma through the first night. The next day, Jemma drank seventeen big jelly glasses of water and had spent most of the day with the covers drawn up over her head. Alex was worried and called the hospital. The doctor assured her that such behavior was not abnormal after a brain injury. All that water had to be dealt with, so she was back and forth to the bathroom, but at least she was walking, with help.

She became obsessed with her hair, and repeatedly braided it, then unbraided it. Alex combed it as best she could, but her thick hair needed to be properly washed and she wouldn't be still long enough to let them. They were all in her bedroom when she suddenly perched herself on the side of the bed, then stood, wavering in the process. Everybody sprang into action. She ignored them and braided her hair.

"Let not your heart be troubled, neither let it be afraid," she said.

Spencer was exhausted.

"How on earth are you going to start basic training like this?" Alex asked.

"I don't know. Maybe they'll send me home," he said.

Jemma stood again and took a couple of steps toward the door. They let her go. She ran her hands over the door and spoke, her head resting on it. "Each day I go to my studio full of joy; in the evening, when obliged to stop because of darkness, I can scarcely wait for the morning to come... My work is not only a pleasure, it has become a necessity. No matter how many other things I have in my life, if I cannot give myself to my dear painting, I am miserable."

Spencer stared at her, a shiver running through his body. It was a quote by a French artist, Bouguereau, from an art history paper she had written two years earlier. She drank more water and stared at the glass as though it were a new concept, turning it over in her hands. What was going on in that precious head of hers? He had hoped that she would at least recognize him before he had to leave, but that was wishful thinking on his part. She unbraided her hair and quoted Emily Dickinson.

He went for a walk. He was going about this all wrong. How could he forget that her first love was her art, and, most likely, her second was to dance, third would have to be the Zephyr. He was lucky to even be on the list.

Spencer and Alex led her to the alley and stood waiting with her, at sunrise.

Jemma played with her hair until she heard the horn zipping past the station. She stopped for a second, then went back to her braiding. As the Zephyr approached, Jemma took them off guard and bolted up to the tracks on her own. They grabbed for her, but she was gone, adrenaline propelling each step. She stopped short of the rail bed.

Spencer was there, too, his feet firmly planted and his arms around her. She lifted her chin and closed her eyes. Spencer had never been this close to a moving train. He held on to Jemma like a child on the edge of a cliff. Her mouth curved into a half smile as the last car had passed.

"Jem?" Spencer asked, hoping for a further response.

She opened her eyes and looked down the tracks to the fast disappearing train, then went back to her hair.

"What did she say?" Alex shouted from the alley.

"Nothing," Spencer said.

They put her to bed, thinking she might be tired from the run to the tracks, but she was out as soon as they turned their backs. She went to the living room and sat in Papa's chair, rubbing the cut velvet arms.

"I think this is progress," Lizbeth said. "What if we showed her some of her art?" Lizbeth guided Jemma's fingers over the grand *trompe l'oeil* she had painted in the kitchen and over the painting of the cardinals in the good bedroom while Spencer raced to his house and got Papa's portrait that she had made for him when he was in Florence. He went to Trina's, too, and got the painting of the three friends as children and brought it back, along with Trina. Jemma was asleep by then. He paced the floor under the empathetic eyes of the women.

"What if this doesn't work?" Alex asked.

"Play 'Candy Man.' If anything could bring her back, that would be it," Trina suggested.

Jemma stirred in her sleep, bringing them to the foot of her bed. She sat up and drank a glass of water. Spencer brought the paintings to her. She reached for the one of Papa and felt the canvas like a sightless person, then gazed past them to the curtains waving in the breeze. "Let not your heart be troubled, neither let it be afraid," she said and covered her head with the quilt again.

Spencer, for lack of a better idea, stuck his head under the quilt with her. They all heard the faintest giggle before she conked out again.

Spencer emerged from the quilt. "At least she can laugh," he said and went to the couch. "Maybe she would like to see the cardinals in the pecan tree."

When she woke up, he led her to the trunk of the old tree and pointed out a red bird hopping amongst the leaves. Jemma never even looked up; she was too fascinated by the tree bark.

Sandy came over to join the vigil. "She and I used to say that amnesia was fake, something created by desperate soap opera writers. I wish I could make a movie of this because she won't believe it," she said to Spencer. "If it weren't so pathetic, it would be hilarious."

He drilled her with a hard look, then went out to the porch swing and sat with his head in his hands.

Trina joined him. "Spence, Brother Cleo would like to pray over her, but only if you want him to."

"Sure, tell him that would be nice. Jem would like that."

"I'm serious about the 'Candy Man' dance. I'll make everybody leave. Jemma loves dancing with you. Have you tried letting her paint or draw?"

Spencer sat up. "I should have thought of that. Her art supplies are all in her suitcase, ready to take on the honeymoon." He went inside and got out the brushes and watercolors she had so carefully packed for the honeymoon. Jemma was back in Papa's chair, running her hands over the arms again. Spencer set up her easel and a sheet of watercolor paper. He filled the little containers with water and mixed the colors as he had seen her do so many times.

"Jemmabeth?" he asked. "Would you like to paint?"

She looked at him, expressionless. "Yes."

Alex put the paintbrush in her hand and held the big palette for her. Jemma stood in front of the blank paper. Spencer guided her hand to a rosy red on the palette and dipped the brush, then took her hand to the paper. Jemma turned her gaze on the brush that was in her hand. She moved it in a circle on the paper and stared at her creation. Dipping the brush first into the water, then another color, she filled in the circle with geometric shapes. She sat back in Papa's chair, still holding the brush.

"It's the kaleidoscope window." Spencer smiled at her, even though it looked like the work of a preschooler.

❧

Lizbeth left the room. She could not bear to see her Jemma like that. The artist who had won a coveted fellowship in one of the world's best art schools was painting like she did when she was three years old. Lizbeth was glad that Cam at least did not have to suffer through this ordeal. He would have been devastated. Jemmabeth would come out of this; she had survived that wreck for a reason.

The kitchen had overflowed with casseroles and baked goods from folks all over the county since the accident. Lizbeth had given most of them to Willa for distribution at the Bethel church. The flower garden and home place mural that she had painted on the kitchen walls, the *trompe l'oeil*, served as a daily reminder of Jemma's spirit.

Lizbeth sighed, then went through the mail. She hadn't paid it any mind since the accident. There were so many cards for the family and a large package from Jemma's school in Paris. She took it to Alex, who promptly opened it and caught her breath. It contained several copies of a French magazine with a perfect likeness of Sandy and Martin on the cover. Alex gave a copy to Spencer, who took it to the hollyhock patch, where he stayed for a while.

❧

Spencer walked to the tracks. Jemma had such an affinity for them. He didn't even try to understand it. Everything she did fascinated him. Melanie had said it well. *"She is a creature of the arts, and we don't think like other people."* God had spared her life, and it was selfish of him to want more at this point. The doctor had said it could be a long process, so maybe he should be praying that there was no permanent damage. She had to love him, under all those scriptures and quotes.

"Spencer. How's our girl doing?" Brother Cleo's voice carried across the tracks.

"Come on over," Spencer said, waving.

They went to Jemma's room. She was out from under the quilt, but braiding again. Everybody but Spencer sat at the kitchenette. He paced around the backyard.

Brother Cleo opened the door after a full hour had gone by. Nobody knew what to expect. They did not expect a miracle, only encouragement.

Alex hugged him. "Thank you."

"She's a sweet child with a heart for the Lord, and He's gonna take care of her. She sure does like to quote the Scriptures. You call me anytime, and I'll drive down from Amarillo. Now, I mean that."

❦

Sandy went to get Spencer. "You need some rest. They're going to eat you alive at boot camp."

"So be it. I won't leave her," he said stiffly.

"Look, with Soap Opera Amnesia, Jem won't know whether you are here are not. You might as well be sleeping on your own bed and having your last bit of freedom. Go on home. When she gets well, you can say you were here the whole time."

Spencer stared her in the eye. "Sandra, now is not the time for your flippant attitude. I know you're hurting like the rest of us, so just cut it out." He walked past her and into the house.

Sandy went behind the little building that Jemma's grandpapa always called his "car house" and cried. Not because Spencer had chewed her out—she probably deserved that—but because her best friend was not right and her own life was about as far from perfect as it could get.

❦

Spencer sat with Jemma, reading a depressing book he had bought about brain injuries. It put him to sleep. He woke up to see Alex and Trina in the corner of the room, setting up Jemma's old portable stereo and a few records.

Alex came to his chair and whispered in his ear. "You go eat supper. I'll stay with her. When she wakes up, see if she'll dance with you, okay?" Alex patted his arm. It was his last night in Chillaton.

He had to be in Amarillo at eight sharp the next morning.

An hour went by before they appeared in the kitchen, headed to the bathroom. Spencer went to her room to wait. Alex brought her back and closed the door.

Jemma sat on the side of the bed. Her old chenille robe was knotted at her waist and she was barefooted. She undid her braids and redid them. Spencer sighed and sat next to her. He was dying to kiss her.

"Jem, would you like to dance with me?" He moved a stray lock of hair out of her eyes.

"Yes," she said in a monotone.

He put on "True Love's Ways." He helped her up and put his arms around her. She was so thin and moved like a junior-high boy at his first dance, not exactly the satiny smooth girl who could dance all night. The song ended and she stood there, seemingly unaware of anything. The next record dropped. It was their song. At the first notes of the harmonica, she looked right at him, like she did at the Zephyr when it moved down the tracks. His heart jumped. He held his hand out to her and she took it.

They danced out of sync with the rhythm, but at least she moved and kept her eyes on him. When the song finished, they stared at each other until Spencer had to look away. She was sweating, and the water pitcher was empty. He opened the door to see the faithful three peering at him from the kitchen. Jemma was still sweating in the center of the room, so he went to fill the pitcher for her.

"Listen," Alex said, over the sound of the water spilling out of the faucet.

Spencer turned it off. "Candy Man" was playing again. He dropped the pitcher and raced to the room. Jemma turned to him and held out her hands. He ran to her and kissed them, then started their dance. They danced again and again, and each time she moved a bit more like herself.

He looked her in the eye. "Jemmabeth Alexandra Forrester, I love you."

She looked down, breathing hard, then raised her chin. "I keep it in mind?" she said, and went back to bed, drawing her quilted shroud over her head.

Spencer turned to the doorway and smiled. She was on the right track.

❦

Lizbeth went to her at sunrise. The head wound was healing and the downy hairs that had sprung up around it would perhaps cover the area. Nobody would ever notice unless it was Nedra, scrutinizing her hair. It was Lizbeth's prayer that she would come back to them, that she would again paint like the masters, dance on those tracks, laugh at Lester's stories, and move like satin when she danced with her love. She touched Jemma's hand. "Sugar, Spencer is coming to tell you good-bye. I thought you might wear something besides that old robe."

Jemma sat up in the bed, picking at the Lone Star quilt that was spread over her.

Alex came in. "Good morning, sweet pea. I've got a wonderful bubble bath ready. You'll like it."

She let them get her ready, then sat in Papa's chair, chewing on her upper lip. Spencer arrived and sat on the couch while Buddy B waited in the Corvette to drive it home.

"I have to go away, Jem," he said, holding her hand. "While I'm gone, I want you to get better. I want you to paint me a picture, and I want you to wear your ring again," he said, slipping it on her finger. She raised her hand to the light and the stones glittered. Suddenly, she left the room and he followed her outside. She sat on the porch swing, hiding something in the folds of her skirt.

They had spent many hours in that swing ever since Lizbeth and Cam had moved into town. He pushed off and let the clinking of the extra chain fill the silence as the honeysuckle blossoms sweetened the air around them. He knew she loved that fragrance. "Here, baby, can you smell it?" he asked, breaking off a few blossoms and tickling her nose with them.

She giggled, making him grin, so he did it again. She wrinkled her nose and sniffed, then put the blooms in her pocket. "What do you have there?" he asked, pointing where her skirt was clutched in a knot. She shrugged but moved her hands away to reveal the Starry Night music box.

"Would you like for me to make it play?"

"Yes," she said and let him take it. He wound it and opened the lid. Jemma closed her eyes and smiled at the familiar sound of "I Will Wait for You." She looked at Spencer from the corner of her eye, then turned to face him. "I think of thee."

He caught his breath. She returned the music box to the folds of her skirt and stared down at it again.

He turned her chin. "Jem, do you remember other things?"

"No."

He was accustomed to that answer. "Do you remember love?"

"Yes."

"Do you remember us?"

"I remember a cowboy."

Spencer's face fell. Surely Paul was not stuck in her head. "What was his name?" he asked, not really wanting to hear the answer.

"Candy Man."

He kissed her and she warmed to it, but not like the old Jemmabeth. She looked aside, embarrassed.

"I have to leave, Jem."

"No."

"I have to serve in the army for a while, and I will be away from you. I'll miss you so much."

She touched her fingers to his lips. "Are we married?"

"No, baby, not yet."

"Oh."

"I have to go now. Buddy is here to take me to Amarillo."

"Will you kiss me again tonight? I like it."

"I will come back and kiss you."

"Deal," she said, nodding.

No matter what else had been tough in his life, this was the hardest thing he had ever done. He stood in front of her and held her hands, palms up, and kissed them.

She concentrated her gaze on the little scar on his chin, and chewed on her lip. "Don't leave. Stay and kiss."

"I love you, Jemmabeth," he said, no longer able to control his voice. "Good-bye." He kissed her one last time, then turned toward the truck.

"No!" she yelled, stamping her foot. He ran back.

"Love you." She gave him the honeysuckle bloom, wilted and crushed from her pocket. She kissed his hands the same way he had kissed hers, then whispered, "Spence."

Chapter 10
The Bride

Jemmabeth stayed in bed for two days, covering her head with a quilt even though, like Sandy said, the summer heat was bad enough to make her own mascara run. Neither Alex nor Lizbeth could coax Jemma out. There were no more scriptures or quotes, she wouldn't eat, and they were worried sick about her.

It was before dawn on the third night that she noticed Jemma was gone, but Alex did her best to keep her wits. Not wanting to wake Lizbeth, she maneuvered in the dark, searching each room and the front porch. She went to the backyard, hoping to find Jemma in the hollyhock patch, but then she saw her. She should have known. Jemma sat on the rails, huddled like a beggar. Alex was about to call out to her when she heard the sobs.

"Sweet pea," Alex said softly, moving to the cool steel rails next to her. "It's Mom."

Jemma reached for her hand. "Spence is gone, isn't he?"

Alex nodded.

"Mom, what has happened to me?"

Alex exhaled. "You were in a serious car accident, honey. We nearly lost you."

"Was I alone?" she asked, searching her mother's face.

"Yes, honey, you were alone."

"Did I hit somebody?"

"You hit a truck, but the driver wasn't seriously hurt." They heard the train and stood up. Alex stepped away, down the embankment, but Jemma turned toward the light coming down the tracks.

"Jem, come on. This is dangerous," Alex said.

Jemma moved off. "I'm all right, Mom. I'll be there in a minute."

Alex took a few steps, then waited. The Zephyr sped past, picking up speed as it left town. Jemma's hair and nightgown fluttered in its wake. She watched until it was out of sight, then turned and walked back to the house with her mother.

❧

Later, when Jemma was alone, she opened her dresser drawer and took out the velvet box containing his wedding ring. She'd had it specially engraved with Scottish thistles twining around the white gold band. It was beautiful, like him. She laid it carefully in the music box as the last few notes played. Now it was her turn to wait for her man like he had always waited for her.

❧

The artist's brain began to function properly. She had yet to paint, but she began to see things with an artistic eye again. She spent time alone with people she loved, just to reassure herself that she was becoming who she used to be. Trina took her out to Plum Creek and they talked under the cottonwoods. Nothing, though, could fill the void left by Spencer's absence. Nobody could tell her exactly how they parted. She had some memory of it, but that was not good enough. Rats. She needed to look him in the eye and make sure that all was well between them.

"Jemmerbeth," Lester said as they sat on his porch, "do you have any recollection about that old wreck you was in?"

"I remember picking up Bibles at the bookstore and that's it."

"That young Buddy B told us that he figures the Dodge helped save your life, it being so heavy and all."

"Where is the Dodge now?" she asked.

"Your daddy had it hauled off as far away as they could get 'er, I reckon. That's a fine little car that Spencer got for your gram, though."

Jemma stared blankly at the vacant lot across the street.

Lester shifted in his chair. He still wondered if she was all right in the head. Alex must have thought so, or she wouldn't have gone back to Arizona.

"Are you gonna be headin' down to Dallas soon?" he asked.

"I don't know. Mother and Daddy don't think I'm ready."

"What are you thinkin'?"

"I haven't started painting yet, Lester. How dumb is that? I can't go to art school and not be able to paint."

"Have you give it a try?"

"No. I'm scared. Even my new sketchbook is empty."

He wished he hadn't asked about Dallas. "Have you heard from Spencer?"

"Not yet, but I'm hoping he can call next weekend."

Their conversation was interrupted by a shout from the street. An oafish woman with bulging tapestry bags yelled at them as she approached.

Lester stood and cupped his hand behind his ear. "What's that?" he yelled back.

"Timms?" she shouted and lumbered nearer his driveway. Her hair flew around her head like a rusty wad of steel wool and her heavy, dark dress could easily carpet Lester's living room.

"I'm Lester Timms. What can I do you for?"

"Hanna," she said, jabbing her thumb toward her chest. "Your bride." She scowled at Lester. Lester turned three shades of maroon and walked out to meet her.

Jemma watched with great interest from the porch.

"Who iss she?" the woman asked, pointing at Jemma. "You got kids? No kids." She waved her finger in Lester's face.

Jemma leaned on the porch rail, straining to catch every word. The woman outweighed Lester by at least a hundred pounds. Lizbeth came out on her porch to see what the hubbub was. Lester started toward the house and tried to take one of the bags.

The woman jerked it back and rutted her head at him. "You go. I got bags."

Lester's face was a mixture of Elmer Fudd's and Wile E. Coyote's on a bad day.

"What iss this girl?" She wiped her forehead on her skirt, then set her bags on the porch and walked up to Jemma. "You are his?" she asked, jerking her head toward Lester, who was stammering explanations. Her heaving bosom rivaled that of Eleanor Perkins, who, up until this moment, had the most ample in town. The buxom newcomer was in dire need of deodorant.

"I am Jemmabeth Forrester, and I live next door. Who are you?" Jemma offered her hand. It might as well have been a toad the way the woman looked at it.

"Hanna Fitz," she said. "I am to be his bride. I am from the old country."

"Ah." Jemma swallowed her giggle.

"I've been meanin' to tell y'all about my mail-order bride," Lester said. His ears were the same color as Hanna's hair. He turned to the woman. "Come on in, Hanna, is it? That ain't the name on the picture I got." Lester strained to lift one of the bags. Jemma set it inside.

"So you will go now," Hanna said, with her hands on her hips and brown eyes peering into Jemma's. "I have business with this Timms." Her upper lip glistened and massive beads of sweat had collected at her hairline and on her nose.

"I can see that you do." Jemma winked at Lester, whose knuckles were white against the porch railing. The breadth of his body would be no match for even one of her legs.

Jemma skipped down the steps but not before she had one last look at the mail-order surprise who retreated into Lester's house with her navy wool dress undulating behind like a defective parachute. She was a sight.

⚜

There was no rest for Lester. He didn't even pick up his own mail. Lizbeth and Jemma had to pick up his and theirs as well as the *Chillaton Star*, but they were having a high time listening and watching. Hanna charged from room to room like a freight train and her voice carried like the fire station's noon whistle. Lester was seen off and on as he emptied buckets, boxes, and carried stacks of newspapers and magazines to the trash barrel. After a few days observing this hard labor, even Jemma and Lizbeth were exhausted.

Trina came for a visit. "Do you think he'll really marry her?" she asked as Lester hung out gigantic undergarments on the clothesline.

"Not if he knows what's good for him," Jemma said.

"Poor Lester. How humiliating. I'm not sure he got what he bargained for," Lizbeth empathized. "I hope she's feeding him."

Jemma giggled. "There may not be much left when she finishes with a meal."

"Do you know that is the first time I have heard you really laugh since the wreck?" Trina said.

"Maybe I'm getting back to normal. Have you heard from Le Claire?"

"That's why I'm here." Trina grinned and held up a letter. "I have been accepted and classes start September third. Nick is nearly as excited as I am."

Lizbeth and Jemma jumped on her with hugs.

"I *will* pay you back someday, girl. I promise. Are you going to be able to go by the end of August?"

"Obviously, there's no use in me going if. . ." Jemma couldn't say it.

"What?" Trina asked.

"I'm too scared to paint, but at least I have an idea for a new piece. Maybe I'll work up a sketch to see how it feels. You can stay with Helene even if I can't go. She's anxious for the company."

Trina looked to Lizbeth for help.

Lizbeth lifted her granddaughter's chin. "Sugar, you are going to be back to normal in every way. I believe that. The good Lord will not allow the gift He gave you to be wasted. His plan will unfold. You just remember that scripture about strength."

"What scripture?" Jemma asked.

"You gotta be kidding me," Trina said. "You pounded us with Bible verses all this time, but now you don't know one?"

"Maybe you needed to hear them." Jemma laughed again. "I'm sorry, Gram. I just don't remember."

"I can do all things through Christ, which strengtheneth me," Lizbeth said.

Jemma looked out the window. The verse roused her memory. "I will paint tonight. I feel it in my heart, but I hope I can put it on canvas."

The sketchbook had been an albatross for her. If she messed up in that book, she would not touch her brushes. She closed the door to the car house and switched on the lights. She walked in circles around the big canvas. Her old red cowboy boots set side-by-side, full of brushes. It was too much.

She opened the door and went up to the tracks. She lifted her face to the starry sky and whispered the verse again, then gathered her hair on top of her head and took a deep breath. Tomorrow could be the day she'd hear her sweet man's voice again. He should be her husband now, rather than her boyfriend. Rats. She knew he must have suffered after the accident. Everybody said that he was there every minute they would allow. Bless his heart.

Her brainwaves seemed retrievable tonight, unlike many times since the wreck when complete thoughts seemed to float away from her. It was time for her to put it to use before it left her again. She had missed the exhilaration of passion, in her work and in her heart. She missed him. She looked down at the car house. Spencer had it all redone after the tornado ripped it in two, and now the lights were shining, ready for her to begin again.

Lizbeth awoke to the sound of water running in the bathtub. She sat up and called Jemma's name as the clock chimed five times, blocking out her voice. She pulled her robe over her nightie. A dim light shone under the bathroom door.

"Jemmabeth, are you all right?" she asked with some concern.

"I'm sorry, Gram. I just wanted to relax and get the paint off me," Jemma said. "I didn't mean to wake you."

Lizbeth dared not ask more. "That's fine. I needed to get up and read my Sunday school lesson again." She switched on the kitchen light.

"I'll go with you to church, but this evening I want to hear Brother Cleo," Jemma said.

"That's fine. I'll go with you tonight." Lizbeth lit the burner and got the percolator going on the stove. She sat at the kitchenette, reading her lesson. A light came on at Lester's house. It was in the back bedroom, his room. She knew they were sleeping in separate beds because Hanna never pulled her shades. She watched as Lester slipped down his back steps and out of sight behind his garage.

Jemma emerged from the bathroom in her old robe with a towel wrapped around her head. She gave Lizbeth a hug. "I did it, Gram. I painted all night. I want to see what you think. C'mon." She tugged at her arm.

"Sugar, I'm not even dressed, and you are barefooted. You could step on a goat's head sticker or a snake out there."

But Jemma was determined and coaxed her to the car house. She unlocked the door and turned on the lights.

Lizbeth's heart skipped a beat. "My goodness, sweet child of mine. Where did you ever get this gift to paint but from the Lord?" Lizbeth studied the piece. "Why did you choose to paint him?"

"It's burned into my head."

"My, my. Brother Cleo spent a good amount of time on his knees with you, and it's fitting that you paint him like that."

The door behind them creaked, sending them both a few inches off the floor.

"Lester!" Lizbeth yelped. "What are you doing in here?" She gathered her housecoat around her like a mummy.

"Shhh," Lester whispered, "that woman will hear you. Listen, I gotta talk, and I ain't got much time. Mornin', Jemmerbeth. Well, I'll be Uncle Johnny. I see that you are gonna be goin' back to school in Dallas with that fine paintin'. Did Miz Liz tell you that we had us a circle prayer for you?"

"No, but I remember Brother Cleo and his words from someplace."

Lester walked closer to the canvas. "Well, if that don't beat all. You've still got it, Jemmer. You've got it even better, if that's possible."

Lizbeth sneaked to the door. "I need to get dressed, so if you'll excuse me," she said, pulling on the handle.

Lester was against it in a flash. "Oh no, Miz Liz, you can't leave me in my hour of need. Brother Cleo'll be havin' another circle prayer—only it'll be for me this time."

"Let's go around the other side of the house," Jemma said. "I don't think she can see us if we come in the east door, through the hollyhock patch."

"That woman can see through brick and steel," Lester said, his eyes still like Elmer Fudd's.

They crept around the dark side of the house and into the east door, as planned. Lizbeth and Jemma dressed while Lester hid in the quilt closet.

Lizbeth cleared her throat. "Come out, Lester. I'm not going to talk with you in there."

"It would mean a lot to me if you would, Miz Liz," Lester said, his voice muffled into the stacks of quilts.

"I'll stay in there with you, if y'all want me to," Jemma said. "Just so I can hear the phone."

She went to the kitchen and got chairs for them. The closet was long and narrow, so they had to sit facing each other. Jemma sat on the floor. Lester's face had taken on a pink tone ever since Hanna's arrival. It didn't really suit him. Something else was different, too.

"What became of your moustache?" Lizbeth asked.

"That woman," he said.

"Lester, did you send off for her like a packet of flower seeds?" Lizbeth narrowed her eyes.

He nodded. The tips of his ears changed from pink to red.

"Where did you find her?"

"In the back pages of that *Ring of Truth* magazine. The ad said, 'The woman of your dreams.' Well, sir, I didn't plan on no nightmare. Her name's different, plus she don't look nothin' like her picture."

"Isn't that a political magazine?" Jemma asked.

"It's how I keep up with the Republicans. 'Know the enemy,' is what I always say. That could be in the Good Book, too."

"Looks like the Republicans pulled one on you," Lizbeth said, trying not to laugh.

"I paid three hundred dollars to bring her over. My old truck cost less than that, and she's grieved me a hundred times more than that pickup. I ought to sue somebody, but I ain't sure who. Probably the Republican Party."

"Maybe she just doesn't know how things are done in America," Jemma said.

"All she does is give me work to do and chew me out. She's got Beelzebub's temper on her. We ain't even talked about our future, heaven help me."

"Your future?" Lizbeth asked. "It seems to me that when you send off for a mail-order bride, you have set your course for the future."

Jemma yawned. "I think we should get to know her better. Maybe she's scared or lonely."

"Well, sir, I don't know about the lonely part, but that woman ain't scared of nothin'."

"I think you're right, Jemmabeth. We'll have her over for supper tonight. You make sure she comes, Lester."

Lester tapped his foot on the wood floor and scratched behind his ear. "I ain't sure that I want to keep her. No offense, Miz Liz."

"You will make good on your promises, Mr. Timms," Lizbeth said without hesitation.

Lester rose slowly. "I should've been happy just gettin' your mail, Miz Liz, and drivin' you to the post office and whatnot. Once you up and got your own license, I couldn't even do that for you. Now all I've got is my tales, and she's probably gonna put the quietus on that. At least my chinchillers was good to cozy down with at night, but I ain't even interested in sharin' a meal with this big 'un. She's fixin' to put me in the ground." He picked up his chair and left.

Lizbeth stared after him. "I suppose I'd better get ready for church. I'll have to come right home and get busy since we're having company tonight."

❧

Jemma sat by the phone, half asleep. The stupid wreck had stolen their wedding from them. Was that a part of God's Great Plan, or was it her punishment for falling for Paul? When the phone did ring, she was dreaming that the Zephyr was in a race with Spencer. She fell back on the bed at the sound of his voice.

"Hi, Jem, do you know who this is?" he asked, not sure if she would have the answer.

"I sure do. Hi, Daddy," she teased.

Spencer was silent.

"Oh Spence, I'm sorry. I'm so bad. I love you, I love you, and I miss you."

He laughed. "I love you more. Now you sound like yourself."

"My head is better, but my heart's in bad shape. I wanted to be your wife by now, babe. It's another thing for you to forgive about me."

"Jemmabeth, don't ask me to forgive you for nearly dying. I'm just glad that you know who I am and remember loving me."

"I not only remember, I think about you and dream about you day and night. Are they being mean to you and teaching you how to shoot?"

"It's about like you would imagine—kind of like an evil football camp with guns. I don't want to talk about it. I want to talk about you. Are you painting?"

"Yes, sir. I finished my first piece this morning."

"Not another one of me, I hope."

"Hey, I love to paint you, but this one is of Brother Cleo, praying for me, I guess. It came from some fuzzy place in my head. Spence, we need to see each other. I know that I wasn't right when you left."

"You're telling me. I need to hold you and kiss you and dance with you. I need to look in your eyes and see if you are really okay."

"If I'm not 100 percent, I'm close. Hey, Trina got accepted to Le Claire. Now if I can just convince Mother and Daddy to let me go back there myself."

"That's great! How's the church coming?"

"It's really nice. Your design is beautiful."

"Next will be the chapel for the nursing home. I guess that'll have to wait until I get out. I'd better go because I'm getting looks from people in line here."

"Oh Spence, kiss me through the phone. I love you."

"I love you, too. You be careful. Don't get a second concussion. You know that the Corvette is waiting for you when you are ready to drive again. Just call Buddy B. Is Sandy still there?"

"You're too good to me. Sandy left today to be with Martin's parents in Tyler."

"Well, maybe you will get well fast enough to go to school next month. Gotta go. Love you. Here's your kiss."

"Bye, babe," she whispered.

Then she ran to her room and cried. Again.

Hanna came early, without Lester. "Timms, he iss working. He will not be here."

"Really?" Lizbeth turned a suspicious eye on their guest. "That's too bad. I made his favorite dessert, too."

Hanna lifted lids off the pots on the stove. "More salt," she said, dipping a stubby finger in the potatoes. "Too much onion," she said as she sampled a corner of the meat loaf, fresh out of the oven.

Lizbeth pulled herself up to her full height. Nobody had ever criticized her cooking before. Ever. "We might as well begin. Let's bow our heads for grace."

Hanna frowned. "Who iss this Grace? Too many women around Timms. Iss not good."

This could be a fun night, Jemma thought, as she struggled to concentrate on the blessing. Hanna's lack of deodorant deserved a prayer, for sure.

"Hanna, what old country are you from? I have a friend who was stationed in Germany." Jemma smiled like sweet cakes.

"You haff no need to know this." Hanna took an extra portion of Lizbeth's homemade rolls.

"I think my granddaughter is being polite, Miss Fitz, is it? Good manners are the mark of a lady in this country."

"Too much talk in this country. Not enough work. I will teach Timms this."

"We thought it would be nice to get to know you a little better since we will be neighbors," Lizbeth said, her lips forming a sickly smile.

Hanna's head was bowed low over the fried okra while Lizbeth spoke of the variety of churches, a choice of the North or South Chillaton Quilting Clubs, the library volunteer group, and all the amenities offered a new female resident of Chillaton. Jemma ate her corn on the cob and wiped the butter off her chin. Hanna did not bother to clean hers. It was a stretch to imagine her volunteering for library duty.

"In the old country, I haff eight sisters older than me. My mother, she had a sickness. I take care of her until she died. Now it iss my turn to go the ways of the worlt. Timms iss to be my husband, no? He iss not your husband. You find your own. I go home now to see if Timms has done his work. No more talk."

Lizbeth planted her tea glass with a thud that reverberated down the metal legs of the kitchenette. "Miss Fitz, you are in America now. That alone is a privilege. How you got here is another story. I don't know all the details about mail-order brides, but I do know this. Lester Timms is a fine man. He brought you here with his own money. You should be grateful for that. If you don't know how to show gratitude to another human being, then I will be glad to help you. I have no romantic notions about Mr. Timms, but he is a good friend to me, and I will not tolerate him being mistreated.

We can live as good neighbors, or you can go back to where you came from." She took a breath. "Would you please pass the potatoes, Jemmabeth?"

Hanna dipped her tongue to her chin and cleared the last bits of butter from it. She maintained a steady gaze at Lizbeth. "You haff the big talk. I do not hit this Timms with pots. It iss not as you say. You and I will not be this good neighbor. We will liff in the big city. I am going the ways of the worlt. Timms will be my husband and not your friend. Good-bye, American old lady." She rose and left, slamming the screen door, but not before she scrounged the last of the rolls.

Jemma exhaled and turned to Lizbeth. "She has to go."

Lizbeth finished her meal in silence. Jemma wasn't quite sure what to make of it, but she cleared the table and did the dishes. Lizbeth sat in Papa's chair and read her Bible, marking certain pages with dainty, crocheted crosses.

"Gram, are you all right?" Jemma asked when she could stand it no longer.

"Oh sugar, I'm sorry to have neglected you since supper, but I had to collect my thoughts and prepare my heart."

"For what? Hanna?"

"For battle. I was angry with her, as you could probably see. I needed God's Word to calm me down. Now I know what I must do."

"Do you need an assistant?"

"The battle will be with my temper, Jemmabeth. I am going to follow the Scriptures to deal with that woman. We must stand by Lester, but we cannot lose sight of the fact that he brought her here and she is God's child, just like the rest of us."

"You're a better Christian than I am, Gram. I'd send her back."

"I would, too, but that's not an option. The Word says to love your enemies, do good to them that despise you. Now that should be a hefty goal in this case. No pun intended, mind you."

Jemma leaned down to kiss Lizbeth's cheek. The Moonlight Over Paris perfume she always wore, especially with company, was wasted this evening.

Lizbeth patted her hand. "You run along and paint. I'm going to work on a quilt."

Jemma went to the car house and sat on the stool, staring at the floor. She had chosen to take the Christian walk when she was in the third grade, but she really didn't know anything about it. She was on more of a Christian crawl. It seemed to her that almost everyone was better at living their faith than she was. She sighed and placed a blank canvas on the easel. Lester had made her so many while she was in the hospital. He did not deserve to be treated like dirt. Gram had a plan and she always carried through on things. Jemma should stick to painting now that she knew she could still do it.

⌘

A week later, Lester rapped at Lizbeth's front door in the dark of night, his face plastered against the oval glass.

Jemma got out of bed and put on her robe. "Lester, did you fall or something?"

He had a hefty bruise on his cheek and a black eye.

He shuffled inside. "Could I sleep on the couch, Jemmerbeth? That woman is after my hide. No offense, but she got in my bed tonight. I don't even know when she did it, seein' as how I was dog-tired from my chores. First thing I knew, I had rolled plumb to the other side of the bed. I dreamed that I was helpin' push the Dodge out of a ditch when I woke up and found myself next to her big backside. Imagine the gall of her invadin' my sleepin' quarters without matrimony. I ain't goin' back to my own house until she's gone, and you can bank on that."

Jemma got a pillow and some quilts. She spread them on the couch and kissed Lester on the forehead. The bruises were plentiful. Papa's clock struck three as she lay in bed. The woman was a criminal to do that to Lester. Rats on her. Surely Gram would see that now. She dozed off thinking about Spencer and how much she would love to invade his sleeping quarters.

Lizbeth did not know what to do. She thought her plan had been going well until this.

"Miz Liz, I know you had a fancy to wear her down with good deeds and kind words, but all it's doin' is making her think you're, no offense now, 'an old American donkey,' to use her exact words. I figgered you was goin' by the Good Book, but the way I see it, the good Lord never had no notion of that woman. I'm thinkin' she's a twin to old Beelzebub himself."

Lizbeth poured herself another cup of coffee and sat at the kitchenette next to Jemma. "Where do you suppose she thinks you are now?" She eyed the bruises on his face.

"I left the car down by the Ruby Store. I'm supposed to be buyin' groceries this mornin'. She's got the place stocked up with vittles. You'd think the Russians were comin' tomorrow."

Lizbeth shook her head. "I have been praying for Hanna's heart to soften and for her to open up to friendship. Maybe it hasn't been enough time."

"No offense, Miz Liz, but I don't know how much longer I can hold on," Lester said, his shoulders sagging and his neck slung out like a vulture's. "I can't even conjure up a good tale to tell these days. 'Course there ain't no time to tell one anyway. I thought I put in my fifty year down to the station. I didn't know that I was gonna have to start toein' the work line like this in my sunset years with a big ol' rhino breathin' fire at me."

"What would she do if you pretended to be sick?" Jemma asked.

"I already tried that. She poked me with a broom handle until I had bruises all up and down my ribs. I'm tellin' you, she's a mean one. Yesterday she smacked me so hard that I fell plumb off my chair. I got this shiner from workin' too slow to suit her."

Lizbeth went to the window, her jaw set.

"She hit you with a broom?" Jemma asked, just to reiterate.

"Yes ma'am, then come hence to usin' her fist right across the back of my head. Give me a headache, for sure." Lester rubbed the back of his neck. "There's been other things, too." His voice cracked.

"She told us that she didn't hurt you," Lizbeth said. "She's a liar to boot."

"She said she didn't hit him with pots, Gram. Maybe we didn't ask the right questions. I say we call the sheriff on her."

"Well, I know the good Lord would not want this to continue." Lizbeth's lips were in full pucker. "What do you say, Lester?"

"I ain't one to go whinin' to the law, but I don't know what else to do. I got my own self into this pickle, but I thought I'd get me some company. Instead I got me a rattlesnake from the *old country*, wherever the Sam Hill that is."

Lizbeth smacked her hands on the table. "Lester, we are going to go see Dr. Huntley first, then we'll go to the sheriff with this. I think your safety is in danger, and Hanna needs help as well."

"It will take forever for a trial or some other legal action. I'd like to try something else," Jemma said.

"What's that, sugar?"

"Well, Hanna was so concerned that first day about Lester not having any kids. We might run her off if we convinced her that he does have kids. Have you told her that you don't have any children?"

Lester shook his head. "We haven't talked about nothin', except my chores and my money."

Lizbeth frowned. "These are serious charges we'll be making against her. I don't know as she needs to be run off to harm someone else."

"Nobody else would be thickheaded enough to take up with her," Lester said, feeling his ribs.

"Let me just try this, Gram. I could get things started today," Jemma said. "Lester could stay at Willa's house because Hanna would never look for him over there."

Lizbeth nodded. "I suppose we have to be the Lord's hands on earth. If Hanna's goal was to come to America, she has done that much."

"Her goal is to *go the ways of the worlt*," Lester said, "and I'm ready for her to take off."

"The ways of the world are sinful, right, Gram?" Jemma asked, hopeful that her grandmother was lending her full support to this.

Lizbeth twisted her wedding ring. Cam would have tackled this predicament with a cool head and a Christian heart. She had to do the best she could without him. "All right; I'll take him to Willa's myself. Lester, I'm going to hang some sheets on the line for cover. Then you sneak around the hollyhock patch and out to the car. I'll be along directly. First, though, I'm calling the doctor for an appointment for you."

Lester exhaled. He stood and put his arms around her neck. It was a first. "No offense, Miz Liz, but I had to give you a hug of appreciation. I've been kindly in a bad way lately, and I hope you don't mind the gesture."

Lizbeth recovered quickly and lowered her voice. "Since Jemmabeth is here with us, I find nothing wrong with a hug once every few years between old friends. You're a good man and a good neighbor to me. I've told Jemma how you sat up with us while she was in the hospital. We all care for you very much, and we'll see this through. Don't worry about Hanna any more. Now I've got a call to make and some sheets to hang."

"Lester, get in the closet and read the *Star*. I have some business to take care of myself." Jemma ushered him out of the room. She made her list and timetable. It had to be perfect because Lester didn't have a phone so Hanna would have to come to Lizbeth's house to take the call. She waited until Lizbeth took Lester to the doctor's office before making the first one. "Sandy, I need you to do me a favor," she said.

Sandy was quite willing to participate.

Jemma went to Lester's house and knocked.

Hanna lumbered to the door, wiping her forehead on her arm. "I'm too busy for you," she said, stopping short of the screen door. "Timms iss not here. Go away."

"You have a phone call at our house," Jemma said, her voice like an angel's.

"Phone call? I haff no calls." Hanna frowned. "Iss it the government of America?"

"Could be. It sounds important. I think you'd better take it."

Hanna made a disgusting noise in her throat, opened the door, and spat just past Jemma's foot. "I haff no time for this telephone." She grunted her way down the steps toward Lizbeth's house. She picked up the receiver and yelled into it, "It iss Hanna Fitz."

Jemma could imagine Sandy's response on the other end.

"What iss this? Timms iss not missing. He iss here. He iss getting food." Hanna's face changed from ruddy to fire red as the fury rose and settled in the shafts of her hair. "Daughter? No. No visits. I go now. No visits." She slammed down the receiver and made for the back door, ignoring Jemma and squawking in a foreign language.

Buddy B and Twila came by right as the noon whistle blew. Twila had borrowed six little nieces and nephews, as instructed. Jemmabeth watched from the porch swing. The crew stood on Lester's porch waiting for Hanna to answer the door.

"What iss it? Go away. Timms iss not here," Hanna shouted from inside.

"Hey, we need to see Granddaddy. He hasn't called in weeks and he was supposed to babysit tonight," Buddy yelled in the door. Twila's nieces and nephews pressed their faces to the screen. Perfect.

"Shoo, shoo!" Hanna poked at them with her infamous broom. "No babies, never."

"Oh yes, he keeps them all every Friday and Saturday—both nights, too," Buddy shouted. "We've got the baby in the car. She fixin' to need a diaper change real quick."

"Granddaddy takes care of his great-grandkids," Twila said, getting into it.

Hanna slammed the door in her face. Twila, Buddy, and their entourage went to the back door and started up again. Hanna pulled all the shades.

⋙⋘

Jemmabeth watched Lester's house like a real-life Nancy Drew while Lizbeth drove over to Willa's with a couple of pecan pies. She walked home because they would need the car for the next phase.

Hanna stayed in the house until bedtime, then appeared. "Old lady!" Hanna yelled in the back door.

Lizbeth was already in bed, and Jemma was writing to Spencer at the kitchenette.

"Are you talking to me?" Jemma asked.

"I need that old one," Hanna said, coming in the door, uninvited.

"That's a rude way to talk about my grandmother, Hanna. I won't get her until you show a respectful tongue in your head."

"Where iss Timms? You are hiding him." Her beady eyes darted around the room.

"Did you hit Lester?" Jemma asked.

Hanna stopped and looked Jemma up and down. She puffed out her cheeks and folded her arms. "Timms iss my business. I am to be the wife."

"You may have to marry him in jail because that's where you will be living if you ever touch him again. We have laws in America to protect people from being beaten."

"Iss my business, not yours." She returned Jemma's glare.

"No, it is the business of the great state of Texas and her people," Jemma said, widening her eyes at Hanna. "I suggest you go home and think about that."

Jemma couldn't sleep. She heard Hanna running bathwater before the 6:23 Zephyr came through. Jemma got dressed and waited in the hollyhock patch. At promptly seven o'clock, Trina drove up with Willa in the backseat of Lizbeth's car. After some maneuvering, Willa was up the steps and standing tall on Lester's back porch. She knocked hard with her cane.

Hanna came to the kitchen window and peeked out. Spying Willa, she ducked into the shadows.

Willa knocked again. "Ain't no use in hidin'. I ain't leavin' til you open this door."

Jemma was impressed with her tone.

Hanna cracked the door open. "Timms iss not here. He has run away."

"Is that so?" Willa leaned into the screen. "It don't matter anyway because I've got a piece of paper here that says him and me are legally man and woman. I heard around town that you was movin' in. Well, if you know what's good for you, you'll hightail it out of this county, maybe out of the state. I've got Lester Timms just where I want him. C'mon out here now and show yourself."

Hanna ventured a longer look. Willa peered in the glass at her, too, her generous caboose sticking way up in the air. Trina sat in the car, mesmerized, as was Jemma.

"Enough pussyfootin' around. Either you show yourself, or I'm callin' the sheriff on you," Willa said.

"I am not knowing that Timms has a woman. He iss a liar to me. I come to this place to go the ways of the worlt, and I find nothing but talk and lies. Americans are all the big liars," Hanna said from behind the door.

"Enough said. I'm comin' in. There's just so much of this hogwash that I can take." Willa pulled back the screen and twisted the doorknob. It was locked. She blasted the door with her cane. Just as she did, Lizbeth came across the driveway.

"Help my life, Willa, what are you doing? You're going to scare poor Hanna to death," she said, her tone like butter frosting.

"This woman is insultin' the U.S. of A. and tryin' to commit a crime by marryin' Lester. She can either get herself on the next train out of town, or I'm fixin' to have a go at her right now."

Hanna appeared in the door again. "This crazy woman goes away. I do nothing wrong. It iss Timms that goes to jail!"

Jemma joined them on the little porch. "Hanna, I'll take you to the train station. You can catch the next train to California. There are lots of jobs there and it's on the ocean, too." They heard words in a foreign language that didn't sound complimentary to anyone. "I will give you some money for the trip," Jemma offered.

All became quiet on the other side of the door. "Money iss good," Hanna said.

"You get your things together, and I'll be back in an hour." Jemma saw a few frazzled copper hairs emerge from around the corner of the glass.

"Crazy woman go first," Hanna said.

They all left, not knowing which one she thought was the craziest. Jemma and Trina sat in the metal chairs in the hollyhock patch. When Trina could stand it no longer, she erupted in laughter.

"Shhh. She'll hear you," Jemma said, barely able to hold it in herself.

"I can't help it, girl. Mama should get an Academy Award for that. I don't know how she did it."

"I know. She was perfect. Everybody was, except you. You didn't have to do squat."

"Hey, I had to sit in the car and pinch myself to keep from laughing the whole time."

"Well, it was worth it to protect poor Lester. Did you see all those bruises on his face? She could be in jail for that."

"Yeah, I'd like to chase her around with her own broom."

"What's he doing at your house? Where did he sleep?"

"I gave him my bed, and I slept with Mama. She snored all night long. Creepers, it was bad. When we left, he was doing some hammering around on the porch. It could use some handyman work, that's for sure."

"Oops, there she is. I'll see you later."

Hanna was early, and the same two bags that she came with were bulging in her grip. Jemma went for a tour of Lester's house. She didn't see anything out of place, but then she didn't know his things all that well, either. "You had better not be taking any of Lester's belongings because I would have you arrested as a thief, too," Jemma said in a bold move.

Hanna begrudgingly unbuckled one of the bags. She took out a silver cup, a lace collar, two teacups, and an ivory shoehorn. "There. We go now."

"Open up the other one, too."

The big woman snarled but unfastened the second bag. She took out a small satin purse, a porcelain doll, a painted fan, and a book. "You are this mean woman," Hanna said.

"Why am I the mean one? I did not beat a helpless old man and then steal from him. Go on—get in the car before I change my mind."

"You giff the money now," Hanna said with an evil eye.

Jemma had seen the evil eye before, and it had no effect on her. "You get in the car *now*." She pointed the way.

Jemma waited at the station until she saw Hanna seated on the moving train. She had bought a one-way ticket to Los Angeles and had given her plenty of her own money to eat and sleep for two months. She thought that Spencer would approve of spending her money that way. If she didn't have Lizbeth's car, she would have danced down the tracks to get home. Lester had been spared the misery of being painted into a corner with no recourse. Jemma knew that feeling to some extent from her summer fling with Paul. Now she couldn't wait to get home and wait for her soldier man to call.

Chapter 11
Sunflowers

S pence!" She closed her eyes and fell back on the bed, propping her feet on the headboard. "I thought you'd never call. I miss you so much."

"Hey, baby. I am dying to see you. Are you still making progress?"

"Yup. In fact, I talked with Mom and Daddy, and I'm going to Le Claire next week. I can't wait. I've done two paintings since you left."

"I'll come to see you in Wicklow then. Can y'all get everything in the Corvette?"

"I'm shipping most of our stuff, but I'm about to run out of money. I think I'll have to get a job when I get there."

"I'll take care of you, Jem. You just write checks on my account. You don't need to work."

"You're sweet to do that, but we aren't married yet. I want to use my own money, unless I have an emergency. Remember, my grandparents are paying all my expenses this year. So I'll pay Trina's tuition and her books out of my savings. I've kept that much back, but I gave some of it to Lester's mail-order bride."

"His what?"

Jemma told him the whole story. He laughed at first, then like everybody else, got serious. "She should have been reported, but I guess it's too late for that.

"I decided this called for quick action. Besides, Gram felt kind of sorry for the woman. I think she must have been raised the same way she treated Lester."

"She needs help then," Spencer said.

"They wouldn't have done anything but keep her in the county jail. Then when she got out, she would have been right back on Lester's doorstep with a vengeance."

"Well, what's done is done. You did well. Brains and beauty all rolled into one. Your picture gets lots of comments around here. Most of the guys think I have a movie star's photo. They can't believe that I have a fiancée who looks like you do."

"Oh brother. I don't look too hot with this weird spot on my head. I have to figure out a way to comb my hair over it. Rats. A comb-over at my age."

"You could be bald and look good."

"Spence, when are we going to get married? I want to invade your sleeping quarters."

"You have no idea how much I want you to do just that."

"So let's get married."

"Jem, you know that I will probably wind up in some foreign place."

"How will they decide that?"

"They gave us a bunch of tests, so I'm sure those scores determine placement."

"Well, that's no help. You ace all tests."

"When do you think we should try the wedding again?" he asked.

"Sandy said they give you some time off between your first year and your second year."

"Maybe I'll get stationed in Europe like Martin did. We could live on a base there." He didn't sound too convincing.

"You really think you might go to Europe? That'd be fun."

"Baby, we have to face the fact that I may get sent to Vietnam."

"Oh Spence, I can't think about war, not now, when we're almost happy." Uh-oh. Was that Miss Scarlett talking? At least she didn't add *fiddle-dee-dee*.

"I have to go now. I'll call you next week."

"I'll be at Helene's. I love you."

"I love you, too. You are everything to me. You take care. Bye."

❦

Jemma sat in Papa's velvet chair, eating pie with Lizbeth. "I can't imagine what it was like for you to have all three of your sons in uniform at once. How did you stand it?"

"We simply went on with life and worked harder and longer. Your papa and I consoled each other and, of course, Julia was a distraction, but I would have crumbled without Cam."

"I don't have Papa."

"You will hold up, honey. You have to trust in the Lord."

"I just don't understand how God could let Luke and Matthew be killed. I know you must have prayed every minute for their safety. Doesn't God hear the prayers of righteous people?"

"I am not that righteous, Jemmabeth, and His ways are not always our ways. We have to pray for strength to endure whatever answer comes."

"Then why pray?"

"We pray because the Word says to never give up and bring all our needs to Him. We are told to believe that we will receive what we ask for. In my heart of hearts, sugar, I knew that my boys wouldn't come home. That's not to say that it wasn't a shock when we lost them, and goodness knows we still grieve over them. When I prayed for their safe return, it was with a heavy burden of doubt. We loved those boys and they brought us great joy, but when they left, I had a gnawing feeling that they were part of a much greater plan of sacrifice and justice. I tried to take some comfort in that thought, but it was small."

"Maybe Spence is part of something bigger than our plans for the future. But I don't get it. I tried to have a good attitude about him being drafted, but Vietnam seems like a trap."

"God doesn't give us more than we can handle. We may struggle, but that is part of living on this old earth."

Jemma moved on the couch with her grandmother. "I want to be with Spencer as his wife, Gram. I want to love him in that way."

"I know you do, honey, and that's good because it's the way God made us. It will happen."

Jemma gazed into her grandmother's eyes, so like her own. "Do you have that heavy feeling of doubt about Spence? Please tell me."

"I believe you and Spencer will have a life together. He is not my flesh-and-blood child, and I don't mean to sound like one of Lester's gypsy fortune-tellers, but I have a good feeling about things."

"I don't see why I had to have that wreck. All things are supposed to work together for good for those who love the Lord. Where's the good in an accident?"

"Sometimes we never know the good that comes of bad. I do know that joy often follows pain, and Helene told me once that joy follows you around. I believe that, too." She stroked Jemma's hair, making sure not to touch the area that had been shaved.

Jemma drew a long breath and stood. "Enough of this sad talk. I have to get busy packing and painting. We need to have some fun around here before Trina and I leave. Should we go out to Plum Creek or the Salt Fork?"

"Let's go to the river," Lizbeth said. "I heard that Plum Creek is not running just now. We need rain."

They heard a loud engine roar out front and then the little *do-ink* knob sounded on the front door. Lizbeth peeked out. "Who on earth could that be?"

"Just so it's not Hanna, that's all I can say," Jemma said.

A heavy-set black man stood in front of them, cowboy hat in hand. "Ma'am, my apologies for showin' up like this. I'm Joe Cross from down Sweetwater way. I'm the truck driver that was in the wreck with Miss Forrester. I wanted to stop by and see how she's comin' along."

Jemma moved in front of Lizbeth. She opened the screen door and looked into Joe's eyes. She slipped her arms around his neck, and he returned the embrace. They stood like that for several minutes, interrupted only by an occasional sniff.

"Thank you for coming," Jemma said.

Joe took out a bandana scarf and wiped his eyes. "I'm on a run to Los Angeles, but I'm real glad to see that you are up and at 'em. You sure had everybody worried there for a while."

Lizbeth shook his hand. "It's very kind of you to check on Jemmabeth, Mr. Cross. Promise me that you'll come by for a meal on your way back. Jemma is leaving for school this Friday, but I'll be here and I'd love to visit with you."

"Yes ma'am, I'll make it a point to do that. I'll call first, though." Joe shifted his weight and looked down at his hat. "I have a confession to make. I kept one of them little New Testaments. I hope you don't mind. It was the one that I had near me before the ambulance got there. It sort of inspired me to speak a scripture in your ear."

Jemma had a sudden chill. "What scripture?"

"My own favorite, John 14:27: 'Let not your heart be troubled, neither let it be afraid.'"

Jemma joined him after the first word. It was the verse she had repeated more than any others. "Mr. Cross, I never tried to learn that verse; you taught it to me out in that ditch."

The three of them stood in awe for a moment.

Joe shook his head. "Well, it was no more than anybody else would've done. I brought you somethin', though. Hold on." He walked to his big rig and came back holding a coffee can full of sunflowers, still on their roots. "I dug this clump up close to where it happened. A batch of 'em were sort of like a pillow for your head when I found you."

"Mr. Cross, you are an uncommon man," Lizbeth said, tears brimming. "We are eternally grateful to you. We'll pray for your safety on the highway and for your family."

"Please, call me Joe. I live with my mother, but she's in real poor health. I have to leave her with my sister when I'm drivin'. I suppose it's worth it because I make good money on the road. Speakin' of which, I'd best be goin'." He turned to Jemma and nodded. "Good luck at your school."

Jemma kissed his cheek. "Thank you."

"Bye, now." He started up his truck and pulled away, leaving the two women standing on the porch.

Jemma spoke first. "Let's plant these on Papa's grave."

"Your papa would've liked that. I'll water them now and then, and Scotty will take care of them, too."

Willa was wallowing in the dumps. She wanted Trina to go to school, but she wanted her home more. "You'd better figger out some way to come home once a month, you hear me?" she said as they laid out the food at their river picnic.

"I know, Mama, I'll do the best I can," Trina promised.

"I'll look after your mama," Lester said. "I owe all you ladies for rescuin' me in my hour of need."

"Willa, what exactly was that piece of paper you were waving around in front of Hanna?" Jemma asked.

"Yeah, Mama, the one that supposedly said you and Lester were man and woman, whatever that means." Trina giggled.

"That was some paper I found on the seat about Lizbeth's new car. It worked good, though."

Lizbeth lifted a brow. "I didn't know you could stretch the truth so well."

"It wasn't no stretch—we are a man and a woman. All I had to do was think about how that creature had beat Lester's old bones around. She's lucky I didn't snatch her baldheaded."

Lester considered that a compliment and took an extra-big spoonful of potato salad. He hadn't eaten this well in a month.

"Are you all packed up, girl?" Trina asked as they dished up Lizbeth's homemade ice cream for dessert.

"Yeah, just about."

Trina gave her a sidelong glance. "Have you driven a car yet, Jem?"

"I made it fine to the cemetery and out to the home place. I'm okay. Maybe we could take turns."

Trina grinned. "Ooh. I get to drive a Corvette."

"Of course they say that the police are attracted to red cars. You'll have to watch out for that lead foot of yours." Jemma looked out at the Salt Fork of the Red River, recalling other times and another someone who liked to drive a little too fast. Maybe he could be a driver for the big brass in the military. Surely *they* didn't get shot at.

Chapter 12
Harbingers

Jemmabeth and Trina whipped out of Chillaton as the sun was coming up. Spencer's Corvette was packed solid, and the girls were ready for school in Big D.

Helene was waiting at the garden gate with Chelsea. She had fresh flowers in their rooms and lunch on the table. Jemma ran to call Lizbeth to say they had arrived in one piece.

Trina was one big smile. "I can't believe I'm gonna be living in this beautiful house."

"Thank you, dear. I am delighted to have you girls here. I'm sure you haven't eaten a bite on the road, so let's be seated, shall we?" Helene put the final touches on the table setting, then fiddled with her new hearing aid.

"Come here." Trina beckoned, then lifted the fat, white glob of fur into her lap. "So this is the famous Chelsea. I always wanted a cat. We seemed to only collect stray dogs and kids at Mama's."

"Well, a certain spoiled feline has the run of things around here." Helene lowered her voice. "Tell me about our Jemma."

"I think she's back to normal," Trina whispered.

"Good," Helene said. "I was so concerned."

"Everybody was, but she's ready for school, and she drove most of the way here."

Jemma came back into the room. "Okay, stop talking about me. Let's eat, then I'm looking in the *Wicklow Weekly* for a job."

"Me, too," Trina said. "Do you think there's any housecleaning work in Wicklow, Helene?"

"Most assuredly. This town is growing way beyond my liking. Will you be sharing transportation?"

"I don't know how that'll work," Trina said.

They didn't have to spend much time on the few want ads in the local paper. Helene suggested they place their own advertisement for cleaning services. Trina jumped at the idea, but Jemma hoped a certain lawyer would not be looking in the classifieds. They got plenty of calls and worked out a schedule so that they could clean houses on Tuesday and Thursday afternoons, when neither had classes.

Jemma's former garage apartment once again became her studio, and she wasted no time getting to work.

⋘⋙

Spencer was due out of basic training in two days and she could barely stand the wait. He would be flying into Love Field at ten thirty. She was there at nine o'clock with flowers and a smile that wasn't about to leave.

Spencer craned his neck to see the airport coming up. Landing at Love Field always seemed as though the plane was going to touch down on a freeway. They had to circle a few times as they waited their turn, then made the final approach, flying low over a small lake. She would be there, looking out the window of the arrival gate. He was nervous. There was a lot to talk about. He had left her when she was barely lucid, yet she seemed fully recovered now. She was back in school and back in the town where her cowboy boyfriend of two summers ago lived. He couldn't worry about that. He walked down the ramp and saw her.

"Spence!" She ran to him and he picked her up, much to the enjoyment of the other passengers. Their kiss lasted from the arrival gate, down the corridor, and to the escalator. "I love you," she said.

"You look fantastic. Let me see the scar." He lifted her hair. "That'll heal up and be gone before you know it." His eyes were fastened onto hers, and they both tripped off the escalator at the bottom.

"Let's get married, right now," she said.

"Okay. First let me get my bags."

"I mean it. I want to go on the honeymoon," she whispered. "This engagement is too long."

"You think I don't agree?" Spencer's heart hammered at the idea.

"Couldn't we just get married, not tell anybody, and then get married again when you are discharged? By the way, you do look good in that uniform," she said, playing with the buttons on his jacket. "C'mon, let's say 'I do.'"

"Would you really want that?" Spencer asked. "To get married in secret?"

Jemma drew back. "Yes, I would."

"If we do, then everybody will know it is for one reason and one reason only."

"Nobody would care."

"I care. Marriage is not just a license to go to bed."

"Whoa. Did you become a prude on me at boot camp?"

"Not quite, but I've heard nearly every seamy joke known to man."

"Tell me one," she said, taking off his cap to check out his crew cut.

"I will not. Your cute ears are way too precious. We'll make our own stories in our own time, Jem. I don't want you to think for a minute that this wait will not be worth it."

She pouted for a second, then suddenly hummed the birthday song to him. "Happy birthday, late, again, but I hope you got my package."

"You bet. Thanks. That was your gram's divinity, wasn't it?"

Jemma raised her chin. "It's mine now because she showed me how to make it. Did you like the sketchbook?"

"I do. It's like looking into your mind."

He drove the Corvette to Wicklow. They kissed at every traffic light and stop sign. After Spencer was settled in at Helene's, they sat in the conservatory with her. "I'm sorry I ran Trina out of the house," Spencer said.

"I don't believe it was a problem, was it, Jemma?" Helene asked.

"Are you kidding? She was excited to stay with Nick's parents. She's been working hard at school. I told her to slow down, or she was going to burn out."

"Show me your paintings," Spencer said. They went to the garage apartment and she showed him Brother Cleo, a pickup kicking dust alongside a wheat field, and a large piece, in progress, of Joe Cross. "How do you know him?" he asked.

"He came by Gram's before I left. He said a scripture over me when I was unconscious, and I guess it was one of the scriptures I said when I was coming back to earth. I know that I hadn't learned it before because I checked my Bible to make sure. I had underlined all the verses I memorized in my Bible; that one was not one of them."

"Amazing."

"He brought me sunflowers, too. They still had roots, so we planted them at Papa's grave. He said I was lying on a clump of sunflowers when he found me."

"What a sweet thing to do for my girl," he whispered.

"I can't believe you're in this apartment. I'm so glad to just touch you. Come over here to the daybed. I want to wrestle with my military man."

Spencer couldn't turn her down. The little daybed creaked as they sat on it. "Are you sure this thing can stand us both on it?"

"Yeah, are you sure you can stand this?" She jumped on him with a wrestling move. "I call this one The Cinderblock. What do you think?" She held on to the mattress with her hands on one side, and hooked her feet underneath it on the opposite side. She was dead weight across his chest.

He laughed until he couldn't breathe. "Time out, woman. Let's have a little respect for the military."

They sat in the garden by the Tiffany rose with its pungent fragrance. He decided to go for it. "Jem, I want you to know something. I think we should marry when I'm not under any pressure by the United States Government to be somewhere at any certain time, and when we're not worried about whether I'm going to be shot at. My life is not going to be my own for a while."

She assumed a pout, full-blown. "I think that I want to have you as my husband and all the privileges that go with it. If that means a weekend honeymoon, that's okay with me."

He turned her chin. She knew that was a signal of serious business.

"Jemma, I want you more than any man has ever wanted a woman on this earth. Do you understand that?"

She nodded.

"I'm saying that if we get married just so we can have sex, that would defeat our honor in a way. When we made this promise, we didn't even know what we were doing. Now we know that it was right, and we should also know that sex is not a good reason to marry. Call me a prude if you want to."

"You're different, Spencer. You've changed."

"I haven't changed when it comes to you. When you were in the ICU, I had a lot of time to think. Loving you has been my life's joy. Sex is only a part of married love, Jem. I want to sleep next to you and feed you when you're sick and take turns rocking babies with you. I know that I still haven't recuperated from your accident, and I've just been through some intense stuff that's only going to get worse, but I am committed to this ideal. As far as setting another date goes, well, when we have our wedding night, I want to concentrate on you and on our life together as a couple. I don't want to have all this military stuff in the back of my mind. Maybe I'm wrong, but just think about it, okay?"

"Okay," she mumbled, knowing that she would do whatever he said. She reached for his hand. "Right now I want to have some fun with you. Let me show you my school, then we can go dancing. What do you think? I'll wear the dress you like."

"I like all your dresses," he said, exhaling, "but I need out of this uniform."

"Are you going to slip into something more comfortable?" she asked, giving him the look he loved.

He pulled her close. "I love you, Jemmabeth. Thanks for listening to me."

❦

They toured Le Claire. She showed him every little nook on the campus. He couldn't help but feel somewhat jealous of all the places. It was there, after all, that she had gotten it in her head to break up with him in the first place. He didn't mention it, but it was on his mind.

"What kind of music do you want?" she asked.

"You choose. I like it all with you."

"Even country?" She drew the vowels out.

He laughed. "Well, almost all."

Jemma had heard about a place on a lake with an outdoor dance floor. It was already rocking when they got there. Lanterns were strung all around, casting a subtle glow on the dancers. There was no band, just a disc jockey in a covered booth above the crowd. They danced to every song, working out their tension on the floor. Stevie Wonder sang "I Was Made to Love Her," and next was "Light My Fire." The accident hadn't taken any edge off her ability to dance like the old days, but they had moved way beyond the Chillaton Stomp.

Two hours had passed before Spencer even checked his watch. Finally, they had a slow dance so he could hold her to him: "I Never Loved a Man" was the one to end on. He wanted to make her his wife and be alone with her, but he had already voiced his opinion and she had agreed to it. He had spoken from his heart, but the rest of him dissented.

Helene was asleep. He knew it would be so easy to bend the rules with Jemma. He knew he wasn't the only one thinking about it because she had the same look in her eyes.

"Spence," she said, holding his hands, "it's hard having you in the room next to me. Remember when I told you that I wanted to invade your sleeping quarters like Lester's mail-order bride did? I still do, even more now, but I know we have to keep our promise." She kissed him, and her breath was warm against his neck. They had never broken their vow even just a little. Nobody would know. She pulled away and looked in his eyes. "Besides, we would be different, wouldn't we? We would always know. Is that what you're thinking?"

"Baby, I am thinking the same things you are, despite my principles, but I need to have the hope of marrying you to keep me focused, no matter the situation. You told me that you had to get that cowboy out of your mind because you were just made that way. Well, I am just made this way. I need to wait to marry you to keep me going. You're right; when I almost lost you in the hospital, it did something to me. We've waited so long that now I want to see it through as an honor to you and to our love. I want to do what's right by God's Word. If we are to walk in the Spirit and lead Christ-centered lives, we have to try to be righteous and pure."

She touched his face. "Spencer Chase, you must be the only man on earth who would say that. I'm pushing you into a corner with my hormones. Okay, when is the earliest that we can marry? Tell me and I'll do it."

"Don't throw a fit, but, like I said, I would like to be free of the military. That means the end of next year."

It was instant. She threw up her hands. "Next year! Rats! Why did I have that wreck, why? It ruined everything for us." She stamped her foot like she was two years old.

"No. It delayed things, but it didn't ruin things. We may never know why, Jem. I know that two more years will be tough. Look at me; I'm shaking right now."

"That means we will be twenty-four years old. Everybody will make fun of me for being an old maid."

"They wouldn't dare. You could marry anybody you want, anytime."

"I don't want anybody but you, and it looks like I'll be an old maid until then."

"Well, it's not like we don't have some good times. I know a few things that still give you a thrill, old maid." Spencer threw her down on the leather couch and proceeded to prove his point. She giggled and kicked off her shoes.

❧

The next day they went to Six Flags Over Texas and stayed until dark. It felt like they were in junior high again. Jemmabeth was fearless, and Spencer tried to keep up with her. They were such goofy pranksters. He told the staff at the Jamboree that it was her birthday. They called her up on stage and sang to her. She got him back by turning his name in as a lost child, and it was promptly announced over the park's public address system.

She told him about her delivery girl disaster at the flower shop and pointed the building out. He got a big kick out of it, as she knew he would. He went in and bought a similar ceramic deer and some roses for her while she sat laughing in the car. They ate a burger at The Best Burger Stop in Texas. It didn't bother Jemma at all that she and Cowboy Paul used to hang out there. She knew the owner recognized her by his smart-aleck smile.

They took Helene out to dinner, but mostly just sat around and talked. She painted, and he watched her. They went for walks around Helene's property, which was no short stroll.

"Where would you like to live?" Spencer asked as they sat in the garden that night, trying to see the stars.

"It doesn't matter to me. I can paint anywhere. You'll be the one with the career choices."

"I guess we'll have to live wherever I can get a job. I'd like to be close to your family, but who knows?"

"I thought you wanted to live in Europe."

"That was before your wreck. Now I think family is everything."

"You've never had a desire to be famous, have you?"

"I think everybody wants to create something fantastic."

"I suppose. I never really thought about it. You aren't going to open up an architectural firm in Chillaton, are you?"

He laughed. "Maybe you and I should go into business together. I could design buildings, and you could paint murals on the ceilings."

She had waited long enough. "When will you know your assignment for the next year?"

He took a deep breath. "I already know it, baby," he said and bit his lip.

"Well, let me have it."

"Fort Wolters, near Mineral Wells."

"What happens at Fort Wolters?"

He held her hand. "They train helicopter pilots, Jem."

Chapter 13

Heart Pieces

The Le Claire senior art students were eager for their first exhibition. It was to be held at the Dallas Museum of Fine Arts. She was glad to have something to pour her heart into. It took many soothing words from Spencer to calm her down after he broke the news to her about his assignment. They both knew he wouldn't be flying helicopters in Europe. She was trying to put it out of her mind, for now.

She had six paintings for the exhibition: *Joe Cross; Brother Cleo; Mirth*—the name she had given the watercolor of Carrie, Trina, and herself as little girls; *Dusty Business*—the pickup on the road by the wheat field; *My Cowboy*—Spencer on the train tracks; and *The Ways of the Worlt*—Hanna holding her tapestry bags.

Professor Rossi, her favorite teacher at Le Claire, was pleased with her choices. "You should be having your own show, Jemmabeth. It will happen after this. . .you wait and see."

"I am working on a painting of your friends in Florence," she said, frowning at a brushstroke of copper in Hanna's hair.

"The Grassos? Ah, they will be happy to hear of this. We will have to send them a photograph when it is complete. Are you working on it at your home? I have not seen it at your station."

"Yes, at home. The one at school is of my mother. Do you like it?"

"She is *bella*. Now I see where you learned that smile. Who is this creature with the fiery mane?"

"She is from the old country. She came to America to go the *ways of the worlt*."

"It appears she is looking for trouble."

"It's a long story, but it ended well. I'll have to tell you sometime, but right now I have to help clean a house in Wicklow."

The professor clicked his tongue. "It will not always be so with you, Jemmabeth. Someday you will be living like royalty."

438

She smiled. "I'd just like to be living on a military base right now, but that's not going to happen." She waved and ran to meet Trina.

—◈—

"Check this out," Trina said, showing deep dimples as she handed her a letter.

"Wow!" That is terrific. You'll have to call Gram tonight so she can tell your mom. How did you get to be a featured designer so fast?"

"They pick somebody from each level. I represent the first level students."

"I knew you had it in you. Congratulations."

"Is Spencer coming to the show?"

"Yeah. I'm picking him up Friday night."

"I hope Nick can come. He and I don't get to see each other much."

"That's the pits. You move to the same county, and you still don't see him."

Trina shrugged. "He doesn't have a car, and I don't either."

"Well, that needs to change." Jemma started thinking. "What happened to his uncle's car?"

"He hates to ask for it. Nick has a lot of pride, so I guess we're a team in that department."

Jemma slammed on the brakes and made an illegal U-turn. "We'll go by his place right now."

Trina held on to the dashboard. "Creepers. You're nuts when you get an idea. I wish Nick and I could afford to get married, but he won't discuss it. You're so lucky to have Spencer. He was so worried about you in the hospital. When you were in the ICU he went in to see you every hour, around the clock. He even asked if he could sit outside your door. Mama said that the nurses didn't let him, though. Hey, did you know that you were naked in the ICU?" Trina grinned.

"What?" Jemma jerked the steering wheel to get back in her lane.

"I saw you, girl. They couldn't cover you up completely because of all the monitors."

"Spence saw me like that?" Jemma blushed at the thought.

"Come on, you'd just been in a head-on collision with a semi. Even Miss America wouldn't look good after that."

"Even so, he's not supposed to see anything until we get married," Jemma said, without joining in the laughter. In fact, she was getting a little ticked off about it.

"Maybe that's why he kept going in so often." Trina giggled. "Oops, I'm sorry. That was a tacky thing to say."

Jemma was in a snit, and Spencer had better have a good defense.

⋘⋙

"Okay, sir, tell me how to fly a helicopter in ten words or less," Jemma said as he pulled out of the base.

"Nah. Tell me how to paint." He leaned over for another kiss. "I'm starving. Let's stop at the first restaurant we come across."

"You're the boss. Just so I'm at the museum by six o'clock tomorrow night."

They stopped at a Mexican food place. Jemma played with her food, thinking of how to ask. Finally she rolled her eyes and simply said it. "Spence, did you or did you not see me naked in the hospital?"

He glanced at her. She was serious. "Maybe. What's it worth to you?"

"Spencer! That's not fair. You take off all your clothes right now and let me have a look."

The diners in the next booth bugged their eyes at them.

"I have to have more suitable surroundings," Spencer said. "You'll have to come up with a better plan than that."

"Did you see me or not?"

"I'll never tell."

"You will tell me right now, or we'll never leave this place."

He looked at her out of the corner of his eye.

"So, you did see me. Quintuplet rats. I can't believe you did that. You should've covered your eyes. I was unconscious, for Pete's sake. Aren't you ashamed?"

Spencer went nose-to-nose with her. "Jem, I'm teasing you. Yes, you were naked, but when I walked in the room I almost threw up when I saw you. Your sweet body had been laid bare to help save your life, but I only looked at your face, I promise. Your daddy and I stood over you and said a prayer. Every time I went in, I was in such an emotional state that you could have had Roy Rogers and Trigger in the bed with you and I wouldn't have noticed. Now there. Okay?"

Jemma backed off but was pouting. "I didn't want you to see me until we got married. I didn't want you to see any naked women until we get married."

"I don't buy girlie magazines, if that's any consolation."

She couldn't help but smile at him. "I'm sorry. I know you're a good boy, but I bet you saw something."

Spencer finished his meal. "Well, you do have a cute belly button," he said, laughing and dodging her punches. "Just a joke, wild woman."

The senior show was a success. Professor Rossi was right. An art gallery manager in Highland Park Village called and scheduled a meeting for Monday afternoon right before they left to go back to Fort Wolters. She was to bring her portfolio. Jemma was radiant with the thought of her own show. Helene was on the phone, telling Lizbeth and Julia within minutes, and Spencer was content to listen to her talk about it all the way back to the base.

Jemma bought groceries and went to the post office to pick up stamps for Helene. She stuffed them in her purse and started out the door, still fiddling with her purse.

"Well, hello, darlin'."

His voice made every hair on her arms rise at full attention. She gazed right into the clover green eyes of Paul Jacob Turner, the embodiment of her "summer of the wild cowboy fling," and the source of all her heartache with Spencer. He was taller than Spence and as handsome a cowboy who ever drove a pickup truck. English Leather cologne trickled inside her head.

Her voice came out silly, like it always did when she was around him. "Hi, Paul. How are you?" She looked away toward the Corvette, as though Spencer could be watching.

He stood way too close. "I'm much better, now that I've seen you," he said, always the charmer. "I heard you were back in town. How about going out for a burger sometime?"

"No, thanks, I'm engaged." She flashed The Ring.

"That's some hunk of jewelry," he said, looking her over. "I assume it's the high school kid, huh?"

"He's graduated from college and is in the military now." Jemma narrowed her eyes.

"Is he far, far away yet?" His beautiful smile had not changed one bit.

"What does that mean?" she snapped.

"It means maybe you and I could hang out sometime—you know, just talk."

"Excuse me, Paul, but you and I were supposed to talk at the coffee shop at Love Field over a year ago. Remember? You went to Las Vegas instead."

"You're not holding that against me, too, are you?"

"I'm not holding anything against you. I never think about you anymore."

"Well, I bet you will tonight, darlin', because I'll be thinking about you." He touched her chin. "Looking into those golden eyes has lifted my spirits like nothing else could. You're still the one, Jemma."

She left and didn't dare look back. It was as though she'd seen a rattler up close. Paul Turner knew how to quicken her pulse. She wiped her chin where he had touched it and sat in the Corvette for a minute. He would not weasel his way into her life ever again.

⋘⊷⋙

Paul watched as she drove away, his heart pounding. He'd never realized how much he had missed her. Even his bones ached. As long as there was a breath in his body, he would try to win her back. He had wanted to see her smile, hear her laugh, and talk about her art. That might take some doing, but she had reacted to his presence. He knew when a woman did that, and this was no ordinary woman. This was his one and only, his joy, his darlin' Jemmabeth. To hold her and kiss those sweet lips, that would make him feel good about life again. She was the only woman who had ever done that and the only one decent enough for his father to hound him about. There was always hope that she might forgive him and allow his love back into her heart. He lifted his Stetson and ran his hand through his hair. He was too old to cry anymore.

He cranked up the eight-track tape. If she'd known how many hours he'd spent grieving over her, maybe she would've come back to him long ago. They might even have babies by now. He opened his eyes wide and blinked back the tears that had cropped up behind his lashes. He couldn't help it. He loved her from an innocent and gentle place way down deep inside himself—a place where nobody else had ever been and where love lasts a lifetime.

The Gallery at Highland Park was just as exclusive as the shops along the Champs Elysees in Paris, but the owner, Annette Lawson, had a definite Texas accent.

"Please, call me Anne. We are excited at the possibility to showcase your art, Miss Forrester. I understand that you were the Girard Fellow at Le Academie Royale D'Art in Paris last year."

"Yes, it was a fascinating experience." Jemma watched as Anne thumbed through her pieces.

"I was told that most of your work was sold at the Academie exhibitions, but I am very impressed with what's left. These are amazing. You're very prolific."

"I paint every day."

"Do you have other pieces like the one used for the cover of *Nouvelle Liberte*?"

"How did you know about that? I've never seen that magazine in Texas."

"Carlo Rossi told me. He is an enthusiastic admirer of your work."

Jemma smiled. "I have others in that mood, but I don't include them in my portfolio."

"Oh, and why is that?"

"They are very personal reflections and not for sale."

Anne's eyes brightened. "I want to see them. We can price them so that they won't be sold, but it will enable clients to gain a deeper perspective of your work."

"I suppose I could bring them by tomorrow after classes." She regretted the idea already. Rats.

"Bring everything. These are excellent, and it will be a fabulous show. Simply fabulous."

~❧~

She was back the next day with her private watercolor collection, pieces that she had never shown anyone. Anne examined each one as though she considered buying it for herself. "These are exactly what I'm looking for. You have bared your soul with them."

Jemma didn't respond. Most of them were too close to her heart for display. She wasn't sure that she wanted to share them with the world.

"I have catalogued the pieces you brought yesterday. Please look over the list and sign at the bottom. I assigned a value to each, subject to your approval, of course. The gallery's commission is included and defined in the paragraph above your signature. Now, let's just quickly title these. A brief description will do. We should begin with number nine."

Jemma flipped through them, heavy-hearted. "Number nine is a girl laughing. Number ten is a girl holding a firefly in her hands. Eleven is a boy and girl kissing. Twelve is a girl looking in a mirror as she brushes her hair. Thirteen is a boy and girl dancing in the moonlight. Fourteen is a girl crying in bed. Fifteen is a boy in a scout uniform. Sixteen is a girl walking on a train track. Seventeen is a bride. Eighteen through twenty-two are all of a soldier."

"Exquisite. Why haven't you exhibited them before now?"

"Personal reasons," she said, staring at them.

"I see. Rest assured, we shall do something special with them. It's such a pleasure to see your work."

"Yes, ma'am. When will the exhibit begin?"

"In five weeks. Is that good for you? I'm having to make some schedule changes, and I need time for advance publicity, etcetera."

"Sure. You said that you would overprice my private collection. Why price them at all? Can't they just be exhibited?"

Anne flashed a patronizing smile. "It is a policy of the gallery that all the pieces in a show be available for purchase by our clientele. Otherwise, we would be a museum. This is a profit-making venture for all of us, Jemma. It protects both your best interests as well as ours. I'm sure that you understand the business side of art. Have you ever considered hiring an agent?"

Jemma shrugged, having forfeited her options by bringing

them in the first place.

"Besides," Anne continued, "you can always paint more."

She left the gallery feeling as though she had just forsaken part of her heart and truly bared her soul, like her body in the ICU. She hit the steering wheel with her fist.

She drove back to Le Claire to pick up Trina. They went straight to their housecleaning job and didn't get home until six o'clock. Jemma flew up to her studio, reached under the daybed, and took out a portfolio case. She removed three watercolors. The first was of Gram, sifting the earth of the home place through her hands as it blew back against her legs. The second was of Spencer as she remembered him in the first grade, front tooth missing and holding an Easter basket. The third was of Papa playing his fiddle. Those would never leave her.

Lizbeth sipped her coffee, eyeing the folded quilts in the oversized closet. There were thirty of them, at least. She had no room left on either side of the narrow, high shelves, and she had no specific plan for any of them. As soon as she finished one, she began another, like Robby reading his comic books. There were even more quilts under the good bed and in the top of Cam's closet. She was no different than the squirrels that ran around the backyard, storing up nuts. At least they planned on eating them to keep from starving through the winter. She had no such excuse, and it was a sin to keep these useful creations folded in plastic.

She was never one to brag, but the quilts were of the highest quality and very pretty. She was a master quilter, one of the best in the Panhandle, and consistently voted president of the combined North and South Chillaton Quilting Clubs. Alex always wanted her to enter some in the county fair, but Lizbeth never had the desire to enter a competition, unlike Julia's compulsion to enter any and all contests. Sewing the pieces to create a pattern had kept her mind busy. She was blessed that arthritis had not hampered her work as it had some of the club members. Now it was time for her to put these cotton creations to good use. They were not pieces of her heart, like some quilts she had made.

As she walked over the tracks to Willa's house, she was struck by another, even more exciting idea. It made her smile, then grin, much wider than she had in a good while. The sign that read DOES IRONING AND GUARANTEE HER WORK was hanging straight, thanks to Lester. She knocked on the door. Willa's radio was playing.

"Miz Liz, come on in here. I'm glad to see your smilin' face. We gotta stick together since them girls left us."

Lizbeth sat at one of the kitchen chairs and Willa plopped down across from her. "I don't know what I've been doing since Jemma left, to tell the truth," she said. "The days blend into one another. It takes me a while to get over her leaving because I've come to think of her as my own. I don't know if that's good or bad."

Willa nodded. "My baby sure is havin' fun at that school. She took to that dress-makin' right away. I hope she'll like it in that fancy pants world."

"She will. Trina has spunk and talent, just like Jemma. It's funny how those two came together when they did. I believe that's all part of God's Great Plan, don't you?"

"I do. I believe just that. Now if she can get her man worries out of the way, she'll be doing all right."

"I thought Trina and her young man were practically engaged."

"Well, you and me both thought that, but I think old St. Nick has cooled his heels in that department. I told her to get some backbone. Women go through all kinds of misery in this old world, and she'd better start buckin' up for it."

"Willa, I have an idea and I'd like your help, if you don't mind."

"You ain't needin' me to scare off another one of Lester's women friends?"

Lizbeth laughed. "No, not quite. I do want to get some things out of my house, though. I'd like to offer most of my quilts to folks that are in need. I wondered if your church has a system for that kind of thing. My church has a fund set aside, but no real goods for helping out."

"It'd be nice to keep folks warm this winter. I'll talk to Brother Cleo when he comes down Sunday. I'm sure we can work somethin' out."

"I'm sorry I didn't think of this sooner. I thought I would give half to my church and the other half to yours."

"Well, poor folks is the same, no matter the color. It's mighty fine of you to use your talent for good deeds, Lizbeth."

"I don't know what I was thinking when I put them away. You'd have thought I was outfitting a small army."

"Speakin' of which, how is Spencer doin'? I sure do hate it that he's gonna be flying them old whirlybirds in that nasty mess. I know Jemma is gonna go out of her mind worryin' over him."

"I think she'll be coming back to Chillaton while he's in Vietnam. I don't know if I can be any consolation to her, Willa. I prayed for my boys to come home safe and sound and it wasn't in God's Plan. You'll have to help me take care of her."

"Spencer'll get through it. Them poor children have had a time of it tryin' to get together."

"That's true. I guess I'd better run. I'm going to talk to Brother Hightower at my church about the quilts. Oh, by the way, come over for dinner on Sunday. Lester will be there, as well as a new friend of ours that I want you to meet." Her heart beat a bit faster as she said the words.

"I'll be there if you cook roast beef," Willa said, laughing.

"I'll have Lester come over to get you."

"See you Sunday, then. I'll bring cobbler."

⋙◈⋘

Lester was right on the dot to pick Willa up. He was a punctual man. He'd run most of his life by the clock at the train station. To most folks, a minute here and a half minute there might not matter much, but it did to a stationmaster.

"What's that big truck doin' here? Did Lizbeth order somethin' special for dinner?" Willa asked as they pulled into his driveway.

"That would be Mr. Cross's rig. He's the man who was drivin' the truck when Jemmerbeth had that wreck. He's a right nice feller," Lester said. "He could be one of them angels folks talk about."

Lizbeth met them at the door and was very talkative. "Come right in, Willa. I'm so glad you could make it. Let me take that cobbler. Hmm, it's still warm. I'd like for you to meet Mr. Joe Cross. Joe, this is my good friend, Willa Johnson. She makes the best cobbler anywhere."

Joe grinned as he shook her hand. Willa smiled and raised her brow. "I'm thinkin' I need to give you a hug instead of a handshake, Mr. Cross. You saved our girl's life from what I hear," she said and gripped him with a bear hug. Joe, somewhat surprised, hugged her back. They exchanged a number of glances as the meal progressed.

"Well, now, Mr. Cross, I never knew nobody who drove a truck for money. Tell us about the truckin' business," Willa said.

"Please call me Joe. Ain't much to tell. I drive my rig across the country and back, east to west, but mostly west these days. It's a good livin', but it's kinda lonely, too."

"Joe lives in Sweetwater." Lizbeth passed the rolls but avoided Willa's eyes.

"I had me a time in Sweetwater once," Lester said. "I went down for the Rattlesnake Roundup. That was about the wildest time I ever had without the company of a lady friend."

"Lester. . ." Lizbeth gave him the schoolmarm eye.

"No offense, Miz Liz, I just mean that I wouldn't dream of takin' a lady to no rattlesnake hunt."

"I can understand that, Lester," Willa agreed. "No lady I know would be hankerin' to go, neither."

Joe shook his head. "I reckon it's a good idea to get shed of as many rattlers as possible, but I ain't never been to it. I'd rather ride to Los Angeles with a load of hogs in the back and a couple more in the cab than to try and catch a rattler."

Willa laughed. "What do you do for entertainment in Sweetwater?"

"I'd have to say that I like to play my daddy's fiddle just about as much as anything."

"You're a fiddler?" Lester perked up. "I'm a French harp man, myself. Miz Liz's dearly departed husband and me were mighty good for a back porch duet. He was a fiddler, too. Do you have yours with you?"

"I take it everywhere I go. It's good company. It never gives me any back talk and stays put, too," Joe said with a laugh to rival Willa's.

"Maybe you two could give us a concert after we have some of Willa's cobbler," Lizbeth said as she cleared the table. "Wait until you taste it."

"I'll just run over and get my harmonica," Lester said. "If you ladies will beg pardon."

Willa watched as Joe helped Lizbeth with the dishes. He was a good-sized fellow, tall, with big bones. She liked that in a man. "Are you a churchgoin' man, Joe?" she asked, surprising herself.

"Yes, ma'am. Sometimes I'm out of pocket, you know, and I can't get to my own church, but I can usually find some place to stop about church time and read my New Testament and spend some time with the Lord."

"Lizbeth told me that you said some scriptures over Jemma. That was real Christian of you. Not many folks would have seen clear to do that." Willa was recalling anything she'd ever heard about him, and putting that with what she was seeing right then, too. It was an impressive combination.

"That poor child had New Testaments flung all over the place that day. It reminded me of one of my favorite verses. The good Lord impressed me to say it out loud while I was bearin' down on her wounds. I expect He heard a lot of prayin' that day."

"Well, all the same, we are grateful for everything you did, Joe," Lizbeth said.

"Were you in that old war?" Willa asked.

"I served in the Second World War and Korea, too, ma'am. I was a cook in the Coast Guard. I've made more meals on water than on land." He laughed and dried the last of the pots and pans.

Lester came in the door warming up on his harmonica in the living room. Joe excused himself and went to his truck to get his fiddle, leaving the two women alone.

"I'm surely glad to get all those quilts into needy hands, Willa. Thank you for helping me do that. It was so silly to have them collecting dust all these years—a sin, really." Lizbeth kept her eyes on the broom as she swept. "I'd like to do more along those lines, but. . ."

Willa cleared her throat, putting a halt to the speech. "Miz Liz, I ain't no fool, and I can see plain what you're doin' here."

"Oh?" Lizbeth banged the silverware as she placed it in a drawer.

"I just want to say that I think you've got a good eye for menfolk," Willa said.

Lizbeth dried her hands on her apron and held her arms out to Willa. They hugged each other tight.

Willa stepped back and grinned at her. "Now let's go see if he can play as good as he looks."

⊰❦⊱

Trina bent down to get a better look at the newspaper clipping on Helene's bulletin board. "Do you ever look bad in a picture, Jem?"

"Yuck. I look like I'm mad."

"Nah. You look like Bridgette Bardot with brown hair."

"That's the second time somebody said that to me. Doesn't she have buckteeth? Anyway, I'm glad to get that interview over with. I don't like talking to reporters. They can leave out part of what you say and give it a totally different meaning."

"I thought the article was quite nice, Jemma," Helene said from the dining room.

"She can really hear with her new hearing aid, huh?" Trina whispered.

"By the way, dear, the gallery owner called about half past four. She needs to speak with you before she closes." Helene handed Jemma the note.

Her show had just opened, so the owner couldn't have much to say.

"Hi, Anne. This is Jemma Forrester. Did you need to talk with me?"

"Jemma, yes. I. . .ah, hope this is not too upsetting for you, but my assistant sold two of your watercolors this morning."

"Really? That's great! Now I've sold three pieces and the show has just been open for two days. I guess the newspaper article helped."

"Actually, the two watercolors were from the group that we had overpriced, hoping that no one would buy. The client paid two thousand dollars for them."

Jemma's smile evaporated. "What? You have to be kidding. Which two were they?"

"Number nine and number ten were sold, and the client put a hold on number twelve."

"I don't remember the numbers. What were the titles?"

"Let's see. Number nine is a girl laughing, number ten is a girl holding a firefly, and number twelve is a girl looking in the mirror as she brushes her hair. They are all self-portraits, I assume. I hope the sale is acceptable with you. You have my apologies."

Her stomach rose to her throat. "May I ask the name of the client?"

"Of course. I have that right here. His name is Paul J. Turner."

Chapter 14
Secrets

Jemma hadn't said much since they left Helene's, and Trina knew why. "So what's your plan, girl? Are you going to let him keep the paintings?"

"What I can do about it? He paid the asking price. I guess he's just like any other buyer, even though I don't want him to have them, and I dread telling Spence about it. Good grief."

"Paul's after you, huh?"

"He just wants my art as a trophy."

"Maybe he really loved you. Even cowboys gotta have somebody to love."

"I don't want to think about it now. Tell me about you and Nick."

"Same old, same old. We never get to see each other. I think Nick must be overwhelmed with his internship. He's keeping some crazy hours. We never go out because there's the car thing."

"I'm sorry, Trina. I'll take you to see him right now." She made her famous U-turn at the next block.

Trina held on to the dashboard. She already knew that Jemmabeth Forrester was about the best friend anybody could have. Now she thought she might also be the craziest.

Nick lived in the shabbiest side of Dallas. Kids played in the litter and discarded furniture that dotted the premises. Young men leaned against buildings, engaged in suspicious conversations while old men clumped together, laughing and arguing on tumbledown steps.

"I'll wait here," Jemma said.

"No, you come with me and say hello. You haven't seen him in a long time."

His apartment was like all the others except for a card, neatly thumb-tacked to the door that said NICHOLAS FIELDS, ALMOST AN M.D.

Jemma laughed. "Some of your work, huh?"

"Yeah," Trina said. "I hoped it would cheer him up, but like I said, he's too serious." She knocked on the door that appeared to have been in several fights of its own and lost. Nick came to the door, his glasses perched on the end of his nose.

"Trina, honey! Oh hi, Jemma. You should've told me y'all were coming. This place is a mess."

Trina kissed him. "I wanted to see you, so Jem brought me by. We can leave if you want."

"No, no, come in. I'll get these papers cleared off so y'all can sit down. I'm glad you came."

Jemma didn't really know Nick very well. She had been around him a few times and liked him. He was a veteran, but before Vietnam, and now he had graduated from Southwestern Medical School and was an intern at Parkland Hospital. The apartment was bare, but neater than she expected for a bachelor. It was organized and functional, like Spencer's room in Florence. "How's the internship going?" she asked.

Nick pushed up his glasses. "I'm working myself to the bone."

"I was thinking that when Spence comes this weekend, maybe we could all go out. You know, on a double date."

"Yeah, that would be nice, but I may be at the hospital all weekend."

Trina put her arm in his. "Oh, c'mon, Nick. We never get to do anything."

"Well, think about it," Jemma said. "It's going to be girls' treat night. Maybe we'll cook for you guys and watch a TV movie. How does that sound?"

"I might be able to do that. I'll see what my schedule is like."

"Listen, y'all, I need to run to the drugstore a minute. I think I saw one down the street."

"Yeah," Nick said. "It's about two blocks north of here."

Jemma winked at Trina and left. She drove around a while and stopped at Walgreen's, just to stay honest, and bought some bubble gum. It wasn't the sort of neighborhood for taking a stroll or she would have stayed gone longer. She drove back to the apartment parking lot and read a chapter in her *Great Masters* book.

It took a while for someone to answer the door, and she saw that as a good sign. It was. Nick had his glasses off and was grinning at Trina. "I'm sure grateful you brought my girl by. I'll check the hospital schedule and try to get over to Wicklow whenever you say."

"I say as soon as the sun comes up on Saturday," Trina said and waved Jemma out the door ahead of her.

⊰◈⊱

The foursome sat down to a splendid meal in Helene's dining room, complete with candles and cloth napkins.

"This is quite a feast, ladies." Spencer grinned at his favorite chef.

"We eat like this all the time." Jemma gave him The Look that drove him crazy.

"So, Nick, how are things in the world of interns?" Spencer asked.

Nick nodded with a mouthful of steak. "It's okay. I think I'm wearing a little thin on sleep and energy. Maybe this meal will fix me up. What's the latest with your bird training?"

"He won't talk about it." Jemma shoved Spencer's arm. "It's all hush-hush."

"It's no secret. But I need a break from it when I'm with you."

"Do you think you'll be seeing a lot of combat?" Nick asked.

"I think I'm going to be flying Medevac."

Nick folded his arms on the table. "The Dust Offs are unbelievable."

"Explain, please." Jemma frowned at the new terminology.

Nick pushed up his glasses. "The Dust Offs are the medical evacuation team. They fly in and pick up the wounded. I guess there's no sweeter sound than a Dust Off coming when you're down."

Spencer kept eating. He could feel her eyes on him.

"Where'd they come up with that name?" Trina asked.

"The blades kick up a lot of dust," Nick said.

"Is it the worst job in Vietnam?" Jemma asked.

"Baby, I don't think there are any good jobs there." Spencer reached for her hand.

⊰◈⊱

Jemma and Trina cleaned up the kitchen while Spencer showed

Nick around Helene's place. She insisted they take her husband's red, classic MG roadster out for a spin.

"Got a question for you, Nick," Spencer began.

"I can't give medical advice yet," Nick shouted over the wind.

"My dad has a car dealership in our hometown. I'd really like to help Trina with her own transportation, but I don't think I can do it without your help."

"What do you have in mind?" Nick leaned in for the explanation.

"I want you to let her think that it's yours, but that she can use it whenever she has the need. She and Jemma are not going to always have the same schedule, plus Jem will be graduating in the spring. She will probably stay with her grandmother in Chillaton."

Nick shook his head. "You two have done so much for Trina already. She'd have a fit if she knew about a car."

"I'm not going to be the one to tell her."

"I don't want to lie to her," Nick said.

"Then just tell her that I loaned you the money for a car and that will be the truth."

"Man, you don't need to do that. I can make it with the bus and my uncle's car."

"Nick, I have the money, and I have a father in the business. We can get it at cost. Please let me do this for y'all. It's a loan, remember."

"Trina told me that you were a nice guy, but this is too much." He exhaled. "I sure would love to be able to see her more often and not stand around waiting for the bus to get to Parkland."

"Then it's a deal." Spencer pulled into the Wicklow Piggly Wiggly parking lot.

"Some deal, all right." They shook hands. "Thank you, Spencer. I'll pay you back as soon as I can."

"Forget it. C'mon, it's your turn to drive this beauty," Spence said and changed seats with him.

❧

The night was cool and clear when they stopped to watch the stars on a lonely dirt road outside of Mineral Wells. They spread their quilt on the hood and found Orion.

"Do you think we have guardian angels?" Jemma asked, pulling another old quilt up over them.

"What does the Bible say about that?" Spencer wrapped his arms around her, and they gazed at the sky.

"I don't know. I'll have to look it up, I guess. If we do, I'll feel better about this Dust Off thing."

"Baby, don't worry about that. I have to do my job—whatever it is. Maybe I will be able to help somebody. God is going to bring me home to you. I really believe that."

Jemma looked him in the eye. "Spence, I love you so much, but it scares me that I had the wreck and we didn't get married. Why did that happen if we are supposed to get married?"

"All I know is that I'll come home to marry you."

She had to get it out. "Babe, I have to tell you something."

"Okay, shoot."

"Paul bought two, maybe three of my paintings. He spent two thousand dollars for them. If he buys the third, it will be three thousand."

Spencer wasn't expecting such an announcement. It took him a minute to recuperate. "Which paintings?"

"They're all of me," she whispered.

"Of course they are. I should've known."

"The gallery thought they wouldn't sell at those prices."

"Looks like he wanted them really bad."

"I'm not going to paint myself anymore."

"I thought I had your first self-portrait. You gave it to me in Flagstaff, remember? Never mind. Just so he doesn't try to get the real thing. That's not something we have to worry about, right?"

Jemma pressed her nose against his. "I said I'd done some other self-portraits, but no one had ever seen them, until now. I have no interest in that man. If you want me not to worry about you coming home from this war, then you have to promise me that you will not worry about Paul Turner."

He liked it when she got heated up. "Hmmm. You have to keep your end of the bargain, though." They resumed their stargazing and talked about their future, after Vietnam, after he came home.

⚜

Paul bought the third painting and the Gallery exhibition earned Jemma enough to forget all about cleaning houses. She also received advance commissions for three portraits. They couldn't be any harder than her Lillygrace grandparents' portrait had been. The first portrait was scheduled for a sitting at The Adolphus Hotel in downtown Dallas. She'd never been there before. She did know that if someone had permanent residence in a ritzy hotel, they were loaded. The arrangements had all been made through the Gallery staff. The patron was a rich old foreigner, she assumed, a Mr. Laup Renrut. She thought that was the funniest name she had heard lately, and had one last giggle over it in the elevator. She knocked on the door, and it opened at her touch into a luxury suite.

"Hello. I'm Jemmabeth Forrester, here to do some sketches for a portrait," she called to the empty room.

"Hello, darlin'," a familiar voice said from the bar.

Jemma's heart stopped. Paul was sitting on a bar stool, his green eyes drilling a hole in her from across the room.

"What are you doing here?" she asked. "I'm supposed to meet someone for a portrait sitting." Her jaw hung open.

He grinned and sauntered to the door, all six foot five of him, and shut it. "Mr. Renrut, I presume? C'mon, Jem, it's me, backwards. I want you to paint my portrait. No harm in that, right?"

Jemma was frozen to the spot. He slipped his big arms around her and halfway kissed her. She jerked back from him and wiped her mouth. "How dare you, Paul! How dare you. This is inexcusable. You tricked me."

"I thought you would get a kick out of this. Have you lost your sense of humor? You always did look good when you were ticked off, Jem. Now come back over here and let me finish what I started." He sat on the tapestry couch and patted the cushion next to him. He looked trimmer than he did when he came to see her at Lizbeth's. Nobody could deny he was a sensational buckaroo, and clearly he knew it.

"Forget it. You've gone to a lot of trouble for nothing. I am not going to paint your portrait so that you can seduce me into your little trap. I'm in love with Spencer, and we're getting married."

"Not any time soon, honey. He's gonna be in another world before long." He relaxed on the couch and stretched his long legs out over it. His boots hung over the arm. "Have you forgotten what it was like between us? Well, I haven't. Every time I look at those paintings of you, I want you even more." He pulled his hat down low over his eyes and moved his hands as though directing oncoming traffic. "You aren't married yet, and I'm giving it all I've got. This old boy's back in the saddle again."

Jemma turned on her heel and flew to the door. He had locked it every which way, but she managed to get them all undone. Paul was off the couch like he had roped a calf, though, and leaned against the door, making it impossible to open.

He touched her cheek. "It's only me, Jem. Won't you let me see if your hair still smells like flowers? I miss you. You're my destiny."

She shook her head to move his hand. "Get away from this door, or I'm going to scream. I mean it."

He looked down at her through his thick, black lashes. "Jemmabeth, I love you. Just give me a chance. You loved me once. We both know you did. It was that night of no mercy that messed us up."

She looked him in the eye. "I was swept away by you, yes, but I didn't love you. We had a great time, but you lied to me. I love Spencer with every part of my being." He traced around her lips while she spoke, further getting on her nerves. She swatted at his hand. "There is no hope for you and me. You'll find someone else if you look in the right places. I'm sorry. I don't want to hurt your feelings, but you'll have to get on with your life."

He touched her forehead with his lips. She wiggled around and plastered her back against the doorknob. He moved a stray lock of hair off her forehead. "You are a thing of beauty, darlin'. I would change my life for you."

"Change your life by going to church, Paul. Then good things will come your way."

"Didn't come here for a sermon. I want you in my life, nothing else." He couldn't keep his hands off her. "Give me one more chance," he whispered and moved his hand to the back of her neck.

Jemma eased her hand behind her and yanked on the doorknob. He held it shut with one snakeskin boot. She gritted her teeth. "There *will* be somebody else. You won't find her at the Handle Bar, though."

He looked right into her eyes. "Would you at least let me have a good-bye kiss?"

"No." He was way too big for any of her wrestling moves. "All my kisses are for Spencer."

"There's bound to be a spare one for old Paul." With that, he pinned her arms to the door and pressed his lips to hers. Jemma's ears were ringing, she was so mad. There was a time when she would have melted with that kiss. It was that good.

Paul pushed his hat back. "Now tell me. What's he got that I haven't got?" He was so close she tasted English Leather.

Jemma blew out his kiss. "My heart, Paul. Spence has my heart."

"I hope he knows what he's got."

"He knows that I love him. I always have and always will." She reached for the doorknob again, and he laid his hand on hers as she opened the door.

"If you ever need anything, anything at all, darlin', I'll be there for you. I mean that."

"I need you to leave me alone!" She flew down the hallway.

"Good-bye, Jemmabeth Alexandra Forrester," he said, leaning against the doorway, *Hud* style.

Jemma did not look at him again. "Good-bye, Mr. Renrut," she hissed. "Maybe you should get a kiss from your ex-wife."

"I'll be seeing you," he whispered and watched her disappear into the elevator. He went back into the suite and slumped in a chair. What a stupid move this had been. It only served to make her mad again, exactly the opposite of what he had hoped for. In the future, maybe he should plan these things in a sober state of mind, but it hurt too much that way.

She chewed on her lip all the way home. How could she have been duped like that, and how on earth could she tell Spencer? She had just told him not to worry about Paul. He had enough to worry about, but she also didn't want to keep any secrets from him. She needed to talk to somebody. She wanted to call her mom, but her parents didn't know the whole story about Mr. Turner. They didn't know that he was not quite divorced while he was dating her.

Jemma hadn't known that particular part of the story either, until it was almost too late and the guilt nearly broke her in two. Then it dawned on her how to get some straight talk.

❧

"It's about time you called your old aunty. How are you, and how is that sweet Spencer?"

"Do Dah, I need your advice." Jemma told her the latest. Julia knew everything that had happened with Paul. She had even hired a private investigator to check him out before the whole thing was over that summer.

"A sore loser," she said. "He can't stand it that he wasn't the better man. I see your predicament, sugar. I'll tell you this much. It never pays to harbor a secret, even if it's tough in the telling, but the jolt won't last long. Now, I can't make this decision for you, but I know from experience that each secret is like a brick and the withholding of it is the mortar. After a while you have yourself a wall built up between you and your man, and that's a wall you don't need. Tell Spencer what happened. If you don't, you'll start thinking that you did something wrong. You've already been down that road—feeling guilty when you were completely innocent."

Jemma sighed. "Thank you, Do Dah. You're a wise woman."

"Call me Julia, and I'm not a wise woman. Your gram is a wise woman. I've made so many mistakes that it's like opening a file cabinet to ask me for advice. Don't sell Spencer short, honey. That boy has grit and he can handle this. Let me know how it goes, and I'll be seeing you in a couple of weeks for Christmas."

"You're coming to Chillaton? I thought you always went to England for Christmas."

Julia coughed. "I'll see you, sometime, sugar." She hung up, leaving Jemma alone on the line.

❧

"Let's go to Dallas tomorrow morning. I need to do some shopping," Spencer said as they drove away from the base.

"Sure. That'll be fine." She had already chewed several antacids.

He caught on immediately. "What's happened?"

She bawled like a two-year-old. "I'm so sorry. Rats. I didn't want this to happen."

Spencer pulled into a roadside park. They stood beside the car, holding one another until she stopped crying. "Is it your health?" he asked.

Bless his heart. If only it were that simple. "No, I'm fine. It's Paul."

Spencer made no remark as they sat on a picnic table and she spilled the story. He held her hand the whole time, staring at the highway and chewing a hole in his lip. "It's cold, baby. Let's go home," he finally said.

He turned on the radio. Jemma watched him out of the corner of her eye and knew that he was livid. The Corvette fairly flew along the highway. Spencer liked to drive fast, but this was angry fast. The red and blue lights rotated behind them. Neither said a word until the officer left him with a warning ticket in his hand. It was a good thing Spencer had on his uniform.

Jemma spoke first. "If you are mad at me, I'll just die."

He put the ticket in his wallet because it was the least of his worries. "I'm not angry with you, Jem. I love you."

"You look mad."

"Yeah, well, that may be true. Let's take Helene and Trina out to dinner tonight."

"Trina is in Dallas, as usual, now that Nick has a car, and Helene has gone to the opera with a friend tonight."

"Then you and I will have peanut butter sandwiches and snuggle on the couch."

She grinned at his ability to move on from sticky issues. "It's a date," she said, but noticed the change in him.

❧

"Good morning, Jemma," Helene said. "I see that the Corvette is gone. Where is Spencer?"

"I don't know. We're supposed to go shopping in Dallas this morning. Maybe he went to get gas or something."

"I've been up for an hour and I have yet to see him."

Jemma went to the conservatory and stood in the door. He was not altogether himself last night.

Helene took her hand. "Come along, dear, let's have a cup of tea and visit. Tell me about your latest painting."

He had gotten the address from another Turner in the phone book, claiming to be an old military buddy who wanted to see Paul. At least part of that was true. Jem had said he was in the army. He just hoped that he could recognize the guy from Jemma's sketchy, year-old description. It was getting chilly in the Corvette, so he started the engine again to warm up. As he did, a tall, good-looking man emerged from the house and retrieved the newspaper from the lawn. Spencer decided to take a chance.

"Hey, how's it going? Aren't you Paul Turner?" Spencer asked, approaching him.

"Yeah. What's up?"

Spencer extended his hand. "I'm Spencer Chase, Jemmabeth's fiancé, and I think we need to talk." Paul was taken aback. He stammered as he repeated his name and sheepishly clasped Spencer's hand.

"You're going to get cold out here, man. Why don't we go inside?"

"No, uh, whatever you have to say, you can say out here," Paul said, looking past Spencer toward the Corvette. "What's on your mind?" He folded his arms across his bare chest.

"Well, Jemma is on my mind most of the time, and from what I've heard, she's on yours, too. The thing is that she has made a choice here, between you and me. I think we need to respect that choice, don't you, Mr. Turner?"

Paul leveled his eyes at Spencer. "I think all's fair anytime, anywhere, Mr. Chase."

"No, that's where you're wrong. Since you care so much for Jemma, I would hope that you would honor her happiness. We both know that she is worth risking everything for."

Paul looked away.

"What you may not know is that she almost died last summer in a car wreck. She was in a coma for almost two weeks. When she was semi-conscious, there was only one name she said and that was mine. If she had said yours, sir, I'd say that we have a fair race on our hands, but she didn't. I fully realize the pain that losing her can cause, but I'm asking you to be a gentleman, and back off." Spencer always did have a way with words.

The news of Jemma's accident clearly took him by surprise. Paul shifted his weight and looked Spencer over, checking to see why he was the preferred one. "I respect what you've said, but Jemma was the best thing that ever happened to me. I don't see what you have to lose by a little competition. If she still feels the same way when you get back from 'Nam, maybe I'll back off then."

Spencer clenched his jaw. "If you continue to bother Jemma-beth and make her uncomfortable, uneasy, or in the least bit upset, I will insist that she gets a restraining order against you. I'm sure you learned about those in law school."

Paul turned toward the house. "You, sir, are on my property. Get off," he snorted over his shoulder.

"You are on my fiancée's nerves. You get off, Mr. Renrut," Spencer said, standing his ground.

Paul slammed the door, but not before Spencer saw one of Jemma's paintings hanging on the wall inside.

⋙◈⋘

She met the Corvette as he pulled in Helene's driveway. Spencer got out and leaned against the car. She put her arms around him. "Where have you been? I was about to start looking for you."

"I had some business to take care of," he said, then kissed her with a healthy dose of enthusiasm for the early morning hour.

"I could take some more of that." She nuzzled his ear.

"Let's eat and get going on our shopping." He didn't elaborate on the exact business he had before breakfast and she didn't ask. She told herself that it must have had something to do with Christmas gifts. He was so good at surprises.

⋙◈⋘

They spent the day in Dallas and stopped at a pizza place before driving back to Wicklow.

"So where were you this morning, Spence? Is it a secret?"

"I went to see Mr. Renrut."

She bugged her eyes at him. "You didn't. You confronted Paul?"

"Nothing happened. I just told him the truth. That you chose me over him, and that he had better leave you alone or else."

"Or else what? Did you go fisticuffs?"

"Or else we're getting a restraining order against him."

"Wow! I wish I had been there. Why didn't you let me go with you?"

"This is between him and me. You are the victim."

"I love you, Mr. Chase. You are my hero once again."

"Yeah, well, he'd better leave you alone, and I'm serious."

"I'm sorry, babe. He's a nice guy. He just can't help himself, I guess."

"Whose side are you on?"

"I didn't mean it like that, Spence. I simply mean that he may have loved me."

Spencer gave her a look she hadn't anticipated and ate his pizza.

"Now wait." Jemma turned his face toward hers. "I love you. Maybe I shouldn't have told you about this."

Spencer shrugged. "I guess you could have kept it a secret if that's the kind of relationship you want to have."

Jemma put her hands on her hips. "What does that mean? I want to be with you as your wife. I want to have your babies and grow old and wrinkled with you and watch the stars from our rocking chairs. That's the kind of relationship I want to have with you."

A little boy in the next booth peeked over at them.

Spencer puffed out his cheeks. "I misspoke—big-time. I didn't realize how jealous I am of him. I just wish that he had never kissed you or whispered sweet things in your ear or even looked at you with those green eyes of his. Forgive me, Jem. I didn't know he would affect me this way. I think it makes me feel like that song of Roy's. Remember 'Running Scared'? Plus, I saw one of your paintings hanging on his wall and that got to me. His idea is to try and win you back while I'm in Vietnam. That was too much for me to handle."

Jemma held him close. "Let's go home, babe. I want to hold you without an audience."

❧

"Miz Liz, I got them lights strung all across the porch, but when I plugged 'em in, they didn't work," Lester said, his ears the color of frozen eggplants.

"Well, that's okay. Those lights are older than electricity anyway," Lizbeth said as she iced Spencer's favorite cake. "We'll make do with what we have."

"Did I ever tell you about the time that the sheriff let the jail-birds decorate the courthouse for Christmas?"

"No, I don't believe I've had the privilege of hearing that story." She probably had, but it was of no use to tell him.

"Well, sir, it was during the second war and the county didn't have much money to spend on decoratin'. The sheriff had the inmates stringin' popcorn with needles and thread. Old Mrs. Chase, Spencer's grandma, donated about five bushels of cranberries, so they had to string them, too. It sure was a sight 'cause back then them fellers had to wear them black-and-white-striped suits. It was real funny to watch. The Callister twins was doin' time for makin' moonshine out to their daddy's old Windy Valley place. 'Course their daddy was as guilty as they were, but he took off to the next county on a horse and the sheriff didn't have enough gas to chase him. Chancy and Chauncy was them twins' names. They were about as ugly as sin, poor things, and flat-out had no sense at all. Them boys ate half of the popcorn and hid most of the cranberries in their cells and kept them there for weeks."

"What on earth for?"

"Moonshine. Their old daddy started visitin' them real regular like. What nobody knew was that he was slippin' things to them, ingredients and stuff for brewin'. They even had themselves a hot plate and whatnot in their cell. Them boys whipped up a batch of cranberry moonshine in a mop bucket. They kept it hid in a contraption down the commode tank, no offense, Miz Liz. Ever one of them inmates was drunk and sick when the sheriff got to work one mornin'. The twins got themselves another six months for that mischief."

Lizbeth sprinkled the remainder of coconut on top of the cake. "Lester, how do you remember all these stories?"

"Well, sir, after that incident, the sheriff hired me to check out the cells one night a week for mischief makin'. I could sniff out that sort of thing. That's how I got enough money to buy my cuckoo clock. Had it on layaway down to the Household Supply for a long spell. It still works, even after makin' that cuckoo racket all them years."

She stood back to look at the cake. It was her best recipe—coconut crème. Spencer could almost eat the whole thing by himself.

"Jemmerbeth and Spencer still don't know what's going on around here?" Lester asked.

"I hope not. Julia said she almost slipped and said too much to Jemma. I imagine Jemma might smell a rat if she was paying attention. Everybody should be coming in tonight. Trina and Helene will be on the last train from Dallas. You can still pick them up, right?"

"Yes ma'am. I'll be there right after I pick up Willer, but if them young'uns are flyin', they could get here right fast."

"They can't leave until Spencer gets in from Mineral Wells. He's meeting Jemma in Dallas, then they'll fly here together."

"What else do you want me to do?"

"Sit down and have a cup of coffee with me, Lester. You've been working hard all week. The place looks good, thanks to you."

"My pleasure, Miz Liz, always a pleasure."

Lizbeth poured them each a cupful from the percolator. "What do you think about Willa and Joe?"

"I like him a lot. He's right good on that fiddle, not as good as Cam, of course, but downright decent."

"I bet he shows up here during the festivities. I think he's pretty sweet on Willa, and I think the feeling is mutual."

"She's a good woman, and he saved our Jemmer's life. I think they'd make a nice couple." Lester reached for a cranberry muffin. "How do you think her girl is gonna take it?"

"Trina will be fine. She wants her mama to be happy. Then she won't have to worry about her so much."

Lester took a big sip of coffee and tapped his foot on the linoleum. "Now don't be takin' this wrong, Miz Liz, but ain't it kindly peculiar how you and me took up with Willer and Joe, them being colored and all."

Lizbeth set down her cup. "Where are you heading with this, Lester?"

"Not sure where I'm headin'. I just was thinkin' that in our younger days, shoot, probably even when Cam was alive, nobody our age would've mixed with colored folks."

"I suppose you're right about that. Of course that doesn't mean it was the right thing to do."

"Well, sir, I've come around to that way of thinkin' myself. We all got the same innerds and the same laugh and the same sense about what's right and wrong. There's bad white folk and real nice colored folk and vice versa. I get teased down to the barber shop about bein' friends with Joe and Willer, but I'm to where it don't bother me none."

Lizbeth smiled at him. "I think the next step for you and me is to stop calling folks 'colored' and learn to say 'black.'"

"That's nothin' but fair. Our bunch has picked 'white' for a color and their bunch can have 'black.' I reckon the whole caboodle of us could be called 'colored.'"

They both chuckled at his assessment.

"Oh my, I hear a car," Lizbeth said.

"Gram!" Robby ran in the back door, his blue eyes shining.

"Help my life, child, what are you doing here so early?"

"We left last night. Mom and Daddy took turns driving. Hi, Lester. May I have a muffin, Gram?"

"Help yourself, honey."

"Merry Christmas!" Jim strode across the room to give his mother a hug.

Alex was right behind him, hugging Lester. "We couldn't stand it. We had to get here and help."

"Let me look at you. Aren't you worn out from driving all night?" Lizbeth asked, taking their coats.

Robby took a second muffin. "They took turns snoring in the car, too."

"I did not snore," Alex said. "Have you heard from Jemmabeth?"

"She called last night. Spencer arrives in Dallas about 5:30 and their flight to Amarillo gets in around nine o'clock."

"I made a big sign for Jem and Spence," Robby said, running back to the car.

"Do you think she knows?" Jim asked.

Lizbeth raised her brow. "If she does, we have Julia to thank. She slipped and told Jemma that she would see her this weekend."

"What got into her? I thought she was the big secret keeper in the family," Jim said.

"She's getting old, like the rest of us, I suppose. She thought Jemma was distracted and may not have noticed."

"Oh, Jem notices everything." Alex rolled her eyes.

Robby came in with a bang from the screen door and flopped a roll of butcher paper on the floor. "See? Jem's gonna love it." He began unrolling the paper, revealing large, red letters—*SURP.*

"Let's wait, son, and I'll help you tack that up." Jim set down his coffee and helped Robby reinstate the noisy paper.

"It says, 'Surprise Jem & Spence!'" Robby grinned. "It's big, too."

"I can see that," Lizbeth said. "You did a fine job."

"Hey, young'un, you want to go with me to buy some popcorn?" Lester asked. "Maybe we'll stop by the drugstore for some comic books and a shake."

"Yeah! Let's go. Okay, Mom?" Robby turned puppy dog eyes on Alex.

"A milk shake this time of the day?" Lizbeth asked.

"Sure, Robby, you go have some fun. It's been a long trip." Jim winked at Lester. "I know what you're thinking, Mama." Jim put his arm around Lizbeth as they watched Robby grab Lester's hand. "He is the spitting image of Luke, right down to that giggle."

She smiled. "He is indeed."

❦

Julia and Arthur were the second to arrive. She was certain that Jemma hadn't caught on to the party plans. Arthur immediately went shopping. When he came back, the kitchen was overstocked with food. He also bought every string of Christmas lights in town. Jim and Lester were busy all day. Carrie and Philip dropped by for a quick visit before heading to The Judge's, and Alex went so far as to extend an invitation for The Judge to join them. Arthur had a few words to say over that idea, quoting Shakespeare's *Macbeth* concerning his wife's high school flame. Alex even called Max and Rebecca Chase, too. Rebecca was almost gracious, if not somewhat inebriated, but declined. Max, however, accepted their offer and promised to bring flowers and something for the punch. Alex assured him that the punch was fine as it was, but that flowers would be very nice.

Ted and Trent Lillygrace had just returned from a month in

Europe. They were tanned and fit, like country club men. It was easy to see that Ted and Alex were siblings, but Trent resembled his mother, who had deserted him as an infant for money. Robert and Catherine Lillygrace, completely overdressed and oblivious to it, stayed in the living room visiting with Arthur. The Christmas tree in the living room was inundated with gifts, and Robby had inspected each one. His banner was strung across the ceiling and went the length of the room. The air was filled with the sweet smells and sounds of the holidays and the excitement of a surprise party for everyone's favorite couple.

Jemma and Spencer would have to rent a car in Amarillo, then it would take them an hour to drive to Chillaton, so they were expected around ten thirty. Cam's clock had just chimed ten when Lizbeth finally sat in Cam's chair. She had been in the kitchen for a week, but now she could relax and wait like the rest.

"What if they stop to eat?" Trent asked.

"Jemma will be hot to get home. They won't eat," Trina said.

"I hope they don't come in the back. It looks like a parking lot in the alley," Ted added.

"Spencer always pulls in front," Lizbeth assured them all.

"I hear a car now." Alex moved to the front door. "My goodness. It's a semi-truck. Why would a big truck be coming here?"

"Oh mercy," Willa said and moved to the door. Trina joined her, and Lester was not far behind.

"What's going on?" Jim bent his head to peer out the oval window in the door.

"Willa, I think maybe you'd better have Joe move his truck out back," Lizbeth called out from the living room.

"I'm two jumps ahead of you, Miz Liz. Trina, come on and help me to the gate." Willa opened the door and stepped onto the front porch.

Alex turned to Lester. "Is that the truck driver that Jemma hit?"

"Yes ma'am," Lester said. "That's him all right, and he's a good'un."

"I'd sure like to meet him," Jim said.

"You'd better ask Miz Liz about Joe. I'm not sure what all I can say at this point," Lester said and ducked back into the good bedroom.

"What's going on, Mama?" Jim asked.

"I think you'll find Joe Cross is one of the nicest men around. I'm sure you'll see plenty of him this week."

The big rig started up again and moved down the block. They heard it pull to the alley behind Lester's house. It wasn't long before the group came in the back door. Trina's eyes were on Joe, and his were set on Willa. He took off his cowboy hat and shook hands all around. "Sounds like we've got us a party tonight."

"Thanks to you and the good Lord." Jim patted Joe's back.

Joe grinned. "No, sir, I didn't do nothin'. It was all the Lord's doin's."

"Car coming!" Robby yelled. "Should we turn the lights out?"

"Are you sure it's them?" Carrie asked. "I can't see."

"It's a big car," Robby said. "It looks like old people, though."

All was quiet as someone rapped on the oval glass.

"Why would they knock?" Trent asked.

Alex opened the door. "Come in. We're so glad that you decided to come. Max, would you mind moving your car to the back of the house? We want to surprise the kids. Thank you."

Lester melted into the woodwork. He and Max Chase had history over a used truck, and Lester wasn't keen on making small talk with him. Spencer's mother, Rebecca, once a beauty herself, had on way too much makeup, and it was not applied quite right. Reeking of alcohol, she snickered and smirked at the introductions. Alex offered her coffee and a chair, both of which she accepted.

"Car!" Robby yelled again. "Oh boy, it's them."

The gathering held its collective breath. Through the lace curtains, most could see Jemma and Spencer walk to the front porch in the glow of the new Christmas lights. Spencer was still in uniform, and Jemmabeth was full of giggles.

"When they open the door, count to three, then yell," Alex whispered.

"Yuck, they're kissing," Robby whispered, causing stifled ripples of laughter through the house. The doorknob turned, and the door creaked open.

"Good grief, it's so dark in here," Jemma said.

"*SURPRISE!*" came the thunderous response, along with every light in the house being turned on.

Jemma shrieked and the house went dark.

"Way to go, Jem," Robby yelled back. "Now you ruined Christmas."

"What's going on?" Jemma asked.

"Somebody get a flashlight. I think we've blown a fuse," Jim shouted.

"Daddy? Where are you?"

"Just a minute, sweet pea," Alex said, laughing. "We'll have to try this again."

Mumbles and laughter rose up from various rooms.

"I think I saw Carrie," Spencer said.

"I'm over here," Carrie called.

"So am I," Trent added in a falsetto.

"Me, too," Robby said. "I can smell your stinky perfume, Jem."

"I can smell your stinky socks," Spencer countered, causing another round of laughter. The lights flickered, then went off again.

"Turn off the outside Christmas lights. That'll help," Trent suggested.

"Leave it to an engineer," Alex said.

Lester could be heard fumbling for the front door. At last the house lights all came on. Spencer and Jemma were speechless. They were surprised for real.

⊰◈⊱

"Mom, was this your idea?" Jemma asked as they ate Lizbeth's cake.

"I'm guilty." Alex gave Spencer a hug.

Spencer watched his own mother, whose glazed eyes were on Jemmabeth everywhere she went.

"We all wanted to be together before our favorite soldier takes off for parts unknown," Julia said.

"As well as fatten him up," Helene added.

"There's going to be another soldier in the family now," Ted said with his arm around Trent.

Spencer sat back. "Oh man. You got yours, too."

Trent shrugged. "Yeah. Crazy, huh?"

"I'm being transferred to a different base," Spencer said.

Ted nodded. "Getting you ready for nighttime and bad weather."

Alex cleared her throat. "So, did we surprise you kids?"

"You did. Y'all are good." Jemma said, still thinking about Spencer flying in bad weather.

"We hoped Sandy could come, but she is meeting Martin in Hawaii right now," Alex explained.

"Yeah, she called me last week. He's almost done over there. Would you like some more cake, Mrs. Chase?" Jemma asked, still on Spencer's lap.

"*No.*" Her volume made everybody jump. "Can't you find your own chair to sit in?"

Jemma hopped off and Spencer stood. "Maybe you would like some more coffee, Mother."

"Let's go home, son," she said. "We have plenty of chairs there."

Alex intervened. "I wish you could stay longer. You know what? Jim and I would love to take you home, if that's okay. I'd like to see your antiques. We'll be right back, sweet pea." She touched Spencer's hand. "I know you are tired, Spence." Alex was so smooth and thoughtful that the devil himself would have a hard time resisting her.

⎯⎯◈⎯⎯

Spencer's dad was working the crowd, and he had cornered Ted Lillygrace. During the Second World War, Max Chase had never left the United States while Ted had flown missions over half of Europe.

"That was the last time anybody had to tell me what two paper clips in a coffee cup meant. You have to learn the pet peeves of the commanding officer, that's for sure." Max laughed harder at his story than his audience did. Lester had sidled up while Max was telling his tale. His beady eyes reminded Lester of a pet mouse he'd had as a youngster, only the mouse wasn't nearly as obnoxious. Finally he couldn't stand it anymore.

"So, are you still passin' off junkers as fine automobiles to elderly folks and then lyin' about it?" Lester said.

"Mr. Timms." Max hustled him aside. "I'm learning more about you every time I see you."

"Well, sir, I'm learnin' more about the devil every time I see your sorry hide around town." Lester's ears colored up.

Max looked around, maintaining a smile. "Mr. Timms, I made

that little mistake up to you. Now, it's time to forgive and forget. Let's be upstanding about things."

"I just want you to 'fess up and say you were wrong and that you're sorry. You can take them last few words any way you want."

"I sent you the money back and gave you the truck. I don't want you interfering in my social life like you did. People don't know all the facts when you say things like that."

"I'll be happy to oblige them. I can do it right now, if you like."

"No. Look, I'm sorry that I misrepresented things to you. I probably got them down wrong to start with."

"I didn't hear the word *lied* in there anywhere." Lester clicked his dentures.

"Okay, okay. I'm sorry that I lied to you about that old truck. Now, are you satisfied? Let's not spoil the kids' party over this."

"Mr. Max-a-million Chase, I forgive you," Lester said and put out his hand.

❧

Max drew back at the sudden change of attitude, but he shook Lester's hand.

"The Good Book says to forgive so you will be forgiven. That's what you should do, too, Max-a-million. You need to ask forgiveness from the Lord and forgive yourself for all your skirt chasin' and lyin'. You need to forgive your good wife for drinkin' herself into a hole over you, and you sure enough need to forgive yourself for bein' such a pitiful excuse for a father to that fine boy in there. My pa used to tell us young'uns to straighten up and fly right, and I suggest you do the same. I'll be prayin' for you, mister." Lester turned to join Joe Cross, who was tuning up his fiddle.

Max Chase, who never considered himself as the object of anybody's kindly prayers, stared after Lester. His mouth had gone dry, and his throat seemed to have knotted up under his necktie. He looked around for Spencer and found him in the kitchen, talking to Robert Lillygrace. He stood next to him and, for once, did not enter the dialogue. Instead he slipped his arm around Spencer's shoulders.

Spencer looked at his father, smiled, and then carried on with his conversation. Max admired the way his son spoke. He never had heard him curse, and he could throw nickel- or five-dollar words around as needed. People liked Spencer and he was, unlike himself, a prince of a man. That's what people used to call Max's father, too. Max took a deep breath. Lester had rattled him. At least he hadn't yelled at him like he did that day at the dealership and called him Max-a-million-skirt-chaser, but Rebecca still did, upon occasion.

⋘⋙

Joe Cross fired up his fiddle. Lester pulled out his harmonica and the group sang along. Only Papa's presence could have made Jemmabeth happier. She stood between Spencer and Carrie as they all sang "White Christmas."

Around one o'clock, the older ones got sleepy and headed off to the That'll Do Motel. The Lillygraces insisted on staying in Amarillo, so they had an hour's drive ahead of them. A few sturdy souls stayed up talking even later. Spencer and Jemma sat in the living room with Trina.

"Do y'all think Mama's in love with Joe?" Trina asked point-blank.

"She acts like it to me," Jemma said. "What do you think, Spence?"

"I like Joe, and if he can make Willa happy, why not?"

"It just took me off guard, you know." Trina yawned. "I'd better get home. I'm beat. I'll see y'all tomorrow."

"I'll take you home," Spencer offered. "I need to go, too. Who knows what's going on at my house?"

Trina stood with her hands on her hips. "I think I can walk across the tracks. Sit down, soldier." She gave him a gentle push. Spencer landed in Jemma's lap, quite on purpose. Trina sneaked out while they were giggling. Robby was sound asleep in Papa's chair or he would have protested. They watched the lights on the Christmas tree. Papa's bubble lights were Jemma's favorite.

"Do you think we'll have our own little tree year after next?" she asked.

"Yup. It probably won't have that many presents under it, though."

"I won't care; just so we are married."

"It will happen. Give me a kiss because I want to go home and talk to my dad. Did you see him put his arm around me tonight? I don't remember him ever doing that."

"No more lovey-dovey stuff," Robby mumbled. "Go home, Spence."

"You little wart. I'll take care of you tomorrow," Spencer said, rolling him onto the floor. Robby wandered off to the kitchen, where his parents and uncle were still talking.

"Good night, babe. I love you," Jemma said, then watched his car lights disappear down the street.

❧

"Uncle Art, how do you like it at That'll Do?"

"It's completely underrated, Jemma, and I think your aunty is quite taken with it, right, Julia?"

"Heavenly days. We have a cigarette burn on our blanket, we almost had to build a fire in the bathtub to heat the place, and don't get me started on the bathroom."

"We'll survive. You're looking fit, Jemmabeth. Are you feeling your usual perky self these days?" Art asked.

"I had some headaches for a while when school first began, but they went away."

"I didn't know about that, young lady. You should have told me," Alex said as she distributed orange juice.

"I had Trina's boyfriend do some research. He said if they didn't go away that I should see a doctor. Good advice, I thought."

Everyone laughed.

Julia drank her coffee and looked toward the tracks. "I think we have a wedding coming up. Willa and Joe make a real cute couple."

"What's this I hear about Spencer being transferred to another base?" Arthur asked. "Where will he be going?"

"Fort Rucker, Alabama," Jemma replied. "That means I can't see him every weekend. We've been lucky that he has been so close to Dallas."

"You'll make it, dear," Helene said. "War is a horrid mess, but many soldiers come home. I know that is a constant worry, but you must carry on."

Arthur loaded up his plate with biscuits and gravy, then paused. "There is a quote, Jemmabeth, from my favorite wise man, Mark

Twain. 'All war must be just that—the killing of strangers against whom you feel no personal animosity; strangers whom, in other circumstances, you would help if you found them in trouble, and who would help you if you needed it.' Tell that to your young man so he can remember it in times of need."

Jemma wrote it in her sketchbook.

"Don't you love Art's photographic memory?" Julia whispered to Jemma. "It comes in handy for so many things—except my checkbook balance." She kissed her husband on the top of his balding head.

"At least Spence won't be shooting at anybody if he's flying a helicopter to rescue people."

Jemma's comment was met with silence.

The rest of the men came in the back just as Spencer came in the front door, and everyone rallied to change the subject. Jemma, however, wanted reassurance that her dearest would not be killing people, nor would anyone try to kill soldiers in an aircraft with a red cross painted on both sides.

❧

The Negro Bethel Church had another surprise for Spencer. The congregation gathered to thank him and have a blessing to officially open the doors to their new building.

After the reception, Spencer and Jemma stood in the church holding hands. "It's beautiful," she said.

"It's nice, really nice. I would make a few changes if I had it to do over."

"I always think that about my paintings."

Spencer walked around, touching the wood and examining the stained-glass window. "I like it. It has the feel that I was hoping for."

They talked, sharing ideas and enjoying the solitude of the church. It was Spencer's first real project as an architect and it was built to God's glory.

Family and friends dined and laughed their way through four days of glorious Christmas celebration. Carrie and Philip took the opportunity to announce their engagement. On the last day of his leave, Jemma and Spencer went for a drive to Plum Creek in his new black Sting Ray convertible. It was a safe and easy thing for

Max to upgrade his son's Corvettes, but the gesture was sorely lacking as a relationship builder.

They had spent many precious hours at the creek with Jemma's family. In December there was no water left to qualify it as a creek. Only a dry bed remained, packed with rippled sand where the water had marked its course. They sat under their favorite tree and exchanged Christmas gifts. Jemma placed a sterling silver cross on a chain around Spencer's neck. Spencer gave her a new watch to mark the time until he came home and a rare copy of Emily Dickinson's poems. They took turns reading the poems aloud until the cold evening air engulfed them, forcing them home.

❦

It was a quiet ride to the airport. Jemma sat as close to him as she could. "You'll tell me when I can come, right?" she asked as they neared the Amarillo city limits.

"I'll call you tonight and every night that I can. I just don't know how long I'll be in Georgia. They are training us to fly tactically."

"What exactly does that mean?"

"It means low level, instrument flying, combat-type training."

"Combat? I thought you were going to be rescuing people."

"Jem, they have to train me for any circumstance. I have to be ready to defend myself. You don't want me ignorant about that, do you?"

"I guess not."

"When I leave Alabama, I'll have my wings."

"You already have wings because you are my angel." She traced around his ear and played with the short hairs at the back of his neck. "My sweet dearie thee. I think I'll write a poem to you and use that."

"Sweetness is in the eye of the beholder, my dearie."

"Is that why you called me a mean woman all those times?"

"Mean can also imply average, you know."

"Hey, that's not sweet talk coming from an angel. Look, it's snowing," she said.

"You be careful driving back. Don't take any chances, okay?"

"It's melting as soon as it hits the road. I'll be fine."

Spencer found his seat on the plane and peered through the

477

window. He couldn't see her through the snow. But as the aircraft rose into the sky, he knew she was watching. He touched the silver cross through his shirt. He would see her again soon, but never soon enough.

Chapter 15
Change of Heart

Max Chase's car was in Lester's driveway when Jemma got home. "He's been here for an hour already," Alex whispered as her daughter came in the back door.

"What does he want?" Jemma asked.

"Nobody knows. He keeps asking when you'll be back."

Jemma went to the living room, where Max was visiting with Uncle Art. He cut his conversation short and took Jemma into the foyer.

"I need to talk with you, if that's okay," he said, his eyes looking right into hers. They were not the pewter gray of Spence's. They were dark and shifty, like his wife's.

"Sure. We could go to the porch if you want." Jemma put her coat back on.

Max, the glad-handing car dealer, stepped outside and shoved his hands in his pockets. He studied the porch floor like it was of the greatest interest to him.

"Someone told me the other day that I have been a pitiful father to Spencer. Has he ever said anything like that to you?"

Jemma blinked. Her first thought was to tell him the truth, but she decided on a different approach. "Spencer is a man of great conviction and character. I'm not sure where he learned those traits."

Max raised his eyes to hers again. "What does he say about me, Jemmabeth? I need to know."

She spoke without hesitation. "Spencer feels that he has been raised by Harriet. I don't see how you could argue with him on that point. He's a precious man, so someone has done right by him."

Max exhaled and rubbed the back of his neck. "I know he is a good boy and I had nothing to do with it. I'm scared spitless for him now. I never thought he'd be put in this kind of danger." He walked to the porch swing and sat down, holding his head in his hands. "I don't like it, but I don't know what to do. You're a good Christian girl. Tell me this. Will God punish me for my sins by taking Spencer away from me?"

Jemma's face flushed, despite the temperature. She had never considered such a thing. "What makes you say that?"

"I don't know much about the Bible, but I do remember a verse that goes, 'The sins of the fathers will be laid on the children.' That's what scares me. It's not that boy's fault that I've lived a feckless life, and I don't know what I can do about it at this point."

Her stomach hollowed out. This could not be right. Spencer had too much faith in his safe return. "Maybe you should visit with my friend, Brother Cleo. He knows a lot about the Bible."

"You mean that colored preacher?"

"I mean Brother Cleo. If you don't want to talk with him, then talk with the Presbyterian minister. I don't know his name."

"Surely you don't think that I know him." Max sniffed. "I barely know where the church is. I'm not too sure about talking to a colored preacher, though." Max studied the porch floor again. "Where is this Brother Cleo anyway?"

"He's in the kitchen," Jemma said, her mind a swirl of scriptures and conversations she'd had with Spencer about his dad over the years. She felt sorry for Max, though, and sat beside him on the swing. "Spence has such faith that his future will be with me."

Max's shoulders began to shake, and Jemma put her arm around him.

"That boy is all I have," he mumbled into his hand. "He was such a cute little guy. All I can think about now is how I missed all those years with him. I was out running around on his mother. Now it's too late."

Jemma lowered her voice. "There is also a scripture that says: 'With men it is impossible, but not with God—for with God all things are possible.'"

Max drew a quivering breath. "Do you think God knows that I'm sorry?"

"I know He would hear your prayers."

"It's been over twenty years since I prayed. I don't think I can."

"Sure you can. Just talk to Him. Get on your knees somewhere private and talk like you are talking to me."

He shook his head. "My father told me that I was going to regret my life someday, and he was right, as usual. No matter what happens to me, I don't want to hurt my boy."

"You pray about it. When Spence comes back, you can build a whole new relationship with him. I know for sure that he is a forgiving person. In the meantime, you might try to talk to your wife and ask for her forgiveness, too. She has suffered all these years just like Spence." Jemma hoped that the woman had a forgiving bone in her body.

Max didn't respond to that idea. There was too much pain already on the table with his alcoholic wife. "Spencer has been lucky to have you and your family all these years. I think I would have lost him if you had died in that wreck." Max studied her face, then reached for her hand and patted it. "Thanks for talking to me. Maybe we could we do this again sometime."

"I'll look forward to it, Mr. Chase."

"You call me Max. Maybe someday I can become likeable to good people like you. It might make Spencer proud of me."

"I'll pray for you."

"Now I've got two people praying for me. I guess I'd better go do some praying of my own." He stepped off the porch. Jemma followed him, pulling her jacket around her in the sudden cold wind. He turned to her and smiled, a little like his son.

She watched him leave and marveled at how quickly she had fed him spiritual advice. Maybe she was learning to walk. She went inside and rubbed her hands together in front of the heater.

"What was our Mr. Chase up to, Jemmabeth?" Arthur looked up from his book.

Jemma sat on the couch next to Papa's chair. "He is worried about a scripture and what it could mean to Spencer's safety."

"Oh, and what's that?" Arthur leaned forward.

"The sins of the fathers are to be laid on their children."

He took a quick draw on his pipe. "A similar reference would be from Exodus, part of the Ten Commandments. It was a warning to those people who hated God and worshipped graven images instead. God said that He would hold that sin against even the third and fourth generation. I think our Mr. Chase is actually quoting the Bard."

"What do you mean?"

"Shakespeare used that line in *The Merchant of Venice*. Act three, I believe."

"Uncle Art, you are too much." Jemma jumped up to hug him.

"Think nothing of it, my little artist. By the way, I haven't seen your portfolio in a long time. I've missed all of your shows and I need to make it up to you and to me. What say Julia and I come to Dallas and see your work this spring?"

"Deal. I'm working on some things now for my senior exhibition. I would love for you to come. Thanks, Uncle Art."

"Whatever for, dear girl?"

"For keeping up with the Bard and knowing the Old Testament."

❧

"Baby girl, come here and talk to me," Jim said.

Jemma closed her sketchbook and went to sit by her father in the living room.

"What or whom are you drawing?" he asked, putting his arm around her.

"Spencer, of course. I probably have five hundred sketches of him. I miss him so much."

"I know. Hey, just remember that I went overseas and I came back."

"I also know that your brothers didn't."

He watched the bubble lights on the tree. "He's going to be all right, honey. I know it, in here," he said, laying his hand on his chest. "Sometimes. . ."

The telephone rang, and she was off the couch before Jim could finish his sentence. He smiled when he realized that it was Spencer. Her hushed conversation brought tears to his eyes. He asked God to cover Spencer with His protection and to have mercy that he would not meet the same fate as his brothers. That thought shrouded all optimism.

❧

Ted poured himself a cup of coffee. "Lester, thanks for letting all of us invade your house."

"I didn't have to do nothin'," Lester said. "Miz Forrester here done all the work. You'd better sit down, Miz Liz, or you're gonna give out before breakfast."

She frowned. "You just drink your coffee, Lester. I'm having fun. Would you care for some more biscuits, Trent?"

"No thanks, I'm doing fine. Jemma, when will you see Spencer again?" Trent tapped his fingers on the table in the same way he had fidgeted through the weekend.

"I don't know. He said that he might not have much time off from now on. He's heard that something big is about to happen in the war."

Trent shook his head. "Too bad that doesn't mean we are withdrawing."

Ted laid his hand on Trent's shoulder. "I'll warm up the car so we can get going. Thank you, Lizbeth, for the best home cooking I've ever had. It was great seeing you, Jim. Don't work too hard." He grasped his brother-in-law's hand. "We really need to do this again. I have that beach house going to waste in California. Do you think we could get this bunch out there?"

"Sure we could. You just set the date."

"Jemmabeth, keep your spirits up and paint. I'll be thinking about you." Ted kissed her cheek and walked to the car with his sister.

"Trent, do you think a monkey would be a good pet?" Robby leaned on his arm with a new book about primates.

"Well, you turned out okay. I don't know what kinds of stuff your parents had to put up with to train you, though." Trent laughed and dodged Robby's good-natured jabs.

"When do you report for basic training?" Jemma asked.

"January 15." Trent pinned Robby's arms to his side.

"Where?" she asked.

Robby ran off and Trent exhaled. "Fort Drum in upstate New York."

"I'll be praying for you, too." Jemma hugged him good-bye. She was going to have to make a prayer list the way things were going.

❧

Jemma and Alex went to Lester's to clean and strip the beds after everybody left. Lester followed them around in protest. "I was fixin' to do that. I'm a good housekeeper."

"We want to help, Lester. You did us all a big favor, and now we want to return it." Alex kissed his forehead. He blushed and sat down in the nearest rocking chair to watch. He put his fingers on the spot where she kissed him and grinned.

"I'll work on the front room; Jem, you work on this one," Alex called from the hallway.

"Lester, have you ever heard anything from Hanna?" Jemma held a pillow with her chin while she peeled off its flannel case.

"No, sir, I never have. Good riddance, I say. I don't know if I've ever thanked you, proper like, Jemmerbeth."

"No thanks needed. She's lucky that we didn't turn her in." Jemma said, still second-guessing the decision to let her go. "Did you notice anything else missing?"

"Oh, this and that, but nothin' to fret over." Lester folded his hands in his lap as the rocking chair made soft thumps on the linoleum. "Jemmer, I had me a talk with our friend Mr. Chase the other night."

Jemmabeth stopped her work for a second, then continued. "Really? What kind of talk was that?"

"Well, sir, I've had a few things stuck in my craw for a good while, and I sort of told him how the cow ate the cabbage. You know, how he needed to get right with the Lord."

"What did he have to say?"

"Nothin' much. I didn't want to go to my grave without tellin' that man to make amends."

Jemma smiled and leaned over the back of Lester's rocker. She rested her head on his. He smelled of shaving soap and Brylcreem. "Lester Timms, I love you," she whispered.

Lester reached for her hand and patted it, much the same as Max Chase had done.

⌇◈⌇

"I'll miss you, Mom," Jemma said as they packed Alex's suitcase.

Alex didn't want to start crying too early. She fanned her eyes. "After you graduate, we want you come to Flagstaff for a while, okay?"

"Sure. I think I'll spend part of the year with Gram, though. I want to try to help Spencer's mother. I don't guess I'll ever get to call her by her first name."

"Don't worry about that, honey. She's not responsible for her actions, poor thing."

"Where did Max meet her? Spencer never talks about his mother."

"They met at college. Neither graduated, but they went to Rice a couple of years."

"Rice? I thought that's where the smartest of the Texas smart go?"

"According to your daddy, Max qualified for that honor, but he's never applied himself to anything. Of course he didn't last at Rice. He did, however, meet Rebecca. I think she is the oldest one in a family of girls. She's a Houston native. That's about all I know. You'll have to ask Spencer the rest."

"I'll ask Harriet, their housekeeper."

"I think Harriet is more than a housekeeper around there, honey. She has kept that family together and raised Spence."

"I know. I should visit her. Maybe tomorrow, after you leave. It will help me keep my mind off missing y'all. Something else I want to ask you: why has Uncle Ted never remarried?"

"I think he's had lots of lady friends, but he got burned with Trent's mother and he's never gotten over it."

"He's so good-looking and sweet. Maybe I'll have to fix him up sometime."

"Good luck. I've tried and it's never worked out. Some men keep trudging along as bachelors and, pretty soon, they're too old to find anybody. Those were my exact words to him before they left."

"Yeah, I know the type." Jemma thought of Paul. For the first time ever, she felt sorry for him.

❦

Jemma and Robby stayed up way past his bedtime sketching monkeys. That's all he wanted to talk about. Jemma showed him how to keep the proportions right, but it didn't matter. After all, they were drawing primates.

It seemed that just as she went to sleep she heard the alarm go off in the good bedroom. She heard her daddy talking in the kitchen about snow. Jemma stretched and woke up Robby, who was asleep on the old army cot beside her bed.

"I don't like the looks of this," Lizbeth said. "The highway can be treacherous when it's this cold. Son, you be extra careful. Maybe you should wait awhile."

"We'll be all right, Mama. Don't forget I grew up in this country. Besides, once we get to the New Mexico line, they actually try to clear off the roads. It's only between here and there that I'll have to watch it."

Alex shivered. "When did it turn so cold? I don't remember it being like this last night," she said, hugging Jemma to her side. "Robby, do you have all your stuff in your duffel bag? All your Christmas gifts and books?"

"Yes ma'am." He yawned.

A light came on in Lester's house. He knocked on the window and waved. He had on his big white nightshirt, and his hair was sticking up in the back.

"Bye, Lester," Robby yelled. He scraped together a nice snowball and tossed it at Jemma as she helped load the car.

"You little monkey," she shouted, chasing him around the car with a snowball of her own.

"Just like old times." Jim grinned. "Come on, Robby. Let's go."

"Dust that snow off before you get in the car," Alex said. "We love you two. Sweet pea, we'll see you at graduation."

Lizbeth retreated to the porch, and Jemma waved from the driveway as the swirling snow became more evident in the headlights of the Rambler. Jim honked and they drove away.

Jemma's heavy heart couldn't stand many more good-byes. "Are you going back to bed, Gram?" she asked as they stood, helpless, in the kitchen.

"No, sugar, I like to read some scriptures and have a quiet prayer time when family leaves. You go on and get some rest."

"I think I'll read, too. I'm a little worried about this storm."

The two women went to their separate rooms and opened their Bibles. Jemma turned to the scriptures she knew best for comfort. Lizbeth began, as always, on her knees, confessing her sins and praising God for the precious gift of her children, her grandchildren, and her beloved husband. Despite her admonitions, she had faith that her little family would make it home safely.

⋘◈⋙

"I think Mama is going to get married before I do," Trina said, drying the dishes. "Have you seen how they look at each other? Even Brother Cleo has been teasing her."

"I hope it doesn't really bother you," Jemma replied as she washed the last of the pots and pans. "I guess they just hit it off."

"Well, the way Mama tells it, she didn't have a choice. Somebody fixed her up with Joe." Trina rolled her eyes toward Lizbeth, who was busy paying bills.

"Is that right, Gram?" Jemma asked. "Did you get things started with Willa and Joe?"

"I think they make a nice couple. Joe Cross is a good, Christian man." Lizbeth tore out a check and carefully addressed an envelope, making the girls wait for more information. She marked *paid* on the bills, closed the Hoosier cabinet drawer, then turned to face them. "Now, who can say otherwise?"

Trina shrugged. "Not me. He's a real sweetheart. I just never thought Mama would find somebody that she would get so silly about."

"Love changes people sometimes." Jemma smiled. "Have you and Nick talked about a date yet?"

"Nope, but Carrie's beating both of us to the altar."

"I wonder what The Judge thinks about that."

Trina shrugged. "Carrie told me that he's gonna give her away at the wedding, but I'll believe it when I see it."

Jemma bit her lip. She'd believe her own wedding when she saw it, too.

Chapter 16
Good-Bye Again

I was beginning to wonder if you had a new girlfriend or something." Jemma pouted into the phone in Helene's conservatory.
"If I had a spare minute, Jem, you would have been the first one to know it."

"You sound exhausted. I bet you could use a good backrub."

"Don't even mention that to me. I'd love one."

"So, when can I come?"

"I'm in a unit that is on a fast training track. They are giving us a double dose of everything. I only get half a day off on the weekends. When I'm not flying, I'm studying. I don't see how we could work it out."

She couldn't respond for a minute, because she was about to cry. Then she managed, "Why are they rushing your training? Are they going to send you over there sooner than we expected?"

"I don't know what they're thinking. It's a military mystery."

"It's because of those test scores. They think you can handle anything."

"You know how sorry I am about this, baby."

"I know. I had a bad feeling about this move anyway. You don't think your next trip will be to Vietnam, do you?"

"I think they'll send us to Fort Sam Houston next. That's where we'll get the Medevac training."

Jemma brightened. "I could go there and stay with Do Dah and Uncle Art. We could even see Carrie."

"It's not in Houston, baby. It's close to San Antonio."

"Oh. How long?"

"Four to six weeks."

"Then doomsday."

"I don't know. My tour of duty in Vietnam should only be a year, but I guess they'll do whatever they want."

"I'm telling you, Spencer, it's all because you are so smart. I didn't know your parents went to Rice."

"Yeah, well, they didn't stay long. Why the sudden interest in my parents?"

"Mom told me. Everybody says hello and that they all miss you."

"I miss you more than anything on earth. Tell me what you were doing when I called and what you're wearing. Then I have to go. There's a line waiting behind me to use the phone."

"I was painting, and I'm wearing your old gray sweatshirt and a pair of jeans."

"I bet you look beautiful. Is your hair in a ponytail?"

"Yup. I love you, Spence. Be careful."

"I love you more. Good-bye."

He didn't call often. She got up earlier in case he was flying at night and could call when he got in. It was before six, though, on a Saturday morning when she heard it ringing. She grabbed it, hoping the noise didn't wake anybody else up. It was Sandy. Jemma almost didn't recognize her voice.

"Sandy?" Jemma asked. "You sound weird."

Sandy cleared her throat. "I'm okay. I just wanted to say hi."

Jemma yawned. "Before six in the morning? I can barely hear you."

"Sorry. I'll let you go back to sleep." Sandy sniffed.

"Don't worry about it. I need to paint anyway." Something was up. Jemma just knew it.

"I'm sorry I gave you such a hard time in Brussels, you know, about y'all sleeping in separate rooms. More people should try that. It might help even after the wedding."

"What's going on with you and Martin? Are you pregnant or something?" Jemma asked. The awkward prayer request Sandy made in Brussels had never been brought up again.

"NO. I am not pregnant."

Jemma held the phone away from her ear. Sandy had her old cheerleader volume going, and went on about not being like everybody else and having babies so soon. There was no need to yell because Jemma totally agreed. She was certain that she didn't want to divide her attention with a new baby as soon as Spencer got out of the army. She wanted him all to herself for a long, long time.

Sandy talked nonstop, then the call was over. There was definitely something wrong in Martyland.

⤜❦⤛

She unlocked the door to her studio above Helene's garage. This was her evening and weekend refuge. She inhaled the fragrance of her tools. Propped against the walls were six paintings ready for the show. Two sisters from the local flower shop were staring a hole through her from one canvas, so she turned that painting to face the wall. A sleazy guy leaned against an angelic fountain while he smoked a cigarette. Mr. and Mrs. Grasso, on the other hand, sat smiling as they ate gelato. Just for the memory, she had painted a section of Monet's garden at Giverny. She had given it considerable thought before doing the painting because his garden had been done to perfection by its owner and numerous others. Jemma had kept this one small and detailed, showing a single flower as the focal point.

Her favorite piece this time around was of two pigeons at Notre Dame engaging in a courtship dance. The sunrise cast a golden light on the male's rust-colored feathers. The last one she had finished before Christmas was of Papa reading the Bible in his maroon velvet chair. She was almost finished with a large portrait of her daddy in his uniform as a young soldier. It reminded her of Spencer as he boarded his flight to Georgia. She sat on the daybed and cried until she could pick up her brushes and begin again.

It was almost suppertime when she decided to take a break. The room was losing natural light anyway. Thunder rumbled in the distance and the distinct fragrance of wet earth wafted in the window as she closed it. Caruso blared from Helene's gramophone in the conservatory. Jemma cleaned her brushes, capped her paints, and grabbed her keys in a hurry to help Helene with the evening meal. She heard the crunch of tires on the graveled driveway and assumed it was Trina coming home from her cleaning job. It wasn't.

She recognized the baby blue pickup immediately. *Paul.* Jemma raced back up the stairs. She left the lights off and hunkered down inside. Helene would handle the situation when he knocked on the door *if* she had on her hearing aid and *if* Caruso's song had ended. Jemma's temples thumped. It wasn't as though Paul would do her harm. No, he was a loving cowboy. Rats.

The rain brought the wind with it. The accelerating patter on the roof camouflaged his footsteps on the stairs, but not for long. She caught her breath.

"I know you're in there, Jemmabeth Alexandra. I just want to talk," he said. "Come on, I'm getting wet out here."

Realizing she hadn't locked it, Jemma reached for the dead bolt just as he pushed the door open. She smelled liquor as soon as he stepped inside. "What are you doing on the floor, you sweet thing?" His sleeves were rolled up, and his black hat was low over his eyes.

"Paul, I'm expecting someone any minute."

"Ah, that must be why the lights are off. You wouldn't be hiding from old Paul, now would you?" He braced himself against the door and folded his arms across his drenched chest.

"Why would I do that? We used to be friends."

"Friends?" He laughed. "No, my love, we were more than friends. I'm sorry you got hurt in a wreck, darlin'. If I'd known about it, well, I don't know what I would've done. Right now I really need to talk to you about my feelings. I've been lonesome for you."

"We could talk, I guess, but I don't want to do it here. Let's go to your truck," she said. Dumb, dumb. He wouldn't fall for such an obvious trick.

"Nah. Here's good. Let's start off with a little sugar, though," Paul said as the dead bolt thudded at his touch. He started toward her, pushing his hat to the back of his head. His soaked white shirt clung to his skin and he needed to shave. A smile spread across his perfect lips, and he reached for her.

She dodged him, knocking off his hat in her dash for the door. They scuffled and he picked her up. She was kicking like crazy as he laid her on the daybed and fell over her. She was helpless.

A flash of lightning lit up his emerald green eyes. His hot beer breath was all over her and his mouth was against her ear. "Jem, all I do is think about us. I was so happy with you. Just give me something to hang on to. I need you. I keep you in my mind and in my heart, but I want the real thing." His stubble scraped against her skin.

She turned her head to stop him, but it was useless. He kissed her. and she could taste the devil's nectar.

"Does that kid know how beautiful you are?" he asked, slurring the words. "I've missed those honey-colored eyes. I do love you, Jemmabeth Forrester. I love every single thing about you. If only I hadn't messed up so bad I could've been your husband by now."

The sad thing was that he was right.

"I can't breathe, Paul. Please get up. I don't want to have to scream."

He faked a pout. "You're always threatening me. I just want to hold you." He traced around her lips. "Besides, I don't think anybody could hear you, my darlin'. I may have had a few too many, but I know thunder and hard rain when I hear it. It's kinda romantic. Doesn't it make you want to snuggle, Jem? You were a good snuggler." He kissed her again, holding her wriggling chin.

"Get off me. I have something to tell you." Jemma held her breath, hoping she took him off guard.

"A secret? Later. I don't want to talk now." He buried his nose in her hair and inhaled. "You still smell like flowers."

She coughed and pushed on his broad shoulders. "If you love me, you'll stop this."

He nuzzled her neck because he knew that always got her tickled, but not this time. She turned her head and ground her teeth. If she ever smelled English Leather again, she would throw up.

Paul propped himself up on his elbow and touched her face. He eased off the daybed and ran his hand through his hair. She had seen him do that a hundred times when they were dating.

Jemma stood, trembling.

"See, now you're cold. Let me warm you up," he said, holding her to him. His wet shirt had soaked into her own. Footsteps on the stairs startled them both.

"Jemma!" Trina's voice was loud and clear from the landing. "Let me in." She yelled again and pounded on the door. Jemma glanced at Paul, who looked like he had just dropped his triple-dip cone on the pavement.

"You said we could talk," he pleaded. "If nothing else, give me a good-bye kiss and I'll go. I don't want to have to steal it from you."

The clatter from the door was constant. Jemma's face was hot, but she wouldn't kiss him. He sensed it and wrapped his arms around her like a python, kissing her sweetly. She wiped her mouth and looked him in the eye. "Now *go*." Her words sprayed across the room as she unlocked the door and heaved it open. Trina stepped in, with wild eyes darting from Jemma to Paul.

"What's going on here?" she asked, standing next to Jemma, who stared at the floor, breathing hard.

"Not a whole lot, thanks to you." Paul squared his hat, then tipped it to Trina. He moved again to Jemma, lifting her chin and wiping the tears with his finger. "Sorry, darlin'," he whispered. "I just want you to love me again. Don't hold this against me. I need you to make me a better man." He ran his finger down the bridge of her nose and left.

The door stood open, allowing a rainy mist to creep into the room. Jemma sat on the daybed and sobbed.

Trina held her. "If he hurt you, I'm calling the police."

"Let him go. I'm okay."

"Helene will be worried if we aren't there for supper."

"I can't let her see me like this." Jemma wiped her eyes.

"Helene's a sharp cookie, Jem. She's gonna know. C'mon, you're freezing. Put this blanket over you." Trina helped her up. "You sure he didn't hurt you?"

"No. He just made me mad."

"Spence will have him thrown in jail when he hears about this," Trina shouted over the storm as they descended the stairs. Jemma stopped in front of her and took the blanket off her head.

"Spencer doesn't need to hear about this, Trina." The rain ran down her face and dripped off her chafed chin. "Okay?"

Trina shrugged. "He's your man, but you'd better think about it, girl. You don't want to keep little secrets. I've heard you say that."

Helene opened the back door. "You two look like sodden pups. Come inside this minute," she yelled over the storm. "Was that Mr. Turner's automobile I saw pulling away just now?"

Trina raised her brow and looked at Jemma.

"Paul paid me a visit, Helene," Jemma said, the tang of his kiss still in her mouth.

"Oh my. Whatever for?" Helene turned her attention to Jemma's downcast eyes. "Has there been trouble afoot while I was singing with Enrico? I think perhaps you should get out of those wet clothes, the both of you. We shall take dinner by the fireplace. Run along now."

They ate in the study. Helene knew how to put problems in perspective and how to ease Jemma's heart and mind. The three of them talked into the night. Jemmabeth knew that Paul never intended to harm her. What she didn't fully realize, until that night, was how truly desperate he was for her love. It was more than a contest for her affections or a practical joke. Helene sensed it, and Trina saw it firsthand. The one thing Jemma knew for sure was that she longed for Spencer.

⋙⋘

Monday evening, Jemma and Trina drove home from Le Claire just as the Granny's Basket station wagon was exiting the driveway. Jemma recognized Sister, the co-owner, at the wheel. Helene met them at the door. "You have some flowers, dear," she said to Jemma.

"Oh wow." Trina gaped in disbelief at the display in the kitchen.

Jemma joined her, and the three of them admired the elaborate arrangements of flowers. "Rats," she said to herself, knowing exactly who'd sent them.

"Here is the card, dearest." Helene handed her the small envelope.

It didn't take Jemma long to read it. She passed it to Helene with Trina looking on.

Once again, I've played the fool.
Forgive me for loving you.
Paul

"That boy's got a big problem." Trina sniffed one of the lilies.

Jemma played with her engagement ring. "Let's take these to the nursing home."

"Sure," Trina said.

The three of them loaded the flowers into Trina's car and drove across town to the Wicklow Sunshine Center. Then, at Helene's suggestion, they ate supper at the Catfish Hut by the lake.

Jemma fell asleep as soon as she laid her head on the pillow that night. Her dreams were filled with a golden-haired soldier dancing like velvet with her in the moonlight, and there were no secrets between them.

⋙⋘

At Fort Rucker, Spencer flew at night as much as he did in the day. Sometimes he wound up talking with Helene because she was the only one at home, but it was Jemma's voice he wanted to hear. Having photos of her and wearing the cross she gave him were not enough. He concentrated on the work at hand. The sooner he got to Vietnam, the sooner he could come home to her.

"I got my wings, baby," he said on the phone. "I know you are just jumping for joy, aren't you?"

"I am proud of you, Spence. I know you've worked hard, and I'm glad you made it through all that training. I really am sorry I wasn't there to see you get your wings. You should have told me."

"I want to see you. I'm off for three days, so pick me up at Love Field tonight. I'm coming in at ten thirty."

"I'll be wearing a black dress. Trina made it for me."

"I'll be wearing my wings. Love you."

Jemmabeth knew that it was time for her to tell him or save the story for after Vietnam. They didn't need any brick walls.

⋙⋘

She decided not to tell him. Things were too perfect to distract him with another Paul story. Every minute was precious because they knew there was only one more step to go before quicksand.

They sat by the pond behind Helene's house. "Spence, I can't even imagine how hard it must be to fly a helicopter. I hope you know how much I admire you. That your superiors must have recognized your smarts and your calm, cool self is no surprise to me. I've known that since the first grade."

His eyes were the same color as the old gray sweatshirt he was wearing. He smiled. "Thank you, ma'am. Flying is actually fun. I know it won't be fun once I get in the thick of things for real, but it comes easy to me now. You have to use your hands, your feet, and you are constantly making decisions."

"Maybe you are descended from weavers or something like that.

My freshman year we visited a weaver and saw a demonstration of an old, hand-operated loom. The guy's hands, feet, and eyes were in motion all the time and his coordination was incredible."

He smiled at the innocence of such a comparison. "I guess you could make that association with flying a helicopter. Experienced pilots are the incredible ones, though. It's an honor just to be around them. They have a lot of intestinal fortitude because rescue helicopters are easy targets." He knew he shouldn't have said it as soon as the words spilled out.

She gave him a wild look. "I thought that was why they painted that big red cross on rescue helicopters, so they wouldn't get shot at. Now you're telling me they are easy targets?"

He tried to back out of it, but the damage had been done. She pouted for a while, then changed the subject, even though it took a lot of effort for her to move away from the topic.

"Lie down so I can give you a backrub," she said. "Are you going to give up architecture for aviation?"

"Yeah, right." His voice was muffled in the quilt. "I can't wait to get back to the drawing board. How about you? What have you been painting? C'mon, let's go look at your work." Spencer took her hand in his and held it all the way to her studio.

Queasiness gripped her as she unlocked the studio door and they stepped inside. She felt the weight of Paul's body that rainy evening, and she could still taste his devil kisses. Spencer's presence was an even heavier weight on her conscience. She did not want to keep this secret from him, but she did, and they discussed her paintings instead.

❧

"It seems like you just got here," Jemma said as they drove back to the airport.

"Time goes by too fast when I'm with you. You look so good, Jem. I think you are back to your old self now. I see the difference in the way you walk and dance."

"Really? I didn't know that I was ever any different. I've sure gained all the weight back that I lost. I'm ready to arm-wrestle any of your old girlfriends." Jemma flexed her biceps.

"Then you will have to wrestle yourself. I don't have any old girlfriends, unlike you, with your old boyfriend hanging around."

A twinge ran through Jemma's stomach and darted into her throat.

"Has he bothered you any more?" Spencer asked.

She didn't know what to say. She had decided not to bring it up. She hadn't considered that he would.

"Jem, has Paul shown up again?" Spencer could barely keep his eyes on the road as he tried to read her face. "He has." He took the next exit and pulled off the road. He held her hands in his. "Tell me right now. We're not having secrets. I know he's a desperate man because I understand the stakes."

She broke down and couldn't say a word.

"Okay. I'll call an attorney and check on a restraining order," he said.

"Spence, don't call an attorney. I think he's going to leave me alone now. I really do. He's not a bad person."

"He wants you, baby, and I don't want him harassing you. If you don't tell me exactly what happened, I'll assume the worst."

"Which would be what?" She wiped her nose on the back of her hand.

"That he tried some other stupid stunt to see you. Am I right?"

Jemma didn't know what to do. Spencer was much too smart and perceptive to let it drop, plus he loved her too much to do that. If Paul was going to continue with this obsessive behavior, maybe he did need a restraining order slapped on him, but then it could ruin his career and that was about all he had. She didn't hate him, and she knew that he loved her, still.

She could not look Spencer in the eye. "He came to Helene's and wanted to see me. We talked about him leaving me alone. He apologized and left."

"Look at me, baby." Spencer turned her face toward his.

"You don't need to know all the details, do you? He didn't scare me or anything."

"What exactly did he do?"

She looked him in the eye. "Spencer, you are about to go to the other side of the world and spend a year tackling the worst thing you have ever done in your life. Let me handle this situation. If you can fly into jungles and pick up wounded soldiers while the enemy shoots at your helicopter, I think I can take care of Paul. He's not a mean person, and I don't want you to worry about this anymore." She swallowed, hoping her bravado had convinced him.

Spencer looked out the window, then turned to her. "Jem, if anything should ever happen to you, I'll never forgive myself, and I don't say that lightly. You know this guy better than I do, I'm sorry to say, but I don't want him touching you. I trust you, but I don't trust him at all."

"I'll be all right. I only have a few more months left. Then I'll be going home."

"That's when things happen, baby, when you are about to go home."

"I hope you are not speaking self-fulfilling prophecy."

"I don't believe in that, but I do believe in you."

She exhaled. "I can handle Paul."

Spencer paused, then slammed the car into gear and peeled out. Only the good Lord kept the highway patrol from seeing him fly the Corvette to the airport.

❧

"This is not going to be like Alabama, is it?" Jemma asked as they sat on the floor, waiting for his flight to be called. "We will get to see each other, right?"

"I'll be up here every weekend that I can," Spence said, his head resting in her lap. "I wish we were back in Paris so we could neck right here."

Jemma suddenly threw her sweater over them and kissed him until she got tickled. Spencer sat up and tossed off the sweater. "We'll never see these people again," he said and kissed her like they were still on Pont Neuf, over the Seine.

❧

The Senior Spring Exhibition was crowded, and Spencer was on his way. Trina and Nick volunteered to pick him up at Love Field. The Exhibition was a formal affair, so Trina had designed Jemma a new white satin dress. It was very sleek and sophisticated; she was just glad she could fit into it. She wore her hair up and put on as much makeup as she could stand. She watched the doors for Spencer, but

Paul got there first. Helene saw him and went straight to tell Jemma, who was talking with Professor Rossi and the Dean.

"He has a date," Helene whispered. "Just carry on." That was some consolation. At least he wouldn't be cornering her and demanding affection that she had no desire to give. That would be the least of her worries if Spencer saw him.

She had ten paintings on display. A *Dallas Morning News* reporter asked Jemma for comments about her art and took a few photos. "Who's your favorite artist?" the reporter asked.

Jemma hated that question. "I don't have one."

The reporter nodded and walked away.

"She has so many that it's hard for her to say," Paul offered from behind her. She turned and was practically in his arms. "Hello, darlin'. You're looking like a movie star tonight, and I don't mean Trigger, either." He grinned and put his finger on the tip of her nose. He was dressed in expensive cowboy duds, complete with a black Stetson that he took off and held at his side. He was definitely movie-star material.

"Aren't you with a date?" Jemma whispered, looking around for Spencer.

"Oh yeah, she's here somewhere. Look, Jem, I apologize for my behavior at your place the other day. It was pathetic and inexcusable. I don't know what came over me." His long, black lashes masked those green eyes as they roamed all over her. "That's not who I am, and you know it."

"Paul, we are over, done, finished. I'm going to marry Spencer as soon as he gets back from Vietnam," she said through a stiff smile.

"Assuming he comes back, you mean," Paul said, tight-lipped.

"Just go, please. Spencer will be here any minute, and it's not fair for you to spoil things for us."

"I thought this was open to the public. I want to buy one of your new pieces." He scanned the crowd.

"Don't do this to yourself. Find somebody else and love her."

"I love you. I've been out there looking for a long time, and you are my heart's desire. There will be nobody else—ever."

"If you love me, leave me alone. Spencer is everything to me.

There is no room for anybody else in my life. Now go, please, before he gets here."

A curvaceous redhead swaggered up next to him and slipped her arm in his. "And who might you be?" she asked Jemma with a syrupy smile.

Paul never even looked at her. "This is the famous artist, Jemmabeth Alexandra Forrester. She and I go way back, don't we, darlin'?"

"Really? I like your paintings," the redhead gushed, still smiling. She turned to Paul, brow raised. "I think Paul already has some of your work."

"Christy likes art. She used to be a model herself," Paul said, not taking his eyes off Jemma. "Now she's a photographer."

"That's nice. If you'll excuse me, I need to meet some of the other patrons," Jemma murmured.

Christy squealed like a stuck hog at Paul's well-placed hand on her derrière. He always did have wandering hands, but Jemma was quicker than Christy, motivated by a certain promise. Of course this particular squealer may have liked his octopus hands.

She moved as far away from him as she could get and kept her eyes glued to the entrance area. Spencer should have been there by now. She could only assume that his flight was delayed or the traffic was heavy. Maybe they would get kicked out if Christy got any louder. Anything to keep Mr. Turner away from Mr. Chase.

"Hey, good looking." Spencer had sneaked up on her. He dipped her back and kissed her. Jemma recovered completely with that.

"I didn't see you come in," she said. "You look great. What took you so long?"

"Dallas traffic," Nick explained, studying Jemma's work. "You're some artist. Wow." He and Trina took off to tour the exhibition.

"Whoa, did you say Trina designed that dress?" Spencer asked. "You're going to give me a heart attack just standing there."

Jemma gave him The Look. She drew a deep breath and sputtered it out. "Spence, don't get upset, okay? Paul is here with a date. Now don't do anything. But I wanted to forewarn you."

Spencer's jaw twitched. "Where?"

"I don't know. They wandered off. Please don't talk to him."

Spencer looked around the room, then straight into her eyes. "You said you would take care of it, and I trust you to do that. He'd better keep his hands off you, though."

"Spence, I don't want this to spoil our evening. Maybe he left. C'mon, let's look at my work." She hooked her arm in his and turned, smiling, toward the main gallery.

"I'd follow you anywhere," he whispered in her ear. Every eye was on her as she passed. To have her love was a precious gift for this earthly life and he knew it. He also knew that Paul Turner coveted that gift for his own.

Professor Rossi appeared out of nowhere with his slender, quiet wife, Carlina. "Hello, Mr. Chase. What do you think of your Jemma's work this season? *Perfezione, sì?*"

"*Ami l'arte, ami l'artista,*" Spencer said and kissed Jemma's hand, palm up.

Carlina Rossi blushed and glanced at her husband. Jemma wondered if the professor ever did such a thing to her.

"Hey, stop that fast Italian. You know I can't keep up with y'all." Jemma grinned at them, then scanned the crowd for Paul and his model friend.

Professor Rossi embraced them both. "We will pray for your safe return, Spencer. You both will be in our hearts."

Jemma saw the glistening in his eyes as they walked away.

"These pieces are amazing, Jem. Just when I think you can't get any better, you add a new dimension to your style." Spencer held her close.

"What did you say to Professor Rossi?" she asked.

"I said 'love the art, love the artist.'"

"Let's run away and get married tonight," she said, meaning it.

Across the room, Paul watched every move Jemma made with a heavy heart. She might never be his again. He could still afford to look at her, though, and buy her work. To have, for his own, the canvas she had touched with her heart and hand was better than nothing at all. "Christy," he said, grabbing her tanned arm, "let's get out of here. How about we stop off for some refreshment before we head home?"

"You got it, cowboy," she schmoozed. "Whatever you want."

"Nope, darlin'," Paul muttered, looking back at Jemma. "I blew that chance a long time ago."

⤞⬥⤝

The family began arriving on Thursday evening. Even though Helene rented rollaway beds and put them all over her house, Trina opted to stay in Dallas with Nick's parents—to get to know them better. Spencer bought tickets for the Arizona bunch to fly down. Lizbeth, Lester, and Willa came on the train. Lester had not been to Dallas since he worked for the railroad company. The train was not punctual enough to suit him, but he soon got over it as he admired Helene's estate. "You could run yourself a small herd of cattle in here and not find 'em for a week," he announced at the supper table.

"I thought you were just a chinchilla rancher, Lester," Jemma said. "I didn't know you were a cattleman."

"Don't bring up Lester's chinchilla ranching days," Lizbeth replied. "He ran into some back luck with that venture."

"No, sir, it wasn't no bad luck. It was the weather. I knew it could ruin a farmer's whole crop, but it never occurred to me that the weather could wipe out my herd."

"We have tornadoes in this part of Texas, too," Helene said. "I don't see the point of the nasty things."

"The point is that the devil himself is throwin' his weight around on this old earth until the good Lord comes back." Willa pointed her finger toward heaven for emphasis. "Have you decided to become a full-fledged believer or not?" Willa pursed her lips in Helene's direction. Only the lovebirds in the conservatory dared make a sound.

Helene smiled. "Jemmabeth and Trina have been diligent missionaries. I cannot say that I have any argument with their message. I'm not quite certain, however, that I want to join a church yet."

"Well, when? You ain't exactly gettin' any younger. None of us are. I'd sure hate to attend your funeral at the undertaker's place of business. That would be a downright shame."

"Helene, maybe you could visit our church in Chillaton the next time you're there," Lizbeth suggested as a little peace offering.

502

"I shall do that. Thank you, Lizbeth," Helene said.

"Hmmph," Willa growled. "Visitin' don't mean nothin'. Anybody can visit. You gotta get your name on the roll."

"I know a kid that has Babe Ruth's name on a baseball," Robby said, much to everybody's relief.

"Really?" Jim asked. "Where did he get that?"

"His daddy met Babe Ruth when he was a teenager. They drew his name out of a big barrel and he won the ball. Cool, huh?" Robby, who wasn't worried in the least about Helene's church status, helped himself to more cheesecake.

"When does Spencer's flight get into Dallas?" Alex asked.

"Seven thirty. Why?" Jemma cast a suspicious eye toward her mother.

"I thought we might go shopping. Since Mother and Dad are in Europe and can't get back for your graduation, they sent a very fat check for us to find you something. I know there are some great shops in Dallas."

"Sounds good to me. Just so we are at the airport in plenty of time. This is the last weekend Spence will have off for a while. He's training with medical evacuation specialists now. How's that for scary?"

⤙❧⤚

They offered to take Willa to meet Nick's family on their way to the shopping malls. Willa was quiet, for once in her life. Alex and Jemma made small talk in the front seat.

"I bet you're excited to meet Nick's family," Jemma said.

"*Excited* ain't the word for it." Willa stared out the window.

Alex took her turn. "I know you must be happy for Trina."

"Trina and Nick have been havin' one of them long-distance things for a while now. I guess comin' down here to school stirred up their feelings again. Now they want to hurry things up."

Jemma decided to risk it. "Are you and Joe getting serious?"

Willa coughed and adjusted her hat. "I think Joe Cross is about the sweetest man I've been around since Trina's daddy. Could be that I've given a serious thought or two about marryin' him."

"Then what are you fretting about? I've never seen you so grumpy." Jemma turned in her seat to look Willa in the eye.

"Grumpy? What's that supposed to mean?" Willa shook her head and returned to her preoccupation with the scenery.

They were in Dallas before she spoke again. "I don't reckon I've been listenin' to myself. You're right. I am actin' like a mule-headed old woman. I think I miss Joe. He's been gone for a week on a cross-country run. I worry when he does that." Willa leaned over the front seat. "It's true what the Good Book says about 'out of the mouths of babes.' 'Course you ain't much of a babe anymore, Jemma, but I thank you for pointin' my problem out to me. It's a good thing you did, too, or else Nick's folks would take me about as well as a dose of castor oil." Willa threw back her head and laughed. Her hat tumbled off her head. She laughed even harder and pitched it in the back of the Rambler. "That old thing needs to go to the trash. I think I need me some new clothes, too. Maybe Trina could whip me up a few dresses, if we can find enough feed sacks to cover this big caboose."

By the time they dropped her off at Trina's prospective in-laws' house, Willa was back to her genial self. Jemma and Alex knew exactly what they were going to buy and it wasn't feed sacks, either. Willa would get her new dresses.

"Thanks for today, Mom. You are such a good shopper." Jemma held up one of her purchases, a cerise linen blouse, as they pulled into Wicklow. "Oh yeah, please stop up here at the post office so I can buy some stamps. I have to get my thank-you notes in the mail."

Alex parked the Rambler across the street from the post office. "What are you doing?" she asked as Jemma took a dive into her seat.

"Rats! It's him—Paul. He just went in the door. Let's get out of here." Jemma covered her head with her new blouse.

Alex turned off the engine and fixed her sights on the post office door. "The famous Paul, huh? This I have to see. I wouldn't miss a chance to see who could steal you away from Spencer."

"Mom. He'll spot me. He has issues. That's his truck parked next to the building. C'mon, you can see him some other time."

"No way. I live in Flagstaff, so hush. Is that him?"

Jemma peeked out. "No, good grief. He's not that old. Wait, that's him with the cowboy hat on."

Paul held the door for an elderly couple and then walked to his truck. He paused, then took off his shirt, pitching it across the seat. Standing beside his pickup, he ran his hand through his hair, put his hat back on, and got in.

Both women watched as he pulled out of the parking lot with Otis Redding blasting from his eight-track tape. He passed within ten feet of them.

"*Mama mia.*" Alex looked straight ahead, her mouth hanging open. She whistled. "My goodness, Jem. My goodness gracious. He's some looker. Anybody could get caught in that web. It's no wonder you lost your senses." She sighed. "Now, go get those stamps."

Alex watched as Jemma crossed the street. She clicked her tongue. Paul could tempt any woman, and her beautiful daughter would be hard for a good-looking cowboy like that to pass up.

As soon as Jemma got back in the car, Alex was ready. "What did you mean by Paul having 'issues'? What's going on?" Alex asked, not starting the engine. Her mouth was set.

Jemma rubbed her forehead. She knew when her mother meant business. Alex didn't know the whole story. Jemma hadn't lied to her parents about Paul, but she hadn't told them everything, either. Maybe now, with her life set for marriage with Spencer, it would be safe to tell.

"Mom, the reason I broke up with Paul was because I found out he had a wife, and I never even knew he'd been married. I was humiliated and ashamed, so I didn't tell you and Daddy about it. Paul loved me and wanted to get married. He still does. He's divorced now and buys my paintings, plus he keeps trying to get me to change my mind about Spence."

Alex was stunned, but she reached for Jemma's hand and squeezed it. "Oh, sweet pea. I'm so sorry that you felt like you couldn't tell us. That must have hurt to keep it inside. Does Gram know?"

Jemma nodded but kept her head down, feeling the unwarranted guilt rising up again.

"I assume Spencer knows?"

"Yes. I wasn't the one who told him, though. Buddy B told him, and he was devastated. That's why we sort of broke up again when he left for Italy. It was such a mess."

"Is Paul harassing you?"

"He's harmless, Mom. I think it's over now. He's not a bad guy, just a ladies' man."

"Well, I can certainly see why." Alex lifted Jemma's chin to look her in the eye. "You were afraid to tell your daddy."

Jemma nodded again.

"I'll tell him sometime after you and Spencer are married. Leave him to me, honey, but you watch your step around this guy. He's magnificent to look at, but that doesn't mean he's not dangerous."

Jemma looked out the window. Life could move so fast. Within ten minutes she had confessed the dreaded truth to her mother, and she'd seen Paul Jacob Turner with his shirt off. Good grief.

⊱⊰

Her family was seated together in the concert hall. It was filled with happy graduates and guests. Jemmabeth sat on the stage with the faculty as the dean gave a welcoming speech. She was nervous, but kept her eyes on Spencer, who grinned at her the whole time. Nobody knew she was going to speak until they saw it in the program. The dean introduced her as the only American to ever receive the Girard Fellowship, and only the second woman to win in seventy years. She had practiced and rewritten this speech for two weeks. Jemma took a breath and began:

"Ladies and gentlemen, distinguished guests, parents, faculty, and fellow students of the arts—rejoice! We have much to celebrate. It is not specifically this ceremony of which I speak, though. It is life itself. It's the air we breathe, the birds we hear, the warmth of a beloved's kiss, the chord struck in perfect tone, words that move the heart, and the subtle blend of pigment to reflect sunlight on a child's silken hair. The very first time you put on your ballet slippers, memorized your lines, rested your bow on the strings, picked up your sketchbook, or loaded your brush, you were commencing on life's unique journey into the finer arts. It's an uncharted journey and not meant for just anyone. Whether we become famous for our skills or fade into a personal world of creativity, what matters most is that we celebrate life by bringing joy or by expressing emotion on behalf of others.

"To connect with one another on a level beyond the mundane is a gift for which we must be thankful. Today, I offer you a challenge. We will never neglect to strengthen the collective spirit of mankind through the arts. Whatever joy or sorrow unfolds in this lifetime, your talent is a vessel for those emotions. Whether your goal is self-expression or shared reflection, you are compelled to create and thereby to engage your talent. We have been blessed, and it is required that we enrich what little time we have on earth with those blessings.

"We must practice our craft, regardless of our personal circumstances, in order to uplift or calm the beleaguered spirit. The world affords breathtaking and heartbreaking moments, but in between, people carry on. All beings must be able to honor each and every aspect of life either as the artist or the audience. However, we, as artists, are compelled to accept such a task because we are the eyes, the ears, the voices, and the wings of the spirit. As I see it, graduates, our next homework assignment lies before us. Carry on with joy. Thank you and congratulations."

Her family may have started the ovation, but it progressed with vigor. Professor Rossi shouted above the rest. Spencer and Jim competed for the loudest whistle. Jemma, somewhat embarrassed, returned to her place on the stage.

She wasn't seated long until she was recalled to the podium to accept the Miriam Beach Chapman Award for Outstanding Contribution to Fine Arts. She held the crystal statue to her heart and graciously accepted the check from Mrs. Chapman's elderly descendant. It was a prestigious award, open to professionals and students, in all fields of the arts and from all states west of the Mississippi.

The families gathered outside the concert hall, waiting for the graduates. Jemma ran up to them as she took off her graduation gown.

"Your speech was fantastic!" Spencer picked her up and kissed her. "Congratulations on the award, too. The audience wouldn't have paid any attention, though, if they could have seen you in that dress." Her graduation dress, a swirl of lavender and white chiffon, had cutaway arms and a draped neckline. It was miniskirt length. Gram pursed her lips and Jim drew back when he saw it, but Spencer loved it. Everybody crowded around her and talked at the same time.

❦

Toward the edge of the crowd, Paul shaded his eyes to see her, his Jemmabeth, his only true darlin'. She was the eyes, ears, voice, and wings to his spirit and more. How could he *carry on* without her? He exhaled, folded his program in his suit coat pocket, and walked away. He stopped, though, and looked back at the sound of her laughter. It nourished his very bones. How he longed to hear that again and have it meant for him only.

❦

Spencer had rented a room at the best seafood restaurant in Dallas. Jemma ate hush puppies until she was about to choke.

He leaned over to her. "Baby, that dress will give me something to think about when I get back to the base."

"I'll give you something to think about when we're alone," she whispered.

"Hey, watch it. I'm a pilot now. I get to be in charge of the flight plan."

"Maybe so, but we're still on the ground, sir."

"Jem, your speech was so bad it made Mom cry." Robby wrinkled his nose at Alex.

"Those were some awful fine things you said, Jemmerbeth," Lester said. "It'll take a while for them words to sink in, but they'll get there."

"How much money did you get?" Robby asked. "Could you loan me enough to buy a monkey?"

"I think you need to talk to Daddy, mister," Jemma replied. "The award was five thousand dollars."

"No way," Robby said. "Monkeys don't cost much, and you'd have lots left over."

"You talk to Mom and Daddy first, then come to see me." Jemma smiled at his serious tone and the thought of their classy mother hosting a monkey.

Helene had a tent set up on her front lawn, and the group danced until midnight. Even Willa and Lester joined in the Bunny Hop. Jemmabeth and Spencer were the last ones to go to bed. They sat in the conservatory with the caged lovebirds.

"What's this?" she asked. "Another present?"

"Yup." Spencer laid a gold foil-wrapped box tied with a blue velvet ribbon in her lap. "This is for our wedding night."

"Our wedding night? Are we going to elope right now? Oh, it's beautiful, Spence." She drew out the long, light gold nightgown. "It's silk, too. I don't think you are supposed to give me lingerie until we are married." She held it up to her dress.

"I don't care about etiquette after all we've been through."

"Yeah." She smiled at him. "I know."

"Now I can dream about you in this gown. It's almost the color of your eyes," he said.

Jemma pulled the gown over her dress and twirled, grinning at him.

He blew out his breath. "On second thought, we'd better go by the etiquette rules. You want me to survive the night, don't you?"

"I keep it in mind," she said.

Everybody left on Sunday except Spencer. He had one more night. The time had pleasantly slipped away from them. They kissed good night and went to their separate rooms, but he couldn't sleep. She was on the other side of that wall, probably two feet from him. He was the one who chose to wait on the wedding. It was his big idea. She would be taken care of financially—he had seen to that—but she wouldn't have his name, though, and he would never have her, completely, if he didn't come back. The thought of coming home to her would be his goal. He had meant this vow to honor her, but he ached, wanting to love her tonight. He stared up at the canopied bed. He had heard all the horror stories about Vietnam. He knew it was going to be worse than he could imagine. She would worry constantly, and he could only dream about her and do his best to survive.

The knock was so soft that, at first, he thought it was the wind. Then he heard it again. He pulled on his jeans. There was no light coming from under the door. He opened it to find Jemma standing in the doorway, her silhouette lit only by the moonlight. His whole body tingled at the sight of her.

"Spence," she whispered, "thank you for this gown."

He drew her to him. The warmth and softness of her body under that honeyed, silken gown was against his skin for an instant, making him weak. She pulled away from him as soon as they touched.

"I love you, and I want you to remember this moment forever. I had to give you something tonight, my sweet Candy Man, my hero." She disappeared into her room and shut the door. He stood in the hallway for a while in case she returned but knew that she would not.

Chapter 17
Ceremonies

W hen I worked for the Burlington Line, we kept things runnin' on time. There wasn't none of this business about 'mechanical delays' and whatnot. If there was a breakdown on the line, another engine was roped in to take care of it. No sir, we didn't have late troubles." Lester slurped his coffee from the saucer, vexing Lizbeth, and tapped his foot on the linoleum.

"Hold it right there, Lester. I recall plenty of times during World War II that the trains ran behind schedule." Lizbeth set a plate of biscuits and dewberry jam in front of him.

"Well, sir, you could be right. I forgot about that. We had us a shortage of help and a few other problems then, but most days the train run on time. Everybody suffers during a war. I ain't sure them times should count, no offense."

"I don't think enough folks appreciate what our boys are going through in Vietnam right now. If something were to happen to Spencer. . ." Lizbeth sat down and unfolded her napkin.

"Could I say grace, Miz Liz?"

"That would be very nice."

"Lord, for this food and the hands that prepared it, we give our thanks. Amen."

"Amen," Lizbeth added. "Thank you, Lester."

They ate their meal without further discussion. Lester knew that Cameron and her sons were on her mind, and he didn't want to interfere. He surely didn't want her to get down about it, either. He decided to take a chance and break the quiet.

"Did I ever tell you about them gypsies that I met over to France? I've been meanin' to bring it up. I'm kindly worried about it."

"Hmm. . .I don't believe I've heard that one," Lizbeth said as she put the dishes in the sink. "Surely you aren't worried about something that happened so long ago."

Lester leaned forward and pulled a tattered coin purse out of his hip pocket. He opened it and fished out a scrap of something, which he handed to Lizbeth.

"What's this?" It was only a pinch of paper with more cellophane tape on it than writing.

"See for yourself." Lester nodded toward the scrap.

She could barely make out two smudged numerals in pencil. "Are these numbers?"

"Yes ma'am. Them's gypsy fortune-tellin' numbers."

"Who wrote this?"

"A little French woman."

"Your wife, Paulette?"

"No, lawsy mercy, no. This here was a French gypsy fortune-tellin' woman. She was a scary one, too. Had them eyes that look like a couple of shooter marbles. 'Course this was over to France. Like I've said before, I walked all over France. It was at the second Battle of the Marne, toward the end of July. Me and another old boy were on patrol and we come up on this here band of gypsies. They were right smack-dab in the middle of a battlefield that our boys had just finished cleanin' up. Had one of them little outhouse-lookin' carts all painted up fancy with a skinny mule pullin' it. They couldn't speak American and we sure couldn't speak gypsy French, but this wild-haired woman come hence to motionin' for us to sit down on some kegs. We did and she grabbed ahold of our hands and oohed and aahhed and babbled on about somethin'. Gypsies scare the piddly-winks out of me anyway— no offense, Miz Liz. Don't they worship the devil or somethin'?"

Lester wrung his hands under the table but went ahead with it. "I know gypsies claimed to be acquainted with the future; I seen one in a travelin' show once. So I says, 'Are we gonna make it through this here war? How much time have we got left?' She stared at us for a bit with them spooky eyes, then handed me this note with what used to be a sixty-eight on it, just as plain as day. I took it to mean that was how long I had to live. I even asked her, 'Is this how long I have to live?' You, know, we were plumb scared that we weren't even gonna see the next hour."

"Why did you ask her if she didn't speak English?" Lizbeth

asked, her head cranked to the side.

"Well, now, she understood somethin' because she pointed at the writin'. I've sweated through everything it could've meant up until now, and this here's the last straw. Nineteen hundred and sixty-eight—not months, not days, hours, or minutes."

"Did you give her money?"

"Nope. Didn't have no money on us."

"Maybe this figure is how much she wanted for her fortune-telling services."

"How come she didn't give my buddy the note?"

"Maybe you looked like a man of means or like you were in charge."

"No, sir, it's doomsday for me, and that's all there is to it. My time's comin' this July. I just know it."

Lizbeth exhaled slowly. "Of all the foolishness that you've come up with, Lester, this is the most harebrained. How can you ask grace with one breath and profess belief in a gypsy curse with the next? It's hogwash. No wild gypsy woman in 1918 had any more idea about the length of your life than I do this very minute. Now you get out of that chair, throw that silly note in the trash, and go get our mail. I am surprised at you, Mr. Timms. The good Lord is the only one who knows our future."

Lizbeth scooted her chair back and stalked to the front of the house, leaving Lester staring cow-eyed at the table. He whistled under his breath and headed for the door, picking up his hat on the way out. Maybe he got her mind off her men for a while. He wasn't known as the best storyteller in Connelly County for nothing. Besides, he liked it when Lizbeth got riled up. It reminded him of Paulette. . .only she chewed him out in French.

❧

It was almost her bedtime when Lizbeth heard the noise at the front door. Someone pulled the little *boink* knob three times in a row. Only Robby could get away with that. She put on her house-coat and slippers and went to the door. "Willa and Joe, come in this house," she said.

"Sorry to be callin' so late, Miz Liz, but we wanted you to be the first to know," Joe announced, holding Willa's hand.

"Since you played Cupid for us, we figgered you had a right." Willa was grinning like a toothpaste commercial.

"Let me guess," Lizbeth said. "Joe, you got some new tires for your truck?"

They laughed, and Willa put out her hand. "This don't look like no truck tire to me." A diamond ring sparkled on her wedding finger.

"Bless your hearts." Lizbeth hugged them. "When is the wedding?"

"Soon as Trina can get herself up here this weekend." Willa's smile was as wide as Joe's.

Joe shrugged. "I don't believe in waitin' around. Willa might change her mind."

"This calls for a celebration. How about supper tomorrow? I'll invite Lester. Will Brother Cleo be in town by then?"

"Yes ma'am. We're meetin' tomorrow afternoon to talk about the weddin'. It'll be real simple, though. Just a few folks."

"Well, I'm really happy for y'all. I knew that it was meant to be. I'm glad you came into our lives, Joe. God bless the both of you," Lizbeth said, tickled at the Lord's work.

Willa leaned toward Lizbeth. "We want you to stand with us, and we won't take no for an answer."

"It'll be an honor. Now let me see this ring again."

⋘◊⋙

Before she went to sleep, Lizbeth knelt beside her bed and thanked her heavenly Father for Joe Cross and Willa Johnson. Joe, for saving her baby girl's life and Willa, for being her dear friend who had lived so near, yet was a world apart from her for such a very long time. She prayed that the good Lord would forgive her sins of omission, one of which was not looking beyond those train tracks, drawn like a thin line of demarcation in a town that professed to be filled with Christians. It had been her sin and her loss to honor that line, if not in word, at least in deed.

⋘◊⋙

Spencer had two weeks off before he was to ship out. They decided to spend a few days in Flagstaff with her family and the rest of the time in Chillaton. It was Jim that suggested they all go camping.

They hiked, played board games, and sat around the campfire talking. Robby kept them laughing. Spencer and Jemma got in plenty of stargazing, too.

When it was time to leave, Alex fell apart at the airport. Spencer had been like a son to them for most of his life. She and Jim wanted to believe otherwise, but they couldn't be certain that they would ever see him again.

Robby said it for all of them. "Spence, you are like my big brother. If you croak in Vietnam, I'll miss you a lot. Maybe you could hide somewhere."

"I'll be careful, I promise, Rob. You write to me and tell me about all your girlfriends."

Robby grinned and nodded. "I only have two, but I'll write if you will."

"I've heard that deal before," Jemma said, "and you don't keep your end of it."

"You aren't a soldier, though. You're just a sister," Robby said in his own defense.

Jim took Spencer aside and talked in hushed tones until their flight was called.

"Good-bye, Spencer. We love you." Alex was crying again. "We'll see you soon."

"I'll be back," Spencer said. "Look what I have to come home to."

⚜

Lizbeth tried to give them all the privacy she could at her house. Spencer spent the mornings with his mother and once he went with his dad to pick up a car in Lubbock.

"I think my dad is changing," he said. "He actually listens when I talk, and he keeps hugging me. What do you suppose caused this sudden interest?"

"Maybe he realizes what a treasure you are," Jemma suggested.

"Maybe he wants something," Spencer said.

"I want something," she said and kissed him.

They went to pay their respects to Papa. The sunset was always more vivid from the cemetery, and they lingered on the wrought-iron bench next to his grave.

"We're going to be buried together even if we're not married,"

515

Jemma said. "I'm going to have them write our story on the tombstones."

"We *will* be married, Jem. I'll come home."

"I bet a lot of guys have said that to their sweethearts down through history." She rested her head on his shoulder. "Not all of them could keep their promises. It's out of a soldier's hands."

"I know I will, baby, I feel it here." Spencer took her hand and put it on his heart. "Remember to check on my mother for me now and then."

"Spence, she can't stand me."

"She'll come around. Remember, it's usually the liquor talking when she's mean. Go see Harriet, too. She's taking this really hard. I don't want you to sit around and be sad for a year, either, so I told Buddy B that maybe you would be in his band if he asked you really nice."

Jemma sat upright and blew her hair out of her eyes. "You what? I'm not going to be in a band. That'll be the day."

"When you say good-bye, yeah," Spencer sang and grinned at her.

"Oh funny. Don't be throwing old Buddy Holly songs at me. How could you even consider such an idea as me singing with his band?"

"It might be fun for you. You could laugh at Wade and Dwayne's stories. That's always worth something. I want to think of you laughing and singing and dancing. I don't want to picture you moping around and crying while you try to paint. See, you're pouting right now." Spencer tickled her until she smiled.

Jemma ran her hand over Papa's marble stone. "Papa would be sad that you're going off like his sons did. Gram said he never got over that, but he never talked about it. She thinks it would have helped them both if he had."

"We are going to talk about everything, okay, baby? No secrets."

Jemma winced as that rainy afternoon in Wicklow slipped across her mind.

"Hello?" Spencer waved his hand in front of her face.

"I agree." She closed her eyes and listened to a meadowlark in the pasture next to the cemetery, then jumped up. "Let's go see the ducks."

They walked down the steep slope to the pond.

Jemma shared her sunflower seeds with the flock. "I don't think I can stand to see your plane leave, Spence. It's bad enough seeing you walk through that gate and disappear." She pounded her fist into her leg. "I hate this war."

"I hate it, too, but there's nothing we can do about it."

"I've already written so many letters to congressmen. I guess now I'll have to start making speeches and leading protest marches."

"You do whatever your heart tells you to. Of course you might do more good by coming up with ideas to rejuvenate the neighborhood across the tracks. That's just a thought."

Jemma looked at him and smiled. "You are a sly one, aren't you? You have a smooth way about you, Spencer Chase. I'm just glad you use it for good and not to get women."

"You are the one I wanted, and you are the one I got," he whispered and kissed her, gentle and sweet.

⋘⋙

They went to Plum Creek. There was water running, but enough to go wading. No minnows were to be found, though, so they resorted to their cottonwood tree.

"Pray with me, Spence." Jemma held his hand, and they knelt on the sandy bank where she had danced the first time he had played his guitar for her.

"Heavenly Father, I give You praise for Spencer, Lord, and I ask that You watch over him and bring him home to me. I ask this in the name of Jesus. Amen."

"Let's marry ourselves right now," he said, and took her face in his hands. "Jemmabeth Alexandra Forrester, you have always been my adored one, and I take you now to be my beloved wife. Before God, I give you my heart and my life. I will cherish and honor you above all women as long as we live on this earth."

Jemma did not look away as she collected her thoughts. "In the presence of our dear Lord, I promise you, Spencer Morgan Chase, that I will love you and adore you as my husband from this moment until I breathe my last. No one but you will ever fill my heart and my life." Her voice, soft with emotion, came out as a whisper. "I promise to cherish and honor you above all men, as my only and dearest love."

They embraced under the tree that held their names, carved long ago in childish fervor.

S M C + J A F

It was his last day. They went to Willa's church and heard Brother Cleo's sermon on God's mercy. Afterward, Brother Cleo called them up front and the congregation had a prayer circle for Spencer's safe return. Brother Cleo gave him a pocket Bible study guide with notes in his own hand.

After lunch, they sat on the grass at the city park. "I used to play here when I was little," Spencer said. "I stayed at Harriet's house a lot then, and she would let me walk over here by myself. I looked for horned toads. When it rained, this ditch was full of water, and that's why these little bridges are scattered around the park." He tossed a stone in the direction of one of the small stone structures. "I bet the WPA built them when they built the high school stadium."

"Hey, you take one of these little stones and throw it in a river over there, so Chillaton will make a mark in Vietnam." Jemma folded his hand over a pebble shaped like a jelly bean. "I remember the Easter egg hunts our class had. Have I ever thanked you for sharing your eggs with me?" she asked, twirling a long-stemmed cloverleaf under his nose. "Have you ever seen a four-leaf clover?"

"I bet the odds of finding one of those are slim to none," Spencer said as he tuned his guitar. "If you find one, I'll take it with me to Vietnam and then I'll bring it back home to you."

"Deal. You play, and I'll look." She crawled to a new spot and began her search.

Spencer was on his fourth song when she screeched. He stopped and joined her on the ground. She held it up. "Ta da! Now you owe me, big boy, and I'm going to collect."

"I think you cheated. I've never seen one except on a greeting card." He touched the delicate leaves. The veins reminded him of hers that night in the hospital. "Incredible. Okay, little Miss Lucky, I'll keep my end of the bargain. When I bring it back to you, we'll frame it and set it out to tell our grandchildren this story."

She smiled at him. "Do you want seven letters a week or one really long one?"

"Whatever you send me will be perfect."

"I want to know what you want. I'll be all cozy at home. Who knows where you'll be. Tell me, please."

"One long, long letter. It will give me something to look forward to."

"You know I'm going to go crazy, don't you? I'll start feeling guilty about old stuff, and you won't be here to forgive me for the thousandth time."

Spencer took her sketchbook away from her and flipped to a blank page. He scribbled something and handed it back to her. "There. Every time you bring that junk up in your brilliant brain, read this, but wait 'til I leave to read it the first time."

She gave him The Look and smiled. "Sometimes I think you are not of this world, Spence. I do believe you are an angel."

"Baby, I'm no angel. If you knew what goes on in my head when I'm thinking about you, the angel idea would be out the window."

"Play some more. I want to remember everything about this day," Jemma said, lying back on the grass. She opened the sketchbook and carefully placed the clover inside. She closed her eyes while Spencer played "Dream Baby."

He watched her every move because she was the baby of his dreams.

⟨⟩

"I think God made the stars just so you and I could look at them," Jemma murmured as they lay on the hood of the Corvette at the river that night.

"Maybe. I think He might have also wanted to give us a map to get around in the dark. Remember, Jem, when you look at the stars, no matter where I am, I'll watch them, too."

"Did you pack the moon I made for you? Can you say the words on the back?"

"'Near or far, I am where you are.'"

"Good. I wish I could send you messages in the stars. Wouldn't that be cool?"

"Make up one now and choose the star. When I look up, I'll remember the message."

"I choose the star of love, Venus. That's what Charlotte Brontë called it."

"The morning and evening star. Good. Give me a backup."

"Orion, our old standby."

"What's the message?"

"I think of thee." She turned to him and touched his cheek. "Of course."

He smiled. "Let's dance."

She took his hand. They moved to the music of crickets and bullfrogs and the beat of their hearts. She could not look at him; instead she watched as the moon cast their shadow onto the hard-packed earth. It was the same earth that Papa coaxed a life out of with his cotton crops. It was the same earth that held Papa now. She could not bear for her life's greatest blessing to join Papa in that dirt before their time together had even begun.

"Please don't leave me and be lost to the stars," she whispered.

He lifted her chin. "Jemmabeth, if I ever leave you, it will be to become the stars for you."

"No," she said, her voice quavering. "Surely that cannot be in God's plan."

❧

They slipped the clover between two sheets of plastic cut from a cheap wallet they bought at the airport gift shop. Spencer taped it on all four sides and put it in his own billfold. He knew what she was thinking. "I'll bring it home. You just paint, okay?"

She looked away.

"Remember, in six months, I'll get R&R. So you get a bikini. We'll be in Hawaii before you know it." He was trying hard to get her to smile because that's how he wanted to remember her, but he couldn't even get her to talk. "What is your next painting going to be?"

She shrugged and pouted.

"Jemmabeth, talk to me. You don't want me to go away thinking you were mad, do you?"

She looked at him like a cornered kitten. "I'm not mad. How

could I ever be mad at you? I'm just trying not to cry."

"We're both going to cry. So talk to me, please. Tell me that you will think about singing in Buddy's band."

"Spence, I am not going to sing in a silly band with Wade Pratt and Dwayne Cummins while you are risking your life in Vietnam."

"I only ask that you think about it. It would make me happy to know that you're full of life. Besides, it's a decent band."

"I'm full of life all right. I wish we were married so I could show you."

"I know you are. All you have to do is stand there and I know it. Remember, don't open your birthday present until the real day."

"I won't." She twisted The Ring. The first call for boarding was announced and panic set in. "Do you have everything?" she asked, just to have something to say.

"No, but I can't stuff you in my bag," he said in an attempt at humor. "I love you, Jemmabeth." He kissed her palms, the way she liked.

She clamped her hand over her mouth before it contorted into misery, but then she moved it away and grabbed his face. "Don't die, Spence. If you do, I'll never marry anybody else. I want you to know that. You are my only husband, and I'm so sorry that I ever caused you pain. Remember that I love you."

He kissed her one last time. Jemmabeth let him go, then closed her eyes so she could not see him disappear, but relented. He turned to the gate and looked back, straight into her golden eyes. She forced a smile, and he winked at her.

She ran outside and watched his plane taxi down the runway and wait for clearance to take off. The jet lifted off and glinted in the morning sun. Jemma waved both arms. She knew that she was nothing more than a speck on the ground, but it gave her something to do besides cry.

She trudged back to the car and sat there. The corner of her sketchbook stuck out of her purse. She opened it to the page where he had written. She read aloud:

"My dear Mrs. Chase,
I'm glad you checked the competition because you will never

*have to wonder again. We were meant to be together, and so it
shall be.*

> *With all my love,
> Your Mr. Chase*

⋙∙⋘

August 16, 1968

Dearest Jemmabeth,

*I have arrived on the other side of the world. By the time
you get this, I will probably be doing what they brought me
over here for. This is a busy place. We can hear artillery in
the distance. I hope it stays there, but I think we'll be flying
right into the thick of it. Don't spend all your days worrying
about me. All will be well.*

*I want to get this in the mail, so I'll write again when I
have more time. Say hello to Gram and Lester. If you have a
chance, please visit Harriet.*

*I hope my father doesn't become a problem for you. He must
be operating on guilt these days. Think about the band because I
promise those nuts will make you laugh if nothing else. Remember, I'd like for you to give it a try.*

*Here's what I have to keep me company: my Bible and
the pocket study guide, your old sketchbook, the lock of hair you
gave me in Italy, the ribbon I took from you at the airport that
bad summer, the four-leaf clover, my silver cross necklace, the
blue moon you made me, and twenty photos of you. Oh yeah,
and the pebble from the park. I'll be glad when it's you keeping
me company, all night long.*

*I tried to see you in the parking lot at the Amarillo airport,
and I think I did.*

Watch the stars tonight, baby. I think of thee always.

Love you, Spence

⋙∙⋘

Spencer got his fat letters and there were surprises in every one.
His favorite was the letter that was written on a life-sized picture
of her on butcher paper. She had Lizbeth trace around her, then
she painted her form with watercolors, cut it out, and wrote him

love poems all over the back of it. She wrote like she talked—full of fun and in a stream-of-consciousness. He knew she was going out of her way to be cheerful. The letters always ended in words of abiding love. She was a brilliant artist, an irresistible woman, and she was almost his wife. He was about to doze off when Paul suddenly crossed his mind. If something happened and Jemma were left alone in the world, would he step in and take care of her? She had said she wouldn't marry anyone else. Spencer fell asleep with that bittersweet thought.

⌘

Carrie's wedding was small, informal, and pretty, like her. There were staff members from the physical therapy center and two of her mother's sisters from out of state. Eleanor, Carrie's longtime caregiver, wouldn't travel to Houston because the humidity bothered her sinuses. Jemmabeth and Trina wore tailored, matching dresses of periwinkle shantung silk and each carried a white rose. Carrie's dress and veil were lace-covered white satin, worn by her mother when she married The Judge. A dozen cornflowers, the color of her eyes, made up her bouquet. Philip never took his eyes off her throughout the ceremony. Jemma watched The Judge because she knew he was struggling. She had exchanged hot words with him when he fired her, but now her heart went out to him. Probably he would become even more attached to the bottle after the wedding.

Carrie was radiant. When Jemma had first met her, Carrie had no life at all. Even her appearance was an afterthought back then. Now her long, blond hair was pulled back into a French twist, and she had learned to use makeup nearly as well as Sandy. She had come to look like her mother's portrait, but with an added measure of impishness.

"Well, girls, who would've ever thought this would happen?" She grinned at her husband.

Jemma gave her a hug. "I'm so glad that you came to Houston, Carrie. At the time, though, I was majorly ticked at your father for sending you." Everyone took a sudden interest in the punch, and someone faked a cough. Jemma turned to find The Judge standing at her elbow.

"I agree with that," The Judge said. "Coming to Houston gave you new life, Carolina. Just look at what Philip has done for you. You are out of your wheelchair."

Jemma turned to Carrie and crossed her eyes in amazement. For The Judge to agree with her was an astounding event on its own, but for him to compliment someone in the same breath was unheard of. Maybe he did have to love whatever and whomever his daughter did, like Carrie had once told her.

Philip was enjoying the moment. "She has a long way to go, sir, but we'll get there, won't we?" Carrie agreed by kissing him and it wasn't a peck, either. She held her arm out to her father and balanced herself between them.

"Who needs wheels when I've got my two favorite men to hold me up? Now, let's get on with the honeymoon." Philip scooped Carrie up and The Judge followed behind and carried her walker to a waiting limo. Trina and Jemma tossed rice as it pulled away. The Judge waved on even after the limo disappeared around the block. He finally let his hand drop and it hung at his side.

Jemma turned away. She wanted to be in that car with Spencer.

⚜

He got her letters and stretched out on his cot. Just seeing her handwriting made him feel good. In junior high, she slanted her words so much that they all looked as though they were sliding into home plate. Their freshman year in high school, she had dotted her *i*'s with little circles, but now her words were flowing and clear, free of embellishment, just like her. He liked reading the letters until he had them memorized.

November 14, 1968

My dearest Spence,

Gram and I have a kitten. Lester found a whole litter in his garage. This one is black with little white patches on its nose and feet, and I've named him Vincent (Van Gogh) because one of his ears got a chunk bitten out of it by something. We need one around here because you know how Gram hates mice.

Do you think that we could have our studios in the same room? I don't want you to work in an office. I want you to work at home with me, unless you could give me a corner in your office so I could paint. I suppose oil paint and brush cleaner fumes might bother your clients, so maybe I will only use acrylics and watercolors in your office. It's just an idea.

I hope you are getting enough sleep. I read an article the other day about how lack of sleep affects your decision-making and motor skills. Please go to sleep right now instead of reading this letter.

It occurred to me that I haven't seen your mother in a long time, so I am going to get up my nerve and pay her a visit. I'll let you know how it goes. (It probably won't.) I'm glad you liked your birthday divinity and it wasn't ruined. I hope they don't open all your packages. They probably ate some of it.

You don't really think that I am going to buy a bikini, do you? I wouldn't wear it anyway. I never liked changing clothes in the dressing room for basketball, so I doubt that I would feel comfortable in a bikini on a beach. You'll just have to be satisfied with my old one-piece in Hawaii.

Spencer stopped reading when he got to that part. Seeing her in a bikini right now was something he wanted to think about because he was weary of war. He rolled over to take her advice and catch some sleep before they got called out again. It was a heart-wrenching, never-ending cycle.

~⚓~

Jemma was in Flagstaff for most of November, but it didn't feel like she was home. She missed Chillaton, and Alex could see it.

"We are so glad that you came, sweet pea. It's good to see your head on the pillow in the mornings. Robby is so happy to be around his big sister."

"I know, Mom, and I'm sorry to be such a drag. Maybe I just need to be where I was with Spence last. I love y'all so much, but something's missing."

"You've grown up, and you're ready to build your own nest." Jim poured himself a last cup of coffee before heading off to work. "Don't worry about it because we'll take what we can get. Right, honey?" He gave Alex a good kiss for an old married couple.

Robbie squeezed his eyes shut. "Are they done yet? Monkeys don't kiss like that. They are way cooler than people."

Jemma visited Robby's class to talk with them about art. He wore a Sunday shirt for the occasion. She demonstrated background, foreground, horizon, and vanishing point. They went outside and sketched a scene, then painted it with water paints. She watched Robby to see if he had the artistic spark she had at his age. He had a spark all right, but it didn't seem to be for art. It was for sports and talking. She should have known that anyway. He was the junior team manager for their daddy's football team, he could keep up with an adult conversation, and could match wits with anybody. She loved being around him. He made her think everything was going to turn out fine.

"I want to be called Rob now," he announced at the supper table one evening.

"Really?" Alex asked. "What brought this on?"

"Spence calls me Rob and since he's not here right now, I want everybody else to do it until he gets back."

"I think Spencer would like that. You should write him and tell him about your name change. I'm mailing him a big letter tomorrow," Jemma said.

"How does he like army food?" Jim asked, passing the roast beef.

"I don't know. We've never talked about it," Jemma said.

"Yeah, they only talk about kissy stuff. 'Oh Spencer, you are so handsome and strong. I hope you don't have a new girlfriend in Vietnam,'" he said in a high-pitched voice.

"You little rat. You've been reading my letters." Jemma put down her fork in mock indignation.

Robby looked at her and grinned. "I wish. Then I could have some really juicy stuff to tell everybody."

"Maybe I should tell who you sat next to—every chance you got—at school the other day, *Rob*." Jemma gave him a *hardee-har-har* look, bringing a little color to his cheeks.

"Well, now I have to know," Alex said. "I thought you still liked the little Wilson girl."

"Nope. Things change, Mom. I don't want to get tied down.

If the right girl comes along, I want to be available." Robby ate another roll in two bites.

"Available in the fourth grade?" Jim asked. "Are you even chewing your food, young man?"

"Yes, sir," he said and gulped. "Jemma and Spence were boyfriend and girlfriend all their lives, except for that old guy she liked. I have to be ready."

They all laughed at that, except Jemma, who winced at the reference to Paul. Would he never go away?

⤌✦⤍

She returned to Chillaton and tried to get back into her routine. Lizbeth still allowed Lester to bring the mail, and Jemma received a very belated letter from Robby. She smiled at the drawing of a saguaro cactus on the back.

October 28, 1968

Dear Jem,

How are you? How is Spence doing? I am writing Gram a letter, too. We are getting stuff ready for your visit next week. Do you think it is okay to pray for a monkey? I have been learning about jungle animals at school. You know that my favorite animal is a monkey and I want one really bad. On the back of one of my comic books it says I can order a monkey for $12.00. I have been saving my money and I have $9.00 so far and Mom owes me $3.00. I am going to order one because they are so cute. I have to go now. Write me back. I am helping Daddy for 25 cents.
Love,
Your Bother (crossed out) Brother

P.S. Don't tell Mom or Daddy. I am going to keep the monkey in my room. I have made him a bed. I am going to call him Ro Ro, the way I said my name when I was littler.

P.S. Again. Do you know that money and monkey are kind of spelled the same? This is a long letter, huh?

Jemma laughed until she couldn't any more. He hadn't mentioned the monkey idea at all when she was there in November. She considered whether or not she should tell her mother about the monkey plans or let it slide, in the hopes that it would never happen. She read the letter again and saw the date on it: *October 28th*. She checked the postmark—*December 14th*—five days ago.

"Gram, I just got this letter from Robby and I think it deserves looking into."

"Oh yes. I got a cute letter from him, too," Lizbeth said. "He wrote it in October, but your daddy jotted a note on the back of the envelope saying that he just found it the other day and stuck it in the mail."

Something told her to call home. She gave Lizbeth the letter to read while she dialed long-distance and gave her parents' number to the operator.

"Daddy. Hi, it's Jem. What? Uh-oh. I hope Mom is okay. Good grief. The Christmas tree and the presents, too. Yuck. Her new curtains, the ones she had specially made? Poor little guy. No, no, I meant Robby. Sure, I'll talk to him. Love you, too, Daddy. Hi, Rob. I'm so sorry. Well, I'm sure he'll be happy at the zoo. I miss you, too, sweetie. So, Santa is bringing you new curtains for the living room." Jemma winked at Lizbeth. "Okay. Tell Mom I love her when she wakes up tomorrow."

"What on earth happened?" Lizbeth asked.

Jemma hung up the phone. "Ro Ro, the monkey, arrived yesterday. Robby wasn't home so Mom opened the shipping box and the little thing bit her, climbed up the Christmas tree, and swung over to sit on the light fixture until it got too hot. His next perch was her new valance and curtains, which he tore up and pooped on. Finally, he ripped into the Christmas packages and started throwing poop at Mom. He went into the kitchen and hid in the cabinet until Robby got home and tried to catch it. When he did, Ro Ro bit him, too. Daddy came home and the police were there with a cage and asked Robby all kinds of questions about his comic book. The monkey bit a policeman, too. I guess everybody but Daddy and the monkey were crying all the way to the emergency room. They have to make sure that the monkey doesn't have rabies. If he doesn't, he'll be sent to a zoo somewhere. What a mess. I feel sorry for everybody, including the monkey, but it is hilarious."

Lizbeth snickered, then shook her head and laughed, long and loud. Jemma did love to see her laugh.

Spencer had saved the package until Christmas Day. Opening it would be his celebration. He had just returned from a candlelit service attended by a lonesome crowd of soldiers. Inside the box was a Christmas tree made from small strips of green fabric meticulously tied together on a wire, tree-shaped frame. She had tied red bows on every branch. He could see Lester's handiwork in the wooden base. He set it next to his photos of her. She also sent him a ukulele "to practice for Hawaii." At the bottom of the box was a small photo album filled with pictures of Thanksgiving and a snowy mountain scene in Flagstaff. Jemma and Robby had made a giant snowman, and the Flagstaff newspaper put a picture of it on the front page. The clipping included a short interview with Robby. His comments made Spencer smile, but the picture of Jemmabeth made him ache to hold her.

Chapter 18
Peace

Gram handed her the phone, "It's for you, sugar."

"Jemma, it's Buddy B. Hey, remember in high school when you and Sandy sang backup for me at the talent show?"

She'd wondered when he would call. "Nope. I don't remember that." She did, but it was more fun to say she didn't.

"Spence said you might like to do it again."

"We were freshmen and you were a senior. You know that you intimidated us into doing it because you're her big brother."

"That's true, but this is my side business now, and I can pay you. We do gigs, you know, all across the Panhandle and over in Oklahoma and New Mexico. Next Friday, it's a dance at Lido, then we've got the Travis High School Valentine's dance in three weeks, and a junior college ball in March. This summer we've got the Goodnight Trail dance. Oh yeah, and the King Cotton Days festival next October."

Jemma sat on the bed. "Whoa. Busy schedule, but I have things to do on Friday nights. Besides, Spence will be home next August."

"C'mon, Jem, help me out here. Sometimes it's a Saturday night. I'm talking cash, and Spence wants you to do it."

Jemma lay back on the bed and put her bare feet on the headboard. "All Buddy Holly songs, I presume."

Buddy snickered. "Shoot. You're way behind. We're doing everybody's stuff now."

"Why do you need me so bad?" Jemma asked. "I thought you had Leon singing backup."

"He's sick of it. Besides, I need a little spice in the show."

"You think I'm going to add some spice for you? Wait until Spencer hears this."

"If I didn't have Spence's blessings, I wouldn't be calling." Twila yelled something in the background. "She wants you to wear that dress you wore in Sandy's wedding. You were a knockout in it."

"If you want spice, find The Cleave. I don't think Spencer knew that you wanted spice."

Buddy exhaled. "Just say you'll do it. At least try it once. Remember, I gave Carrie her big break. Just come to one rehearsal. That's all I'm asking. Come over to the house tomorrow night for supper. You've got that certain something that will bring in the guys."

"You're scaring me, Buddy."

"Just kidding. I'll see you tomorrow night, okay?"

"Maybe."

⚜

She knew it was going to be a bad day when she saw the mass of hair coming down the sidewalk by the post office. The Cleave was home from Europe.

Missy Blake flashed her most spiteful smile at Jemma, like she'd been saving it up. "Jemmartsybeth, how weird to see you because I dreamed about Spence last night. I hope he's not getting shot at or something. I've been thinking about writing him, so I got his address from his mother. My letters will be like a...something...of hope to him in his...."

"Trash can?" Jemma suggested. "Write all you want. I don't think you'll be getting an answer, though. Spence and I are engaged, as in to be married." Jemma held up The Ring.

Missy rolled her eyes. "Really. Engagement rings are ho-hum these days. Couples live together first. That way there's none of that crybaby stuff if something better comes along. Oh yeah, like a *beacon* of hope to him in his...what's a word for, you know, being sad and scared all at the same time? I heard it on the radio the other day."

"I'll see you around." Jemma turned toward the post office.

"I just got back from a year in Madrid. That's in Spain."

"I know where Madrid is, Missy. I didn't know you spoke Spanish. You barely passed Mr. Smalley's class in high school."

"I didn't have any problems. The guys there are all hunks and talking wasn't exactly at the top of our list, if you know what I mean."

"Yeah, I know exactly what you mean." Jemma shoved open the door to the post office.

"Tell Spence to write me back. I'll send him a care package with some surprises in it," The Cleave yelled.

Jemma didn't look back, but she did chew on her lip. She knew The Cleave's idea of surprises. Their junior year at CHS, Mollie Sykes threw a "come as you are" party and Missy showed up in skimpy baby-doll pajamas. The boys went cuckoo until Mrs. Sykes called Missy's father to come and get her. Nobody believed that The Cleave was dressed for bed at six thirty at night, anyway. It put quite a damper on the party for the rest of the girls. Spencer, bless his heart, never left Jemma's side to check out Missy's arrival and further antics. He was truly every girl's dream boyfriend. Now he was fighting in a war a world away from her. *Misery* or *despair*—either word might have been what The Cleave heard on the radio. She was never known for her vocabulary, but she was remembered for those baby-doll pajamas. Rats.

❧

The Buddy Baker Band consisted of: Buddy B—vocals and rhythm guitar; Leon Shafer—lead guitar; Dwayne Cummins—bass guitar; and Wade Pratt on the drums. They weren't too bad and had played for many dances at Chillaton High School before branching out. Buddy was probably right, though: it was time to add something to the group.

Leon, Dwayne, and Wade were already there when Jemma arrived at the Bakers' house. The prospect of a meal was always a good incentive for single guys.

"Hi, Jemma, come in." Twila gave her a hug and shoved Wade's feet off the coffee table as she walked by. The boys were too busy wolf-whistling at Jemma to say hello. She didn't mind because she had known them all her life, and they had yet to make a good impression. They were a scraggly bunch with good hearts. Dwayne and Wade had barely scratched their way out of CHS. Now they were hanging out together just like they were still in junior high. If they hadn't joined the military right after graduation, they'd be in Vietnam, like Spencer. Instead, they were looking for wives and eating greasy food from the truck stop and still wearing crew cuts, except for

Leon, the smartest one, whose blond hair was fast becoming a pony-tail. "Come on back here in the kitchen and talk to me," Twila said.

"Did you guys come early for the free food or to get in some extra practice?" Jemma asked the crew. "You probably need it."

"We just came to see you, sweet thang." Dwayne made kissing noises at her and bugged his muddy blue eyes.

"Where's Buddy?" she asked.

"He's running late from work, as usual," Twila said from the kitchen. "He called from the dealership about ten minutes ago and said he has to finish up a job, then he'll be right home."

Jemma set the table while Twila talked about her day at Nedra's. The most interesting conversation, though, was coming from the living room between Dwayne and Wade. Leon, a man of few words, was watching television. Jemma needed a good laugh and Spence said these two would provide it. It really didn't matter who was saying what. The story was the thing.

"Were you at the game last night? I tell you what, we got our-selves a ball club this year," Wade said, jabbing his finger into the air for emphasis.

"Shoot yeah, we got us some neegroes," Dwayne shouted to-ward the kitchen.

Jemma gave him a dirty look.

"This is the best team I've seen in thirty years. What we been needin' all along is some colored boys to rebound," Wade added.

"That is so pathetic," Jemma replied. "Are you a bigot or what? Besides, you aren't even thirty years old. How could it be the best team you've seen in thirty years?"

Wade took a big drag on his cigarette and pondered this new word she'd thrown at him. "Bigot? Are you talking about my height or somethin'?"

"Oh brother. You both sound like you just fell off a turnip truck," Jemma yelled.

Dwayne stubbed out his cigarette. "You been spendin' too much time with the coloreds. Nobody that I know grows turnips, at least not on this side of the tracks."

They fell silent, turnips having no hold in cotton country. Tur-nip greens, maybe.

"I like to have fell off my seat at the game Friday night when somebody said Lorena Hodges was goin' to stewardess school. You remember her?" Wade asked.

"Oh yeah," Dwayne said, "but you gotta be kiddin' me. What airline would take her on?"

"One of them big ones. Braniff, maybe."

"Man, I hope the people that hired her ain't the same ones flyin' the planes. They gotta be hard up for help."

"Remember when we set her up with Jeeber McCleary for a homecomin' dance?"

"You know, she didn't look half bad that night."

"Maybe if you were comin' toward her and not behind her."

"That'd be like watchin' two pigs fightin' under a blanket." Wade hooted at his own perceptiveness, then they were both quiet, reflecting on his exquisite example.

"Whatever become of Ethan Sears?" Dwayne asked. "I'll never forget him claimin' he roasted a mouse once down at the park, then ate it."

"He made a preacher," Wade said. "Then he come up sellin' vacuum cleaners and made good money at it so he gave up the preachin' business right quick."

"Did the devil get at him?"

"Somethin' did. Maybe he figured his name would help him get rich."

"In the preachin' business?"

"No, dummy, in the vacuum cleaner business. You know, Sears. As in Sears & Rareback."

"Oh, like Monkey Wards. I get it. How's that help?" Dwayne's upper lip curled in puzzlement.

Leon stood and faced them. "If you're gonna buy an appliance, you might come nearer buying it if you thought it was from Sears." He went outside.

"Yeah, yeah, I see what you gettin' after. Reputation," Dwayne said.

"I hadn't seen Ethan since high school."

"Me neither. All I know is that Lorena must've lost a whole lotta bohunkus to be making a stewardess or else some plane is gonna be flyin' low with her on it."

The door flew open and Buddy B entered. His voice boomed when he was excited, just like Sandy's. "Supper about ready, hon?" he asked and gave Twila and Jemma each a peck on the cheek.

Dwayne leaned back in his chair, stretching and shouting. "What are we havin' tonight, little woman?"

"Turnip casserole," Twila shouted back, much to Jemma's delight.

Buddy B gave her a list of all their songs. There were check marks by those that she was to sing harmony with him, and stars by those that she was supposed to sing dumb backup lyrics.

"Hold it, Buddy," she began. "I'm not doing that bop, bop, bop, bop business on 'Fade Away.' I'm sorry, but I think it's stupid."

"Hey, you're not the star here, Miss Priss," Wade said.

Buddy filled his plate. "That's okay; you don't have to do the bop part. Just hit the tambourine, but when you are singing harmony, don't step on my speci-alities."

"Your what?"

"My speci-alities. Like when I break my voice like Buddy H did. You know, like ah-hoo on 'It Doesn't Matter Anymore' and way-uh-hay-hay-hay on 'Everyday.'"

"Oh brother," Jemma said. "I thought you weren't doing just his songs anymore."

"I've kept a few of the best," Buddy said.

"Yeah, Jemma, it's his signature stuff and it's his band," Dwayne said in a sing-songy voice.

Buddy winked at her.

"Do I get a break when I'm not singing?" she asked.

Everybody laughed.

"No, sweetness, don't ever leave the stage. We take a break halfway. Just move around to the music and that'll drive 'em wild. Now, when I sing the part about Cupid shootin', you act like you just got shot—in the heart."

Jemma stared at them cockeyed and started to laugh but thought better of it when she saw Buddy's deadpan face. "Show business," she said under her breath.

⊷◍⊶

She was chewing a hole in her lip as she watched the Lido High

School gym fill up. She wiped her damp hands on her poodle skirt. Buddy B came over and gave her a pep talk. He had on his black, horn-rimmed glasses that had no lenses. "Don't worry about anything, Jem," he said as he combed his recently dyed hair. "You've nailed every song at rehearsals so relax and have a good time. The girls are all gonna be wishin' they were you, and the guys are all gonna be wishin' they were your boyfriend. Just sling your hair around and do some of those moves you've got." He grinned. "They'll be hollerin' for more."

Jemma considered what her own boyfriend might be doing at the moment. Whatever it was, it couldn't be much fun. This was his idea, for her to sing with Buddy's band, so if it would give Spence a little happiness, she'd better do it and do it well. Buddy would most likely be giving her boyfriend a report.

Buddy's list was unnecessary now, but she laid it on the floor by her microphone anyway. Buddy could read the audience and give them what they wanted and what they had paid for. The lights came up on the stage, and he started his introduction to the crowd.

"Jemma," Leon whispered, "turn on your mike."

She did and bumped it at the same time, but nobody seemed to notice. Buddy wailed out, "Well-ll-ll. . ."

The night was crazy. Jemma added the spice, as Buddy had predicted, and the audience loved her. She had to admit it was fun. If Spencer wanted her to do it, she'd give it a try because there wasn't much else to do in Chillaton when your man was far away. The so-called Peace Talks in Paris didn't make her think that he'd be coming home sooner than expected, either.

⋙⋘

Her flight was late into the Honolulu Airport. Spencer paced from one end of the terminal to the other. He stopped at the big window and peered skyward, but it was too foggy to see anything. What if her flight was cancelled or the plane ran into trouble? No. This trip could not get messed up for them, like other times, other places. His nerves were just like they were on his first solo flight. He was very good at what he did, but he was not cut out for the emotional strain. Dealing with the continual agony of the wounded, and the gory aftermath of weapons inflicted on the human body was too much.

Transporting young men his own age, or even younger, in plastic bags was slowly killing him. It had taken a toll on his spirit and he couldn't let it go. He wanted to help save as many lives as he could, but he also longed for the peace of his childhood with happy playmates and Harriet reading him a story until he fell asleep. Now scenes of an especially horrific nature had left a permanent imprint. The hideous sound of gunfire and the sickening smells of combat were becoming the norm for him. He didn't know if he could ever speak of this time, even with her. He needed joy, light, enchantment, warmth, and peace. He needed his Jemmabeth.

His heart pounded as the passengers finally began filing through the gate. She was in the middle of them. She didn't cry like he thought she might, but instead dropped her bags and ran to him, yelling his name the whole way. They embraced and kissed in the center of the crowd until nobody was left but them. "Aloha, baby. Welcome to Hawaii." He took the lei off his neck and put it around hers.

"Let's go to the hotel," she said. "I want to hold you for a week."

They checked into the Ilima Hotel near Waikiki Beach. Each had their own room, but he had filled Jemma's with bouquets of flowers.

"They are beautiful, Spence, thank you," she said. "Now, this is what I came for." She dove at him, knocking him flat on the sofa. He was ready. They were on the couch for an hour before Jemma sat up. "Whew. I've missed you. Let's get married right this minute."

Spencer pulled her to him. "Nope. In six months, I'll be home and we'll have our big wedding with family and friends."

She rested her head on his chest and pouted. "Please, Spence, I want to get married. Willa's married, Carrie's married, Sandy is married, and here we sit in a hotel in Hawaii, going insane. Give me the speech again."

"I need to wait to get me through this."

"If we were married, though, you would have us getting together when you get out to look forward to. Am I going to lose my irresistible charm once you marry me?"

"You will be even more irresistible. It's just the way I am, baby. Remember your old cowboy theory?"

"Of course I remember that theory, but you are my only cowboy now."

"You had to get him out of your mind, though. You said it was just the way you were made. Well, I have to have the most important event of my life and the big prize that comes with it as my reward for finishing this job. It's just the way I'm made."

Jemma banged her head on his chest in exasperation. "Aarrgghh! Okay. I'll drop that idea for now, but I had to try. So, how does this fit into your little plan?" She whispered something in his ear and then nipped it. She jumped up, giggled, and ran to the opposite end of the room.

"You're a mean woman, Jemmabeth Alexandra. I'll show you what I think of your idea." Spencer chased after her, but she crawled over the top of the bed. He grabbed her foot and there they were, on the bed, in a heap. Spencer caught his breath and looked into her eyes that were the same color as a tiger's. She gave him a half smile and he couldn't help but kiss her. "C'mon, get up. I know when I'm being lured into your trap." He stood. "Let's go for a walk on the beach."

"Spoilsport," she said. "This beach can't be any better than Plum Creek."

The beach at Waikiki was not Plum Creek, but it would do. They felt the sand under their bare feet for an hour. Not until it began to rain did they decide to go back to the hotel. Their days were spent talking and walking. Their nights were filled with dancing and necking, but they slept in their respective rooms.

On their last day, they rented a car and drove around the island. A spectacular sunset materialized and waves pounded the shoreline. He played his ukulele for her and they watched the stars. It was a heavenly night that would be over much too soon.

"Spence," Jemma said as they sat in her room, "I want to ask you a favor."

"Anything."

"I want you to sleep with me tonight," she said, smoothing his hair.

"Jem, don't do this."

"Now just listen to me. I really mean sleep, to be together while we sleep. It will be the same as stargazing on the hood of the Corvette. Nothing will happen, I promise. I want to have that memory for the next six months. I want to wake up in the night and kiss you. I'll be good, really, I will." She hoped that didn't sound like Miss Scarlett.

Spencer walked around the room. He came back to the sofa, looked at her, then smiled. "Let's brush our teeth together, too. We've never done that."

"Thank you, thank you." Jemma jumped up and got her toothbrush and loaded it with toothpaste. He went next door and got his.

They said their prayers, then curled up on the couch in their jeans with their shirts tucked in, and made plans for their wedding and their future as man and wife. It was the most peaceful feeling that Spencer could remember. It wouldn't be easy for him to have her perfect body against him all night, but it would be worth it to have her breath intermingle with his. It was about as far away from a battle zone as he could get.

"I'm always amazed that I can love you more than the last time I was with you," Spencer whispered, long after she thought he was asleep.

She snuggled even closer until her hair tickled his chin. "I adore you, Spencer Chase. Good night."

"Sweet dreams, baby." He closed his eyes and prayed that the good Lord would bring him home so that he could spend tens of thousands of nights with her.

At daybreak, Jemma turned to see if he was awake yet. He wasn't. She wanted to touch him but knew he needed the rest. From the instant she saw him at the airport, she knew that he was stretched to his limit with this job. He wouldn't say so, but she could tell that he had been living with terror and it was consuming him. She was so grateful that he had given in to letting her rest beside him. Jemma laid her hand on his arm and asked God to keep him safe until they could hold one another again on their wedding night. She memorized every detail about him as she watched him sleep until the sun was in the sky.

Only a few hours later, Spencer watched the plane take her

away and leave him to face the months that lay ahead.

⋙⋘

Lizbeth and Jemma had been looking forward to Julia's visit for weeks. Having her around brought a burst of excitement to everybody's world.

"I wonder if Julia knows that the revival starts Sunday," Lizbeth said. "I don't think I'll go. That Ryder fellow is the evangelist, and I don't care for his style at all, not one bit."

"It's that slick hair and all the jewelry," Jemma said with a mouthful of biscuit and jam.

"Well, he brings in crowds of backsliders, plus he fills up the pews and the offering plates. My father would have called him a Soul Tinker."

"Mom said that he was tinkering around with Paula Sharpe the last time he held a revival here."

"I heard about that at the beauty parlor and I hoped that wasn't true. I hate to see a man who claims to be doing the Lord's work doing his own dirty work instead."

There was a shuffling at the screened-in porch as Lester laid the mail inside the back door, then shut it. "Get in here and have coffee with us," Lizbeth shouted, still peeved with Brother Ryder.

"Is your sister up yet?" he asked, peering through the screen.

"No, it's safe." Jemma grinned. "You aren't scared of Do Dah, are you, Lester?"

"I just like to give that woman a clear track."

"Tell us what's going on downtown," Jemma said.

"Well, sir, Son Wheeler is down in the dumps. Seems that his two full-growed daughters have up and started their own restaurant where the old feed store used to be."

"How nice," Lizbeth said. "I wondered what was going in there."

"It may be nice for the town, but Son don't look at it that way. He's got a good business goin' for hisself at the drive-in burger place. He was down to the post office this mornin', and he looked like he'd been shot in the foot." Lester took a slurp of coffee.

"And?" Lizbeth pressed.

"Seems that these gals are from his first marriage and they've both been livin' down to Corpus. The wife, she passed on, and left them all the alimony money that Son has been sendin' her for all these years. They decided to move here and start up a restaurant to give Son some competition. Appears they don't much cotton to him and the way he done their mama."

"What kind of restaurant is it?" Jemma asked.

"It's a sit-down place with menus at every table."

"Well, I think it's good that we can go somewhere to eat besides the truck stop," Lizbeth said.

"Son ain't happy about none of it, but especially since them gals is plasterin' up a big billboard advertisement right next to his burger joint and it's even got lights on it. The place is supposed to open tomorrow."

"What's the name of the new restaurant?" Jemma asked.

"Daddy's Money." Lester shook his head. "Ain't that a fine howdy-do name for a eatin' place?"

Lizbeth was distracted by a letter with an official-looking return address. She took it to the living room and opened it. Her face softened into a smile. At long last, good news.

Jemma's twenty-third birthday came and went like an empty passenger train. Everyone tried to make it special, but they all knew what she really wanted. She got out all his letters and read them again, then went to her dresser and picked up the pretty package Spencer had given her at the Amarillo airport. She sat in the porch swing and opened it with care, afraid that even tearing the paper could somehow cause him harm. She knew better, but lately she had become weird about such things. Spence's hand had last touched the box inside, making even that dear to her. It was small, so her guess all along had been that it contained jewelry, and she was right. A gold bracelet lay curled inside the velvet liner. The delicate chain flanked a design just like the heart necklace he had given her, only this one did not have a diamond in the center. Instead, it had initials—JAC. She smiled and traced it. He not only had a way with words, but with initials, too. She put it on her wrist and leaned back to admire the combination of letters. How she ever got so lucky to have him love her, she would forever wonder.

❧

Jemma caught up with Twila in the grocery store. "Hey, I haven't seen you at Nedra's lately."

"I quit," Twila said flatly. "Nedra wanted me to work on the hairpieces, and I tried my best. She didn't tell me that you couldn't wash the fake hair like you do real hair. I guess I ruined a bunch. They looked like cow patties when I was done with them. Nedra had a hissy fit at first, talkin' about all the money I had wasted and how those old ladies were going to look half bald until she could order some more, 'specially that old Gramma Knuckle. She yelled at me in front of everybody and said that it didn't take a genius to wash a wig. Then she told me to stick with sweepin' and runnin' the cash register if I wanted to keep my job. When I told Buddy B, he said to quit."

"How are y'all going to make it on his salary?"

"Eat beans, I guess. I'm gonna go talk to Dr. Benson today and see if he'll hire me for that dental helper job he's got in the *Star*."

"Don't you have to go to school for that?"

"I don't know. He said he would use me for little stuff until he gets a real nurse or whatever you call 'em."

"Good luck, Twila," Jemma said. "Call me whenever you want to talk."

She called that night. "I didn't understand some of the questions on the application, Jem. Like, 'Does your spouse work?' I took it up to Dr. Benson and said I didn't know I had one, so how would I know if it was workin' or not?"

Jemma clamped down on her tongue. "Oh Twila. Did Dr. Benson laugh?"

"He liked to have died laughin'. I was so embarrassed. I still don't know what was so funny. I'm not askin' Buddy, though, because he'll laugh at me, too."

"Buddy B is your spouse, Twila."

"He is? Oh. Well, he'd better be workin'. See, Jemma, I need you there when I take these tests."

"Did you get the job?"

"I'm workin' tomorrow. He showed me what I have to do. It's kind of like workin' at Nedra's, only it smells funny, like the hospital."

"You'll do fine."

"I hope so. Otherwise I don't know where else I can find a job."

⋘⋙

Twila called again during lunch the next day. "I got sent home."

"Oh Twila," Jemma said.

"I fainted. Dr. Benson wanted me to hold this little doodad in this old man's mouth to suck out the blood and spit while he yanked out a tooth. I started out okay with my eyes shut, but he told me to watch what I was doin' and as soon as I opened my eyes, there was blood and yucky spit and he was pullin' with these pliers and I couldn't help it; I just went down. I fell right across the old guy's chest. I guess they had a hard time pullin' me off him."

"I'm sorry. Are you fired?"

"He didn't say that in so many words, but I got the feelin'. I did okay before that happened. You remember the old guy that used to run the hardware store? He wears false teeth and I guess one of the teeth was loose, so he tried to fix it at home with something real strong. He glued his uppers to his hand and had a hard time drivin' to the office. It was real funny but I didn't laugh, honest. I was professional with him. Dr. Benson gave me some stuff to get rid of the glue then I cleaned him and his teeth up good as new, and he left happy. Now I have no job."

"Talk to Nedra. I bet she would take you back. She didn't fire you."

"I know. Buddy's gonna blow his stack when he hears about me faintin'. That would've been a nice job except for the icky parts."

"He'll be okay. Buddy's a good guy."

"I'll go see Nedra. Thanks, Jem."

Jemma hung up the phone and collapsed into laughter. She had never heard Twila talk so much in her life, but it was worth every word. She couldn't wait to write it all down for her own, soon-to-be spouse.

⋘⋙

The revival banners were hung from tree to tree and the church was packed. The newest member of the revival team came down the aisle and sat at the organ. He played a chord, then hushed up the congregation with a hopping rendition of "When the Saints Go Marching In." At the last note, Angel Ryder appeared at the pulpit, Bible in hand. The mood in the sanctuary was much the same as

543

right before the referee blows the whistle at the kickoff in a football game.

Lizbeth opened her Bible and read to herself. Julia looked around the sanctuary.

A dazzling smile spread across Angel's face. "Welcome to the Lord's House. Praise God! Yes, yes. How y'all doing tonight? Let me hear you say amen," Angel thundered.

The congregation wasn't quite revived. They were used to Brother Hightower's mild-mannered sermons. It had been a year since Angel Ryder had held a revival in Chillaton. He lifted his Bible above his head and leered out at the pews and did a double take, like nobody was there. "Let-me-hear-you-say-*amen*," he repeated, with gusto.

The congregation obliged, somewhat more enthusiastically. Lizbeth and Jemma exchanged glances. Julia closed her eyes.

Angel nodded approval. "Now let's get started with a song that everybody knows. Brothers and sisters, leading the music this week will be a good friend of the Lord's, Frankie Franco."

Julia stretched her neck a little toward the action.

Frankie stood and bowed, then moved to the piano.

Angel looked thoughtful. "Say, Frankie, I've been wondering, what kind of name is Franco, anyway?"

Frankie leaned into the microphone that was rigged up on the piano. "A-mer-i-can." The words oozed out of his mouth like an announcer at the Fourth of July bingo tent and resounded into the street.

"Well, that's what we all are this morning—Americans. If you love your country, raise your hand. Good. If you love your family, raise your hand. Yes, yes. Now, if you love the Lord, rise up, brothers and sisters, and start singing page 153 in your hymnal."

Frankie crooned the hymn into the mike. He sounded a little like Dean Martin. Lizbeth stood and began singing in her sweet soprano and Jemma sang alto. Julia didn't sing, but held her hymnal high and kept her eyes on Frankie.

Angel made a sizable impression on the congregation with his sermon on the sinful ways of man. Three humble souls went down to the front of the church wanting to be saved, and a half-dozen more went down to rededicate their lives to the Lord. He closed with the announcement that he would be preaching on a different sin every night that week. He emphasized that it was each person's Christian duty to bring at least one sinner, each preferably linked to the sinful topic of the evening. When the offering plate was passed, it was already brimming over by the time it reached Lizbeth's pew. One of the deacons got a fresh plate to pass to the next row. Julia, who normally dropped in a large bill, didn't. The service had gone on for over an hour, and, after the final hymn, Julia asked them to wait for her on the front steps.

"What's she up to?" Lizbeth whispered.

"Maybe she's making sermon suggestions to Angel."

"I wouldn't put it past her."

They waited as the revived filed out of the church, shaking hands with Brother Hightower and squinting into the sunlight. Several men clustered under the trees and fired up their cigarettes, inhaling deeply after the long sermon. Most children ran around under the big elms while others clambered up the brick railings that flanked the steps so they could jump off before their parents yelled at them. Almost everyone paused to say hello to Lizbeth and visit for a few minutes. Finally, the only conversations to be heard were chirps high in the branches of the old trees, and only a couple of cars remained.

"Jemmabeth, would you go check on her?" Lizbeth asked, more suspicious than worried. Jemma turned to go inside but was met by Julia, Frankie, and Angel. Lizbeth caught her breath and looked skyward.

"Sorry, y'all, that it took me so long, but I've invited these gentlemen out to eat with us girls," she said, smiling at the slick-haired duo. Their white suits and wide, loud ties made them ready for carnival work at best.

Angel extended his hand to Jemma. "And who might this be?"

"This is my great-niece, Jemmabeth, and this is my sister, Lizbeth."

"Well, beauty runs in this family, isn't that a fact, Frankie?" Angel said, laying his other hand over Jemma's, too.

Frankie nodded, giving Jemma a thorough inspection. "C'mon, let's go. I'm starving."

They all climbed in Julia's Cadillac DeVille. Lizbeth and Jemma got in the backseat. Lizbeth sat wooden-faced. "You can just drop me off at the house," she said.

"No, you are going with us, Lizbeth." Julia rounded the corner heading toward Daddy's Money. "We are going to have a good time." She winked at her niece in the rearview mirror.

Daddy's Money was full of the after-church crowd, mostly Methodists and Presbyterians. The Baptists still had not warmed to the thought of going out to eat after Sunday morning services. Lizbeth puckered her lips and folded her arms across her chest. They got the last big table, a corner booth.

"Well, now," Angel said, "tell us all about yourself, little Miss Jimmybeth Foster."

"Forrester," Lizbeth corrected, "Jemmabeth Forrester."

"Ah." Angel nodded.

Julia put on her reading glasses and looked over the menu. "Jemma is an artist. You would be wise to invest in her work someday, if you can afford it."

The waitress brought water to the table and took an immediate liking to Angel and Frankie. "How are y'all doin' today?" she asked, cutting her eyes at them.

"The question is," Angel said, "how are *you* doing?"

"I'm just great, what can I get for y'all?" She concentrated her attention on the sullen Frankie.

"We'll all have the special, sweetheart, and I'm paying," Julia said. "Bring us some iced tea, and for dessert, we'll try your Mama's Fudge Pie."

Angel leaned back in the booth and loosened his flashy necktie. "I can see that you are a take-charge woman, Miss Julia."

"Mrs. Billington," Julia said, putting her glasses away.

"Ah."

"So, Mr. Franco," Julia said, "what do you think of our little town?"

Frankie waved to the waitress for a refill. "I prefer Brother Franco."

"Is that so," Julia said.

"We consider it an honor to be called *brother* in the good Lord's service. It keeps us humble," Angel said. He was still hot from the pulpit and gave a brief, yet disquiet, sermon on the rigors of circuit evangelism. Jemma was sure that some of the Methodists left before their desserts were served because of it.

Lizbeth cleared her throat and shifted on the slick plastic seat.

"How long have you been preaching?" Jemma asked.

"Thirteen years." Angel pushed back a twirl of hair that had somehow escaped his Brylcreem. "The time has flown by, praise the Lord." The stone in his ring was the same size as Julia's.

"Brother Franco, how long have you been in the good Lord's service?" Julia asked.

"We started out in this business together," Angel answered, giving Julia a pious look.

The waitress arrived with five plates of chicken-fried steak lined up both arms.

"Now that's a real talent you've got there, girly-girl," Frankie said.

"Help my life," Lizbeth said, looking at her plate. "That's enough to feed Cox's army."

"A toast." Angel raised his glass without response from the odd assemblage. "To the fine-looking, generous women of Texas."

"Hear, hear," said a man in the next booth.

Jemma nudged Lizbeth's foot with hers. A smile played in the corners of Julia's mouth, but the men concentrated on the meal before them.

Julia picked at her steak. "You know, my husband is Arthur Billington," she began. "We own several retail stores around Texas. Maybe you have heard of Billington's in Houston, Dallas, or maybe San Antonio?"

Angel shook his head. "Can't say as I have, but I don't shop much on the road."

"Where's home for you, Brother Franco?" she asked.

Frankie frowned. "Are you a reporter or something?"

"I'm trying to satisfy my curiosity," Julia said.

"I'm not much on curiosity." Frankie dabbed at his chin with a napkin.

Julia continued. "Arthur and I were in Las Vegas last summer for a buyers' convention."

Angel winked at Jemma. "The devil's playground."

"We stayed away from the playground, Brother Ryder, but I do remember a poster in the convention center elevator advertising a Frank Franco and Frankie's Naughty Mamas performing nightly in some casino bar."

Angel's fork slipped and hit his plate. Frankie swiveled and faced Julia, who dabbed at her mouth with her napkin.

"What are you up to, lady?" Frankie was on the edge of the booth, one leg bouncing wildly.

"Now, let's not get upset." Angel lowered his voice and looked around. "Nobody wants trouble." He shook his head slightly at Frankie. "Maybe we should call a cab."

"This is not Vegas. If you don't have a ride in Chillaton, you walk," Julia said. "You two are fixin' to have some bumpy roads ahead of you if you don't watch out."

Jemma realized that she had been holding her breath and she suspected Gram had, as well.

"What are you suggesting?" Angel asked with a maniacal grin.

"I suggest," Julia said, "that you give every penny of the offerings that you collect this week to the church's fund for the poor. What do you think about that, Brother Ryder?"

"I think you are out of line, sister," Frankie spewed through clamped teeth.

"I believe that the Lord has His own ways of taking care of the poor." Angel eased his way toward Frankie, who was already standing, cracking his knuckles. "Let us take this situation to the Lord in prayer, sisters." He quickly knelt on the linoleum with his hands folded on the booth's plastic upholstery. "He'll reveal His divine consideration to me real quick, always does."

"No consideration required," Julia said. "I've already told the good pastor and the head deacon that those are your wishes. The pastor will announce it tonight at the evening service. He was very impressed with your generosity. Good afternoon, brothers." She spread a hot roll with the melting pat of butter beside her plate. "Now, I'm about ready for some of Mama's Fudge Pie. Aren't you, girls?"

Angel stood, adjusted his suit coat, then wiped sweat off his upper lip before moving toward the exit. Frankie eased out the door and onto the sidewalk. Jemma watched as Angel and Frankie gestured wildly at one another before slithering down the street.

Lizbeth blew out a low whistle. "Julia, you never cease to amaze me." She began to chuckle as the waitress plunked down five dessert plates.

"I told you this was going to be fun." Julia closed her lips around her first bite of pie.

"Do Dah, I wish I could be you for just one day." Jemma giggled with relief and admiration.

"The feeling is mutual, sweet girl. I'd like to be your age again. Let's get going on this dessert. We've got extra now."

⁂

Buddy's band was waiting to rehearse for the next dance.

"So, Jemma, are you fixin' to have your own act?" Wade asked. "That was some heavy stuff you were layin' on the other night."

"Excuse me, my own act?"

"Yeah," Dwayne said, "I didn't know good little church girls knew how to dance like that."

Wade added a *ba-dump-bump-chhhh* on the drums.

"We know a thing or two," Jemma said, a tad embarrassed.

"Y'all shut up and leave her alone," Leon yelled. "You done real good, Jemma. You've got that Peggy Lee kinda voice. You've got the moves, too. It's all in the shoulders, isn't it?" He took his eyes off the television momentarily. "I'm sure sorry that Spencer had to go to 'Nam."

Jemma was somewhat taken aback by this sudden display of chivalry and compliments. "Why, thank you, Leon."

"No thanks needed," he said, going back to his TV show.

"Didn't you go to some fancy-pants school in Dallas?" Dwayne asked. "Did they teach you how to fold napkins like birds and stuff?"

Jemma went in the kitchen to say hi to Twila, ignoring him.

"I just want to know if they really have buck-naked girls for you to draw," he shouted, then snorted.

"You'll have to get accepted to art school to find that out," Jemma yelled back.

Twila stopped laughing and leaned in close to Jemma's ear.

"Do they have naked men, too?"

"Yeah, but things are sort of covered. You couldn't pay me enough money to model for an art class," Jemma whispered.

"Hey, what's going on? Y'all ready to hit it?" Buddy B burst in, smelling like axle grease. "Hi, hon," he said, giving Twila a peck on the cheek.

"Is that the best you can do?" Jemma asked, hands on her hips.

Buddy took off his jacket. "What'd I do wrong? I just got here."

"Where's the romance? Is that what becomes of married couples?" Jemma asked.

"Oh, that was just the warm-up." He dipped Twila off her feet and laid a huge smacker on her. Twila looked as though she'd been dunked in a tank at a carnival game.

The boys all whistled.

"Now that's more like it," Jemma said.

"Let me grab a bite to eat and I'll be right out. Y'all go ahead and warm up with 'Mustang Sally.'"

"You sure got Twila all warmed up," Dwayne said on his way to the garage.

Wade got a chuckle out of that and raised his brow at Twila, who threw a wet dishrag at him. Leon went outside for a smoke.

"Jemma, can you come here a sec? I've got an idea that I want to run by you." Buddy B motioned her into the kitchen. He heaped his plate with corn bread and black-eyed peas. "Looks good, hon," he said and dug in.

"Here, I'll clean up the dishes; you go eat with your husband," Jemma said as she pushed Twila into a chair. "Buddy, you were great on 'Candy Man' the other night. You should do more Roy Orbison."

"I just might do that," he said. "Listen, I thought we might try you comin' up to my mike for harmony on 'That'll Be the Day,' and 'He Will Break Your Heart,' then we'll take turns on 'Stand by Me.' I want to work on some Aretha stuff for you to try solo, too."

"Solo?" Jemma whirled around from the sink. "You want me to sing solo?"

"You've got the voice for it. What do you think?"

"Good grief."

"I think it'll go over real nice. Like you and me are in love or somethin'." Buddy jabbed at Twila with his elbow.

Twila elbowed him back. "Hey, if you were singin' with anybody but Jemma, I'd fix your clock."

"I'm going to the garage." Jemma dried her hands on her jeans. "Y'all need some time alone."

Wade and Dwayne were already out there, relaxing and catching up on Chillaton caveman gossip, which was Jemma's exact reason for leaving the kitchen. Leon was outside, still smoking. Jemma picked up a year-old *Chillaton Star* and pretended to read it.

"So, did you hear about old man Huff?" Wade asked.

"I thought I went to his funeral," Dwayne said.

"What? He was pullin' a trailer full of hogs to Amarillo last Friday. You know that hill right before the big house where they made that movie?"

Dwayne frowned. "You mean on the highway with the cotton gin on the left or on the Farm to Market that's on the right?"

"The highway. Anyway, old man Huff is coming down the hill when his own trailer passes him, just as smooth as you please. Whole thing come unhitched and rolled right on by him in the other lane."

"What about the hogs?"

"They were givin' him the pig eye as they went past. He liked to have had a heart attack. He slammed on the brakes first, like that would do a lot of good. Then he chased the trailer down the highway until it rolled into that big windbreak on the old Davis place."

"Man. Was anybody else on the road?"

"Highway patrol car. Threw the book at him."

"Old people shouldn't pull trailers."

Jemma had moved to a stack of magazines, discards from Nedra's Nook, and thumbed through several. Spencer was right—these two made her smile.

❧

The next night, Buddy B was on time for rehearsal. "I've got about the best news we could get," he said with a grin.

"We're splittin' up?" Dwayne asked. He and Wade enjoyed guffaws over that.

"Western State wants us to play for their weekend homecomin' dances next fall. We could headline. It's somebody's big reunion."

"How much are they payin' us?" Wade asked.

"Five hundred bucks."

"American money?" Dwayne asked amid whistles of disbelief.

"There's a hitch, though," Buddy B said.

"They don't want you to sing." Dwayne cracked another one.

"Some of them are comin' to Chillaton to hear us play for the prom."

"We're auditioning?" Jemma asked.

"Looks like."

"Then let's get goin.' I got me some TV to watch later," Leon said.

Leon and Buddy worked out some new arrangements while Jemma caught the Dwayne and Wade Show.

"Hey, did you hear about Sherman Ray?" Dwayne began.

"Nelson or Fisher?"

"Nelson. He wrecked his car. It went airborne out by the bridge in Windy Valley."

"Is he dead?" Wade sat up with renewed interest.

"Too dumb to die. He never knew what hit him until he woke up in jail the next day. His face was all swoll up, though."

"They put him in jail?" Wade asked.

"Problem was they didn't know what to do with him because he had about five fake driver's licenses on him. The deputy couldn't figure out who he was to call his folks. He had just made one for Donna Sitton, so I guess they knew that wasn't his name."

"How's that?" Wade raised his brow.

Dwayne lowered his. "Donna is a girl, bonehead. What's the matter with you?"

"Oh yeah. I heard she was datin' old Chick Mason."

"Chick's in the doghouse right now. He won't be datin' nobody for a while," Dwayne said.

"The doghouse? I heard he'd been sleepin' in the outhouse again." Wade snickered. "That was about the funniest story I ever heard. How did Chick get to be so ignorant?"

"Same way you did," Leon said, ready to rehearse.

Wade looked up. "How's that?"

"All the brains get used up in the first few kids born." Leon winked at Jemma. "Everybody knows that."

Wade and Dwayne considered the possibility of that being a scientific fact, since neither was the oldest in their families.

⋙

The Cleave leaned against the bank teller's window where Jemma waited for her deposit receipt. "We keep bumping into each other. It must be bad. . .uh. . .that stuff. I've been studying other religions. Spencer is probably our connection. I know he loved my care package because I sent him lots of expensive chocolate and a girlie magazine that I know soldiers always crave. One of my sorority sisters is in it. I could've been in it, too, but I was in Madrid."

Jemma's scalp prickled. "He hasn't mentioned it."

"Well, of course not, silly. Why would he tell you how much he's enjoying looking at Shelia Thompson? She's got plenty to look at, too—not like me, but okay. I'm expecting a letter from him any day."

Jemma took her deposit slip and walked away. Her face had to be the same color as Missy's fingernail polish. Spencer wouldn't open anything from The Cleave. He just wouldn't.

"Karma!" Missy yelled from the teller's window.

She turned back to the cashier, Durinda McAfee, and flashed her perfect smile. "I've been studying other religions."

Durinda popped her gum. "That so? Well, now, I bet the angels are singing an extra hallelujah chorus to hear that. Next, please."

Chapter 19
Dearest

July 22, 1969

Dearest Jemmabeth,

I'm looking at the watercolor you sent of Plum Creek and thinking about the vows we said there. Let's use them in our real wedding. The words came right back to me. I miss your laugh and your kisses, but I think I've fallen for this tempting girl who lives under my bed. She's getting premature wrinkles, though, from spending most of her life all folded up.

Your letters are the carrot that gets me through the week. I read an old one again each night. I told you way back about the guys over here calling me "cowboy." Now somebody has painted a cowboy boot kicking the VC on the side of our chopper, and the other day there was a sign taped to the chopper door that said Do Not Disturb—Cowboy at Work. It's good to have some humor around this place because there is an overload of suffering and death. We're all wound tight. This is a world I hope our sons never have to know, Jem. There are some real heroes over here. My crew is incredible. I don't know how they keep it together, but they do. We fly all hours of the day and night. Many of the wounded are in such bad shape that they don't make it. It's hard, really hard.

I hope you're painting. I'm expecting a twenty-piece show when I get home. That's great news about the Girard Fellows exhibition in Paris and the commission for another magazine cover, but it had better not be of me. Just think, we'll be married the next time we visit Sainte-Chapelle. By the way, I tossed that little pebble into the Mekong River while we were on a mission. Chillaton has landed, just like Neil Armstrong on the moon! What did you think about that

*event? Everybody got quiet around here as we listened to the
radio. It's as though part of life's mystery has come undone now
that we've touched the moon.*

*Keep knocking their socks off in the band! I would love
to hear you. I'm so glad that Dwayne and Wade keep you
laughing. It won't be long until I'll be home. I just know
that everything will be all right. God is with me every step.
I watch the silvery stars every night as I think of thee, my
beautiful love. You are more than in my heart. You are the
marrow, the strength in my bones, Jemmabeth, and that's
what keeps me going.*

Always,
Spence

Jemma sat in the Corvette in front of the Chase castle reading
his letter again. She put it in her purse and stared up at the turrets
that Spence so disliked. Spencer's grandfather had built the house
to please his grandmother. For her own part, this was Jemma's third
visit to check on Mrs. Chase like Spencer had requested. On the
first visit, Rebecca Chase opened her bedroom door just enough to
hear the conversation in the foyer below. It was almost humorous,
as though nobody could see her through the crack. The second visit
proved no better. Jemma told herself she was doing this for Spence,
but she knew in her heart that she was doing it for her own reasons.
She couldn't bear for his mother to dislike her.

She went up the steps and looked back toward town. The crows
on the barbed-wire fence stared back at her like some Shakespear-
ean omen.

Max answered the door. They were equally surprised to see one
another. "Jemmabeth, come in. Is everything okay?"

"I was about to ask you the same thing. I thought you would
be at work."

"If you're looking for Harriet, she has the day off." Max glanced
toward the kitchen as dishes clattered to the floor. "Have a seat,
hon. I'll be right back."

He disappeared into the dining room, and Jemma looked
around at the furnishings and décor. The house had been featured

in *Southern Comfort* magazine a few years back, which further embarrassed Spencer. She turned at the onset of an argument followed by shouted obscenities blasting out of the kitchen. Max reappeared, pulling Mrs. Chase behind him.

"Becky, come say hello to Jemmabeth. You two need to get to know each other since we are going to be family pretty soon," Max said, like there was no history between them.

Jemma looked away. Mrs. Chase was still in her nightgown. Her hair hadn't seen a comb in some time, and she had spilled something down the front of her gown.

"Hello, Mrs. Chase," Jemma said, unable to look directly at her. Rebecca protested with no small amount of profanity to Jemma's presence and stumbled toward the stairs. Max ignored her and tried to engage in polite conversation about Spencer. Rebecca inched her way up the stairs, holding onto the handrail. She was almost to the top when she lost her grip. She slipped and plummeted back down. Jemmabeth screamed and raced to the bottom of the steps.

"Becky!" Max shouted, touching her shoulder.

"Don't move her," Jemma said. "I'll call Sheriff Ezell; he'll get an ambulance. Don't move her." She darted around the room, looking for a phone.

"There's one in the kitchen," Max yelled, still hunched over his wife's body.

The ambulance took her to Amarillo, to the same hospital where Jemma had been in a coma. Mrs. Chase was not in a coma, but she had broken her arm and dislocated her shoulder. She wouldn't be drinking for a while.

"You don't need to take me home. I'll hop on the Zephyr and be there in no time," Jemma said to Max in the waiting area.

"I'm sorry this all happened. I should have paid more attention to her. It's just another example of my useless life." Max looked out at the courtyard and rubbed the back of his neck. "You know she was a beauty in her day. Of course you couldn't tell it now, but that's where Spencer got his good looks."

Jemma had been waiting for the right moment. "You know, Mr. Chase," she began.

"Please, call me Max. I'd really like that." She noticed that his hair was getting a little gray around the temples.

"Max, this might be the perfect time to get Mrs. Chase into an alcohol rehabilitation program. It could be a blessing that she's in this situation. I'm sorry she got hurt, but maybe you could use this time to get her some help. She could become that beautiful person again."

"Yeah, I've thought about that a lot lately. Spencer has been asking to get her some help for years, but I don't want him to know that she's in the hospital now. The doc says that she'll recover, so let's not worry him, okay?"

"Of course. I totally agree, but please consider taking her straight from here to a treatment center. That would make Spence very happy."

"There's a good one in Waco. I checked it out a couple of months ago. I'll make some calls." He smiled at her. "C'mon, at least let me drive you to the train station. I don't know when the next train will be heading to Chillaton."

"There's one that gets into town at 9:04," Jemma said. "Max, thank you for taking care of Spence's mother."

"Well, before she was his mother, she was my wife. We had a lot of fun. . .until the drinking started. It's time I did something for her."

Jemma and Lizbeth went to the cemetery to work on Papa's grave. Afterward, Jemma walked to the pond below the Chase mausoleum. The ducks weren't there. Maybe they were hiding in the cattails. As she started back up the path, a helicopter flew overhead. Jemma's heart stopped. For one crazy second, she thought it might be Spence. She didn't cover her ears as it passed; she wanted to hear the sounds that he might hear. It wasn't a fat Huey like he flew, but its blades made a whirring, chopping sound and it moved through the sky like an ugly dragonfly. She closed her eyes and strained to listen as it faded away. He would be home soon.

The sun was low and a thin drizzle chilled the air as Spencer and his crew ran to their chopper for the fifth time in sixteen hours. He pulled the trigger and waited for the engine to take hold. The wind was off their tail because he could smell the burnt jet fuel.

Thirty more seconds and the turbine engine, with its increasingly loud whine, would spin up to full rpm. Spencer preferred to wait several minutes to make sure everything was working right, but with guys down and waiting for them, he could be ready to pick his bird up and fly in much less than that. The crew was exhausted. His co-pilot was John Davis from Pennsylvania. The crew chief was Allan Porter, whose hometown was Milwaukee, and Shelton "Skeleton" Taylor, the best flight medic in the army, was born and bred in Kentucky. They had flown enough missions together to be like family. Now they were concentrating on getting in and out of this hot landing zone as quickly as possible and bringing back as many soldiers as they could hoist.

Spencer picked up the Huey slowly, stopping just above the ground to check things out, then hovered to the take-off pad. He got clearance and took it up to altitude.

"Giddy up, cowboy." Skeleton gave a thumbs-up and a weary grin.

Spencer made contact with the troops in the landing zone for an estimate of casualties and to see where Charlie, the Viet Cong, was concentrated. The gunship team assigned to cover them was also on the radio. In a half hour they were both over the pickup point. The ground unit was in a wooded area flanked on one side by a field of tall grass. Porter began lowering the hoist cable through the canopy of trees. The gunship radioed that a hostile missile launch pad had been spotted.

Spencer was scanning the area and talking to the gunship pilot when, like a bolt of lightning, a massive fireball lit up the sky right in front of his chopper. Instantly, all contact ceased from the gunship. Spencer gasped and Skeleton called on the Almighty. They shuddered as the gunship debris pelted their chopper and its fiery smoke left sinister trails in the twilight. John called in the hit while Porter continued with the cable.

Spencer drew a quick breath and talked to the guys on the ground. "The cable is still coming. Get ready."

As the words came out of his mouth, a large volley of small-arms fire penetrated the engine. The big bird reacted to the hit, shaking violently, then dropped in altitude like a giant boulder.

Spencer held it as best he could. There was no time for a May Day call. An RPG round blasted through the cockpit window. Flames burst into the cabin as the crippled Huey slammed into the trees, nose down. Within seconds, the only sounds that remained were the sickening shift of metal against metal and the hiss and crack of an inferno. Thick, black smoke curled upward to the heavens, its tentacles clawing at the stars.

Chapter 20

In the Stars

Jemma stopped by the post office to mail Carrie a letter.

Paralee Batson, the postmistress, stubbed out her cigarette and leaned over the window. "Spencer sure has dropped off in the mail department. You two are still an item, aren't you? That Blake girl has been sendin' him a right smart amount of letters and packages. I had half a mind to lose them in the trash barrel." Her cat, H.D., lifted his head and twitched an ear for Jemma's response.

"Oh, you'll never have to worry about that again, Paralee," Jemma said and gave H.D. a pat. He stretched and jumped off the counter. "I guess Spence is really busy now. It's almost time for him to come home. Then you'll get to come to our wedding."

A right smart amount of letters and packages, huh? Rats. She was considering a few wrestling moves that The Cleave could sure write about.

Paralee raised her Joan Crawford brow. "I'd better be findin' me a dress to wear, then. The mister and me might go up to Amarillo next week after he gets his social security check. Don't let Spencer get in a rut of watchin' too much TV. That's about all my mister does these days. He likes them game shows. If it weren't for the beauty parlor, I wouldn't have nobody to talk to at all. Not countin' folks who come in for their mail, of course. On the other hand, hon, you can get some good ideas for fashion off them soaps. I got my little TV in the back, you know. Just the other day, I told Nedra about a new hairdo that I saw on 'As the Stomach Turns'—that's what the mister calls it. She's gonna fix me up just like that actress for your weddin'."

Jemma had never seen Paralee's hair combed out in her life. If not tightly wound in brush rollers, her silver locks were frozen in the same shape as the rollers and corralled under a hairnet.

"I bet you'll look very pretty at our wedding. I'll see you, Paralee."

"If you get a letter from Spencer, I'll give you a call," Paralee shouted.

Jemma went next door to buy her favorite shampoo at Nedra's Nook. Twila, recently rehired, waited on her.

"Come outside," Twila said and pulled her to the sidewalk. She glanced around and lowered her voice. "I need your help with somethin'. I'm tryin' to get p.g."

"Well, don't look at me," Jemma said, laughing.

"Ow." Twila's face contorted into a knot. "Hold on a minute."

"What's wrong with you?"

"Sorry. I was ovulatin'."

"You can't tell when that happens. You were in pain just then."

"I get this little twinge in my side."

"Left or right?"

"Sometimes it's both sides, so I'm thinkin' that would be twins."

"Twila, have you talked to your doctor about this?"

"No. I read about ovulatin' in a magazine here at Nedra's."

"I think you should check with your doctor and not a beauty parlor magazine. That isn't the way things work. I'm a girl, and I've never had twinges like that."

"Well, it's gotten stronger right after Buddy and me started tryin' to have a baby."

"How long has that been?"

"Almost two months."

"You don't have to get twinges to get pregnant. You don't even have to be married to get pregnant."

"All I know is that you can't get p.g. without ovulatin'. I'm ovulatin', but I'm not p.g. yet."

"All the more reason why you should see a doctor."

"I was hopin' that you would ask your doctor for me," Twila said, grimacing again.

"You need to see Dr. Huntley now."

"I'm not going to a man doctor for this kind of stuff."

Jemma took Twila's hand. "Twila, those pains in your side could be something else. My doctor is a man and he's very nice."

"Is he an old man?"

"He's not as old as Dr. Huntley."

"How much does it cost to see him? We've been savin' up for a baby for five years."

"Don't worry, I'll pay for it."

"I don't want Buddy B to know about the twinges. He's already worried why I'm not p.g."

"I'll get an appointment for you, and it'll be our secret, okay?"

Twila winced again.

"I'll call today," Jemma said firmly.

They went to Amarillo that week. Twila had a monster bladder infection that had gone on far too long, and she was pregnant. Twila rode home with her hands on her belly and a silly little smile.

Jemma grinned at her. "Now aren't you glad we went? You wouldn't have known about the infection, and it might have hurt your baby."

Twila nodded. "Buddy is gonna be so happy. I can't believe I'm p.g. If it's a girl, we'll name her after you and my mother."

Jemma dropped Twila off, thinking of Buddy's reaction to the great news, and headed home to see if there was any mail from Spencer. There wasn't. She hadn't heard from him in two weeks. Max was due back soon from an auto show in Detroit and a visit to see Mrs. Chase in Waco. Harriet was in North Carolina, visiting her sister. Jemma assumed that the army was getting all they could out of Spence before he was discharged. He only had two weeks left until he would be coming home to her. Then they could have their wedding at Plum Creek before it went dry and the trees lost their leaves.

❧

Jemma had the feeling that maybe Shorty Knox had been peeking in the car house window for a couple of days, but she hadn't seen him. It was nothing to be frightened about, but she knew that Spence wouldn't like the idea of the town peeping Tom watching her paint again. The last time he'd hung around, it was to rescue Jemma's paintings before a deadly tornado swept through Chillaton. Spencer had made it up to Shorty by installing a color television with its own generator at his dugout. He had all but given up his peeping career after that.

She saw him on the fourth night. He grinned at her and she

waved at him, then went outside to say hello. He was nowhere to be seen, but under the window was a dirty scrap of cardboard held down by a rock. She got goose bumps when she saw the crude stick drawing of a girl with a paintbrush in her hand. Spence would have to hear about this.

That same evening, besides her usual bags of groceries, she carried a giant box full of Big Chief tablets, pencils, and crayons to Shorty's dugout and left them next to the generator. There were other things to do in life besides watch television and peek into people's windows. There was art.

⟨⟨⟩⟩

It had rained for three days in a row. Lizbeth had used the dreary weather to bake. "Sugar, I'm going to make some fruit pies for the wedding and freeze them in that new chest freezer that Julia bought me. What do you think? Is it tacky to serve thawed pies?" she asked.

"It might be tacky if they were still frozen." Jemma laughed and put her arm around Lizbeth while she went through the mail. "I don't know why I haven't heard from Spencer. He's so faithful to write every week and I sent him that big birthday package."

"Maybe his letters got misdirected. You'll hear soon, I'm sure."

Lester came in the back door for his mid-morning coffee. "That kitty cat dragged up a snake this mornin'."

Jemma drew back, big-eyed. "I'm not going out the door if there's a snake around."

"It's just a garter snake, no more than a cat's plaything." Lester helped himself to a cold biscuit with his coffee. "It's pretty much dead now. 'Course you can't be too careful when it comes to dead snakes. Ask Bernie Miller about that. Here 'while back, he was movin' some old lumber at his mother's house and uncovered a rattler. He picked up a two-by-four and give it a wallop. It was a big 'un, too, about this long, accordin' to Bernie." Lester held his arms out as far as he could reach. "Anyway, he was gonna skin it for a belt, so he put it in a gunny sack in the back floorboard of his Hudson. He come hence to drivin' back into town when he heard a rattlin' sound. Bernie thought it was the old Hudson, but it turned out to be the rattler. It was coiled up in the front seat floorboard until it struck at him and nipped his boot. Bernie slammed on the brakes and jumped outta the car while it was still rollin'. Got himself all scratched up. Never did find the rattler."

"How did it live through a hit by a two-by-four?" Jemma asked.

"I expect he just winged the critter. It most likely woke up in the sack, kinda woozy. Bernie could've been a good inch or so off since he's just got the one eye. I never could figure out how he cuts hair so good. 'Course all them young fellers get crew cuts. He just has to aim his electric shaver at their heads."

Jemma peeked around the screened-in porch. "I have to work in the yard today, too. I hope Vincent doesn't find any more reptiles." She shivered. "I hate snakes. They are evil."

"I got some other news, too. The Burlington Line is droppin' the Zephyr passenger service startin' New Year's Eve. Not enough folks ridin' these days. I know how much you love that train, Jemmer, so I thought it was best that you heard it from me."

Jemma stared at Lester, hoping he was joking, but he looked at his coffee cup and tapped his foot.

"I've seen that train come and go a thousand times. It won't be the same without it," Lizbeth said, watching her granddaughter.

Jemma went outside and wandered to the tracks. Since she was old enough to point, she had loved that train. The Silver Zephyr was beautiful and powerful. It held such mystery, anticipation, and exhilaration. What would all those strangers do now? Looking down on life in miniature from a jet wouldn't be the same as seeing into the eyes of the people who lived in those towns below. Blurred glimpses of unfamiliar faces would be no more. There would be no reason to dance on the tracks because nothing special would happen if she did. Freight trains offered no romance or mystery. Jemma sat on the rails and cried. The world was changing, and their sweet kitty had touched evil, all in the same day.

❧

She was pulling weeds around Papa's rosebushes when she heard the car drive up. It was Harriet. She broke down as soon as they embraced. Jemma saw the mustard-colored envelope in Harriet's hand. Every muscle in Jemma's body tightened and her stomach rose to her throat. Lizbeth came outside and searched their faces, then put her arms around them.

Harriet could barely speak. "I'm sorry to bear this news to you, my girl. I just now got back in town, and found this in the Chases' front door." She held out the envelope with *Western Union* on the front. Jemma recoiled, letting it drop to the ground. She clenched her fists inside Papa's big work gloves and they fell to the grass beside the letter.

Lizbeth picked up the telegram and slipped her arm around her granddaughter's waist. "We'll read it together, honey. Come over to the porch swing."

"I can't," Jemma whispered.

"You have to, Jemmabeth. You owe it to Spencer."

Harriet sat in a wicker chair next to the swing, her hands covering her mouth.

Jemma's hands trembled as she unfolded the telegram. She scanned it in silence, then threw it on the swing and bolted inside the house.

Lizbeth read it.

THE SECRETARY OF DEFENSE REGRETS TO INFORM YOU
THAT YOUR SON, WO1 SPENCER M. CHASE, FAILED TO
RETURN FROM A RESCUE MISSION 23 JULY, 1969. WO1
CHASE IS NOW CLASSIFIED AS MISSING IN ACTION.
THERE WERE NO OTHER SURVIVORS IN THE INCIDENT.

Lizbeth took Harriet's hand and led her inside. The two of them sat on the couch and cried. She heard Jemma being sick in the bathroom, then the slam of the back screen door. Lizbeth excused herself and looked out the kitchen window toward the tracks and saw Jemma. Her first instinct was to go to her, but decided instead to give Jemma some privacy. That's what she had needed when her telegrams had come about her dear boys. She said a quick prayer, then returned to the living room to comfort Harriet.

❧

Jemma was blank. She turned east on the rail bed and ran to the city limits and stopped. On the horizon she could see the Chase castle and felt the bile come up in her throat again. She screamed his name and planted herself in the middle of the tracks until she heard the 3:37 blow its horn. The steel rail was blistering hot in the August sun, but she ran her hand along the smooth metal surface. She didn't turn even when she felt it coming. She didn't care what happened to her. It blasted its horn. A rabbit, startled by the shrill whistle, paused in the rail bed not far from her, and then hopped off. Her own life didn't seem all that important, but when the rails vibrated hard against her hands, Jemma moved off, too. The engineer yelled at her, but she didn't even look up.

⋙❦⋘

Lester and Lizbeth made their way down the tracks after Jemma had been gone for over two hours.

"I should have comforted her," Lizbeth said, picking her way through the rail bed. "I thought she needed some time alone, and I surely needed to collect my composure. That was downright foolish of me."

"She's gonna be all right, Miz Liz. Jemmerbeth is rock-solid." Lester sniffed. "What are you thinkin' about Spencer?"

"Well, at least they haven't found him, but I know the pain of hoping against hope, only to get the next telegram with the worst of all news."

"I know you do, Miz Liz. I can't see the good Lord lettin' this happen to your family again. No sir, I just can't figger on it."

Lizbeth gasped. "There she is, Lester. Oh my." Jemma was curled up like a ball of yarn on the rails.

⋙❦⋘

The three of them talked through suppertime. Lizbeth pleaded with her to eat something.

"I'm not hungry," Jemma said. "I'll sit outside for a while."

"Jemmabeth, you must at least drink some water. It's not good for you to go without fluids." Lizbeth filled a tall glass for her.

Jemma sat on the steps, holding the glass in her hands. She had to make him drink fluids when he was sick in Florence. What if he were thirsty now? She could not get the date out of her head—it was July 23, exactly a year after their wedding date that had ended in disaster. It could not be in God's plan for him to lose his dear life on that same date. It hurt her heart that she had not known for all this long time. Jemma bit her lip thinking of conversations where she had laughed or made jokes or times she had neglected her Bible study. Spencer could have been fighting for his life while she was thinking of wedding cakes.

She had forgotten to look at the stars tonight, and she had a dumb thought. If, in God's mercy, Spencer was safe, he might send her a message there. Jemma moved to the grass and searched the heavens. There was the moon with a part of its mystery now gone, like he'd said. She found Venus, then prayed to the good Lord that she would not have to inscribe *I Think of Thee* onto a cold marble stone. Before she could finish her prayer, a Cadillac slammed to a halt in front of Gram's gate. Max Chase jumped out, leaving the door open and the car running. He didn't see Jemma sitting in the grass as he barreled up to the front door.

"Max," Jemma said, getting up slowly. "Bad news?"

He turned and collapsed in her arms. "I just got home and Harriet was waiting with the news. How could this happen? He was so close to coming home. I thought maybe the Lord was going to spare my boy," he said, sobbing without shame. "I've been praying hard for it."

"The letter said that he is missing, though. They have not found him, and that should give us hope."

"I remember when your daddy's brother was missing in action. They even had prayer vigils at the church. Look what happened to him, to both of those boys. Families all over the country have prayed for their kids in wars. This is my fault. I told you that the sins of the fathers would come out on the children. That sweet boy of mine could be suffering some kind of torture because of me, if he's still alive."

"We don't know that he's a prisoner, Max. We don't know anything, really. He told me in his last letter that he was sure he'd make it home. I've decided to believe that, too."

Max shook his head. "It's my fault."

"Does Mrs. Chase know?"

"Oh no, hon. She doesn't need to know anything about this. They evaluated her and put her right into rehab. She's got enough worries."

Jemma wiped her cheeks. "He told me once that things happen just when you think you're safe."

"What are we going to do?" he asked.

"Pray. That's all we can do. Spence is smart and he wants to come home more than anything. I know that even smart people get killed and captured, but we have to trust that God's Great Plan includes him coming back to us."

"He can't be dead." Max tilted his head back and groaned. "My mother always called dying being *lifted*—such a funny thing to say, huh? But Spencer can't have been lifted. He's got to know that I'm trying to change."

Jemma put her arm around him. "Let's think of Spence being lifted by angels, Max, but only to safety for now."

Lizbeth opened the front door. "Jemmabeth, there you are, sugar. Your folks are on the phone. Come in, Mr. Chase, and have some coffee with us." Much to Lizbeth's surprise, he did. Lester was even more surprised to see him, and he was especially shocked to get a hug from Max-a-million Chase.

Jemma went to bed just before dawn. She had talked with Max until they were hoarse. She searched his face for Spencer, but Max had none of Spence's mannerisms or wit, but he was suffering, and he was his father. It gave her strength to offer him hope.

She had read so many stories of inhumane treatment for Americans held captive by the Viet Cong and their allies. She prayed that Spencer be spared such horror. In fact, each breath became a prayer. Jemma's head ached and her nerves buzzed as she crumpled across her bed. She was still wearing her gardening clothes, Papa's old overalls, but she didn't want to get under the covers anyway. The lace curtains billowed out with an early morning breeze and touched her face. He could not be dead. She would have felt something when his life left him, and she would have seen him in the stars.

~❦~

Lizbeth stood in the pouting room with the door shut. She had been on her knees for an hour. It had been the same when they had gotten the telegram with the news that Matthew was missing. She had spent almost every waking minute in prayer then, too, but

Matt's death didn't mean that she shouldn't pray for Spencer's life. It was different to be the mother, but it was all agony of the heart. She wanted to lift this burden from Jemmabeth and take it upon herself. . .if only that were possible. Jemma had shown great faith for one so young, but nobody should have to go through this sickening wait.

She closed up the pouting room and set about cooking breakfast. She could make it in her sleep. Now her hands worked at it without a single thought propelling them. Jemma wouldn't eat anything, but Lester would. Since they got the news, Lester was with them most of the days and into the evenings, as were Willa and Joe. . .bless their hearts.

Cameron would have grieved himself sick over this. He loved Spencer, and Jemmabeth was his jewel. She held fast to the countertop and said one more prayer that the good Lord would have mercy on this sweet boy. She asked that it could be within The Great Plan for him to come home in one piece and, most assuredly, not in a box. She heard Jemma playing that sad song again on her stereo: "Praeludium and Allegro" was the name on the record. Lizbeth sat at the table, her head in her hands. She wasn't sure that Jemmabeth was the only one who might fall apart if they got that second telegram. Cam had kept her from crumbling before, but she would have to be the strong one now.

✧

As had become her habit the past week, Jemma spent part of her day praying in the chapel that Spence had designed. She prayed for Harriet and Max, too. Max had taken a week off from work to stay in a motel in Waco. He was taking this hard. Jemma prayed that God would heal Mrs. Chase and that she and Max could start over, somehow. Most of her prayers were for her beloved. If she didn't have faith about this, she was still on her Christian crawl, rather than her walk.

This particular evening, she sat in the hollyhock patch and read Emily Dickinson's poem that compared hope to a little bird that never gives up and is a constant comfort to all. Emily always spoke to her heart.

It had been weeks since the crash, but Jemma's faith rested in the God of the universe, the author of The Great Plan. Her everlasting hope lay with Spencer and his determination to return to her. Spence was her hero, whatever happened. She laid the book across her lap. The hollyhock stalks bobbed and swayed, heavy with white, pink, and maroon blossoms. She had been there so many times with Spencer, laughing and flirting. Flowers might be blooming where he was, too. The little scar on his chin came to her mind. It had taken forever to heal when it happened, but it was smooth against her fingers in Hawaii. She had caused it at recess in the fifth grade when she went up to knock the basketball out of his hands and came down with a bit of his chin instead. He had teased her about scarring him for life. She wondered what deeper scars he bore now.

She wanted to walk with Spence in Papa's cotton fields when the plants were loaded with pink and white flowers. Someday they could pick just enough cotton at harvest for a little quilt to lay their babies on. Their children should be like him, steady and even-tempered. The boys might all have gray eyes like their daddy. The girls could be a little like her. No. None should be so stubborn, wishy-washy, and prone to pouting. She did not pout their last night in Hawaii. That memory, tucked in her heart, could not be their only time together.

Jemma looked at her watch. The Zephyr would be coming soon in the early autumn twilight. She would miss seeing its passengers as they lingered over an evening meal when the Burlington big shots closed it down. Those diners were the subject of her latest painting. She walked up to the tracks and sat on the rail. Joe's dog barked a couple of times, then gave up. The lights from the football field cast a faint glow in the western sky. The CHS band was playing the fight song. How could people around her carry on without knowing if Spencer had breath? The Johnson grass by the tree row had gone to seed, and the evening breeze ruffled through it, stirring the heads into a raspy chatter. Jemma gathered her skirt around her legs. She picked up a twig, twirling it between her thumb and finger, then drew a heart in the dirt.

When she and Sandy were younger, they had danced on the tracks to see who would be the last to jump off before the train got too close. She hadn't danced since the telegram came. It hadn't even occurred to her. The 9:04 blew its whistle at the station, and she moved off the tracks to wait for it.

The Zephyr passed by, picking up speed. Its horn changed tones as it moved past. Jemma returned to her seat on the rail, now hot through her skirt. A grasshopper flew up from the sunflowers and landed on her. She brushed it off and watched it recover. Gram would be home soon from her Bible study circle. Jemma dusted the back of her skirt and faced the breeze. The gentle wind parted her hair, and she felt a slight prickle where the scar remained from her wreck.

She closed her eyes and hummed "Candy Man," moving like the hollyhock stalks with their heavy burdens. Crickets had begun their night rhythm and a flock of birds resting on the telephone lines overhead kept curious eyes on her. She could almost hear Spencer saying her name on the warm wind. It gave her a chill to think that he could be calling out to her somewhere. She stopped and peered into the dim horizon, then closed her eyes and resumed her solitary dance.

It came to her again, but his voice was not in her head. It was drifting down the track. Her eyes popped open and her body tingled at the familiar form heading toward her.

"Spence!" she screamed. She ran, her feet flying over the rail bed.

The flock of birds took flight, too. Spencer, sprinting full speed, dropped his bag somewhere along the last fifty yards. They collided, like two shooting stars whose collective radiance overshadowed Venus and dazzled the heavens. He held her, breathless, and they peered into one another's eyes—golden and pewter, fastened together for life. They trembled, first in disbelief, then in laughter.

He was not lost among those stars, not while she could hear the beat of his heart above her own. Praise God.

Chapter 21
That'll Do

The Cotton Festival and Fourth of July committee members sprang into action to celebrate the return of Chillaton's native son. Spencer would have none of it, though, unless all the veterans in the county were honored as well. The cars in the parade were courtesy of Chase's Cadillac & Chevrolet. The Lion's Club served hot dogs and cherry pie to every citizen who could get to the courthouse lawn and delivered to those who couldn't. Congressman Cyrus Millsap made a speech and, to everyone's surprise, presented Willa with a posthumous Purple Heart to honor Sergeant Samuel Augustus Johnson, 92nd Infantry, for his actions in WWII. The crowd became suddenly quiet at this honor for a brave Buffalo Soldier who was born and raised just across the tracks, and whose widow had, at one time or the other, ironed their clothing.

A tearful Willa embraced Lizbeth. "I know this come from your doins', Miz Liz, but my words ain't good enough to thank you."

Trina couldn't manage to say anything. The moment was too close to her heart.

Spencer told his own story with his usual good-natured poise and humor at least twenty times. The Amarillo television stations and newspaper were there. The Judge showed up and was in line for hot dogs right alongside Shorty Knox.

When they got back to Lizbeth's house, the phone was ringing. It was the Lillygraces.

"Dear boy, you must tell this story once more. I know you are weary of it, but we want to know all the details. Everyone was so worried," Robert said.

Spencer clasped Jemma to his side, where she had been since he came home, and they sat on the floor in the good bedroom. "I don't mind telling you my story, sir. We were on a mission to hoist some wounded who were pinned down by snipers in a wooded area.

We were at the LZ, the landing zone, but a missile hit the gunship that was supposed to cover us, wiping it completely out. We were continuing with the rescue when our chopper took a major hit in the engine and dropped about the same time that another missile exploded in the cabin. I lost my whole crew."

Spence exhaled and there was a long pause before he continued. "My leg had a gaping rip in it, but I could still move. I felt around in the smoke for the hoist cable and inched my way down it until I couldn't hold on anymore and fell into some bushes. By some miracle, I was able to crawl into a big field of elephant grass and hide. I just kept crawling and praying. I heard shots again and knew that they were still in the area so I sweated it out in the grass until right before dawn. It was quiet because I remember hearing birds, then I got it stuck in my brain that we'd heard of guys encountering cobras in elephant grass. I thought that would be a great way to die in 'Nam. I was in shock, for sure.

"My plan was to get back across the field where we went down and get with any unit that was still in the woods. My arm throbbed and was so swollen that I figured it was broken. I made a sling with my belt, and I had gone about a hundred yards when I heard the VC yelling in the woods where I was headed. I got out my map and went the opposite direction for a couple of hours. I crossed a stream and came up on a cluster of shacks, a village of sorts. There were women cooking outside and little kids running around, but I didn't see any VC. The villagers were eating, so I decided to stay put. My arm was giving me fits, and I had lost a lot of blood from my leg wound. I thought that if my unit was looking for me, I needed to stop moving. The whole day, I never saw any men around the area, so I got my nerve up and moved closer to one of the shacks. I could smell food, and I would have eaten anything at that point, believe me.

"The last thing I recall was watching the sunset. When I woke up, some little kids had found me. I kept thinking about Gulliver and the Lilliputians and cobras. I was out of my head. I just knew they were going to turn me in to the nearest VC, but I was wrong. One of them went to get an elderly woman and a skinny teenage girl. They helped me into her hut and put me on a floor mat. The old woman was in charge of the whole village, or so it seemed to me. They fed me and made a splint for my arm and dressed my thigh. I drank some hot tea or something and fell asleep. The next morning the hut was full of women and children watching me. There was one man there, though. He was probably ninety years old. He came to check me out, too. I guess I must have been out of it for a week."

"How did you communicate?" Robert asked.

"My crew's *mamasan*, who cleaned our quarters, taught me some of her language. Anyway, I tried to explain to the teenage girl that I needed to get back to my people. I could hear choppers in the distance off and on, and sporadic gunfire, so I knew we had a unit around the area. I guess I was at the village about three weeks. They were very kind to me. I taught the kids some songs that we used to sing in Sunday school. The grandma really liked the silver cross that Jem had given me before I left home, so I gave it to her. Then one morning she woke me up before sunrise and walked with me to the woods on the other side of their village. Grandma waved me off with the girl, and I just hoped we weren't walking into a trap.

"The girl walked for about an hour with me, then pointed toward the hills and said for me to go over them. I took off my boot and gave her all the money I had hidden there. She disappeared into the jungle. I got out my survival map and tried to figure out where I was. I made my way across a river and got up in the hills. It seemed to take forever. About dusk I was sighted by one of our assault helicopter units. I was never so happy to see a Huey aimed at me. They picked me up and took me to their camp. The doctors checked me out and said nothing was broken. Two weeks later, I was running down the tracks to my beautiful fiancée."

"It's a shame the army didn't tell Jemmabeth that you were safe," Catherine said.

"Yes ma'am. Jem and I talked about that, and I think there was some military miscommunication."

Jemmabeth reached for another tissue and blew her nose.

Robert cleared his throat. "I see. To what do you attribute this fascinating survival story, Spencer?"

Spence rested his head on the edge of the bed as he considered the question. "There was a scripture from Isaiah that stuck in my mind. 'When you pass through the waters I will be with you; and through the rivers, they shall not overflow you: when you walk through the fire, you shall not be burned; neither shall the flame kindle upon you.' Brother Cleo used that verse in his sermon the last Sunday before I left. Now that I'm home, I recall an appropriate quote from Mark Twain, too, about war and strangers helping you. Those women helped me survive, and I'll never forget them. Oh, and I also had a four-leaf clover that my fiancée had given me." He grinned at her.

"You are an intrepid young man, Spencer. We are so grateful that you are home. Jemmabeth has been distraught, as we all have. We shall be seeing you in a few days for the wedding. Until then."

"Yes, dear. We are anxious to see you and give you a proper welcome. Do give Jemmabeth a hug for us," Catherine said. "Godspeed."

Spencer and Jemmabeth stayed on the floor by the good bed and relaxed in one another's arms.

"I didn't tell your grandfather one other thing, Jem," Spencer said.

"What's that?"

"You have the most delicious lips and eyes the color of honey."

"Is that what you didn't tell him?"

"Nope, but it's true. I also didn't tell him that I kept thinking about holding you in that silk nightgown, and how that thought helped carry me out of the jungle."

"I'm glad I could be of service, sir." She saluted.

"You'll never know, Jem. You'll just never know," he said and kissed her. "That first night, when the smoke lifted, the stars were brilliant. I was so shook up about my crew, the gunship team, and all those wounded that we didn't get out. Those images will always be in my head, I suppose. I had to concentrate on you to keep my wits. I went through our whole conversation we had at the river, the night before I left. *I think of thee*, remember? I know this sounds crazy, but I saw it in the stars, baby, I really did."

She cradled him, like she did in Hawaii. He was thin, but he was home.

"The earth is a big place and there are lots of good people on it," he said, his cheek buried in her hair. "Somewhere there's a little grandma who made this day possible. I honor her tonight, too."

"Maybe she was an angel."

"Maybe so." It had crossed his mind.

❧

The wedding plans were easy. All they had to do was get out the old list and follow it. This time, though, Spencer went with her everywhere. There were no hitches. Everything was perfect and everybody came, right down to Uncle Arthur and all the Jenkins sisters.

On the eve of the wedding, the sunset was all Hollywood. There were no fishing trips, just one big party. Lizbeth presented them with the wedding ring quilt that she had made two years before. It was in shades of yellow and gold on a tiny blue floral background. The fabric in one corner was solid cornflower blue. Jemmabeth knew it was meant to be for Papa's twinkling eyes always watching over them. She draped it over herself and Spencer as cameras snapped.

❧

In the early morning sunshine, Jemmabeth appeared under the cottonwoods on her daddy's arm. Melanie played "Morning Has Broken" as they walked along the creek to the old cottonwood tree. The sight took Spencer's breath away. Jemma and Trina had designed her two-piece wedding dress of vintage French lace over cream-colored Italian silk. It was nothing like the gowns Miss Scarlett wore. The skirt was slender, encircled by burgundy and pink beaded flowers and golden leaves, and a long, silky train was attached at her waist. The strapless bodice was fitted and the scrolled neckline showed off Spencer's wedding gift—a double strand of pearls embracing a ruby heart. Her auburn hair cascaded over her shoulders and was crowned with a wreath of rosebuds and forget-me-nots attached to the veil that flowed behind her like a misty lace confection. She carried a bouquet of fragrant roses, sweet peas, cornflowers, and one small sunflower. Her great-grandmother Forrester's lace handkerchief was tucked inside the bouquet.

Trina, her maid-of-honor, was "looking fine," as Nick put it, in the gold crepe silk dress of her own design. The fabric was embroidered across the bodice and hem with burgundy and pink rosebuds. Sandy's matching one was pewter, the same as Spencer's eyes, and

Carrie's was the color of Scottish heather. Each carried a cluster of heather, tied with an ivory velvet bow. Robby was Spencer's best man. He didn't try any monkey business, and he looked quite handsome in his tux.

When Jim gave her to him at the rose-bedecked altar, Spencer whispered something in her ear, then they repeated the vows from their private ceremony. Brother Cleo said, at last, "I now pronounce you man and wife."

Spencer picked her up and spun her around. The guests clapped and yelled like it was the winning touchdown at homecoming.

Melanie played "Josefin's Waltz" and "Archibald MacDonald of Keppoch"—Papa's favorite songs. Jemma and Spencer danced the first dance alone as Melanie played "I Will Wait for You." Nobody said a word, but there were constant sniffles from the crowd.

Things lightened up when Buddy took over. The band was cookin'. Buddy played his harmonica and sang "Candy Man." The fire that had glowed for almost eighteen years was burning its brightest when the newlyweds danced.

After a few more songs, Spencer took the microphone. "This one's for Jemmabeth Alexandra Chase." He sang "Pretty Woman." Jemma laughed and danced with Robby, cutting her eyes at Spencer, whenever she could, to give him The Look.

The band got a big kick out of Spencer singing to her, especially Leon, who nodded his approval. Spencer, looking like Prince Charming once again, danced with every woman there, so it was a good thing that Missy Blake wasn't invited. Jemma did the same with all the guys. Uncle Art knew how to move for a man his age and Max showed her where Spencer got his dancing skills. Helene and Lester waltzed solo when Melanie played "*Un Coin Tout Bleu,*" a French song that Helene liked. Nobody knew Lester could dance like that. Lizbeth assumed he had learned with his Methodist wife.

"Jemma," Paralee Batson yelled, "if the U.S. of A. government would use its own postal service instead of Western Union, I could've got the news about Spencer to you quicker. You know that, don't you?"

Jemma waved.

Paralee sniffed and touched her hair. Nedra had combed it back behind her ears, just like the twin on *As the World Turns* who showed up after eight years of amnesia. It was perfect, just like her new dress and this wedding, which would be the hot topic at Nedra's until Christmas.

Lester was keeping Lizbeth company when Jemma came to say good-bye. "Bless you two, in your new life. I don't suppose you'll be comin' back to live with your gram anymore, but we'll sure miss you," he added, giving her a hug.

"Thank you, Lester, I'll miss you, too." She took Lizbeth aside. "Gram, you know that nobody in this world is more precious to me than you. Of course, that's not counting my husband." She saw him across the crowd and blushed a little.

"I know, sugar, the feeling is mutual. I see that you gave him a new Bible."

"Yes ma'am. I wanted it to have the right date on the cover. I also gave him a new silver cross to wear."

Spencer came to get her.

"Gotta go," Jemma said, kissing Lizbeth's soft cheek that was laced with an extra dose of "Moonlight Over Paris" perfume. "We'll be back in three weeks. Maybe you can live with us someday! You, too, Lester, because you never know what The Great Plan has in store," she yelled as Spencer tugged her away from the happy group. Jemma got inside a makeshift tent and changed into her traveling outfit.

She threw an extra bouquet into the clump of hopefuls and Lester caught it, but promptly handed it over to Trina. They escaped ahead of the rice in their new silver Corvette, a gift from Max, and drove to the cemetery. They walked to Papa's grave, holding hands. The sunflowers were in full bloom this year.

"Here we are, Papa—Mr. and Mrs. Spencer Chase," Spence said.

"We just wanted to introduce ourselves," Jemma whispered and laid some of the flowers from her bouquet at the base of his headstone. She kissed her fingers and touched his name.

❧

"When does our flight leave for Scotland?" Jemmabeth asked, turning her attention to other things in the car.

"Not for four hours," Spencer answered, trying to concentrate on the road.

"Four hours? It just takes an hour to get to Amarillo."

"I know," he said.

They had just passed Main Street when he suddenly made a left turn and pulled into the driveway of the That'll Do Motel. He parked, jangling a room key in front of his giggling wife. He opened her door and stood for a moment as a breeze swirled her hair around her face. He growled, then lifted her out of the car and carried his bride inside, closing the door behind them. He opened it once again, just wide enough to hang a ragged, handmade sign on the doorknob.

DO NOT DISTURB—COWBOY AT WORK

Taste of Gold

Jemma
Book Three

Dedication

For
Mother and Daddy

Sweet Attitude

✦

Texas wind, like a pack of coyotes,
Not truly evil, only nature's due.
Yet hear it howl as earth is hurled
Toward the humble and those vain few.

Is there no escape for its victims?
Must they endure relentless pain
Like hapless, fenced-in cattle,
Hearts and heads lowered in the rain?

Not me. I'll not cower at the threat
Of giant dusters nor deadly twisters;
No dark sky gloom for me foretold.
I'll kiss, instead, the honeyed dawn
For the bittersweet taste of gold.

—Jemmabeth Chase

The good folks of Chillaton are talking
about newlyweds Jemmabeth and Spencer Chase
and how crazy in love they are.
But not everybody's happy about it. . . .

Chapter 1
Married Men

Darrell Nelson, class clown of '61, aimed the spotlight at them in the gym bleachers, and Spencer and Jemmabeth Chase squinted into the beam. Spence grinned, then laid a second kiss on his wife, before she had her breath back. This moment would be the hot topic at Nedra's Beauty Parlor & Craft Nook for weeks, so Spencer figured he might as well enjoy himself. Darrell was supposed to be setting up to highlight the homecoming queen, but he couldn't resist exposing the popular newlywed alumni instead, eliciting wolf whistles from their peers, mixed with shocked gasps from the more aged alumni seated below.

❧

On the gym floor, a pair of dark eyes followed the couple's every move, and red lips coiled into a wicked smile. So what if Jemmabeth Forrester had finally become Mrs. Spencer Chase? Nothing was ever set in stone. Things could always change and Melissa Blake was up to any challenge, especially when it came to Spencer.

Melissa, covertly known in high school as The Cleave for her magnificent bosom, edged over to talk with Twila Baker for lack of excitement and an escort.

❧

"You forgot your name tag, Missy. Here, pin this on." Twila shoved a CLASS OF '63 label at her. "I thought you were engaged to a doctor. What happened?"

"I don't use Missy anymore. I'm Melissa now, remember? I've been Melissa for several years." The Cleave threw back her mane of blond hair. "It didn't work out with the med student. He said he was too busy for partying. Twila, you really should get your nails done since you work at a beauty shop." She rolled her eyes toward the bleachers. "What's the deal with those two? Nobody acts like that once they're married."

Twila didn't like The Cleave bossing her around, nor did she care for her tone about the newlyweds. She smiled up at them. "They are the most romantic couple ever. It's like a fairy tale."

"I don't know why I'm asking you, one of Jemmartsybeth's fan club. Anyway, it's more like creepy," Missy said. "It's not like they haven't been boyfriend and girlfriend since birth."

"I wish Buddy and I could say that." Twila patted her generous stomach. "Of course, we have other things to think about now."

"If they keep it up, Jemma's going to be borrowing your tent tops before she planned to. Getting pregnant is the ultimate disaster for people like me. It ruins your figure and you get little stretch marks that don't look good in a bikini." The Cleave turned to check out a young male teacher.

"That guy's married, Missy. How would you know about stretch marks, anyway? I've never looked good in a one-piece, much less a bikini. I bet Jemma does, though. She's got the figure for it."

"She's too tall. I'm about as tall as you can get and still look. . . what's that word. . .to men."

Twila raised her shoulders. "Half naked? No, I reckon that's two words."

"You don't even know what I'm talking about. Vul. . .vul. . ."

"Vulture? Vulgar? How come I know more words than you do? I didn't even get to college."

"*Vunerable.* That's it. I still look vunerable to men," Missy said. "Jemma probably won't even let him dance with anybody else."

"I never heard that word before. You sure you're sayin' it right?" Twila counted the ticket money again, making sure the bills were all facing the same way. She hoped Missy would leave, but she parked herself, instead, on the edge of the table. An elderly attendee dropped her jaw at Missy's miniskirt.

"Everything always goes so perfect for Miss Artsy," Missy said. "It's like she has some special secret or something, and don't throw that religious junk at me either. My mother heard that she and Spence go to the colored church about half the time. She also says that if Brother Hightower had any backbone, he would have them kicked out of his church for praying across the tracks. My family doesn't need church. Daddy says he's just as close to God watching *Goldfinger* as he would be if he were listening to some idiot trying to make him feel guilty. Anyway, where's Jemma's Twinkie? I wish she'd had a baby. It would have totally ruined her figure."

"Sandy's livin' in Idaho. Marty got a job up there on a potato farm, working for his uncle, but I don't think Sandy likes it very much. How about you, Missy? What are you doing now that you've graduated from UT?" Twila paused to take ticket money from a cluster of blue-haired ladies.

"Twila, can you say Mah-liss-ah? You should get a frost job on your hair. It would soften that dishwater-blond look." She fingered her own flaxen tresses. "I work for an accountant in Amarillo, and my boss says that he couldn't make it through the day without me."

"Oh, that's right," Twila said. "I heard your mom say that you were wastin' your education in the copy room. Are those machines hard to run?"

"I may go out to Hollywood and get in the movies. It wouldn't be all that hard since my daddy owns nine movie theaters now—he has the connections." Melissa turned her attention back to the bleachers. "Look at them. Too bad she didn't marry that cowboy from Dallas. I heard he's a wild man."

"Give it up, Missy. You never had a chance with Spencer and you know it. You always were so jealous of Jemma."

"Shut up. I've never been jealous of anybody." Missy curled her lip. "I just remember how good he looked in his football uniform."

"Guys all look alike in those."

"Then you weren't looking very well."

"I only had eyes for Buddy B." Twila squinted toward the stage where her husband's band was setting up. "Anyway, Spencer is married now, so it's too late."

"It's never, ever too late." Missy cut her indigo eyes again at the Chases.

Twila's baby kicked as Melissa Blake, the only girl in their class who could afford braces, eased off the table and slithered away.

Twila rearranged the name tags and smoothed her new maternity top over her middle. She had to be doing something right. The homecoming committee had put her in charge of the registration table for the third year in a row. She moved her chair under her own handmade sign, 1869–1969: ONE HUNDRED YEARS OF CHILLATON HIGH SCHOOL. The sign wasn't easy to make, either, what with her big belly and all. Not to mention she had to do it over after Leon Shafer told her there was no apostrophe in *years*. Smart aleck. No wonder he was still single.

The old gymnasium glistened with twisted maroon and white crepe-paper streamers, gold balloons, and gold confetti that littered the hardwood floor. Early alumni, who would rather not sit on concrete bleachers and endure the chilly autumn football game, had dutifully signed their name tags. They engaged in hushed conversations on folding chairs that lined the gym, waiting for the onslaught of the after-game crowd and the musical gyrations that would follow.

A wayward sparrow had also entered the gym. It repeatedly propelled itself into a closed window, thus stirring some excitement for those with corrective lenses. The janitor and Buddy Baker finally guided it to an open pane. Ladies fresh from Nedra's Beauty Parlor and Craft Nook heaved a collective sigh of relief that their various shades of lavender and blue coiffures would not be soiled from above. This brush with anxiety, however, would be given some verbal attention because nothing much escaped Nedra's Nook. The sign in the window put her gossip mill on the map: HAIR'S WHERE IT ALL BEGINS. Twila waved at Buddy B and grinned so wide that she loosened the spit curl from her cheek that Nedra had plastered with Aqua Net.

Unless they were preoccupied marking off days in the county jail, graduates showed up faithfully to the CHS Homecoming. Legendary reunion stories of selflessness and sacrifice were handed down like family legacies. On one such occasion, the notorious Donnie Pitts, class of '58, snuck out of the county facility by hiding in the jail Dumpster when he was trusted to empty the trash. He rinsed off in the river and showed up at the 1960 CHS homecoming celebration, only to be arrested by Sheriff Ezell during the first dance. Cleta Naylor, class of 1899, claimed she hadn't missed a homecoming in seventy years, but had passed away a month shy of this one. Her parting words were cordial expressions of regret to the homecoming committee. That was how Panhandle people did things. This year would be no exception as far as Twila could tell. She had already collected well over three hundred dollars, and the evenin' was young, as they say in Texas.

Twila kept an eye on Jemma and Spencer, but not so they'd notice. Like she'd said, they were the perfect couple, always had been. Jemmabeth had that long, wavy auburn hair that Twila had always wanted, plus she'd been Miss Everything at CHS. Now she was putting Chillaton on the map with her art but was still a sweet girlfriend. It was only her second month to be Mrs. Spencer Chase, Mr. Everything. He was, in everybody's opinion, the cutest boy to ever graduate from CHS. Besides being the quarterback, he was consistently class favorite, class president, and finally, class valedictorian. Now that he was over twenty-one, he was the richest man in the Panhandle. Sometimes Twila dreamed about being married to him herself. In her dreams they traveled all over the world inspecting the humongous buildings he had designed as an architect, and every night he proposed to her all over again because she was so beautiful and smart.

Spencer and Jemma emerged from the bleachers and visited with some of the older alumni. All heads turned because there was just something about them. They were such good people, Twila thought, but things had not always been perfect for them. Jemma nearly croaked in that wreck, then Spencer went missing in Vietnam. Missy just saw what she wanted to. What most people didn't know was that the couple had made a promise in the eighth grade to not fool around until they were married. That's probably why now they couldn't carry on a decent conversation without looking around the room to find one another. It wasn't pathetic at all; it was their reward for keeping the promise.

Twila scratched her belly. She and Buddy B tried to have a pact like that, but it was too hard to keep. They'd been married now for six years, so surely it was safe to have a baby and not get talked about at Nedra's.

The Buddy Baker Band blasted out their first number, "Try a Little Tenderness." Buddy B had added a little zip by pulling in Toby Watkins to play the saxophone. Leon Shafer, Dwayne Cummins, and Wade Pratt had been in Buddy's band since high school. It wouldn't be homecoming without them.

⊰❦⊱

Jemma and Spencer moved onto the floor, never losing eye contact and moving, as always, like smooth satin. Spencer wore his signature black turtleneck, and Jemma's long legs were tucked into knee boots topped with a leather skirt and a white silk blouse, both purchased by her husband.

"Go home with me, woman," he said over the music.

She gave him The Look. "I keep it in mind," she said, using their private joke from an old Paul Newman movie.

The gym filled quickly after the game. The Cleave followed Spencer to the refreshment table when Jemma finally took a break.

"Hi there, old married man." Missy poked a manicured finger into his chest. She moved in close so that her neckline displayed her namesake. "Wanna dance? Unless, of course, you aren't allowed to do things like that with me anymore." Her eyes roamed around his face.

Spencer smiled, somewhat. "I'm probably allowed, but I think I'll sit this one out."

"C'mon, are you scared of her? There was a time when you weren't."

"Nope. Not scared, just don't want to, Melissa. Thanks, anyway." Spencer walked away to have a few words with Darrell, the spotlight man.

⊰❦⊱

Missy was ruffled. Spencer had never really dated her, but when he and Jemma broke up for a year in college, she had gone out with him a few times. She should have seized the moment then and hooked him somehow, but he never had had eyes for anybody except her old archrival, the ever-present Jemmabeth Forrester. He could have at least danced one little song with her. It wouldn't have killed him.

⊰❦⊱

"Jemmabeth Chase, come on up here," Buddy B schmoozed into the microphone. "Until recently, Jemma has been singing in our band. Let's give her a round of applause and maybe she'll help us out one more time." The band played the intro to "Chain of Fools."

Jemma stepped up to the mike. The saxophone sounded good. She took a deep breath and let loose her husky alto voice. Spencer didn't think he would ever get over being her husband. He was practically in a trance when she finished.

He led her outside and pinned her against the bricks. "That's it. We're going home or to the river. Take your pick. Did you sing like that when I was in Vietnam?"

"Sure. It was your big idea, mister," she said. "You wanted me to sing with the band so you could think about me being happy."

"I didn't know you would be belting out soul music and making every guy in the gym grin like Gomer Pyle."

"I looked right at you the whole time."

"I know, but the gym's not exactly empty. You are too much for me to handle." He ran his finger under her chin. "Now let's go home. I'll warm up the 'Vette."

"Nope. Buddy's gonna play 'Candy Man' in a minute, and I've been looking forward to it."

"We can dance at the apartment. Mr. Orbison sings it better anyway." He knew the pout she was giving him. "Okay, just 'Candy Man,' then we're gone." The wind kicked up and flapped a homecoming banner against the building. Jemma's hair swirled around her like an open umbrella. He kissed her again.

"Cut that out and let's go back inside," she said and dragged him away just in time for their special version of the Chillaton Stomp.

Melissa Blake left when Spencer curled his finger at Jemma as she danced around him. He never even took his eyes off his bride to check out Missy's new red miniskirt. She'd bought it just in the hope that he would.

Meanwhile, the frazzled sparrow blinked and shook his head again. The world remained somewhat out of focus since his collision with the window. He hopped along the telephone line a few feet, then darted off, away from the loud gymnasium and its tricky windows. The sparrow's path was aligned for a few blocks with that of a silver Corvette. They parted ways at the flashing red light where Main

Street met the state highway to Amarillo. The little bird rested on the line again as the Corvette's tires squealed into action below, headed for home.

≈∞≈

Lizbeth Forrester and Lester Timms were an hour early, as planned. Now they had plenty of extra time to spend in the waiting room of the Amarillo airport. On top of that, the loudspeaker blasted out the news that the flight was going to be late.

Lizbeth had chosen to wear her best Sunday dress. She would be wearing the same outfit to church the next day, and was relieved to see nobody else from Chillaton was at the airport. She paced around with her Sunday purse dangling securely from her folded arms.

Lester adjusted his wedding/funeral tie and double-checked that his new white shirt was tucked into his khakis. He'd been yakking nonstop. "Like I've said before, Miz Liz, when I worked for the Burlington Line there weren't near as many late runs with the railroad like there are with the airplane business. No, sir, we kept things goin'." He squinted and checked his gold watch for the tenth time.

"We've been over this before, Lester. The trains were not always punctual. That's just your convenient memory at work. Besides, you were the stationmaster. How could you keep the trains on time? Wouldn't that be the engineer's job?" Lizbeth touched her hair to see if Nedra had sprayed it well enough to withstand the steady surge of Panhandle wind predicted through the weekend.

"Well, sir, you'd be surprised. There was the ticketin' of the passengers. That's a whole other story. I took care of the mail—comin' and goin'. Now, that was a job and a half, and I was the signalman to boot. When them trains come through, I was one busy feller, and if I was the least bit behind, they could get even behinder."

"I suppose you were rebuilding the track when there wasn't a train coming."

"No, sir, that was somebody else's job. I had to do the bookwork, you know, keepin' account of folks and packages, plus there was the telegraph to run. Did I ever tell you about the time that I caught Shorty Knox rummagin' through the parcel post cart? We like to have scared each other to death."

592

The arrival of the flight interrupted him.

"I think I missed that story," Lizbeth said, watching the attendants open the double doors for emerging passengers.

Lester felt his silver moustache again for crumbs. It wasn't often that a man his age got to shine in the presence of two fine-looking widow women.

Helene Neblitt, dressed in a royal blue linen suit with her white hair impeccably tucked into a bun, was one of the last passengers to appear. She adjusted her hearing aid, then smiled.

"Hello, my dear ones," she said, coming toward them with outstretched arms. "Lester, you are looking quite dapper today," she added in her Cambridge-educated accent.

Lester blushed. She always made him feel like he was Errol Flynn.

"Helene, you never look like you have been traveling. How do you manage that?" Lizbeth asked.

"It's my English upbringing, I suppose. We were so proper that neither a wrinkle nor a wisp of hair would dare appear, unbidden. I am quite grateful to be away from the bustle of Dallas."

"I'll fetch your bags, Miz Helene; you two ladies just relax." Lester strode off, carrying himself upright as best he could. He admired Helene's perfect posture and didn't want to look any older than he was.

⁕

An hour later, they sat around Lizbeth's shiny chrome and yellow kitchenette in Chillaton, drinking coffee and catching up on things.

"So, tell me, how are Jemmabeth and Spencer?" Helene asked.

Lizbeth smiled. "They are the happiest pair you'll ever see. It'll make you feel good just to be around them."

"Married life sure does agree with them two, and it don't look like it's about to wear thin, neither." Lester tapped his foot on the uneven black-and-white-checkered linoleum. "I never had that kind of lovey-dovey feelin' last this long with any of my women folk, exceptin' maybe Pretty Paulette." He shifted in his chair and blushed at that memory.

"Jemma and Spencer could have one of those romantic marriages that one reads about now and again," Helene said. "When may I expect to see them?" The way she said *Zhemma* instead of Jemmer enchanted Lester.

"They'll drive down from Amarillo tomorrow. She's anxious to tell you about their honeymoon in Scotland. I think she has more than a few painting ideas from the trip. My Cameron always wanted to see Scotland. It was his parents' homeland. I think Jemmabeth wanted to go there because of that. She's just like her grandfather, I suppose." Lizbeth smiled at the thought of Cam in his father's kilt on every holiday, worn sometimes just so she could pretend to be irritated with him for showing his legs.

⚜

Across the tracks, Joe Cross put the last of the dishes away and changed into his Sunday-go-to-meetin' shirt. His wife sang in the bathroom as she finished up her primping. He smiled. He didn't know how good things could be in this world. The Lord had heaped blessings on him, but letting him marry Willa Johnson in his early middle years was the best one of all. Willa made him laugh, cooked better than he ever did in the Coast Guard, danced like a Methodist woman, and best of all, she had a heart for the Lord.

"What are you thinkin' about, Joe?" she asked, peeking around the door.

"You. I was countin' my blessings, and you're all of 'em rolled into one."

"Come here and let me kiss you for that."

He went. He'd be a fool not to take her up on that offer.

"You are lookin' mighty fine tonight, Mrs. Cross. Maybe we should just stay home, lovey."

"We'll be home early. I gotta go see Miz Helene and find out how my baby's doin' at that fancy school. Ain't nobody nicer than them two white women. They're my travelin' buddies, too. Both of 'em got college degrees. Did you know that?"

Joe nodded and helped her down the steps, then tucked the cobbler she'd baked under his arm. It was still warm.

"You sure you don't want to ride over?" he asked.

"No, sir, I'm walkin'. The doctor said I needed to work this old leg, and I'm gonna do it. Now, you see if you can keep up with me." She took off at a slow but steady pace across the road and up toward the tracks. They might as well have been teenagers the way they carried on, but she loved it.

⟨⟨⟩⟩

"I thought I could hear somethin' besides Texas being spoke," Willa shouted through Lizbeth's back porch screen. She came inside and spread her arms like an eagle, then lifted Helene's petite frame off the floor.

"You are maneuvering much better," Helene said. "What has become of your cane?"

Willa laughed. "Don't need that old stick now that I had me some work done on my hip. It pays to marry a rich man," she whispered.

"Drivin' a semi don't exactly make me a rich man, lovey." Joe set his cowboy hat on the foldout kitchen stool and smiled at the women, wondering if they'd seen him carrying on with Willa on the tracks. The floor creaked as he moved to stand beside her.

"Here, you two have a seat," Lizbeth said. "Joe, would you like some coffee?"

"Thank you, ma'am, I'd be obliged. Willa's been spoilin' me with her cookin'. My mouth was waterin' the whole time I was carrying that cobbler. How are you doin', Miz Helene?"

"Everything is lovely, thank you. Marriage seems to be the rage around here. I guess I'll have to find me a companion," she said.

Lester cleared his throat. "I hear lots of hammerin' across the tracks. How's your project comin' along, Joe?"

"We're movin' ahead right smart with the remodelin'. 'Course I'm not here all the time, so it's been a slow deal."

"Folks are gonna start callin' it the Cross castle," Willa said. "It'll be the finest thing ever built in colored town, that's for sure. Exceptin' Spencer's chapel at our church, of course."

"How's Latrina doin', Miz Helene?" Joe asked.

"She's doing well and sends her love. She's very involved with a project of her own right now or she would have come with me."

"It's sure good of you to let my baby girl live with you like this. She's gonna be all cultured up by the time she graduates from that clothes designin' school. I just hope she can find a job," Willa said. "She may have to start cleanin' houses again."

"Quite the contrary, Willa. Trina is very talented. There must be something about your little village that nurtures artistic giftedness to have three outstanding young people emerge from it."

"Panhandle wind," Lester said. "It starts whippin' Chillaton's young folks into shape as soon as they draw breath, sorta like one of them sculptor fellers."

Lizbeth excused herself and went to check the extra bedroom one more time. She wanted everything to be perfect for Helene's stay. She fluffed the pillows again, then walked through the "good" bedroom—hers and Cam's. It was the nicest one, but there was no privacy for a guest since it connected the living room to the kitchen.

Cam liked to tease her about their quirky little house, but she loved it for that very reason. She touched his photograph on the dresser. He would have enjoyed Helene's company, but he really would have gotten a kick out of Willa and Joe, if only he'd taken that first step across the tracks. Lizbeth often wondered if she would've ever made their acquaintance herself, if it weren't for Jemmabeth's example. Lizbeth sighed and returned to the kitchen. She uncovered Willa's cobbler and passed out generous helpings, then scooped out some for herself. Willa's was always better than hers, and she couldn't figure out her secret. Maybe she could get Joe to tell her.

"Willa, you should enter your cobbler in the fair this year," Lizbeth said. "It's by far the best I've ever tasted. I don't suppose you are willing to share your secret, are you?"

Willa laughed. "Ain't no secret, Miz Liz, just habit. Mercy, them fussy ladies don't want no colored woman stickin' her cobbler on the same shelf as theirs. Joe and me went to the Cotton Festival last month. It was all they could do to let us look at them pies and whatnot. I don't want to stir up no trouble."

"Fiddlesticks," Lizbeth said. "I know all the womenfolk who enter that contest and they are all good, Christian people. You should give it a try."

"Sometimes the Christian folks are the last ones to come around to things, Miz Liz. You know that," Willa said. "That's exceptin' Jemma. Them two girls was brought together by the good Lord Himself."

"All I know for sure is that you are supposed to be calling me Lizbeth on a regular basis. It's taking you a good while to come around to that. I'm going to start calling you Miz Willa if you don't watch out."

Lester raised his brow at Lizbeth. He knew that tone. Funny that she never gave him trouble for calling her Miz Liz. It had to be something about him being a man and her still loving Cameron. He wondered, too, if Cam Forrester ever knew what a lucky old boy he was.

Jemma couldn't wait for Spencer to wake up. Being with him as his wife was more than she could stand. It sometimes made her feel guilty. She wrote her new name on his back, waking him up.

He turned over and smiled. "Mornin', my love," he mumbled.

"I'm going to cook breakfast for you. Do you want cereal or toast?" she asked.

"Hmmm. . .they both sound so delicious, but way too hard for my baby to cook. How about we just snuggle? We can pick up some doughnuts on the way to Chillaton."

Jemma stood up on the bed and hit him with her pillow. "I can cook toast! You take that back." She whacked him again. He grabbed her ankles and threatened to yank her off her feet if she didn't stop.

An hour later, they had forgotten all about breakfast and had to hustle just to arrive at Lizbeth's in time for lunch.

Helene could see what everyone was saying about the new-lyweds. They stopped in the hollyhock patch behind the house, laughing and kissing, before they came in. She knew that feeling but hadn't felt it in decades.

Jemma shared her honeymoon photo album and her sketchbook with the group. "I'm working on some portraits that you will like," she said. "Time seems to have stopped in some of the Scottish villages. Our favorite, of course, was Kilton. That's where Papa's family came from. There's even a little castle right on the shore."

"It's not ancient, but it's old enough," Spencer said, rubbing Jemma's shoulders. "It's for sale, too, in case you're interested, Lester."

"How do you like living so close to home?" Helene asked.

"It's great," Spencer said. "Of course we don't really care where we live right now. We're just happy to be together, finally." He refrained from kissing her in front of the silver-haired group, but he considered it.

"Spence just took the architectural job in Amarillo because they were so good to him during his internship there. We won't stay there long."

"They're too conservative for my style, but it's good experience for an upstart like me." Spencer winked at Lester, who liked to call him that.

"Are you thinking of starting a family anytime soon?" Helene asked.

"No." Jemma's inflection made Lizbeth flinch. "We are going to enjoy one another's company without any distractions for a long time."

"I see," Helene said. "Well, don't wait too long, my dears. Nebs and I regretted our decision to postpone that part of our lives."

"I haven't seen Vincent around today," Jemma said, making sure that the baby topic didn't continue.

"Oh, that cat roams all over the neighborhood. He'll show up." Lizbeth opened the door to the walk-in pantry and brought out a three-layered, coconut crème cake, Spencer's favorite. He whistled and made room on the table for it.

"Jemmerbeth, have you made your Gram's coconut cake yet for your mister?" Lester asked, accepting a fat piece for himself.

"No, sir. I haven't learned how to make much of anything yet. Do you think he looks thinner?" She squeezed Spencer's biceps.

"You were learning culinary skills quite well when you were in Wicklow," Helene said. "As I recall, you prepared a whole meal in the continental style, with a little help, of course." Helene savored her first bite of cake, eyes closed in appreciation. She couldn't see Jemma giving her the signal to hush about that summer.

"Jemma's getting ready for her next show right now. She'll take on cooking skills when she has the time," Spencer said.

"Nice one," Jemma whispered.

Spencer looked up with a mouthful and grinned. Jemma touched his chin where a stray shred of coconut rested and put it in her mouth. Spence widened his eyes and raised his brow. She wrinkled her nose at him.

Lizbeth watched their antics with a sudden longing for the early days of her own marriage when she and her Cameron had teased and flirted. She understood Jemma's impassioned reply to the question of starting a family. As much as Lizbeth loved her babies, she would have enjoyed another few years of foolishness with Cam.

"Vincent caught two mice today, both at the same time, Jemma," Helene said, as the great hunter himself took a seat on the windowsill outside. "I saw him carrying them around."

"How did he accomplish that?" Jemma asked.

"I'm not quite sure, but my Chelsea could take a lesson from him. She does nothing all day but sleep."

"Well, sir, you've got your mousers and your moochers. I had me a time once with some cats," Lester said. "I was between womenfolk when it happened. Must've been between Bertie and Mae Ella. No, sir, I take that back. It was after Zippy run off and, after a few years, The Judge give me the go-ahead to look around for a fourth one."

Lizbeth cleared her throat.

Lester hooked his thumbs under his suspenders that he had only recently begun wearing to hold up his sagging pants. "I took a notion to join the ladies' bridge club, and they seemed real pleased to have me. When it come my turn to be the host, I had the house cleaned up good, and plenty of vittles on the sideboard. All was well until out of nowheres a field mouse come hence to waltzin' across the floor. It sat up on its haunches and grinned right at us. Now you can imagine how embarrassin' that would be in a refined social situation like a bridge club gatherin'. All my prospects for a missus lifted their feet and squealed. That mouse just kept on grinnin' like old Beelzebub himself. I chased him off, but the damage was done." Lester shook his head and tapped his foot on the linoleum.

"Where's the cat in that story?" Lizbeth asked.

"It's comin'. I had me a bigger problem than just the one mouse critter. Seems like word got out that old Lester's place was a rodent hotel. So I come hence to lettin' folks around town know that I was in need of a cat. Well, sir, in one day's time I had me a dozen. I never saw another mouse, but then I had me a cat situation. I took a notion to use 'em to my advantage. I went down to the five-and-dime and bought a sack full of ribbons and tied a bow around every one of them cats, which wasn't easy. I loaded up three at a time in my truck and drove from one bridge-playin' prospect to another and give each one of them ladies a purrin' pet for a present. It was a big hit."

Spencer smiled at Jemma. "Does this mean that the way to a woman's heart is through a cat?"

"I wouldn't go that far, son. Them ladies must have talked amongst themselves because not a single one of 'em would give me the time of day after a week or so. I got kicked out of the bridge club, too, but at least I got rid of the mice. I know how you hate the varmints, Miz Liz."

"I had no idea that you enjoyed bridge, Lester. I'm a founding member of the Wicklow Bridge Club," Helene said. "Find us two more players and we're set. But not to worry, dear, I already have a fat feline at home."

⧫

Paul Turner pulled the baby blue pickup into his driveway. He set his briefcase on the kitchen table, hung his Stetson on his great-grandmother's hall tree, then sank on the couch to pull off his new boots. They were killing him. He should've broken them in around the house instead of the courtroom. He leaned back against the cushions and stared at the painting of the girl holding the firefly. She remained his heart's only desire. She made him laugh and feel good about himself until she found out that he was a married man. Actually, he was a separated man, not that such a detail mattered to a good Christian girl like her. It was over with before he could get his mother's ring out of the safety deposit box at the bank. He hadn't lied to her, but he hadn't exactly told her the truth, either. That was his everlasting shame and that's how he had lost his Jemma.

The phone rang, but he let it go. It was probably one of his sisters checking up on him. They would have loved her, too, but he could never risk introducing them. They might have let it slip about his pending divorce. He stretched and looked around his house. No amount of substitutes could fill the void she'd left and he had tried, too. She had made the place come alive with her joy that summer, and she never even stepped foot in it.

Paul unfolded the *Dallas Morning News* while his TV dinner cooled off. He flipped through the sports pages, then, as usual, scanned the arts and entertainment section. There it was on the first page: JEMMABETH CHASE SET TO SHOW AT THE GALLERY AT HIGHLAND PARK. His heart jumped, and he spread the newspaper on the coffee table.

He read it twice, then cut it out and put it on his fridge. It didn't matter to him that she was a married woman now. He couldn't wait to see her.

⁂

Jemma knocked on the bathroom door. "Spence, I found some photos of soldiers in Vietnam. Could I use them for the French magazine thing? I need to give them several to choose from. Is that okay?"

Spencer emerged, drying his hair with a towel. "Sure, I haven't had the heart to look at them since I got back. Use whatever you need, baby."

Jemma grinned. "I'm counting to two and you'd better be back in that bathroom with the door locked, or you're going to be in trouble. One, one and a half."

"Two," Spencer said and was almost late to work.

⁂

The extra bedroom was becoming a canvas jungle. She wanted to save space for Spencer to have a desk in the corner. It was her plan to fix up a little office for him, but she had spent all her time on the landscapes and portraits for the Dallas show. The French magazine, *Nouvelle Liberte*, had given her a deadline for the Vietnam pieces. It had only taken her two weeks to paint the five photos she had selected. Three were action scenes, showing Spencer's Medevac team working on the wounded. One showed a member of the team resting on the ground, holding the hand of a young man on a stretcher, and she was just finishing up a group portrait of Spencer's crew celebrating Christmas around a little wire and fabric tree that Jemma had mailed to him.

He came in late. Jemma hadn't even noticed the time, nor had she stopped, even for lunch. "What do you think, babe?" she asked and moved away from the easel for his response.

Spencer sank to the floor and leaned his head against the wall. He started to speak, but instead, covered his face with his hands.

She dropped her brush. "What have I done? Oh Spence, I'm so sorry."

He tried to say something about being okay, but a fiendish moan shifted around in his throat and then unleashed itself with a fury. He sobbed and Jemma cradled him until it was over. The apartment was totally dark when they stopped talking. It was the first time he had really shared his grief over the horrendous attack on his helicopter and crew in Vietnam. He had confided the details of his own rescue before but always avoided the deaths of his Medevac team members. Jemma had never pressed the topic on the advice of her daddy, Jim. It came out just as he had said it would, when least expected.

They went out for hamburgers and got home late. He was staring at the painting when it was time for their nightly prayer. "Those poor guys. They worked their hearts out." He exhaled and took her hand, then read Psalm 4:8 aloud: " 'I will both lay me down in peace, and sleep: for thou, Lord, only makest me dwell in safety.'"

Jemma bowed her head. "Heavenly Father, we thank You for delivering Spencer from certain death in a time of war. We thank You for the men and women who worked so hard to rescue soldiers despite the dangers, and we pray for the families of those who didn't make it home, that they might find peace in their hearts. Amen."

Chapter 2

English Leather

Jemma took her paintings to Lester's house so he could build shipping crates for them and Lizbeth watched. "Which one do you like best, Gram?" Jemma yelled over Lester's pounding.

"Help my life, honey, do I have to choose?" She moved around the room, studying them again. "I like the whole lot. This one is really nice, but I just don't understand how you can paint yourself so well."

Jemma put her arm around her grandmother. "That was easy. Spencer took a hundred photos of me on our honeymoon. I liked the old guy who is showing me the dance step in this painting. He was full of the dickens."

"All of them old fellers look like they're getting' a kick out of watchin' you dance, Jemmer. Did Spencer get kindly jealous?" Lester asked.

"Everybody in that pub was three times our age. It was fun, though."

"A pub?" Lizbeth arched her brow. "Isn't that what they call a bar over there?"

"Yes ma'am, but sometimes it's the only place you can get a meal. At night they had great fiddle music, too. Gram, we didn't drink."

Lizbeth sniffed. "Well, back to my choice. The lady hanging her wash while the children play in the basket reminds me of your daddy. Jimmy loved to get in my laundry basket when he was a baby. I like these, too." She pointed to the four pieces of village children.

Lester stopped hammering. "Nobody asked me yet, but I prefer the boat captain, myself. I helped out on a boat one time. I'll have to tell you about that job. It didn't work out too well, seein' as how I'm not a sailin' man. That castle is mighty good, too. It's like we could just walk in them big doors."

"Thanks. I already sent the watercolors for the magazine to choose from. They are all of soldiers in Vietnam. Mom just told us that my cousin, Trent, will be getting out in January."

"That's wonderful, sugar. I know his father will be glad of that. Isn't he an engineer?" Lizbeth asked.

"Yes ma'am, but they had him calculating formulas to blow up roads and bridges while he was in Vietnam. He didn't get to build anything. Uncle Ted is throwing a big welcome home celebration at his beach house in California. He wants y'all to come, too."

"We'll have to see about that. Lester and I are getting on in years, aren't we?" Lizbeth shouted.

"You bet; these crates will last for years. You'll be fat and sassy with ten young'uns before these wear out, Jemmerbeth," Lester shouted back, banging away.

Lizbeth snickered, then motioned for Jemma to follow her to the car house, Cam's name for their garage, where Jemma had created so many of her masterpieces before she and Spencer married.

"Look at this," Lizbeth said and placed a Mason jar in her hand. "I found it on one of the chairs in the hollyhock patch."

Jemma unscrewed the lid and took out two folded sheets of Big Chief notebook paper. "Oh Gram, these are drawings that Shorty Knox has done. How sweet. He's trying to draw flowers, see?"

Lizbeth frowned at the scribbles. "Hmmm. If you say so. I hope he's not snooping around here again."

"Don't worry, Gram. With his TV and now his drawing hobby, he's too busy to take up the peeping Tom business."

Lizbeth pursed her lips.

Jemma smiled. "Besides, I owe Shorty a lot. I'll draw him something and put the jar back on the chair. He'll like that."

⊰⊱

Jemma met Spencer at the airport. It was like they'd been apart for a month rather than all day.

"Mother's coming home the week before Christmas," Spencer said as they drove home. "She looked better than I've ever seen her, but who knows? She's been living in that halfway house for six months, but once she gets home, she may fall back into her old drinking routine."

Jemma thought back to the time at the country club's New Year's dance when Rebecca Chase, not totally drunk, gave her a verbal lambasting for breaking up with her son. "She could surprise you," she managed at last. "How's your dad doing?"

"Surprisingly well. He's going to bring her home himself and he's taking off a week from work to help her adjust. He really turned on the charm in Waco, but it makes me nervous—like he's up to something."

"I think your dad has changed his ways, Spence. He and I had some good talks when you were in Vietnam and I like him."

Spencer frowned at her. "Are you sure he wasn't trying to hit on you? I wouldn't put it past him."

"Spencer! He was really sweet and remorseful. He was afraid that you would be punished for his skirt-chasing sins and never come home."

"Yeah, well, he *has* been decent to me since I got home, but I bet it won't last. It'll be a contest to see what happens first—Mother gets drunk or Dad gets a new lady friend." He threw the Corvette into another gear and they flew down the highway. Jemma looked over her shoulder to see if there were any police cars trying to keep up.

❧

"Rats. I don't want to go alone," Jemma said, throwing toiletries in her makeup bag. "It's not fair for them to make you change your plans. It's our first time apart."

"I agree, baby, but I'm the low man on the totem pole. It'll be exciting when you get back. Just think about that. You call me as soon as you get there and every morning and night."

Spencer insisted that she fly and rent a car in Dallas for her show. He also wanted her to stay in a hotel and not go to Helene's. Cowboy lawyer Paul lived too close to Helene. Paul was the only competition that Spencer had ever worried about. Those feelings were history now, but it crept around in Spencer's mind, especially when she went anywhere near Dallas.

They compromised on her accommodations. She stayed Friday night with Helene and Trina, then Saturday, the opening day of the show, she booked a hotel room near the airport so she'd be ready to get home Sunday evening.

～✦～

A persistent drizzle seemed to bring out the art patrons. Jemma visited with the last few attendees on the soggy evening and looked around for Anne, the gallery manager, to say good-bye. She spotted a reporter from the *Dallas Morning News* and ducked behind a group of patrons. She did not enjoy being interviewed nor did she like being photographed by anyone but family. Someone else, however, touched her arm.

"Hello, darlin'," Paul said. "Are you trying to hide from me again?"

Jemma caught her breath. He was every bit as good-looking as the last time she saw him. His six-foot-five frame was leaner, too. His hair was a little longer, and those devil eyes were even greener. He had on his usual cowboy formal attire—white Western shirt, bolo tie, boots, and black felt hat. English Leather remained his aftershave of choice. She couldn't help it; her scalp tingled and her tongue twisted. "Paul, I'm just about to leave."

He grinned at her. "I like your work, but I like the real thing even better. You are one breathtaking woman, Jemmabeth." He moved a lock of her hair away from her forehead. She felt his hand touch her waist. A slight movement at her elbow caught her attention, and the flash of a reporter's camera brought her out of her daze.

"Miss Forrester," the reporter began.

"Mrs. Chase," Jemma corrected him.

Ignoring the correction, the reporter carried on with his questions. Jemma was polite but gave no details in her responses. She was aware that Paul had remained by her side and continued to keep his hand on her waist. She moved it away with her elbow, but it went right back and stayed there until the reporter left.

"I know you're glad that's over. At least he didn't ask who your favorite artists are," Paul whispered, implying a former awareness.

Jemma turned on him, her golden eyes narrowed squarely on his. "Move your hand, Paul." He complied, displaying his hands innocently. "Thank you," she said and hurried toward the exit.

He walked alongside her. "I just like to check on you, darlin'. I'm not breaking any laws. I keep up with that, you know. Besides,

I'm one of your best customers."

"Then as a lawyer, you should know you walk a fine line between friendliness and harassment toward me." Jemma picked up her pace.

Paul moved in front of her as they reached the foyer. "Look, Jem, I did what you said. I tried hard to find somebody to love. I even went to church once. There is nobody else I want. I know you love your husband, so what would it hurt for you to spend one evening with me? We could go to the Best Burger Stop. You'd be in control, I promise."

"No. I don't have anything to say to you. I don't love you, so get on with your life. Good-bye." She shoved the revolving door and stepped into the blowing rain.

"Jemmabeth, wait." A jet screamed above them in the night sky. "You don't know what it's like for me. Okay, I messed up by not telling you that I wasn't quite divorced, but you were so innocent. I was afraid I'd lose you. Now I've lost you anyway."

"It wasn't in God's plan, Paul," Jemma shouted over her shoulder. "I never stopped loving Spencer. You just stole my attention for a while. Now, please, leave me alone."

"C'mon, Jem, I've made a wild ride of this life. The women I've had meant nothing to me, but it was different with you. I loved you, darlin'. You wouldn't let me try anything, and I liked that. I need that feeling again. I loved being with you and just talking. What's the harm in that now?"

Lightning flashed, silhouetting the buildings, and raindrops freckled her face. He wiped them off her nose.

Jemma recoiled at his touch. "Go back to church, Paul. Maybe you'll find God. At the least, you might find a good woman there, but don't try your tricks with her."

"She won't be you. I can't help it that you put a spell on me. I can't shake it even after all this time. Besides, I have to tell you something," he said, touching her chin. "I need to explain more about that night of no mercy."

"Yeah, right. You mean the night of big truth? Why don't you write it on a business card and mail it to me? No, mail it to my husband. I bet he'd be interested in what you have to say, but I'm not."

"You hold that against me, too, don't you? I did everything wrong."

"Look, I've tried to be patient with this obsessive behavior of yours, but it's getting old. Now move; you're blocking my car."

"I love you, Jem," he said as she unlocked the door and slid in.

He bent down and pressed his hands against the window like a little boy looking in a candy store.

She rolled it down a little. "Paul, please, I have the life I want with Spencer. I adore him. We've been through this before, and it's time to let it go. You can't spend your whole life chasing after me. Remember the fireflies? You can't keep me bottled up like this in your head. You need to give me my freedom."

Paul squatted beside the car, head down. Rain dripped off the brim of his hat. "I know." He raised tear-filled eyes to hers. "Even though I was drunk, those last kisses I took from you have lasted me a long time. Could I have one while I'm sober?"

"No! What kind of wife do you think I am? I'm sorry that you can't find somebody to love, but I won't feed your fire. Good-bye, Paul."

She took her foot off the brake and let the car roll. He stood up. She backed out and left him standing in the parking lot.

❧

Spencer met her at the airport with a rose. His arms felt so good around her. "I missed you, baby. Are you tired? I don't think I've ever seen you like this, not even after the Lido game when you scored thirty points."

"Yeah, I guess I might be tired, but I'm glad to see you, too." She rested her head on his shoulder so he couldn't see her eyes. "I think I need some sleep."

"I can't believe I'm hearing this after our first full weekend apart." He felt her forehead. "You really must be getting sick or something. Get thee to bed, woman," he said as they pulled into the apartment complex.

❧

Jemma crawled under the covers. She decided not to tell Spence about the encounter. She didn't want Paul interfering with their bliss, as though she weren't worrying about it already.

Spencer lay beside her, stroking her cheek. "I hope you have sweet dreams and feel better tomorrow."

Rats on her worries; she couldn't resist him. Jemma reached for his face and kissed him. Big-time.

⁂

The apartment was quiet when she got up the next morning. Spencer had said something about an early appointment. She put on his robe and went downstairs, yawning. She got out the cereal and dumped some in her bowl, spilling a little of it on the counter. Popping the spilled bits in her mouth, she turned to get the milk and choked.

Taped to the refrigerator was a clipping from the *Dallas Morning News*. The photo was very clear. *Jemmabeth Forrester,* the caption read, *and an unnamed companion at The Gallery at Highland Park.* Paul was right beside her, his hand on her waist.

She ran to the phone with her heart pounding in her ears. Spencer's number rang, but he didn't answer—probably on purpose. She threw on some jeans and a paint shirt and raced to the bus stop, barefooted, just as it pulled away. She went home and called a taxi.

The smartly dressed secretaries looked up as she burst into the office. "I have to see Spencer."

"May I say who wishes to see him?" the older one asked, like they didn't recognize her.

Jemma was in no mood for games. "His wife."

There was an exchange of smug glances that she didn't miss.

"He's in a meeting right now, but I'll show you to his office." The younger of the two led the way to Spencer's corner of a vacant conference room. Jemma walked the floor for half an hour. She touched the things on his desk. Right by his phone was their wedding picture and next to it was a photo of her in the first grade wearing her red cowboy boots and a frilly dress. All she could think about was that telegram saying he was MIA. This was going to spoil their joy and change things. Tears, long overdue, poured out. She sat in his chair and tried to quell the urge to throw up.

The door opened and closed.

"Jemmabeth. I suppose we are going to talk about something," Spencer said with the same chilly voice that he had when he left for

Italy three years ago, when he had found out the truth about Paul.

Jemma jumped up and rattled off her side of the story, replete with wild gestures. "Spence, I swear to you that nothing happened in Dallas for me to be ashamed of, I promise. He showed up just as that photo was taken and put his hand on my waist. Babe, you have to believe me. He followed me to the parking lot and wanted to talk. I told him to go to church and to forget about me. It's the newspapers. They always assume things and get mixed up. I am so sorry. You know that I love you. Please forgive me for not telling you. I just wanted the whole thing to go away."

Spencer didn't move. Jemma wanted to hold him, but the iceberg that sank the *Titanic* loomed up between them. His phone rang, but his glare never wavered.

"I thought we were going to be honest in our marriage, Jem. I'm curious to know why you decided not to tell me about this. If I'd known, it wouldn't have been such a shock to see it in the newspaper. Can you imagine how that photo made me feel?"

Jemma clamped her hand over her mouth and nodded. She had messed up again. They were perfect until now, and it had to be her that ruined it. She was back to her Miss Scarlett days. She wanted to throw herself out the window. Instead, she got on her knees, like the beggar that she was. "I told you a long time ago that I don't deserve you. I'm just a fool. I tried to protect your feelings and instead I hurt you. I didn't want to spoil how we are, were. I am bad, Spence. I am a mean woman, just like you've said before."

Spencer sat on the floor next to her, keeping an arm's length between them. "You can't protect my feelings by hiding something like this from me. I'm a big boy, and it's not like I'm going to shoot the guy or something. We could've handled this together, like adults."

"I forgot about the photographer," she sobbed.

"Jem, that picture isn't the worst of this. It's that you kept the whole thing from me. I trusted you to take care of him, but Paul is obsessed with you and you don't seem to understand the danger of that. Besides, I don't think you know how I feel about him. I think he's a sorry jerk, but you obviously still have feelings for him or you would let me get a restraining order against him."

The crying came to an abrupt halt. "Excuse me? I do *not* have feelings for him! That is absolutely untrue." They both stood, and she looked him in the eye. "I didn't want him butting into this beautiful life we have, so I didn't tell you, and now look what's happened. You are my life. Paul came along back when what I really needed was you. I feel sorry for him now and that's it. I can't believe that you would even say such a thing! Don't you know me?"

Jemma turned toward the door and didn't stop. She was careful not to slam it, though, as she had been known to do when steaming mad. She even forced a smile at the secretaries as she left to prevent further looks between them. She bawled in the cab home, then tried to paint.

It was almost nine o'clock when she heard him. She'd gone to bed at eight to avoid another scene and had cried herself into a red-eyed mess.

Spencer turned on the television and watched mindlessly as shapes and colors flashed by on the screen. It was their first real fight since he had gone to Florence and left her to choose between him and Paul. When he opened the newspaper and saw the photograph, he was shot straight through the heart. He knew she loved him and he believed her story about the picture, but he didn't understand why she hadn't warned him. A friend of Jemma's told him once that artists don't think like other people do. He knew that. It was with her heart that she painted and that was the same way she lived her life. He had let Paul get to him. He wasn't mad at Jemma because he knew her too well. He didn't need anybody to tell him that she functioned on emotion. He was angry with Paul.

He went upstairs to their room and could tell that she was breathing through her mouth. He knew she had been crying all day until her nose was clogged. Their apartment normally smelled like paint and brush cleaner. He liked that smell because it meant she was working. He hadn't seen much progress on the easel today. She'd taken a bath, though. The tub still had a puddle of water left over, and he smelled her floral shampoo.

He'd spent the day thinking about how close to death she'd been after that wreck and what his life would've been like without her. Now, to be in their bed without holding one another was a first.

He had wanted her when she was his girlfriend and desired her while she was his fiancée, but they had denied themselves that privilege and reserved it for their married life. It had intensified their emotions and their physical relationship beyond his expectations. For the first time since their wedding night, he wasn't sure that she would want him to touch her. She had left the office madder than he was.

❦

Jemma had turned her back toward the door when she heard him coming up the stairs, and she held her breath as he came into the room. He didn't call out to her, but he did ease into his side of the bed. She listened to each breath he took and closed her eyes to hold back the tears. She hadn't felt this anxious since he was in Vietnam. He was hurting now and it was all her fault. Triple rats. Would she ever use her brain just once?

She didn't know how long she could lie there and not turn to him and beg again for his forgiveness. Sandy had accused her once of being born just to hurt him. That wasn't true, but he might never again look at her in public like he was ready to go home and love her. She sniffed and wiped her eyes.

He laid his hand on her arm, giving her goose bumps. She touched his fingertips. Spencer moved her hair and kissed her cheek, wet with tears.

She grabbed his neck and held him like a drowning woman. "I'm sorry again, Spence. I didn't mean to hurt you. I'm so stupid."

He put his finger on her lips, then moved it away and kissed her. It was the sweet, tender kiss of atonement.

Chapter 3
No Trouble At All

It was almost daybreak, and Jemma knew that she must look horrid after crying most of the day before. She tried not to wake her husband as she slipped out of bed and into the bathroom to check. Good grief. She appeared to have run into another truck. She put a wet washcloth over her face, hoping it would help, but it didn't. Spencer knocked on the door.

"You okay, Jem?"

"Yeah. I just look like I got beat up, that's all."

"Come back to bed, baby. I love you no matter what you look like."

"If you see me, you might kick me out of the house." She opened the door and stood there, looking pathetic.

He grinned. She did look bad.

She went back in the bathroom and shut the door, holding the washcloth under the faucet. Her head hurt, too. She squeezed out the cloth and opened the medicine cabinet to get some aspirin. Her birth control pill packet fell out on the countertop. A chill ran from her scalp to her toes. She raced to the bed and stood beside it with the dripping washcloth in her hand.

"I meant for you to get *in* the bed," he said, pulling her down.

"Spence, I think I'm in big trouble."

"What?" He sat up, wondering what she was going to tell him now.

"I forgot to take my b.c. pills for three nights."

"That's it? Well, what's the worst thing that can happen? We'll have a cute little baby. It was no trouble at all as far as I'm concerned." He snickered into the pillow.

"No! I want us to have a long time together before we have a baby." She threw the washcloth at the bathroom door. "Rats!"

Spencer got out of bed and held her. "Don't worry about this,

Jem. Whatever the Lord gives us, we'll be grateful. It won't affect our feelings."

"I know, but once you have children, you can't focus totally on each other. You won't be able to change my mind about this."

"I understand what you are saying, but there's nothing we can do about it now. We can't take back last night."

"I've caused this trouble, though. I've done it again."

"Jemmabeth. This is not trouble. This might be a change of plans, but to have a baby with you would be fantastic. You may not even be pregnant. Now hush and come back to bed."

She blew her red nose. "How did I ever get so lucky to have you love me?"

"It's not luck that brought us together, Jem. It was God's plan that you talk about."

"Maybe you're right. I'm probably not pregnant." She slid under the covers.

"I know one thing. You'd better go take that pill, woman," Spencer mumbled.

Over the next few days, the secretaries became used to Jemmabeth's unannounced entrances. "Hi," she'd say and point to his door. One of them would indicate if he was busy or not. She got the go-ahead this trip.

Jemma knocked on his door. "Mr. Chase," she said in a secretarial voice from the door. "Would you run away with me? I think I love you."

"Sure. I've been thinking the same thing about you. Just don't tell my wife. She has a terrible temper," he said. "Come here, you."

She sank into his lap. "I have to show you my letter." She waved it in front of his nose.

"A show in New York? How did this happen?"

"Anne, the gallery owner in Dallas, has connections with the Sabine Gallery in Manhattan. Can you believe it?"

"What are the dates again?" Spencer flipped through his desk calendar.

"It's your birthday weekend. If you can't go, it could be another year that we won't be together to celebrate."

"That's so far down the road. I'll talk to Mr. Chapman today and see what he thinks. Congratulations, Jem. I'm proud of you."

"Maybe I won't do it if you can't go."

There was a knock on the door as one of the secretaries stuck her head in with a patronizing smile. She had interrupted them on purpose. Probably wanted something to talk about at her coffee break.

"Mr. Chase, there's a call for you. I didn't want to disturb you, but it's important." She shrugged at Jemma. "Business."

⁂

Jemma cooked everything exactly the way her new cookbook said and was quite pleased with herself. It was ready way too early, though.

She called him anyway. "Babe, could you come home early? I cooked supper."

"It's only four thirty. Is this a special occasion and I forgot?"

"Nothing special. I guess I miscalculated the time and cooked all this stuff too soon. Maybe I can reheat it or you can eat it cold. Which do you want?"

He laughed. "I'll come home as soon as I can. You paint until I get there."

He managed to get home early, and she watched every bite he took. "Well?"

"It's good, really. I'm very impressed. I think you have raised ham to a higher standard." Spencer took a big swig of sweet tea.

"You're implying that ham is lowly food to start with." She jumped up and got the cookbook, propping it up in front of his plate. "See," she said, reading the title to him: *Elegant Meals for the Newlywed Chef.* I thought you would like it."

Spencer tried to hide a burp. "I don't know how you did all this and had time to paint, too. I really appreciate such a delicious meal." He burped again.

"Why do you keep burping? Is something wrong with the ham?"

"Maybe it's just the end piece. It has a little kick to it."

She looked at her recipe book again. "I did just what it says. See—'wash ham thoroughly.' I used plenty of Ivory liquid on it, too. Then I—"

"Wait. You put soap on the ham?"

"Of course. I just read you that part. 'Wash ham thoroughly.' I do know how to wash things." Their eyes met, then she burst into a fit of laughter. "Good grief! How dumb of me. Can you believe I did that? I must not have rinsed all the soap off. I did notice some big bubbles around the ham while it cooked."

Spencer finished off his tea and refilled it. They both laughed so hard that they wound up on the kitchen floor, propped against the cabinets. Spencer had developed a strong case of hiccups, too.

"There's dessert," she said and took out a mixing bowl filled to the brim with tapioca pudding from the fridge. "Ta da. I doubled the recipe so we could have it several nights. It's kind of runny, though."

"Did you wash the tapioca first?"

She set the bowl on the table and punched his arm. "I did not! You'd better not ever tell anybody that I put soap on that ham. Promise?"

"What's it worth to you?" he said with a loud hiccup.

She dumped the ham in the trash and turned to him.

"How about I take you out to eat tonight?" she said and parked herself in his lap. He tried to kiss her, but the hiccups got in the way.

"Maybe the tapioca would help get rid of those."

"Sure. It looks great. Dish me up some of it." Spencer eyed the contents.

They sat on the couch and ate.

"I hope we never have another day like when I got back from Dallas," she said. "I was afraid that you weren't going to look at me ever again the same way. I thought I had ruined our perfect marriage."

"Jem, there is no perfect marriage. If humans get married, it won't be perfect. It might seem so, but it's not. If they never fight or disagree, one of them is always giving in and not saying what they really think. They hold it in for fifty years. We're not going to have a perfect marriage, but we will always have perfect love for one another."

"What wasn't perfect about us until I messed up?"

"We were still on our honeymoon. The marriage hadn't kicked in yet. I don't mean that ours can't be closer to perfection than all the rest."

"Good," she said.

Spencer put the dishes in the sink and stood in the doorway. "Jemma, we need to make a promise."

"Whatever you say."

"We will tell each other everything. Even if the telling is going to cause pain or words between us. Can you agree to that?"

Jemma slipped her arms around him. "The problem is that I don't want to hurt you. I've caused you enough pain to last our whole lives. I don't like keeping secrets from you, but I feel like some things are better off stopping with me. Does that make any sense?"

"You know that secrets have a way of creeping out and causing more trouble than the telling would've. Most of your secrets have revolved around Paul anyway."

"He's really not a worthless person. I have a lot of sympathy for someone whose love is not returned because that's what I almost did to you. Paul goes around trying to get women to go home with him, looking for love. There's no reason for you to be jealous, but I may run into him again sometime. I think we should just count on it. That way, it won't be a major ordeal."

Spencer swallowed and rested his chin on her head. "Do you promise that you will tell me when that happens?"

"I promise."

"You will tell me everything? No more secrets?"

Jemma looked up at him and offered her hand to shake on it. "I will if you will, but does that mean I have to go back and tell all the old ones now?"

"There are more?"

"There are details. I don't think you are going to like them, but I'll tell you if you have to know," Jemma said, dreading it.

"Let me think about that. Maybe last weekend was enough for now."

"Good." She pulled him over to the couch. "We're still in the making-up stage anyway."

Spencer awoke before sunrise to an odd scratching noise, followed by a low moan. He shot up in the bed, thinking something else had happened.

"Jem?" He could see the light coming from under their closet door. He opened it to find her wearing the gold silk gown he had given her for their wedding night and standing in a pile of discarded clothing. "What's going on, baby?" he asked.

She exhaled and gestured at a heap of clothes at her feet. "I can't find anything to wear that will make me look like a sweet little wife to your mother. I don't have a single thing." She turned to the rack of dresses still left and scraped them across to the reject side. "Nope, nope, nope, see what I mean?" She groaned. "I need Mom here to figure this out."

"Jemma, what you wear is not going to make any difference to my mother. I always thought it was the liquor talking, but I think she's jealous of you. Wear whatever you want, or we'll stop on the way out of town and get you a new outfit. How does that sound?"

"It sounds hopeless, because we both know she's never going to like me."

"Well, you're perfect to me." He kissed her until the hanger in her hand dropped to the floor just prior to their own descent.

⬥

The Chase castle, as it was known around Chillaton, loomed on the horizon just outside town, near Citizen's Cemetery. Spencer's grandfather had built the Texas Gothic mansion to cheer up his wife. The Chase patriarch, being long on money and very short on design experience, had created a bitter architectural pill for Spencer to swallow. The interior, redone by a former lady friend of Max's from Atlanta, was of such elegance as to be featured in *Southern Comfort* magazine the year before. Max had added a swimming pool off the back of the house for Spencer's eighteenth birthday. It was the only one in Connelly County, except for the old one at the Chillaton Country Club.

Harriet, Spencer's Irish nanny who had raised him according to the cowboy code of honor, opened the door. "Ah, my favorite couple," she said. "Come into the den, my dearies. Your folks are waiting."

"Then why didn't they come to the door?" Spencer whispered in Jemma's ear. She took a deep breath.

"Ya'll come on in." Max Chase greeted them with his Cadillac dealer's smile. He was tall, like Spencer, and nice-looking, too, but not exactly handsome. "You sure smell good, young lady. What's that you're wearing?"

"It's something Spence gave me," Jemma said, glancing toward the leather throne.

Rebecca made no effort to get up from her big wing chair. Spencer went to her instead. She didn't let go until Jemma boldly came up beside him.

"Hello, Mrs. Chase. It's good to see you." Jemma said, leery of saying much else.

Rebecca shifted in her chair and looked away. Jemma retreated to the couch and kept her eyes on Spencer as he joined her.

"So how are things in honeymoon haven?" Max asked with a big grin.

"Fantastic." Spencer squeezed Jemma's hand. "How are things here?"

Rebecca trained her dark eyes on her new daughter-in-law. They were not the beautiful gray eyes of her son; hers were blue, but she did appear more together than Jemma had ever seen her. Her makeup was on straight and her blond hair was whipped up in a rich lady's style. She must have had it done in Amarillo because Nedra's Beauty Parlor & Craft Nook only churned out two hairdos, both guaranteed to last a week, and this was neither of them. Maybe Nedra's was only good enough for the drunken Rebecca, Jemma thought, almost smiling. Her mother-in-law held her glare.

Even Max, not known for his social intuitiveness, must have sensed the tension. "We're doing good, good. We were just discussing taking a little second honeymoon cruise ourselves, weren't we, hon?" Max stood behind Rebecca and massaged her shoulders. She reached for his hand and he took it, both flashing major diamond rings.

"Supper is ready whenever you folks are," Harriet said, giving Jemma a smile.

"That's what we needed to hear. Thanks, Harriet," Max replied.

Spencer led the way to the dining room with his arm around his wife. He pulled her chair out for her and whispered in her ear, "Hang in there."

Jemma decided that Rebecca's evil eye was even worse when she was sober.

"Are you getting used to Chillaton again, Mother?" Spencer asked.

Rebecca sneered at Jemma. "I understand you had a creek wedding. I don't think I've ever been to a farm ceremony like that. I wonder, did you kneel at a feed trough, and am I to assume there were cows and other barnyard animals loitering about?"

Jemma traced around the edge of her plate. Spencer put his hand on her leg under the table. A mischievous thought came to her.

"Well, there was the mule I rode in on." She giggled.

Max got a big laugh out of it. Spencer grinned at Jemma's valiant attempt, but Rebecca found no humor in it at all.

"How clever. You probably used some homemade lasso to rope my son and drag him to your little ambush since we all know that you nearly married an elderly cowboy."

Jemma was ready to crawl under the table.

Max cleared his throat. "Actually, Becky, it was a beautiful wedding. Jemma was a real lovely bride."

Spencer looked straight at his mother with a tolerant smile and took Jemma's hand. "I'm sorry you couldn't have been there, Mother," he said, his voice calm but chilly. "I'm sure you remember that Jemmabeth and I have been in love for a long time. We've been through a lot and feel blessed to be married now. I know you'll want to share our happiness, so that you can be a part of our lives." The last bit was very clearly stated.

"No need to bristle, son," Rebecca said. "I was only making conversation."

Harriet appeared with the main course. The men dug in like orphans in *Oliver Twist*, but Jemma wasn't sure she could eat under the resolute eyes of a condor. She was just glad that she'd remembered to throw on extra deodorant.

❧

They had talked about their first Christmas together since the eighth grade, and their apartment glowed from two blocks away. Inside, Jemma strung popcorn and cranberries across all the windows and made a wreath of cedar boughs, cranberries, and gold velvet ribbon for their door. Spencer's idea was to hang mistletoe from every overhang, and to make certain none of it went to waste, either. It was a newlywed Christmas, for sure. *Nouvelle Liberte* had sent her a few copies of its holiday issue with her watercolor on the cover. It was the painting of Spence's Medevac team gathered around the tree. She hid it from him. He didn't need any more reminders for a while.

"I don't want to go to Twila and Buddy's party this year," Jemma said on their way to Lizbeth's for the annual family gathering.

"Why not? I thought you liked seeing everybody." Spencer slowed down as a state trooper car came toward them on the highway.

"I don't want you dancing with The Cleave." Jemma watched the patrol car over her shoulder.

"Oh, come on, Jem. I won't dance with her. I learned my lesson."

"That's no answer. It sounds like you like dancing with her but you won't, just to keep me happy."

"That's not what I meant, baby."

"That's what you said."

"Let me rephrase that. I don't want to dance with Missy. I learned my lesson about letting her drag me into it. How's that?" He grinned and tickled her pouty lips. "She really gets to you, doesn't she?"

Jemma turned up the radio and sang along with Joni Mitchell. Spencer turned his attention to the road. He knew when to let her stew.

❧

"Mom!" Jemma yelled, opening the door before the car stopped.

"Sweet pea!" Alexandra Forrester yelled back as they embraced in the driveway. "You look so happy."

"We are," Jemma said.

Spencer figured he was out of the doghouse and could concentrate on his young brother-in-law clinging to his leg and his father-in-law shaking his hand. They joined the happy crowd inside and opened presents and stuffed themselves with food.

"I sure do like this fancy art book. Thank you, Jemmerbeth." Lester ran his fingers over the slick pages. "I ain't never been to a art museum before, exceptin' the railroad museum over to Dallas when you graduated from college. I need to see these up close, I reckon."

"Most of those are in Italy and France, but New York has a good museum. How'd you like to take a trip up there?"

"No ma'am. I ain't gonna go where folks talk too fast. I'll just enjoy this book for all it's worth. You know, Jemmer, if you'd lived at the same time as all them old I-talian painters, you would've been even more famous than them because your paintings look more like real people. The way them boys painted, the heads didn't fit with the size of the rest of 'em. See what I mean, like this one right here."

"Why, thank you, Lester. Some art historians believe that because the Church was so powerful during that era, art couldn't be too perfect or else the general public might worship it like a graven image. At least that might have been the Church's fear, and that kind of worship would be breaking the second commandment."

"Well, don't that beat all. I'll have to set on that thought for a spell. You're talkin' about the Catholics, I figger. In other words, they come hence to sayin' 'Paint like a young'un or we'll be comin' to get you.'"

"I'm not so sure they said it like that. Now, don't hold this old theory against the Catholics, Lester. There are good people in all churches."

"All churches don't have just one feller tellin' how things is gonna be. Your Lillygrace grandparents over there ain't Catholic, are they?"

Jemma turned and smiled at her hoity-toity grandmother and grandfather. They smiled and nodded.

"No, Lester, they are Episcopalian," she said.

"Close enough. I sure get some pig-eye looks from 'em." Lester shook his head and wandered off with his book. Her little brother, Robby, joined him and listened to Lester's quaint explanation about each piece. Mercifully, he left the pope out of the conversation.

"Baby girl." Jim motioned for his daughter. "Let's go for a walk." They bundled up and walked to the Ruby Store and bought a couple of bags of marshmallows for the hot cocoa that would appear in the evening.

"I miss you, Daddy," Jemma said.

"I know the feeling. Maybe when I retire, we'll move back here.

I need to take better care of Mama. How's she doing?" Jim asked.

"Gram seems fine to me. She stays busy with church work and quilting."

"Good. The holidays always get me wondering what things would have been like if Matt and Luke had lived. I think about how they might have turned out, who they would have married—that kind of stuff. Maybe you and Robby could have had some Forrester cousins." He exhaled. "The Lord's been really good to your mom and me. We have two wonderful children. Papa would be so proud of your work, honey. We all are."

"Y'all did a good job of raising me. You always encouraged my interest in art."

"Papa and Gram half raised you. I'm just grateful that you have Spencer to raise your own kids with. As for me, I couldn't have found a better woman than your mother. She's everything to me. The older you get, the more you look just like her. Listen, do you hear a fiddle? That gives me a shiver because it sounds like Papa's warming up."

"It's Joe. He's pretty good, too." Jemma stopped at the front gate. "You were right about Spence and the helicopter crash, Daddy. All his pain came pouring out one night."

"That happened to me when you were a baby. I was rocking you and all of a sudden it hit me about Luke and Matt. Your mother had to put you in your crib for me because I fell apart. We talked the rest of the night on the floor beside your bed. It never really leaves, though. Your head clears up somewhat, but your heart, well, it can't forget." His voice broke. "Let's get inside and enjoy some music."

She put her arms around him. Jim wiped his eyes and held her. She kept her daddy's words tucked in her heart.

⌇

"Old Lady Chase, telephone," Robby yelled over the music. Rats. Jemma knew who it was—Twila. She didn't want Spence to think she couldn't handle Missy, so they went.

It was the same old crowd with the usual chips and dip, but instead of dancing, everybody was fussing about babies. They seemed to be all over the house, like puppies. Jemma smiled politely every time somebody plopped one in her lap so they could have a free minute. Even Twila's walk resembled that of the ducks at the cemetery pond.

Spencer grinned at her. "You do look good with those little ones, Jem."

"Somebody else's, if you don't mind. This is a boring party. I'm ready to go whenever you are."

"Well, if it isn't the lovebirds." Melissa Blake's micro-miniskirt rode up even higher as she leaned across Spencer to plant a kiss in the air near his quite rosy cheek. He jerked his head back to avoid a near-collision with her cleavage, but she brushed against his neck anyway.

Missy smiled as her Chanel rose up like steam off a waffle iron. "Oh Spence. That turtleneck is the same color as your eyes," she said and gave him a real peck right on his earlobe.

Jemma's stomach did a flip.

The Cleave placed a well-manicured finger on the corner of her own mouth. "You've got some food right there on your lip, Jemma." She winked at Spencer. "Some party, huh? I've been to car washes more exciting than this."

Spencer choked out a laugh, and Jemma gritted her teeth.

"Remember when we washed your Corvette at my house and you sprayed me with the hose?" Missy shook back her hair. "My T-shirt was totally drenched. I'll never forget what you said. Are you still a bad boy even though you're married?"

For one evil second, Jemmabeth considered throwing up on The Cleave's boots. Jemma had been on the all-state basketball team a few years back, and she still had good aim.

They left within five minutes. Jemma stomped to the car way ahead of him.

Spencer grabbed her arm. "Okay, before you start. You were dating Paul when I went out with Missy. Keep that in mind, Jem, and yes, we washed my car, but I wouldn't have said anything to her that was memorable. Now, let me have it."

Jemma pried his hand off her. "Did you spray her with water until her shirt was drenched? How dumb. You can see what she has without going to all that trouble." She got in the Corvette and slammed the door. The windows frosted over immediately.

Spencer walked around the car and took a deep breath before getting in.

◄◎►

From the kitchen window of the Bakers' trailer, The Cleave pulled the curtain back just a smidge and blew a kiss as the silver Corvette peeled out.

◄◎►

Jemma was as far on her side of the bed as she could get. She hadn't said a word in the last two hours. Spencer scooted up against her, and she had no place to go but the floor.

"Jemmabeth Alexandra," he said, "please don't be mad about this. It's old stuff. I was hurting and she was around. Even if I did squirt her with a hose, at least I didn't consider marrying her like you did Paul. Do you really think that I would make some suggestive remark to Missy? Give me some credit, Jem. Why would I do that when who I really wanted to see in a wet shirt was you? I've told you before—The Cleave was just a distraction from my misery. We never even went parking. C'mon, turn around and wish me a Merry Christmas Eve." He moved her hair and kissed her neck.

"What precisely did you say when you sprayed her?"

"I probably said 'bombs away' like we used to say when I was a little kid and we threw water balloons at the park. That's all I can figure out."

"Did you open the packages she sent you in Vietnam?"

"I did not. I threw them in the trash, along with the letters."

She looked over her shoulder at him. "Why did you need to put water on her at all?"

Spencer kissed her shoulder. "You want the real truth? I wanted to see what she would look like if that famous hair of hers was soaked."

"Promise?" Jemma asked, half smiling.

"Cowboy's Code of Honor promise."

Jemma turned over and leaned on her elbow. "What did she look like? Bad?"

"Like a wet Pekingese."

"Smooth talker."

"Heartbreaker," he said and kissed her pouty lips.

"Wait. I've come up with a new wrestling move." She stood up on the bed.

"I assume that you are about to demonstrate it."

"Yup. It's where I'd like to put her if she ever touches your face again."

"Where's that? On the floor?"

"Nope. Between the jaws of. . .The Waffle Iron!" she said as she fell on him. She jabbed him with her elbows and knees like a maniacal typewriter.

He couldn't stop laughing long enough to defend himself.

Chapter 4
Plan B

So, is this going to be the trip where I get to see you in a bikini?" Spencer yelled from the bathroom as Jemma dug through her summer clothes to find something suitable for a warm beach weekend in California.

"Nope. I would just as soon wear my underwear as a bikini," she said, throwing things in her suitcase. "We are going for a welcome home celebration for Trent—not a swimsuit style show."

Spencer stuck his head out the door. "Would you really wear your underwear on the beach? I'll need a private showing of that first."

She threw a sneaker at him, hitting the door as it closed.

⦿⊱⊰⦿

Jemma's hair swirled in the breeze off the Pacific the same as it did in the wake of the Zephyr passenger train when it used to stream down the tracks. The waves lapped against her ankles and shifted the sand beneath her. She had hoped to see moonlight reflected on the water, but the moon was shrouded by a thin blanket of clouds. She wrote their names in the sand, encircled with a heart, then put her hand on her belly. She would make an appointment as soon as they got home. The tide erased their names, and Jemma blew out her breath. There wasn't room in that heart now for another name. Someday, but not yet.

"Hello, beautiful." Spencer eased his arms around her waist. "What are you thinking?" The tide enveloped them and they stood ankle-deep in salt water.

"I love you," she said. "That's what I'm always thinking."

"Sorry Trent and I went on for so long. He's really a great guy; but after all, he's your cousin. You'll be glad to know that he looks you in the eye when he's talking business, too, even though he's not a Forrester. His philosophy and mine are a match, Jem. We're talking about getting together and forming a company. Architecture and engineering would be an exciting combination. We both have the financial resources to stay afloat through the lean times. What do you think?"

His enthusiasm made her answer easy. "I can't imagine two nicer guys getting together to design and build things. It's a super idea."

"There's something in your voice, though. Are you okay?"

"Everything is fine." She turned back to the ocean and chewed on her lip.

⁓❦⁓

"I bet I can beat you to that next dune, Jem," Robby said. "Loser buys ice cream, okay?"

"Robby, you don't have enough money to keep that bet." Jemma laughed.

"I do, too. I brought some money. I've been working hard to buy a new bike." Robby's blue eyes shone like Papa's.

"I'll take you up on that bet," Jim said. "See if you can beat an old man with a bad leg."

They took off. Her daddy was no match for a ten-year-old. Jim came back with ice cream for everybody. "Come on, Rob, let's find some crabs." The two Forrester men walked ahead of the ladies.

"Sweet pea, what do you think about your cousin and your husband having a business together?" Alex asked. "They are spending a lot of time planning things, that's for sure."

"I think it's great. There was a time when I didn't like Trent, but I didn't really know him. I love him now."

"He is so much like Ted. My brother is a gentle, smart, big-hearted man. Thank goodness Trent is nothing like his absentee mother. Now tell me what's the matter with you. I've seen that faraway look in those pretty eyes."

"I may be pregnant, Mom."

Alex stopped. "So soon? You always said you wanted to wait a few years. What happened? Did you forget to take your birth control pills?"

Jemma nodded. "I'm trying not to think about it, but it's driving me nuts. I want to be alone with Spence and stay crazy. We waited and were good all those years. That's what I want right now."

"Things don't always go as planned." Alex wiped a cone crumb from her daughter's chin.

"Spence already gave me this lecture. Just because I know the facts of the matter, it doesn't change my heart."

"Your heart will melt when you see what you and Spence have created. Trust me. Besides, you may not be pregnant. Now tell me about your art. What are you working on?"

Robby ran up to them, giggling over some sea creature that he held out for his mother's reaction. Jemma again turned her face toward the ocean breeze to dry her eyes.

"I've spent so much time with Trent, I feel like I have neglected you." Spence laid the blanket on the sand, and they cuddled up to watch the stars.

"Yeah, well, maybe you'd better start making up for it, mister."

"Any suggestions?" He kissed her palms, for starters.

"Hmm. I'm not the one in trouble here. You'll have to come up with something on your own." Jemma resumed her stargazing.

Spencer nuzzled up to her ear and whispered in it, sending her into a giggle. He loved the way she closed her eyes and threw back her head when she laughed. She had done that since he first knew her. Things like that lingered from her childhood and had endeared her to many, probably even Paul.

Spencer turned her chin toward him and kissed her. "You are precious to me, Mrs. Chase," he said, pulling the blanket over them as a ship out on the Pacific blew its melancholy horn. The sound mingled with the hypnotic pulse of the surf and their conversation.

He had an hour's worth of drafting to finish, and, as he was the only one left in the office, he chose to ignore the knocking on the main door. It didn't stop. He exhaled and went to see who could possibly need an architect after office hours. It was Jemma. She leaned against the door as she kept a steady rhythm with her knuckles. Spencer unlocked the door and she fell against him, crying. He helped her to a couch and got her a box of tissues.

"I'm pregnant." She blew her nose, then threw the whole tissue box at the wastebasket. "Rats, rats, rats! I didn't want this to happen. Now we'll be like all the other old married couples who have a kid to take care of and we won't be crazy newlyweds anymore. I'm not ready for a baby. I still want to be wild and free with you. It's all my fault for being irresponsible with the stupid pill. I do *not* want to be pregnant!"

"Whoa. Well, we knew it was a possibility." He chose his words carefully. "It'll be okay, Jem. I know we didn't plan it this way, but think about the little life growing inside you. We made it together. It's our very own baby, and we want it to be loved from the very beginning, don't we?"

"I know all that stuff and I want to have babies. I just didn't want to start so soon. I'm still celebrating us."

"We'll still be us. We'll love each other like we do now."

"No, we won't love each other the same way. We can't be free. Our focus will be on the baby, not us. We'll be a trio. I know the baby will be cute and an extension of our love. I'm not arguing with you. It's just. . .I never stop messing things up." She retrieved the tissues and went to his office, flopping in a chair.

Spencer drew her limp body toward him. "Jemmabeth, I agree with you that this is not Plan A, but it is not the end of the world as we know it. It's just Plan B. We will make it a new part of our joy, though. If we've created life, then we are going to celebrate that. You get a smile on your face and we are going out for dinner and dancing. C'mon, let me see that beautiful smile."

Jemma stared at the carpet. He waited. She looked out the window while he wiped the tears off her cheeks. Without warning, she jerked away from him and bolted out of the room. Spencer followed her to the restroom and leaned against the wall as the joy of morning sickness in the evening took its toll. He had a feeling that maybe she was right; things were going to change.

Chapter 5
Sealing the Deal

A nother month passed and they didn't tell anyone the news. "I hope you aren't going to be like this the whole nine months," Spencer commented over dinner.

"What? You mean the throwing up?" She slammed down a milk carton, causing little droplets of milk to spray up on her face. Without so much as a giggle, she wiped them off.

Spencer raised his brow. "Nope, I'm talking about the big pout that has taken over our lives. I think it's been long enough."

Jemma poked at her baked potato, then stabbed it with her fork and flew upstairs. Spencer exhaled and trudged up after her. Their bedroom door was shut. At least she hadn't slammed it.

He knocked and found her sitting on the side of the bed. "Jem, I want us to be happy about this. You are carrying our firstborn. We don't want to create any bad memories of this special event. Our baby can't change the timing. I'm ready to tell everybody and start making plans. Besides, we could be having fun right now while we're still alone."

Jemma was dry-eyed for once. She reached for his hand. "I know you're right, babe. Just tell me what to do and I'll do it."

"How are you feeling?"

"I'm a little better. There are some smells, though, that make me sick to think about them. Like bacon and mayonnaise. Yuck."

He kissed her. "Let's go look at baby furniture."

"How can you be so patient with me, Spence? I don't want to be this way, but we saved ourselves for all those years, waiting until we got married. I wanted to relish this—this golden time, with just you and me. Do you know what I'm talking about?"

"I know that, Jem, and I really do understand. Our schedules and solitude may suffer, but the passion between us is permanent. I think we need a little vacation. Let's go somewhere romantic. I haven't had much time with my wild lady lately. In fact, I haven't even seen her around."

She looked up and gave him a grin. "How much romance can you stand for the next six months?"

"As much as you can dish out, woman," he said as they fell back on the bed.

❦

They called Alex and Jim that night. Jim was ecstatic and Robby decided to be called Uncle Rob. Alex was still choosing between Gran and Gramma when they hung up. Lizbeth expressed her excitement and vowed to get started on a quilt, but Jemma detected a certain something in her response. Jemma had voiced her opinion too many times about waiting to have a family, and she knew Lizbeth remembered those remarks.

Spencer wanted to tell his parents in person. "I think it'll be all right. Mother needs to see you anyway. Just remember that I love you, and it won't last long."

"Will you still love me when my belly is hanging over my knees?" she asked, playing with his tie. She looked up and bit her lip.

"Jemmabeth, I would love you even if you gained fifty pounds and never lost it."

"Liar. You might love my personality, but you would get a roving eye."

"Never. Now hush up and get dressed." He gave her a swat on her behind. He watched as she chose what to wear to see his mother. It was a major ordeal and an amusing sight, but he would never tell her that. He just loved to watch her do anything. The pregnancy had thrown her into a spin, but she was bouncing back. An hour later, he helped her hang up all the rejects and she was ready to go. As he watched her, he hoped that their baby would be a girl—the spirit and image of his golden-eyed love.

❦

Max and Rebecca were late returning from a drive around their ranch. Harriet was the first person that Spencer wanted to tell anyway. She was jubilant.

"I should have known, my girl. You have that special look. Motherhood is written all over you," she said and patted Jemma's hand.

Jemma wanted to hear that particular observation about as much as she wanted to see her mother-in-law. Spencer kissed her as soon as Harriet left them alone in the den. Jemma pulled her black skirt down as far as she could and adjusted the Peter Pan collar on her white blouse.

Spencer smiled. "You look like an English schoolgirl. Stop worrying. You know she is going to say something rude, so just expect it."

Jemma jumped as the back door opened and Max's voice tumbled down the Italian-tiled hallway. She sat up straight and held her breath.

"Spencer, my man." Max gave his son a bear hug. "You look good. Married life is the way to go, huh? I guess that would have something to do with you, young lady."

Jemma smiled at Max as Rebecca embraced her son. "Tell me all about your work, Spencer," she said, taking him to the matching leather armchairs.

Spencer walked instead to the sofa and sat by his wife, grinning. "Before we talk about anything else, Jemma and I have some news." He couldn't hold it any longer. "We're having a baby."

"Well, I'll be." Max laughed and clapped his hands. "So I'm gonna be a granddaddy, huh? I guess I'd better buy myself a how-to book for this deal. Wow! I figured you two would be honeymooning for five or six years."

Jemma cleared her throat to get rid of the lump that was rising in it. Rebecca pursed her lips and stared out the bank of windows that overlooked the swimming pool.

"Becky, what do you have to say about this news? Won't it be great to have a baby around the house?"

Rebecca raised her chin and turned her gaze on Jemma. "So, I guess you've sealed the deal now, as they say in the car business."

Max flashed a shaky smile. "That's not very nice, Becky. The kids are sharing something special with us, and you should be happy for them. I know I am."

Rebecca's face twitched. "I suppose we should be grateful that you waited until you were married to get pregnant; that way we can be relatively certain that it's a Chase."

Jemma was off the couch and out the front door before Spencer could stop her. He came back into the den, his gray eyes set on his mother. "If you don't care for Jemmabeth, Mother, then you don't care for me. She is my love and my life. When you look at her, you're looking at me, and when you speak to her, you're speaking to your son. Until you treat her with respect and honor our marriage, I won't be back to your house. That's a promise. Good-bye, Dad; it was good seeing you."

Spencer caught up with Jemma at the cemetery gates. She could move when she wanted to. He stopped the car and held her. They walked to Papa's grave and sat on the bench.

"I can't go there anymore. Please don't ask me to," she said.

"That's a promise. Mother is acting like a bitter old woman, and she has nothing to be bitter about. She needs to get back into counseling or something. Let's go see Gram. We'll take her to Daddy's Money for dinner."

Jemma said a prayer over her papa's grave. He would have loved having a baby around the house, but he would not have liked Jemma's belated attitude over her impending motherhood.

They pulled into the driveway and sat in the car for a while, talking. Spencer stepped over to Lester's house to invite him to dinner. Lizbeth and Jemma sat in the porch swing. The honeysuckle vine was dry and brittle behind them, waiting for spring. Jemma had avoided her eyes, but Lizbeth put her arm around her grand-daughter as they considered the bittersweet twists in life. It had been the same for her and Cameron. God's Great Plan was not always in tune with that of His children, but His was always the perfect way. Lizbeth had known that, too, but it hadn't made the acceptance of motherhood any easier while their hearts were still on fire for each other all those years ago.

～◈～

Jemmabeth stepped out of the elevator and walked down the shiny hallway to the nurses' station to ask for directions. There was no need to because the window was right there. She approached it much the same as when she entered the room where her mother-in-law sat in her leather throne. When Jemma's eyes fell on the bassinettes filled with pink and blue blankets, she melted. It was the same feeling she had the first time she heard *Praeludium and Allegro*. One of those cribs would hold their own little one with Baby Chase written on a pastel tag. Her hand moved to her heart as the smallest newborn near the window made a sucking motion with its pink lips and turned its mouth toward its own tiny fist. A wave of reconciliation swept through Jemma's body, ripping out her old attitude and leaving behind a sparkling new one. More than anything else in the world, at that very moment, she wanted to be a mother.

✦

"I'm in here, babe," Jemma yelled from the extra bedroom. "Come and see what you think." She wiped her cheek, but the paint was still wet on it. She surveyed her day's work. Spencer, impeccable in his sports coat and turtleneck, walked in the room and whistled. Jemma had on Papa's old overalls and a bandana scarf tied around her head. He kissed her and the paint smudge transferred to him. They were branded as expectant parents.

"What's all this? I thought we were going to paint it together." Spencer looked around the room—stark white when he left for work, but now the color of butter.

"I couldn't help it," she said. "It went really fast, and I think it's perfect for the baby's room. We can buy unfinished furniture and paint it sky blue. I have some ideas for a *trompe l'oeil*."

"I'll bet you do." He grinned at her. "You look fantastic."

"Check this out." She whipped out a book of baby names. "I thought we could look at it after supper. Rats. I forgot to turn on the oven. Do you want dirt pie or water casserole for supper?"

He gave her a sneaky look. "I don't want any supper," he whispered. "I've been a bad boy, and I think you should send me straight to my room."

"Well, now, I'm real sorry to hear that," she said in her Scarlett O'Hara voice. "I'll be up in five minutes to check on you. You'd better be in that bed, too. Or else."

Spencer stopped on the stairs. "Or else what?"

She grinned and wiggled her eyebrows at him. He took the stairs two at a time.

✦

The phone rang while she was finishing up a painting of Max. He had his foot on the front bumper of a Cadillac with a cigarette dangling from the corner of his smile. One hand was on his knee and the other was in a price-haggling gesture. She put her paintbrush behind her ear and answered.

"Stop painting and start packing," Spencer said.

"You're kicking me out?" she asked.

"No, I'm running off to Mexico with you."

"Mexico? You're kidding. What's down there?"

"Puerto Vallarta, that's what. We leave tomorrow morning."

"I'll get the suitcases. Spence, thank you." She kissed the phone.

Jemma took a breath and felt her cheeks. She hadn't been quite right the last couple of weeks. It felt something like the flu coming on, but it never did. That was her big fear, that she would get sick and make the little one sick, too. She put her hands on her belly and closed her eyes. She hoped he looked just like his daddy, right down to the cowlick and those pretty gray eyes. She pulled out the suitcases. The first thing she threw in was the *Big Book of Baby Names*.

❧

Nothing would do but for him to buy her a bikini in Mexico.

"I can't wear this," she said, looking in the mirror in their room by the beach. "I'm starting to show."

Spencer lay on the bed watching her. "I like it. You wouldn't wear one in Hawaii either and you weren't even pregnant then. C'mon, do it just to humor me. You're a knockout in it."

She put it on and stood up on the bed. "Me, Amazon woman, come to take you to my cave. Will you go in peace, or must I drag you?"

He grabbed the ties on the sides of her bikini. "Now what does Amazon woman have to say?"

She couldn't do anything but giggle. He had missed that about her.

❧

They took a boat ride to see the South Shore. It was a romantic tour but endured on rough waters.

"It's a good thing you are over that evening sickness or this could be a disaster," Spencer said, tracing around her lips.

She nodded, wincing. Her head throbbed and the strange

tingling sensation that had bothered her both nights they had been in Mexico returned. Maybe it was the drinking water.

Spencer stood between the boat captain and Jemma, easing his hands onto her stomach. "I want you to know, Jem, that this little life growing in you only makes you even more beautiful to me. Don't ever forget that."

"I won't. I'm really excited and happy now, Spence. I want him to be you, all over again."

He kissed her, making her forget about her other chills for a moment.

⩗

They were slow dancing in the hotel ballroom after supper when Spencer stopped. "Jem, do you have a fever? You feel really warm to me."

"I'm not doing too well, babe. Maybe we should go back to the room. I'm kind of dizzy," she said as he felt her forehead. She lost her balance and leaned against him.

"You wait here. I'm calling a cab."

⩗

"Sorry, Spence. We were having such a good time. I don't want to spoil it," she said as soon as they took the thermometer out of her mouth. The nurse spoke in Spanish but comprehended the couple's anxious looks. A young doctor read Jemma's chart and gave instructions to the nurse. She wheeled Jemma away, motioning for Spencer to stay put.

The doctor introduced himself in English and offered Spencer a chair. "It is of concern to me that your wife has had these symptoms for almost a month and that she is so far advanced in the pregnancy. We cannot detect a fetal heartbeat, so it is possible that the fetus has died and did not abort naturally. Your wife has all the symptoms of septicemia, which left untreated, can be fatal." He put his hand on Spencer's shoulder. "We will run some lab tests quickly, and I must examine her. She is normally healthy?"

"Yes, very." Spencer couldn't think straight. He rubbed his forehead and stood. Thoughts of death riding in his chopper during Vietnam filled his head and made his stomach turn. How could their baby be dead and threatening Jemma's life?

The doctor left to examine her. Spencer circled the waiting area several times. He needed to touch her fingers like he did when she'd had the wreck and nearly died. Jemma would take this hard, very hard, and he had to be with her.

The doctor returned with confirmation of his fears. "As I suspected, this is most certainly a missed abortion; that is, the fetus has died, but none of the tissue has been expelled, and it is causing your wife to become ill."

Spencer took a breath and resorted to his Medevac pilot demeanor. "How can you be sure that the baby is dead? Are there other tests?"

"I know the fetus is dead. In Mexico City they could perform tests to be completely certain, but your wife is becoming more seriously ill by the hour. I don't know if you should risk that delay."

"What do you recommend, sir?" Spencer searched the doctor's eyes.

"We have already started her on antibiotics, but it is necessary to evacuate the uterus to assure the septicemia will subside. I will need you to complete some paperwork so that I may perform the procedure."

Spencer nodded. He could not let Jemma die. "Could I see her first?"

"Quickly, please," the doctor said and took him to her.

She turned her tear-streaked face at the sound of his footsteps and raised her head off the pillow to reach for Spencer, pulling the IV stand with her. The doctor stepped out to give them privacy as they grieved before he loosened all that remained of the life they had created.

Chapter 6
A Sharp Blow

Lester and Lizbeth stood outside the apartment door. Their knocks went unanswered, so Lizbeth turned the knob. "Hello, sugar. It's just us," she shouted up the stairs.

"Maybe she's stepped out for a minute," Lester said.

"No, no. Spencer said she won't leave the apartment. She must be asleep." Lizbeth looked up the long steps to their second-story bedroom. "Jemmabeth. It's Gram and Lester."

Jemma appeared at the top of the stairs in her old chenille robe.

"Hi, sugar," Lizbeth said, trying to conceal her shock at Jemma's appearance. "We thought we would drop by for a little visit. I brought you a couple of casseroles, too."

Lester backed away into the living room, twisting the brim of his hat.

"I'll come down in a minute," Jemma mumbled. She turned and closed the door behind her.

"Oh my." Lizbeth shook her head. "Oh my."

Lester headed for the door. "Miz Liz, I'm thinkin' this is a time for woman talk. I just can't see clear to me bein' around for it. I'll wait in the car. No offense."

"That's fine, Lester. Here, take Spencer's newspaper with you. I'll be out directly." Lizbeth took off her hat and set to work washing dishes. She did not expect her precious girl to be in this shape. Spencer said things were bad, but she had no idea it would be to such an extent.

She was about to go up and check on her when she heard the door open and footsteps on the stairs. Jemma's bare feet stuck out from the bottom step. Lizbeth put the broom away and joined her granddaughter on the stairs. Her beautiful hair seemed to have barely survived an eggbeater attack, and she still had on the robe. Her arms hung at her side and her glassy eyes remained fixed on the carpet. Lizbeth put her arms around her. She held her until her arms trembled with her own sense of grief for Jemma's pain.

They were still there when Spencer came in the door with Lester.

⊰◈⊱

"Hi, Gram," Spencer said, but his attention was on his wife. He rubbed her back. "Lester and I were saying that we would like a hamburger. I'm going to change clothes and get us some food." He bit his lip and squatted in front of Jemma, brushing her hair out of her face. "Hey, baby," he whispered. "I'll be right back. Would you eat something, just for me?"

Lizbeth pulled herself up by the handrail and disappeared into the living room.

"Y'all go on," Jemma mumbled. "I'm not hungry." She turned and went up the stairs.

Spencer walked with her. "Gram and Lester are here to see us. I know you don't feel good, but maybe you could come back down and visit for a while. We don't want them to worry."

"Do you think they're talking about me?" she asked.

Spencer frowned. "It would only be words of love. We all want you to get well."

"Everybody knows it's my fault that our baby died. That can change the way people feel about you," she said.

"Jem, nobody thinks that but you. Remember the doctor said that one out of four pregnancies ends in miscarriage. It happens to a lot of people. It just happened to be our first."

"No. It's me. I didn't want to be pregnant. I didn't want to have the baby, so look what happened. It's no different than everything else that I've done. I'm so sorry, Spence. You should have married Michelle Taylor. I don't deserve to have your babies. I should have died instead of that little precious child. Everybody is thinking that."

Spencer massaged the bridge of his nose. "I'll see if they can come back another time. I don't think we're ready for company."

Jemma got in bed and pulled the covers over her head so she couldn't hear them talking. She did hear the front door close and his footsteps on the stairs again. She folded the pillow over her face and held it there until he left the room.

⊲◈⊳

Lizbeth kept her thoughts to herself on the trip home. Her head was full of Cameron and her heart fluttered, still, at the thought of him topping the little rise by the home place at day's end. At the windmill, he would remove his hat and beat it against his leg to get rid of the dust of his labors. Those tiny particles, caught in the golden light of dusk, majestically floated back to the earth.

It was on a rainy afternoon when she'd told him they were going to be parents. Thunder rolled as they had snuggled in the storm dugout warmed by the glow of the kerosene lamp. He was quiet at first, then his smile crinkled up his sparkling blue eyes. "Thank you, Lizbeth, for giving me the pleasure of your company these months," he said. "I didn't know such joy was to be had. Now we'll start the business that the good Lord has given us, that of raising Christian children."

She had cried, not wanting their time alone together to be over and not sure she was ready for this new business of raising children. She wanted the unexpected pleasure and fun of just being Cam's wife to last forever. Then, before she understood what it really meant, motherhood had enveloped her with its strong, sensible, and loving arms.

Lester's words invaded her thoughts. "Jemmerbeth's had a real sharp blow to her heart, hasn't she, Miz Liz? I feel right sorry for her, but she'll come out of it okay. There ain't no shame in grief."

Lizbeth stirred in her seat and watched as a tractor made a turn at the end of a cotton row and lowered the contraption behind it into the earth. "Yes, she'll be all right, but it may take some time. She'll need our prayers."

"Yes ma'am. I've already started," Lester said and cleared his throat.

⊲◈⊳

Alex was about to take a cab to the apartment when she saw him in the airport crowd. He forced a smile, but it didn't last long. At the apartment parking lot, they sat in the Corvette even though Spencer saw Jemma looking out the window of their place.

"What did the doctor say?" Alex said, blowing her nose.

641

"She's been going to the best psychiatrist in Amarillo. He says that Jem is dealing with guilt coupled with depression."

"Guilt? Whatever for?"

Spencer watched as Jemma moved away from the window. "She didn't want to be pregnant. She was mad when she found out because she had a hard time with the idea of us giving up our romantic lifestyle. That lasted the whole first trimester. She did come around and was happy about it, but then, well, you know the rest. At first I thought she was just sad, but that's not all of it." His voice broke. "Now she is convinced that the baby didn't live as a punishment for her attitude."

Alex took his hand. "Spence, this will pass. The Lord will use this to His glory, somehow. Don't let Jemma's misery make you lose sight of who she really is, son. She loves you and probably thinks you're disappointed in her. You know that Jim and I love you like you were our own. We will work through this. I'll never forget your patience when she was in that coma. She's still that same precious Jemmabeth; don't hold this against her."

"I could never hold anything against her. She's in my every thought. I just can't help her through this one. I don't know how. It hurts too much for both of us when she keeps feeling the same, day after day."

"That's why I'm here, honey. I will take up the slack now. You need some rest and probably some food. Let's go see our girl."

"I'd better warn you," Spencer said as they got her luggage out of the trunk. "She never sleeps."

He unlocked the apartment door, but Jemma was nowhere to be seen. Alex was shocked when they found her in the closet, cornered, like a wild kitten.

"Sweet pea." Alex dropped to her knees and held her. "Jem, I haven't seen you hide in your closet since you were a little girl in need of a spanking."

"I'm tired, Mom. I'm so tired and I can't sleep because when I do, I see my baby. I've been bad and I can't make it good," she said and glanced up at her with sunken eyes.

Alex blinked back her tears. "Put your head in my lap, Jemmabeth. Let's talk about when you were a little girl."

Spencer sat on the bed, listening in the dark. He wiped his eyes. Alex had done what he was unable to do. She could speak to Jemma without the memory of conception, the pain of their private loss, and his constant fear that Jemma was slipping away from him altogether.

⊰❦⊱

Alex brought them fresh hope. She took up residence on the sofa bed, and Jemma began to sleep and eat again. Spencer wrote his wife love notes and words of encouragement and left them on their bathroom mirror. They were always gone by evening. She sat with him and let him hold her hand but never looked him in the eye. He had put the baby furniture in storage before Alex came and had carefully returned Jemma's art supplies to the butter-colored bedroom. Jemma had not touched her paints since Mexico, nor had she really touched him.

⊰❦⊱

Jemmabeth let Alex drive the Corvette and played with her hair all the way to Chillaton.

"You haven't been to Gram's house for a while," Alex said as they passed the city limits sign.

"I'm nervous," Jemma said, "and I can't think straight." She knew that she was getting on everybody's nerves, but they just didn't understand; she had let them all down, especially Spence. Now strange ideas had sprung up in her head lately, corners of thinking that frightened her, so she tried not to use her brain too much—but her heart was hurting from all the extra effort.

"Goodness, Jemmabeth, you have lived with Gram for the last few years. It should be like home to you."

Jemma didn't answer. She stared out the window. It wasn't only that she had caused the miscarriage of their baby. What she could never make anybody else understand was that, by doing so, she was responsible for literally losing a part of Spencer. The last time she was in Gram's house, she had life growing inside her. Looking Gram in the eye now would be further admission that she was guilty of wishing away that little life.

Lizbeth had lunch all ready for them. Lester didn't come. He had gone to the barbershop instead.

"Sugar, you look so pretty today. Is that a new dress?" Lizbeth said as they sat around the kitchenette.

"Yes ma'am. Spencer bought it for me." Jemma kept her eyes on her plate.

"How is that boy? Is he still keeping long hours?" Lizbeth asked, exchanging glances with Alex.

Jemma blurted it out. "I'm so sorry about the baby, Gram. I should have rejoiced that God blessed us and instead I acted like a brat." She relaxed into a heavy sigh.

Lizbeth reached for her hand, letting the words come softly, in all tenderness. "You know, Jemmabeth, when I found out that I was expecting Matthew, I threw a wall-eyed fit the first time I was alone. When he died in the war, I considered those feelings I had way back then, but I wanted to be with your papa in our golden time, and that was all. It wasn't the idea of motherhood that made me angry. . .it was that it snuck up and invaded our honeymoon. I think you had the same feelings, too. I saw it in your eyes. Those ere honest feelings, but they didn't kill your baby, sugar. It is the never-ending, hard row to hoe in life that did it, not you. I'm sure you've been on your knees about this. Now it's your husband that you must consider. You know, Spencer came to see me last week. He is struggling hard with this guilt you have, honey, and he feels sort of shut off by it. Don't make holes in your marriage over this."

Lizbeth raised Jemma's chin. "Nobody would ever consider blaming you for this, least of all that sweet boy." Lizbeth pushed her chair back and bent down to rest her cheek on Jemma's, leaving a trace of her Moonlight Over Paris perfume on her skin.

The day brightened. Jemma even smiled at Lester when he brought the mail, then she drew some cats and dogs for Shorty and put them in the Mason jar in the hollyhock patch. She remained quiet on the way back to Amarillo but asked Alex to stop at a plant center near the apartment. She bought a small rosebush called "Tiffany" and set it on their balcony. Alex didn't ask why; she was just glad of the little spark returning to her girl.

<◦>

They waited at the airport.

"Thank you for coming," Spencer said as Jemma paced around

the waiting area.

"She's so nervous," Alex said. "I guess that's better than depressed and stressed. I have never seen her like this."

"Jem's gone through a combination of just about every emotion there is lately. I just pray that she'll come back to me. It's almost like she's angry." Spencer craned his neck to see where she was.

"No, Spencer. She isn't angry with you. She has to get past this guilt. Jemma's embarrassed and ashamed about things only she understands, but she's going to be all right. You start praying with her again. She is still the girl you've always loved," Alex said as the first boarding call came for her flight.

Spencer looked at her much the same as he did when he came to pick Jemma up for their first real date.

Alex hugged him. "I love you, son. You call us any time, okay? There's my girl." She waved Jemma over. "Good-bye, sweet pea. We'll be back before school starts. You get going on your paintings."

Alex had to pull away from Jemma's embrace.

"Bye, Mom. Hug Daddy and Robby for me. Thank you for everything," Jemma whispered.

Neither said anything on the way back to their apartment. Spencer was getting used to it. He missed her in every way that one soul mate misses another, and in every way that a husband misses his adored wife. Most of all, he missed her joy; it was the source of his own.

Jemma stood on the balcony and looked up at the nighttime city sky. Life hadn't been right in such a long time. It couldn't be good again until she and Spence were happy. She could try dancing on the tracks behind Gram's house like she used to, but in her heart, she knew the only lasting peace would have to come from the Lord. She had to know that Spencer didn't regret loving her. She had never once set out to hurt her hero, her Candy Man, but she always did. She reached for the creamy pink bloom of the Tiffany rose, still in its planting bucket. The petals fell to the floor like miniature butterflies escaping her touch. Nothing she did now turned out right.

Chapter 7

A Gracious Spark

Brother Cleo came to see them the day after Alex left. Spencer knew that it was Alex who had summoned him. He filled the armchair. Spencer and Jemma sat on the sofa about a foot apart.

"I always feel a bond with the folks that I marry, like they're my own children," Brother Cleo said in his rich bass voice. "I know you two have been through a troublesome time. Jemma, the last time I saw you, there was a deep pain in your eyes, and I still see it. Your mama told me that this pain is covering the joy in your marriage."

Jemma raised her head a little. Spencer bit his lip and looked at the floor.

"You told me once that it was a family trait to always look folks in the eye when you mean something," Brother Cleo said, leaning to one side so as to make eye contact with her. "Now, I'm not denying that you are suffering, but we've got to make sure that the devil hasn't picked you up as a pet project and is hoping to mark you and your marriage for life. I don't want that to happen to you two. This sadness that has caught you is not through any fault of your own. It is just life and that's all. It needs a place to go."

Jemma looked at Spencer out of the corner of her eye.

"It's been my practice to have my 'children' repeat their wedding vows during troubled times. Some folks scoff at such, but it's something I put a lot of faith in. So I want us to kneel right now like we did that morning at Plum Creek and pray. Then, if you remember any of your vows, I want you to look each other in the eye and say them again, just like it was the first time. Now hold hands." Brother Cleo's voice left no margin for hesitation between them.

Spencer reached for her hands. Jemma offered one, but he took the other, too. She closed her eyes and felt the warmth of him.

Brother Cleo prayed and when he finished, Spencer spoke as

though they were alone. "Jemmabeth Alexandra Forrester, you have always been my adored one, and I take you now to be my beloved wife. Before God, I give you my heart and my life. I will cherish and honor you above all women as long as we live on this earth."

Jemma's mouth was dry and tears had trickled to her neck. She glanced at him several times until she could steady her eyes on his, but she could only manage a whisper.

"In the presence of our dear Lord, I promise you, Spencer Morgan Chase, that I will love you and adore you as my husband from this moment until I breathe my last. No one but you will ever fill my heart and my life." Even her whisper broke and she took another breath. "I promise to cherish and honor you above all men, as my only and dearest love."

"Amen," Brother Cleo said.

The three of them stayed like that for a while. The only sound was Brother Cleo's heavy breathing. Jemma looked away first.

Brother Cleo laid his hand on theirs. "May the Holy Spirit move in your hearts to give you hope and restore your joy and, may 'the Lord bless thee and keep thee; and make his face shine upon thee, and be gracious unto thee.' You'll find that verse in the book of Numbers, chapter 6, verses 24 and 25." He stood, leaving them still on their knees and holding hands. "I know my way out. I'll check on y'all next week."

She meant to take her hands away from Spencer's grasp, but he held tight. "Jem, I miss you so much. Don't you miss me?"

She nodded. He reached for her and, for once, she didn't draw back. He inhaled the sweet fragrance of her hair.

Jemma focused on his chin, thinking how the little scar there used to feel against her fingers. "Spence, all I ever do is apologize. You're probably sorry that you've loved me all this time. I'm plain worthless." Jemma stood, and he let her go. She went up the stairs and closed the door to their room.

She waited for the sunset on the balcony. He hadn't mentioned the rosebush, but they didn't talk much anyways these days.

A helicopter flew overhead, sending shivers over her. He flew all those rescue missions in Vietnam, only to crash within days of his discharge. God's Plan was to give him back to her then. That glorious evening when he ran down the tracks against a sparkling sunset was etched in her brain.

The sunset on this night was not much to speak of, though. She went to their bed and fell across it, too weary to cry. Her eyes fell on their wedding picture. That was the most perfect day of her life. She had become a woman with him. Now she was his misery. Her old copy of Emily Dickinson's poems lay on the dresser. She picked it up and it fell open to the lines about a sparrow to whom God had given bread, but the little bird couldn't eat it because he was too struck with just having it.

It struck her that she owned this particular crumb, this guilty grief. It had become her *poignant luxury*, as the poetess had said. Maybe Miss Dickinson had meant something else, but Jemma took that thought away with her. She closed the book and stared at the rosebush. Brother Cleo's scripture about graciousness stuck in her head, waking up her brain again. She could use a whole truckload of God's face shining down on her right now.

Jemma got on her knees beside the bed and asked God one more time to forgive her and to help her find her sparkle for life. Maybe He would be gracious and sprinkle some out on her right then and there.

She lay her head on the bed, Spencer's side, pondering the word *gracious*. That adjective had never occurred to her when she thought of the Lord. It seemed to fit in better with Emily Post.

She wound the Starry Night music box that he had given her on her twenty-first birthday and lifted the lid to read the inscription, *I think of thee*. Spence always had thought of her. Since they were six years old, he had put her first and there she had remained. Rats. She had to get over this and make it up to him, somehow, and then maybe the Lord would shine on her. He had already been more than gracious by giving her Spencer's love and she knew it.

She drew herself up and looked in the mirror. "No more silence, no more darkness, as of this very minute," she said aloud.

Guitar music wafted up the stairs and she put her ear to the door, but almost immediately, it stopped. She heard, instead, his approaching footsteps and moved away, afraid of what he might say to her. The door didn't open, but she heard him playing and singing "I

Will Wait for You," the song from the music box, on the other side.

Jemma closed her eyes. The same feeling swept over her that she had when they saw each other after a year—during their big breakup in college—only she was too nervous to open the door this time. She grabbed a scrap of paper and wrote on it, then slid it under the door when the song was over. She stuck the pen under the door, too.

⁂

Spencer picked up the paper and read her words. *Do you see now that I don't deserve you?* He took the pen and wrote quickly, *I see now that you deserve all my love and my life,* then pushed it under the door.

A few seconds later it was returned. *I'm scared that I have lost my sparkle.* He wrote back. *We'll find it together.*

There was no response. He heard a shuffling, then quiet. He sat by the door for a long time before picking up his guitar to start downstairs. The door opened behind him. He turned to look right into her golden eyes. He took a few steps toward her and she didn't move away. They stood close enough to give each other goose bumps.

Jemma took his hands in hers. She kissed them, palms up, and put her head on his chest. "I'm so sorry about our baby, Spence. I will love you forever and always. Thank you for sticking with me, despite everything."

His eyes welled up. "I will love you until I become the stars for you, Jem. Please believe me."

"I keep it in mind, babe," she whispered and kissed him.

The ring of love he had given her sparkled in the moonlight as they began their gentle journey toward hope, healing, and joy.

⁂

He heard her downstairs when he woke up. She hadn't been in the kitchen in six weeks. "Everything okay?" he yelled.

"I'm bringing you breakfast. Stay in bed." She sounded good to him. Five minutes later she came up the stairs with a tray and a big smile. "Hi. I made you a real breakfast, see? No cereal. There's a flower, too. Smell it."

Spencer inhaled the fruity scent of the rose. "Very, very nice."

"That's all you can say about it?" she asked, sounding like her sassy self.

"I wasn't talking about the breakfast or the rose."

She gave him The Look that he had been dying to see. "Eat, and I'll tell you my plan." She climbed on the bed, settling next to him.

"What plan?" he said, folding a whole slice of bacon into his mouth.

"I want to take the rosebush that's on the balcony to Chillaton and plant it at Papa's grave."

"I wondered why you bought it."

"It will be to remember our first child—the one that I, that we, lost."

Spencer put his arm around her. "I think that's a beautiful idea, Jem. Sometimes I think that I don't deserve you."

She smiled and put her finger to his lips. "Everything good that I do, I learned from you, my husband. Everything."

❧

The sun was shining, and there was not a cloud to be seen. They drove through the arched gates at the Chillaton Citizens' Cemetery and waved at Scotty Logan, the caretaker. Spencer stopped and chatted with him. Jemma watched Spencer talk. He was such a good listener and genuinely cared about people. He would be a sweet daddy someday.

Scotty gave Spence a shovel, and they stopped at Papa's grave. Spencer dug a hole in the hard-packed ground. Jemma cut the plastic away from the plant and together they set it in the earth. On their hands and knees they filled it in, patted the soil, and poured four jugs of water on it.

Spencer put his arm around her and prayed, "Lord, we thank You for our blessings, for those we can keep and those that slip away. Help us to cope with the loss of our unborn child. Amen."

They sat in the bench by Papa's grave and held hands. A yellow butterfly landed on the smallest rosebud and rested. Its wings opened and closed for a long moment before it moved away.

Spencer leaned his head against hers. "Jem, you accused me last night of being sorry that I've loved you all these years. I'll tell you what I regret. I regret that I kept my promise to you and didn't try to see you when we broke up in college. I'm sorry that I went fishing the day you had the wreck, and I regret that I couldn't save my crew when our chopper went down in Vietnam."

"Oh Spence, I'm sorry that I ever made you promise such a thing that year. It was so stupid. As far as the wreck is concerned, there is no way you could have known that I was going to run head-on into Joe's truck. Daddy wanted to spend time with you that day anyway, and the helicopter crash, babe, there was nothing you could have done to prevent it. It wasn't your fault they died." Her voice trailed off with a sense of understanding.

"You're never alone again in this or any grief, Jem. I will always be beside you. Please promise me something, though. Say that you will never question my love for you. No matter the circumstances, that will always remain constant. The idea that you're not worthy of my love and devotion will never cross my mind. Promise that you'll never doubt that again." He held out his hand to shake on it. "Look me in the eye."

She squeezed his hand. "I promise that I will never again question your love for me."

"Now, c'mon, let's go see some people and have some Chillaton fun for the rest of the day."

"We aren't going to the castle, are we?" Jemma peered over her shoulder at his parents' house.

He opened the car door for her. "Nope. I'll stop by the dealership and see if Dad's there, but apparently, Mom has some thinking left to do."

They went to Plum Creek and played in the stream. The old cottonwood tree creaked and swayed above them as they relaxed in its shade. They got burger baskets with milk shakes at Son's Drive In, then surprised Lizbeth, Lester, Willa, and Joe with the feast. They visited until dark, then parked at the Salt Fork of the Red River to watch the stars. After spreading the quilt on the hood, they kissed and reclined on their arms to enjoy the sparkling night.

"I miss this, don't you, Spence?"

"There's nothing like it." He took a deep breath and reached for her.

"Unless it's this," she said, snuggling against him.

A shooting star made its way across the heavens. "Make a wish," Spencer said.

Jemma closed her eyes and crossed her fingers.

"Okay, now tell," he said.

"Nope. Then it won't come true. You always do that to me, but you never tell me yours."

They waltzed in the moonlight. Jemma closed her eyes and inhaled the familiar scent of his skin. "I wished for me to go to heaven before you because I cannot bear for you to become the stars for me."

"Sorry; that wish is already taken, only with a different outcome."

She grinned at him. "Maybe when we're one hundred and ten, we'll just take a nap on the tracks, okay?"

"I keep it in mind," he said.

Jemma was now running a tight schedule to be ready for the New York show. They created a drafting corner for Spencer in her painting room. She was usually quiet, and he could get lots of work done, but not always.

"Remember when you got your driver's license and we started going to the drive-in movies?" she asked. "We decided to do everything they did on the screen. I guess we couldn't do that if we were dating now, huh? We would have to break our eighth-grade promise of no fooling around until the wedding night. Movies are going to be the ruin of promises like that. Can you imagine trying to be good kids and seeing all the sex that is in movies now?" She waited for a comeback, but he was absorbed in his work. "Anyway, I want to watch *Saturday Night Wrestling* and do everything they do on that show, okay?" No response. She stared at his back. "Spencer!"

He jerked around in his chair. "What?"

"I said I want to watch *Saturday Night Wrestling*, okay?"

"Sure, baby. That'll be fun."

She narrowed her eyes at him, and her mouth formed a crooked little smile.

"Jem, I've decided that I don't want to build a chapel at the nursing home like we planned," he announced after supper.

Her jaw dropped. "That was supposed to be in memory of Kenneth Rippetoe." Spencer left the room while she was talking so she followed him, dish soap dripping from her hands. "Spence, we have to build the chapel. Kenneth was so sweet and wanted to do something to change nursing homes. Remember his granny?"

Spencer unrolled a set of blueprints on his drafting table. He pulled her in front of the table and she put her soapy hand over her mouth. "A new building? Whoa." She clapped and jumped around the room. "You are too much, Mr. Chase."

He grinned at her old cheerleading moves. "We'll have to find the right person to run it, though. Somebody with Kenneth's tender heart for the elderly. I'm excited to get started on it. I've bought the old nursing home and the land out by the drive-in theater. It's a great spot. We'll phase out the old one and move the residents into the new one."

Jemma watched him talk about the plans. He showed her every door and window. She put her arms around his waist and leaned her head against his chest, hearing his words through his heart.

By Saturday night, the portrait of Harriet was finished and she had the background done for the next one of her feisty, generous Great-Aunt Julia. She kept her eye on the clock and when it was five minutes until nine, she cleaned her brushes and dragged Spencer in front of the television. He didn't mind. Only Jemmabeth could get by with watching such a goofy thing, yet be so serious about her art. He actually enjoyed watching her more than she liked the silly program. It was so very good to have her back.

"Now, remember what we talked about. Be ready," she said with a cocked eyebrow.

Spencer frowned at her. "What's that?"

She was ready. Jock, The Spider, Snyder was pitted against the local favorite, Mory, The Snake, Watts. The Snake came out with his first move a little too slow and The Spider bounced off the ropes and flattened him with his full weight. Jemma forthwith stood up on the couch and landed on an unsuspecting Spencer. He couldn't move. Jemma giggled and rolled off him.

"Have you gone crazy?" he asked, coughing.

"I told you that I wanted to do everything they do on the show tonight. You weren't listening to me, were you? Oops, now you aren't watching." She moved like lightning and was on him with The Claw. Spencer flipped her over and caught her with a leg lock. She was helpless. "No fair," she moaned. "They haven't even done this one yet, you dog."

"All's fair in love and wrestling, baby." Spencer shook his legs unmercifully.

"I can't breathe," she said, her voice vibrating.

"Yes, you can. I'll let you up if you promise to use your skills for good and not for evil."

"I can't do that. I don't know what else may come up on the show."

"Then you can just stay there, young lady," Spencer said and changed the channel.

Jemma curled up in a ball, bit his leg, and escaped up the stairs while he yelped in pain and chased after her.

❧

"Trent is coming this weekend, but he says he'll stay in a hotel," Spencer announced.

"Why? He could sleep on the sofa bed for free," Jemma said, then stuck a thin paintbrush behind her ear as she analyzed Do Dah's left eye.

"I don't think money is an issue with your cousin, Jem."

"Two rich guys, huh? So are you going to form a partnership?"

"If all goes as planned. You're for it, right?"

"You'll be a great team. Whose name goes first?"

"I think 'Lillygrace and Chase' sounds good, don't you?"

"I knew you'd put yourself last. I was just checking."

❧

They celebrated their new corporation with dinner at Cattlemen's, the Golden Globe penthouse restaurant. Jemma took an official photograph of the partners signing a napkin. They decided to begin with an office in Chillaton, just to get their feet wet.

"I can't believe we're going to end up there," Jemma said during dessert. "Actually, I think we used to joke about that."

Trent folded his arms on the table, his dark brown eyes dancing.

"It's my idea. I've never lived in a small town. It's kind of exciting to me."

Spencer and Jemma exchanged looks and laughed.

"You're in for some big cultural changes, man," Spencer said, "but at least you can drive an hour and fly wherever you want, if it starts to get to you."

"Are there any more girls like you left in Chillaton?" Trent asked, his question directed at his cousin, but his eyes on a female diner next to them.

"If you mean smart aleck and stubborn, yeah, I guess." Jemma laughed.

"I mean beautiful and funny."

Spencer pulled her to him. "I got the beautiful one, but there are plenty of funny ones left."

"You'll find somebody. Not to worry. Where are you going to live?" Jemma asked.

Trent shrugged. "I have no idea. Maybe Lester would let me stay with him for a while."

"That'll be something to go from a Park Avenue town house to Lester's place."

Trent leaned back in his chair. "I decided in Vietnam that I wanted to live where life is peaceful. So I changed my goals over there, and I'm learning to appreciate family and friends more every day. You guys are an inspiration to me."

Jemma smiled at that. "Well, we can't promise you that it will be peaceful in Chillaton, but I guarantee it'll be different."

As they left the restaurant, Trent watched his cousin and his new business partner; they had what he really wanted—crazy love. He took a taxi to his hotel.

They drove home with the top down. "By the way, where do you plan for us to live?" Jemma asked, watching the speedometer.

"I think we'd better take a trip and see what we can find tomorrow," Spencer said as the Corvette zipped along the highway.

The flashing red and blue lights behind them made her scalp tingle. Spencer pulled over and knew he was doomed. Nobody gets a warning ticket in a Sting Ray convertible with a fabulous-looking girl in the car, and he was right. The state trooper walked away, and

Spencer pulled back onto the highway much like Lizbeth did when she took her driver's test.

Jemma exhaled. "How many of those can you get? I don't want to be the only driver in the family, but I guess it's kind of a relief to know that you aren't completely perfect."

Spencer chewed on his lip and adjusted his rearview mirror.

⚘

The next day they drove around Chillaton, looking at the small selection of rentals and homes for sale. "Let's take a break and head out to Plum Creek," Spencer said, driving like an old man.

The creek was still. It needed rain just like the cotton crops. This was one of those summers when Papa would have quoted his Scottish gran when she'd say, *The coos need a wooshing.* The cows definitely needed a washing around Chillaton. Even the coyotes were restless and thirsty. Everybody was talking about packs of them yipping and slinking around the countryside, coming close to the city limits. There was a threatening bank of dark clouds to the north, and Jemma was well aware of them. She had been through one tornado and didn't relish trying it again. The rusty windmill by the road groaned as it moved momentarily—against its will. Papa had built it decades ago and it marked the entrance to his and Gram's land on Plum Creek.

Jemma wrote their names in the sandy bank near where they had exchanged their marriage vows while Spencer got something out of the trunk. He was gone for a few minutes, then snuck up behind her and put a gold box in her lap.

"Happy early anniversary," he said and sat next to her.

Jemma untied the ribbon and looked inside. A piece of twine protruded through a hole in the bottom. She pulled the box off and followed the twine down the sandy shoreline to an old stand of cottonwoods, each one a giant. There, the twine was attached to survey stakes in a geometrical shape with one prominent pole in the middle. Attached to the pole was the piece of driftwood that Robby had carved for her hope chest when he could barely spell. Jemma's Place, it said.

She covered her mouth with her hands and turned to Spencer in realization of it all. She jumped on him, squealing in delight. He whirled her around in a circle like they did when they played "sling the statue" in the second grade. They fell, landing in the soft sand. This spot on the banks of Plum Creek would be their home.

❦

Lizbeth waited in the doorway with her arms stretched wide. Jemma and Spencer nestled right into them. "Thank you, Gram," Jemma said. "I love it."

"It was nothing but right for you two to have that spot of land. Your papa would have wanted it this way. I'll make sure Robby has a special place, too. Have you already made the plans for your house?"

"Well, just in the dirt." Spencer laughed. "It'll be something else, though. An artist and an architect should be able to come up with a sensational home. Thanks for letting us stay here until it's ready."

Jemma grabbed his arm. "Come with me, Spence, hurry."

They ran out to the tracks just in time for the freight train. Jemma took a deep breath as it clamored past, then turned to Spencer. "Now touch the rails," she said, putting his hand on the steel. "That's the way I feel about you even when you leave my sight. You warm my heart, Spencer Chase."

"It has to cool off sometime." He tucked her hair behind her ears.

"Yeah, but it's made of metal, and I'm not." She kissed him like they were still in high school.

❦

Lizbeth watched Jemmabeth and Spencer as they walked back to the house. Life shouldn't be so hard toward the end. Cam was her greatest blessing, and she had hoped he would be there with her to make the last of it as sweet as the beginning.

Nobody else had enjoyed Plum Creek as much as Jemmabeth. It was only natural that she and Spencer would inherit that land. When she'd signed the papers, though, Lizbeth's thoughts had wandered to Matthew and Luke. Had they survived the war, perhaps they, too, would have walked their daughters to an altar on its sandy shore. She sighed and set out Spencer's favorite cake along with her nicest dishes and was ready with a smile when they came back in the door.

❧

Jemma had everything packed for New York. Spencer got off early and came home. He presented her with a business card.

"I thought it was going to be Lillygrace & Chase," she said, taping the card to the refrigerator.

"Trent pointed out that if we put my name first, we would show up closer to the front of the listings in the Amarillo phone book," he explained, taking off his shoes.

Jemma snapped her fingers and went into the bathroom.

"Almost forgot something?" Spencer asked.

"I remembered, though," she said and climbed on his back. He stood, and she flopped back on the bed. "Come here." She puckered her lips at him.

"No time for that. We need to be at the airport in thirty minutes."

"Then we have ten minutes to kill, the way you drive." She grabbed him around his waist and pulled him down beside her. "I love you, Mr. Chase of Chase & Lillygrace. We are going to have fun in the big city."

He gave her the once-over. "You look like a New York model. Let me see if you kiss like one."

"Are you going to compare me to Michelle?"

"Nope. Don't even remember ever kissing her. You have erased every memory of every woman I ever dated."

"Nice answer," she said, "because if you had said yes, there would have been big trouble coming down your road, mister."

"You're big trouble anyway. Now let's get out of here. Save this for Manhattan."

❧

Jemma stepped out of the cab and drew a deep breath. Since forever, she had wanted to have a show in New York City. Spencer offered his arm like a true gentleman. "You are stunning, Mrs. Chase," he said in the elevator. "That's the dress you wore for your second exhibition in Paris."

"My, my, what a memory, and don't you do look good in that tux."

They were mid-kiss when the elevator door opened directly into the Sabine Gallery. It was very chic and urban and made for an interesting contrast with her work. She had twenty pieces of varying sizes and mediums for a two-week show that was a part of the "young artists" series at the gallery. It was bizarre to see people she had known most of her life hanging on the walls of a gallery like this, complete with designer lighting. She had painted Leon, from the Buddy Baker Band, rocking out on his guitar, hanging next to Son Shepherd, owner of Son's Drive In, whose cigar was clinging to his lip as he flipped a burger.

Jemma pointed out the painting of Trent and Spencer huddled around the kitchen table in California as they discussed their prospective business venture. The overhead light lent a glow to Spencer's blond hair.

"Oh man, I didn't know you were going to use that one," he said as they waited for the gallery manager to arrive.

"I like it. It's priced way, way high so nobody will buy it, and we can hang it in your waiting room someday," she said.

"I just hope there will be somebody to wait in the waiting room. Actually, I doubt we'll have one. Maybe just a comfortable seating area." Jemma could see the plans already forming in his head.

"Did you get the tickets for *Promises, Promises*?" she asked.

"The matinee was all I could get. Let's go dancing tomorrow night. Trent told me about a place that has a great band."

Jemma raised an eyebrow. "Trent goes dancing? I can't believe that."

"I think he is looking for a woman like the one I have."

"You think he'll find one?"

"There aren't any others," Spencer whispered as the gallery manager, a tall woman with hair like Cleopatra, approached them.

❧

If she met one more celebrity, Jemma would have to sit down. To shake hands with people she used to read about in movie magazines was too much to handle. Now what she really wanted was to dive in to the fancy food table with several luscious-looking items she'd never even seen Helene make. She had her eye on a nice meringue dessert with caramelized fruit around the edges. It looked like an edible sunset.

"Mrs. Chase, I'd like to introduce you to someone," the gallery manager said, just as Jemma was about to take a bite.

Rats. She dusted off her hands and left Spencer talking with the mayor of New York. The manager took her to a cluster of people who were admiring the painting of Harriet.

"Sir, I'd like you to meet the artist. This is Jemmabeth Chase. Mrs. Chase, this is Governor Ronald Reagan."

Jemma swallowed and shook his hand. He was even more handsome in person than he was on the screen, big or little. "It's a pleasure to meet you, sir," she said. "I hope you enjoy my work." He grinned and introduced her to his entourage. The twinkle in his eye reminded her of Papa's. Jemma answered some of the group's generic questions about her art, but the governor was interested in several pieces and wanted to know more about the people she had painted.

⊰◈⊱

Spencer watched her from across the room, as he enjoyed doing in public places. She could converse with kings and queens about her art, but Spencer got a chill when he saw her talking with Ronald Reagan. Lester would get goose bumps, too, when he found out because they shared a secret about the governor. Spencer couldn't wait to tell him that Mr. Reagan had bought the painting of Harriet. He had especially liked it that Harriet was Irish, like him.

⊰◈⊱

"Happy birthday, babe," Jemma said at midnight as they waited for a cab. "We could stay up all night and celebrate if you want to. I'm on a roll."

"Nope. Staying up all night is what we did before we got married." He whispered something in her ear, then gave their hotel address to the cab driver.

"Well, since you *are* the birthday boy." She giggled. "You realize I haven't been with you on your birthday in four years." She gave him a package from her bag. "Here, open this. I can't wait."

Spencer unwrapped the tissue and held up a midnight blue frame with tiny gold stars painted on it.

"It's to frame the four-leaf clover that you took to Vietnam. I painted a star for every night that we missed being together while you were there."

"You have a way about you, Jem," he said. "This is perfect."

"No, you are perfect," she said.

"Did Papa ever tell you about his dream that Ronald Reagan became the president and invited you to the White House to paint his portrait?"

She nodded. "I didn't think about it until the governor left. That's kind of weird."

"We shall see just how weird it is; his dream could come true. You are blessed."

"I'm blessed, all right. I am blessed that you have held me in your heart for all this time and never wavered."

Spencer whispered in her ear again, making her giggle. He tipped the cab driver and they ran inside their hotel.

Lester dusted the bedroom for the third time. If Trent didn't hurry up and move in, Lester would have to sacrifice another undershirt for a dust rag. "I never had me a boarder," Lester said as he watched Lizbeth punch down a fat ball of bread dough. "I ain't countin' that mail-order bride. She didn't give me nothin' but grief. Trent's payin' me a right smart amount of money to lay his head down at my house."

"Are you going to cook for Trent?"

"No ma'am, he told me that he's gonna cook for the both of us. Says it's his hobby. I'm hopin' he ain't fond of Chinese or something. I don't cotton to vittles that a feller's not sure whether he's eatin' plant or critter."

"I'm sure Trent will try to cater to your tastes, Lester. If not, you can come over for leftovers. Have you seen their office?"

"Yes ma'am. You won't recognize that old post office. Them boys have good heads on their shoulders, for rich kids. I reckon I'll just go down there now and see how things are comin' along. I don't suppose you'd like to accompany me, Miz Liz?"

"I can't stay long. I'll have to get back and tend to this bread." Lizbeth got her purse and followed Lester out the door.

Spencer had their house plans tacked on their home office wall so that whenever one of them got an idea, it was easy to make notes, but it was going to be a long time before any ground would be turned at Plum Creek. They were both too busy.

Jemma was getting better in the kitchen. She was using the rose-patterned dishes from her hope chest, and she had discovered casseroles and salads.

"This is good, Jem. What do you call it?" he asked.

"Friday night," she said. "I just make this stuff up. You can put anything in a casserole."

Spencer grinned at her. "You put it in there, baby, and I'll eat it. What a team."

"Have you decided on the paintings you want for the office?" Jemma asked.

"Trent picked the one of Lester in his stationmaster uniform, and I want the one of the little kids sitting on the bench in Scotland."

"You need a landscape, too. It soothes the savage beast."

"Are you calling me a savage beast?" Spencer raised his brow at her.

"Maybe. Want to play King Kong again?" She giggled.

"I don't think I can carry you up the stairs," he said, pulling on her braids.

"So now I'm fat?" Jemma put her hands on her hips.

"No, I'm the one out of shape. How about we play some basketball tomorrow?"

"You're on," she said, begrudgingly leaving the rest of her casserole on her plate.

⊰✿⊱

Trent met them at the office. They let Jemma decide where to hang the paintings. It bore no resemblance to the old post office where she used to go with Papa to mail Christmas packages to Gram's old maid sisters in Houston. The new owners had stripped the hardwood and refinished them with a light varnish. A skylight filled the room with Texas sunshine. The old wallboard had been removed, exposing the original brick construction, and the oak and leather furniture lent a Panhandle flair to the office. Jemma bought a half-dozen giant potted plants, and the place couldn't have looked finer.

Trent and Spencer sat in the comfy armchairs talking about advertising while Jemma put the final touches on things. "I almost forgot," Trent said. "I hired a secretary since you turned that task over to me. She's a friend of yours, so I figured that was a solid reference. She's quite the looker, too, but I'm sure you already know that."

"What's her name?" Jemma asked, holding the last potted plant at such an angle that water spilled out on the polished wood floor.

Trent pulled out a file folder and read from it. "Melissa. Melissa Blake. She'll start next week."

Chapter 8

Hardtack

They sat in the corner booth at Daddy's Money. Spencer puffed out his cheeks and exhaled slowly. "Okay, Jem, what do you want me to do?"

Jemma took a sip of her sweet tea. "All she wants is to have you for her own. That's her goal. It always has been. Now she'll be able to spend more time with you every day than I can."

"Baby, it's the first decision that Trent has made in our partnership. I can't very well tell him to rescind it. I could, I guess, let him know that you are paranoid about Missy and we need to rethink it, and I'll do that if you want me to."

She narrowed her eyes at him, then folded and unfolded her napkin. "Why does The Cleave have to come along and make me miserable? You have to admit that she throws herself at you and she has a lot to throw."

"Everybody in Chillaton has seen enough of Missy to last a lifetime. You know that I'm not interested in her. I've never been attracted to her. Besides all that, Mrs. Chase, you are my wife and you made me a promise, remember?"

"I know that you love me, Spence, but you took her out more times than necessary when we broke up. You sprayed her with water and kissed her."

"You've never caught on to my plan, baby. I only had three dates with her, and I did it hoping that you would hear about it. I was using her to win you back. Did you ever consider that? If not, it was a lousy plan because it has caused me much more grief than it was worth."

Jemma's eyes darted up. "Really. That was it? Why did you have to kiss her to accomplish that?"

"Jemmabeth, you dated half of Dallas for almost a year, plus Paul Turner for about four months. Am I to believe that you never kissed anybody?"

"Truce."

"I am curious to know what you think Missy has that could possibly steal my heart."

"She is assertive and very self-confident. She has a perfect figure—beyond perfect. She hates me. She has all that blond hair, and she is the queen of flirts."

Spencer sighed. "Jem, if you don't remember all the reasons that I love you, I'll tell you again. I love your heart, your laugh, the way you walk and dance. I love your talent, your temper, and your kisses. I love your spirituality, your sense of humor, the way you wear your hair, and those pouty lips. I think *you* are the one with the perfect figure. I love the scar on your head, the way you say my name, the way you sing, and the way you love me. There is no room for Melissa Blake in my heart or my head." He kissed her right smack on the lips even though there were elderly diners nearby.

He wasn't playing fair. "The fact remains that she'll be with you all day and she'll flaunt herself the whole time," she said. "How can you not watch her?"

Spencer raised his hands like an evangelist. "Baby, I'm not going to watch her. I can't help but see her, but watching is something I only do with you. Besides, I want to work at home all that I can. If we get busy enough, Trent can use her, and I'll hire some old lady. It could very well be that Missy is not secretarial material anyway."

Jemmabeth took some consolation in that thought, but not much.

❧

Lizbeth went to the grocery store and loaded up. Spencer had given her more than enough money to feed the three of them for a year. She put the groceries away and checked their room again. It needed fresh flowers; her granddaughter had to have them.

Lester knocked, then let himself in the back door. "I've got the car house ready for our little artist. These young'uns are goin' to give us a boost. I feel it in the air."

"I do too, Lester. How is your new chef working out?"

"No offense, Miz Liz, but he's as good as you are. Well, not quite, but comin' along." Lester thought again. "He can do some things good, but he's still got a lot to learn. He ain't tried bread and cobbler and such yet."

"That's nice," she said, surprising him. Either she was in a rare mood or wasn't listening.

"Did I ever tell you about my pa and the biscuits?" Lester asked.

"No, I don't recall that one," Lizbeth said, humming.

"Well, sir, my pa fancied himself a sharpshooter. He was kindly boastful about it, too. Claimed he could hit a day-old hardtack biscuit thirty foot up in the air, then catch the crumbs from it in his mouth."

"You don't say," Lizbeth muttered, going through her recipe box.

"My uncle lived just down the hill from us. He and Pa were always playin' pranks on each other. So, one Sunday, Uncle Ketch and Pa were going on about who was the best shot, and they come hence to makin' a wager about it. Pa grabbed his bucket of stale hardtacks—we kept 'em for the hogs—and his Winchester. He was all set up in the pasture, ready to prove himself. Uncle Ketch said Pa couldn't shoot three in a row and trap a single crumb in his mouth. Pa did, though. When Uncle Ketch got ready to throw up the third one, I seen him grab somethin' off the ground instead of out of the hardtack bucket. He let 'er fly. Pa nailed it and run around until he got himself a chunk of it in his mouth. Uncle Ketch come hence to laughin' his head off while Pa upchucked all over creation. Seems Pa had swallowed himself a crumb off a cow chip. Uncle Ketch took off down the road as fast as his old paint horse could trot. I'll never forget the look on Pa's face when he come back up to the house."

"What did you say, Lester?" Lizbeth asked. "Were you talking about biscuits?"

"Miz Liz, are you feelin' all right?" Lester looked at her over his bifocals.

"I'm feeling fine. I think I must have missed part of your story, but now I have my recipes written down and organized for Jemmabeth. She wants to learn how to cook from me. Would you like some biscuits and dewberry jam, Lester?" Lizbeth poured him another cup of coffee. "Shooting food seems like a waste of everybody's time to me. I hope you don't take up with such nonsense."

"Good-bye, honeymoon house," Jemma said, sniffing into a tissue. Her voice echoed around the empty apartment. "We had some rough times here, huh?"

"Oh, but we had some really, really good times here, too. Let's have one last dance. May I?" he asked, taking her hand.

They danced around the living room where their first Christmas tree had been and into the spare bedroom where Jemma had painted her way to Manhattan and where the baby furniture had waited. Spencer carried her out the door. "I carried you over the threshold the first time, so I should do the same for the last, right?" He locked it up. "Now, come on, we have a new chapter in our life to unfold," he said and kissed her.

They had borrowed Lizbeth's car for this last part of the move. The Corvette just wouldn't hold enough stuff. Spencer turned on the radio for a distraction. Lizbeth had it set on the Cotton John Show. "Welcome to the best part of a Golden Spread day," Cotton John said in his nasal tone before Jemma switched him off.

"Spence, would you show me where I had the wreck? I've never really seen it."

He was a little surprised because she had never mentioned it before. "Sure, if that's what you want. I'm not all that fond of the spot." He pulled off the road.

They walked around the nondescript ditch. A few sunflowers sprouted among the Johnson grass. Jemma held on to his arm as though the wind could carry her away from him. "Why do you think God didn't want us to get married then?"

"I have no idea, Jem. It's like Gram says, His ways are not our ways."

"The only good I can see from it was that Willa married Joe. Could that have been worth—well, never mind," she said and looked out over the pasture adjacent to the highway. A cluster of Hereford cattle gawked back at her, chewing their cuds. "Let's go."

"Don't you think this is weird to live next door to Trent and see him at the office every day, too?" Jemma asked as they pulled into the driveway. She had not mentioned The Cleave in a week.

"Yeah, but it's only temporary. I'm sure Trent will find someplace else to live. Look at Gram. She's beaming because we're moving in." Spencer got out of the car and gave Lizbeth a hug.

Jemma watched them. She might never have a hugging relationship with his mother. She had hoped that the baby might make a difference, but the Lord had other ideas. She took a deep breath as Spencer opened her door. Maybe he was right. This was a new chapter.

They wanted to see the sunset from their old necking spot at the river after supper. As the Corvette topped the last hill before the turnoff, Spencer slowed up. "Good grief. Somebody hit a deer. We don't have that many around here to spare, either."

"Oh Spence, look!" Jemma pointed to the ditch beside the dead doe. "It's her fawn. It can't even be a day old. Look how tiny it is."

Spencer pulled off the road. "Its leg is caught in the fence."

"We have to do something." She was out of the car before Spencer could think straight.

He jumped out and caught her elbow as she approached the little animal.

"Wait, Jem. We don't want to frighten it any more than it already is," Spencer said. "Let me think."

The fawn made a pitiful noise and jerked its leg. Jemma froze by the front bumper. It turned its brown eyes on her and shuddered. "Hurry, Spence," she whispered.

Spencer grabbed their old stargazing quilt. He motioned for Jemma to follow him. They inched their way toward the fawn. A car sped by on the road, causing the baby to resort to another spasmodic attempt to free itself. Spencer took advantage of the distraction and eased the quilt over its little body. Jemma held the quilt in place while Spencer worked its leg free of the fence wire. They both held tight to the animal, binding it as best they could with the quilt. "Get in the car and I'll hand him to you." Spencer struggled with the fawn as Jemma let go. She ran to the car. Spence laid it in her lap and shut the door.

She covered its head with the quilt, but its sharp hooves dug into Jemma's legs until it stopped wiggling. "Where can we take it?" she asked, holding it against her.

"We'll take it by Doc Evans. Maybe he could keep it overnight in one of his big kennels. He'll know who to call in the morning. Are you okay?"

Jemma nodded, her pulse racing. She could feel the fawn's heartbeat even through the folds of the quilt, and its little body was warm and helpless in her arms. She turned to look out the window so Spencer couldn't see the tears in her eyes.

Chapter 9

Mr. Universe

Lizbeth had her work cut out for her. Jemmabeth was never interested in cooking before, but now it was time to learn. She knew how to plan a menu, but had no clue what to do about it after that. Lizbeth worked side-by-side with her every evening for a month so that supper was on the table at six. The rest of the day Jemma was in the car house doing what she did best, creating masterpieces on canvas.

"Cooking is divided up into science, math, and art," Lizbeth said. "You should like the last of those three."

"It's so time-consuming, though." Jemma frowned at the pie-crust she was about to bake. "I just need to hire you to do it for us. Wouldn't that work?"

"Even so, honey, everybody needs to learn the basics so you can pass them on to your children," Lizbeth said, then wished she hadn't. She recanted. "When the time is right. Now remember to watch the clock, or this crust will get too brown."

Jemma put it in the oven and set the timer. She plopped down in one of the yellow and chrome chairs.

"How's Trina these days?" Lizbeth asked.

"She's fine. Nick told Spencer that he's going to propose at Christmas because he'll be finishing up his internship this spring." Jemma moved to the window as a freight train went by. "She'll be Mrs. Fields by next summer."

"What's wrong, sugar?" Lizbeth asked. "You can't seem to sit still these days."

"I miss Spencer."

"Why don't you walk down there and see him? Surely he's not that busy yet," Lizbeth said.

"I don't want to look like I'm spying on him. He's working on plans for the nursing home and our house. The firm in Amarillo is sending some business this way, too."

Lizbeth lowered her coffee cup. "It's the Blake girl."

"Missy is such a flirt, Gram. I know she wants Spence even though we are married. She spends eight hours a day with him and I don't."

"Jemmabeth, you surely aren't suggesting that Spencer could, for one minute, be distracted by that silly girl."

"He dated her when I broke up with him. She's beautiful. I know he loves me, but he's only human," Jemma said, sketching a passenger train for Shorty's jar.

"Spencer is not that kind of man, honey. If anybody should have his eyes peeled, it would be Trent. He's a willing target in my mind. You have every right to go see your husband. I'll watch this crust for you."

The phone rang. Jemma sprang up, hoping it was her man.

"Jem? It's Sandy. Can you talk a minute?"

"Sandy! I haven't heard from you in so long. How are you?" Jemma asked. Sandy broke down. Jemma hadn't heard her cry since the tenth grade when Marty broke up with her for a week. "What's wrong?"

"I'm leaving Marty. It's horrible. Everything has gone to pot. I can't do this anymore," she moaned.

"What happened?"

"Marty is messed up. He is moody and ticked off most of the time. I'm afraid that he's going to explode."

"Has he been to a doctor?"

"Yeah, right. He won't go anywhere except to a bar."

"Well, he'll come around. It'll be all right." Rats. That sounded pathetic.

"No. There's more." Sandy took a deep breath. "He has a girlfriend."

Jemma gasped. "He wouldn't. He's too crazy about you."

"He's crazy all right, but not about me. I've gotta go. I'll be home this weekend. Don't tell anybody but Spence, okay? Jem, never take anything for granted."

Jemma hung up the phone and went back into the kitchen. "Gram, I'll be back in an hour." She took off running toward the tracks and the Chase & Lillygrace office.

◄◊►

The office reeked of Chanel No. 5. The Cleave opened Spencer's office door holding some papers and laughing. Jemma's face prickled.

"Well, look who it is." Missy bent over her desk to write a note.

Jemma looked away, knowing the scoop-necked dress would reveal more than she cared to see.

"I assume you're checking up on Spence. We'll be finished with this in about an hour," Missy said, her miniskirt barely covering her thighs. "We've had our heads together over this all day."

Spencer came out of his office. "Hey, Jem, come in. Melissa, you can finish that up yourself sometime."

Jemma glared at her. She even wanted to stick her tongue out, too, but didn't. Spencer closed the door behind them and gave her a good kiss as they sank into his chair.

"What was so funny to make Missy laugh?" she asked.

"Oh. I told her that miniskirts and low-cut tops are not allowed, as in the dress code, and she said that she hadn't read the code. I reminded her that she had signed it, but she claimed that her dress shrunk in the laundry. She thought that was hilarious. I wasn't laughing because I included that dress code just for this very reason." Spencer studied Jemma's face. "What's up? You have a look that worries me."

"Sandy is leaving Marty."

"No way. What happened?"

"She said he's mean, drinking, and has a girlfriend."

"He's been known to be a hothead, but man, this really shocks me. They were always so tight." He lifted her chin. "What happens to other people has nothing to do with our relationship. Remember the promise."

Missy opened the door. "Sorry. I thought you might want to look these over. It's the bid from the contractor in Lubbock." She flashed her perfect smile at Spencer.

"Melissa, always knock before you come in my office, and if my wife is with me, don't disturb us at all. Got it?" Spencer said, his voice low and direct.

"Sure. You're the boss." She turned to leave, then came back.

"Listen, Jemmabeth, this is so weird, but one of my closest sorority sisters went out a few times last Christmas with your old boyfriend, Paul Turner. Isn't that just too wild? She said he's the sexiest hunk ever, and he confer. . .confron. . .*told* her a few things about you. I thought you'd like to know that." Her lips puckered up, delighted in her own revelation.

"Why don't you leave a little early today, Missy?" Spencer said, his tone now chilly. "Remember the dress code tomorrow. This is your third warning. When Trent gets back from New York, we will all sit down and review a few things. Are we clear on that?"

Missy left with a triumphant toss of her mane.

Jemma was still in his lap but dry-mouthed and wilted. Spencer's arms were around her, and they had not loosened during Missy's little scene. "Don't let it get to you, Jem. I'm the one who has to deal with those memories now."

Jemma nodded. She closed her eyes and moved her fingers over his hand. He was the most patient person on the planet, but there was a healthy portion of melancholy in his voice. She exhaled and slid off his lap. "I'm making you a pie for supper. I'd better go home and finish it."

He smiled. "Go home and paint. I'm not worried about your cooking like Gram is. I'll see you in a couple of hours or you can stay here with me. Forget the pie."

"No. I'd better get home. I miss you, babe. I hope you can work at home someday. I love you."

When Jemma stepped out of his office, The Cleave was pretending to tidy up her desk.

Jemma paused, then moved right up next to Missy, so close that her nostrils were filled with Chanel. "You know, *Missy*, I read the other day that when men see a large, exposed bosom like yours, it only reminds them of their lactating mothers. In other words, it makes them want to go eat pizza or a burger. You might think about that if you are hoping to hook a man with cleavage. You could be transporting them mentally to Son's or Daddy's Money with that very dress. Sometimes less is more, if you catch my drift. If you are thinking large, maybe you should invest in a really big dictionary for your desk; the word you couldn't think of was *confided*."

❧

Spencer, listening from his chair, grinned broadly at Jemma's spunky rebuke. He laid the papers on his desk and leaned back, thinking of the afternoon of their wedding—the first time he ever saw his sweet wife's body. That moment was something he would never forget. He put the papers in his drawer and turned off the lights in his office. If he hurried, he could still catch Jemmabeth and give her a ride home.

❧

Jemma and Sandy sat in the Corvette at Son's Drive In. Sandy's hazel eyes held none of their old fire and her makeup was not exactly perfection, which was even more shocking. Her frosted blond flip was droopy, and she had not touched her favorite food, French fries.

"It got so that I couldn't figure out what to say to him," Sandy said. "You know me; I'm sarcastic, but it's just for fun. He always liked that about me. I even tried to tone it down, thinking that might help. If I said it was a rainy day, he would take it personally and jump all over me, then sulk about it. If I asked him to take out the trash, he growled at me and gave me the evil eye the rest of the day. He made sure I had gone to bed before he came home at night, but if I mentioned it, he would leave the house and slam the door behind him."

"What about the drinking?" Jemma remembered the time Marty got suspended from CHS for drinking and fighting under the bleachers during a pep rally.

"I think the heavy drinking started in Vietnam. The MPs arrested him one night. He drank when we first got married but never alone at a bar. He met his girlfriend at one."

"I'm sorry, Sandy. Y'all always seemed so much in love. I never thought this could happen. Do you think it was the war that changed him?"

"All I know is that I am not one to stay around if somebody hits me. I don't care even if he is Mr. Universe. I could work through the girlfriend business, but not his temper. I would have come home sooner, but my daddy would have killed him if he'd seen what Marty did to my face one night."

"Good grief." Jemma squeezed Sandy's hand. "You should've

had him arrested."

"He would've gotten out and done it again."

Jemma couldn't shake the idea of Martin qualifying as Mr. Universe—not if she were one of the judges. "Has he called yet?"

"Nope. He doesn't care. Besides, I'm sure she's moved in with him."

"What's she like?"

"She's kind of mousy with narrow eyes and a big bust," Sandy said.

"Like The Cleave?"

"Kinda, but The Cleave has those long legs and all that hair. This one gets by on just being loosey goosey. The girlfriend business doesn't bother me that much anymore. Isn't that weird? I think he may have fooled around in the army, too."

"Good grief, Sandy. I can't believe this is happening. Life changes so fast."

"Believe it, Jem. It can happen to anybody. Marty's on a path of self-destruction, and he can go straight there with his girlfriend for all I care."

"Do you still love him?"

Sandy sniffed and stared at the flashing neon sparks above Son's sign. "The well is dried up in that department. He used it up with his surly temper and his fist. I can take a lot, but he dished out too much. It wasn't fun anymore, and now it's over."

"Just like that? You don't even want to try and work it out?"

"No. Once he started the punching and kicking, I looked at him with new eyes. I don't care how long we've been together. The last time I saw him, he came home drunk and slapped me for scratching an old 45 record he had. Get this: The name of the song was 'If Jesus Came to Your House.' I accidentally scraped it when we were packing to move to Idaho, and he knew that. Some of the things he said to me will hang in my ears for the rest of my life, even if he apologizes on his knees." She drew herself up. "But I will never be mistreated. You know me better than that."

"Good grief, Sandy, nobody expects you to put up with getting hit, but surely you feel something for him. Maybe you're being too hasty. Let your heart rest awhile. Remember me and my stupid decisions."

"You had to be there, Jemma. I'm not sentimental like you. I don't hold on to things like you did with that cowboy of yours. You're not still carrying a torch for him in the back of your mind, are you?"

"I am not!"

"Just curious. My mom sent me your picture with some guy in the Dallas paper right after Christmas. If that was Paul, it's no wonder you fell so hard. He was something else. He'd win Mr. Universe even over Marty."

"Yeah. That picture was a bad deal. I guess he's obsessed with me or something."

Much to Jemma's relief, Sandy changed the subject. "Do you know of any jobs around town? I need money."

"You could have been Spencer and Trent's secretary, but The Cleave got that job."

"You're kidding me. Spence hired her? No, wait, I bet your cousin hired her. His tongue was probably hanging out as soon as she walked in the door," Sandy said. "I bet that's driving you nuts."

"I'm trying to be cool, but you know she only wants to flirt with Spence."

"Maybe she wants to be your cousin-in-law. Don't worry, though. You have Spencer all to yourself."

Jemma laughed at the *cousin-in-law* part. "What's next for you?"

"I don't know. You and Spence don't know what it's like to be married and broke. If things had been different, I could have put up with living on a potato farm in the middle of nowhere. Listen, I need to get home. My mom is worried sick about all this."

"Here, take this." Jemma slipped a hundred-dollar bill into Sandy's hand. "You can pay me back sometime."

Sandy looked at the money for a second, then burst into tears.

Jemma dropped her off at the Bakers' house. She sighed and watched as her best friend since nursery school trudged up to the steps and waved. How could love be so easily whipped around in the wind? Jemma had doubted her love for Spencer when she met Paul. Were it not for the good Lord's Plan, she might have been Mrs. Turner now. She had a sudden urge to see Spencer, so she dropped by his office. The Cleave was typing but stopped when

Jemma slipped past her. She probably didn't want her to see how many mistakes she was making.

"Nice skirt." Missy eyed Jemma's hand-me-down silk that sported a couple of holes. "Still working on the bohemian thing, huh? Ever think you could be embarrassing your husband? He's such a professional."

"It's amazing that you consistently remember the word *bohemian*, when so many others escape your brain, Missy. Anyway, I don't really care about fashion," Jemma said. "I wear what feels good. I like cotton and silk."

"You should get that colored friend of yours to help you. It's weird how she's making something of herself, going against the nature of the coloreds. Maybe she'll save the government some money and won't be having a bunch of babies to get more money in her welfare check like the rest of them." Missy returned to her typing.

Jemma's throat tightened. "Your comments about Trina are unfounded and unappreciated, Missy. What would you know about welfare? Your daddy owns every dinky movie theater in the Panhandle." She lowered her voice. "It's not the natural order of things, Missy. It's not *nature's due* or something. I'd like to see how you would have turned out if you were born black in a white world."

"Me? Black?" She laughed. "It's nothing but right for some to be born less than equal to us. Deal with it. Hey, I bet Spencer has never sprayed your T-shirt with water and said, 'bottoms next' to you."

Jemma took a step toward Missy's desk with the full intention to slap her just as Trent emerged from his office. "Hi there, Jem. Spence and I thought it would be fun to catch dinner and a movie tomorrow in Amarillo. How does that sound to you?"

"Sounds great," Jemma said. The Cleave had been spared a slap or The Claw once again.

Spencer appeared and put a folder on Missy's desk, then turned his attention on his wife. "Just the woman I'm looking for. Come into my office."

Jemma took a breath to regroup.

"See you tomorrow night then," Trent said.

"How do you like your new house?" Jemma asked over her shoulder. "Lester misses you."

"It'll work for now. I'll have you two over soon. The painters are finishing up today," Trent added as Spencer guided Jemma into his office and shut the door.

"We are not leaving this office until we finish these house plans." Spencer unrolled their dream home. "We need to be alone again."

"You design it and surprise me." She reached to straighten a big painting of Plum Creek that hung over his drafting table. "I'll like anything you come up with, except your obnoxious, ignorant, big-mouthed secretary who thinks you said 'bottoms next' when you sprayed her with water."

He laughed. "Missy has a problem with words. She makes typos all the time. Now come on; I'm not doing this by myself. We are designing it together. What do you say if we push the deck out just a little more here." He pointed to the spot on the plans, then took off his tie, unbuttoned his shirt, and rolled up his sleeves. "We need to break ground this month."

Jemma picked up his tie and looped it around his neck, pulling him to her. "First things first, mister."

❧

Trent picked them up in his new convertible. Jemma and Spencer sat in the back. "You aren't going to put the top down, are you?" Jemma asked.

"No. Melissa probably wouldn't like it if the wind messed up her hair." Trent laughed.

Jemma's googly eyes bored a hole in the back of Trent's head. "*She's* coming?"

"Yeah. I haven't been out with anybody since I moved here." Trent pulled up in front of the Blakes' colonial, redbrick house. It took up half the block. "I'll be right back," he said and went to the front door.

Spencer held up his hands. "I had no idea he was going to ask her. Just make the best of it."

"There is no 'best of it' with Missy. Why don't you tell him that I can't stand her?"

"I know she's always acted witchy toward you, but don't let this ruin the evening, baby. Trent deserves some fun."

"Well, The Cleave knows how to dish that out. Ask any boy in our class."

"Except me," Spencer said. "Remember, I was only gambling for your attention."

"Are you two necking already back there?" Missy asked as she burst into the car, bringing her Chanel with her. "Jemma, that color sort of washes your skin out." She smiled over the back of the seat at Spencer. "Anything looks yummy on you, though, Spence."

The evening was ruined as soon as Jemma saw her. *Witchy* was putting it mildly. Missy overwhelmed Trent. If Jemma caught her ogling Spencer one more time, though, she was ready with The Claw, The Sleeper, and a full Cinderblock. The Cleave would be a good name for a wrestling move. She could clamp one hand around Missy's mouth while the other applied a thick coat of mayonnaise to her hair, just to settle an old score.

"Do you have your house plans ready?" Trent asked as they waited for their sundaes after the movie. Missy rested her chin on his shoulder while he talked. Not exactly first date behavior, in Jemma's opinion. How could they go back to an office relationship after that?

"Yeah, almost. The excavation starts next week. I want to get rolling on it before Thanksgiving," Spencer said.

"How exciting," Missy gushed. "Let's go see the building site. Maybe we could have a picnic there tomorrow. That would be kind of…homespun. We could splash around in the water. I have a crazy new bikini, or I could wear a T-shirt and cutoffs." The T-shirt part was directed straight at Spencer.

Jemma's mouth twitched.

"We're busy tomorrow," Spencer said quickly, squeezing Jemma's hand under the table.

"Well, then we could go, huh, boss?" Missy breathed in Trent's ear. Trent gulped.

"There's a lock on the gate," Spencer said.

"There must be a key then." Missy took the cherry off Trent's sundae and held it by the stem as she ate it with her perfect teeth. *Fangs,* Jemma thought.

Spencer changed the subject by discussing the movie they'd just seen while Missy laughed way too loud and traced around Trent's ear with her long, red fingernails. *Witch Claws.*

It was a painfully long ride home. Jemma watched helplessly as The Cleave tried every move she had on poor Trent. Probably 99 percent of it was for the benefit of those in the backseat. Jemma spent the last half hour of the trip with her eyes closed but her ears wide open.

⟞⟐⟞

Jemma could not let it go. "That was totally unethical. I think Missy should always call y'all Mr. Chase and Mr. Lillygrace."

"I don't know what Trent is thinking, but we'll talk," Spencer said with an audible yawn.

"He doesn't have a chance and you know it. The Cleave has a plan. If she can't get you, she's going for him and wants you to watch." Jemma turned over. "Remember, I'm the only show you watch."

He turned over. "Are you about to put on a show for me?"

"Maybe. Is Gram asleep?"

"She's snoring. What are you doing?"

"Shhh. I need to work out my frustrations with some wrestling moves. You are going to get what The Cleave deserved all night long. Get ready, mister, and keep your voice down." Jemma assumed a grappling stance on the cool floor. Her husband stifled his laughter as best he could until she hit him with The Cinderblock.

Chapter 10
Hauntings

The wind rattled the car house windows and whipped grains of sand against the glass. On days like this, even the birds took shelter. Nedra would use up several cans of Aqua Net on her patrons today. Jemma, however, stood on the tracks and surveyed the houses on the other side. Her ponytail flew at her side like a flag in a gale. Missy's comments and insinuations about welfare haunted her heart. Rats on Missy's ignorance, but her own indignant words were worthless unless she took some action. Lecturing The Cleave about inequality was one thing, but Jemma hadn't done anything, really, to help the situation, either. Maybe the Holy Spirit had laid this burden on her heart for a reason. How long would it take for things to change if left to the natural order of life in Chillaton? There was no pride for anyone picking up welfare checks. Pride came from working hard and doing the job well.

Jemmabeth walked with her head down, against the wind, along the rails to further survey the neighborhood. She waved at Joe as he hustled into his house with the mail. Jemma smiled. He and Willa were so happy that nobody saw much of them these days. She had invited them over for supper several times so she could show off her new cooking skills, but they always gave some excuse to stay home. Jemma knew that feeling. She hoped that she and Spencer would always have it. It was fun living at Gram's, but it was not the unabashed freedom they had enjoyed at their own apartment.

She plodded down the tracks for a while until she saw a For Sale sign stuck in the middle of the cow pasture across from Shorty Knox's dugout. Her scalp tingled at the thought, and the sign quivered in the wind. She memorized the number, then ran down the tracks to Main Street. She burst into Spencer's office without asking Missy, but he was on the phone. Jemma paced around his office until he hung up. She landed on his lap.

"This is a pleasant surprise," he mumbled before he kissed her.

She jumped off and resumed her pacing. She took the rubber band out of her hair and played with it as she talked. "You know that things are far from equal in Chillaton, and nobody wants to change anything. They just sit around and gripe about it, as though it's part of our destiny—like enduring the wind or something. I think we have the resources to make a difference. So, I want to buy a little land across the tracks and start some kind of business to help that neighborhood become independent of welfare. There's a for sale sign in a pasture there right now, and I think it's a sign from God. What do you think?"

Spencer blinked. "Now tell me this again."

Jemma started over, adding bits of heartfelt philosophy here and there. Spencer nodded, jotted a few notes, including the number of the Realtor, then smiled. "I understand what you are saying and I agree, but something like this would take a lot of planning, Jem. What kind of business are you thinking about?"

"That part I don't know. I suppose I need to do some research to see what skills are floating around over there, but we have to do something, babe. I mean it's not right for some of us to be so content while others are hurting, you know? I just can't accept that nothing can be done. I want everybody to feel good inside about living here," she said, then got distracted by his eyes. "I love you, Spence." She kissed him like they hadn't seen one another in a month.

"Let's go out to the river, my little thinker," he said.

"Tonight?"

"No, right now."

❧

Willa's old 'tunia path was no longer the dirt lane with perennial petunias planted in old boots. Jemma and Trina had rescued all the boot planters they could carry when a tornado ripped through town. Joe had changed that when he laid out flat, smooth rocks in a curved design. On both sides he had created flower beds lined with bricks. The porch was graced with a railing, as were the steps leading up to the front door. The roof that had been damaged by the tornado was new, as was the addition Joe had begun on the back and side of the old house.

Willa stood at the ironing board. The old sign that had advertised her business from her porch post for years—DOES IRONING AND GUARANTEE HER WORK—was now hung nonchalantly above her rocking chair.

She threw up her arms when she saw who was knocking. "Come in this house, child."

"Your place is looking so good," Jemma said.

"It's been way too long since I seen you, sugar," Willa exclaimed. "Set yourself down. You know this ain't gonna be my kitchen when Joe finishes his project. This'll be the laundry room, he says. I'm gonna have me a whole room to do the wash and my ironin' jobs. Don't that beat all?"

"Where is Joe?" Jemma asked.

"He had to run to the lumber yard for somethin'. That man is the hardest-workin' human I ever saw." Willa laughed. "He can't sit still, except for lovin' on me." She covered her mouth and giggled.

Jemma smiled at her own knowledge of that kind of man. "I need your help, Willa. Is there one thing that folks in your neighborhood know how to do better than anything else?"

"Law, child. What kind of a question is that to start off with?"

"I have to know. Let's say that just the women were all in business together. What is a skill that they would have, other than cooking?" Jemma leaned forward for the answer.

"Are you workin' for some TV game show? My ol' noggin ain't even been turned on yet today." Willa puckered her lips and considered the question. "I can see you're set on a quick answer. Hmm. . .folks over here makes nearly everything they wear. I reckon that's what you'd call a skill. 'Course we been workin' the land ever since folks needed help, too."

Jemma wrote it down. "Hand sewing. Does anybody know how to run a sewing machine?"

"Gweny Matthews and, of course, my Latrina. What you got cookin' in that pretty head of yours?"

"I want to start a business over here to help families get off welfare."

"Oh, for land's sake, sugar, that ain't gonna happen. It would take a miracle."

"I believe in miracles, Willa. I'll see you later and we'll talk more."

Jemma dashed out of the house, down the path, and across the train tracks.

Willa shook her head and turned back to her ironing. "That child's headin' for nothin' but disappointment, but Lord love her for tryin'."

⌘

"Maybe what you should do next, Jemma, is have a meeting and see if the neighborhood is interested in such a venture. It would have a better chance at success if you have their support," Trent said as the three of them sat in the conference room.

Spencer nodded. "I agree. If this is going to get off the ground, it'll need the whole community behind it. At the earliest stages, maybe we could use the basement of the Bethel Church and, of course, pay rent and all utilities for it."

Jemma had written everything they said on her notepad. "Want to come over for supper tonight, Trent? I'm cooking Gram's Cornish pasties. It's an old family recipe with meat and potatoes that are folded up in pastry," she said in culinary triumph.

"Thanks, but I'm cooking for Melissa tonight at my place. I'll take a raincheck. You guys should come over later, if you want." Trent yawned.

Jemma nudged Spencer's leg. "You two are really mixing business and pleasure," he said.

Trent drew in his chin. "Oh. I hope that's not a problem."

Jemma turned to Spencer. He grimaced and stammered. "I trust your judgment, man. But I do think we should keep things as professional as possible in the office." He avoided Jemma's evil eye. "You know, Missy and Jemma were. . .rivals in high school."

"Yeah, Melissa told me there was some intense jealousy coming at her, but I assumed you've worked through it by now." He grinned patronizingly at his cousin.

Jemma stood, pushing in her chair. "I'm going home and get started on supper. Thanks for the suggestions. See ya'll later."

She flew through the door and past Missy, who was watering the plants as the sun cast a glow through her cascading, Breck Girl hair.

⁂

"Sugar, you look like you are about to pop." Lizbeth wiped flour off her granddaughter's chin.

"I need the Lord to forgive me, Gram. I think I hate someone." Jemma stirred the potatoes, then sat down at the kitchenette. She twisted her fingers through her hair and gazed out the window.

"The Blake girl again." Lizbeth clicked her tongue. "Nobody is all bad. That girl must have something to like about her."

Jemma looked up at Lizbeth. "Not to my knowledge. Now she is dating Trent and she told him that I used to be jealous of her. I know she is a tramp, Gram. Do you know what that means?"

"Well, I think I can come up with an idea or two. Didn't Spencer take her out a few times? I find it hard to believe that he would have had a date with that sort of girl."

"Spencer is naïve about Missy, but not half as naïve as Trent is. I can't let this happen to my only cousin, but I don't know how to stop her."

"I assume you've prayed about this."

Jemma nodded. "I don't know what to do. I think I want to hate her. I know that's an awful thing to say."

"Then pray to love her." Lizbeth saw the twinge run through Jemma. "It's in the Scriptures. The fifth chapter of Matthew, verse 44. Loving your enemies is never easy, but you must do it or you are never going to mature in your Christian walk. The Scriptures also tell us to praise God in all things. We are quick to ask Him for things, but often we neglect to praise Him. Praising Him in a bad situation can be even harder than loving your enemies. I don't mean to preach, Jemmabeth, but when things seem at their worst, remember that verse."

"Would you watch these potatoes for me, Gram? I'll be right back." Jemma left the house and went outside, sketchbook in hand.

Lizbeth opened the screen door. "You keep an eye on those clouds, Jemmabeth. They look like trouble brewing to me. Could be a twister or a duster heading our way," she yelled.

Jemma waved back and stepped up on the rails in the bitter wind. Lizbeth went back to the kitchen and watched her through the window. She was not a child anymore. She was a woman with a loving husband and the loss of an unborn child still haunting her. Dealing with this jealousy and anger could possibly make her life easier and increase her testimony for the Lord. Lizbeth herself had never known jealousy with Cameron, but she had known anger at his passing. It lingered over her like a swarm of locusts. She had scriptures of her own—committed to memory but not yet fully realized in her heart.

⚜

Spencer's car pulled in the driveway. Lizbeth met him at the back door.

"Where's the chef?" he asked.

Lizbeth nodded toward the tracks. "She's doing some thinking, son. Just let her be. She'll come in directly."

Spencer turned to the tall windows and saw her. The wind swirled her hair around her as she clutched her arms against her chest. "She's upset about Missy," he said, "and probably with me, too."

"For all her beauty and talent, Jemmabeth still has some doubts about herself, honey, and she's not over that miscarriage. She needs more time and your love." Lizbeth patted his back and tended to the supper.

Spencer stayed at the window watching her as she sat on the rails, now writing in her sketchbook. A half hour later, she was still there. He went outside and sat next to her, putting his coat over her shoulders.

"How's my girl?" he asked. "Are you composing a poem?"

"Maybe."

"Am I in the doghouse for saying that you and Missy were rivals in high school?"

"Maybe."

He sat next to her. "Bad choice of words on my part. I know that Missy is a royal pain and a big flirt. Are you writing a poem about her?"

"Not exactly." She closed her sketchbook and smiled up at him. "I'm not Emily Dickinson, but it makes me feel better." She grabbed his hand. "Let's go in. We have some Cornish pasties to eat."

Chapter 11
Revelation

Jemma burst into his office again. "They want me to teach a two-week seminar in Paris!"

Spencer was on the phone but gave her a thumbs-up. She danced around until he hung up, then grabbed his neck.

"I like what good news does to you," he said. "I have some of my own. That was your uncle Arthur on the phone and he wants us to come down and discuss two expansions of Billington's. One will be in Austin and the other will be their second one in Houston."

"Congratulations! We can see Carrie while we're there. I miss her."

"I've missed you all day long." He pulled her to him. "When's Paris?"

"The last two weeks of November. I guess that's the bad part."

"I think that's when we will be wrapping up the nursing home. I don't know if I can go with you or not. I'm sure there will be plenty of loose ends to tie up and everybody will be wanting their money. It's kind of my project."

"Trent can handle it."

"If he's back from California. The day before Thanksgiving is when we are making our presentation for the mini-mall in Sacramento. It's a big deal for us."

"It's okay. I can go alone. I'll just hook up with some Frenchman and he'll take care of me. *C'est la vie.*" She shrugged.

"Oh yeah? Well, *such is life* for me to be in love with a famous artist. C'mon—let's go celebrate at Plum Creek. They should have some walls up by now."

"Where are you two going?" Missy scanned Jemma's painting jeans and old sweatshirt.

"Personal information," Spencer said, much to Jemma's amusement.

"It's weird to see it coming to life, isn't it?" Jemma asked as they walked under the cottonwoods. "I guess that's the way all your projects are, though."

Spencer ran his hand across a piece of lumber. "Yeah, I love it."

He took her for a tour of the house and she stopped in a corner of the kitchen. "Wait, what's this? I don't remember this on the plans." She took two steps up a narrow stairwell.

He grinned. "This is my little surprise. I thought we might accidentally need a pouting room like Gram's. I threw it into the plans, just in case. What do you think?"

"I think I love it, you sneak. It looks like the hidden steps up to the Sainte-Chapelle."

"I'm putting in some stained glass so whoever needs to pout can cheer up quicker."

"Well, I wonder who that will be?" Jemma kissed him. "I love you, Mr. Architect. Maybe I'll pout even more since you made me a special room for the purpose."

"C'mon, let's finish the tour," he said and led the way up another stairway to their shared studio. "This is the room where the renowned Jemmabeth Alexandra Chase paints her masterpieces. Notice how the light changes from dawn to high noon then to the setting sun by the perfect placement of windows."

"Ah, but over in this corner of her studio is where the prominent architect, Spencer Morgan Chase, envisions timeless structures."

They left the studio and went downstairs to a large room that curved along the creek.

"Here, ladies and gentlemen, is the happiest room of all. It is within these walls that Mr. Chase tells Mrs. Chase how much he loves her every night." He curled his finger at her.

Jemma backed up in mock defense. "What if somebody is still around?"

"They will be trespassing. Come here, woman."

A flock of geese floated across the sky, paying no attention at all to the giggling activity directly below them on the banks of Plum Creek.

⟫⟪

"Mother has invited us to supper," Spencer announced as he stood in the car house admiring her latest work, a piece showing the town postmistress, Paralee Batson, leaning over the counter in the old post office checking the weight of a package. "This is great, Jem. I like it that her tongue is sticking out just a bit and that her cat is staring at those scales."

Jemma cleaned her brushes. "It's sort of *Saturday Evening Post*. Now what's this invitation all about? I'm not sure I'm ready for your mother yet."

"I'll be there to protect you. She called the office and told me that she's doing the cooking herself for the first time in fifteen years." Spencer looked around at some of the other pieces. "Wow. You've been churning out the work, haven't you? Who's this pianist?"

"That's Melanie Glazer's fiancé. I wanted to thank her for playing that sweet violin music at our wedding." Jemma turned off the light. "When do we eat?"

"Six thirty. So that guy is the reason that you double-dated while we were still going steady. Melanie needed your help to catch him."

"You know I'll regret that until the day I croak. C'mon, there's not much time for me to find something to wear. Rats."

Spencer waited while she dragged out one dress after another to hold up in front of the mirror. "Jem, it's already six o'clock. You take a quick bath, and I'll pick something out."

She pouted into the bathroom. Spencer picked up all the discards and hung them up. He slid a few dresses around on the rack, then pulled out a black dress her mother had given her and laid it on the bed.

"Not that!" she shrieked when she came back. "Your mother will think I'm a floozy."

"I love that dress on you. It's very sophisticated and she will be impressed," he said, kissing the back of her damp neck.

"Maybe you should start choosing all my clothes. The Cleave always says that I'm stuck in a bohemian rut." Jemma slipped into the dress and dabbed on some lipstick. She shook her hair and ran her fingers through it.

Spencer watched, mesmerized by such beauty carrying his name. "Missy is jealous of you and that's that. She's harmless."

⌘

"The chimes of doom," Jemma whispered as Spencer rang the Chase castle doorbell. "Nobody rings the doorbell at their own house."

"This is not a normal house."

Max Chase came to the door. "Vah-vah-voom, daughter-in-law, you look spectacular." He grinned at Jemma.

Jemma jabbed Spencer with her elbow. "See, *floozy*."

"Son, it's so good to see you, sweetheart." Rebecca rearranged the centerpiece flowers on the dining room table. She embraced him, then turned to Jemma, exhaling. "You look nice this evening, Jemmabeth." The words came out of her mouth like lukewarm breath on an icy morning, but they came out.

"Thank you." Jemma turned to Spencer, wide-eyed.

"Let's eat." Max pulled out a chair for Rebecca. "Your mother's been in the kitchen all afternoon."

It was a gourmet meal. Rebecca was very talkative, and Max was his usual jovial self.

"I've been going to church," he whispered as he and Jemma cleared the table.

"Good for you. Does Mrs. Chase go with you?"

"Oh no, hon. She's not much on religion. I think her family belonged to the church of the firstborn atheist or something like that. She's being good tonight, huh? No catty remarks."

Jemma nodded as Spencer came into the kitchen. "Mother wants us to have dessert by the fireplace. She says you can serve it. I'll help."

They had lemon tarts and coffee. Jemma stuck close to Spence's side.

"Have you seen my new Caddy?" Max asked.

"No, but it probably looks just like last year's model," Spencer said.

"Take a look for yourself." Max and Spencer headed to the garage to view the Cadillac, leaving Jemma and Rebecca alone.

"The meal was delicious, Mrs. Chase. Thank you for inviting us," Jemma said, her eyes on the coffee table.

"I've been thinking about your miscarriage, Jemmabeth," Mrs. Chase said, taking Jemma off guard. "You may not be aware that I lost three babies before my Spencer was born."

A chill ran over Jemma. She looked right at Rebecca, tears gleaming in her eyes. "I didn't know that. I am so sorry."

"People underestimate the fracture it leaves in a woman's heart. I understand that you struggled with some of that yourself." Rebecca stirred her coffee.

"Yes ma'am. I wanted more time to be alone with Spencer when I found out I was pregnant, and I wasn't excited at all. When the baby died, well, I blamed myself." Jemmabeth glanced at Mrs. Chase, surprised by her kindness.

"Nonsense. Miscarriages just happen sometimes. I'm sure you will be one of the lucky ones who turns right around and carries the next baby full term." Rebecca set her cup on the table. "I realize that Spencer has always loved you. He is a rare person who gives his love for a lifetime. I know that I have been rather cold toward you, and I want to change that about myself. I don't want to lose my baby after all these years of being a useless mother to him. I trust you will bear with me." She paused. "My therapist says that I'm jealous of you, of your relationship with my son. Maybe there's some truth in that, and if you are of the same opinion, forgive me, please."

Jemma placed her hand lightly on Rebecca's shoulder until Spencer and Max's laughter trickled down the hallway. She moved back to the couch and exchanged unsteady smiles with Rebecca. Jemma considered how extraordinary it must be to suddenly wake up and realize that your child has grown from a toddler to a fine man without your assistance.

❦

Julia met them at the Houston airport. "Look at you two. The honeymoon is still going, isn't it?" she asked in her straightforward style. Her hair, as always, was a little too red.

"You are always right, aren't you, Do Dah?" Jemma slid her arm around her great-aunt's naturally well-padded shoulders.

"Here's the deal. I don't want to hear the name Do Dah mentioned the whole time you are in Houston. I'm going to break you of that habit if it's my final act on this old earth," she proclaimed.

"Do Dah!" Spencer said, arriving with their luggage, "I'm so glad to see you."

"*Julia.* Call me Julia for three days in a row and I'll buy you supper at the best restaurant in Texas."

"I don't know." Spencer grinned. "Do Dah is a cute name."

"It was cute coming from my nephew's mouth when he couldn't do any better, but not from two fully grown adults. Now let's get moving. Arthur wants you delivered by ten o'clock sharp, and he's a man bent on punctuality."

Spencer was right on time. He and Arthur met behind closed doors until noon. Jemma and Julia went shopping at Billington's. "Let me pay for it, sugar. I get everything at cost. You can reimburse me when I'm old and dotty."

"You'll never be like that, Do—Julia."

They drove back to Julia's mansion in the classy River Oaks area of Houston.

"Now tell me about this business you are trying to get started across the tracks. Are you sure you'll have enough workers?" Julia wagged her finger at a driver who cut her off on the freeway.

"I hope so. I can't sit around and wait for change in Willa's neighborhood. Things are so pitiful over there. They need some pride, and I think pride comes from working hard and doing your job well, don't you?" Jemma said as they entered the gate to Julia's home.

"That's true, but folks may be scared off by a white girl coming in and changing things. You'll have to take it slow and easy. Get it going, then fade out. Do you have enough funds to get it off the ground and take a loss for a while?" Julia parked the car and unloaded their packages. "Art and I would be happy to help. He's a believer in projects like this."

"Spencer says we'll be fine, but I have no clue about business. I hope he's going to talk to Uncle Art about it while we're here." Jemma surveyed the lavish home. "Your home is even swankier than my Lillygrace grandparents' home in St. Louis."

Julia laughed. "That's good to hear. Come look at this." She led Jemma down the shiny marble hallway and pointed at her portrait on the wall, now encased in an ornate frame. "We get so many compliments on it, sugar, you could make a fortune in Houston. Everybody likes to see themselves captured in oil, no pun intended, and hanging in their own foyer."

"I want to paint Uncle Art, too. I just need about an hour's worth of sketches when he has the time."

"We'll make the time. I was going to ask you when you could do just that. It looks egotistical for an old hen to have her portrait up without her rooster. My old sweetie needs to slow down. We both could stand to shed a few pounds, but we love to eat. Speaking of which, let's go see what's for supper."

"I'd forgotten how pretty this part of Houston is," Jemma said, looking out the bay windows. "Doesn't somebody famous live in this neighborhood?"

"You must be thinking of old Ima Hogg. She's the daughter of Jim Hogg, the governor during Texas's Wild West days. Ima's done a lot for the state, and her gardens are something else. I doubt she got much dirt under her fingernails, though. Anybody can have a gorgeous garden if you hire enough people to work on it. I know that firsthand." Julia was never one to pass out compliments lightly.

"I need to paint my other great-aunts, too. Would they like that? I feel funny coming here and not visiting them. I don't know them at all."

Julia snorted. "Those old maids wouldn't waste their time on portraits. All they do is watch TV and fuss about housework. Let them be, sugar. I know them."

After supper, Jemma sketched Arthur in the study that night while he advised them on their project, and she got more than her hour's worth of sketches. "What you need for a cottage industry is enthusiasm and commitment over time. Of course, this may not be a typical cottage industry, but you should treat it like one, initially. If the products are appealing, it could take off. We will certainly be interested in giving the goods a go," Arthur said, puffing on his pipe. Jemma put down her work and gave him a good bear hug of appreciation.

⋙⋘

Carrie came to the door using her walker. Her blond hair was cut in a pageboy, and her twinkling blue eyes were still full of mischief.

"They're here, Phil," she yelled. "I'm so glad to see y'all."

Spencer picked her up for a hug and Jemma waited her turn. "You look so good, Carrie. It must be the Houston climate."

Spencer and Philip shook hands and the foursome settled into the living room of their modest home. Jemma sat on the arm of Carrie's chair.

"Phil and I would like to get out of Houston, actually. It's too big. You know what I'm used to, and Chillaton is the size we want. Now that I have my own built-in therapist, I can live anywhere. I'm up to three hours a day with my walker. What do you think of that?"

"I think that's fantastic," Jemma said. "Are you looking for a job in rehabilitation therapy, Phil?"

"Maybe," he said, looking at his wife.

Jemma put her arm around Carrie. "You've done wonders for this little twerp, that's for sure. The first time I ever saw her I thought she would be tethered forever to her circus cannon, that iron lung. Now look at her—Mrs. Suburbia."

"That's all because of you, Jem. If you hadn't made my dad angry with your crazy ideas and that portrait, I never would've met Mr. Philip Bryce, and I definitely wouldn't be using a walker, even if it is only for part of the day. Plus, I never would have danced with your husband," Carrie added, grinning at Spencer.

"I can't imagine why such a beautiful piece of art would make anybody angry," Spencer said, studying the portrait of Carrie striking a pose in a tutu. "I remember he thought Jem was mocking her, as if that could ever happen."

"I think The Judge felt like she was giving Carrie wild ideas." Philip laughed.

"I was painting her spirit," Jemma said. "She told me once that she could do whatever came into her head. She could even fly, if she thought it up. Of course, there was also the little matter of me arranging for Carrie to go to church as well as play with Buddy's band at a dance. Actually, the dance infuriated him, right, Carrie?"

"None of that matters now. I have Phil, and I'm able to take care of myself! Let's eat. I'm starving." Carrie struggled upright with her walker, refusing all offers of assistance.

❧

"Phil, do you have any background in management?" Spencer asked while the girls were away from the table.

"I'm the supervisor for the hospital's rehab unit, why?"

"Do you have a certain age group that you like to work with?" Spencer added, evaluating Philip's interest.

"I like them all." Philip leaned toward Spencer. "Do you know of a job opening somewhere?"

"Maybe. Jemma and I are looking for a manager for our nursing home. It's almost complete, but the person we're looking for has to have the same compassion for the elderly that the building's namesake had. He was this kid in high school that was a good guy, but he was always on the fringes of the teenage social scene. His family struggled to make ends meet, then his dad died. Kenneth delivered groceries even before he had his driver's license. He became an Eagle Scout and hoped someday to run a nursing home, but he and his mother were killed in a tornado that ripped through Chillaton a few years ago. Jemma had a real soft spot in her heart for him. Now we're about to open this home in his name, and I think you could be just who we're looking for."

Philip nodded. "My mom died in a nursing home. She's the reason I went into rehab therapy. She had several little strokes and eventually lost control over her life." He tapped his fingers on the table. "Let me talk this over with Carrie. I don't know how she'd feel about going back to Chillaton and her father."

"Oh sure, but let me know as soon as you can."

Jemma and Carrie came back laughing. "So what have you two been talking about? You look suspicious to me," Carrie said. "It's so good to be with y'all. I'd love to be back home in Chillaton with my husband. You two are lucky."

Jemma smiled at Carrie's declaration, but Philip and Spencer grinned at each other, big-time.

❧

Jemma waited until 7:30 to begin, but there were still only five women present for her first meeting, including Willa. "I could've told you this, child, but you didn't ask me," Willa said, behind one of the handouts that Jemma had passed around. "People are plumb scared of change. They'd rather be worse off than a skunk with their liver draggin' than to figger out a new way to do things. It's just the way life is, at least on this side of them tracks."

"Be that as it may, we're going to try." Jemma stepped in front of the pews. "Ladies, thank you for coming tonight. As you know, I'm here to share a business idea with you. I need your input to see if it could work, though."

A large woman with white streaks in her hair spoke up. "What kind of business? Me and my man, Terrill, is already takin' care of things at the Dew." Jemma had seen her before when she went with Trina to the Dew Drop Inn—a combination grocery store, dime store, and social center for the neighborhood. Bernie Miller, Chillaton's one-eyed town barber on the other side of the tracks, owned it.

"I was thinking of a small business that creates handmade items, like quilts and rag rugs, those kinds of things," Jemma said with a sparkling smile.

A pencil-thin, white-haired woman shifted in her seat and spat something into a can. "Ain't nobody gonna pay for no rag rug. Have to be crazy to do that."

"Maybe we should introduce ourselves," Jemma said. "I'm Jemmabeth Chase. I know a few of you from church."

"They call me Grandma Hardy, and that's all you need to know," the white-haired woman said.

Willa cleared her throat.

"You know me, I'm Bertie Shanks, Shiloh's sister." She pointed to Terrill's woman. "I'm real interested in this idea of yours if it'll pay off in the long run...that's what I want to know." Bertie's voice was high-pitched and kept going in a soft whirring sound, connecting her words like a remote control car.

The last one to speak was a young woman with coal black eyes that had not left Jemma's face since the meeting began. "My name's Gweny Matthews. What's in this for you?"

"Nothing," Jemma said. "I want to make sure it gets off the ground, but the idea is to turn the profits back into the community, back to you."

"You mean we won't get paid?" Gweny asked.

"Oh no. Of course you'll get paid. That's how the community

will benefit. You can be more independent," Jemma looked at the group for any encouragement.

Willa spoke up. "What the child is sayin', girls, is that the gov'ment might not have to buy your groceries and whatnot. Now, I know Jemmabeth. She's sweet and for the most part, smart. Her and my Trina have been friends for a good while now. I think we should at least see what she's got to say."

Jemma held nothing back. She told them just what Uncle Art said and explained how she and Spencer would be involved. When she finished, she asked who would like to give it a try.

Willa spoke up. "Sugar, you know old Willa here can't sew nothin' for nothin'. I can iron what gets sewed, but I can't help you none with a needle and thread."

Bertie and Shiloh both volunteered. Gweny and Grandma Hardy said nothing.

Jemma sighed. "Surely there are more ladies who can sew in the neighborhood. We'll need a bigger crew to get much done."

"They's all busy," Grandma Hardy said. "We'll let 'em know what you got in mind."

"Thank you; that would be great. Please see what everybody thinks. Maybe you could encourage more people to come," Jemma said. "We could brainstorm."

"I ain't gettin' out in no kind of storm," Grandma Hardy said with a solid hit in her can.

Gweny eyed her like a guard dog. "How much would we get paid?"

"Minimum wages, I suppose, until we see what the profits are, then everybody would share in that," Jemma said. "Unless we have more interest than we do tonight, though, we couldn't really fill an order for my uncle's stores."

"Just how much will you be sharin' in the profits?" Gweny asked.

"Not at all."

"What kind of orders are you talkin' about?" Bertie asked.

Jemma brightened at the interest. "My uncle said that he would like to try a dozen quilts in one store, and if they sell within a certain period of time, he would double the order and expand the quilts to another one of his stores, too."

"Her uncle's got four real fancy stores," Willa added.

Gweny left with the others but not before she gave Jemma one hard, last look.

"Whoa. That was a tough crowd," Jemma said as she and Willa cleaned up the juice and cookies.

"I told you, honey, folks don't like change. If they see a white girl tellin' it to 'em, that's even worse."

"That Gweny looks so familiar to me. I must have seen her before."

"She's been around for a few months. She's Weese's little sister. You gotta remember him."

"Really. Well, I'll never forget Weese. I was afraid of him when I first met y'all."

"That's the one and only. Shot off his mouth more times than not. He's out of the military now and brought his little sister with him to Chillaton. Appears he got his high school diploma and is tryin' to go to junior college. Don't that beat all? I figgered he'd get himself killed in Vietnam, but I think he's too pigheaded or ornery for even the devil to take him. Anyway, Gweny looks out at folks just like him. Kinda scary, ain't it?" Willa brushed the crumbs off her dress. "I gotta get home to Joe, sugar, but I need to lock up. Joe and me are in charge of the church key this year."

"I think Weese hated me, the way he talked," Jemma said, gathering up her things.

"Aw, he hated white folks in general. He's drivin' back and forth to the power plant now. Got a good job over there. Don't worry about him, sugar. He's come home like a three-legged dog. I think he got the peewiddles scared out of him in that war. Let's go, honey. I miss my man." Willa held the door open for Jemma, motioning her through.

"Isn't Trina coming home this weekend?" Jemma asked.

"She ain't comin' home until she graduates. She sent me a dress for the ceremony. Come over tomorrow and I'll show you. That girl's good. I don't know where she got it, but she can dream up Sunday-go-to-meetin' clothes even for a big old barn like me."

"I know she's busy, but I really need to call her."

"You ain't keepin' secrets from old Willa now, are you?" Willa locked the door, then gave it a good tug.

"No secrets, just in need of sewing machine advice."

"Then you're headin' down the right track for that. Sleep tight, Jemma. Say hello to Miz Liz for me." Willa headed toward her house and Jemma, lost in thought, waved good-bye as she crossed the tracks.

Lizbeth met her at the door. "How did it go?"

Jemma hung her coat on the hall tree. "It was a pitiful turnout. I hope this all works out. Did Spence call?"

"Not yet. He probably had a late meeting or something, but Buddy B called. Twila had a little girl or maybe I should say a big girl. She weighed over ten pounds. Buddy said they named her after his mother, Twila's maiden name, and you."

Jemma grinned. "That's great! I'll have to go see her. What's the baby's name?"

Lizbeth was about to burst. "You know how everybody calls Mrs. Baker 'Sweety' and Trout was Twila's maiden name, and, well, I suppose you can tack 'beth' on to just about anything. They named her Sweetybeth Trout Baker."

"Can you imagine her name being called out at graduation?" Jemma giggled. "Do people ever bake trout?"

They howled until their sides ached.

"I made hot cocoa. Would you like some?" Lizbeth produced a bag of marshmallows.

"That sounds good. I should have served cocoa at the meeting. Maybe it would have warmed them up. How long does it take to make a quilt, Gram?"

"Oh my. Let's see."

"Wait." Jemma jumped up from the table. "I'll be right back. I need to call Trina."

❧

Lizbeth wrapped her hands around her cup. Lester came in the back door.

"Don't you knock anymore, Mr. Timms?"

Lester went back outside and knocked. She had to laugh. "Come on in and have some cocoa with us."

"I don't mind if I do." He draped his coat on the back of his chair. "I think a storm's comin' in. It's downright cold tonight. I don't see Spencer's car. Where is that boy?"

"Los Angeles. It just amazes me how young folk take an airplane everywhere they go these days." Lizbeth offered him the cookie jar. "Help yourself, Lester. Jemma made them today, but she took most of them to her meeting."

"Well, sir, I've been thinkin' about this business across the tracks. If it's a quiltin' business they're considerin', don't it make sense to get your quiltin' club in on it?"

"I don't think that's the idea, Lester. Not that I wouldn't help if asked, but it's supposed be a neighborhood venture." Lizbeth lowered her voice. "Something special to take pride in."

"You think it'll fly?"

"Anything's possible with the Lord."

"Here are my flight numbers, the Academie's number, and my hotel number. Call me whenever you can. It doesn't matter if I'm asleep," Jemma told Spencer, tucking a piece of paper in his pocket.

"I'll put this in my desk and I'll keep another copy in my wallet. It'll be like you are with me everywhere I go." He put his arms around her, starting the good-bye kisses a little early.

The Cleave moved away from the door just as they opened it.

"If anybody calls, I'll get back with them tomorrow," Spencer told her.

Missy shook back her hair, like a horse slinging its head at the bit. "I thought you were expecting to hear from Trent this afternoon. Nice suit, Jemma. I had one just like it about three years ago. I gave mine to the Salvation Army. Wait; maybe that's where you got yours. How weird."

Neither Jemma nor Spencer answered and went straight to the Corvette.

"She makes me sick. Aarrgghh!" Jemma shuddered, then inhaled. "Okay. How come you don't have a new Corvette this year, babe? What happened to your dad's perennial gift?" Jemma asked as they turned onto the highway. Spencer tried to hide his grin.

"I told Dad that he needed to stop giving me cars. I'm a big boy now. Maybe we should buy something different." He adjusted his rearview mirror, working hard to look nonchalant. "I was thinking about us buying matching motorcycles."

"Spencer Chase, don't even think about that. You know I have a problem with motorcycles. They are deadly. I will never forget the sight of the Kelseys sprawled across the road when Mom and I came upon them. When those deer ran out, they never had a chance on that machine."

"Okay, okay. I'm sorry I brought it up, but you know I like cycles."

"You should have gotten that out of your system in Europe. Say you won't bring it up anymore. I love you too much."

"I won't bring it up anymore. I'll miss you, baby. You take care of yourself in Paris. Don't go out at night alone and all that. We haven't been apart this long since we got married."

"Say that again and I'll start crying. When we're apart, do you think more about the dumb things I've done or the good things?"

"You've done some good things?" he teased. "C'mon, Jem, I think about holding you again and that's the truth."

An hour later, he raced to the parking lot to watch her plane shrink into the clouds. He'd meant to let her take his four-leaf clover with her, just in case she needed it. It was with him in Vietnam when his chopper got shot out of the sky. He drove home in silence, wishing already he had gone with her.

Chapter 12
Blindsided

Paris coming into view was one of Jemma's favorite sights, but that would not be the case today. Gloomy clouds shrouded the city, and it didn't stop raining until late afternoon. She walked past cafés, whose rain-slick chairs were turned upside down on the tables waiting for the sun. As usual, she had not slept well after her long flight and had talked way too long to Spence on the phone. She drank some coffee, loaded with cream and sugar, to wake her up, then walked to Le Academie Royale D'Art. There was really no need for the coffee; she was invigorated the instant she stepped inside to meet with her old supervisors.

Peter, her onetime liaison when she was the Girard Fellow, met her in the hallway. "Jemma, my dear, you are perhaps even more beautiful. It must be matrimony that has done this to you. Ami and I insist that you come for dinner while you are here, *oui?*"

She gave him a Texas hug. "Of course I'll come. I can't wait to tell y'all about my life." Jemma thought everyone should say her name like the French did—*Zhemma*.

She met her former Girard advisor, Louis, and the Academie Director. "Here is my syllabus, Monsieur Lanier," she said, after they had all exchanged pleasantries. "I've already given a copy to Louis and he approved. I'd like to mingle with the students and see how they approach their work. I want to listen to their thinking today, so that I can address their questions when we begin tomorrow." Jemma waited for his response as he thumbed through the pages.

Monsieur Lanier played with his moustache. "Ah, very nice. The pupils also wish to observe you as you work and exchange ideas about perspective, technique, and the unique voice in your art," he said in his impeccable English.

Louis raised his finger, as was his habit. "What we are seeking, Jemma, is a certain essence of personality that all of your work has—

the voice. Is this voice something that can be, how do you say. . . fostered. . .or does it only spring from the heart? We shall explore the answer. I strongly believe that it comes from your heart, my dear."

"However," Monsieur Lanier added, "we can, with your permission, listen to your heart, as you exercise that voice."

She smiled. "I do believe that artists can train their thinking to include something extra in a portrait that adds the spice, the zest. You can get caught up in realism to the point that characters look alive, but boring as all get-out. Of course, some people are just plain boring. Everybody can have a little zing in their personality, even if you have to give it to them. Believe me, I've done my share of zinging."

The men laughed. "Perhaps we should call your seminar 'Zinging with Zhemma,'" Monsieur Lanier quipped. "This will be a fascinating time that will be gone before you know it. Did your husband accompany you?"

"No, he had other responsibilities, but he wanted to, very much." She sighed. "Let's get going with these artists. Who is the Girard Fellow this year?"

"A very talented young man from Russia. I think you will like his work. It has this zing you speak of," Louis said as they left the director's office.

         ❧

Jemma had the class's eyes at her first brushstroke and ears after her first Texas vowel. Peter interpreted for her and she stayed late every night. After the third night, she knew most of the students' names. Her own piece was taking shape. It was a large portrait of Marie, the Academie's secretary, sitting behind stacks of paper at her desk. Marie was massaging her own neck and watching the leaves outside her window. Jemma spoke intermittently, when she had made a conscious decision related to Marie herself or the inanimate objects in the piece that would enhance the viewer's understanding of Marie's emotions.

Louis and Jemma collaborated until half past eleven with a student who was struggling with a concept in his own piece. "It is so good of you to come, Jemma," Louis said as they descended the steps from the studios to the main entrance. "Your passion will be contagious with our students. Have you been well?"

"*Oui,* I have been very well. Marriage has made me complete," she said as they walked out the massive Academie entry door.

Louis smiled. "Your husband is most fortunate."

"No, it is just the opposite," Jemma said. "I'll see you tomorrow."

Louis frowned as Jemma turned down the sidewalk toward her hotel. "Jemma," he said, coming alongside her, "perhaps I should see you to your accommodations. There have been ah…how do you say… *agresseurs* nearby in recent weeks."

Jemma laughed. "Aggressive people? Don't worry. I can take care of myself. I know some wrestling moves."

"Are you certain? It is no bother for me. Let me call a taxi for you."

"I'll be fine." She waved. "It's just four blocks from here, and I need the exercise."

Jemma yawned and glanced at some young men playing bongos under a tree just a block from her hotel. She smiled, thinking about Robby and the bongos that he had included in his Christmas list. She decided to write to him as soon as she got to the hotel.

She checked her watch as she passed under the streetlight. It was almost midnight. Suddenly she became aware of heavy footsteps behind her and quickened her pace. It was too late. A wrenching blow to her back lurched her forward, and she fell hard on her face. The agonizing pain in her nose was followed by a choking gush of blood.

There were two of them, pinning her arms down as they dragged her into the alley between darkened buildings. She struggled and screamed as a hand was clamped over her mouth. The men scrambled around her. Jemma landed a solid kick against one, causing him to yelp in pain. The other pressed his knee into her stomach and spoke low, grating French in her face.

Jemma writhed under his weight. She held her breath as a third man appeared in the dark. She coughed, gagging on blood that oozed down her throat. The new arrival grunted and yanked the men off her, simultaneously slamming each against the wall.

Jemma rolled on her side and tried to stand. Her ankle gave way. She wobbled up, lost her balance, but managed a few steps, spewing blood that flowed from her nose. The third man shouted something in English, and they all ran past her as she stumbled into the street.

The lights down the block swirled in front of her. Her nose throbbed and her back hurt like fire. She hobbled toward the lights, shaking uncontrollably.

"Wait, darlin'," a voice thundered behind her.

She froze.

Paul moved in front of her and gathered her up in his arms just as she fainted.

Jemma woke up in a fog. She didn't know which hurt worse—her nose, her back, or her ankle wrapped in tight bandages. Muffled conversations drifted in and out of her aching head. She heard French and a thick Texas accent, engaged in a discussion over her condition.

"She had a serious concussion a couple of years ago. Wouldn't that make her more susceptible to another one?" a familiar voice asked.

"Ah, she is awake. Let me speak with her," the Frenchman said.

Jemma responded to a series of questions and an eye exam to his satisfaction. The doctor explained that she had been given pain medication and she would remain in the hospital overnight for observation, then left her in the room with Paul.

Jemma blinked at the ceiling as he came over to the bed. Rats, rats, rats.

"Hello, my darlin'," he whispered and took her hand. "Sorry you had such a scare. If I see those cowards again, I'll kill 'em. Guaranteed."

Tears rolled down Jemma's cheeks. She tensed at his touch and withdrew her hand from his. She coughed up a gross blood clot and glanced at her unlikely nurse. "I have no idea why you are here, Paul, but thanks for whatever you did," she whispered. "I think you saved my life."

"No thanks ever needed," he murmured, dabbing at her chin with a damp cloth. "The police came by earlier and I told them all they needed to know. I just hope they catch those scumbags before

I do," he said through clenched teeth. "How are you feeling?"

"Like I've been in another wreck. Is my nose broken?"

"The doc says no broken bones, only deep bruises and swollen tissue. You are going to be black and blue by tomorrow."

"What about my ankle?"

"Sprain." Paul pulled a stool over beside her.

"I need to call Spencer."

"Wait until morning."

"No. I want to call him now. I'm getting up." She grunted to her elbows and fell back on the pillow.

Paul patted her arm. "I'll find a phone. You don't move."

The effects of the pain medication took hold as she sat on the side of the bed. Paul returned and she squinted up at him. She had forgotten how tall he was. "You have blood on your shirt. Are you hurt, too?" she asked.

"No, darlin', it's from your cute little nose. I thought we'd struck oil there for a while. I pinched it all the way to the hospital. Come on, I found you a phone down the hall, but there are lots of nurses lurking around out there." He helped her off the bed. "I think the doc ordered bed rest, so we'll have to sneak out."

Jemma had not realized she was wearing a hospital gown until the cool hallway air hit her bare back. She gasped and clutched the gown around her. She hadn't forgotten about Paul's wandering hands.

❧

The Cleave answered Jemma's call in her usual velvety tone. "Chase and Lillygrace. May I help you?"

The operator asked if she would accept the charges. The Cleave paused, then lost her kitteny voice. "Yeah, I guess."

"Missy," Jemma began.

"*Melissa.*"

"I need to talk to Spencer, Missy. It's an emergency."

"Spence is not here. They've gone to a meeting in Amarillo. By the way, I'm cooking for both of them at Trent's place tonight."

Jemma could see her smirk clear across the Atlantic. The drugs were taking over or else she would have had a pertinent comeback.

"Then interrupt the meeting. Spencer needs to call me in Paris immediately." Jemma read the number on the pay phone. "Read it back to me, please." She was drifting off by the second, but held on until Missy repeated the number. She handed the phone to Paul, who hung it up for her. That was the last thing she remembered.

⁂

Jemma awoke to another foggy French conversation between a different physician and Paul. She could not focus long enough to see the men clearly.

The doctor checked her pupils and asked her a series of questions. "You are her husband?" he asked Paul.

"No." Paul struggled with the words. "We're. . .old friends."

"You are feeling better, yes?" the doctor asked Jemma.

She nodded.

"Eat some food, then perhaps we will dismiss you. You will rest today, of course."

"I'll see to it that she does," Paul said.

Jemma rose up to protest, but went down again. "Did Spence call?" she mumbled. "I need to call the Academie, too; they will be worried."

"I've already called the school, Jem. Everything is taken care of. They were very concerned about you, though." Paul moved the bed up for her and adjusted the pillows.

"How did you know to call them?" Jemma touched the tip of her sore nose and ran her hands through her hair. "I must look like a witch."

"On the contrary." Paul sat on the stool beside her. "You look like an angel." He hadn't changed the bloodstained shirt.

"Paul, why on earth are you in Paris and how did you, of all people, show up to rescue me from who-knows-what?" She tried to look him in the eye, but her swollen nose was in the way.

He smoothed his overnight stubble. "I came to see you. I'm not ashamed that I was. . .well, watching you from afar, as they say."

"You're good at that, aren't you?" Her breakfast was set up in front of her on a tray. She picked at the food and drank the juice. "Stop looking at me. You're giving me the creeps. There's a name for people like you."

He grinned. "Oh yeah. What's that, Guardian Angel?"

"*Obsessed.* Did you stay in here all night?"

He nodded.

"Oh great. Spencer is going to blow his stack. Can't you see how wrong it is for you to keep this up? Have you seriously considered your behavior?"

"Darlin', I told you; I'm under your spell."

"Arrgghh! Paul! There is no spell. Listen to me. I love my husband, and I always have. This obsession is hopeless."

A nurse interrupted and took her blood pressure, which was up, and her temperature, then gave her a form to fill out, in French. Jemma hoped that she hadn't agreed to a lobotomy.

"I bought you some clothes since your others were ruined," Paul said, setting a bag and her own purse on the bed. He left the room as Jemma opened the bag and took out a blouse and a miniskirt. Leave it to him to pick out a miniskirt. The tags were still on them. She dressed and did what she could to her hair. Her nose was skinned up and its size rivaled W.C. Field's. She had bruises all over her, and everything that had a nerve ached.

She limped to the door and opened it. "Did Spencer call? You never said."

Paul was leaning against the wall, his black cowboy hat pushed back. He looked her over and sighed. Two nurses walked by and gave him admiring, giggling glances. He tipped his hat, then turned to Jemma. "No calls, ma'am. I asked at the nurses' station. Let's get out of here. I hate hospitals." He held her arm as they entered the elevator.

"That's not like Spence." Jemma bit her sore lip. She had a sudden urge to phone him again, then recalled vaguely that The Cleave said she was cooking supper for Trent and Spencer. Spence wouldn't eat with Missy. She must have been dreaming.

"Do you want some real food, darlin'?" Paul asked as he flagged down a taxi.

"Paul, stop calling me *darlin'.* I am not your darling. You shouldn't even be in Paris," she said, holding the miniskirt down as she got in the cab.

He raised his brow. "Do you know what might have happened to you last night if I hadn't been here?"

Jemma exhaled and looked out the window. "I know. It's weird that you were in the right place at the right time, but my husband is not going to understand this at all. He wants to have a restraining order put on you."

"I'd do the same thing if I were him, but we're in Europe, darlin'. I don't think a restraining order would hold up over here."

"Paul, you and I are not going to have a rendezvous or something just because you saved my life. . .or at least my virtue."

He turned his beautiful, green-eyed gaze on her. "Preserving your virtue is something I would give my life for, Jem. Watching you sleep last night will be one of my life's sweetest memories."

Jemma held on to the door handle in case he tried something. Paul told the driver an address in French, and they were dropped off at a café.

Jemma looked at her wrist. "Rats, my watch is gone! It must have fallen off in that alley last night." Her nose stung at this added insult. "Spence gave me that watch before he went to Vietnam."

"I'll look for it," Paul said. "I bet those creeps stole it. You can't be walking around alone in a big city at midnight, Jemma. It's dangerous. I seem to remember you doing the same thing when I first met you, but Paris isn't exactly Wicklow, my darlin'."

"I can't believe they took my watch. What happened to my clothes, anyway?"

"The police took them. They were ruined," Paul said, his hand in the small of her back.

Jemma moved it away. "Just order me some tea and toast. I've got to talk to my husband." She inched her way to a pay phone and called Lizbeth's number.

"Hi, Gram. Sorry to wake you up," she said, holding her voice steady. "Is Spencer there?"

"No, sugar, he spent the night with his folks. Are you all right?" Lizbeth asked.

"I'm okay now, but there's been a little trouble. Could you have Spence call me at my room, please? I'll be there in an hour," she added.

"What's wrong, Jemmabeth?" Lizbeth's voice crackled over the phone.

"I'm all right. Spencer can tell you, but I have to go now. I love you." She hated not telling her everything, but she had to tell Spence first.

"I love you, too, honey. You take care."

"Wait. Gram, did Spencer eat out last night?"

"Why, yes, I believe he planned to eat with Trent."

A large lump crept up her throat. She said good-bye and turned toward the café. It was all she could do to walk.

"Maybe we should take you back to the hospital. I'm not so sure you're ready for the outside world," Paul steered her to her chair.

"I'm okay. I just need to sit down."

Paul's eyes were on her every move. She knew it but didn't care. She only wanted to know if The Cleave had cooked up something more than dinner for her husband.

⊰⊱

"I don't need you to babysit me, Paul," she said, even though he had practically carried her from the café to the taxi. "I appreciate all you've done, really, but now you have to go home," Jemma said as they stood in front of her hotel room. "I'm not going to invite you in." She narrowed her eyes at him. "It really wasn't wise for you to follow me across the ocean like this."

"I'd follow you anywhere if I thought it would change things." He reached for her, but she caught his hand to push it away. He took her off guard and kissed her fingers, looking at her with his eyes half-closed under those lashes black as night. "Even if I find somebody to settle down with, Jem, it'll be you that I'll be lovin' the whole time. That's a solemn promise."

She wriggled her hand out of his grasp. "How did you know that I was in Paris?"

"Apparently you have some competition yourself, back in that little one-horse town."

Her scalp prickled. "What do you mean?"

"All I know is that I got a phone call from a breathy sorority sister of some old girl I took out. She said if I'd like to be alone with you, I should whip over here to France. She gave me all the details, right down to the school, your flight number, and hotel. Sounds serious, darlin'."

Jemma's face burned. "Good-bye, Paul," she said, controlling her voice. "I'll pray for you. I have to tell Spence about what happened, and I don't know what he'll say or do. Now go home." She turned her attention to getting her key in the door. The Cleave was all she could think about.

Paul seized the opportunity. He pulled her to him and kissed her, full on the lips.

Jemma panicked and dropped her keys. She pushed hard on his chest, but he had her face firmly in his big hand and she had nowhere to go. Her nose still ached from the attack and now her mouth hurt from this.

After the longest time, he backed away and smiled, not with a smirk, but in a sweet way. "I love you, Jemmabeth Alexandra, and I'll see you whenever and wherever I can. Stay safe for me." He walked down the hallway and paused before taking the stairs. "You'll always be the only one," he said, "my darlin' Jemma."

Jemma wiped her mouth and cried. This was the worst twenty-four hours she had endured since Spence was reported as MIA in Vietnam. She leaned her forehead against the door to let a wave of nausea pass. The phone was ringing in her room as her trembling hands struggled to get the key in the lock again.

"Spence!" she yelled into the receiver.

"Jem, what's happened?"

His voice unleashed a torrent of emotion.

⁓⚬⁓

Spencer's temples throbbed as he pulled up to Trent's house. He blew out his breath, then rang the doorbell.

Trent answered. "Hey, Spence, what's up?"

"I need to talk to Missy." Spencer's voice resembled a pilot's when he gives the warning just before upcoming turbulence. Heavy turbulence.

"Sure, come in," Trent said, big-eyed.

The Cleave was curled up on the couch, barefooted, watching television. She ran her tongue around her lips at the sound of Spencer's voice and fluffed out her hair. "Hi, Spence. I thought old married men weren't allowed on the streets this late." She flashed her perfect smile.

Spencer's jaw twitched. "Did Jemma call me yesterday morning and ask you to get in touch with me immediately?"

Missy puckered her lips and peered up at the ceiling. "Let's see. . .oh yeah, I guess she did. I totally forgot about it. I just got busy, plus y'all were in Amarillo all morning," she said with a follow-up smile and indigo eyes that shifted from steely-eyed Spencer to big-eyed Trent.

"Did you call Paul Turner and tell him Jemma's flight number and the address of her school and hotel in Paris?" Spencer asked.

Missy turned to Trent, who stood with his arms folded and his gaze now stuck on the floor. She shrugged. "Of course not. I don't even know those things."

"Mr. Turner told Jemma that a sorority sister of one of his old girlfriends called him and gave him all of that information. You have a sorority sister who dated Paul Turner, but you had to go through my desk to get those other details." Spencer's breath whistled through his teeth. "As far as I'm concerned, you are fired, *Missy*," he hissed. "Trent, Jemma was assaulted in Paris and called me from a hospital yesterday. I just got off the phone with her, and she told me the rest of the story. I trust you'll do the right thing." He shot one last look at The Cleave, then left.

Jemma sat in her room all morning, afraid that Paul would be waiting for her somewhere outside. She felt stronger, physically. Her heart was hurting, though. She needed to have Spencer's arms around her, but it would be ten more days before that could happen. Her head reeled with questions. How could so many things she touched wind up hurting people she loved? The Bible said that things work together for the good of those who love God or something like that. Why would it be good for her to be attacked and for Paul to be the one to come to her rescue? Now she would have to tell Spence everything because she promised not to keep secrets from him. That would only serve to hurt him more. Maybe she should break that promise and not tell him everything. It couldn't make things easier for Spence to know that Paul had sat up with her all night in a hospital room. Who knew what went on in Paul's head while she slept in that hospital gown? There was nothing to do but to paint. Paul surely had to be on his way home by now.

Jemma said a prayer, took two aspirin, and changed clothes. She peeked into the hallway, locked her room, and gingerly made her way to Le Academie. She stayed on the other side of the street, away from that awful spot. She could have taken a cab, but Papa had always taught her to face her fears.

⪦⪧

Spencer hadn't slept since her call. Twice now he had stayed home while she went away, and twice there had been trouble with the cowboy. What kind of man was Paul? Spencer didn't have to give that question much thought. Jemmabeth Alexandra was, to both of them, like fresh air. They needed her, but he couldn't share her with another man, even if she were only shared in Paul's mind. He wasn't sure if he could bear periodic visitations from an obsessive old boyfriend as though he were no more than a wayward uncle. At the same time, he couldn't very well get angry with a man who saved Jemma from some terrible fate. Now didn't seem like a good time to ruin the guy's reputation with a restraining order, either.

Why did the good Lord let Missy contact Paul? Maybe this was a warning from Him that this big-shot architect husband was a little too busy. He should have been the one to rescue his own wife, but Mr. Busy Architect was in Texas. If he had gone with her, like she wanted, she wouldn't have been attacked in the first place. Mr. Selfish Architect Husband. He couldn't wait to hold her and know that she was really all right. He closed his eyes and tried to pass the time with sleep.

⪦⪧

Jemma stood at her window and sipped hot tea. She caught a glimpse of herself in the mirror. Both eyes were black, and her nose was still like a sausage. Spencer had said he would call, but the phone hadn't rung. She set the cup on a small table and took out the letterhead stationery from the desk drawer.

Dear Robby,
    I hope you are having a good time. I am in Paris teaching

a class for two weeks. Are you sure you want bongos for
Christmas? They can be very annoying. When you get in
high school, take French. There are important words that you
might need to know when you travel to Paris.

She was interrupted by a knock on the door. Her pulse shot up, thinking it could be Paul. Rats! She decided not to answer and instead sat motionless on the couch.

A movement by the door caught her eye. She crossed the room and reached for the envelope that had suddenly appeared on the floor. *You need this more than I do now* was scrawled on the envelope. Puzzled, she opened it. Inside was the four-leafed clover that she had found for Spencer just before he left for Vietnam. He had taken it from the starry frame.

"Spence!" she yelled and flung open the door. They were like two trains appearing out of the fog and smashing into one another. She didn't even care if the collision hurt like the dickens. He held on while she sobbed into his shirt.

They sat on the couch for hours. Jemma told him everything that she thought he could stand. "I can't believe you are here. I wanted to come home, but I didn't want to disappoint the Academie."

"You have to be in a lot of pain, baby." Spencer scrutinized her face.

"My nose doesn't look too good, huh? I'm taking aspirin for my back and ankle, but I'll be okay now that you are here."

"I should have been here all along. I can't believe Missy pulled such a stunt. I guess she did us a bittersweet favor."

"I think when we get home you should teach me more French," she said. "Louis warned me that there were *agresseurs* in the neighborhood, but I thought that meant aggressive people."

Spencer hung his head. "Oh Jem, I'm so sorry. You're learning French the hard way." He exhaled. "What makes Paul think that he can follow you around, anyway? He can't keep this up. I'm grateful that he was here and all that, but, it's not right. It's sick."

"I don't know, and I don't get why the Lord used him to help me this time. Now it's like we are indebted to him in some twisted way."

"That's a scary thought." Spencer smoothed her hair. "I fired Missy, then drove straight to the airport. My clothes probably stink," he said, smelling under his arms.

"You are the best thing I've seen since I left home."

When he kissed her gently, she only hoped he couldn't taste the last kiss that had been on her lips. For a while, they forgot their woes.

Chapter 13
Details

Spencer, always keeping busy, spent the next few days visiting architectural firms in Paris and working from the hotel room. "I like walking you to the Academie every day," he told Jemma. "It's like we are in grade school again."

"In grade school, we couldn't do this," Jemma said and kissed him as they stood on the Academie steps.

Monsieur Lanier passed by and smiled. "*Bonjour,* Jemma and Spencer."

Jemma waved without stopping her business with her husband.

"There is a concert at Sainte-Chapelle tonight. Want to go?" Spencer asked as she wiped the lipstick off him.

"You bet, mister. I'll try to finish early. I love you." She grinned and disappeared inside.

Spencer headed back to the hotel to call Trent.

Trent answered the phone himself. "How are things in Paris? How's Jemma?"

"Better. I see you are taking calls yourself. What happened with Missy?"

"Hey, I like to have fun as much as the next guy, but not at the expense of my cousin's welfare and our firm's security."

"Good riddance. She's always walked a thin line, but I was hoping she had grown out of it by now."

Trent cleared his throat. "Did that old boyfriend of Jemma's assault her?"

"No, no. It was a couple of French thugs. The cowboy sort of saved her life." Spencer toyed with his pen, not ready to share the details. "Listen, I've made some great contacts in Paris. I figure since I'm here, I might as well see what's going on. I think I may have sparked some interest for our business."

"No kidding? Well, I have nothing keeping me home at night.

If there's traveling to be done, I'm your man." Trent laughed.

"Are you and Missy still seeing each other? It's really none of my business; I'm just curious."

"No way, not after this fiasco. She was beginning to get on my nerves, to tell the truth, and this episode was just evil. I get the feeling that she's spent some serious time making dumb guys like me happy. We're going to have to find us another secretary, though. I've pecked out a couple of letters, but my typing skills are about like Robby's. Any suggestions?"

Spencer sat back on the couch and rubbed the bridge of his nose. "You know what? Call out to my dad's car dealership and ask for Buddy Baker. See if his sister, Sandy, has found a job yet. She won some kind of typing contest when we were in high school. She's good friends with Jem, and is going through some hard times right now."

"I'll do it. I think I met her at your wedding. I'd better go now. The other line is ringing. Keep up the good work. We'll see you soon. Give my love and apologies to Jem."

Spencer got the phone book out and made his list for the day.

The orchestra was warming up as they found their seats. "This has to be the most incredible setting for a concert," Jemma whispered.

"There's nothing like perfect Gothic architecture to put you in your place as a mere mortal," Spencer said. The evening light filtered through the ornate stained glass, reducing the two of them to tiny glass jewels like those inside a kaleidoscope.

She touched his hand. "Spence, how much detail do you want to know about this whole incident?"

"There's more? About the assault or about Paul?"

"Paul," Jemma whispered.

He looked away, his jaw tight. "For you to ask if I want to know about the details means there are some things you don't want to tell me."

"I don't want to hurt you, babe. It's nothing horrible, but it would be hard for me to tell it. I will if you want me to, since we made our promise."

"Why would I want to get hurt? I should take comfort that

God is going to handle things, but it's tough being a mere mortal. More details that you'd rather not share, huh? I guess I'll have to give that some thought."

Jemma tried to enjoy the concert and forget about those details, but she couldn't. She watched him, her sweet Candy Man, the whole time. If he chose to know, she would have to think of the gentlest way to tell him. They didn't talk much during intermission, but he finally looked her in the eye and nodded. She squeezed his hand and took a deep breath. They might as well have left at that point.

❧

At the hotel, Jemma asked Spencer for the key to their room in the hallway. She put it in the lock and turned to him. "This is what happened right here at the door. I said, 'Good-bye, Paul. I pray that you won't keep this up. I'll tell Spencer everything and I don't know what he'll say or do. Go home. You can't follow me around even though you are the hero this time.' Now you grab my shoulders, Spence, and pull me to you no matter what I do, okay?"

Spencer yanked her to him with more force than she expected.

"Now kiss me," she said.

She felt him shudder at the word. She pushed on his chest with all the power she could muster. She had expected a tentatively executed response, given her recovering condition. Instead, he kissed her hard, much harder than Paul had a week earlier. She didn't wipe her mouth as she had with Paul but looked away from Spencer's blistering stare.

"That's it," she said, "except the key fell out of the door."

"I'm not sure I like your little melodrama," he said at long last. "So your hero collected his reward, did he? Would you like it if I was on the receiving end of that kind of passion from, say, Michelle Taylor?"

"Her name came up really fast, didn't it?" Jemma fired back, disappointed that he didn't get the point of her reenactment. "I wanted you to see that I couldn't help what happened."

"Did you like it?" Spencer's voice had an unfamiliar tone.

"His kiss?" She glared at him, shoved open the door, and flung her purse on the bed.

719

Spencer was right behind her. "It's my worst fear, baby, that you did like it and you will miss it someday." He touched her face.

Jemma pulled back from him, sniffing. "Never, Spence. I wiped my heart clean of him a long time ago even if he keeps popping up. You are my precious husband. I tried the rest but you won, remember, babe? I love you, and I want nothing more, ever."

Her golden eyes were on him. He had called them tiger-eyes in the third grade and made her mad. Every time her temper flared they glowed. Now they were brimming with pain, and he was fast becoming the source of it. He buried his face in her hair and inhaled. She smelled of paint and flowers. He tucked her hair behind her ear, and made a trail of warm kisses down her neck. "Remember our first time, at the That'll Do Motel after our wedding?" he whispered in her ear.

"Of course," she said.

His chest rose and fell against hers. "Let's reenact that event because I remember all of those details," he said, "and those I liked."

Jemma smiled. "Me, too." Then she kissed him, long and sweet, ignoring all pain.

❦

Their flight was delayed out of Paris. Spencer watched as she sketched passengers in the waiting area. He would never tire of seeing her brain work. She could take just a few pencil marks and re-create a complete stranger from fifty feet away. In ten minutes, the stranger would come alive with personality and have facial details that most people wouldn't have noticed for days.

Jemma looked up and smiled. "Where did you and Trent eat dinner before you left?" she asked, remaining quite serene, considering the question.

"What?" Spencer wasn't ready for quizzes. "Oh, Dad took us to Amarillo. He wants to get to know Trent better."

"Just the three of you?"

"Yeah. Why?"

"When I called you the night of the attack, Missy told me that she was cooking supper for y'all," Jemma said and held her breath.

Spencer put his arm around her. "Jem, she knows just what to say to you, and you fall for it every time. We do have to find a new secretary, though. I told Trent to check with Sandy."

"Great idea. That would be nice for her." She gave him The Look, then whispered something in his ear. He took a deep breath and got in a little more necking time while they were still in the City of Love.

"Where did they come up with a name like this for a restaurant?" Philip asked.

Spencer laughed. "Our local burger joint, Son's, is owned by a character who sent alimony to his ex-wife for years. When his daughters grew up, they came to Chillaton and started this place with the proceeds, out of spite. Thus the name—Daddy's Money."

"It used to be a feed store, but now it's Son's biggest competitor. His daughters don't even live here," Jemma added.

"All we need now is for Trina to move back and the circle will be complete." Carrie surveyed the plastic flower arrangements in empty gallon pickle jars.

"I can't wait to see her wedding dress," Jemma said as Spencer and Philip talked business. "Not to mention our gowns."

"You have no idea how happy we are to get out of the city. We've been praying about it. Phil is a strong believer in prayer," Carrie whispered.

Jemma nodded and reached for her hand. "Me, too. Sometimes that's all we have."

"Are you getting over your miscarriage, Jem?"

Jemma bit her lip. "Mom says that time heals pain, but that hasn't happened yet."

"Phil and I want to start a family, but not for a while. Of course, I don't know if I can even get pregnant. If not, we're going to adopt."

Jemma nodded and watched Spencer talk. His wedding ring, a gold band engraved with Scottish thistles, glinted in the restaurant light. He was to her like the beat of her own heart. He turned briefly toward her and smiled, warming her inside and out. Someday they would have babies, too; then maybe her guilt would fade away. She didn't want to ever again bring him pain.

"Call me every night, okay?" Jemma asked as they sat in the boarding area. "I'm nervous about Paul. The Cleave may tell him every time I'm alone, simply out of spite."

Spencer held her hands. "Jem, you told me he would never harm you. Is that not true?"

She looked away. "He wouldn't do me any harm, but he is desperate for me to love him. You know that I don't, right?"

"I'm not worried about your love. It's just him and this is his last chance. If there is one single problem, no matter how much you protest, I'm going to a lawyer. Don't look at me like that, either." He reached for his briefcase. "That's my flight. I'll call you when I get there. Give Trina a hug for me and smile. I'll see you next weekend."

Her lips were made for the perfect pout. "I'll miss you, Spence." She looked up at him like a sick puppy.

"Aw, baby, don't do this to me just as I'm leaving. You know I have to go. I'll be back before you know it." He whispered in her ear, making her smile, then was gone.

◦◦◦

Jemma went through the skirt sale rack at Kidwell's Department Store in Amarillo. Trina probably wouldn't approve of some of the styles she was considering. She pushed apart two bohemian skirts to have a better look and revealed another customer on the opposite side of the rack.

"Missy."

"Jemmartsybeth."

Their eyes locked for an instant, and without giving it a thought, Jemma stepped between the skirts and stood squarely in The Cleave's face. "How dare you try to undermine my marriage," she said, the words swarming out of her mouth.

Missy looked as though she might throw up, but it was actually the beginnings of a smile. "I don't know what you're talking about."

"I'm talking about you and your constant flirting with Spencer, and now you've tried to stir up trouble with Paul Turner."

"Oh sorry. Did you ever consider that Spencer might like my attention? I know he did at one time."

Jemma's mouth twitched. The Claw would work, but she'd seen Bull Von Tersch wrap his opponent's long hair around his neck in a new move called the "The Calf Roper" last weekend. It would be a satisfying way to drag The Cleave around Kidwell's.

"How about this, Missy? You leave my husband alone, and I won't run for cheerleader anymore, and, let's see, I'll decline the football and prom queen elections. Would you like to step into my little time machine and get rid of some of your pent-up jealousy?"

"Ouch. The pain. Like I ever cared about your popularity. But it would be only fair if I could have had my turn with Spence. You have no idea what I'm capable of doing for his happiness."

"News alert, Missy. Spencer is completely happy."

"That's not what I heard. It's all around town that he wants a baby and you can't give him one."

Jemma swallowed hard. She had no comeback, and The Cleave gave a soft snort, knowing she'd struck gold.

"I could give him all he wants. That's a proven fact, twice over," Missy said.

"Really. A proven fact." Jemma's eyes lit up like bonfires. "If you ever try another stunt like you did by contacting Paul, I will call the Women's Prayer Circle at your parents' church and tell them exactly what you just told me. I'll picket your father's movie theaters with big signs telling just exactly what a flirtatious tramp you are."

The Cleave took a step toward Jemma until their perfume mingled. "You loser. Leave my parents out of this. They've never done anything to you."

"They gave birth to you, Missy."

She slung back her hair. "I'm Melissa now. Get that through your thick skull. I suppose it's all clogged up with unused baby names, though. Too bad."

"You know what, Missy? The real reason I can't remember to call you Melissa is that I don't care about your real name; all I can remember is what we all called you in high school."

"Still in high school. What a constituted toad you are. So, what little nickname did you think up for me?"

"The Cleave, short for 'cleavage,' which you threw in everybody's face until it became boring. People were laughing at you, and they still are. Even the guys call you that. I hear them. Respect is something you've never had, and it's something you can't steal, either. The only way you could get it now is by turning to the Lord."

"Ding, dong, missionary time. Don't give me your bull. I'm not interested. You just sit back, Miss CHS, and watch me get what I want. I'm not down and out yet, and your little threats don't scare me. Here, why don't you buy all these hippie skirts; then people can laugh at *you* even more." With that, she hoisted an armful of skirts off the rack, dumped them on the floor, then twisted off like she was leading the CHS band off the field at halftime. Jemma replaced the skirts and left.

She sat in the parking lot while her body buzzed with emotion. She had lost her temper and tried to feel better about it by bringing in the Lord. All her Bible verses and prayers hadn't done her a lick of good when confronted with Missy. She bounced her head against the steering wheel. The Cleave was a clever liar. Those hateful things she had said about Spencer being unhappy were lies. How dare Missy mention their lost baby. If she brought all this up to Spence, it would give power to the lie. She knew her husband, and he was anything but unhappy.

Jemma started the car. . .and turned it off. She winced, then prayed out loud, "Please, please, forgive me, Lord, for losing my temper. Help me learn to control it better. . . ."

She blew her nose, then burst into a giggle. *Constituted* toad. Missy herself was the embodiment of a *conceited* toad.

Rats. That wasn't exactly a Christian thought and right after a heartfelt prayer, too.

Chapter 14

Clever Mrs. Baldwin

Trina's class threw their hats in the air, then she scrambled to find hers for the refund. Her family and friends had yelled louder than anybody's, digging her dimples even deeper as she clutched her diploma. She made her way through a sea of purple graduation gowns until she found Nick. Jemma caught the moment with Spencer's fancy camera.

"I hope I did that right," Jemma said. "He showed me how to use it, but I was packing."

"Jemmabeth!" Professor Rossi, always Jemma's most vocal fan, embraced her. "Where is your husband? I was hoping to see both of you."

"He's in California. He has a project there, and he couldn't come on this trip. How are you? You look happy, as usual."

"My wife and I are leaving next week for Italy. Come, I have someone you must meet. I trust you have been working hard."

"You know me. I paint every day, all day. I have thirty pieces that are just sitting around, waiting to be loved by someone other than me."

"Not to worry," the professor said. "I have the solution." He escorted her to a cluster of people talking with the dean. One member of the group was a distinguished, slender man, impeccably dressed with a rosebud in his lapel and a moustache that appeared painted on. He smelled like sandalwood, but his face bore a slight resemblance to that of a mustachioed rat.

"Don't tell me," he said in an accent similar to Helene's, "you must be the young American artist that everyone is talking about—Forrester-Chase, is it?" He bowed slightly and held her hand by the fingertips, his eyes on her lips.

Professor Rossi laughed. "Ah, the English, always hyphenating names. Jemma, this is Mr. Howard-Finch, owner of the Finchgate

Gallery in London."

"It's a pleasure to meet you, Mr. Finch. I visited your gallery on my honeymoon." She released his hand, but he tugged her to him.

"Call me Thornton, please," he said in a glib tone. "Rossi, here, has been extolling your praises, madam." He lowered his voice and spoke in her ear. "He assures me that you are exactly what we need for our next one-man, pardon, one-woman show." His hand slid to her waist. "How may I see your portfolio?"

"Jemmabeth lives in a small village in the far reaches of Texas," the professor explained. "Perhaps you could meet her somewhere. Jemma, what is the nearest airport?"

Jemma's words stumbled out. "Uh, Amarillo."

"Of course, Spanish for yellow. See what arrangements you can make, Thor. I have her telephone number. You will not be disappointed; you have my word," the professor said just as the dean called him back to the group.

Thornton scanned Jemma's face and came to rest on her eyes. "Such unusual eyes. You must have some hot French blood in you. I knew a girl in Paris with eyes like that." He smiled. "She was a dancer." He raised an eyebrow. "Do you like to dance?"

Jemma turned to Professor Rossi for help, but he was still laughing with the dean. "My husband and I like to dance." She forced a smile. "Do you really want to see my portfolio?"

His brow arched. "Indeed. I know you have shown in New York and studied in Paris. What harm could there be in it? You may surprise me, and I like surprises." He winked. "Though, I must warn you, our gallery is very discriminating. Our shows attract collectors and buyers from all over Europe. We pride ourselves on featuring only those established and emerging artists whose work is preeminent and thoroughly dynamic. I have business this week here in Dallas and then on to Houston. Rossi says that he has one of your pieces. I shall see it later at dinner. If I like it, I'll be in touch." He lifted her hand but kept eye contact as he pecked it. "I surely like what I see before me now. I assume you have been told before that you are a stunning woman."

Jemma looked away from his shifty little eyes and back, exhaling. "Thank you. I'll look forward to hearing from you."

His mouth curved into a smirk. "We shall see." When he pursed his lips, his scrawny moustache folded up like bat wings.

Jemma walked away, feeling his eyes still on her. She wished she had worn a different dress, but Trina had made this one just for her. It was too short, too tight, and too purple at the moment.

The Fields, Nick's family, threw a party for Trina. Lots of laughter came from the corner where Willa sat with Nick's parents. They had big things to discuss about the wedding. Nick and Trina were both only children in their families, so their parents wanted everything to be special all around.

Lizbeth and Willa took the Trailways bus home. Jemma stayed to help Trina move her belongings back to Chillaton. Jemma cleaned out some of her own things that she had left in her old studio. She looked around at the place. There weren't nearly enough memories there with Spence, and that was all her fault. If she hadn't gotten it in her head to see if there was somebody else that she was destined to love rather than him, her life would have been simpler now. Most of her Wicklow memories revolved around Paul, and they weren't all good, especially the thought of him pinning her to the daybed, hungry for kisses and reeking of hot beer breath. She gathered up her things and locked the door behind her. She missed her husband, especially with the memory of Paul Turner ferreting into her brain.

"I'll never be able to thank you enough for Le Claire," Trina said as Jemma helped her pack. "Do you know what I'd be doing right now if you hadn't paid my tuition?"

Jemma feigned concentration. "You would have stopped being so stubborn and gotten a scholarship?"

"I wasn't being stubborn. I just didn't want some rich person giving me money and knowing nothing about me. I guess you and Spencer are rich, though, huh?" Trina packed each of her design sketchbooks as though they were fine china. She glanced at Jemma. "Jem, did I make you feel like you had to help me go to school?"

Jemma wrinkled her nose as though a skunk had sprayed the room. "What are you talking about? You are my talented, sweet friend, and I wanted you to get the training you deserve. You always think I operate on guilt, but I don't. I'm not sure what drives my decisions. I'd like to think that the Lord uses me sometimes to do His will. I know He uses Spence."

"Yeah, but it was you, girl, who gave me the money. You've got a fine heart that drives you, and you don't even realize it. I'm the one who should feel guilty about whining over my situation back then. Right now all I can offer you is my talent, so from now on, I'm designing your clothes with my Le Claire School of Fine Arts degree. I think you need a fresh style."

Jemma laughed. "What's the deal with everybody talking about my clothes? I'm happy with what I have."

"Oh. Is that why you keep griping about that Blake girl calling you a bohemian, and that you don't have anything to wear except what your mom hands you down or what your snobby grandmother or Spence buys for you?" Trina grinned, her dimples set. "It doesn't take your Nancy Drew to figure out that you need help."

Jemma sighed. "You're right, as usual. When we get to Chillaton, you can go through my clothes and get rid of everything that doesn't meet your designer standards. There. Does that make you happy?"

Trina taped a box shut. "It would make me happy if I knew where Nick and I will end up after his residency. I want to live in a place where I can think. I don't want to be in a crazy city full of pressure and ego. You know what I mean?"

"I know that Spence felt the same way and look where we ended up. It amazes me that he and Trent have so much business with an office in Chillaton. They do spend a lot of time flying around the country, though. Did I tell you that they now have a client in Paris? Maybe y'all can move back home like everybody else is doing. It works for us."

Trina pooh-poohed that. "You think all those blue hairs would let Nick even check their blood pressure? That would be a miracle."

"Don't say it like that."

"I know, you believe in miracles and so do I." Trina went back to packing. "So you think I can make a difference with your neighborhood business idea? Sorry nobody showed up for the first meeting."

"A few came. I'm taking it slow. I don't want to scare anybody off."

"Speaking of scary, I suppose you know that Weese is back, and he brought his sister. She looks just like him and has the attitude. Mama said he got his high school diploma and somehow got into a junior college. Maybe he'll be a wiser Weese. Have you seen him yet?"

"I saw his sister. Her name's Gweny. She came to the little get-together I had. I wonder if Weese still hates me."

"He was all talk. Don't worry about it."

"Ladies," Helene called up the stairs, "lunch is served."

"I'm going to have to start running laps." Trina patted her stomach. "Helene is a good cook. I'm going to miss her and this beautiful place. I've been so lucky."

"Just like me," Jemma said, putting her arm around her as they went downstairs. "Now let's talk more about my new wardrobe."

They discussed all the aspects of outfitting a portrait artist in colors to suit her mood and fabrics that felt good to her. Helene set her hearing aid a little higher and listened with delight. She, who had never had children of her own, had come to love these two young people, their families, and their circle of friends. It had been a panacea for her the last few years, and she did not want it to end. "Trina," Helene asked, "how did you meet Nicholas?"

Trina giggled. "*Nicholas* sounds so funny. Sorry, Helene." She cleared her throat. "I got a basketball scholarship to a junior college when I got out of high school."

"A scholarship?" Jemma said.

"Yeah. I know what you're thinking, but it was only a dinky one. I had to pay most of the tuition and expenses myself. Anyway, Nick and I worked at a burger place in Dallas. Nick had been in the army and was starting medical school. We just hit it off."

Jemma narrowed her eyes. "You never told me he was that much older than you."

"Hey, girl, he still wasn't as old as *Paul*." Trina whispered his name.

"I challenge you to a duel for that. Outside in an hour. Bring your basketball."

"You're on." Trina grinned and had a second helping of Helene's broccoli quiche.

Helene tapped her teacup with a spoon. "A toast." The girls raised their glasses of cold sweet tea, which Helene had begrudgingly made for them. "To the three of us as we begin—or continue, in Jemma's case—new chapters in our lives." She clinked her cup against their glasses, then took a sip of hot tea and returned to her seat, her expression quite serene. Jemma and Trina still held their glasses aloft.

"Wait a minute, Helene. What's all this 'new chapter' business?" Jemma asked.

"Are you getting married or something?" Trina asked.

Helene dabbed at her mouth with her napkin and chuckled. "No, dear, I am not getting married, although I have not dismissed the idea."

"What, then?"

"I am moving to Chillaton. Lizbeth has invited me, and I have accepted. We are going to be flatmates. I will get to hear all the Lester stories that I want, and I can play Nana to all Lizbeth's great-grandchildren, when they arrive."

Jemmabeth and Latrina embraced her at once.

"Moving to Chillaton is a brave move for an Englishwoman," Trina said. "You know who your neighbors will be across the tracks. Wait 'til Mama hears about this."

"Lizbeth and Willa have known for the past year. They were sworn to secrecy. Now that you have both moved on, I want to keep you in my sight, so I'm carrying on as well."

"What about your home?" Jemma asked. "How can you stand to leave it?"

"That's the sad part. Perhaps if anyone needs a place to stay, it can serve as the That'll Do Motel for Wicklow. Nebs would be amused at such nonsense."

❧

Jemma and Trina played basketball in the driveway. Helene had installed a goal just for her boarder's amusement. They worked out until Trina quit.

"Ha!" Jemma announced. "I'm finally in better shape than you are."

"You and Spencer have been chasing each other around the house for over a year. I've been slaving away in school and eating Helene's rich food. What are you looking at?"

Jemma's attention was on the road. A baby blue pickup had

stopped near Helene's driveway—*Paul*.

"Inside, quick," Jemma said. "Don't look at him."

They went in and locked the door, giving Helene specific instructions to not answer if he knocked. The three women huddled around the conservatory windows peeking through the panes. After several minutes, he drove away.

Trina shivered. "That was so creepy."

Jemma flopped in an armchair. "If he does one more thing, it will put Spence over the edge. Paul has to back off."

"Do you think it would help if I talked with him, dear?" Helene asked. "I know his father, slightly, from Neb's legal dealings."

"That old boy could step on you like a sugar ant, Helene," Trina declared.

Jemma was still watching out the window.

"Of course," Trina added, "you might die happy, lookin' at him."

"I don't know what will ever help." Jemma sighed and slumped back into the chair.

"You should introduce him to that Blake girl. They would be the perfect couple," Trina suggested.

"Y'all don't leave me alone, okay?" Jemma paced around the room.

Trina and Helene exchanged glances, and Helene put her mind in Clever Englishwoman Mode.

The next morning, the girls went for a run around the Wicklow High School track. When they got home, Helene and her red MG were nowhere to be seen.

"She must be at the supermarket. There's a new one down by the highway," Trina said.

Jemma wasn't too sure about that, but kept her ideas to herself.

Helene sat in the law office. She was not as calm as she thought she would be. The secretary was pleasant enough and had even offered her tea. She didn't drink it, though. It was that awful brand Americans buy just to be on the safe side with the odd hot tea-drinking guest. She adjusted her pearls.

"Mrs. Baldwin? Mr. Turner will see you now." The secretary

smiled as she picked up Helene's teacup. "Wouldn't you like to take your tea with you?"

"No thank you, dear," Helene said, concentrating on the task at hand.

Paul was on the phone with his back to the door. Helene seated herself and surveyed the room. It was impressive, but with a somewhat melancholy, perfunctory air. Her eyes came to rest on a watercolor self-portrait of Jemma laughing. It hung directly behind his desk next to a large, vibrant painting of a river flanked by rolling meadows of bluebonnets. She remembered that piece, too. It had been a gift from Jemma to Paul before his secret was found out. Helene knew also that he had paid a thousand dollars for the watercolor and another two thousand for others she didn't see in the office. She took a deep breath. This was not going to be easy.

He did the same double take that Helene had enjoyed watching in silent movies as a child. In her younger days, her heart would have quaked at the sight of such a splendidly handsome man, but not now, and especially not after all she knew about him.

She extended her hand. "Hello, Paul. Your office is quite nice."

He pressed his hand to hers. "Helene. Are you using an alias these days?" he asked, recovering, and turning on the charm.

"Baldwin is my maiden name. I use it sometimes for legal documents and such." Helene sat forward in her chair, straight as a hatpin. She concentrated her attention on a small watercolor of flowers on his desk, another of Jemma's works. "I'm here, Paul, out of concern for Jemmabeth. As you know, she is very dear to me."

"She is to me, as well." He leaned back in his leather chair, watching her.

She knew those eyes of his could mesmerize even an old sort like her, so she returned to the watercolor and weighed each word. "I'm not sure that you comprehend what has happened. Jemma has committed her life to Spencer and that will not change, dear. She is not a woman to be twisted about like a university girl anymore."

"What's your point, Helene? I've heard speeches like this before."

"My point is that all of us who love Jemma want her life to be full of joy and as peaceful as possible. If we impede that joy, we become a negative influence on her life, and also on her art, since

I see that you enjoy her work. Unfortunately, you have managed to jeopardize her happiness. I don't mean to become threatening, Paul, but I do know your father, and I have made an appointment with him as well, as soon as we are finished here. I truly hope that you will be able to convince me that our Jemmabeth is not in any further danger of your harassment. Perhaps you have already confided this troublesome behavior to your father, but I am prepared to help you in that revelation, should you need such assistance."

Paul drummed his fingertips on the desk, his face solemn and his voice low. "Coercion doesn't become you, darlin'. My father has a heart condition, and it could kill him to hear this. Regardless of what you think, I have never harmed Jemmabeth. I love her. Just because she chose the kid over me doesn't change that fact. Remember, I saved her life in Paris."

"I am well aware of that situation, and nobody denies that you kept her from a ghastly fate. That incident, however, was coincidental to your obsessive nature. Harassing her does not send a message of affection. I have, myself, witnessed her fear and anxiety over your actions. You have infringed on Jemma's pursuit of happiness, and I believe that is assured us in the *Declaration of Independence*. I have dual citizenship, you know."

Paul leaned back in his chair and stared at her. His green eyes matched her emerald earrings. "Don't talk to Dad, Helene. Like I said, he's had two heart attacks in the last three years." His voice quavered, and the room became quiet.

He finally stood and moved to sit on the corner of his desk. Trina was right; he truly was a large chap, and he could quite possibly squash her like an ant.

"I am not ashamed to say that I adore Jemma," he said. "She's as close to perfection as a woman could ever be. If I've frightened her, as you say, I'm sorry. Ironically, nobody understands my feelings for her except the husband kid. To be frank with you, ma'am, she's the only woman, besides my mother, that I've ever respected. I just want to be near her whenever I can, to see those golden eyes and to hear her laugh. I like the way her hair. . ." He ran his hand through his own.

Helene spoke quietly and with unforeseen tenderness. "I

understand your affection for her, dear. She is an extraordinary person, but you mustn't put your desires above hers. It is not fair to her, Paul. Surely, as a lawyer, you can see that. What do you say, then? If you can assure me that this nonsense will stop, I shan't keep my appointment with your father." She kept her breath steady and her eyes on the watercolor flowers.

"You are asking me to give up all hope, Helene. What is a man without hope?"

"Hope is always inside us, Paul, but such hope must abide only in your heart and not infringe on this dear girl's joy. She is worth more than that to you, is she not?"

He brushed his cheek with his thumb. "I need to always know, somehow, that she is safe and lacks for absolutely nothing."

Helene put her hand on his. "I can write to you now and then, if it would be of any consolation to you."

He nodded. "The first time I ever saw her, she was dancing in this very room with a vacuum cleaner. She stole my heart that night, and it's never ticked right since. I've handled things all wrong, but I do know that she cared for me, once. My miserable past caught up with me at every turn. It was the chance of a lifetime, and I blew it."

"Nevertheless," Helene said, "Jemma believes the Almighty has His own plans for us all. It would appear, then, that you are meant to find another woman to love and let her be. Do carry on, dear boy." She looked directly at him, ill-prepared to find this beguiling man in tears.

"I will let her be, if possible," he said, "but I will never love anyone the way that I love Jem. How could I? You know her. She is the rose in a garden of daisies."

Helene could not disagree. There was nothing more to be said. She reached for one of his business cards. "Good day, Paul. I wish you well," she said, and meant it.

"Helene, you've got a lot of guts, pardon my French, to come here and talk to me about this. Jemma brings out something in people, and they do things for her that normally they might not. Promise me that you really will keep in touch."

"I shall. I am a steadfast woman, and you are quite right; I would do anything for her." She offered her hand. He took it in his and held it for a moment.

"By the way, darlin', our rights are guaranteed by the *Constitution*, not the *Declaration of Independence*. Just for future reference," he clarified with a feeble smile.

"I did say that I have dual citizenship. At my age it's difficult to keep historical things from two countries straight." She closed the door on his vacant stare, then dabbed her eyes with her lace hanky after tucking his card into her purse.

⟡

Jemma waited in the garden by the fragrant Tiffany rose. She closed her eyes and inhaled. The rosebush they had planted by Papa's grave would duplicate that scent this summer. Such a heavenly creation stirred hope in her. Their merciful Lord might bless them again with a baby.

Her eyes popped open when she heard the MG rolling down the lane. Helene waved and pulled it into the garage. She emerged, dressed in the same aqua blue linen suit she had worn to Trina's graduation.

"Such a lovely morning," Helene called from the gate.

"Yes," Jemma said. "What business took you out so early in your new suit?"

"Personal business, much like a mission trip. You wouldn't interrogate a missionary, now would you?" She gave Chelsea, the cat, a quick pet and went inside.

"So does this mean that you're ready to join a church?" Jemma asked, following her down the hallway.

Helene removed her suit coat and set her handbag on the hallway telephone table. "Perhaps that will be one of my endeavors when I move to Chillaton, but for now, dearest, we need to make plans for dinner. Remember, Nicholas and his family are our guests. Where is Trina?"

"She's upstairs sketching some dresses for my new wardrobe." Jemma watched Helene scamper up the steps like a twenty-year-old. Jemma peered after her for a second, then turned to find Chelsea sniffing at Helene's handbag. It tumbled to the floor with a thump, spilling the contents and sending Chelsea into a speedy exit down the hall. Jemma collected the scattered things: keys, wallet, coin purse, and a damp handkerchief.

That's when she saw it. She read it to be sure, but there was no need. It was just like the other one hundred or so cards that he had sent her in hopes she would call him after he'd played with her heart. Jemma placed it back in the bag and returned to the garden. Chelsea jumped in her lap as she sat again by the Tiffany, pondering the significance of it all.

⋙⋘

Trina's car was so loaded that they thought the tires might go flat.

"Now, Jemma," Helene said, "you must come back to help me move when the time arrives. You will do that for me, won't you?"

"I will. Just call out my name and I'll come running, like the Carole King song says."

Helene twisted her hearing aid. "What's that, dear?"

Trina shook her head. "Jemma just needs to see Spencer, that's all. Thank you for so many things. Someday, when I'm famous, I'm gonna make it up to you two ladies for everything y'all have done for me."

"How about a burger on the road for now?" Jemma asked as she readjusted a couple of boxes in the front seat. "Bye, Helene and Chelsea. Chillaton, here we come." Jemma squeezed behind the wheel and honked the horn.

Trina shouted out the window as they rolled down the lane, "See you at the wedding!"

Helene stroked fat Chelsea and sighed. Were it not for her own plans to move to their village, the moment would have been too heavy for her to bear.

Chapter 15
Coming Attractions

Lizbeth was at Nedra's Nook for her weekly appointment, and Jemma was trying out a new home hair dryer for the first time. Her long, wavy locks flared out en masse and the bathroom emitted an odor of singed fur. She heard him at the back door.

"Jem?" he yelled.

"She's not here," Jemma answered and appeared in the bathroom door. "It's only me, wild woman." She ran around the kitchenette to land on him.

"Now," he said, catching his breath, "who are you, and what have you done with my wife?"

Jemma giggled. "You, sir, are early. See what you get when you arrive ahead of schedule? This mess is the result of something called a blow-dryer. It's more like a blowtorch if you ask me. I bought it at Kidwell's."

Spencer closed the back door. "You sure make my old shirt look good, but I don't think Lester needs to see you in it."

Jemma perched herself on the kitchenette table, grinning. "Guess what? Trina is going to make me a whole new wardrobe. She says I need a 'fresher look,' whatever that means."

Spencer stood close to her with dreamy eyes.

Jemma giggled. "Now, Mr. Chase, before *you* get fresh, remember, Gram could walk in at any moment."

"Well, come on, then, help me unpack, but we are going straight out to the house. I have paint choices for us. Are you ready for that?" Spencer offered his hand, and she jumped off the table and followed him through the good bedroom to theirs.

"The question is, are you ready for this?" She pushed him on the bed and held him down with a sleeper hold. Spencer overpowered her and got her in a tremulous leg lock. Even her teeth chattered. She couldn't stop laughing.

"Give up?" he asked.

"Yes!" she rattled.

Spencer stopped, his legs weak, and Jemma sat up. Her hair was even wilder than before.

"Remember," she said, "I have to practice my moves for Thor, The Lech. *If* he calls, I have to meet him with my portfolio, and *if* you aren't with me, I'll have to fend for myself."

"Oh, I'll be there all right. I'll knock that boutonnière right out of his lapel for him." Spencer took off his tie.

"Oooh, tough guy, huh?" Jemma whispered, smoothing the front of his shirt. "I dare you to try that leg lock again because I'm ready for it this time." She looked up at him and bit her lip.

Spencer responded with his own whispered ideas.

"Hello, anybody home?" Lizbeth called from the kitchen.

Jemma dashed into the closet to finish dressing. Spencer, ever the gentleman, went to see the lady of the house.

They sat under the cottonwoods discussing paint colors. She knew it would be an odd time to bring it up, but she had waited as long as she could.

"Tell me something, babe, and don't spare my feelings."

He raised his brow. "I get the feeling that this is not going to be about paint."

"Are you unhappy that we don't have a baby yet?" she asked quietly, looking straight into his eyes.

He put the color strips down. His answer came slowly, as if he were turning over the source of this question in his mind. "This life of ours could not be happier, Jem. Well, maybe if our house was finished and I could chase you around more. That might make me happier. What's going on?"

"I was just wondering."

"Yeah, I believe that one. Look at me. Who has been messing with your brain?"

She should have kept her trap shut. Rats. "I saw Missy in Amarillo. We sort of had a confrontation, and she said a bunch of things."

"Like what?"

"She said that everybody in Chillaton knew that you were

unhappy because I couldn't give you a baby, and that she could because she's already had two abortions, and that I can't remember to call her Melissa because my head is full of unused baby names." She threw her arms around him and bawled. "I wanted to take her hair and choke her with it. I am so bad, Spence. Don't chew me out, either. I know that she's a liar and that she gets to me, but it was the first time I'd seen her since Paris and I just—"

"Jemmabeth. If we never have a baby, it won't be some kind of a blemish on our marriage. The way I feel about you is enough to keep me content for a lifetime. To have a child with you would be a blessing, but I don't have any secret desires to produce an heir or something. I won't give you any lectures about Missy, but I want you to think about this the next time you see her: Pretend she has hooves, horns, and a tail because I do believe that the devil uses her to get to you. Promise me that you will give that a try."

She glanced up at him, wiping her nose on the back of her hand. "Are you mad at me for asking that?"

"Maybe. Let's make up and see if that helps. Do you understand how I feel about us and babies?"

She nodded and hugged him.

He held her tight. Someday, surely Missy Blake would get her comeuppance.

⋘◈⋙

"You look like Doris Day sitting at that desk," Jemma said as Sandy hung up the phone.

"I love this job. If I don't get fired for spouting off about something, I could work here forever." Sandy stood and danced around in her hot pink pantsuit. "Like what I did with part of my first paycheck? I made it myself." Marriage had not packed any extra pounds on her petite figure.

"I like it a lot better than the dance hall stuff The Cleave wore."

"I heard that she got another job in Amarillo. You'd think that they would call here for references." Sandy sharpened pencils for her bosses.

"I doubt she listed this one for that very reason. Have you heard anything from Marty?" Jemma watched Sandy out of the corner of her eye.

Sandy mouthed the words, "I filed for divorce last week."

"No regrets?" Jemma whispered back.

Sandy shook her head without hesitation. "Anybody hits, I quit. Even if it's Mr. Universe." She went back to the electric pencil sharpener, her perfect makeup still looking good in the air-conditioned office.

Jemma watered the plants, something she hadn't done when Missy was the secretary; then again, maybe she should have and denied The Cleave the opportunity to lean over the pots. "How do you like working for Trent?"

"He's so shy." Sandy lowered her voice. "Hard to get to know, but I guess that's okay. He's cute, but that's probably a prerequisite just to be in your family."

"Easy does it; you're still a married woman."

"Hi, cousin," Trent said, emerging with a stack of folders. "Sandy, would you please call these people and ask for their bids for the job numbers listed on the files? Remind them the deadline is Monday."

Jemma sat on the corner of Sandy's desk. "So, Trent, are you back to your lonely days now that Missy is gone?"

Trent blushed. "I'm keeping busy. It's amazing how Spencer and I have so many clients. Nobody even complains about our location. Of course we meet them at their offices. Our travel and phone expenses are going to be off the charts when tax time rolls around. I just made another call to Paris."

"What do you think of your new secretary?" Jemma asked. "You know she won state in typing."

Trent turned red again. "She's great. Goes by the dress code, too," he said, with a quick look at Sandy. "Well, I guess I'd better get back to work. See ya, Jem."

"Did you see how embarrassed he was? Too shy." Sandy got busy on her assignment.

"Hi, baby, are you ready to go?" Spencer turned off the lights in his office, then dipped Jemma back for a kiss. "Sorry I took so long."

"Kissing is not suitable for the office," Sandy replied.

"Your comments are unsuitable for the office." Spencer grinned and kissed his wife again. "We're leaving this joint. If a call comes from New York, be sure to get their mailing address, okay?" Spencer grabbed Jemma's hand and his briefcase.

Jemma waved on their way out the door.

"What's going on in New York?" Jemma asked on the way to Plum Creek.

"We may get a shot at a chapel design for a new hospital. The plans didn't include it, and some lady gave a big chunk of money to add one. She doesn't like the original architects and won't give her money to them. It's a mess."

"Maybe you could specialize in chapels." Jemma braided her hair.

"That would be nice, wouldn't it? Okay, I have to tell you something, and I don't want you to get upset."

"The sooner you tell me, the sooner I can get over it."

"The firm we would be working with in New York City is the firm that Michelle Taylor is with." He said it fast and waited.

Jemma looked out the window. It was her turn to trust now. Spencer had set a very high standard in that department. They passed two mile markers before she spoke. "I know that you love me even though she is an aggressive, possessive woman. Is she married yet?"

Spencer exhaled. "I can't answer that. All I know is that when Trent and I researched the firm, her name was on the list as Taylor." He reached for her hand. "You are taking this well."

She shrugged. "I'm trying to put faith into action, but let's don't talk about it anymore. Same rules I have with Paul. You call me if anything happens."

"Nothing is going to happen."

"Just don't let her touch you. Remember she called me a she-hick, a *shick*."

"I remember you called her a fool in French. What if she wants to shake hands?" He grinned.

"You may only salute, soldier," she said, giving him The Look that he loved.

⚜

This time the pews at the Negro Bethel Church were full. Word had gotten out that Latrina, college graduate and fashion designer, would be there.

"Some of these women are from Red Mule and Pleasant," Trina whispered.

"That's okay with me. If they're interested in making this work," Jemma said.

"How come there ain't no cookies?" Grandma Hardy called out.

"Hold your horses, Grandma," Willa yelled back. "There's sandwiches when the meetin's done."

"Thanks for coming, ladies. I hope that this big turnout means you are all interested in making a go of the project," Jemma said as the crowd quieted down. "I have arranged for you to have ten sewing machines, and Trina has chosen the fabric. She will help with the details of the machines and the actual quilting. I hope everyone signed the sheet at the back table."

Gweny sniffed. "Some can't write. You should've known that." Murmurs of agreement sputtered around the room.

Jemma's face reddened. "Oh, I'm sorry. If you'll tell me your name, that will do. I want to make up a work schedule as a guide, so everybody will have something to do."

"What's your job?" Grandma Hardy asked.

"I'll drop by when I can, but I have my own work. I don't know how to quilt. I'm an artist," Jemma said almost apologetically.

Bertie Shanks raised her hand. "Who's gonna be the boss?"

"You're lookin' at her," Willa announced proudly. "I don't want no fightin', neither."

The group who knew her laughed and relaxed.

"Me and my husband, Joe, are takin' a real interest in these goin's-on, and Brother Cleo is lettin' us use the basement here at the church during the weekdays. My baby, Trina, is gonna give sewin' machine lessons every day startin' tomorrow at eight in the mornin'. Now if all of us pull our weight, we can make us some grocery money that don't come from the guv'ment. It can't be no harder than pickin' cotton. Now, in the past, I've been thinkin' that Jemmabeth here had fertilizer in her head, but after she told me and Joe the details, I seen the light. I'm ready to go on it, but I ain't no quilter neither. I can iron, so I reckon that means I can iron out problems if any come up."

More laughter.

Trina showed the ladies her original pattern ideas. They voted on their favorites and broke into smaller groups to argue about fabric colors and quilting styles. Most had been quilting since childhood, but never with material like Jemma had purchased. They ran their hands over the bolts and cast their first approving glances her way.

Jemma had done her homework, with Lizbeth's help. The North & South Chillaton Quilting Club President had even calculated bathroom breaks into the plan. It paid off. Jemma taped the schedule, drawn on Spencer's oversized drafting paper, on the basement wall, as the whole group descended downstairs for sandwiches and sweet tea. They looked over the sewing machines resting on the folding church tables with oohs and aahs. Lester and Joe had made four quilting frames that were suspended overhead like giant spiderwebs. The air was tinged with excitement and high hopes. The women from Pleasant and Red Mule would only be able to work two days a week, when they could all pile into the back of a truck belonging to Teeky Samson's son. He would drive them over and only charge gas money. Jemma said she would pay him for his trouble.

"My Joe's gonna keep the books, so y'all be sure to make your mark on the days you work. We'll all be on the lookout for each other, so keep everybody honest. Now I think we should have ourselves a prayer over this business," Willa said, and the group joined hands, except for Gweny Matthews, who took her sandwiches and left. "Lord Almighty, we give You thanks for this food and the hands that prepared it. We come to Your holy feet, Lord, and lay down this here plan for a quiltin' business. If You want to bless it, Jesus, we'll know that's what You think we should do. Also, we ask You to bless Jemmabeth, Lord, for comin' to us with this here notion, the machines, and the cloth. Help steady our hands to Your glory and to get off welfare. Amen."

Shiloh Favor approached Jemma and smiled. "I just wanna say that me and my man, Terrill, think this is a fine idea. Lots of folks think it's gonna flop, but if nobody never tries nothin', then nothin' never gets better. That's all I've got to say on it." She lifted her chin and left.

"Thank you, Shiloh," Jemma said to her back. She turned to

Trina, blinking back tears. "Let's eat. Are there any sandwiches left?"

"Nope. What wasn't eaten was taken home. Mama wants to get out of here. Joe comes home tonight from a run to L.A."

"Then we'll go to Daddy's Money." Jemma cleared off the refreshment table.

"Let's just go to Son's." Trina shook the tablecloth over the wastebasket. "I still get looks at Daddy's Money. Nobody can see me that well if I'm sitting in the car at Son's."

Jemma was taken aback. Chillaton had come around faster than this, surely. Still, Trina avoided her eyes. Rats. Double ugly rats. Maybe it hadn't. The momentary silence between them was broken by a freight train clamoring down those tracks that still divided their little town.

"So, what's the plan?" Jemma asked, turning toward Son's. "Are you going to work for a design house?"

Trina laughed. "I doubt it. One of my professors helped me put together a portfolio, though. She sent it to a few places for me. I might as well get used to the idea of living in a ghetto and being Nick's assistant."

"Don't give me that. You're a fantastic designer. Something will come along. A ghetto? Good grief, Trina."

"I have thought of a label for myself, but don't tell anybody. It's my initials, *LJF*, with the *F* coming off the *J*; you know what I mean, like the *J* is a flagpole? I want to keep the Johnson in there to honor my daddy."

"I do like it. You get started on my clothes, and I'll tell everybody they're from the *LJF* label. Thanks for your help on this project, Trina. You made all the difference."

"Mama's the one who made the difference. It's great to see her getting out and having something to do besides ironing. Joe is a real blessing to her. I wish we'd had him twenty years ago."

"Do you think all those women will show up on Monday?"

"Yeah, I do. Out of curiosity, if nothing else. Hey, maybe we could shoot some baskets before we eat. I need to trim off a few inches before my wedding."

"You're on." Jemma did one of her famous U-turns and headed to the high school tennis courts. They both loved the old hoop without a net on the side of the concrete court. It was there that they had first become friends.

Jemma called Do Dah and Uncle Art as soon as she got home. "It should be interesting," she said. "Do you want me to send the first quilt for your approval when it's finished?"

"I trust your judgment, Jemmabeth," Arthur replied. "If you like it, I'll like it."

"Go ahead and send the first one and we'll put it in a window display with a 'Coming Attractions' banner. That'll stir some interest," Julia, ever the thinker, added.

"I defer to my better half." Arthur chuckled. "Good idea."

The women were waiting on the church steps when Jemma drove up on Monday. Willa arrived about the same time and unlocked the door. After a bit of confusion about chairs and coffee cups, they got started. Jemma left them under Willa's watchful eye. It was up to the Lord now. She didn't know what else to offer.

Chapter 16
Chased Out of Town

"Hey, Mrs. Chase," Sandy said, knocking on the door to Spence's office.

"Yeah." Jemma turned from the color chips spread all over Spencer's desk.

"There's some Englishman on the phone with three first names. He wants to talk to you." Sandy lowered her voice. "Must be Thor."

Jemma bugged her eyes at Spencer, who gave her a thumbs-up. Sandy and Spencer listened as best they could while Jemma made the appointment. She took notes and hung up the phone.

"Well?" Sandy asked. "We're dying here. What did he say?"

Jemma shrugged. "I'm meeting him at his hotel room. I have to bring six pieces, blah, blah, blah. Y'all don't want to hear all of that. I guess I'd better get home and get busy."

"When is this happening?" Spencer asked.

"Today," Jemma said, palms up.

"Baby, we can't go today. We have to meet with the painters this afternoon about our house. Call him back and be assertive."

Sandy snickered. "How about I call him back and be assertive? Jemma has to get fired up to be assertive." She strode back to her desk.

Spencer held Jemma's shoulders. "I don't want you going alone. If you call him back, he'll see that you are not intimidated by his position and power. Just try it."

"He's only going to be in Amarillo for a few hours, Spence. He got this room just to look at my work. I can handle him. You know what my choices are for the house. I'll hurry back. The painters can't even buy the paint today. They'll have to get it in Amarillo." Jemma looked him in the eye. "This is a major opportunity for my career. I can't let it slip away."

Spencer traced around her chin. "Every time I don't go with

you, something happens that I could have prevented. I don't want that to be the case today."

"I'll be all right, babe. Right now I need to get out of here and load up the car. I don't think the paintings will fit in the Corvette. What should I do?"

"We're going to have to get another vehicle. Ask Gram if you can borrow hers for today. I'm sorry, Jem. I really wanted to be there with you."

Jemma picked up the phone to call home, then changed her mind. "Rats. Gram's gone to her quilting club meeting for the day. I don't have a clue where. Maybe Lester could take me. At least I would have a man along." She giggled and grabbed her purse. "I'll see you tonight."

He watched her leave before picking up the phone.

❧

Lester was busy in his shop. The paintings were too large for his car, too, and she couldn't risk transporting them in the back of his old pickup.

"That Buddy B feller that works for Spencer's dad has a big truck. He tows folks' cars with it. I'd give him a call," Lester suggested, slapping his overalls to get rid of the sawdust.

Jemma ran to use Gram's phone.

"Sure, you can borrow the truck," Buddy said. "It's kinda beat up, but it will get you there. Just come on down and get it. Are you sure you don't want to talk to Max? He'd let you take something off the lot."

"Oh, I hadn't thought of that. Do you think he would mind? I guess that's his business, huh?"

"Yeah, and you're his daughter-in-law. He's always bragging about your art. Let me put you through to his office. Hang on." Buddy B had a way of talking her into things.

Max came on the line. "Hey, beautiful, how are things? Buddy tells me that you need some transportation to Amarillo, and I've got just the thing."

Within ten minutes, Max was in the alley, ready to load the paintings from the car house. He was driving a new turquoise and white 1969 Suburban. It was perfect. "I don't have anything to do this afternoon. Would you like some company?" he asked with a sheepish grin.

"Spence called you, didn't he?"

"Right before you did. Come on, we haven't talked in a while. Let me go with you."

Max loaded the last big canvas into the Suburban. Jemma climbed in the passenger side. "I may need moral support anyway," she said.

Max drove like Spencer—way too fast. "Now who's this guy we're going to see?"

"He is the owner of a very prestigious art gallery in London. If he likes my work, he could offer me a one-woman show. This is a great car, Max. Thanks for coming to my rescue."

"Anytime. Now, tell me about your new house. I'm trying to talk Rebecca into taking a drive out there to see it."

"Really?" Jemma asked, thinking of her last conversation with her mother-in-law. "Spence is talking with the painters today. I love the house. It is a little of both of us, mostly in the Craftsman style. Of course we wanted to make it as perfect as possible, knowing our professions. It's sort of in the shape of a four-leaf clover—so, not pure Craftsman," she said, sketching it for him in her book. "The center is called a 'great room' with a kitchen, dining room, and living room all rolled into one. It has a really high ceiling, then the bedrooms and bathrooms all branch out from there. There's a spiral staircase leading up to our shared studio loft and a spot for stargazing. Spence added this tiny little room with stained-glass windows for me to pout in—that's a long story. Oh, it's all so fantastic. Coming up out of the deck is a big cottonwood tree that we carved our names on in grade school. Isn't that sweet? We'll have a big party, I'm sure, when we move in."

Max watched her draw the house plans. "You and my boy were just meant to be together, weren't you? You're like some fairy-tale couple," he said, then was quiet for a long minute. "I'll tell you something that I've never told anybody before, not even Spencer. I used to sneak into his room when he was a little boy and kiss him good night. We all know those were the beginnings of my bad days, the times when I chased after every halfway decent-looking female in six counties. It made me feel better about myself to see him lying there, so peaceful and perfect, and know that he was part of me. He was the best of me, if there is any. I'd look around his room and learn about his life. As time went by, I'd go through his homework and see how he was thinking. He was a smart kid. From the time he was little, though, he kept pictures you'd drawn and tacked them up around the room. Isn't that something? He loved you even then."

Jemma smiled. "Max, you need to tell this to Spencer. It would mean a lot to him."

"No, I don't think I could handle that. I might start bawling or something." Max checked his rearview mirror.

"Maybe it would be good for both of you to talk about those years," she said quietly. "It could ease some of the pain. Think about it, okay?"

Max nodded and looked in the mirror again. "I guess I'd better slow up. We've got company."

The state trooper turned on his lights. Jemma looked back and shook her head. She knew what was going to happen next. These Chase men.

"May I see your license and registration, sir?" The trooper tipped his hat.

Max pulled out his wallet and obliged.

"Mr. Chase? The Chevy dealer in Chillaton?" the trooper asked.

"The one and the same, sir." Max perked up at a potential reprieve.

"Well then, you should know better than to drive a vehicle without tags on it." The trooper smiled at Jemma. She looked away.

"Shoot," Max said. "I was in such a hurry to pick up my daughter-in-law here that I forgot to tape this on." Max reached in the backseat and showed the officer the dealer's plate.

"Jemmabeth?" The officer took off his glasses. "I guess you don't recognize me. I'm Jeeber McCleary. You were a couple of grades behind me in school. I married Lorena Hodges."

Jemma raised her brow and leaned in for a better look. "Oh, hi, Jeeber, I do remember you. I thought Lorena was a stewardess working out of Dallas."

"Naw, that didn't happen. Too many rules about her weight. I tell you what, Mr. Chase. I'm gonna give you a warning this time, but you need to get that license stuck up on the back window ASAP." Jeeber tipped his hat and grinned at Jemma. "Tell Spencer hello for me and that I'm glad he got out of 'Nam in one piece. I heard about his close call."

"Tell Lorena hi for me, too," Jemma said as he walked back to his car.

"Whew." Max exhaled. "If there's one thing I don't need, it's another ticket. It's a good thing your pretty face sticks in a fellow's mind. Now if I can get this to stick on that back window."

Jemma took some tape from the wrapped paintings and plastered it onto the license plate. It almost lasted to the city limits before dropping free.

◈

They pulled into the parking lot of the Fairmont Hotel. It was the best that Amarillo had to offer. Jemma went inside and called up to his room. "Mr. Howard-Finch? It's Jemmabeth Chase. I'm downstairs. Would you like for us to bring my pieces to your room now?"

"Us?" he asked. "Please, call me Thornton. Yes, now is fine. Do come up, *alone* preferably."

Max loaded up a luggage cart, and they took it to the room. Jemma set the paintings up while Thornton moved around them. He scrutinized every detail while smoking a cigarette at the end of an ebony holder.

Max called Jemma to the door. "I'll be right back, hon. I have to get something to keep that plate on the window. Won't take but a couple of minutes."

Jemma nodded.

Thornton backed away from a painting of Weese leaning against Willa's porch, holding a bottle. "I would have to say that your work is truly brilliant. It goes beyond mundane portraiture and exudes a 'slice of life.' Articulate for me your objectives, my dear."

Jemma folded her arms. "I want the viewer to experience the subject's life. I want an audience to breathe the same air as the subject, to feel his skin, and to hear his voice—literally and figuratively," Jemma said, her eyes on Weese.

Thor put out his cigarette and moved to the piece showing Sandy, looking out the window of a car, her hazel eyes reflecting disappointment and determination. "Fascinating eye treatment. You tell me everything I need to know through them."

Jemma smiled. "When I was a little girl, Papa, my grandfather, would give me a stack of *National Geographic* magazines to copy. The eyes in those photographs inspire my brush. I want that one detail to be perfect."

"You have succeeded admirably." He ogled Jemma as she commented on the other pieces, moving nearer as she spoke. Then he touched her arm. "I think I've found my one-woman show," he said, his lips moving curiously. "There are but a few particulars to discuss." He slipped his hand under her hair to stroke the back of her neck.

Jemma jerked her head at his touch. "What are you doing? Cut that out."

Thor made a fist around her hair and pulled her to him until his cigarette breath filled her nostrils. His thin lips skimmed hers just as she raised her right foot and hooked the back of his knee with a walloping blow. Thor's leg buckled, and he stumbled to the floor. Jemma scrambled to nab him and hold him down with The Sleeper hold. She knew how to react to The Calf Roper. Thornton never knew what hit him.

"I shall have you arrested for this, you wench," he gurgled. "Let me go immediately, or I shall call for the police."

"You'll have a hard time reaching the phone from here, sir," Jemma warned.

They stayed on the floor until Jemma thought he was going to faint, but she knew this man needed to be taught a lesson. She had just the moves to accomplish that.

"Let me up," he whispered. "I'll not press charges if you do as I say now."

"I may press charges myself, Thor," Jemma said, her voice rising. "How do I know that you won't try something else?"

"My word as a gentleman," he whispered.

"Well, that's no good. Any other ideas?"

"I won't touch you." Thor rolled his eyes up to look at her.

Jemma let him go only because he looked like he might throw

up. Better him than her.

He coughed and sat up. One of his tasseled, leather loafers had come off in the scuffle. He fumbled around on all fours, then staggered up. He lit a cigarette and sneered at her, blowing smoke. "My, my, my, that was some demonstration of brute strength."

Jemma wasn't listening. She opened the door and set her paintings on the cart in the hall.

Thor reclined on the bed and watched with interest. "I misspoke earlier. Your work is by no means suitable for my gallery." He flicked ashes in a cup. "I can assure you that it will be unsuitable for any London venue, if you grasp my meaning."

Jemma put her purse on her shoulder. She shut the door and rolled the cart toward the elevator, trembling.

The doors opened and Max stepped out. "Done already? Sorry it took me so long."

Jemma nodded and stared at the carpet.

Max touched her shoulder. "What's wrong, hon? Did things not go well? Is the guy blind or something?"

Jemma put her hands over her face and cried. Max consoled her as best he could all the way to the Suburban. She spilled out the story once they were inside. He lurched open his door and disappeared inside The Fairmont. Jemma yelled after him, but it was of no use.

She sat with her eyes trained on the lobby doors. After about ten minutes, Max-a-Million, as Lester called him, came back to the car, breathing heavy and shaking his hand. Jemma didn't know what to say.

Max grimaced in pain, then started the engine. "Well, I'd have to say that Mr. Thornton or Finch or whatever his name is has been thoroughly *Chased* out of town, and I think we should go celebrate. What do you say, Mrs. Chase?"

Jemma blew her nose and started laughing. Max joined her, and they were still laughing when they pulled up in front of Meyer's Ice Cream Shoppe. They compared tactics and ate their banana splits in mutual admiration.

❧

Back in Chillaton, Spencer did not think it was funny. He was angry.

"Do you see what happens when you are stubborn? We're lucky he didn't try something more than kissing. What's the deal with everybody trying to kiss my wife, anyway?" He took a deep breath and looked at her.

She sat head down, playing with the embroidered design on her skirt.

Suddenly he changed his tune and lifted her chin. "Baby, I'm sorry. Here I've been yelling about him and haven't even considered your feelings. Something better than his gallery will come along. He was just bluffing you with those threats. He can't blackball you from every gallery in London. He's an idiot."

Spencer had taken the humor out of the situation and had her thinking about other things.

Jemma sighed. "I'm going home. I'll see you later."

"Oh no you don't. You are staying right here with me. I'll be finished in a minute. I should have been there instead of Dad. I'm the idiot."

She waited and relived Thor's speech. Her day was clouded with "maybes." Maybe he could keep her work out of London. Maybe she was too stubborn. Maybe she shouldn't have put the Sleeper on him—maybe she should have just stuck with The Claw.

⋘◈⋙

That night Spencer edged up against her back. "Are you mad at me, Jem? I'm sorry about what happened with Thor." He put his chin on her arm and felt around for her lips. "Yup, big pout. I thought so. Is it me or him?"

Jemma faced him. "I did what I thought was best. You made me feel like everything I did was wrong."

He smoothed her hair. "I was just angry with myself for not going. It's kind of funny to think about my dad punching somebody. He's never been in a physical fight in his life."

"Me neither," she said and turned back to the wall.

"That's not true. You've been practicing on me for years. Now Thor knows what it's like to suffer under your power." He made an unsuccessful attempt to tickle her. "The more I think about it, the funnier it gets. A snobby gallery owner being taken down with The Sleeper hold by the most beautiful artist on the planet is actually hilarious. I guess I'm jealous that you would use that hold on anybody but me." He nibbled on her ear.

She smiled, but not so he would notice.

"Is it possible that you could demonstrate what happened now that we're alone?" Spencer asked. "So, he was coming at you like this," he said, moving in front of her and making the old bed squeak, "and then you knocked him flat and put The Sleeper on him?"

Jemma rose up from her side of the bed and flung her body across Spencer, knocking the breath out of him. "This is what I should have done to him." She giggled.

Spencer's voice was rather weak. "Not the Waffle Iron again," he said, shaking with laughter. "This is too special for anybody but me. I deserve it, I guess. Have mercy, O great one."

Jemma got off him and sat up on the bed. "Do you think that if I don't make it as an artist, I could be a professional female wrestler?"

Spencer hung his head and laughed even harder, making Lizbeth's snores change rhythm. Spence lowered his voice. "Well, I don't think there would be any question as to you being a female wrestler as opposed to a male one. What would you call yourself?"

"I'm thinking about The Big Hurt. Do you like it?" She grinned at him in the dark.

"I like it. I think you would have a large fan club, too. Maybe Thor could turn pro, too, and y'all could tour together. I could be your mercy man, the one you practice new stuff on."

"That's all the mercy you get." She kissed him until they fell off the bed and landed on the cool hardwood floor without missing a beat of their activity.

❧

Lizbeth finished blind-stitching her latest quilt, a rose and cream floral pattern. She tied off the knot and spread the quilt on the good bed to check her work. It was one of her best, and made especially for their second anniversary. Jemma and Spencer could use it in their new guest bedroom. The hammering from Lester's shop was more than she could handle for the fifth day in a row. She went out the back door and yelled at him.

He came out, his overalls and hair covered in sawdust. "Morning, Miz Liz." His hands were shoved into his pockets and a hammer hung off the loop at the side of his overalls.

"Lester Timms, what are you doing? I haven't asked you for nearly a week now, hoping that you would volunteer the information. If I know what the secret is, maybe I can tolerate the noise." She held her hairdo down in the wind.

"Well, sir, I'm sure sorry for the aggravation, but I'm on a business adventure," Lester said, not divulging anything.

"What kind of venture?" Lizbeth asked, her mouth pinched to one side.

Lester dropped his head and poked at a stone with his work boot. "No offense, Miz Liz, but you scared me off from sharin' business secrets with you a while back."

"I assume you mean the chinchilla ranching thing."

"Yes ma'am. I was hopin' to get this new adventure up and runnin' before givin' out any details." Lester paused and looked out over the tracks. He took off his glasses and rubbed his eyes. Between sawdust and Panhandle grit, he had a mouthful to spit, but not in front of her.

"You aren't going to tell me, are you?" Lizbeth raised her brow. "What if I promise not to make light of this one?"

Lester folded his arms and gave her a sideways look. "Is that a fact now, Miz Liz? No disrespect, but I know how you get around that kind of promise."

"I'll be gentle. I might even have a suggestion or two. Fiddlesticks, Lester, what's going on in there?"

Lester whipped back the door to his shop. The fresh air scooted inside, then curled back, full of sawdust. His transistor radio blared out the early morning news. He turned it off and picked up a cedar box the size of Jemma's hope chest. It was polished to a fine sheen and the hinged lid was decorated with a sculpted rose.

Lizbeth smiled. "Are you going to sell hope chests?"

Lester set the box down and rubbed his chin. "I hadn't thought of that; maybe I'll give 'er a try. Anyway, these here are gonna be coffins." He gestured to several more of various sizes at the back of the shop.

"Coffins? My stars."

"For critters," he said, avoiding her eyes.

Lizbeth drew in the dusty air and coughed. "Critter coffins? You mean for cats and such?"

He nodded. "Cats, dogs—of course they'd have to be them kind of dogs that folks carries around, but whatever takes an owner's fancy. That's what I'm namin' my company, too. Critter Coffins. You caught on right fast, Miz Liz. It's plain that you're a college girl."

Lizbeth shifted her weight. "Well, now, Lester. I think you've come up with a halfway decent idea this time. I know lots of folks who are silly about their pets and might take you up on this notion."

Lester brightened. "Well, sir, I come upon the notion down to the barbershop. Pud Green was saying how his missus's Siamese up and died on her, but she had to bury it in a plastic cake holder. It had a lid on it, but that just didn't seem right to me. I come home and got me some ideas on paper, then went to the lumberyard. This cedar is topnotch wood. Jemmer drew me some flower designs, and the rest you see before you."

Lizbeth ran her finger across the rose. "Maybe you should put an ad in the Amarillo paper. There are probably a lot more small pet owners up there than in Chillaton. Most farmers don't go for house pets and whatnot. They keep working animals."

"That's a fine idea, Miz Liz. I'll send the paper some money and get that goin'. I sure do appreciate your support. Now that my secret is out, I think I'll put me an ad in the Chillaton paper, too."

"I wouldn't do that if I were you, Lester. I think I'd wait until the idea catches on in Amarillo, then go ahead with it here." Lizbeth walked to the door. "Now that I know what all the commotion is, I can handle it better. Good luck, Lester. Are you coming over for coffee later?"

He picked up a screwdriver. "We'll see, Miz Liz. I need to finish off what I've started here. You go on without me for now." He eased around the corner and spat.

Lizbeth went home and sat at the kitchenette. She sipped her hot coffee and grinned. She made sure the liquid was all the way down, then laughed for a full minute. When the laugh subsided, she wiped her eyes and drank the rest of her coffee. One last chuckle took her to the window as a tardy freight train rattled past. Vincent, her mouse-catching, snake-killing cat jumped up on the windowsill and settled down for a snooze, but not before looking up at her with loving eyes. Lizbeth cleared her throat and poured out the rest of her coffee.

Chapter 17
Prizes

Have you heard anything from Thor Hyphen-Hyphen?" Trent asked.

"No." Jemma stabbed her chicken-fried steak at Daddy's Money.

"We're not sure that we care, either." Spencer winked at Jemma.

"Spencer told me about your wrestling match." Trent laughed. "I wish I could have seen that. Can you imagine our grandparents' reaction to that story?"

"I hope they never hear about it, but I'm out of luck for a show in London," Jemma said.

"That's not true," Trent fired back. "I'll bet that you have a show in London before this time next year."

"Really? I'll take that bet. Loser buys burgers at Son's Drive In." The cousins shook on it.

"Shhh…you're not supposed to mention Son's in here," Spencer whispered.

"Did Spence tell you that we may hire an interior designer to consult with us on a few projects?" Trent asked.

"No," she said. "He didn't."

"Not my idea. Talk to your cousin." Spencer pointed at Trent.

"Are you looking for anybody in particular?" Jemma asked, shooting her husband the evil eye.

"I don't know. Why? Do you have somebody in mind?" Trent asked, watching a new waitress with interest.

"Le Claire might have some graduates looking for jobs. Their interior design department is very good," Jemma said.

Trent nodded. "Thanks, I might check that out. I've already talked with someone in Dallas, though. She's coming up to meet us Monday."

"Tomorrow?" Jemma asked.

Spencer held up his hands. "Hey, this is all his deal. I won't even be in the office tomorrow. My flight leaves at nine forty in the morning."

"Hers gets in at nine fifteen. Maybe you'll run into her at the airport," Trent said.

Spencer smiled weakly at Jemma. He could tell this topic would entail further discussion.

❧

"When were you going to tell me about hiring an interior designer?" she asked as soon as they got in the car.

Spencer gave her The Look that she normally gave him. "Jemmabeth Alexandra Chase, do not be jealous of someone that neither you nor I have seen and with whom we are only consulting. I'm telling you, this is all Trent's idea. He thinks we need to jazz up the mall in Sacramento. Personally, I think it looks great."

"I am not jealous. I just like to know about your business, that's all."

"Oookay," Spencer said, starting the Corvette.

Jemma reached over and turned off the engine. "What does *oookay* mean? Do you think I am a jealous wife? Just tell me." Her nostrils flared a bit.

"I think you don't give yourself enough credit for being the only woman on this earth that I could ever love. You also believe that if any women, other than Twila Baker or Eleanor Perkins, come into my line of vision, I check them out with the serious notion of comparing them to you."

"Well?"

"What do you honestly think, Jem?"

"That you can't help but check them out because you are a man."

"I can't help but see them because I have two eyes, but I don't look at them with the eyes of a man seeing a potential lover or something. I'm not Thor. Do you want me to wear a blindfold all the time?"

"Maybe." She turned toward her window.

The Corvette was quiet. An elderly couple came out of Daddy's Money and pulled away in their car, but not before they had a good stare.

"May I start the car now?" Spencer asked.

"Sure," she said, her voice cool, although she was still rather hot.

"You'll have to drive, then."

"Why?" She swiveled toward him.

Spencer sat facing the steering wheel with his tie wrapped around his eyes and in a knot at the back of his head. Jemma laughed so hard that her sides ached. He knew just how to handle a sticky situation.

⋙⋘

They drove to the river and got on the hood of the Corvette to watch the stars.

He kissed her, and they lay back on their old stargazing quilt.

"Baby, how do you think I felt the first time I ever saw Paul?" he asked when he had her securely wrapped up in his arms.

"What kind of question is that?" She could barely turn her head, he held her so close against him.

"When I saw that guy, my heart fell. I knew that this big hulk of a cowboy, the best-looking man I'd ever seen, had held you close, tasted your pretty lips, and whispered things in your ear that probably gave you chill bumps. I knew that he had to know that your hair smells like flowers, and he had looked on you with the desires of his heart, body, and mind, just like I do. I knew, too, that you had considered giving me up for him, and, to this day, he still wants you. That's what I still have to contend with. I will always have to share those feelings with Paul because we have you in common. Jem, I want you to remember this for the next one hundred years. Granted, I have kissed lots of women, but only because you broke up with me twice. You will never have to hurt in your heart for any of those other reasons like I did and still do. Whether a bearded lady comes to work for us or a bombshell from Hollywood takes over as secretary and sits across my desk every day, stark naked, you will never have to know the pain I feel sometimes. That's a promise."

She felt like dirt and couldn't speak. When she did, it came out in a whisper. "I'm so sorry, Spence, as usual. Remember, before Vietnam, you wrote in my sketchbook that I didn't have to carry that guilt around anymore. You said it was like I had just tried all the rest and you won first prize. There was never even a contest, babe." She struggled around to look at him, her voice shaky. "You know if I could erase that time in our lives, I would, but Paul just keeps showing up, doesn't he, twisting the knife? How can I ever make it hurt less?"

"By learning not to be jealous of other women. At least that way I won't feel like you don't trust me or believe my wedding vows to you."

She sniffed. "I try, Spence. I do well sometimes and other times I flop. Don't give up on me. I guess I don't think I'm worthy of you. Maybe I'm just one of those people who always needs reassuring," she said and turned back to the stars.

"I'll reassure you, baby. But give me some credit when it comes to admiring and loving you, and only you, okay?"

"Okay." She kissed him, hoping to lessen the hurt that came with Paul, Mr. Summer Romance Everlasting Pain. To her credit, she succeeded, too.

⁂

"Is this the last load?" Buddy B asked, wiping sweat off his forehead.

"That's it." Lizbeth looked around at her house. She was excited for these precious children to have their own home. Her lonely days would return, but not for long. Helene would be moving into Jemma's old bedroom before Christmas. Of course, Helene was not Jemmabeth, but they would keep each other company.

"Gram, come on and ride with me," Jemma yelled from the back door.

Lizbeth grabbed her purse and her headscarf. She moved as fast as she could to catch up with her long-legged granddaughter. "Is Lester coming?" Lizbeth asked.

"He's already gone with Spence," Jemma said as she backed her new Suburban down the driveway. "Lester is going to inspect the house and see if the builders knew what they were doing."

"Honey, do you think we could check the mail? Things have been so busy around here that Lester didn't get to the post office today. I hope they're still open."

⁂

Jemma ran back to the car with two letters. "Paralee says hello. Here's one for you and one for me. Yours is from Do Dah and mine is from Le Claire." She ripped the end of the envelope. "I wonder who. . .oh wow. Oh wow! An art gallery in Florence is offering me a show. I can't believe this. The owners saw my work—oh, how sweet—at the Grassos' house. I had given them a couple of pieces. The Grassos are the ones who got the whole thing put together, through Professor Rossi and the gallery in New York. Professor Rossi wanted to surprise me after the London deal fell through. Do you know what this means?"

"Something wonderful, I'm sure."

Jemma closed her eyes and held the letter to her heart. "It means that I have what it takes to go across the Atlantic and show my work as an artist, not just a student artist. It means that I'm on a roll, maybe." She clapped her hands like she did at her third birthday party when Cam played a Highland tune on his fiddle and she danced for him, whirling around until she fell down, laughing.

"Jemmabeth, you may be a Chase now, you may be a Forrester and a Lillygrace, but underneath all that there remains a Jenkins girl. We are strong and have what it takes to keep standing when all else falls down. I'm proud of you, sugar. Now let's go tell that husband of yours."

On a wet evening with tornado alerts all over the television, they had their housewarming party. The JEMMA'S PLACE sign was officially nailed above the front door and Plum Creek was up to its banks. Alex and Robby surprised them by showing up the night before. They had seen pictures of the progress, but the real thing took them by surprise. "Cool, way cool." Robby scrambled up the spiral staircase.

Lizbeth stood on the deck, keeping an eye on the storm. This was the way Cam would want their Plum Creek to be remembered, as the joyful home of this precious couple. Someday they would bring their own babies home to grow up in this house. Lizbeth didn't choose to wax melancholy at such a happy occasion, but Cameron remained in her head, always, and that fact was bittersweet comfort these days.

"Gram!" Robby burst into her thoughts. "Come on, I want to show you something in the pouting room. You're not too old to climb up there, are you?"

She laughed. "Let's see if I can make it, young man. Maybe a good pout is just what I need."

❧

"I hope you have flood insurance," Sandy said. "You know that all this rain will bring out the snakes."

"What snakes?" Jemma asked. "I told Spence to get rid of every snake out here and he told me he did."

"I'm hopin' y'all got a 'fraidy hole that will hold all of us," Willa said, holding on to Joe as they came up the steps with a cherry cobbler and a shoe box full of petunia plants. "Here you go, sugar. Now you'd better not let these babies of mine die." She kissed Jemma and stood wide-eyed, gawking at their home. "My lands, child, you've gone and built yourself a mansion. Wait 'til Trina sees this."

"I'm glad you approve, Willa. Come in and let me show you around." Spencer took her hand and led her into the sunken Great Room with its double-sided, river-rock fireplace separating the kitchen and dining room from the den.

Rebecca Chase sat on the suede couch, holding a coffee cup. "Mother, have you met Willa Cross? Willa, this is my mother, Rebecca."

Willa put out her hand. Rebecca paused momentarily, then took it with a stiff smile.

Spencer grinned at the scene. "I'm giving Willa a tour, Mother. Do you want to join us?"

"No, I'll wait for your father. He's showing that old fellow, Lester, something just now." She picked up a magazine and flipped through it.

"Rebecca," Jemma said, bringing Sandy to her, "this is my friend, Sandy. She grew up with Spencer and me."

"Of course I remember you, Sandra," Rebecca replied, suddenly friendly. "Didn't you marry that Skinner boy? What was his name?"

"Martin. We're divorced now—well, almost divorced. It's nice to see you, Mrs. Chase. Spence and Jemma have a fantastic home, don't they?"

Rebecca nodded. "It has Spencer written all over it, and of course, Jemma, too," she said and went back to her magazine.

"What's the deal with her?" Sandy asked. "She acts like she's got hemorrhoids or something."

Jemma giggled. "She's trying to be sweet. I guess it's tough when your reputation precedes you. Don't you just love this house? I think it's incredible."

"It is, Jem. I'm really happy for y'all. I also think that painting of Spencer is incredible. How come you got him, anyway? Everybody wanted Spence. Look at those eyes." Sandy stared up at the painting that Jemma had titled "I Think of Thee," when she had her first show as a student in Paris. Spencer's guitar lay across his lap, and he was stretched out under a big cottonwood tree at Plum Creek.

"He wasn't in favor of hanging it in here, but I threw a fit."

"I bet you did. Show me this studio you've been bragging about." They climbed the stairs to their shared space. Sandy whistled. "Oh wow. It's nearly all glass. You are going to burn up in here. We'll find a little scorched spot on this pretty hardwood floor and that'll be what's left of the famous artist. You should just go ahead and sign a spot now."

Jemma laughed and pressed a button as window shades covered the glass.

"Nice," Sandy said. "You've thought of everything."

"Look through here." Jemma turned a telescope toward her. "We don't have to get on the hood of his car for our stargazing."

Sandy took a little framed drawing of a flower off Jemma's worktable. "Who did this—Robby?"

"Nope. An old friend of mine who recently got into art."

"Now for the biggie." Sandy lowered her voice. "Show me the bedroom."

They met Willa and Spencer coming out of the master suite. "Mercy, child, that room is somethin' from a movie. I ain't never seen nothin' like that."

Sandy stepped in and looked around, bug-eyed. "Cheezo. Did you two make this up? Don't answer that. So this is what happens when you have a no-fooling-around-until-we're-married rule, huh? I wish I'd done that. Of course we never got past the two-room trailer-house dream." She touched the lighted, stained-glass pillars that flanked the French doors. "So you can just walk out to the deck whenever you want? What a prize y'all have given each other."

Jemma sat on the bed and rubbed her hand across the silk bedspread. She looked out at Plum Creek and the cottonwood tree protruding from the deck where their initials were still visible. "Yeah, I guess you could say that this is one of our prizes, but the best prize is that everything is new every day with Spence."

Sandy sat next to her. "I hope that someday I'll find love again."

"You will. Just remember to be still and watch for God's blessings. It took me a while to learn that. Now, let's go eat my first attempt at baking Spencer's favorite cake, if it's not already gone."

"Wait." Sandy grabbed her arm. "I have to tell you what I did last night."

"Okay. This is not a confession about messing up the bookkeeping at the office or something, is it?"

"Oh please. This is something I am proud to tell. Remember when you and I were always comparing our hope chest stuff? You had those dishes with the roses on them, and mine had daisies. Well, about eleven o'clock last night I drove out to the river, opened the trunk, took out a box filled with those dumb daisy-patterned dishes and chucked them, one by one, into the Salt Fork of the Red River. It's up to its banks, too, with all this rain. Each time I heard that stuff shattering in the water, I began to feel like a new woman. I never want to see anything Mr. Universe touched ever again."

Jemma frowned. "Whoa. I guess it was worth it if made you feel better."

"It did, trust me."

"They really shattered? Weren't all your hope chest dishes Melmac?"

"What's your point?" Sandy asked. "Plastic was all I could afford."

"Never mind. Coconut crème is calling."

⋙❦⋘

Alex helped give tours, as did Robby. His style was short and to the point. His favorite place was the pouting room with its stained glass and window seats. He didn't have many customers, which was fine with him. As soon as the storm cleared, he went outside to catch frogs.

"Sweet pea, why is there no art in your bedroom? You have

several pieces that seem perfect for those walls," Alex asked, after everyone had gone home.

Jemma took off her shoes and propped her feet on the deck railing. "I know, but someone doesn't want to use them." She took a sip of her tea.

"All she wants are giant paintings of me," Spencer said. "I don't want to get up every morning and see myself everywhere." He grabbed Robby and held him upside down. "This is a shakedown, mister. Give up all illegally gotten Plum Creek frogs."

"This is cool." Robby looked around. "Keep doing it."

Spencer dangled him over the deck rail. "How do you like this, then?"

"I love it. Your old man arms are shaking, huh? I can feel it from way down here," Robby teased. "Hey, I think I see a snake."

Alex and Jemma both jumped up. "Spencer!" they yelled in chorus.

Robby was hoisted to safety, then giggled and ran off with Spencer chasing after him.

"You have a lot to be thankful for, Jem," Alex said as they sat listening to the crickets and leftover frogs.

"I know, Mom." Jemma put her arm around her mother. "I am well aware of that. God's Plan just gets better."

Chapter 18
A Wonder

Trina and Nick's ceremony would be at her church and the reception at Willa's house, followed by dancing on the deck at Plum Creek. Spencer was cutting it close. His flight was due in from New York just an hour and a half before the ceremony. Jemma paced the adult Sunday school room in her *LJF* designer dress of emerald green brocade. Carrie tried to keep up with her for a while with her walker.

Spencer stuck his head in only seconds before the music began. "Hi, gorgeous, I'm here. Don't trip walking down the aisle," he said and shut the door before she could throw a shoe at him.

Trina's gown was a dress designer's, for sure. The bodice was fitted cream satin with hundreds of tiny seed pearls covering it in the shape of *fleurs de lis*—to remember the postcard her daddy had sent her from Paris when she was a baby. The waistline was a gathering of English netting from the skirt that clasped to form a rose at her side. Her skirt was slender, like Jemma's had been. A veil fluttered behind her with a scalloped hem upon which even more seed pearls had been hand sewn. She wore her hair swept up in a bun, with the veil attached. She was beautiful.

Jemma and Spencer left the reception early to make sure that Buddy B's band was set up on their deck and that all the refreshments were ready.

"You haven't asked if Michelle was in New York City," Spencer said as they necked in the kitchen. "This dress is outstanding, by the way." He held her back for a better look.

"I'm trying to be good, like you said."

"I didn't have to salute her. She came in late to a meeting and left before it was over. Her services were not required, I guess. I think she just wanted to make an appearance," Spencer said, wishing suddenly that there was no party scheduled at their home.

"And? How did she look?" Jemma asked.

"The same, but Michelle is not my big news. The woman next to me on the flight from New York to Dallas is the features editor of *Panache* magazine—you know, the men's magazine that no man buys. Anyway, she wants to do a story about me. She said the magazine is about men's style, but that it's women who buy it."

"You mean the magazine with all the pretty boys striking poses next to their motorcycles and airplanes?"

"I wouldn't say pretty boys. They're just guys who are supposed to have been somewhat successful and dress well. Which of those descriptions do you disagree with about me?"

"Neither." She pulled on his tie and kissed him. "You fit all of those, even the pretty boy part. I'm proud of you, babe. I really am. But no wife in her right mind wants her husband flaunted in a magazine for other women to drool over. When's all of this going to happen?"

"She's supposed to call me. It may not work out. I don't know. It was just kind of flattering, I guess," he said and went to open the door for their first guests.

"Spence." Jemma grabbed his arm and went nose to nose with him. "I'm thrilled for you. I am married to the handsomest, brightest architect in the universe, plus you have impeccable taste."

"Go ahead and say it; you know you want to."

"Okay," she said, wiping lipstick off him, "you married me, didn't you?"

"Feel better?"

"Yeah." She grinned as she opened the door.

They didn't want to take away from the wedding couple, but they had to dance when Buddy B played their song. Lizbeth was once again embarrassed by their antics, but nobody else seemed to notice. Lester asked Trina for a waltz. Lizbeth smiled, thinking that never would have happened ten years earlier, not in Chillaton, and not with Lester. Jemmabeth had made the difference. She had opened up their hearts and minds to what it is to be a friend and to love like Christ. When the dance was over, Buddy B called Jemma up to the microphone to sing with him, but he tricked her into a solo. Jemma sang some low-throated song about love that would have made Cam blush. Spencer seemed to like it, though. Lizbeth exhaled and had a second cup of fruit punch.

Trina asked Jemma to sing a song that was a favorite of Nick's—"How Sweet It Is to Be Loved by You"—but Jemma wouldn't do it unless Spencer sang with her, which he did, in his sweet way, and the newest newlyweds had the floor to themselves. Nick's family was a dancing crowd, too, filling up the deck. It was a good thing that Trent was a structural engineer and was involved with all the details of the house.

Lester got up his nerve to dance with Helene. Lizbeth sipped her punch and watched.

Afterward, he came over to her. "Miz Liz, I'll just come right out with it. Would you care to dance?" His silver moustache seemed extra trim in the moonlight.

Lizbeth considered it for a second. "Lester, if we danced, things would never be the same between us, would they?"

Lester scratched behind his ear. "No ma'am, I reckon they wouldn't, but it never hurts for a fella to ask." He walked away.

"Lester," Lizbeth called after him. He came back, his expression hopeful. "I've never danced in my life. I would step all over you," she added in a whisper.

His face relaxed into a grin. "Maybe I'll have to teach you sometime."

Mr. and Mrs. Nicholas Fields went to the microphone. "We want to thank all of y'all for coming tonight to share our happiness," Trina said. "We especially thank our parents and the Chases for the wonderful celebrations."

Nick moved in to speak. "Thanks to Spencer and Jemma for lots of things they've done for us. We'll be leaving in the morning for our honeymoon in Acapulco, thanks to those two, again. We appreciate every last one of y'all. My grandpa must be doing somersaults in his grave to see the beautiful mix of the colors here. Life is good."

Trina tossed her bouquet, and an embarrassed Trent caught it. His red-haired date, a chatty interior designer from Dallas, raised her brow at him.

❧

"That was fun," Jemma said as she picked up the last stray napkin off the deck.

"No, this is fun." Spencer carried her to their bedroom. He pressed a button, and a skylight opened up above their bed, revealing the starry night. "You look great in that dress. You'll have to wear it to Florence for the opening of your show."

"I'm not going if you can't go with me, and I mean it."

"I'm getting tickets tomorrow. I'll go, no matter what."

"There's a shooting star. Did you see it?"

"Nope. I'm looking at my wife."

"This life we have is a wonder," she said.

"Yeah, it's almost scary."

"Ummm. I liked singing with you tonight."

"I liked listening to you sing Aretha. I'm just glad we're married so that the boys in the band don't whistle at you like they used to."

"Oh, they still do, but not so you can hear it."

"That magazine thing doesn't bother you, does it?"

"No more than the guys' whistling bothers you."

"It bothers me some."

"The magazine bothers me."

"How about you sing something for me now?"

"Like what?"

"Leon said your voice is like Peggy Lee's, so how about 'Fever'?"

"What will you give me if I do?"

"A new pair of cowboy boots."

"Red?"

"Yeah."

Jemma stood up on the bed and sang, silhouetted in the starlight. She didn't even get to make it through the chorus.

❧

The *Panache* magazine editor called the next week. She and a photographer would be arriving on the last flight into Amarillo on Friday night. Jemma didn't want to dwell on it, so she painted from dawn until Spencer came home. Plum Creek was perfect for her work. Jemma walked across the room to analyze the painting. The man's back was all that was visible of him, but the ebony cigarette holder gave his identity away. He stood in the aisle of a wrestling arena, wearing his tasseled loafers. She liked it.

"I thought you were going to work at home when we got married," she said later, setting a masterpiece salad in front of Spencer.

"I know, and I will, too. I just have to get squared away first, kind of get in a rhythm. Maybe next year."

"Maybe never," she said. "Isn't there anything you can do at home? You could do your drafting here, but it's all the phone calls you think you have to take, isn't it? I know it is because Sandy told me."

Spencer looked up from his salad. "You're right, Jem. I just need to commit to working at home. I will surprise you, and you'll be getting sick of me someday."

"Never. I love it out here. It's so peaceful, but it's lonesome without you. All I have are the coyotes."

"There's always motherhood." He grinned.

"Right. That's the solution to every problem, even you working at home." She went to get the steaks and chewed on her lip. She would get an appointment on Monday.

⋘⋙

"When's Jem supposed to get home from Amarillo?" Sandy asked.

Spencer checked his watch. "She said by two. It's four thirty now. I've tried the doctor's office, but they're closed."

"Well, I'm heading home, if that's okay. Jemma got a call from Italy. That's gotta be important, so here's the number." Sandy tapped her message pad and pushed her chair in. She turned to Spencer. "Don't worry. She's probably sitting on a rock drawing a cow or something."

Sandy knew, though, that the road to Amarillo held a sore spot for everybody who loved Jemmabeth. "She'll be here any minute now." Sandy waved and left.

By five o'clock Spencer decided to drive to Amarillo. He locked up the office and started the Corvette. Jemma pulled up next to him, and he knew as soon as he saw her face. Something awful had happened. He got in the car with her, and she burst into tears.

"I've been at the hospital having all these tests done. There's something wrong with me. I thought maybe I was pregnant, but instead, it's this scary thing."

Spencer's pulse raced. "Cancer?"

"No. One doctor sent me to another doctor who said that this happens sometimes after a miscarriage like mine. There's scar tissue in my uterus. I have to go back Friday so he can explain it all. I should have told you, but I wanted to surprise you if I was pregnant."

He held her. "We'll face this together, whatever it is. Let's go home."

❧

The week dragged by. Jemma couldn't paint, so Spencer took her to Amarillo and they bought a dozen rosebushes, a dozen honeysuckle vines, and packets of sweet pea and hollyhock seeds. Willa's petunias were already in the ground. She borrowed Lizbeth's cat, Vincent, to keep the snakes away while she worked. From the time Spencer left in the morning until he came home, she created pocket gardens around the perimeter of their home. When the plants ran out, she called Alex.

"They can work wonders nowadays, sweet pea," Alex said. "You mustn't worry so much about things after you turn them over to the Lord. You can't say out of one side of your mouth that you are trusting Him, then whisper out of the other side that you're scared to death."

"I know. I haven't told Gram yet. After we see the doctor tomorrow, we'll stop by her house." Jemma sat on the deck and listened to the soft ripple of water in Plum Creek. "Mom, surely it's in The Plan for us to have babies."

"Honey, nobody knows what the Lord has in mind. We just have to pray about things and wait to see if our will matches His. There's always adoption. You and Spencer will be parents one way or another. Now you call us as soon as you know something. I'll be home all day tomorrow."

❧

Alex had to hang up quickly so her daughter couldn't hear her cry. Even her own advice was easier in the giving than it was in the taking.

❧

Jemma and Spencer held hands. The doctor was a middle-aged

man, polite but straightforward. "When the physician in Mexico found it necessary to remove tissue from you, the procedure left scars. You may have even had an infection afterward, but that's immaterial now. We need to remove the adhesions, and get you back to as normal as possible."

"Is there a name for this?" Spencer asked.

"Asherman's Syndrome."

Jemma cleared her throat. "Will I be able to have babies?"

"Time will tell. Some women do, and some don't. We'll know more after the surgery." The doctor called the appointment desk at the hospital.

Jemma tightened her hold on Spencer's hand.

"Will next Thursday be all right?" the doctor asked.

Spencer nodded. "Sure. Fine. How long will she be in the hospital?"

"At least two days, barring complications."

"I'll be sleeping in the room with her," Spencer said.

"I would expect that from the looks of you two." He reached across his desk and shook Spencer's hand. "Have you been married long?"

"Not long enough," Spencer said. "Thank you, Doctor."

They went to their favorite Mexican food place. Jemma picked at her food. Spencer tried unsuccessfully to cheer her up. "What happened to the faith in action that you've been talking about? Last night we said we'd give this to the Lord and let Him handle it for us."

She looked at him and shrugged. "I know, but it's different when you hear the words from the doctor."

"Like I said, Jem, it's not the end of the world if we can't have kids. We can stay in this present state of matrimonial bliss forever, or we can adopt, too."

"I wanted to have your baby."

"You think I don't want a wee Jemmabeth?"

"I still feel guilty, I guess, for not wanting to be pregnant when I was. All this just brought it up again. Let's go home. I'm not hungry."

❧

They sat on the deck, talking until after dark. Spencer put on some old records and they danced, all slow ones.

"What did the gallery owner want the other day? I forgot to ask you," Spence said as they moved under the watchful feline eye of Vincent van Gogh.

"He wanted some photos of me. I guess I'll have to dig out those from the New York show."

The phone rang. "Let it go," Spencer said. "It's probably Sandy."

"Or Mom and Daddy. I forgot to call them." Jemma went inside but came right back. "It's for you. The *Panache* people are in Amarillo."

Spencer slapped his forehead. "I totally forgot about them coming." He talked for a few minutes while Jemma played with Vincent's notched ear.

"They'll be here in the morning." Spencer took his seat next to her. "I'm sorry, Jem. This is bad timing, and I know you're not crazy about the whole thing anyway. Maybe something good will come of it. Trent and I might get a great project somewhere."

"Yeah, or maybe you'll get a job as a model."

"If there is anybody around here who could be a model, it's you, woman." He kissed her pouty lips, boring Vincent into sleep.

Chapter 19
Pain with Panache

Jemma followed the two women and her husband all over their house, around the creek, and into the pasture by the road. She couldn't believe they talked him into wearing cowboy stuff. He had only worn that once before, when he'd proposed to her on the train tracks. Now they had him leaning against a barbed-wire fencepost with his hat pushed back on his head.

The photographer got him to unbutton more than the top button on his shirt, too. "Just enough to inspire," she'd said. Spencer snickered and glanced toward Jemma. "Give me that again," the skinny photographer said, taking off her beaded headband. "I like that look."

"I was looking at my wife," Spencer replied. "Why don't we have her in some of the pictures? She is the one with the good looks."

The editor, a willowy woman named Simone with hair nearly as short as Spencer's, turned to Jemma. "Lucky girl, aren't you? Don't take offense, but we like to keep the marital status of our subjects a mystery. The mystique must be preserved to keep the sales up, you see. Sheer business. By the way, I love your art; it's quite brilliant. We must talk later. Okay. Now, Spence, we need intimacy. Say you just woke up—that's fantastic. Now try giving us a pout. Women like that, don't they, Mrs. Chase?" she added in her stilted British accent.

Spencer laughed and put his thumbs in his pockets. "James Dean, huh?"

"We have to get that old windmill in the next shot. Where's the corral?" Simone asked. "After we get some good ones of you in the office, I want sunset shots of you working with your horse."

He laughed again and shook his head. "I've never been on a horse, ma'am, much less worked with one."

The photographer smiled and touched his arm. "Well, Spence,

looks like today will be a first, then."

Jemma dusted the seat of her pants and walked back to the house. She thought it was time for her to paint. Nobody called him *Spence* unless they had known him most of his life. Nobody except these two and Michelle Taylor, that is. She had even called him *Spencey*. Assertive, presumptuous women. Rats on them.

⌘

If she didn't have her surgery to worry about, Jemma would have been in a snit. She hadn't seen Spencer much in the two days that the *Panache* crew had been in Chillaton. She needed to know that they were breathing the same air. He came in late on Saturday night and left before she got up Sunday morning. There was a love note in the refrigerator, but a note wasn't the same as him. She went to church with Gram, then painted until the Corvette pulled into the garage. Jemma gave herself a quick speech and put on a smile.

Spencer came up the steps to the studio and plopped in a chair.

Her pasty smile faded. "Oh my gosh, babe, what happened to you?"

"I fell off the horse. Simone Legree and her evil sidekick nearly killed me with their ideas. This had better be worth it." He opened a puffy eye. "I should've been home with you. I'm sorry."

She tried to sulk, but he was too funny looking. Jemma sat on the floor and laughed. Spencer moved onto the floor with her, moaning. "I'm glad that you think this is funny. I'm never doing it again. Who knew it was so hard to be in a magazine?"

"Oh poor baby. You didn't seem too upset with your Stetson and your shirt unbuttoned."

Spencer's face drooped. "I was just going along with the business. I got what I deserved, I'm sure."

"Well, I guess I'd better be the good little wife and take care of your cuts and scrapes. Stay right here."

"Don't worry, ma'am. This cowpoke ain't goin' nowhere but to sleep."

⌘

She put the finished canvas on the drying rail. He was going to hate it, but she might hang it above their bed without asking. For him to be leaning against a fencepost was one thing, but for him to have cowboy gear on was something altogether different. He looked like a real buckaroo. She caught him for posterity even if the *Panache* photos didn't turn out. Jemma had painted only one button on his shirt undone. She knew her man. Maybe she should hang it next to the one of him on the train tracks, the morning he proposed to her.

The phone rang, interrupting her daydream about Spencer.

"Jemma, it's Gram. I just talked with Alex, sugar. I'm so sorry about your female problem. I know everything is going to work out for the best. The good Lord is going to take care of you."

"Oh Gram. I would have said something, but I didn't want to worry you. Are you mad at me?"

"Jemmabeth, have I ever been angry with you? Of course not. I may have disagreed with you on occasion, but never angry. I want y'all to come for supper tonight. I know you have to be up early tomorrow for your hospital stay, so I've got it cooking, and I've already talked to Spencer."

"I guess we're coming then."

"Oh honey, would you do me a favor?" Lizbeth asked. "If you're finished with Vincent, you might bring him along. I hate to admit it, but I miss him."

"Say no more, Gram. He's as good as home." Jemma looked out the studio window to the deck below where the cat was stretched out, snoozing. She would miss him, too. He had been good company since her husband couldn't figure out how to work at home.

The first thing she saw when she woke up in the hospital was a pair of bright red cowboy boots appliquéd with turquoise flowers. She tried to smile.

"You sure do look cute in your hospital gown," Spencer said.

"My mouth is dry," she managed.

"Drink this water, Jem. The nurse said so."

She sipped her fill, then waved it away. "Is it over? What did the doctor say?"

"He said you're not the worst case he's had. He thinks you'll recover and be fine."

"Babies?" she mumbled.

"Time will tell. Those were his words." Spencer kissed her

forehead. "Go back to sleep. They gave you some painkillers. I'm finishing some paperwork, but I'll be right here beside you, and I won't leave."

❧

As Jemma fell back to sleep, Spencer smoothed her hair and glimpsed the scar that had brought her to this hospital before. He shuddered at that memory. He traced his fingers along the lifeline of her palm. "I love you," he whispered in her ear.

He moved his chair closer to the bed. Even in that sterile place, there was the faintest scent of flowers about her. He watched the rise and fall of her chest. She had to outlive him in their old age, because he could not bear to be without this precious blessing ever again.

❧

"I think I left my passport in my old suitcase. Would you check and bring it when you come?" Spencer asked over the phone, giving orders to Sandy at the office simultaneously.

"Sure," Jemma said, putting on her shoes. "What if it's not there? You are the most organized person I know, so you're scaring me."

"It's there. I just forgot to transfer it to my new bag because my wife was messing with my brain last night."

She giggled. "I thought you would like a preview of the wardrobe that Trina sent me, that's all."

"Yeah. I liked the presentation, too. Stop talking and come to see me. I need some affection."

"Sandy says that we are too affectionate in the office."

"Sandy talks too much. Drive safely. Tell Gram good-bye for me."

"Love you." Jemma hung up the phone and loaded her car.

❧

Lizbeth waited in the porch swing with Vincent for Jemma to arrive. It was too hard to keep up with the passage of time. If she let herself, she could get down about it, but nowadays there seemed to be things to look forward to, like Helene moving in with her in less than a week. Jim's little family would be coming for a visit before school started, and there could be Dr. Huntley's retirement party around there sometime, if he could ever find a replacement.

Lester appeared, holding an orange crate full of cedar chunks.

"Miz Liz, would you have any use for these wood scraps?"

"You could make me a doorstop for the pouting room. I'm trying to keep it aired out, but the door hangs so cockeyed that it won't stay open," Lizbeth said. She had never mentioned that she was the one who nearly knocked it off its hinges the morning Cameron died.

"That's a good idea. Maybe I should make several and add them to my newspaper advertisement. You know, I've offered many a time to fix that door for you."

"Just leave it be, Lester. Have you sold many of your critter coffins?"

"Well, sir, I've sold me enough to break even with the advertisin'. I'm hopin' to get ahead of the game and make some profit. I ain't chargin' nearly what I put into 'em."

Lizbeth stroked Vincent's silky black and white fur. "I suppose you could take comfort in the fact that you don't have much else to do and you might be bringing some peace to folks when their pets pass on."

"That's a good thought, Miz Liz. I suppose you're waitin' for Jemmerbeth?"

The Suburban pulled up as he spoke.

"Lester, would you go with me and drive her big car back to the house?" Lizbeth set Vincent van Gogh on the porch swing. "I don't like sitting up so high in that thing. I feel like I'm driving Joe's semi-truck."

❦

"You're sure you don't mind giving us a ride, Trent?" Jemma asked. "I hate to ruin your Saturday, but the Suburban needs some work done on it while we're gone and the Corvette won't hold all our stuff."

"No, no that's fine. Actually, Sandy's riding up with us, too. She's buying office supplies," he said with a faint blush.

"Oh, I see. Well, you won't get lonesome, that's for sure. She'll keep you laughing."

Spencer came out of his office with his briefcase and a carrier for blueprints. "Yeah, you might want to invest in some earplugs for the trip home," he said, picking up on the conversation.

Jemma elbowed her husband. "Sandy has a good heart, Trent.

Don't let her sarcasm fool you."

"I think I can stand a little sarcasm. It's just a business trip, anyway. You two are the ones off to Italy."

Trent went to the Bakers' door to get Sandy. She had on the hot pink pantsuit that she'd made. Her hair was perfect, and her makeup was flawless. She smiled at Trent, who stood at least six inches taller than Sandy's petite frame. She still had the posture and figure she did when she won the Sew It with Wool competition their senior year.

Jemma watched them. Good grief, was she blind? She should have thought of it sooner.

Spencer saw it coming. "I know what you are thinking, baby. Stay out of it. Trent is hungry for love, and Sandy doesn't need anybody who's hungry. I'm getting in the front seat so you two can talk, and Trent and I can go over some things."

Jemma tried to look innocent. She swatted the seat of his pants as he got out. "You'll regret that, young lady," he said, looking back at her.

She pouted and put her finger to her lips. "Promise?"

⊰⊱

The first stop they made in Florence was for gelato near the Piazza della Signoria. Jemma had been dying for some. "If and when I ever get pregnant, I want this every day for nine months," she said, inhaling the first bite.

"Done and done." Spencer watched her take on ice cream much the same way she enjoyed life. "Stay right there." He took a photo of her with her eyes closed and a gelato moustache. "This is the picture they should use at your shows because it's the real you."

She laughed. "I suppose we'd better mosey on down to the gallery."

"How about we drop off this luggage at the hotel first?"

"Details, details," she said and picked up her multitude of bags.

The Galeria Fiorinzi was near their hotel. The owners, Mr. and Mrs. Fiorinzi, greeted them.

"Signora Chase, what a pleasure to meet you in person." Mr. Fiorinzi bowed slightly. "We were not able to contact you yesterday, but we hope you won't mind a slight change of plans."

Jemma and Spencer exchanged glances. "You mean the opening date?" Jemma asked.

Mrs. Fiorinzi laughed. "No, no, nothing like that. We had a request for a private showing."

Jemma's first thought was of Paul; it just flew into her brain and she panicked. "Who made the request? An American?"

"Ah, yes, very American. Come, you must meet him."

Jemma grimaced at Spencer, and they followed the couple to another section of the gallery where men in black suits and sunglasses stepped in front of them, blocking their passage.

Mr. Fiorinzi gestured at Jemma. "This is the artist. We thought he might like to meet her."

"Please, bring her in." A familiar male voice changed the demeanor of the men.

"Mr. President, permit me to introduce Signora Jemmabeth Chase and Signore Chase."

"Ah, the artist from Texas." President Richard Nixon extended his hand to a dumbfounded Jemma.

❦

They sat on a bench in a nearby park. "Good grief," Jemma said for the umpteenth time. "I can't believe that The President of the United States now owns a painting of Lester building critter coffins. I didn't even vote for him."

"Me neither." Spencer shrugged. "It's an honor, but it took me off guard."

"I think she was the one who loved the piece, though. What did she say, that he reminded her of her grandfather? Lester won't like that comparison at all. Besides, he'll have a cow when he finds out that a Republican has his portrait."

Spencer laughed. "Jemmabeth, you're missing the point," he said, turning her palms up. "These hands that have won basketball games, wrestled men to the ground, and held my heart for nearly twenty years, have created something so beautiful that it caught the eye of the leader of the most powerful nation in the world. Maybe Papa was wrong and it'll be Nixon, rather than Reagan, who wants you to paint his official portrait."

Jemma smiled at that thought.

❧

They visited the Villa Rossa, the Syracuse facility where Spencer spent much of his time as an architecture student. The secretaries fell all over him. He brought that out in people, especially the Italians. At the American Military Cemetery, they laid flowers on her uncle Matthew's grave. Had the war not claimed him, he would be a minister now. Her daddy's other brother, Luke, was killed within months of Matt, in an air raid over Tunisia and buried on the cliffs overlooking the Mediterranean Sea. Someday she wanted to send her parents to both places. For now, Jim claimed he was too busy, but Jemma wouldn't give up because she knew he needed to touch their crosses, just like his mama had done not so long ago.

They celebrated their second anniversary on their last night in Florence, climbing the steps to the Campanile, a beautiful tower next to the Duomo with the best views in town. The last time they had made this climb, they got caught on the third floor right as the big bells tolled. From the fourth floor, the views in every direction were amazing. The Uffizi art gallery, where they had just spent most of the day, and the Tuscany hills called to her. She couldn't wait to get back to her little red boots filled with brushes and paint these memories. Her husband, however, was equally tempting. "Am I the only girl you've ever been up here with?" she asked.

He rested his chin on her head. "You know how you're always saying that you want to protect me from all the facts?"

"It was Michelle, wasn't it?"

"Nope, and don't ask unless you can handle it."

"The Cleave has never been to Florence, has she? Tell me. I won't throw a fit."

"Actually, I've forgotten her name. She was an Italian student and wanted to show me the tower." He glanced at her, briefly, testing the waters.

"Rats. Did you kiss her? You said that you've forgotten about all other women."

Spencer was silent, but with his lips wrestled with a smile.

"Double rats. So this is meaningless. I thought it might qualify as one of those golden moments in our lives."

"Jem, when we are a hundred and one we won't be able to tell the golden moments from all the others. They will all melt into one big, gleaming chunk of gold. We are just getting the taste of it now. Besides, I didn't kiss her like this," he said, then proceeded to melt her pouty lips. "Keep that in mind when you're thinking of golden moments."

"Show me what hers was like," she said.

He gave her a quick peck.

"Promise?"

"Now, Mrs. Chase, do you think I really remember one silly kiss with a girl whose name I don't recall?"

"You shouldn't have been kissing on your first date anyway."

"Who said it was our first date?" He grinned and dodged her punch. "Hang on, hot stuff, and open your present." Spencer reached into his jacket and gave her a small box. Inside was a gold barrette in the shape of a four-leaf clover. "Now you'll always have one with you."

"Happy anniversary, Spence." She slipped a package into his hand, giggling. "It's the pin-pen anniversary."

He opened it to find a gleaming brass pen engraved with his initials. "Thanks, baby; it's very classy."

"Just like you. Remember when you used to wear those shirts in high school with your initials on them?"

"Yeah. Mother was really into initials. I think it was so she would remember who I was when she was drunk out of her mind."

Jemma was quiet. Rebecca Chase had chosen a nasty way to forget her sadness with her husband and lost babies. The devil's nectar had made her miss out on the time with the sweet child she did have, but there was always tomorrow, like Scarlett O'Hara had said.

❧

The *Panache* photo proofs were waiting for them when they got home, and she was dying for him to open the big envelope. He did, with an uproar of laughter. He spread out the glossy black-and-white pictures on his drafting table and called her over. "Would the real Spencer Chase please stand up?" He snickered.

Jemma didn't snicker. The images were fascinating. The camera and some Western duds had transformed her handsome architect husband into an equally beautiful buckaroo. There was a time when she would've danced all night with such a fine example of Panhandle fare. She slipped her arm around his waist. "I don't want any other women to see these. They'll be calling to ask you out," she said and held a particularly good one up to the light.

"You can screen all my calls."

"Nothing good is going to come of this," she said. "What's worse is that hundreds of girls will tack these up in their dorm rooms and offices."

"Girls don't do stuff like that. Besides, this is not me, Jem. You know that." He put the photos back in the envelope. "I need to get to work."

Her lips assumed the position. "You don't know girls very well. I bet The Cleave alone will buy a dozen copies of this issue."

"When you get your lips all puckered up like that, I assume you're ready for a good smooch. Come here." Spencer leaned back on their leather chaise lounge.

"I thought you needed to work," she said, falling in his lap.

"This was the job I was referring to," he whispered and got started.

Helene didn't want her prized collections tossed around in a moving van, so the Chases placed each boxed item with great care into the big U-Haul and pulled it to Chillaton behind their Suburban. Helene had to put most of her furnishings in storage, but it would be worth it to be in such a happy place. She did not look back at her Tudor-style home that her beloved husband had built for her. Instead, she held Chelsea in her lap and smiled. No more dreary days spent alone. She would have the company of dear ones close at hand. Lester would make her laugh, Willa would keep her on her toes, and she could nurture her friendship with Lizbeth, the most spiritual woman she'd ever known. Perhaps it was time for her to consider her own spiritual life. Their small village might be the right place for her to do so.

More than anything, though, she would be near Jemmabeth and share in her life joys. Jemma, the child she longed to call her own, and Spencer, her sweet husband, would be her delight. At the first stop for gas, Helene checked her purse. The business card was there. She would keep her promise to Paul.

Home again, they invited the silver-haired group out for supper. Jemma knew that she was on trial with every meal she cooked. This one was received quite well, and Lizbeth had brought dessert. They ate in the living room.

"Lester," Jemma began, "I have some good news and some bad news about my show in Florence."

Lester sipped his coffee. "I don't know how it could be nothin' but good news, Jemmer."

"We shall see. I sold that painting of you in your workshop to a *very* famous American," Jemma said, choosing an upbeat tone.

He smiled. "Good for you. Is it one of them movie stars? They don't make 'em any more like Jimmy Stewart or Henry Fonda."

"He's a Republican," she added, not knowing the political affiliation of either of the two actors.

Lester frowned. "Bob Hope? I never could figger out why he joined up with that side. I'm bettin' it was all that golfin' that done it."

"No, bigger than Bob Hope. It was bought by the president of the United States."

A perplexed Lester set his coffee cup on the lamp table. "Well, sir, Ike's passed on." His expression evolved into one of great pain. "Not Nixon."

Jemma nodded, and a silence hung over the room. Helene turned up the volume on her hearing aid.

"Doggone it," he said, rising from his chair. He paced to the door and stood for a moment, looking out at the darkening creek, then returned to his chair and slumped into it. After a few taps of his foot, he drew himself up and took another sip of coffee. "Well, sir, he don't know me from Adam. Did I ever tell you about the time that I snapped a photo of a woman in New Mexico and she come hence to yellin' that I owed her two dollars for it? Maybe I'll have to start chargin' you, Jemmerbeth."

Jemma glanced at him. She would just die if Lester were truly upset about the whole thing. He raised his brow, then chuckled. He was joined at once by the rest of them, all very much relieved.

"Bravo, Jemma, bravo," Helene said and basked in the pleasure of her first outing as a member of this fair company.

⬧

"How is Spencer ever going to live this magazine thing down?" Sandy whispered at the office, pulling out her own copy. "Twila said that Nedra's Nook is already going crazy with it. Nedra has a copy at every hair dryer. Did you read the part that says your house is 'sophisticated in design, yet warm, bright, and airy in presentation'? What does that mean?" She folded back one of the pages with his photo on it. "Spence really does look fantastic."

Jemma shrugged. "I suppose we might as well go with the flow."

"What?" Sandy dropped her pen in astonishment. "The most possessive wife in Texas is going with the flow?"

"I am not possessive. What am I supposed to do—share him with everyone? So, how was your trip back from Amarillo with my cuz?"

"Not too bad." She clicked her tongue a couple of times.

"Don't say anything to Spence because he doesn't want either of you to get hurt."

Sandy snorted. "Get hurt? My idea of getting hurt is when Mr. Universe knocks me around. I don't think Trent would hurt a fly."

There was the Mr. Universe title again. Jemma tried not to laugh. "I suggest you keep it quiet if you really are interested. I personally like the idea," she said, then changed the subject fast when Trent opened his door.

"Jem, you're just the person I want to see. Come in here for a second," he said.

Jemma grimaced over her shoulder at Sandy, then took a seat in Trent's office. "What's up?" she asked, hopeful he hadn't overheard them.

Trent leaned across his desk and smiled. "I just heard something that I got a big kick out of, and I'm letting you in on the secret."

She couldn't make eye contact with him. *He must have great ears.*

"Missy Blake is going to run for Miss Texas. Isn't that a hoot? Can you imagine her as the epitome of Texas women?" He stretched back in his chair and laughed.

Jemma was wide-eyed. "You're joking me."

"Nope. I saw her mother at the grocery store yesterday. Missy's won all the preliminary rounds. Her mother is delighted that she's doing something *constructive*, as she called it, but wants to let the newspapers break the news. I think they are worried about polishing up her talent, whatever that is. I couldn't wait to tell you because we know the real Melissa."

Jemma flew to Spencer's office.

He looked up from the blueprints on his table. "You look like trouble to me."

"Trouble's where you find it," she said, closing the door. "I think the Miss Texas Pageant Committee is heading down a troubled road very soon."

"You're a married woman now, my little heartbreaker, and I can't allow you to be in any beauty contests. I'm keeping you all to myself."

"The Cleave is running for Miss Texas."

"Good grief." He laughed. "I wonder if they'll check references."

"What do you think her talent will be?"

"Twirling, of course. The problem will be the question and answer section, and that'll be fun to watch." He curled his finger at her. She made herself comfy in his lap.

"Okay, but you're skipping the swimsuit part," she mumbled and concentrated on the moment at hand.

Chapter 20
Missy Texas

Lester sat in the barbershop waiting his turn. He liked waiting so much that he would gladly let other customers go ahead of him. The barbershop and the post office were the best places in town to keep up with the local happenings. The news was usually fresh, and for the most part, accurate—coming from the menfolk of the county.

Today the shop had too many young people to suit him. Their conversations tended to be about girls, sporting events, and girls. His ears did perk up at the mention of Flavil Capp's name. Flavil was Chillaton's contribution to the state penitentiary system a few years back, and everybody knew he was only two days into his parole.

Toady Ballew was having his turn in the chair. He tilted his head so Bernie Miller could finish up his neck with his good eye.

"Your cousin gonna make it to his mama's funeral today?" Bernie asked, squinting.

"Sure hope so." Toady grunted. "My mama's been cookin' like all get out to welcome Flavil home. She figured he ain't had a decent meal since he left."

"I reckon that's true." Bernie rubbed Crown Wax on his hands and then into Toady's flattop. "A man's gotta give up somethin' when he goes to Huntsville. How much was it that he got away with?" Bernie whisked the chair around and dusted the stocky neck before him.

Toady turned his head from side to side, wrinkling his nose at the mirror, then got out his wallet. "It was something like eight thousand dollars that went missing. Flavil claims to be a changed man now, but my daddy says he ain't gonna hold his breath."

Lester couldn't let that go by. "Somebody ought to tell that boy that if his mama hadn't got bad sick when she did, most likely he'd had himself six more months behind bars."

"Yes, sir, we're all well aware of that fact. Flavil does have himself a girlfriend, though. She's a Sunday school teacher. He got her while he was in the pen. She wrote to him ever' day."

"I reckon that makes her a pen pal then," Lester said, creating a ripple of laughter around the customers. He scooted himself into the chair because he needed to get on home and change into his funeral clothes.

≈❧≈

Lester tried to attend all graveside services. He hated to see anyone laid to rest without a decent amount of mourners. This wouldn't be a big turnout like the 180-car procession that wound around the cemetery when Spencer's grandfather passed on. No, Lacy Capp had been a surly woman with a sorry mister and a good-for-nothin' son. The only respectable thing about that union was the fact that Leemon Capp, her mister, had run off to join the Merchant Marines and never came back. Lacy had worked at the Chillaton Dry Cleaners for twenty years until female cancer claimed her. She raised her ornery son alone and always smelled of naphtha, which to Lester's way of thinking helped keep her single.

Flavil was there all right. Had on dark glasses, a Hawaiian shirt, and shoes like Pat Boone's. His pen pal was hooked on to his arm like a night crawler, too, and she sure didn't look like any Sunday school teacher Lester had ever seen. They whispered in each other's ears during the graveside services, showing no respect at all.

≈❧≈

Flavil was a hot topic at the post office and the barbershop for a couple of weeks. Then everybody lost interest when Carson Blake offered everybody in town complimentary matinee tickets to a double feature Western at the Parnell to celebrate his daughter being a finalist in the Miss Texas Beauty Pageant. Lester loved shoot-'em-upper movies, and especially a free one.

Connelly County had never been represented in the Miss Texas contest, and every resident would be glued to the TV on the big night. It would be hard to find a better all-around swimsuit contestant than Missy Blake.

Jemma was reluctant to host a gathering to watch the proceedings, but Twila was dying to, and did. Sweetybeth was in the center of the room in her playpen and bowls of chips and bean dip were on the coffee table when Spencer and Jemma arrived. Trent, Sandy, Twila, and Buddy B rounded out the audience. Jemma had been nursing a big pout all day but had successfully hidden it from her husband. The Cleave didn't deserve to win anything in her opinion, but beauty contests weren't about dignity or honor; they were just about looks, so The Cleave actually had a chance.

"She'll win the swimsuit part, but the interview will kill her," Sandy predicted.

After the initial introductions and a silly group song and dance, the contestants began the traditional parade to display their physical blessings. The closer it got to Miss Panhandle, Spencer excused himself to make a phone call to a client.

Sandy nudged Jemma. "Smart boy."

Missy must have been working out because she didn't have a single ounce of baby fat anywhere. She knew how to walk, too. Being the CHS band majorette had served her well. The camera didn't linger on her face for long. Spencer came back just in time for Miss East Texas to strut her stuff.

The announcer called out the runners-up, then blurted, "The winner of the swimsuit competition is: Miss Panhandle, Melissa Blake!"

Big surprise. Rats. Jemma looked briefly at her husband. His eyes were already on her. He leaned over and whispered in her ear, "They don't have the best of the best."

Jemma smiled slightly. "Smooth talker."

Buddy B pushed back in his recliner. "Now the fun begins. I heard that Missy's gonna twirl two batons."

Trent frowned. "While she sings or something?"

"Nope." Sandy sighed. "While she wears something short on both ends."

"I heard that the batons are going to be on fire," Twila added.

"Naw, that's Nedra news," Buddy said. "Carson laid down the big bucks and hired a choreographer from New York to plan the whole thing. He even had the music especially recorded."

Trent shook his head. "You can be Miss Texas and just twirl a baton?"

"Two batons," Twila corrected. "Texans appreciate twirlers."

Her routine was well executed, much to Jemma's disappointment. She had hoped that The Cleave would drop one baton and get hit by the other in the meantime. At least she hoped that her hair would cover her face, but Missy was dressed like a cowgirl whose outfit got washed in hot water and shrunk down to nothing. Her hat was fastened to her head with a drawstring under her chin. She pranced and cavorted to a song from *Oklahoma*. Jemma thought that choice alone should have gotten her disqualified. Instead, she came in third in the talent competition.

"Oh brother." Sandy moaned. "Every little girl in the state will sign up for twirling lessons now."

Twila, ever the faithful employee, defended the notion. "Twirling's a sport. Nedra's niece got a twirling scholarship to a college in Louisiana."

After a medley of songs by the pageant orchestra, it was time for the finalists to be announced and interviewed. The Cleave was among the chosen few. She made her phony surprised face that Jemma couldn't stand. Her daddy had probably bought off the judges. If Missy Blake became Missy Texas, Jemma would beg Spencer to move to Scotland.

The camera moved in close to scrutinize each contestant as she pondered the question. The master of ceremonies read slowly, as though speaking a foreign language. "What challenge in your life have you overcome?" The camera lingered on The Cleave as she pursed her lips in profound concentration.

"If she says that being a total jerk has been a challenge, she'll be lying," Sandy said. "It comes naturally to her."

Twila spoke up. "She's not a jerk all the time, is she?"

"Whose side are you on, Twila? The Cleave has a personality problem. Plus she went through Spencer's desk for her own benefit," Sandy said. "Cheezo, it's like she's your best friend or something."

"Well, let's see if Melissa's small brain is working tonight." Trent slipped his arm around Sandy.

The first contestant spoke about her struggle to overcome a learning disorder. The second was studying to become a space scientist despite her meager monetary resources, and the third went for universal peace and how, as Miss Texas, she would strive to overcome world unrest.

Then it was Missy's turn. She slung back her hair and made eye contact with the camera, like a viper. "I've had to deal with jealousy all my life. Ever since I was a little girl, people have hated me because I'm so pretty. Now that I've grown up, it's even worse. Nobody really understands how beautiful people suffer because of jealousy. I've overcome it by learning to just love myself and my God-given beauty. It is only. . .uh. . .native. . .nativity. . .*nature's due* that I be crowned Miss Texas." She arched a brow at the camera and smiled, showing the results of her junior high braces.

Jemma felt like Missy was looking right at her. Twila's guests erupted into laughter.

"There goes the shootin' match." Buddy B spoke for them all.

Jemma exhaled. The Cleave had exposed herself at the Houston Convention Center on tri-state television in more ways than one. No learning disorder, no world peace, no rocket science major—just ego. Even her daddy couldn't fix The Cleave's embarrassing response, and thus Miss San Antonio tearfully wore the crown down the runway. Despite invoking God and using a phrase she had learned from Jemma, Missy came in dead last.

❧

"Uncle Art," Jemma bubbled into the phone, "I just sent you the first quilt, and there are six more almost finished. You're going to be impressed."

"Good," Arthur said. "I'll be looking forward to it. Your aunty has been working with the marketing department to get started as soon as it arrives."

"Love y'all," Jemma said and handed the phone to Spencer. He was to begin the new Billington's in Austin soon and had a list of questions.

❧

Spencer pulled up to the nursing home; it was coming along at a slow pace, unlike their other projects. He probably needed someone else to supervise the construction of it, but he wanted to make sure it was done right. He and Jemma had been praying for a solution. Pinky Simmons and his brother, Skinny Jack, of Jack's Concrete, rolled up next to him in a beat-up '49 pickup.

Pinky stuck his head in the Corvette window. "Hey, Spencer, how's it goin'?"

"This job is taking forever, Pinky. We need to speed things up."

Skinny Jack moved in so as not to miss anything. "I heard you're in one of them girlie magazines. I betcha your pretty wife don't like you gettin' naked for a magazine." He guffawed, hoping to get him going.

Spencer grinned right back at him. "So, do y'all have any ideas for making some quick progress here? I'm open for suggestions."

Pinky took off his straw hat and squatted beside the car. "Money talks, Spencer. Offer Pa a bonus for overtime; maybe that'll light his fire."

"Throw in a copy of that girlie magazine, too," Skinny Jack offered, wheezing with laughter.

Pinky lowered his voice. "You ain't really naked in them pictures, are you, Spence?"

"Of course not," Spencer said. "Now about this project. . ."

Jack Simmons honked his horn and lurched his truck to a stop on the other side of the Corvette. "Nobody said nothin' about a pity party this mornin'. Young Mr. Chase, you best be earnin' some money to pay us with." Jack scratched his enormous belly under his overalls and yawned.

Skinny Jack piped up. "Spencer's gonna give us all raises and nudie magazines if we cut loose on this place. It was Pinky's idea."

Jack guffawed. "Magazines? I ain't sure Skinny Jack here can read, young mister. You might want to change that to something helpful, like cigarettes. I thought you was in some pretty boy's magazine anyway."

Skinny Jack put his arm around his pa. "Don't need to read nothin' to enjoy them kind of pictures. Hold on. Pretty boy's magazine? I ain't wantin' to see no naked bucks like you. You can forget that idea right now." Skinny Jack backed away from the Corvette.

"Jack, we were discussing your slow progress. I might consider a bonus, though, because the target date is already history."

"You boys hightail it on out there and start working before I kick your sorry hides." Jack spat a wad of tobacco into an orange juice can stuck in the front pocket of his bib overalls, then turned to Spencer. "Listen here, sonny boy, you're making me look bad in front of my family when you whine about the way I do things."

"It's not your work quality that I'm concerned about. It's the long lunch breaks, late arrivals, and early quitting times. It's nine o'clock right now, and y'all just got here. The sun has been up for three hours."

"Family comes first with us, young Mr. Chase. My mama's got a rattler holed up in her outhouse foundation. Me 'n' the boys went over there and cemented him in. I ain't gonna have my mama gettin' her hindquarters bit by a rattler, even if it harelips the gov'ner. Besides, your old man's got enough money to hire you some more help so we can get your pretty little place done in time. Nobody's gonna live here anyway, except a bunch of rich old bags." He spat again. "I see no hurry."

Spencer looked him in the eye. "Jack, I have twenty-five elderly men and women who need to move into this building right now. I would appreciate it if you would get your crew over here, on time, tomorrow. Maybe you should spend some of your earnings to get your mother an indoor bathroom."

Spencer backed up the Corvette, and it threw a bucketful of gravel as he left the site.

The bosses and their perky secretary were having lunch in the conference room at the office, courtesy of Son's Drive In new delivery service.

"This is hilarious." Sandy giggled. "Whoever heard of a hamburger place delivering to your door? There are deadbeats in this town who will never have to leave their houses again."

"I think Son is trying to compete with his daughters' place. Daddy's Money is raking in the supper crowd," Spencer said.

"Is it true that Son invented the spork, and that's why he has them on his neon sign?" Trent asked.

"Yeah," Sandy said between bites. "Supposedly, Son developed sporks when he was one of the cooks for General MacArthur during the Second World War."

"Really." Trent drew in his chin. "The names in this town kill me. For instance, why is Buddy called Buddy B, and what's the deal with the two Jacks who are working on the nursing home?"

"If you could call it work," Spencer muttered.

Sandy took a sip of soda. "We call my brother Buddy B to not confuse him with Buddy Holly. His band used to only play Buddy Holly songs. The Simmons daddy is Jack and he's a tub of lard, but rather than call him Fat Jack, folks thought the best thing to do was to call the son Skinny Jack."

"Why not call him Jack Jr.?" Trent asked.

"That's Pinky's real name."

Trent hung his head and laughed. "What that Simmons bunch needs is some competition."

Spencer exhaled. "I couldn't get anybody else to come until the fall, and Jack was the only crew around. They do know how to pour concrete and lay bricks, especially Pinky." Spencer cleaned up his trash and walked to the door. "This is what I get for trying to act as the contractor on this job. It's not my field."

"Don't look at me." Trent held up his hands.

"You want me to do it?" Sandy asked. "I will, because Jack Simmons is a liar. He and my daddy had a major falling-out about five years ago. I'll call around. The new Amarillo phone book just came out."

"Thanks, Sandy." Trent smiled admiringly.

"Yeah, thanks," Spencer added. "I have to get back to the Billington projects, and I've got a hot date tonight." He turned toward his office, but not before he saw the smile that Sandy gave Trent. They weren't even listening to him.

Jemma sat on the edge of the chaise lounge in their study. She smiled at the photograph. She knew that right after they had snapped this shot, her dear husband had been thrown off the borrowed horse that resembled Gene Autry's Champion. She just knew that if the horse had been a Trigger look-alike, it wouldn't have thrown Spence. Roy Rogers remained supreme. She still had his cowboy rules tucked in her wallet.

She eyed the canvas. He would hate it if she did another huge painting of him. She jumped up and got started.

She worked on it all day until she saw the Corvette coming down the county road. Then, tearing off her paint-spattered clothes, she jumped in the shower. She emerged to hear him groaning in the studio.

"Jemmabeth Alexandra, not again. Can't you find something else to paint?" he yelled as he descended the stairs, then came into their bedroom. "Well, hello, good-looking. Are we going out with you dressed like that?"

She grinned. "I paint however my heart leads me, and it led me straight to you today." She went in her closet and began the tedious task of choosing an outfit for their overnight date in Amarillo.

Spencer stood in the doorway. "Let's stay home. We can eat peanut butter and jelly for all I care."

She gave him The Look. "What changed your mind?"

He didn't answer but shut the closet door, leaving them marooned in the dark.

⊰❧⊱

The painting was her new favorite, well, maybe not her favorite, but she really liked it. Cowboy Spencer stood on the banks of Plum Creek holding the sorrel horse's reins. It drank from the stream as Spencer's attention was on the minnows scattering from the commotion. The sun filtered through dust particles, settling behind horse and rider, and the light provided the scene with a regal luminescence. She had just added a dragonfly hovering above the water when the phone rang. It was her cowboy.

"Hey, you, guess what?"

"You're coming home to work, like you promised you would do someday."

"You just watch. I'm going to do it, Jem. But first, here's some news you'll like. Sandy has found somebody from Amarillo to do the brickwork on the nursing home. I've already told Jack, which was very satisfying, I might add."

"Super. How did he take it?"

"He was ticked off and called me an assortment of names. This other crew can be here tomorrow if we need them. Apparently, it's a group of buddies who worked construction in the army and arc just getting started. Sandy found them in the Amarillo newspaper."

"It's an answer to our prayers. I hope they'll do a good job," Jemma said, studying the horse's right nostril.

"We'll keep an eye on them, but the guy gave Sandy several numbers back East to call for references. Sorry, baby, I have to take another call. See you tonight."

Jemma took his advice and did find something else to paint. She had been thinking about this idea for a while.

She walked down their lane and turned east on the county road for ten minutes or so. Making her way across the cattle guard, she passed the windmill and horse tank, then rounded the corner and unfastened the gate to the green field of cotton, the cotton field that Papa had called Jemmalou's, meaning he would spend all the profits from it on her art lessons and Christmas presents, if possible.

At the far end of the turn row, a giant, lone elm tree held many memories for her. In its shade stood a cedar bench that he had crafted himself and placed there for his lunch breaks. Now a hawk was perched on it. Papa would have liked that.

She stopped and sketched the sight, then moved closer until the bird spread its wings and lifted into the branches of the big elm. Jemma peered up into the tree. She caught a movement and there he was, cinnamon feathers ruffling in a sudden cool breeze. His black eyes pierced into hers; then he was off, drifting on the wind until he disappeared in the clouds.

Jemma ran her hand across the wooden bench, then looked out over the field, to see things as Papa might have. She took out her pencil again, making pages of sketches as the wind moved through the cotton patch and moaned in the branches, bringing with it a bank of heavy clouds.

A gust whipped around the bench and peppered her face and arms with sand. She turned her back to it and felt the first drops of rain.

A streak of lightning brought her out of her artistic stupor. She tucked her sketchbook inside her cowboy shirt and walked toward the gate. With every step she took, the storm intensified.

By the time she reached the gate, she was soaked, and the lightning propelled her into an all-out sprint. She knew Spencer would call, she wouldn't be home to answer, and there would be a scolding tonight. She never considered the weather in her plans, so it was always a blessing when things worked out.

She strained to see the county road. All she needed now was to get run over; she'd never hear the end of it, if she lived. Rats. She pushed her hair back from her face and plodded ahead. A horn beeped behind her. She turned to see the smiling, nearly toothless face of Shy Tomlinson. He yelled for her to get in. She ran around to the passenger side to comply, but Shy motioned her to the driver's side.

"Sorry, Jemmerbeth," he said, taking off his hat. "That door ain't worked since 1954. Scoot on across, hon." He ran his hand through his white hair. "This is one miserable storm, but we can sure use the moisture." The smell of old rags and machine oil permeated the pickup. "I suppose you need off at your place. It's sure different-lookin', ain't it? Spencer's a smart feller to come up with such a interestin' house."

Shy was Chillaton's best fix-it man and had done some work for her mom and daddy before they sold their house. She peered out the back window into the bed of the truck. "Your spruce tree looks pretty this year, Shy. This rain will be good for it."

"Sure will. I won't have to water it for a good while. The Lord's blessed me with a special knack for growin' things back there. My melons are coming along, too. Take a look."

Jemma turned again. The cantaloupes made a ring around the tree. The blue spruce was the same size it had been since she was a little girl. Some folks said Shy bought a new one every year and pretended it was the same tree, but she knew he couldn't afford to buy new trees.

They pulled up in front of her house. "Thanks for the ride, Shy. Would you like to see the inside of our home? I have some leftover chocolate cake, and I could make you some coffee." She assumed he could manage those without teeth.

"Oh no, ma'am. I'm way too dirty to go anywhere but to the dump. I'd get mud on your floor, but thanks anyway. I'm sure it's fixed up real pretty in there."

"You can take your shoes off. C'mon. I won't take no for an answer. Besides, I'd like to do a few sketches of you, if you don't mind." She touched her shirt to see if her sketchbook was intact. It was there, and only a little moist.

Shy hesitated, then opened the door into the rain. Jemma skipped up the steps and onto the deck. Shy ambled along behind her. She changed clothes and served him the promised cake and coffee. He wolfed it down, and she gave him seconds.

"Now, you sit right there and let me draw your picture, okay? I'll show you the finished portrait in a few weeks."

He chuckled and rubbed his chin, then sat very still for several minutes. "Last time somebody wanted to make a likeness of me was when I took a notion to grow things in my truck. That was right after them Dust Bowl days. The Amarillo newspaper come down here and wrote a story about me and took pictures. It was plumb embarrassin'."

"This won't be embarrassing, I promise." Jemma flipped the page. The phone rang, and she knew it was Spencer. "Take a look around, Shy. Make yourself at home." She picked up the phone.

"Where have you been?" he asked.

"I'm fine. I just took a little walk over to Jemmalou's."

Spencer sighed. "Do you ever look at the sky?"

"Of course I do, I'm an artist," she said, playing with the cord. "Shy Tomlinson gave me a ride home. He's here now, and I'm doing some sketches of him."

"Tell him thanks for me, but you haven't heard the last of this."

"I know. Love you. Bye." She hung up the phone and found Shy studying the painting of Papa.

"That's some likeness, hon." He shook his head. "He sure was a good man. I first met your grandpa at the hospital. He come in to pray over the sick and afflicted. I'd got myself pretty beat up in The Great War. I was what you'd call a wild young'un up until then, so I figgered the Lord said, 'Okay, sonny boy, you've been askin' for a whuppin' and here it is.' Your grandpa helped me see the light, and I was much obliged. Anytime I worked for him, I did it for free. He always made me chuckle. He said you might as well laugh about your troubles as cry about 'em, and he was right, you know." Shy shifted in his stocking feet. "It sure made me sad about his boys."

Jemma smiled. "I miss him a lot, and I love hearing stories

about him. Thanks, Shy."

"I reckon I'd best be gettin' on home. This is my day for checkin' the roadside for odds and ends. You'd be surprised at what folks throw out or lose along the highway. Last week I was passin' over the Salt Fork bridge and spotted me some real nice dishes washed up on the sand barge. Had little daises painted on 'em. You just never know. Anyways, your place sure is somethin' to brag about. You tell Spencer I said that."

Jemma grinned. It was good to know that Sandy's hope chest dishes had found a deserving home. "Come back anytime." Jemma walked him to the door. The rain had lessened. "I like your pickup garden. It's always fun to see you around town, especially when the lights are on the tree."

"Well, I know folks think I've got a few loose screws, but that's all right by me. I've had me some good tomatoes and melons out of it, except a couple of summers back when somebody messed around with my plants. I figgered it was some kids, out for some mischief."

"Probably. Have you ever been married, Shy?" she asked.

He grinned. "No ma'am. I was kindly sweet on Eleanor Perkins back in the forties, but that woman talks enough to bend a mule's ear for life. No ma'am, never married."

Jemma laughed. She knew he'd spoken the truth about Eleanor. "You take care, Shy. Thanks for rescuing me. I hope you have good luck on the highway." Jemma closed the door and ran upstairs with her damp sketchbook. She had more ideas than she had canvases, and it was time to get busy.

❧

She got up early to take Spencer and Trent to the airport the next morning. They were to meet with Arthur and iron out the final details for the department stores.

"I'll be thinking about you while I paint," she said as they waited.

Spence leaned his forehead on hers and looked into her eyes. "Really? I thought you got lost in your work when you paint, but I'm flattered that you would even try."

"You are the same way and you know it. Once your brain starts walking around those blueprints, there's no room for any other thoughts."

"Mrs. Chase, you are always in my mind. Always." He kissed her.

⋘◈⋙

Trent peeked over his *Wall Street Journal*. He would like to be doing the same to a special someone, and it was at that moment he really cranked the door wide open to his heart.

Chapter 21
Nancy Takes Charge

Jemma stopped by the office to leave Sandy some notes from Spencer. Sandy was sitting at her desk with an expression of doom.

"What's wrong with you?" Jemma asked.

"I may get fired."

"Is this from your crystal ball, or have you been embezzling funds?"

"I'm serious, Jem. The new masonry crew got here right on time this morning."

"That's good."

"You don't understand. There are six of them, and they are all black. I had no idea."

"So why are you getting fired?"

"Spencer and Trent trusted me to get them a good crew."

"Are you insinuating that these guys aren't?"

"I don't mean that. They may be fantastic at what they do. The problem is that this is Chillaton. We are still living in the fifties here; haven't you noticed, Miss Liberal?"

"Look, Spencer and Trent are certainly not going to fire you because a construction crew is one color or another. They aren't going to fire you even if this crew doesn't work out. Your job is secure, so stop worrying."

"Just wait until word gets around about this, Jemma. Can you imagine what Jack Simmons will say or do, for that matter? This is not Dallas or even Amarillo. People around here think Negroes should still be picking cotton and little else. You know that's true, even though they complain about them being on welfare. Now these guys come in and take a job away from local whites. Cheezo. It could be a disaster."

Jemma thought for a moment. "Well, I do know that we can't

live in the past. Who cares if there is a reaction? Let people say what they want. If there is a true Christian spirit in Chillaton, it will all be for the best. Life goes on, and we have to grow up. Prejudice is ignorance, and I think people in this town are smarter than you think."

"You are not a realist, Jem. All I know is that Jack Simmons will stir up trouble. I just hope he doesn't do anybody any harm."

Jemma bit her lip and decided to leave a message for Spencer to call as soon as he got to Do Dah's. Why did trouble always rear its head when they were apart? It had to be the devil. She just hoped the devil didn't wear overalls stretched to the limit over a porker beer belly. If so, she would have to give some thought to a new wrestling move or two or three.

❦

She drove home by way of the building site. The A-1 Concrete and Masonry crew were hard at work. Nobody else was around. At home, she built some canvases and had two completed when he called. She told him the whole story.

He considered it for a minute. "Call Buddy and ask him to get in touch with Leon Shafer. He just got laid off and could use a few extra bucks. Tell him that I need Leon to get the grounds at the nursing home ready for sidewalks and landscaping. It's already been excavated."

"Is he going to be your spy?" Jemma asked, feeling relief already at the decisiveness in his voice.

"Yup. Leon's a good guy, and once he knows the score with Jack, he'll keep a lid on things."

"That's why I love you, because you're so smart."

"You be smart, Jemmabeth. Don't get involved in this. Jack Simmons is not to be trusted."

"I know."

"I mean it. You stay home and paint."

Nancy Drew would not stay home when trouble was afoot.

❦

She had supper with Gram and Helene, then drove to the nursing home site near Blake's Drive In Theater. It was deserted. The A-1 crew had left their mixer and several neatly stacked bags of concrete on the west side of the structure. She parked her Suburban and walked around the site. She had picked the brick color herself. It was a salmon tone with accents of white and black. The A-1 crew had done a good day's work. Leon had been working, too. The front of the building was hand raked and rocks were piled outside the survey stakes. Jemma walked back to her car and was about to get in when she spotted the pickup. Jack and Skinny Jack made one pass before turning in the lot. Their truck idled for a minute, then took off, radio blaring.

So they had heard. Jemma sat in the Suburban and gave some thought to her options. It would be dark soon, and there was nobody to guard the site. Jack Simmons was brazen enough to break the law and do some damage, but Spencer would be calling the house soon to see how the day went. She went home and painted. He called around nine and they talked for an hour.

She sat at his desk, touching his things after they hung up. He had told her again to stay out of the Jack deal. Spencer didn't think Jack would do anything yet, and he would be home soon to handle things. Jemma wasn't so sure. She would just die if Jack pulled a stunt and ruined this crew's chance to do a good job. Rats. She grabbed her pillow, a quilt, and a flashlight, then drove back to town in the Corvette. It would be easier to hide behind the bushes than the Suburban.

Nothing was amiss when she pulled up to the site. She drove the Corvette to the east side of the building and killed the engine behind the stout cedars that separated their property from the Blakes' outdoor theater. She locked the doors, moved the seat back as far as it would go, and tried to sleep. After an hour or so, she dozed off and didn't wake up until just before dawn. She shook her head and opened the door, moving the flashlight around the premises. All was well. She yawned and drove home. There was a light on at Lester's.

She worked on the painting of Jemmalou's until Spencer called. He and Trent had eaten dinner with Carrie and Phil. They would move to Chillaton in the fall, but Phil could come earlier to get things running and screen the staff. Carrie sent her love. They ended the conversation in whispers, speaking of love and longings. She hung up, grabbed her stuff, and headed for town.

The A-1 group had finished one whole side of the building and had turned the corner with the next. Spencer would be pleased. She repeated her routine, and the ticking of her alarm clock lulled her to sleep much quicker this time.

⋙

It was just after two that she heard voices. Her heart thumped like she was playing basketball again. She squinted into the moonless night and detected the outline of Jack's truck. Then she heard Skinny Jack's voice, the wheezy, cackling voice of a *good-for-nothin'*, as Lester called the younger Jack. She had a plan, but it was becoming sketchier by the moment.

Jack coughed and spat on the ground. "Can't you do nothin' right? Give me that sledgehammer. You gotta get a good backswing on it."

"What if the head comes off and falls on me?" Skinny Jack asked. "Did you ever think about that? You could have yourself a dead Skinny Jack. Then you'd have to put up with Pinky all by yourself."

"I'm fixin' to beat the soup outta you," Jack snarled.

Jemma went into action. She turned the lights on the Corvette and pushed on the horn without letting up. The headlights weren't directly on them, but they were close enough.

Skinny Jack ran to the truck and Jack shaded his eyes with one hand while still holding the sledgehammer in the other. He walked a few steps toward her, then abruptly jerked around and dropped the sledgehammer, kicking it behind him. He put his hands in the air.

Jemma took her hand off the horn in time to overhear Jack's words.

"I wasn't doin' nothin'. Me and the boy here were just takin' a bathroom break on our way home from Amarillo. Yes, sir, we'll get right on home. Thank you, sir. Are you new in the sheriff's office? No, sir, I didn't mean no disrespect. You have yourself a good night, sir." Jack lumbered to his truck.

Jemma heard the sledgehammer hit the truck bed, then the cab dipped as he got in and drove away. A big beam of light came toward her and she got out of the Corvette, ready to meet Sheriff Ezell.

"Jemma? Is that you?"

"Leon?" she yelled back.

He clicked off his flashlight and came toward her, grinning in the dark. "What on earth are you doing out here? Spencer will have a fit."

"I thought you were the sheriff."

"That was good, huh? I used some of the stuff I've seen on my TV shows. You can learn a lot from them, you know. Actually, Spencer asked me to camp out here at night until the project is done. I'm on a twenty-four-hour stakeout. It's real exciting. Were you here last night, too? I got off to a late start. *Mannix* was on."

"Please don't tell Spence; he'll croak. I'll tell him sometime. I was just afraid that Jack would pull something, and he would've, too, if you hadn't run him off."

Leon lit up a cigarette. "Well, to tell the truth, I didn't hear nothin' until you laid into that horn. I'm a sound sleeper. I guess this was a two-man job. Excuse me for saying so, Jemma, but you've got a lot of guts, and I sure do respect that. You go on home now. I've got my detective adrenaline going."

She laughed. "I doubt Jack will be back, but you'll tell Sheriff Ezell about this, won't you?"

"Sure will. Law enforcement is a real tight circle. Don't worry. Your secret's safe with me. We're old band cronies anyway, huh?"

"We are. Thank you so much, Leon." She gave him a hug and went to the Corvette. He was standing in front of the building as she drove past. She rolled down her window. "Leon, I want you to know that I appreciate your attitude about the A-1 crew. I know this is a first for Chillaton, and you might take some flak."

Leon put out his cigarette and coughed. "In my book, we're all the same under our skin. Them boys fought just like Spencer did in 'Nam. No difference in 'em."

Jemma bit her lip and waved. She had told Sandy that Chillaton people were smart. They also had some good hearts amongst them.

She waited until she had buttered him up with a good meal and sweet nothings. They sat on the deck barefooted, enjoying the sounds of the evening.

"We need a porch swing, Spence. I miss Gram's."

"I'll have to come up with a plan for that, I guess. You look very suspicious tonight, my love."

"You can't read my mind. It's just that I missed you. I don't sleep well when you are away. I worry about things." The seed was planted.

"What things?"

She watched him out of the corner of her eye. This could turn out badly, and she knew it. "I worried that Jack Simmons might do something evil. So. . ."

Spencer sat up, but it was too late to stop now.

"So, I checked the site both nights you were gone."

"Tell me that again."

"I sort of waited around to make sure he didn't do anything."

There was a very pregnant pause, as in quintuplets.

"Now let me get this straight. I made arrangements with Leon to hang out at the building site twenty-four hours a day, but you went all by yourself to the site in the middle of the night and checked to make sure that a man who weighs twice as much as you, not to mention his crazy son, wasn't committing any crimes there. Is that pretty much it?"

"Well, pretty much," she said, shrinking into the patio furniture. "You should have told me that Leon would be there at night."

Spencer leaned against the railing and exhaled. "Is there more?"

"I was kind of there when Leon confronted Jack and Skinny Jack." She had done it again, but it was a good thing this time. Maybe not all that safe, but a really good thing.

He paced around, then picked her up, took her in the house, and deposited her on their bed. She looked at him, big-eyed and pouty lipped. He left the room and came back with a legal pad and a pencil. "All right, little Miss Smarty Pants, start writing. When you've filled up the page, I'll let you know what's going to happen next." He plumped up the pillows and lay on the bed, arms folded across his chest.

Jemma looked at the words written so perfectly in block letters, like only a draftsman could do. *I scared the wits out of my husband, and I'm sorry.* She looked at him, but he was not smiling. She copied the words, filling every line, and handed it to him.

"I really am sorry, Spence."

He crawled across the big bed toward her until their noses touched. She couldn't help but notice how pretty his eyes were in the soft light of their bedroom. If he weren't so mad at her, she would have told him, too.

"Jemmabeth Alexandra Chase, promise me that you will stop acting on every idea that pops into your head, especially if it endangers your life."

"I don't know if I can promise you that. I thought A-1 needed me. Jack could have stolen their equipment."

"Jemma! What if Jack had hurt you? Leon told me that he and Skinny Jack had been drinking. Didn't you consider that I knew what Jack might do and that's why I had Leon there?"

She hung her head. "Okay. I promise I'll try to be more careful. You have really pretty eyes," she said and gave him the puppy dog look.

"I can't leave you alone. Something happens nearly every time, and you know that I'm going to have to be away a lot with all these projects."

"I could come with you, but then I can't paint as well. I'm sorry I scared you. At least it was all over when you found out. Retroactive scares are easier to handle, aren't they?"

"It doesn't change the facts."

"What's going to happen next?"

"This." He grabbed her in a merciless leg lock.

She giggled and tried to curl around to break the lock, but couldn't. He was shaking his legs and jiggling her insides. She settled for a toehold and bent his foot backward. He yelped and let her go. She slammed him with The Pancake and Waffle Iron combined, but he maneuvered his arms out and pinned her to the bed. They stayed like that for a while, both gasping for air.

"Truce?" he asked.

"Truce," she said, and he let her go.

"Sucker!" She grabbed his ankles, pulling him to the floor.

He landed like a cat and chased her out of the room and up the stairs to their studio loft. "You've had it," he said and kissed her like they were still on their honeymoon. All things considered, they were.

❧

The quilts were finished. Jemma brought Lizbeth over to Willa's house to see them after dark. Lizbeth set right to work looking over the quilts.

Willa laughed. "You sneakin' around? You 'fraid them women will think Miz Liz is the inspector?"

"I just don't want to mess up a good relationship. It's been smooth sailing, hasn't it?" Jemma asked.

"If you don't count all the whinin' about who sits where and choosin' radio stations. Then there was Grandma's spit can that spilled."

"Do Dah and Uncle Art are excited. They have gotten lots of interest from the first quilt I sent. So, what's the latest with Trina and Nick?"

"They've about spent all their money sendin' him on wild goose chases for interviews."

"Don't hospitals pay him back?"

"Some do, but there's a chunk of time in between where there ain't no money in the bank. Joe sent 'em what we could afford, and his folks is helpin', too."

"Spencer and I will send them a check," Jemma said. "I wish they would come to Chillaton. Dr. Huntley is about to retire."

Willa laughed. "Sugar, ain't no white folks gonna let a colored man see them in their underbritches. You should know that."

Jemma nodded, but she didn't really agree. Leon had proven that.

"This is fine work." Lizbeth eyed the last quilt. "The bindings are a little stiff, but the rest is very nice."

"I tell you who's been the biggest surprise in all this business," Willa said. "Gweny. She even come over at night and got the keys to the church from us several times so she could work on them quilts. She's been by once this mornin' already to see if they was ready to mail. Beat all I ever saw. Weese didn't do a lick of work the whole time he lived at my house."

"Maybe she wants extra money. I bet she marked down her time."

Willa shrugged. "No ma'am. She just worked. You gonna take these to the post office?"

"I'll have to get some boxes and pack them first. I'll come back in the morning. Maybe we should give Gweny a bonus."

⊷◈⊶

Jemma saw him as she turned the corner toward the railroad crossing. He was thinner. She slammed on her brakes and backed up. He raised his eyes to her like the same old angry Weese.

"Hi," Jemma said. "How are you? I heard that you're going to junior college. That's great."

He gave a slight bob of his head.

"Your sister seems to be excited about the neighborhood quilting business. I hope you like the idea, too."

"I told you a long time ago that I don't care about you or anything you do."

"You don't know me. I'm only trying to help the neighborhood be more financially independent. Surely you can agree with me on that."

Weese turned suspicious eyes on her. "You don't know squat about bein' poor, otherwise you wouldn't be flashin' your fancy Corvette around here. Why don't you sell it and give the money to Gweny and me? That would make you feel better about yourself. That's all you're lookin' for anyway."

Their eyes locked up. It was a pointless conversation. A monster whirlwind passed between them, needling their skin with sand. A tumbleweed fastened itself to Weese's leg, and the aftermath of the gust left Jemma's hair full of dirt. She rubbed her eyes and he was gone, trudging down the street and spitting the encounter out of his mouth along with the dirt. She exhaled and ran her tongue over the grit that stuck to her teeth.

Weese didn't speak for everybody. It could work out for the women and that's what mattered, despite his opinion of her motivation. The Lord knew her heart.

The next morning Jemma went behind Household Supply and flattened three portable television boxes she found in the alley. She bought wrapping tissue at the dime store and took it to Willa's house. They packed the quilts like eggs in the sturdy containers. Jemma taped them shut and wrote the address on each box. It was an exciting moment, tempered only by the fact that the boxes wouldn't fit into the Corvette.

"I'll use the Suburban. I need to buy groceries, anyway, so I'll be back in a couple of hours to pick these up. Thanks for your help, Willa. We're making history today."

"Let's hope it ain't history like Pearl Harbor. I gotta get this ironin' done. Joe wants me to cut back on my work if the quiltin' business takes off. I can't argue with that. It'll give me more time to spend on him, too."

She and Spencer ate at Son's, then traded cars. Willa was outside sweeping her porch when Jemma drove up. "Ain't no boxes here," Willa yelled. "Gweny done took 'em to the post office herself. Said it was no trouble for her 'cause she had Weese's truck today."

Jemma drew back. "Gweny? How did she pay for the postage?"

"I give her what I had from my secret money jar. I hope that was all right with you, sugar."

"I suppose so. Here, this should cover it." She gave Willa all the cash in her purse. "Boy, Gweny really is trying hard to get things rolling. I guess she wants that paycheck. Well, okay, tell her thanks for me. Uncle Art should get this first dozen next week, and then we'll see how they sell. Keep your fingers crossed."

"Don't be crossin' no fingers around this place. Only the good Lord makes things happen. Ain't nothin' to do with crossin' fingers. Shame on you, child. Maybe you need a good swat with this broom."

"Sorry, just kidding," Jemma said and blew Willa a kiss. "I'll talk to you later."

Chapter 22
Bitter Pills

Her very next piece was of Grandma Hardy, but Grandma wasn't quilting. She was sitting in a church pew, her trusty spit can in her lap. Spencer laughed when he saw it. They had celebrated his birthday early, the night before, in Amarillo. She had given him a cherrywood pencil box for his desk. Lester had made it, but she had designed it and grouted the Celtic knots around the sides all by herself. His favorite coconut crème cake was almost ready for him, too. She was sprinkling the last flakes on it when she heard a motorcycle coming down their lane. It had to be Leon. He was the only motorcycle owner she knew. She put the lid on the cake and opened the front door.

A leather-clad rider got off the motorcycle. Leon was dressing well to be drawing unemployment, and he was also looking extremely good in the leather pants. The rider took off the helmet and grinned.

"Spence?" Jemma's jaw dropped. "What are you doing with Leon's cycle?"

"Excuse me, baby, but *this* is not Leon's cycle. C'mon, I'll take you for a ride."

"You know I don't ride motorcycles. Whose is it?"

"It's my birthday present to myself. I thought I'd surprise you."

The countryside noises around them became suddenly louder as Jemma stared daggers at the black motorcycle. It might as well have been The Cleave grinning at her behind her husband.

"So, what do you think?" Spencer kept a safe distance, as if he didn't know what to expect.

She turned without a word and went inside. He followed her. "What's the matter, baby? Are you sick?" Ignoring him, she went to their bedroom and shut the door. She even locked it. "Jem, open up. Are you mad at me on my birthday?"

She was more than mad; she was livid. She was so furious, in fact, that she had retreated rather than attack.

⚜

He set his helmet on the floor and went through the mail to have something to do. This could be disastrous. He exhaled and sat on the couch. His leather pants felt kind of odd once he got off the cycle. He should've given her some warning, but he knew she would throw a fit. He had always wanted a cycle, and she had fervently voiced her opinion that they were too dangerous. This BMW was his dream. It wasn't like he had a macho desire for power; he just wanted this one thing. She would indulge him, hopefully.

"Jemma, come out and look at it. You don't have to ride it. Please. I know what you're thinking. We should have talked about it, but there was no hope in that idea. You would have vetoed my plans." He paced in front of the door. "Just come out and talk to me."

Nothing. He went outside to peek into the French doors of their bedroom, but they were locked, the blinds tightly drawn. He sat for a while on a deck chair, then went back to his cycle. It had some bug stains on it. He rubbed them off with a chamois cloth from the garage. He got on it and revved up the engine and took off for parts unknown, sans helmet. Maybe she would lighten up by the time he got back.

⚜

Jemma watched him disappear in a cloud of dust. How could he buy something like that behind her back? He knew how she felt about motorcycles. He'd even picked out that stupid leather stuff without her. He must have been thinking about the whole mess instead of working. Maybe his mind was on it even while they were together. Good grief, it was like he had a girlfriend.

She opened the door to the great room and saw the helmet. She gave it a solid, thundering kick, then got a Dr Pepper out of the fridge, staring at the helmet as it wobbled on the hardwood floor. She bit her lip and went back to their bedroom.

⚜

Spencer got it up to 90 on the Farm to Market. He totally forgot that the helmet was at home. Jemma would get over this. He had gotten the same feeling of freedom when he flew Hueys in training,

813

before the reality of Vietnam. It was exhilarating—like he was the wind. She would come around. He slowed down considerably at the crest of the hill above Plum Creek. He pulled it into the garage and went in the house, whistling and feigning hope.

The sunset cast a warm glow on their home, but there was no sign of his sweet wife. She was still holed up in the bedroom. He salivated at the beautiful cake but made himself a sandwich and ate it on the deck, hoping she might come out. This wasn't a major thing. It was just a motorcycle, for Pete's sake. He fell asleep on the couch.

He knocked on their bedroom door the next morning. "C'mon, Jem, give me a break. You told me not to ever bring it up, so I didn't. It's really fun to ride."

Silence.

"I have a meeting in Amarillo this morning. May I at least take a shower and get dressed?"

Nothing.

"Are you okay in there?" It was worth a shot.

He sighed and walked toward the guest bathroom shower.

⁂

Jemma picked through Spencer's wardrobe and put a gray turtleneck, black slacks, socks, and clean underwear outside the door, then shut it, locked tight. The sweet scent of his aftershave brought tears to her eyes, but she blinked them away. He shouldn't have done this.

⁂

Spencer saw the pile of clothes in front of their bedroom door. She was alive. He got dressed, drank a glass of orange juice, and slapped some of Lizbeth's preserves on toast, again eyeing the cake in the glass holder. He ate on the deck again. The onset of autumn nipped at his face. Surely she would come out of that room by the time the cottonwoods turned. He moved to the French doors and peered inside. All he could see were the blinds. He wrote her a note, stuck it on the phone, and left.

⁂

Jemma waited several minutes after she heard the monster disappear over the hill. The house was quiet. She went into the guest bathroom just to be where he'd been. The towels were damp, and his footprints were on the plush rug. If he had a wreck on that thing, she would die. She roamed around the kitchen but wasn't really hungry. Maybe she should call him. She turned toward the phone and saw the note.

Jemma, I love you, not the cycle.
It's only a motor on wheels.
You are my life.
Spence

Rats. Why'd he have to write that? Now she'd have to call him. She climbed the stairs to the pouting room and sulked in their tiny Sainte-Chapelle.

❦

"The Corvette is here, but Spencer isn't," Sandy said on the phone. "What did you do when you saw his new toy? I bet you flipped out."

"So he rode that thing to Amarillo?"

"Yeah, but you didn't answer my question. I'll bet a dollar he slept on the couch."

Jemma sniffed. "I assume you knew about this all along. Some friend you are."

"Hey, I've just known since he rode up on it yesterday afternoon. I sure wasn't going to be the one to break the news to you. I remember the Kelseys, too."

"How did he get to Amarillo to buy it? I suppose that's where he bought the thing."

"Leon."

"Blood brothers. Maybe Spence will grow a ponytail, too." She hung up the phone and painted for a few hours.

That afternoon she took her sketchbook and sat in his chair on the deck. Up until now, Spencer could always get her out of a pout. This time he hadn't even tried—except for the note. It wasn't so much that she hated motorcycles. It was that he had planned the whole deal without including her, and he had to have been considering it for a while.

What had Sandy called her? A possessive wife. She gave that

some thought. At least the thing he'd bought was quiet, unlike Leon's. Quiet, though, wouldn't help if he were in an accident, and the way Spencer drove, he could be propelled through the air at a hundred miles per hour. She shuddered at that image, as well as those of Carol and Bill Kelsey bleeding to death on the road to Jericho, while a buck and two doe grazed serenely in the ditch. Jemma had watched from the car as Carol died in Alex's arms. Spencer Chase knew that story well.

The phone rang, startling her.

"Jemma, it's Leon."

"Oh. Hello."

"It's about Spencer. There's been some trouble near Amarillo."

Her body went limp. She braced herself on the counter and couldn't form anything close to a word. Nausea crept up her throat, and she tried to think of a scripture.

"Uh. You might want to get on up here."

She drew a breath. "Which hospital?"

"Naw, he's not in the hospital. He's at the Big Tex Truck Stop."

"What do you mean?"

"The state patrol yanked his license and impounded his bike. I'd bring him home on mine, but I'm starting a new job in an hour. We just happened to be at the same place at the same time."

"Leon, what are you telling me? Is Spence hurt?"

He laughed. "I guess his pocketbook is gonna hurt. He got clocked at 95 on the highway, and since it's his umpteenth speeding ticket in three years, there's a big price tag to pay. Listen, I gotta go."

"Wait, Leon. Why didn't Spencer call me himself?"

"A man's got his pride, I suppose."

❧

She parked right under Big Tex's waving arm. Spencer was sitting in the window drinking coffee, and he didn't look up when she came inside. She slipped into the booth.

"Hey, babe, know any good lawyers?" she asked, shooting for a light tone. He avoided her eyes and chewed on his lip. She touched his hand. "I didn't know that you'd gotten so many tickets. Have you been keeping things from me?"

He exhaled. "I got one in California and a couple in Houston and New York; you know about the others. I just didn't want to worry you."

"Good excuse. I'll have to remember that one. You're a real menace to society, mister; let's go home."

The Suburban moved along the highway just under the speed limit. Jemma listened to the radio, and Spencer looked straight ahead, holding a large paper sack with both hands like a little boy on his first day of school.

"What's in the bag?" she asked after a long silence.

"My stuff."

"What stuff?"

"The leather clothes and boots."

"Did you wear them to the meeting?"

"No, and it looks like I won't be wearing them ever again."

"I don't know about that. You looked really hot in those pants."

"I should have told you about the tickets. I have a lead foot."

"Well, everybody in town knows that. I'm just glad that you got stopped rather than transported to the hospital or the morgue."

He reached across the seat and touched her shoulder. "Sorry about the cycle, baby. I know it got to you, and I handled that all wrong."

"Me, too," she whispered, then looked at him out of the corner of her eye. His face showed signs of weariness, like it did when he got his draft notice. This day the weariness had sprung from stress of his own making, coupled with the impending embarrassment of the consequences. She touched his cheek, and he immediately kissed the palm of her hand like a puppy starved for its mother.

He slipped his hand under her hair and let it rest at the nape of her neck, tracing his fingers over her skin for the duration of the ride home. The air between them sizzled as Spencer unlocked the front door.

"Spence, I should have. . ."

He pinned her against the river-rock wall and kissed her. She thought she would explode with affection for him. There were no more words, only love.

The morning brought the first frost of the season, but inside the Chase home, life was blissful and quite warm. The coconut crème cake was nothing but crumbs, devoured before sunrise.

❧

Lester hadn't been so happy since his fourth wife, Paulette, had agreed to marry him. Living next door to two cultured ladies, both easy on the eyes, was like breath from heaven for an old fellow like him. Lizbeth watched him with interest. He was sweet on Helene, it was plain to see, and Helene enjoyed the attention. This was working out very well for them all. Helene had brought a few of her elegant belongings to Chillaton, and after a fresh paint job by Jemma, Lizbeth's home was taking on a whole new look. She awoke each morning with a sense of anticipation. It was almost like having Jemmabeth back.

"Lester, do help yourself to another scone. If we were in Devon, you could lavish them with clotted cream and strawberry jam," Helene said, wearing a starched white apron.

"These are delicious," Lizbeth noted. "I think they are an eloquent cousin to our biscuits."

Lester wiped crumbs off his moustache. "Now, if you want somethin' clotted, you need to give a tall glass of buttermilk a try. You crumble yourself up some corn bread in it, and you've got yourself a meal." He stifled a burp into one of Helene's linen napkins.

"How are things in the village, Lester?" Helene asked.

"Well, sir, things are hoppin'. Lots of folks are feelin' bad for Spencer. Drivin' fast don't mean he's a criminal or nothin'. Nobody would ever say a word against that boy. On the other hand, that sorry Flavil Capp's done got hisself thrown back in the hoosegow. He tried to break into The Judge's house, of all places. To top it all off, some pranksters got into Shy Tomlinson's truck and tore up his pumpkins. Throwed 'em on the ground and busted ever' last one of 'em."

Lizbeth shook her head. "Who would do such a cruel thing to Shy?"

"Young'uns got too much time on their hands. If they worked in the fields like we did, they'd be too tuckered out to get into mischief after dark," Lester said.

Helene lifted her teacup, then paused midway. "I do hope our Spencer shall be able to carry on after this nasty bit of humiliation."

Lester chewed on that thought. It hadn't occurred to him that Spencer might let this thing get the best of him.

⋙⋘

"You could hire Lester to drive you around," Jemma said as they drove home from the proceedings. "At least it's been delayed until the end of December. Good thing the judge is going on vacation."

Spencer closed his eyes. "Yeah, but I still can't drive until he decides my fate. I can't believe how stupid I've been. You've married an idiot."

"Maybe this will force you to work at home with me. You said you would. I think you even promised me."

"It's embarrassing. You'd think I was still a teenager."

"You aren't listening to me at all. Now who's the one not turning their problems over to the Lord? Do you need to stop by your office?"

"I might as well get it over with. Sandy will never shut up about this."

⋙⋘

Sandy started singing "He's in the Jailhouse Now" as soon as they walked in the door. "I wonder if we'll lose business over this," she asked, then giggled.

"Are there any calls I need to return?"

"Of course. There's a stack of notes on your desk, and Jemma, your uncle Arthur called, too."

Jemma called him immediately. "Hi, Uncle Art. Did you like the quilts?"

"Actually, that's the reason for my call, Jemmabeth. We've not received another thing from you, and quite enough shipping time has elapsed."

She bit her lip. "I suppose they could be lost," Jemma said, thinking of the women and their dutiful labor. "I'll call you back. Thanks, Uncle Art. Say hi to Do Dah for me."

Spencer was on the phone and Jemma needed to think. Rats. She should have mailed the quilts herself. She had let the women down, and now it was all going to flop. She paced Main Street, battling more than the gusty wind. A '57 Chevy pulled alongside her, and the pair inside emitted lengthy wolf whistles.

"Hey, good lookin', what kind of husband lets his wife walk all over town? Ain't he still got the 'Vette?" Wade Pratt asked.

Jemma exhaled. These two were all she needed in her plight.

"We miss you in the band. Now there ain't nothin' for the guys to look at," Dwayne Cummins added. "That's includin' us."

"Y'all take off. I'm busy right now. I need to think." Jemma pulled her hair back with a rubber band.

"Thinkin's my middle name." Wade gave a thumbs-up in complete confidence. Dwayne kept the car rolling along beside her while Wade continued. "My mama sent me to the store the other day to get some soap, and I was standin' there just lookin' at the wrapper. It said 99 percent pure. That started me to thinkin'. Pure what?"

Dwayne laughed. "Pure soap, you dummy."

"Not necessarily. The guv'ment could be controllin' our minds with some pure chemical."

Dwayne laughed again. "Shut up, Wade. You don't bathe enough to have your mind controlled by no chemicals. What's so important that you've gotta spend all this thinkin' on it, Jemmabeth? You gonna dump ol' Spence and take up with me?"

"I had some packages disappear in the mail." Jemma neared Spencer's office. "I should have mailed them myself, but I let someone else do it."

"Well, I can solve that one," Wade said. "Ask Paralee. She don't mind tellin' you about whatever has passed through her office. Rules or no rules."

Jemma stopped. Of course. She should have thought of that instead of worrying so much about not mailing them herself. "Thanks, guys!"

She went straight to the post office. Paralee, engrossed in *The Guiding Light*, glanced at her. "Hi, hon, I'll be right with you. It's almost time for a commercial." H.D., the cat, stirred, but didn't bother getting up either.

Jemma drummed her fingers on the counter. "It's about those boxes I sent to Uncle Art in Houston."

Paralee turned down the television and leaned across the counter. "I'm sure sorry about Spencer and all them tickets. I reckon he'll be walkin' for a while. He most likely got that from his daddy. Max used to tear around town like a maniac. Now what about them boxes, hon?"

"My uncle hasn't gotten them yet. Isn't there a way to trace them and see where they went?"

"I figger they went right where you sent 'em. That colored girl told me that you changed the address on 'em at the last minute."

"I what? I did no such thing. What address were they changed to?"

"Law, hon. I ain't supposed to tell stuff like that. It's unethical."

"Those were my boxes. I paid to have them mailed. If somebody changed the address on them, isn't that a crime?"

"That could depend on if they did it inside this building. I saw a story close to this very predicament on *Perry Mason*."

"Please tell me. You could save the day, Paralee."

"You don't say." Paralee drew herself up. Her silver hair was still tucked behind her ears, the way she wore it to Jemma and Spencer's wedding, but the rest looked like the curlers had evaporated while leaving every hair still coiled in place. She raised her Joan Crawford eyebrows. "I'll just look up the record of that transaction." H.D. harrumphed as she shooed him off her ledger. "Yesiree, Bob. . .here 'tis. Bonna June Lampkin, P.O. Box 42, Paducah, Texas. I don't suppose you need the zip, do you, hon?"

Jemma scribbled the address on a scrap of paper. "Thanks, Paralee. I owe you one." She was out the door before H.D. could blink.

Paralee made a soft noise at the back of her throat and checked her lipstick and hot pink rouge in the mirror. She drew her thumb and forefinger across the air in front of her. "Paralee Saves the Day," she said. "Nice headline."

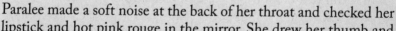

"Willa!" Jemma barrelled into her house without knocking. "Have you seen Gweny or Weese around today?"

"Sugar, what's wrong? I seen 'em yesterday. Gweny was over to the Dew Drop buyin' Fritos and Twinkies. Said they was headed off to see kinfolk. I didn't ask where."

"Gweny sent those quilts someplace else. Uncle Art never got them."

"Now why on earth would that child do such a thing? What's

gonna happen next?"

"I'll talk to Spencer. He'll know what to do."

Jemma started the Corvette and peeled out just like her husband. She rattled off the story to the office crew.

"Maybe she wants to undermine the business," Trent suggested.

"Or sell the quilts and keep the money herself," Sandy said.

Spencer rapped his knuckles on the desk. "This is a matter for the police. I'll call Sheriff Ezell."

"Are you sure you don't want to just *drive* down there?" Sandy snickered.

The sheriff arrived quickly, got all the information, and promised to call if he learned anything. Jemma could just picture him questioning all the women who had worked with Gweny. Maybe she should've handled this herself, with Leon's help. They'd made a good team before.

She waited at Lizbeth's for Spencer to get off work. They sat around the kitchenette as Lester tapped his foot, but with no windy tales on this evening. Helene kept them entertained with stories of her childhood in England. Chelsea and Vincent eyed one another through the window.

"Hot dog!" Lester said, interrupting Helene. "Bonna June. I know where I've heard that name before. She's the gal who was with Flavil Capp at his mama's funeral. I heard him call her Bonna June several times while the minister was talkin'."

Jemma kissed his cheek. "I'll call Sheriff Ezell right now. Lester, you've saved the day!"

Lester beamed. He hadn't saved the day in a good, long while.

◈

"I'm buying a bicycle," Spencer announced as they snuggled up in front of the fireplace. "That way I can get to work without bothering you, and I'll get a good workout as well. I came up with this idea in the pouting room. I seem to spend a lot of time there these days."

Jemma looked him in the eye. "Are you going to wear that leather outfit on your bicycle?"

"Maybe. It's supposed to protect you from road burns."

"Why won't you work here, at home? That was our plan, big boy."

"I know. It's just that I have to go in to the office sometimes."

"Aw, you'll get so cold in the winter."

He moved her hair away from her face. "I love you, Jem."

She smiled and kissed him just as the phone rang.

Spencer sighed and answered. "Hi, Simone."

Jemma rolled her eyes. What now? Another magazine story to get the ladies stirred up at Nedra's? They were probably having a field day already with his license suspension.

"It's for you." Spencer held the phone out to her.

"Hello," she said, then covered her mouth until the conversation was complete. Whereupon she squealed in delight and landed on her husband, knocking the breath out of him.

"I take it that you have good news."

"Simone wants to me to meet her brother in New York City next month to discuss a show at his gallery in London! Can you believe it? He owns a gallery in London. I have to get a slide presentation ready for my portfolio."

"I told you that something good might come out of that magazine fiasco. The Lord takes care of us."

Her mind was already working on the details. She took a breath and put those thoughts aside. "If you lose your license for a year, it could be you getting justice for breaking the speed limit all the time."

"Like you said, it's better than a trip in the ambulance. The Lord knows this is the only way to break my bad habit."

⁕

The phone was ringing when Spencer unlocked his office door. His chauffeur, Jemma, used her best secretarial tone as she answered.

"Chase and Lillygrace. May I help you?"

"Jemmabeth, Sheriff Ezell here. Could you come by my office within the hour? I need you to look at some photos."

"We'll be right there." They headed to the Connelly County jailhouse.

The sheriff laid several sheets of mugshots on his desk. "Look at these pictures, hon, and tell me if you recognize any of them."

It didn't take her long. "I sure do. This is Gweny Matthews and there's her brother, Weese Matthews. I don't recognize anybody else. You mean Gweny and Weese have been arrested? Did they find the quilts yet?"

The sheriff nodded and filled out a form for Jemma to sign. "I think we're on to somethin' bigger than quilt stealin', but I'm not at liberty to talk about it just yet. I'll be in touch."

❧

"What do you think he meant by 'something bigger than quilt stealing'?" Jemma asked as they left.

"You got me. That Weese looked like a surly character. Didn't you tell me that he had a confrontation with you?"

"It wasn't bad. He believed that I was to blame for all his misery. Speaking of misery, Trina and Nick are running low on funds right now. Neither of them have a job yet."

"I'll get a check right out to them. I wonder if he's tried at the Golden Triangle Hospital in Amarillo? I'll mention it in my note. You and I need to go by the nursing home and make a final inspection of the living quarters for Philip and Carrie, then I have to get to work on other projects. Could you help me move some of my files out to the house?"

Jemma threw her arms around his neck. "I can't wait!"

❧

Spencer took slides of her paintings with his fancy camera; then she wrote artist's comments for all twenty-five. She was ready for Simone and her brother. To see Spencer across the studio from her, his head bent industriously over blueprints and to hear his gentle voice on the phone with clients, warmed her heart. This was all she needed to be happy. To those nosy few who continued to inquire about "starting a family," she flashed a polite smile.

They had just started breakfast when the doorbell rang. Sheriff Ezell rubbed his hands together, then tipped his cowboy hat. "Mornin', folks. Hope I'm not disturbin' you, but I figgered you'd want to know about your quilts."

"Did you bring them?" Jemma asked. "Come on in."

The sheriff took off his hat. "Well, you probably aren't gonna see those quilts for a while. They're in the evidence room down in Childress, hon."

Jemma looked to Spencer for help.

"What was the official charge?" Spencer asked.

"Theft, burglary, destruction of property, and possession of stolen money. It appears that your quilts were used to transport over eight thousand dollars to Flavil Capp's girlfriend down in Paducah."

The Chases were dumbfounded.

"The girlfriend broke down and told the whole story. The sheriff down there said that the brother and sister duo never opened their traps. They arrested the whole bunch and Flavil's girlfriend started talkin' fast. 'Course they're all in jail now."

"How did they manage such a thing?" Spencer asked.

"Apparently, Flavil and the Matthews boy burglarized several businesses a couple of years back and stole the money. Flavil got busted for somethin' else, and the Matthews kid was scared stiff and hid the money in old plastic bags from the dry cleaners. Then he snuck around and stuffed the plastic into the dirt around the edges of old Shy Tomlinson's truck garden. Shy never digs around the sides, you know. Anyway, the kid got arrested at the time, but there was no evidence. A judge in Amarillo sort of sent him off to Vietnam. When Flavil got out, they came up with this plan to sew the money in the quilt bindin's and send them to Flavil's girlfriend. Crazy, huh?"

Jemma shuddered. "What am I going to tell the women?"

"Tell 'em there was a criminal in their midst." Sheriff Ezell put on his hat. "Well, there it is. I'm sure sorry about keepin' the quilts for evidence, but we need to throw the book at these turkeys. I'll talk to the district attorney and see if he can do anything, but I'm afraid you'd best get your crew up and sewin' again. By the way, I think it's a good thing that you're doin' across the tracks. Farmin' is changin'. Everything's goin' big agribusiness with more machines and less people. Coloreds are gonna be hurtin' just like whites. Maybe then folks will feel more like we're all in this mess together."

"Why didn't they just take the boxes to Paducah themselves?" Jemma asked, still in shock.

"The girl said she thought that the postal service was a cinch as a hidin' place. 'Course they don't know Paralee Batson too well, either. She never misses a thing."

"Thanks for coming out," Spencer said, shaking the sheriff's hand. They watched the patrol car head down the lane.

Jemma plopped on the sofa. "Rats. All that work for nothing. Those ladies probably won't even be interested after this."

"You might be surprised, baby. They may want to overcome such a mean setback."

"I'd better call Uncle Art. He's going to give up on this project. Maybe the Lord doesn't like this idea, and that's why He let this happen."

"Have faith, Jem."

"I'm trying."

❧

The Bethel Negro Church had a special prayer circle about the quilt trouble. Brother Cleo delivered a stern sermon about fool's gold and the real thing. He quoted from First Corinthians 3:13: "It shall be revealed by fire; and the fire shall try every man's work of what sort it is." Brother Cleo adapted the verse to Gweny, without mentioning her name. He admonished the congregation, the majority of whom had never seen gold of either kind, that when fool's gold is given the test of fire, it stinks and smokes, but when real gold is put to the test, it stands strong. Jemma had never heard him quite so peeved. It had to be because Gweny did the deed in the basement of the church and the whole story filled the front page for two issues of the *Chillaton Star*. After the prayer circle, Brother Cleo gave Jemma a sturdy hug and assured her that the Lord would prevail.

Willa took off her hat on the front steps and fanned herself. "I should've known that pickle-headed Weese was up to no good. I think my old heart was hopin' that he was headin' down a better road this time. Now he's in cahoots with his little sister to boot. I bit the bullet about that young'un so much that now I'm about ready for a new set of teeth."

❧

Arthur requested, on the basis of the quilt she'd already sent, that they try to fill the order for twenty-four. His point was that he'd already had interest from their advance marketing campaign and could sell the quilts quickly. Jemma called a meeting of the quilters. Everybody knew about Gweny and the money.

"Ain't nobody gonna quilt any faster than we did the first time around. Now Gweny's gone, and she had the quickest needle,"

Bertie Shanks lamented.

"You gonna have to get us more help," Grandma Hardy scolded Jemma. "My old bones ain't workin' too well like it is."

"They'd work a whole lot better if you didn't have to take a spit every five minutes," Shiloh said, straight to her face.

"You hush. You ain't too big to whup, girl," Grandma Hardy shouted, then spat extra loud.

"Now everybody just hold it," Willa ordered. "I'm still in charge of this here business. Sure, we need help, but where are we gonna get it? We don't want Amarillo folks comin' down. Let 'em start their own business. We already got Red Mule and Pleasant drivin' over, and that's okay 'cause they go to church here. Who's got an idea?"

Not one hand went up.

"I have an idea," Jemma said quietly. All heads turned. "My grandmother is a quilter. She has volunteered to work here or at her home to help meet the deadline. I don't know how you feel about a white woman working with you, but she has offered. She will not take any money for herself, though. She wants you to know that."

Willa cleared her throat. "I have to speak up about this. Lizbeth Forrester is just about my best friend, and there's no finer woman on either side of them tracks. When she makes a quilt, it comes straight from her heart. I know this notion may not set well with some of you, but I'm all for it. The Lord knows that we need help to make up for Gweny's mess, and Miz Liz is just the ticket."

Someone coughed and Grandma Hardy made another audible deposit in her can.

Teeky Samson stood. "I say that if somebody's willin' and ain't hopin' for no money, we let 'em get with it. I spent too much time ridin' back and forth from Red Mule to let this drop."

"I'm for it," Bertie said.

Willa gave Jemma the nod. "Let's vote on it. All those in favor of takin' on help, no matter what the skin color, raise your hand."

"Just so long as they ain't interested in the purse," Grandma Hardy added.

The vote passed unanimously.

❧

Word spread quickly about Flavil's misdeed and about the fate of the quilts. To Jemma's surprise, Brother Hightower rang their doorbell early one morning. Spencer had taken off on his new bicycle, and she wasn't even completely dressed. She threw on a pair of jeans to let him in.

"Mrs. Chase, how are you?" he asked, choosing to remain on the porch. His thin frame seemed even more fragile away from his pulpit. He had never looked like the picture of health anyway. He was what Papa called "pasty-faced."

"What brings you way out here? Is anything the matter in town?" Jemma asked, somewhat concerned.

"Oh, nothing like that." He fumbled for words. "I, ah, we, heard about the unfortunate business with your efforts across the tracks. The thing is that we, I, would like to help."

"I didn't know that Mrs. Hightower was a quilter. How nice of her."

"That's not exactly what I meant." He exhaled. "When I was a little boy, my grandmother taught me to quilt, knit, and embroider. I was an only child, you know, and she doted on me. I still enjoy all those activities. I've made several nice quilts over the years."

Jemma gulped. Not only had she misspoken, but she'd misjudged the reverend's talents, taking him for a pompous male chauvinist. "Brother Hightower, we'd be delighted to have your help. Gram is working already. Maybe you'd like to join her at the Bethel Church."

"I don't want to intrude, but I would like to help. Could you go with me, perhaps to ease the introductions?"

"Let me change clothes, and I'll meet you there in thirty minutes. Thank you so much." She watched him get into his car and drive away. She smiled. The Lord did work in mysterious ways, indeed.

The addition of Brother Hightower to the group proved to open a door for several members of the North and South Chillaton Quilting Clubs to assist as well. The initial discomfort was replaced by polite conversation, and then, gradually, to commingled laughter. Jemmabeth could not have been more delighted. This had to be

God's plan. She stayed up half of one night painting the scene she'd witnessed for several days at the church. She left Brother Hightower out, though, so he wouldn't be a curious focal point in the painting. The message was revealed in the gentle portrayal of eyes that observed one another with fresh hope and cautious acceptance.

⋘⋙

Jemma concentrated on typing her last artist's statement on Gram's kitchenette. Her old portable needed a new ribbon. She didn't even notice that she had company.

"Hey, girl, what are you doing?" her guest inquired.

"Trina! I'm so glad to see you. What's going on? Where's Nick?"

"He's in Amarillo for interviews at the hospitals. I'm here to quilt. Are you heading to the church soon?"

"Yeah, Helene is baking cookies for everybody. It's great to see you looking so happy."

"You too," Trina said. "I'll talk to you later. Wait, you aren't pregnant, are you?"

Jemma shook her head. "Just happy. How about you?"

"No way, but I'm happy all right. I decided not to worry about jobs as much as Nick does. Maybe he'll get this one in Amarillo. The Lord will bless us with something. Thanks a lot, girl, for the loan. Maybe we'll end up being y'all's maid and butler so we can pay you back."

"Get out of here and go quilt. I'll be over in a minute."

Jemma watched as Trina walked through the hollyhock patch and up to the tracks. It would be a long time before she'd be able to rid herself completely of the shame of never knowing Trina and Willa all those years they had been separated by those tracks. That guilt might never go away.

⋘⋙

They met the deadline, such as it was, set by Arthur. There were six big boxes, taken personally by the whole group, to the post office. Paralee doused her cigarette and recorded each one in her ledger. Jemma even took pictures for the *Star*.

"You put us over the hump, Trina. Thanks for your help," Jemma said as they sat in the empty church.

"I hope this works. If not, then you take some consolation in the fact that you gave it your all. Don't look at it like that basketball game you lost at state, okay?" Trina said. "This project has lifted everybody's spirits and opened hearts and minds."

Jemma reached for her hand. "You're gonna make me cry, but I think this will work. I have faith that the Lord wants it to." She exhaled. "Have you heard from Nick yet?"

"Nope. This is the first time anybody's asked him to come back, though. That has to mean something."

"How about you—any nibbles with your design portfolio?" Jemma asked.

"Aw, I might as well be trying to make it in the NBA. Fashion designers must be a starving lot."

"Have faith. That's what Spencer keeps telling me. Look how this little idea turned out. I just hope they sell all those quilts."

Trina smiled. "They will. What fun to see Gram's friends laughing and eating cookies with Mama's neighbors. Who would have thought it?"

"I know. Carrie and Philip move into the nursing home next week. It would be perfect if y'all moved to Amarillo. Things would just be too good. Have you spent much time with Helene?"

"No, but she's cooking supper for everybody tonight. Lester has his eye on her, doesn't he?" Trina asked.

"Yeah, but she's just a friend, I think," Jemma said.

"Hmm. I believe Lester hopes otherwise."

⁂

"A toast," Spencer announced. "To the newest member of the Golden Triangle Hospital."

If Nick had grinned any wider, his teeth would have fallen right out. "Thanks," he said, drinking his sweet tea. "It's been a lengthy haul."

"We're all proud of you, son," Joe said. "I can't wait to make an appointment. I've got a list a mile long of ailments."

"I won't be taking appointments," Nick clarified. "I'm part of the emergency room staff. You'll have to be in really bad shape to see me."

"Helene, the meal was delicious," Jemma told her. "I'll have to run an extra mile tomorrow to get rid of the calories."

"You look perfect," Spencer whispered in her ear. "Let's go home."

Lizbeth watched them and smiled. It had been such a peaceful night among family and friends. She only wished the rest of her family could be there because she could have no better feeling than to gather all her loved ones under the same roof.

Lester cleared his throat. "I thought me and Joe could entertain for a spell. It's been a while since we tuned up together."

"I like that idea," Helene said. "I'll just tidy up in here first."

"We'll take care of that, Helene." Jemma volunteered. "You go on and enjoy the show."

"Meet me in the pouting room in ten minutes," Spencer said in her ear. His breath tickled her neck, and she raised her shoulder, giving him the eye. He went right to work on the dishes.

"I'll help clean up, too," Trina said.

"No, that's okay." Jemma nodded in Spencer's direction. Trina got the hint and moved into the living room with the others.

"What are you doing?" Jemma asked, closing the creaky door in the pouting room at the appointed time.

Spencer pulled her to him in the dark. "During supper, I was thinking about the time when we were hiding in here and your parents came in the kitchen. Let's try that again."

"You're my kind of man." Jemma attacked him like they were alone in the house. "What do you think about that?" she asked, coming up for air.

"I think we'd better leave right now, or I'm not responsible for the outcome."

She giggled. "I'm not scared. Everybody's listening to the music, and besides, we're married now."

"Okay, woman, you asked for it."

She would never again look at the pouting room quite the same.

❧

"Shy!" Jemma yelled across the street. "I want you to see a photo of your portrait. I'm on my way to New York right now to show it to a gallery owner."

"You don't say? I always wanted to see them skyscrapers. Take a long look at 'em for me, would you?" Shy grinned, showing a wide expanse of gums.

Jemma opened her portfolio on the hood of his truck. "There. What do you think?"

"Well, I'll be Uncle Johnny. That beats all I ever saw. You've got yourself a real knack, Jemmerbeth. Them folks in New York don't know what they're in for."

"Thanks, Shy. That was some surprise about those people hiding that money in your dirt."

"Yes ma'am, them newspapers are wantin' to take pictures already." He pushed his hat back and scratched his head. "It makes me look even more foolish, drivin' around with my garden and eight thousand dollars underneath it."

"Nobody thinks that, Shy. It just makes your truck a landmark, that's all. When I get back from this trip, Spencer and I want to take you out to supper or you could come to our house."

"Thank you, hon. I'll have to clean up real good to go back to your place. Did you tell Spencer I was sure impressed?"

"I did. I have to go now, but we'll be getting in touch with you soon."

❧

"This is pathetic," Spencer said. "I can't even drive my wife to the airport."

"Yeah, but if you were driving, I couldn't do this." She kissed him.

"None of that." Sandy adjusted the rearview mirror. "I don't want any distractions in my chauffeuring duties."

"Get over it," Spencer replied and paid Jemma back.

"I thought you said you would never let me go off alone again."

"Sorry, Jem. I just have to get caught up. I didn't dream that Trent and I would be so busy this early in our career. I think this trip is quick enough so there won't be any trouble, especially with you-know-who."

"I think Helene had a talk with him."

"Really. It must have worked; at least we can hope so. Call me when you get there."

"I will. Don't let Sandy get to you on the way home. Bye, babe."

Sandy waited while he stood beside the car, waving at the plane as it rose into the clouds. Spencer Chase was the most handsome and the sweetest man she'd ever known. Her serious attention however, was on someone else—someone cute and sweet, too. Maybe he wasn't as perfect as Spence, but he was more than able to steal her heart away. She smiled at the thought of Trenton Lillygrace.

Chapter 23

Test by Fire

A h, Mrs. Chase," Simone said. "This is my brother, Jonathan Essex. Jon, this is Jemmabeth Chase."

Jonathan Essex stood eye to eye with Jemma. He wore a black turtleneck like the one Spencer had on when she kissed him good-bye at the airport. She offered her hand and he acquiesced to shake it, to her relief, rather than kiss it. He had dimples; that was the second thing she noticed. He also had a great smile and black hair, like Simone, and eyes like two perfect turquoise stones.

"My sister has been relentless in her efforts to get us together. I must say things look good thus far," he said, raising an approving brow toward Simone.

Jemma smiled politely. "I have my portfolio. Would you like to see the prints or the slides?"

"Right to business, I see," Jonathan quipped. "Let's move down to Simone's viewing room and see what you have, shall we?"

"I'll leave you to it then," Simone said. "Do give Spencer my best." She turned to a cluster of assistants who were waiting for her in the hallway. At least she didn't call him *Spence* this time.

Jonathan pressed the button on the elevator. "So, you're from cowboy country? I've never been to Texas. We've shipped pieces to Houston, I believe. Do you live near there?"

"No. I live at the top of the state. It's an area we call The Panhandle."

"Quaint. Here we are. After you, Jemmabeth." He touched her waist as they walked down another corridor. "Is Chase your maiden name?"

"No, my maiden name was Forrester."

He stopped. "I saw your work in Paris. You were the Girard Fellow, were you not?"

"I was. How nice of you to remember."

He opened the door to a room with a large screen and seats much nicer than the Parnell. "A Girard Fellow. Now I truly am excited to see what you've brought. Please, sit anywhere." He loaded the slides into the projector, then dimmed the lights and turned his turquoise eyes on her.

The images of her work flashed before them. Jemma relived each brushstroke. Jonathan didn't speak until the final piece was on the screen. It was of Grandma Hardy in the church pew.

"Exquisite, darling, simple perfection. You have such a way with eyes. I assume you have heard that before, but I am very impressed. You must show at my gallery. Is this your complete portfolio, or is there more? Don't hide anything from me, because I want it all."

"I have a few other pieces in our private collection, but they will not be offered under any circumstances. I learned that lesson the hard way. What time frame are you considering? If I have a few months, I'll have more pieces. I'm a prolific painter."

He studied her face. "Of course you are, darling. I am on holiday next week in Greece; then we are booked solid until the spring. I might be able to shift things around a bit. What would you say to an April date? Our showings are six weeks in duration and the gallery retains fifty percent of the sales."

"Fifty percent? How do you determine the pricing?"

"You set your price, and we double it. Fair?"

"Sure, if you can get it."

"We can. I assure you. Your work is splendid. Don't be shy about pricing it because it will be irresistible to our clientele." He stood close enough to make her uncomfortable.

Neither spoke for a few seconds. Jemma frowned at the carpet. He massaged his chin.

"Where are you staying tonight?" he asked. "I could ring you up later, and we can meet for drinks to discuss things further. Shall I?"

"I've forgotten the name of the hotel, and I don't drink anyway. I don't even know the name of your gallery."

Jonathan was nonplussed. "You don't drink? Curious trait. My gallery is known as The Lex, short for The Lexington, on Regent Street. Do you know it?"

"No, but I'm sure my grandfather does. He is an art connoisseur."

"Oh, and what is his name?"

"Robert Lillygrace. He owns several newspapers in the Midwest."

"That name does sound familiar, and is he a non-drinker as well?"

Jemma giggled at that. "No, I think he is also a connoisseur of fine wines."

"Perhaps we could meet regardless of the devil's nectar, then. Say, nine-ish?"

She flushed at those familiar words. "Why don't you give me your number and I'll call you?"

"I'm in and out, best let me do the calling. Surely you have your hotel name written somewhere, darling."

"It's The Madison."

"Ah. So you were toying with me earlier."

She blushed, full-blown. "I don't like to give out personal information."

"I see. I'd like to keep the slides for a while, if you don't mind."

"That's fine. I have two sets."

"Until later, then, Jemma." He gave her an admiring glance, then turned back to the slides.

She took a cab to The Madison, staring blankly out the window. She hadn't been attracted to any man since Spencer walked up to Gram's door that summer after Paul. She wasn't attracted to Jonathan, but something nagged at her. Mention of the *devil's nectar* brought up her beginnings with Paul, and she hadn't been able to really look this guy in the eye to see if he was honest. She paid the driver and checked in to her room. Spencer had booked it for her. He had stayed there on his last trip to New York.

She kneeled beside her bed and prayed for an angel to follow her around on this trip. What did happen with Jonathan? Rats. It had to be the devil, or maybe it was the turtleneck like Spence's. Not a single wrestling idea had come up during this meeting with Jonathan, and something about his eyes had gotten to her, too. There was no need to meet with him anymore on this trip. She sat on the couch and stared at the phone.

She picked it up and dialed the long-distance operator. The maid answered. "Lillygrace residence."

"Hi, Margaret, it's Jemmabeth. Is my grandfather there?"

"Certainly, Mrs. Chase. One moment."

Robert Lillygrace picked up the phone. "Jemmabeth, where are you?"

"I'm in New York City at The Madison Hotel. How are you and Grandmother?"

"Fine, fine. How's Spencer?"

"He's great. I need to know something, Grandfather."

"Of course. How can I help?"

"Are you familiar with a gallery in London called The Lexington?"

"The Lex? Oh yes. It's a fine gallery. Why do you ask?"

She exhaled. "I may have a show there next spring."

"What marvelous news, Jemmabeth! Catherine is out at the moment, but she will be thrilled to hear about this."

They visited for a while, and then said their good-byes. Jemma was getting a stomachache anyway. She would have to answer if he called. It meant a show in London. This was silly. She was not attracted to him.

She got out her New Testament and read some scriptures. Maybe this was her test by fire. What was the deal with Jonathan calling her "darling"? She was nobody's darling but Spence's. Of course Paul called her darlin' with every other breath, and he had the same black hair and devil eyes. A therapist would most likely have a name for this.

She took a shower and put on her cowboy pajamas that her mom had sent. Spencer would call before he went to bed. This would be a touchy matter to share with him. Double rats. She bit her lip and turned on the television. A knock at the door made her jump.

"Who is it?" she shouted from the couch.

"Jonathan Essex. I thought you might like some company, darling."

"No. I'm waiting for my husband to call me, I'm not feeling well, and I'm ready for bed."

"Which of those would hamper my visit?"

"All of them."

"Too bad. I was hoping we could talk about your work."

"Thanks anyway, but I am really looking forward to the show."

"As am I, but I do feel rather foolish talking through the door like this."

She picked up her New Testament and walked to the door.

"Good night, Jonathan," she said, her eye wide open at the peephole.

"You have such lovely, golden eyes, Jemma. I don't know what to make of it, but I am very much attracted to you."

"Oh." She stepped back.

"I sensed that the feeling was mutual."

"Well, you must have misinterpreted something, because I'm very much in love with my husband."

"I see. Are you certain that we couldn't just chat for a while? Go over some things about the show?"

"Like I said, I'm not feeling too hot. You can call me when I get home, though. My number is on all the slides."

"Very well." He stood for a moment, mumbled, "Feel better, Mrs. Chase," and left.

She returned to the couch with an overwhelming desire to talk to Spence. As she reached for the phone, it rang. "Spence!" she squealed into the mouthpiece.

"No, dear, it's your Grandmother Lillygrace. I wanted to offer my congratulations on your London show. What a wonderful opportunity."

"Thank you, Grandmother. It's sweet of you to call."

"Does Alexandra know yet?"

"She knows that I'm in New York to talk about it."

"I won't keep you, Jemmabeth, but we are very excited and proud of you. We shall not miss it, and we'll make certain your mother doesn't either."

"I'm sure Daddy would love to come, too."

"Well, of course. We'll make a party of it. Sweet dreams, dear."

"Good night, Grandmother."

"One more thing, Jemma. I would keep my eye on that gallery owner, Jonathan something-or-other. He's a notorious ladies' man, very nice-looking and smooth. That's an established fact around London. The last time Robert and I visited The Rex, he tried to seduce me. A friend of ours told us that Jonathan has specially made contact lenses from Germany, and he wears a different colored pair every day. Now, that's the devil's doings if you ask me. Good night, dear."

Jemma hung up the phone and burst into laughter. The idea of Catherine Lillygrace being hit on by Jonathan was too much. She wondered what color his eyes had been on that night. When Spencer called, she told him everything. It took him a minute to get over it, but, after all, he had his chance to come with her. She wasn't keeping anything from him ever again. Unless, perhaps, she got a speeding ticket. Fair's fair.

⋘⋙

Spencer pulled onto the county road right as the sun came up. Papa's old windmill stood silhouetted against the horizon. He was pedaling right along until he came up behind a combine moving at about two miles an hour. He passed the combine at the wrong spot. Its big wheels splashed pothole mud directly in his face and on his slacks.

"All English art dealers are out to get my wife," Spencer said into the wind as he rode his bike toward town. He wiped his face and pedaled faster. A school bus splashed more mud, and the kids in the back seats stuck their tongues out at him. It would be the pits if he lost his license for a whole year. It served him right, speeding and endangering lives.

At least he could be home more with her, and that part delighted him. What if someday a guy put a move on her and she liked it? No, that could never happen. Jemmabeth was true blue since Cowboy Paul. He and Paul were like characters in an old novel, both in love with the same woman. He hoped the day would come when he didn't worry about the cowboy and his past with Jem. She hadn't told him all the details of their relationship, but maybe that was for the best. If he knew them, he might not feel halfway sorry for the guy. Skinny Jack passed him, too, honking and laughing. The pits.

⋘⋙

Lester and the ladies were enjoying mid-morning coffee and conversation, but Lester had something on his mind. "Roy Bob Sisk told me he saw Spencer riding his bicycle into town early this morning. He said he looked like the old schoolteacher in that Judy Garland rainbow movie. Roy Bob swears that Spencer had been in a mud-wrestling match. I just don't think that boy should have to ride a bike like a young'un for a whole cotton-pickin' year."

"I suppose the law must be equal for everyone," Helene said. "Perhaps the judge will be lenient. You know, in Germany, the autobahn has no speed limit. Drivers may go as fast as their cars will take them. My Nebs frightened the wits out of me every time we went there."

Lester smoothed his moustache. "Looks like the judge could take into consideration that Spencer was in that war and got shot down. It just don't seem right, but far be it from me to tell a judge what to do. Maybe if Judge McFarland was in charge, he'd have mercy on such a fine young man. One of them tickets Spencer got was in Los Angeleez. I didn't know they even had any laws in that town."

"Jemmabeth thinks this will change Spencer's bad habit of speeding. We surely don't want him to wind up having a wreck," Lizbeth said.

"Well, sir, the more I think about it, I should help that boy out." Lester tapped his foot relentlessly while the women exchanged glances.

Lizbeth proceeded with caution. "No one is stopping you, Lester, but we are curious as to what you have in mind."

"You'll see. I ain't tellin' until I get my thoughts collected."

"I admire a man who acts on his convictions. Bully for you, Lester." Helene raised her teacup in his direction.

Lizbeth raised her brow.

❧

"So, did you miss me?" Jemma asked, sitting on Spencer's desk, blowing bubbles with her gum.

"Nah. I think it's good for us to be apart. It refreshes the senses," he answered, concentrating on his slide rule.

"Really? Which sense is that?" She poked at his leg with her foot. "Good grief, your pants look like you've been playing football in them."

He sighed. "I'm going to have to wear old clothes into town and change when I get here. These slacks are ruined."

"Which senses are refreshed when I leave?" She popped a big bubble.

"My common sense. I consistently send you off into the arms of other men. That has to change because it's driving me nuts."

She grinned. "Very good answer. I wasn't sure where you were going with that." She moved to his lap. "Are there any senses that need refreshing now that I'm home?"

He dropped his pencil and turned his full attention on his wife until Sandy knocked on the door.

"Hello in there. Anybody want to go with us to Son's?" she asked.

Jemma and Spencer separated. "No ma'am, we're heading home right now." He smiled at his wife.

"Thanks anyway," Jemma said. "Ya'll have fun."

Sandy and Trent left. He had his arm around her.

Jemma watched them get in his car. "I think it's a done deal. What do you think?"

"I think I'll lock this door and drag you back into my office," Spencer said.

"No dragging required, mister."

❧

Lester had his plan. He wrote it all out and got Paralee to type it up for him. She swore to secrecy and made him several carbon copies, too. The easy way would be to leave them around town at the barbershop and Nedra's, but he was going to do this thing right. He was going door-to-door and pledging folks to secrecy. He should be done by Christmas.

❧

Carrie and Philip sat in The Judge's study. Carrie winked at her husband while The Judge rummaged through his desk. "I'm very pleased that you're going to be living in Chillaton. I want you to know that," The Judge said.

"Well, that's good to hear, Dad. What kind of father would you be if you weren't happy to have us here?" Carrie hadn't lost any of her sassiness since she'd left home. "It looks like you've lost weight. We need to get you some new slacks because those could fall down anytime, and what would happen in the courtroom then?"

The Judge looked up at such talk. Nobody spoke back to him like that. At least not in his chambers. "Yes, well, I have been cutting back on a few things. I hope we'll be seeing quite a lot of one another, so you might like to have an extra key to the house. Eleanor has one, but I know that there is one in here somewhere. Ah, here it is."

Philip took the key and examined it. "It's too bad that you were burglarized last month. Maybe it's time you invested in an upgraded security system. Not many people use skeleton keys anymore."

"I'm well aware of that, Philip. Fortunately, the thief didn't get far with the silver. He probably thought a more prosperous man than myself lived here."

"We've thought it over about your offer to move in here, sir, and. . ."

Carrie finished Philip's sentence for him. "We need our own place, Dad. It'll be important for Phil to be right at the nursing home to keep it running smoothly."

The Judge shifted his bulk in the chair. "I hardly think a two-minute drive would impede such a goal."

Carrie smiled. "We'll see. It might work out later. We may get tired of living and working at the same place."

"You're afraid I'll try to run the show around here, aren't you?"

Philip glanced at his wife. "It's nothing like that, sir. We're still sort of newlyweds, you know. We like being alone."

Carrie rallied. "I think your assessment is right on target, Dad. Let's be honest. You've lived here forever, and I was cooped up in this house for longer than I should have been. I love you, but I don't want to live here anymore. We'll see you a lot. It'll be okay."

The room was quiet; then The Judge pushed back from his chair. "I guess that settles that. I've given Eleanor the evening off. I'm hoping you'll join me at this new restaurant we have in town—Son's Money, I believe it's called."

Carrie laughed. "Correction—*Daddy's Money*. Are you sure you want to eat out? In my whole life, I don't remember ever eating out with you until our wedding reception."

"You may be surprised at your old dad, young lady. I'm out to show you two that there's life in this old boy yet. If Max can stop chasing skirts, I can change my ways, too. Max Chase and I are old poker buddies, Philip. Maybe you'd like to join us sometime."

The two men considered that unexpected offer for a moment. Carrie, not exactly sure what to make of this newfound friendliness in her father, maneuvered her walker between them and down the ramp to their van. She looked around at her father's grand old home. It was a sorry sight. Maybe together, the three of them could resuscitate it. After all, it had seen very little joy in the past twenty years. It was time for a change.

⁂

"Ver gonna haf to make ush a big cawendar, Shhpence."

"What did you say?"

She took the paintbrush out of her mouth and repeated it. "I can't keep up with your projects, and I feel like I'm the last one to know your schedule. Our life is all chopped up into puzzle pieces, so maybe a big planning calendar might help."

He nodded. "Part of it is that I have to depend on everybody else to get me around. You know what I need? A helicopter. I could fly us to every business meeting, with refueling stops, of course. This is a great idea, baby, because I can go places with you. What do you think?"

Jemma had stepped back from her painting to check it out. She looked at him like a scolding mother in church. "Oh great. You get your license taken away for going 90 miles an hour on a dumb motorcycle, then you tell me you want to park a helicopter outside our door so you can be a pilot again and worry me to death that you'll crash somewhere. Where would you park it in town? On the football field?"

"Listen, Jem, this is not all that crazy. If I had a chopper, we could quit messing around with airports and travel arrangements."

"How much does a helicopter cost anyway?"

"I don't know. A couple hundred thousand, maybe more."

She dropped her brush.

"Of course one that size wouldn't have a very wide flight range. Maybe three hours. We could get to Dallas."

"What for?"

"Okay. Forget that idea. I'm stuck with the bicycle and the

kindness of friends and family. I need to just shut up and take my medicine."

"Good. No more transportation creativity. Get to work. Rats. I forgot to call Robby. His flight gets in at eight o'clock. We'll need to leave about six thirty. I'll set the timer on the oven."

"If I had a chopper, we could be there in twenty minutes."

"If you had a driver's license, you could pick him up yourself, and I could finish this piece."

"Speaking of licenses, they passed a new law, and Phil is going to have to pass a nursing home administrator's exam. Hopefully, we'll have the state inspection done about the same time." He watched her as she retouched an area on the canvas. The light that was so perfect for her work was also dancing in her hair. It bounced off cascades of dark auburn and gold, transforming her into a princess like those from the fairy-tale books Harriet had read him when he was a little boy.

She wiped some paint from her hand onto her jeans and turned to him. "What did you say?" Her pouty lips spread into a big smile.

"I said that I love you, Jemmabeth Alexandra Chase. Step into my office, and I'll explain my project dates to you." She walked across the room and kissed him.

❧

Lizbeth sat in the porch swing, moving it slightly. The air was full of early winter, and she was beginning her mental Christmas list. How much fun it was to share her home with Helene. Everything was lighter and happier, especially during Robby's visit. He had kept them laughing and hopping with his ideas. Robby was the image of her Luke. Lester loved that boy, as did Spencer. Spence was going to be a special father someday. Her constant prayer was that the Lord's plan could include her granddaughter bearing a child, if and when He was ready.

She clutched her sweater around her and considered the day ahead. Turkey and all the trimmings for thirteen people—fourteen if Judge McFarland decided to join them. Everything was easy, though. That was another bonus that came with Helene. She was a gourmet cook, but not pushy in the kitchen. She couldn't be; there wasn't enough room. All that was left to be done was bringing in the box of Helene's beautiful china dishes from Lester's shed. It would be a pleasure just to wash them. She stretched her arms and went inside. Only the presence of all her own menfolk could have made this Thanksgiving Day more than it promised to be.

Robby had taken over Plum Creek. For a twelve-year-old, he could certainly rule the roost, but it was a hilarious monarchy, partially due to the fact that his voice was changing. He had also lost his Texas accent, which made him seem somewhat like a different kid to them.

All was bright and shiny fun until Spencer rode his bike into town and Jemma was alone with Robby. She painted while he tried his hand at sketching on Spence's big table. She caught him staring at her, but then he shifted his gaze to the window.

"Jem, I need to ask you something."

"That's what I do best—answer hard questions." It sounded good at the time.

"Is the Bible against smoking?" he mumbled.

Oh great, a growing-up question. Rats. "Do you mean smoking a ham or a turkey?"

"I mean cigarettes."

"I think the Lord wants us to use the brains He gave us and take care of ourselves." Good one.

"Yeah, I know all that, but does it say in there somewhere not to smoke?"

She bit her lip. What happened to the cute little brother who wanted to buy a monkey? She could ruin his life with her answer. If she were walking right with God, He might drop a scripture into her brain right now. She stalled. "You tell me what's going on; then I'll tell you if I know what the Lord had to say about it."

Robby lowered his head. "When I get home, some of the guys are going to go to Kenny Hall's basement and smoke a pack of his big brother's cigarettes. I told them God wouldn't like it, but they said prove it."

The only scripture that popped into her head was the one about gold. She had no idea how to use it. "In the first book of Corinthians it says that everything we do will be tested by fire to see if what we did was good. So that means if you smoke, you stink, and if you stink, God's not happy." She kept her eyes right on his to add some credibility, hoping the Lord would approve of this translation to help out a woman trying to do the right thing.

"Cool. You're sure that what it says?"

"I said that's what it means." She blew out her breath and picked up her paintbrush.

"Jem, how do you think a cigarette tastes?"

"I wouldn't know, Robby, but I guess it would taste like smoke."

"What do you think a real gold nugget tastes like?" he asked, playing with the chain on his gold cross necklace.

She gave that some thought. "Probably all metal tastes bitter, but nobody cares what it tastes like. We like it because it's beautiful."

"Typical girl answer. I care what it tastes like. I bet the real thing tastes sweeter than fool's gold. Ricky Bates brought some fool's gold to church camp, and we busted it with a hammer. That was cool. I even tasted it."

"Do Daddy and Mom know about this smoking party?"

"No, and if they find out, I'll know who told them."

"You're getting a little smarty pants with me, sir."

"I'll be thirteen on my birthday." Robby shrugged and turned his attention back to his drafting project. "Right now, I'm still called a tweenager."

Jemma returned to her painting, grateful that she didn't have a tweenager to figure out on a daily basis.

Robby returned to his drawings for Shorty's jar. Even Shorty would probably notice a decided difference in the quality and the subject matter—race cars.

⁂

Lizbeth invited them to stop by for lunch on the way to the airport.

"Do you ever shut up, Robby?" Jemma asked as they reached the city limits. "If I didn't love you so much, I think I would put tape over your mouth at least once a day."

"I only speak pearls of wisdom," he said, straight-faced.

Spencer grinned. "Well, that's a matter of opinion. If you talk this much at Gram's house, Lester won't be able to get a word in sideways."

"I'll let the old boy talk. He's one of my heroes. He's got style."

Jemma smiled as she turned into their driveway. Lester would love to know that last bit of information. True to his word, Robby only talked half the time, swapping antics and moneymaking schemes with Lester. Everyone laughed and looked forward to Christmas vacation when they could all be together again. Jemma watched her brother; he was no longer the mischievous wart who teased her by reading her diary or the stinker who sold tickets to his friends to watch her sunbathe. Someday soon, he wouldn't consider the taste of gold anymore, but he would buy it for some special girl because it was beautiful. Rats.

Chapter 24
The Kindest Thing

Shy had Christmas lights strung on his blue spruce. Jemma waved at him as she waited for Spencer. The idea hit her hard. She ran into his office.

"I'm nearly done, baby. I promise," he said with a pencil tucked behind his ear and his attention on a blueprint.

"I have an idea."

"I don't think the quilting ladies can fill any more orders. Aren't they working overtime as it is?"

"This is not about quilts. It's about teeth. I want to get Shy some teeth."

Spencer stopped working and grinned at her. "You just kill me, Jem. Let's do it."

"I'll talk to him first. That's probably a wise move, but surely he'll like the idea," she said, then was out the door before he could agree.

Jemma caught up with Shy as he was leaving the hardware store and shocked him with her plan.

He swallowed to get shed of the big lump in his throat. "I ain't sure what to say, Jemmerbeth. I don't rightly know how to turn down such a offer, though. What would I do with a full set of choppers? I might have to change my eatin' habits."

"Then I can do it? Thank you, Shy. I'll get everything set up and let you know."

❦

Shy was stumped. He sat in his truck considering the possibilities of having teeth. Imagine her thinking of such a thing. He looked in his rearview mirror and moved his lips apart. It would be nice to eat corn on the cob again and maybe some store-bought peanut brittle like he'd seen at the five-and-dime. It'd be a fine thing, too, if one of the front ones was gold. Might improve the taste of his cooking somewhat. That child sure was a lot like her grandpa. It was Cam Forrester that gave him the money for his tools to get started in the fix-it business. If Spencer and Jemmerbeth ever needed anything fixed, he'd do it for free until the day he passed, that was for certain sure.

⋘❧⋙

Willa and Joe held hands as they walked across the tracks to Lizbeth's house. Each carried a grocery sack with pans of Willa's cobbler in them. Joe stopped just as they got to the alley. "Lovey, I don't know why the Lord has blessed me like He has, but I want to tell you how much you mean to me. I think about my ol' lonesome life sometimes, and it gives me the shivers to think that you were sittin' right here in Chillaton all them times I drove my rig through here. I just wish we could've been together all them years."

She patted his arm. "Could be the Lord knew that I'd have to touch Sam's grave marker across the ocean before I could let him go and tuck them memories away in a corner of this ol' heart. Now I got all this room for lovin' you, Joe Cross. Bend down here and give me a kiss. No disrespect to Trina's daddy, but you're the best kisser I ever laid a lip on." They set the sacks on the frozen ground and spent a few extra minutes behind Lizbeth's garage before joining the Christmas festivities that lit up her house with food, laughter, music, and love.

⋘❧⋙

Spencer and Trent spent hours at their office with Arthur. There were numerous details to wrap up before construction began in January. Sandy was there every time they were, taking notes and smiling at Trent. When they joined everyone else at Lizbeth's, he introduced her to his dad and his Lillygrace grandparents as his girlfriend. Sandy was not exactly what Robert and Catherine had in mind for their grandson.

"Do you have plans for furthering your education, dear?" Catherine asked.

"I'm thinking of taking some classes at Amarillo Junior College to learn more about computers. The guys want me to bone up on that stuff."

"Oh, I see, and what does your father do?"

"He owns Household Supply. They sell furniture, flooring, and appliances."

"A businessman. That's good," Robert said. "Are you and our Trenton 'serious,' as they say?"

Sandy actually blushed, something Jemma had never seen her do. "You'll have to ask your grandson about that," she said and excused herself to say hello to Carrie.

"Jemma, come and sit by me. We need to talk," Julia said. "The quilts went like hotcakes and honey during the holidays. My idea now is to add some baby quilts and wedding ring patterns. Those will sell during the spring. Of course, babies come all year round, so that should become a staple. How are your business partners holding up?"

"Amazingly well. They had a meeting last week to talk about expanding to a real location. You know Spence and I bought some land just down the tracks. They even named their business—*Stitchers*. There was some hot debate about the name, but I like it. To me, it's a metaphor for stitching hope back into their neighborhood. Corny, huh?"

"Not at all. How's Spencer taking this speeding ticket business? Lizbeth told me that he could lose his license for a year. That has to hurt a busy man like him."

"It does hurt, but he's willing to take it. His court date is next week. He's so sweet. I'll never get used to being his wife, Do Dah. Sometimes I feel like I'm going to pop with happiness."

Julia patted her hand and looked across the room at Arthur. He puffed on his pipe and laughed at a joke that Max Chase was telling. She knew about popping with happiness; it could last a long, long time.

"Lester, where have you been? Joe's been itching to get started. Willa's been leading the Christmas carols a cappella," Lizbeth scolded.

"I had me some business to take care of, but I'm set to entertain now. If I could just have a cup of coffee to warm up and maybe a piece of your pecan pie, Miz Liz."

Lizbeth cut him a healthy piece and set a steaming cup of coffee in front of him, then put her hands on her hips and gave him a good stare. "What's going on? I know you too well. Out with it."

Lester's eyes darted up at her. Her lips were puckered.

"I'd like to keep it kindly quiet, Miz Liz. If you'll step out to the porch with me, I'll let you in on it."

Lizbeth stepped briskly to the screened-in porch ahead of him.

"Well, sir, it's about my idea to help Spencer out when he goes before the judge in Amarillo," Lester said. "I reckon I've been in every house in Chillaton since September. I feel like one of them traveling salesmen."

"Lester, what have you done?"

He drew a sheet of paper out of his jacket and offered it to her. "If you're of a mind to sign this, Miz Liz, you'll be number 2,035 to sign a petition that I'm sending to the judge before he makes up his mind about Spencer's license."

Lizbeth read the petition then scanned the signatures until her glasses fogged over. She put her arms around him, without asking. He stood perfectly still and held his breath. She pulled away and wiped her cheek. "You are a dear, dear man, Lester Timms. Get me a pen."

❧

"How on earth did you keep a whole town quiet about something like that?" Jemma asked, blowing her nose. "I can't believe that nobody has said a word to us. Nedra and Paralee must be about to explode."

"Folks got a lot of respect for Spencer. I didn't hear nothin' bad from nobody except Skinny Jack and his pa. I didn't even ask them to sign, but they was at Pinky's house when I stopped by. I did get a nip on the leg from Pop Whatley's mutt. Bernie Miller put out a page for me at the Dew Drop Inn, too."

"You are certainly to be commended, Lester," Helene said. "This project exemplifies the American spirit."

"Well, sir, if I'd had me a son, I couldn't have done any better than that boy. Things ain't always been good for him, even if he does come from money. Gettin' chased by a few pooch hounds and having to eat some odd vittles for manners' sake was nothin' if it'll help him out."

❦

Spencer sat at his desk. It felt about ten times too big for him. Lester and Jemma had left only minutes earlier, bringing the petitions by before Lester mailed them, and it had hit him hard. Spencer could only manage to hang on to Lester with a tearful, long embrace. Everyone in the office was crying.

It was the kindest thing anybody had done in recent Chillaton memory. It wasn't like Spencer had a deadly disease and needed a kidney or that sort of thing, but he was the grandson of a state senator and the son of a reformed skirt chaser and a recovering alcoholic. He'd gone to war without pulling strings, and he'd brought his business back to his hometown. He was their golden boy, and folks were happy to do what they could. Now it was up to some bigshot judge.

❦

The ribbon cutting for The Kenneth Rippetoe House was on a freezing cold Saturday morning. The license from the state board had come in the mail the day before, but they were still waiting to hear if Philip passed his administrator's exam. They had the ceremony inside. Jemma recited the Emily Dickinson poem that she'd read over the P.A. system when she was in junior high and Kenneth was in elementary school. She only choked up once, at the part about not living in vain. It was engraved on marble plaques, too, in the garden and above the doorway.

They served chocolate cake, Kenneth's favorite. Jemma had eaten his mother's version only weeks before she and her son were killed in a tornado that ripped their old trailer house in two. Now his dream could begin, though, and Philip was determined to make this the best home for the elderly in the state. Spencer and Jemma had done their part by donating this spacious, gleaming facility.

❦

The day of reckoning was upon Spencer.

"Good luck, son," Lester said. "We all know your speedin' days are behind you, and to my way of thinkin', California should've kept them tickets in Los Angeleez."

"Thank you, Lester, for everything. I still don't know what else to say."

"It was my pleasure. I just hope it helps a little."

They got to the courthouse an hour early. Spencer was quiet as Jemma held his hand in the hallway. The doors opened and all the accused filed in. Spencer's name was one of the first on the list.

"Spencer Morgan Chase, how do you plead?"

He cleared his throat. "Guilty, sir."

"Mr. Chase, I have before me one of the most unusual situations I've encountered in my term. Are you aware that the bulk of the citizens of Chillaton have signed a petition to ask the court to reduce the terms of the forfeiture of your license?"

"Yes, sir, I am."

"I also received a very touching letter from a Mr. Timms explaining that you had no knowledge of this petition being circulated."

"That's correct, sir." He sounded more like a soldier now.

The judge leafed through the petition, then looked at Spencer over the top of his glasses. Jemma wondered if that was a requirement for being a judge. Carrie's father had given Jemma a similar look right before he fired her.

"So you were missing in action, Mr. Chase. Where was that?"

"Just south of the DMZ, sir."

The judge nodded. "Mr. Chase, I'm going to have to ask you to forfeit your license for one year, as required by law." Jemma flinched, but Spencer stood arrow-straight. "However, I'm going to suspend six months of that forfeiture. You will also be given credit for the four months you've been in compliance. That means you have two months left from this date before your license will be reinstated."

Spencer nodded. "Thank you, sir."

"Don't let me see you in here again, son."

"Sir, you won't."

Jemma grinned at him and he grinned back, squeezing her hand. They went to eat at Cattlemen's restaurant atop the Golden Spread building.

"I owe it all to Lester," Spencer said. "Bless his heart. What a good man he is, sort of like Papa."

"That's true, but you'd better not get another ticket."

"Can you imagine? Never again. I'm a changed man."

"That's what Flavil Capp said, too." She clicked her tongue, then smiled.

❦

Helene had kept her red MG roadster in Lester's garage, but lately, she'd been taking it to the post office and out for spins around the county. Lizbeth wasn't nearly as prone to riding in the cold air like Lester was. He loved bundling up and zipping along the Farm to Market Road with the Englishwoman. He liked everything about her and wished that she'd let him bring her mail to her like Lizbeth did.

❦

Jemma had fired up the heater in the car house once again so she could paint on those days that Spencer had to be at his office. She had added six more pieces to her portfolio for the London show. Jonathan Essex communicated only through his secretary, but everything was on schedule for April. The show would open on her birthday.

Helene knocked on the car house door. "Care for a break, dear?" she asked, nodding at Jemma's progress.

"What do you have in mind?"

"I was thinking of driving out to the river. We shan't be but a few minutes. I want to snap a few wintry photographs."

"Sure. Just let me clean up."

"I'll be in the car."

Jemma liked to watch Helene operate. She had such perfect posture and composure, but her eyes twinkled in such a way that Jemma knew she was a corker in her youth.

Jemma directed Helene to a place she and Spencer knew very well. It was their special stargazing spot. Helene took several photos with her old-fashioned camera.

"Dear, would you please look in the glove compartment and bring me another roll of film?" she called out from the little cliff that overlooked the Salt Fork of the Red River.

Jemma opened it and found the film. She also found something else. A letter from Paul.

❦

After a week passed, Jemma still didn't know what to do about her discovery. It wasn't clear if this was something to worry Spencer about or not, but she couldn't let it go. Rats. This could be another test of fire like in Corinthians, but she had to ask Helene.

So they met at Daddy's Money.

Helene's hearing aid screeched as she adjusted it. "How nice to have lunch with you, dear. I do like the country ambiance at this restaurant."

"Yes ma'am. It's country all right." Jemma stirred her Dr Pepper with a straw. "Helene, I need to know why you have a letter from Paul in your car."

It was the first time Jemma had ever seen Helene rattled.

"Oh my. I suppose I should have told you about my correspondence with him."

"Maybe so."

"You see, dearest, I went to Paul before I moved here and pleaded with him to stop harassing you. He touched my heart, that's all I can say. Truly. I agreed to let him know, now and again, how you are getting on. I consider it to be no more than a small kindness on my part, but I must have left one of his responses in the MG. I am so sorry."

"So he writes you back. I can't believe that."

"Yes, dear, he does. Such a pitiful fellow and so passionate about you."

"Don't you feel weird doing this? I mean, I appreciate your point of view, but it just seems like you're on his side or something."

"No, no. Not at all, Jemma. I think Paul is a man who needs a mother figure, of sorts, and I'm just trying to help him see his life in a different way. You and Spencer are like family to me. Paul is but an incomplete man."

Jemma lowered her eyes. She had never heard it put quite in those terms. "That's not my problem, though."

"Most assuredly not. Would you care to read the letter? I don't mind."

She would be like the fool's gold in Brother Cleo's sermon if she said yes, plus she'd have to tell Spencer. That wouldn't be good. "No, thank you," she said, but her spirits were dampened by Helene's choice of words.

❦

Helene drove back to Lizbeth's. Jemma returned to the car house, but Helene remained in the MG and opened the glove compartment. She read it again.

February 1, 1972

Dear Helene,

Thanks for your letter. I'm glad you are enjoying living with Mrs. Forrester. She seemed like a real sweet lady. I've been busy here. My father has turned more of his caseload over to me. I think he'll retire soon.

I read in the Dallas paper that Jem will be having a show in London this spring. I know she's always wanted one, and I'm sure it will be a hit. What is she painting now? I'd like to add more of her work to my collection, but it seems to make her even madder at me when I do.

I'm thinking of buying another place with more room for horses, and maybe invest in some cattle. The airport authority for the new Dallas airport is buying up everything around here. My own family sold a prime section to them, and I represent several of the other land owners myself, so, you can see that the airport is certainly helping my bank account. This area is going to boom when they get that thing built.

I hope Jemma is well and happy. Maybe I'll run over to London when she has her show, but I won't bother her. I'd just like to see her face and maybe hear her laugh. Thanks for all your advice.

Best wishes,
Paul

Helene sighed. She had nothing but good intentions with this postal relationship. However, it certainly was not worth the look she'd seen on Jemma's face at lunch, nor the worry that she herself was enduring over his potential attendance at the London show.

❦

"Happy Valentine's Day, baby," Spencer said, bringing her breakfast in bed.

Jemma sat up, giggling at her husband and his red swimming shorts and angel wings. "Where on earth did you get those?"

"I grew them just for you."

"Did you stop at one of those tacky shops in Amarillo?"

"No way. Sandy borrowed them from her niece. She was an angel in the Christmas pageant." He sat on the bed beside her and flapped his wings with a little yarn pulley.

She laughed and set the breakfast aside. "Well, Cupid, what else can you do?"

"I thought you'd never ask."

Willa had been thinking for weeks about the best way to approach Helene about her salvation. If she was going to live in Chillaton, she should be in church, and not just in the pew, but also in the Lord's fold. Lizbeth agreed, but she was a more patient woman than Willa.

"Miz Helene, I might as well not beat around the bush about it. The time has come for you to choose the Lord," Willa said, sitting across the kitchenette one morning.

"I know, Willa. I have that on my agenda."

"On your what? The Lord don't show up on no agenda. You could get yourself killed drivin' around the county, then where would your *agenda* be, then? Hush puppies. Nobody never said such a thing around here."

"Perhaps I used the wrong term. I realize I have some decisions to make in that area, but I'd like to speak with a minister first."

"Brother Cleo will speak with you. He'll be here tomorrow."

"That would be nice, but I prefer to talk with Reverend Hightower."

Willa turned to Lizbeth, whose startled look spoke for them both, but Willa couldn't keep quiet. "Well, I never. Who knew that on top of bein' unchurched, you was one of them racists? I'd best be goin', Miz Liz, before I say somethin' I can't take back."

Helene laughed out loud. "Heavens, Willa, it has nothing to do whatsoever with Brother Cleo being a black man. He's a fine orator and completely worthy to be my spiritual counselor. I'm surprised you would think such a thing. The whole of it is that I have this ghastly fear of drowning, and I know your church submerses new recruits. I want to see if this Reverend Hightower follows the same policy."

The room was quiet when she finished. Then Willa let loose with one of her belly laughs, and Lizbeth followed. "Whew, you had me gettin' hot there for a minute," Willa said and gave Helene a bear hug.

~⊗~

On the first day of spring, Helene Baldwin Neblitt was accepted into the Chillaton Presbyterian Church, the church of Spencer's grandfather. Her infant baptism sufficed in their eyes, and a righteous celebration was held at Spencer and Jemmabeth's. Trina and Nick drove down from Amarillo to eat cobbler and homemade ice cream on the deck. Plum Creek babbled along as they visited.

"I need to talk business before you go to London," Trina said. "Do you think anybody in Stitchers could make some dresses for me?"

"They're good with straight seams on the machines, but I'm not sure any of them are ready for dressmaking. Maybe after a year or so. Why?"

"A boutique in Amarillo likes my designs and is willing to let me put some on consignment. If they sell, I may need some help."

"That's great! You should talk to Sandy. She makes almost all of her own clothes, and she won the state Sew It with Wool contest in high school. Show me the designs you're going to use."

"Only if you give me a preview of your London show."

"I have photos, but the paintings are gone. We shipped them two weeks ago."

"Is Spence going with you?"

"Yup. He wants to check out the guy who put some moves on my grandmother Lillygrace and me. It's going to be a blast."

~⊗~

They were dancing to "Only the Lonely" when Twila called to ask if they could watch Sweetybeth while she and Buddy went to the movies. Jemma would have graciously declined, but Spencer said they would be happy to help out. He told Jemma that it would be fun to play Mommy and Daddy for the evening.

He was not quite as enthusiastic thirty minutes later as Sweety-beth screamed her lungs out. Her reddish hair and complexion made her look like an angry rosebud, and the two of them scrambled through the mountain of stuff that came with her to try and figure out how to make her happy. Nothing worked. Jemma changed her diaper, offered a warm bottle of milk, sang, and rocked her. She wailed on. Spencer played his guitar, made silly noises and faces, all to no avail.

As a last resort, they packed everything up and drove around in the Corvette. It worked; she fell asleep with her pacifier hanging limply from the corner of her mouth.

They circled The Parnell until Buddy B and Twila came out, laughing and holding hands. Spencer honked at them and woke up Sweetybeth, who sucked cheerfully on her pacifier as though nothing else had happened.

"Oh my precious, you look just like your daddy," Twila said as she took her from Jemma. "She's cutting teeth, but you'd never know it. Yes, yes, honeybunches, how's my Sweetybeth?" she cooed to her daughter. "Did you hear the news? Missy got a contract to be a Breck Shampoo Girl. Somebody from that company saw her on the Miss Texas pageant. She'll be in magazine ads this summer. Mr. Blake has a big poster about it in the lobby of The Parnell."

Jemma sighed. "Good for her. She's very proud of her hair, and it's beautiful."

There was a hush as the rest of the group absorbed that comment.

"Look at that—our Sweetybeth's grinning at you two. Now you've done it. She's gonna want to spend every Saturday night with y'all," Buddy B said.

Spencer and Jemma exchanged alarmed glances. "We need to get home. We'll see y'all around," Spencer said and revved up the Corvette like he was going to peel out. He didn't, but it crossed his mind.

⚜

"Spence, do you think Shorty Knox knows that it was you who gave him a television?" Jemma asked as they enjoyed the quiet drive home.

"What on earth brought that up?"

"Shorty has a smile like Sweetybeth. I just want him to know, that's all. Maybe he thinks we never thanked him for saving my paintings from the tornado. Do you think he's made that association?"

"He knows, Jem. I taped a photo of some of the paintings to the TV screen. He made the association, I'm sure of it."

She reached for his hand. He and Shorty were both heroes to her. One slightly more than the other.

Chapter 25
Heartfelt Visions

The Suburban was packed and ready for Lester and the ladies to drop them off at the airport for their flight to London. Trina had made four new outfits for Jemma and had completely revamped her wardrobe after a shopping spree in Amarillo. Now there was even a special section of Jemma's closet reserved for visits to the Chase castle. She picked through it for the third time.

Spencer slipped his arms around her waist and waited. "Remember, these all have Trina's stamp of approval. You just close your eyes and grab something. It'll be perfect because it'll be on you."

She closed her eyes and put one hand on his and the other she held blindly out and took a hanger off the rack.

"Now, that wasn't difficult, was it?" He pulled his turtleneck over his head.

"That's easy for you to say. All you have to do is choose between turtleneck colors." She gave him The Look that he loved.

"Don't start something that we don't have time for, Mrs. Chase."

"Zip me up, will you?" She held her hair up and turned her back to him.

"Oh no you don't. You can reach that zipper all by yourself. I'll go back the car out."

"Rats," she muttered. It was no use to buy time. She might as well get it over with. Maybe Rebecca would be in another good mood tonight.

❧

"Hello, you two sweethearts," Harriet said as she answered the door. "Don't you look pretty, Jemma, my girl."

Rebecca greeted them in the study. "We're having your favorite, tonight, Spencer—chateaubriand, hearts of artichoke and tomato salad, and cheese soufflé. Hello, Jemmabeth." Rebecca was one of those Texans who had trained herself to say *tomahto*.

Max gave Jemma a wink. She wanted to say something like, "How funny, we just had that last night," but she didn't. Spencer nudged her toward his mother. Jemma bent down to Rebecca's chair and gave her a peck on the cheek.

"So you lovebirds are flying the coop tomorrow, huh?" Max asked.

"You bet," Spencer said. "We've waited a long time for London. Jem has added several new pieces to the show that the gallery hasn't seen yet, and they are outstanding."

"We really should have Jemma do our portrait, Max. We keep putting it off and I don't know why." Rebecca set her glass of V-8 juice on the coffee table. "I'm sure you will enjoy London this time of the year. I know we will."

Jemma's eyes widened as she turned to Spencer.

"What do you mean by that, Mother?" he asked.

"I mean that your father and I are going over for the show." Rebecca drew herself up in triumphant glory for taking them totally off guard.

Max stood and took his wife's hand. "Some shocker, huh? Becky cooked this idea up all by herself, but I have to say I'm looking forward to it. Let's eat, folks."

"When are you leaving?" Spencer asked.

"Day after tomorrow, of course; we don't want to miss the grand opening." Rebecca nodded sweetly at Jemma, whose eyes were the size of a plump artichoke heart.

Supper was surprisingly pleasant. Rebecca talked to Jemma more than she'd ever bothered before. Jemma figured that some therapist had earned his pay to turn her around like this.

"Jemmabeth, I'd like you to see the art that we inherited from Spencer's grandparents," Rebecca said. "Come with me, please."

Jemma shrugged at Spencer, then followed her mother-in-law up the stairs.

Max put his hand on Spencer's shoulder. "Don't worry, son. We won't be barging in on Jemma's spotlight. I know how much this show means to her."

"That's fine, Dad. I'm just surprised that Mother wants to attend."

"Your mother's a decent woman. If there's any fault to be laid concerning her personality, well, that probably rests squarely with me. At least that's what I've been told."

Spencer put his arms around his father. "I love you, Dad, and I respect you for saying that."

Max couldn't speak but sniffed and blew his nose. "I almost had us a whopper of a land deal last week. It's probably just as well that I got outbid. We would've looked like Panhandle land barons or something."

"What deal was that?"

"Spence, you need to get out of that office more. Old Marvin Jacks put the Lazy J up for bids right after Christmas. Some cowboy lawyer from Dallas made the winning offer. He got himself one good chunk of dirt, too. That place is spread out over three counties. 'Course it'll take a good while to iron out all the details. Marv's a tough man to deal with when it comes to a dollar. . .what's wrong, son? You look like you just saw a ghost."

Spencer puffed out his cheeks and exhaled. "I sure hope not, Dad, believe me." He sat on the couch and stared at the floor while Max talked about the price of cattle.

❧

Lester loaded the batch of critter coffins in his pickup for the delivery trip to Amarillo. He'd made a fair amount of money on this adventure, but nothing to brag about. He'd kept good books on the business, too. Right down to the postal stamps. The government was charging way too much for stamps these days. If a feller had to buy more than a couple, he could ruin a good quarter doing it. Besides, he'd never figured on this being such a solemn business. After all, the deceased was only critters. Now he understood why the Boxwright Brothers had them sour faces. Maybe the time had come for him to make fewer coffins and more hope chests.

He could make a special one for Helene. That thought put a grin on Lester's face. He took his time detailing it and presented it to her with a big red bow on top, just as Lizbeth entered the room.

"Why, Lester, this is lovely. Whatever is it?" Helene asked.

"Folks around here call it a hope chest. Young ladies come hence to puttin' things aside in it, hopin' for a husband. You know, table linens and what not. I thought you might like to have one to keep your fancy English things in. No offense about the husband part."

"No offense taken, Lester. I shall treasure it. Jemma had one when she lived with me in Wicklow."

"Cam made it for her when she was about to turn sixteen. I watched him do it."

Lizbeth raised a brow at the conversation and eyed Helene, then Lester. "Lester," she asked, " have you heard anything about a community retirement party for Dr. Huntley?"

"No ma'am. All I heard is that he's gonna keep his office open until they find a replacement. Seems to me nobody wants to throw a party for him if he's not retirin' just yet. The funeral parlor is changin' hands, though. I don't suppose them sourpuss Boxwright Brothers will be gettin' no retirement party." Lester chuckled.

Lizbeth smiled somewhat. "So many families have gone through their doors in grief."

"Well, sir, I recall one time when a family went through them doors as mad as all get-out."

Helene was always ready for a yarn. "Do tell, Lester."

"The Boxwright Brothers had all them kids, a dozen between 'em, and the whole batch was as wild as jackrabbits, too. The girls weren't so bad, but them boys was always a whiff away from the hoosegow. The only car they had between 'em was an old Packard hearse. Well, sir, them boys was well taken with the young ladies and never went out with the same one twice in a row. Seeing as how there was so many of 'em, they come hence to fussing over the hearse. The oldest of the cousins, Byron and Basil, was all set for a double date. In the meantime, their daddies was all set, too, but for widow Selma Henderson's service. Selma must've been over a hundred years old when she passed on. They had her loaded up and in the hearse for the trip to the church the next mornin'. Well, sir, that night, them two boys took off in it without askin' or lookin' in the back, neither. The Meachum twins was waiting on 'em over to Goshen way, so that old Packard was flyin' along the county road when they smacked right into the Salt Fork bridge. The back door of the Packard flew open and Selma slid out and down to the water. Them brothers had sealed her up good and tight because it never come open. The cousins got banged up bad, but Selma's coffin floated in the Salt Fork all the way down to Pleasant. Her folks come into the Parlor with a shotgun and pointed it right at them boys' daddies. It took the sheriff, a new coffin, and a complimentary chapel service includin' floral displays to persuade them to lay down their double barrel. I figger Byron and Basil didn't hear much in the way of compliments from their daddies for a spell. I heard that them boys went into the insurance business down near Bowie."

"You have a plethora of oral history, Lester. Someone must transcribe these anecdotes for posterity," Helen said.

He hadn't understood a thing she'd said, but he tapped his foot and smiled. He did admire an educated woman.

There was no time for making inquires about the sale of the ranch, and Spencer didn't dare ask Lester as they drove to Amarillo. It had taken all his concentration to keep this anxiety to himself. Paul wasn't playing fair. If he really had bought the Lazy J, the only option for Spencer was to take his precious wife and move as far away as they could.

The expanses of green burst into view as they emerged from the thick cover of clouds. Pieces of London loomed up like one of Spence's miniature shopping mall models back on the conference table in Chillaton. For reasons she'd never dwelt upon, London had been the place most elusive to Jemma's artistic connection. She'd shown in Paris, New York, Florence, Dallas, and now this beautiful city was about to welcome her, she hoped, like Gram's flowers in the springtime. She reached for Spencer's hand and held on for the landing.

At The Lex, Jemma stood next to a chic banner, "Visions from the Heart—Works by The Artist, Jemmabeth Chase" while Spencer took her picture. She had an irrepressible urge to take the banner home with her.

"Ah, Mr. Chase." Jonathan Essex bowed slightly and forged a smile. "It's a pleasure to meet you, I'm sure. My sister tells me you are an up-and-coming architect. How nice to have two artists in the family. Although I suppose artistic temperaments could ignite more readily."

Spencer shrugged. "That might be the case in some relationships, but with us, the only thing ignited is passion." He kissed Jemma's hand, then looked squarely into Jonathan's violet eyes.

Jemma thought she would melt with joy over that comment as the three of them toured the gallery. She differed with only a few placement choices, but overall, the exhibition was perfect.

A skinny young gallery manager named Fiona followed them and took notes. "If you don't mind me saying so, I have an odd feeling as though the subjects are somehow acquainted with me, but, of course, I've never been to Texas. It's the eyes. They are quite unique. Where did you train in order to capture such intensity?"

"In a cotton patch with a stack of *National Geographic* magazines." Jemma grinned at the memory.

"Lovely," Fiona said and wrote that in her notebook.

Trina had made Jemma a royal blue silk dress with a short jacket for opening night. Her hair was swept up and fastened with a bejeweled clip that Spencer had given her for Christmas. The prime minister and his wife were scheduled for a private showing, without Jemma's prior knowledge, requiring that Jonathan accompany her for an hour. Her parents, her grandparents, and her in-laws waited in the reception area. Jemma, however, kept an eye on Spence because she sensed that he had something on his mind.

Spencer watched her float from piece to piece in animated conversation. She loved to talk about her work and no audience fazed her. She was just as composed with celebrities as she was with Shy Tomlinson. He couldn't have Paul diffusing that radiance. It was hard enough watching Jonathan place his hand at her waist as they moved around the gallery. She shook hands with the dignitaries, then turned her eyes on her husband. His heart jumped up at that. When the doors opened to the general public, she was able to be with him again.

They made small talk with interested patrons and she was pulled aside for more photographs and the press questions that she disdained. "Who influenced your work? Is there one piece that represents your style more than others? Do you have a particular modern artist whose work you admire? What's it like to be from a small village in Texas and show your work to world leaders? What inspiration would you offer to young artists? How do you explain your artistic gift? Your work depicts the common man. How do you explain its popularity?"

The last question caught her ear. "Our world goes by too fast, and the human spirit often gets trampled. As an artist, I feel that whatever gifts I may have should connect audiences to those small moments in life that they might otherwise miss. There is no such thing as a common man or woman in my opinion. Each of us is uncommon, and I hope one of my pieces will open a heart to a different perspective or attitude. That would validate my efforts."

Spencer and the rest of their family hung on her every word.

❧

Jim exhaled and surveyed the crowd. His baby girl had made all this happen. She had gone through countless pencils, paper, crayons, and paint sets to get to this point. He had scolded her many times for not doing her chores or her homework and choosing, instead, to create art. Now she was reaping the rewards.

He moved through the gathering to tell her that. "You make your old daddy proud, baby girl. Look at this place. It's incredible. I only wish Papa could be here. This is too much for an old country boy like me to handle."

She giggled. "I'm so glad you came. Lots of these people just want to be seen at a show. You know that I paint because I have to, because it is given to me by the Lord. If people want to spend thousands of dollars or pounds on it, who am I to stop them?"

Jim lowered his voice. "Thank you, Jem, for sending your mom and me to visit Matt and Luke's graves. I don't know how that'll play out, but I think it'll be good for me."

"I hope so, Daddy. Gram did it, and I know she's glad. We'll be praying for you. I have to find Spence now. Love you."

She rushed off, leaving Jim behind. He sighed and brushed his cheek with his hand. *The world goes by too fast.* He had heard that all his life, but now he realized that it was true. Even his little girl had noticed.

❧

Rebecca Chase was right at home with the Lillygraces, but Max hung out with Spencer. "When did you know that Jemma was this good, son?"

"You know I've loved her art since the first grade, but then I've loved her all that time, too; I'm biased."

"She nails everybody she paints. It's almost spooky. I wish that slick crook she wrestled to the floor would show up. I'd like to give him a taste of my fist again. Do you think he knows about tonight?"

"I'm sure he does. Dad, do you know the lawyer's name who bought the Lazy J?"

"All I know is what I've told you. I didn't think you'd be interested, or else we could've put our money together and outbid him."

They were interrupted by The Artist.

"What do you think? Crazy, huh?" She kissed them both. "Come on, you two. Let's get some fancy little sandwiches." She hooked her arms in theirs, and they walked to the reception area. "Guess which painting Mr. Prime Minister bought?" She popped a canapé in her mouth.

"Just so it's not of me," Spencer said.

"Nope. I wouldn't have sold him those. He bought *The Sermon and the Can*, the one of Grandma Hardy sitting in the pew with her chewing tobacco can. Isn't that hilarious? He said that was his favorite."

"Did you get to shake his hand, Spence?" Max asked.

"Only when my wife introduced me."

Jemma grabbed a handful of mini-sandwiches. "Shy's getting his teeth today, and I can't wait to see him when we get back. Let's go catch up with Mom and Daddy. You come, too, Max."

❧

Across the crowd at the gallery, Alex thought she saw him, but dismissed the idea. Then again, how many men in the world could look like that? She excused herself from Jim and her parents and made her way across the room. There he was. Her first reaction was to tell her daughter, but she changed her mind and moved up next to him as he studied the show's catalog.

"Are you a collector?" she asked, heart pounding.

Paul jumped at the sight of her. "Just this artist."

His eyes were jade green. Despite everything she knew about him, he remained exquisitely handsome. He didn't have on the cowboy hat like he did that day in the Wicklow post office parking lot, but he was wearing boots and English Leather.

"You look familiar to me," she said.

"I was thinking the same thing about you," he replied, studying her face.

"Are you Paul Turner?"

"Are you Jemma's mother?"

"We've never met. I'm Alexandra Forrester." She extended her hand.

He blinked and took it. "You look like her," he said, his voice barely audible. "Your voices are the same. . .I guess you know all about us."

"I do. Are you in London just to see my daughter? She's married, you know."

"Yes ma'am, I know. Please don't say anything to her. It's easy for people to misjudge my intentions, but nobody understands how I feel about her. If I hadn't messed up, you'd be looking at your son-in-law right now."

Alex smiled. "My son-in-law is just over there with his wife. I do have some idea of how you must hurt, Paul, but that doesn't mean you should take advantage of her."

"I can assure you that won't happen. I was only hoping to buy a new piece of her art and maybe catch a glimpse of her, but I guess meeting you comes close. I'll take off. Maybe, if you think it's right someday, you could tell her that we met. She's never out of my mind, ma'am; I'm sorry." Paul put his hand out, and she took it without thinking. He lifted her fingers to his lips, and then was gone.

Alex stared after him, her hand suspended in midair.

"What do you think, Mom?" Jemma asked as Alex rejoined them.

She exhaled before answering. "I think you are a remarkable young woman, Jemmabeth, and you've made all the right choices in your life. I'm so proud of you."

A frown crossed Jemma's brow, but then she smiled. She took her mother's hand—the very one—and they began their own tour of the show.

⊰❧⊱

Paul sat in his rental car. Her mother had thrown him for a loop. She didn't have those honey-colored eyes, but everything else was there. It gave him great peace to kiss the hand of the woman who gave her birth. He hadn't told Alex that, before she found him, he'd been watching Jemma for an hour from another crowded corner of the gallery. He had heard her talking with the press and laughing between her husband and another man. That would have to do him for a while.

He thumbed absently through her exhibition catalog, *Visions from the Heart*. He still wanted her heart, even though it was denied him. For now, he'd have to settle for seeing life through her eyes. He should have paid more attention to her work when there was a chance that she loved him. He traced around her photo on the back page. He'd never shed a tear over any woman other than his mother, until he lost Jemmabeth.

He turned to the page with the painting he had just purchased, *Jemmalou's*. It had surely come straight from her heart because he had read her artist's statement, but then he knew already how she felt about her Papa. It was almost spiritual the way she captured the cotton fields in the hawk's eye. He had been so much in love with her that he'd never realized the depth of her talent that summer in Wicklow. The piece tore at him, but it would also be a great comfort when he moved it into his new weekend ranch house on the Lazy J. He hoped to get a glimpse of her more often now that he owned a place in her hometown.

❦

Alex saw no point in telling anybody, at least not in London. She and Jim knew that Spencer had a surprise for Jemma's birthday, and she wasn't about to let Paul spoil it. She realized that he'd kissed her hand out of respect, and she did feel sorry for the guy, but the Lord had steered her daughter back to Spencer, answering everybody's prayers and shutting the door on Paul. He would just have to buck up. After all, he was a gentleman cowboy. He must know something about riding off into the sunset.

❦

The Lillygraces had booked a celebration table at The Ritz Hotel in honor of the birthday girl. It was a slight upgrade from Daddy's Money. After everyone had said their good nights, Jemma and Spencer took a cab to their hotel, kissing shamelessly in the backseat. By the time they got to their room, she had forgotten it was her birthday.

He hadn't. Spencer unlocked the door, and she stepped in. The entire room was stuffed with baskets of roses, delphiniums, and lilies. Resting on her pillow was a flat package wrapped in gold paper and tied with purple ribbon. She gave him The Look he loved as she unwrapped it, looking a bit perplexed at its contents. "Great photo," she said. "I remember this little castle; it's the one at Kilton. What are you telling me? Did you sneak around and plan a trip to Scotland?"

"Could be."

She pulled him down on the bed with her, nose to nose. "Thank you so much, Spence. It'll be fun to get away for a while. Where are we staying?"

"We can stay in the castle if you like, m'lady."

She sat up, her elegant hairdo coming undone. Spencer took out the clip and her hair fell around her shoulders.

"Okay," she said. "Now what exactly are you talking about? If this is a camping trip, I'll have to go shopping and get some clothes. Everything I brought is uptown stuff. What? Why are you looking at me like that?"

"Turn the frame over."

She crawled over him and retrieved the gift from the lamp table. On the back was an envelope. She opened it to find several legal documents, and, after reading the first paragraph, she flipped to the last page, then dropped the papers on the floor, staring at him. "Spencer Morgan Chase, have you bought that castle?" she shrieked.

"Happy birthday, Jem."

She fell on him, pretending to faint. "How do you think of these things?"

"I think of thee," he said and lavished her with birthday affection.

Chapter 26

Gracious Gold

Julia and Arthur had surprised them with their attendance and purchase of the painting of Shy Tomlinson, whom Do Dah had known all her life. British celebrities and strangers toured the show. After two more evenings at The Lex, the younger Chase couple took the night train to Scotland. "The Hottest Artist in Town," as the *Times* had called her, now slept soundly as the train rocked along, but Spencer lay awake watching as the lights of villages sprang out of the darkness.

The last thing on earth he wanted was for Paul to move to Connelly County, if indeed Paul was the buyer. In his heart, Spencer knew that was the case. He also knew he couldn't take Jemma and flee the situation. No, they would have to stick it out—"like it or lump it," as Max would say. Spencer couldn't control Paul's life, but he would have to have a heart-to-heart talk with the man. Surely it was not still a contest between them for her love because he was certain where Jemma's affections permanently lay. It had to be that Paul needed to be near her, to catch a sense of her presence. He understood that, but he could never again allow him close enough to see if her hair held the fragrance of flowers. That privilege belonged only to her husband. God's Great Plan, as Jemma called it, had to be unfolding, somehow, in this quandary.

❧

"I'm never going back to Texas," she said, taking in the view after their long hike. Rugged hills encircled Loch Tarron, and the tiny fishing village of Kilton nestled along the curve of its harbor. "My great-grandparents were born in this village. I belong here."

"We have a major project ahead of us if you really want to move into our castle," Spencer told her.

Jemma inhaled. "I don't care. Even if we never have any furniture in it, we can come here and sit. Everything just looks good enough to eat. See, even the clouds look like perfectly baked meringue."

"Let me show you something." Spencer took her hand.

They climbed the crest of the craggy cliff that overlooked the castle and loch. He wrapped his arms around her waist, and they turned in a slow circle. The ancient Highland mountains gave way to the sea and the Isle of Skye beyond. The moon spilled into the mist of the loch, and the darkening horizon brimmed with clouds laced in shades of orange and gold.

"I could stay here forever with you," he murmured.

Jemma smiled up at him. "Aye, I keep it in mind, you Englishman."

As the mist moved into the hills, it shifted to a soft rain, forcing them to seek shelter under the tangled branches of an old rhododendron. Spencer spread his jacket on the ground as they waited for it to pass. She lay her head on his shoulder. "Spence, I've been thinking about those verses from Numbers that Brother Cleo said over us. God has been so gracious to us. Sometimes I do feel His face shining down."

A bird moved among the rhododendron, sharing its evening song.

"Thank you, Jem, for loving me."

"I'm the one who owes all the thank-yous in this relationship, let's not forget that. Hey, was something bothering you in London? You seemed a little different."

He avoided her eyes. "It was probably business. I guess I have some of that in the back of my mind."

"Business, huh? Spence, please say that our life will always be full of surprises and of this feeling that I can't put into words when I wake up beside you."

"I know that feeling. It's called joy. I can promise you that our life will always be full of love, Jem, and the rest is a given."

"The rest includes sad times, though."

"That's because we're not in heaven yet."

"This comes close, babe. Who else buys his wife a castle in Scotland? Only you. You are my Candy Man, my hero, and the sweetest husband in the world."

"C'mon, I just happen to have enough money to buy castles. It's not very big anyway, and how do you know who's the sweetest husband in the world?"

"I know things." She kissed the little scar on his chin and couldn't stop. The bird sang again, its eyes darting down at the rhododendron.

The rain settled back into a mist without their notice. Jemma sat up and ran her fingers through her hair.

"Let's see what our castle is like in the dark." Spencer pulled a leaf from her tresses.

She shivered as they edged down the trail. "What happened to springtime in the Highlands?"

"Beats me, but this is like a fairy tale, hen."

"Hen? That's not very romantic."

"I read that when a lad likes a Scottish lass, he calls her 'hen,' and I happen to like every bit of you. Since we are land owners here, I thought I should start practicing the language of the land."

"Well, did ya now?" she asked in her best accent and cradled his face in her hands. "I do adore you, Mr. Chase."

He forgot about cowboys and ranches and kissed her palms as the faint sounds of a fiddle drifted across the loch from their hotel. He drew her close, and they moved to the music. The tide rippled in near the castle, lending its own gentle rhythm to the crisp night air. They lingered for a while, whispering and giggling while the mist rose off the loch and settled around the castle.

She clasped the warmth of his hand. "May the Lord bless and keep thee, my husband."

"May the Lord make His face shine upon thee, and be gracious unto thee, Jem." He rested his head against hers. "Now I'm in the mood for some more of that fiddle music. Let's go."

"Spence, I can't even see the trail."

"Looks like we'll be walking in faith, then." Spencer took her hand and they inched along the path, talking quietly about other things.

Their hushed conversation blended into the mist as it suddenly slipped away to reveal the hillside. Far above, the full Scottish moon, with its golden, smiling face, graciously brightened all that lay before them.

Acknowledgments

Corner of Blue
With thanks to my sons, for their uncommon wit; to my uncle, Johnny Leathers, Mary Wilson, and Kelly Mull for their continued encouragement; to Josh, for his kindness and patience; to Maureen Rowlatt, who inspires me from across the Atlantic; to Ramona Tucker, for believing; to my parents and brothers for their fine humor; and to Dwight, who showed me Paris.

Touch of Silver
Thanks to my family and in-laws—those present and those dearly departed—who have spun many a yarn into gold; to my aunt Charlene, for her humor and splendid memory; and to my bonny friends in the Bon Appétit Book Club with whom I've often laughed 'til it hurt.

Grateful acknowledgment is also made to Chief Warrant Officer 3 Timothy E. Wilkerson, United States Army (retired). Without Tim, Spencer could never have gotten a Huey off the ground.

Taste of Gold
With love and gratitude to my parents, Margaret Jean and Judson Roy Williams, who shaped my early years and softened my view of this world.

Blessings upon my sons—Joshua, Jeremy, Gabriel, and Daniel—who keep me laughing.

Special thanks to Jayne Griffith, Fred and Liz Whitehurst, and, as always, loving appreciation to my best friend and husband, Dwight.

About the Author

Sharon McAnear was raised in the small towns of the Texas Panhandle, where anybody and everybody helped a child know who she was and what was expected of her.

Her beloved *Jemma* series, which introduces some of the lively Chillaton residents, is "more than a love story," Sharon says. "It rekindles a sweeter time when family and friends were everywhere, and you were frequently glad of it. When needed, the good citizens of Connelly County stood ready to help out with chores, form a prayer circle, or stretch the truth about your situation. Take your pick. It was a place where sweet companionship soothed lonely hearts and 'porch company' abounded."

Pictured above with a quilt, handmade by her grandmother Grace almost a century ago, Sharon says, "Both of my grandmothers were accomplished quilters. My mother remembers, as a little girl, watching Grandmother hand stitch the tiny hexagons together for this quilt. It hangs close by my writing desk now."

To the right is Sharon with her scholarly cat, Squirrel—her sharpest critic and most trusted confidante. The pull-out step stool at the left of the photo is from her grandmother Grace's kitchen. In the early fifties, it was bright yellow and always her seat for mealtimes at her grandparents' house. The stool was an upgrade from her previous stack of Sears catalogs.

Sharon now lives in Colorado with her very patient husband, and her periodically dramatic family is scattered around the country. As a writer, she has come to rely heavily upon the frozen talents of Marie Callender and the Grace of God. Well, perhaps only a couple of times a week for Marie.

http://www.sharonmcanear.com
www.oaktara.com

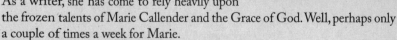